ISBN 978-0-483-70941-6
PIBN 10515772

THE WORKS

OF

G. P. R. JAMES, ESQ.

VOL. III.

THE HUGUENOT.

Dietz. pinx.^t

"STARTING FORWARD INSTANTLY TO HER SIDE, HE SEIZED THE BRIDLE OF
DE HERICOURT'S HORSE, AND FORCED THE ANIMAL BACK ALMOST UPON
HIS HAUNCHES"

THE WORKS

OF

G. P. R. JAMES, ESQ.

REVISED AND CORRECTED   THE AUTHOR.

WITH AN INTRODUCTORY PREFACE.

VOL. III.

THE HUGUENOT.

LONDON:
SMITH, ELDER AND CO., 65, CORNHILL.
MDCCCXLV.

Published by Smith, Elder & C°. Cornhill, London.

THE WORKS

OF

G. P. R. JAMES, ESQ.

REVISED AND CORRECTED BY THE AUTHOR.

WITH AN INTRODUCTORY PREFACE.

"D'autres auteurs l'ont encore plus avili, (le roman,) en y mèlant les tableaux dégoutant du vice ; et tandis que le premier avantage des fictions est de rassembler autour de l'homme tout ce qui, dans la nature, peut lui servir de leçon ou de modèle, on a imaginé qu'on tirerait une utilité quelconque des peintures odieuses de mauvaises mœurs ; comme si elles pouvaient jamais laisser le cœur qui les repousse, dans une situation aussi pure que le cœur qui les aurait toujours ignorées.   Mais un roman tel qu'on peut le concevoir, tel que nous en avons quelques modèles, est une des plus belles productions de l'esprit humain, une des plus influentes sur la morale des individus, qui doit former ensuite les mœurs publiques."—MADAME DE STAEL. *Essai sur les Fictions.*

"Poca favilla gran fiamma seconda :
Forse diretro a me, con miglior voci
Si pregherà, perchè Cirra risponda."
DANTE. *Paradiso,* Canto I

VOL. III.

THE HUGUENOT.

LONDON:

SMITH, ELDER AND CO., 65, CORNHILL.

MDCCCXLV.

THE

HUGUENOT:

𝔄 𝔗𝔞𝔩𝔢

OF

THE FRENCH PROTESTANTS.

BY

G. P. R. JAMES, ESQ.

LONDON:

SMITH, ELDER AND CO., 65, CORNHILL.

MDCCCXLV.

CHARLES RUDOLPHE LORD CLINTON,

My Lord,

ALTHOUGH I, of course, look upon the book which I now venture to dedicate to one whom I so much esteem and respect, with those parental prejudices which make us often overlook all defects, and magnify any good qualities in our offspring, yet, believe me, I feel that it is very far inferior to that which I could wish to present to you. Do not, then, measure my regard by the value of the work, but accept it only as a very slight testimony of great esteem; and, at the same time, allow me, even in my Dedication, to say a few words concerning the book itself.

I will not trouble you or the public with any reasoning upon the general conduct of the story—why I suddenly changed the scene here, or flew off to another character there—why I gave but a glimpse of one personage, or dwelt long and minutely upon another. I believe and trust that those who read the work attentively, will discover strong reasons for all such proceedings; and I am quite sure that much thought and care were bestowed on each step of the kind before it was taken. Your own good taste will decide whether I was right or wrong, and blame or approve, I know, whatever I may plead. The public will do so also; and, as a general rule, I think it best to conceal, as far as possible, in all cases, the machinery of a composition of this kind, suffering the wheels to produce their effect without being publicly exhibited.

run on to follow the history of one character, whenever a less interesting personage is brought upon the scene, will derive little, either of profit or pleasure, from any well-constructed work of fiction. I have, in all my works, avoided, as far as possible, bringing prominently forward any character or any scene which has not a direct influence upon the progress and end of the tale; but I have equally avoided pointing out to the superficial reader, by any flourish of trumpets, that the personage he thinks of no importance is "to turn out a great man in the end," or that the scene which seems unconnected and irrelevant will be found, not without results.

Besides these considerations, however, I trust every romance-writer in the present day proposes to himself greater objects than the mere telling of a good story. He who, in the course of a well-conceived and interesting tale, excites the better part of our nature to high and noble aspirations; depicts our bad passions so as to teach us to abhor and govern them; arrays our sympathies on the side of virtue, benevolence, and right; expands our hearts, and makes the circle of our feelings and affections more comprehensive; stores our imaginations with images bright, and sweet, and beautiful; makes us more intimately and philosophically acquainted with the characters of our fellow-men; and in short, causes the reader to rise wiser, and with a higher appreciation of all that is good and great—attains the grand object at which every man should aim, and deserves the thanks and admiration of mankind. Even he, who makes the attempt though without such success, does something, and never can write altogether in vain.

That you, to whom I inscribe this work, can appreciate such purposes, and will encourage the attempt, even where, as in these pages, it goes little beyond endeavour, is no slight pleasure to me : nor is it an unmeaning or insincere compliment when I say, that though I yield my own opinions to no man, yet I have often thought of you and yours while writing these volumes. I know not whether you remember saying, one day, after we had visited together the school instituted by our noble acquaintance Guicciardini, " that whether it succeeded or failed, the endeavour to do good, ought to immortalize him." Perhaps you have forgotten the words ; but I have not.

Allow me, ere I end this long epistle, to add something in regard to the truth of the representations made in the work, and the foundation on which the story rests. If you will look into the curious " Mémoires Historiques sur la Bastille," published in 1789, (vol. i. page 203,) you will find some of the bare facts, as they are stated in the Great Register of the Bastille, on which the plot of the tale that follows entirely hinges.

Of course I cannot forestall my story by alluding more particularly to those facts; and I have only further to say on that subject, that for many reasons I have altered the names inserted in the Great Register. I have also taken a similar liberty with regard to the scenes of many events which really occurred, placing in Poitou what sometimes took place in Dauphiny, sometimes in Provence. Nor have I felt myself bound, in all instances, to respect the exact dates, having judged it expedient to bring many events within a short compass, which were spread over a greater space of time. I have endeavoured, however, to represent most accurately, without prejudice or favour, the conduct of the French Catholics to French Protestants, and of Protestants to Catholics, during the persecutions of the seventeenth century. My love and esteem for many excellent Catholics—priests as well as laity—would prevent me, I believe, from viewing the question of the revocation of the edict of Nantes, and the consequences thereof, with a prejudiced eye; but when I read the following passages in the writings, not of a Protestant, but of a sincere Catholic, I am only inclined to doubt whether I have not softened the picture of persecution.

" Il restait peu à faire pour exciter le zèle du roi contre une religion solennellement frappée des plus éclatans anathèmes par l'église universelle, et qui s'en était elle-même frappée la première, en se séparant de tout l'antiquité sur des points de foi fondamentaux.

" Le roi était devenu dévot, et dévot dans la dernière ignorance. A la dévotion se joignit la politique. On voulut lui plaire par les endroits qui le touchaient le plus sensiblement, la devotion et l'autorité. On lui peignit les Huguenots avec les plus noires couleurs; un état dans un état, parvenu à ce point de licence à force de désordres, de révoltes, de guerres civiles, d'alliances étrangères, de résistance à force ouverte contre les rois ses prédécesseurs, et jusqu'à lui-même, réduit à vivre en traité avec eux. Mais on se garda bien de lui apprendre la source de tant de maux, les origines de leurs divers dégrès et de leurs progrès, pourquoi et par qui les Huguenots furent premièrement armés, puis soutenus, et surtout de lui dire un seul mot des projets de si longue main pourpensés, des horreurs et des attentats de la ligue contre sa couronne, contre sa maison, contre son père, son aïeul, et tous les siens.

" On lui voila avec autant de soin ce que l'évangile, et d'après cette divine loi les apôtres, et tous les pères et leur suite, enseignent la manière de prêcher Jésus Christ, de convertir les infidèles et les hérétiques, et de se conduire en ce qui regarde la religion. On toucha un dévot de la douceur de faire, aux dépens d'autrui, une pénitence facile, qu'on lui persuada sure pour l'autre monde.* * * *

" Les grands ministres n'étaient plus alors. Le Tellier au lit de la mort, son funeste fils était le seul qui restât, car Seignelay ne faisait guère que poindre. Louvois, avide de guerre, atterré sous le poids d'une trève de vingt ans, qui ne faisait presque que d'être signée, espéra qu'un si grand coup porté aux Huguenots réunirait

tout le Protestantisme de l'Europe, et s'applaudit, en attendant, de
ce que le roi ne pouvant frapper sur les Huguenots que par ses
troupes, il en serait le principal exécuteur, et par là de plus en plus
en crédit. L'esprit et le génie de Madame de Maintenon, tel qu'il
vient d'être représenté avec exactitude, n'était rien moins que
propre, ni capable d'aucune affaire au-delà de l'intrigue. Elle
n'était pas née ni nourrie à voir sur celle-ci au-delà de ce qui lui en
était présenté, moins encore pour ne pas saisir avec ardeur une occasion si naturelle de plaire, d'admirer, de s'affermir de plus en plus
par la dévotion. Qui d'ailleurs eût su un mot de ce qui ne se déli-
bérait qu'entre le confesseur, le ministre alors comme unique, et
l'épouse nouvelle et chérie; et qui de plus eût osé contredire?
C'est ainsi que sont menés à tout, par une voie ou par une autre,
les rois qui, par grandeur, par défiance, par abandon à ceux qui les
tiennent, par paresse ou par orgueil, ne se communiquent qu'à deux
ou trois personnes, et bien souvent à moins, et qui mettent entre eux
et tout le reste de leurs sujets une barrière insurmontable.

" La révocation de l'édit de Nantes, sans le moindre prétexte et
sans aucun besoin, et les diverses proscriptions plutôt que déclara-
tions qui la suivirent, furent les fruits de ce complot affreux qui
dépeupla un quart du royaume; qui ruina son commerce; qui l'af-
faiblit dans toutes ses parties; qui le mit si longtemps au pillage
public et avoué des dragons; qui autorisa les tourmens et les sup-
plices dans lesquels ils firent réellement mourir tant d'innocens de
tout sexe par milliers; qui ruina un peuple si nombreux; qui dé-
chira un monde de familles; qui arma les parens contre les parens
pour avoir leur bien et les laisser mourir de faim; qui fit passer nos
manufactures aux étrangers, fit fleurir et regorger leurs états aux
dépens du nôtre, et leur fit bâtir de nouvelles villes; qui leur donna
le spectacle d'un si prodigieux peuple proscrit, nu, fugitif, errant
sans crime, cherchant asile loin de sa patrie; qui mit nobles, riches,
vieillards, gens souvent très-estimés pour leur piété, leur savoir, leur
vertu, des gens aisés, faibles, délicats, à la ruine, et sous le nerf très-
effectif du comite, pour cause unique de religion; enfin qui, pour
comble de toutes horreurs, remplit toutes les provinces du royaume
de parjures et de sacrilèges, où tout retentissait de hurlemens de

l'un et l'autre par des abjurations simulées, d'où sans intervalle on les traînait à adorer ce qu'ils ne croyaient point, et à recevoir réellement le divin corps du saint des saints, tandis qu'ils demeuraient persuadés qu'ils ne mangeaient que du pain qu'ils devaient encore abhorrer. Telle fut l'abomination générale enfantée par la flatterie et par la cruauté. De la torture à l'abjuration, et de celle-ci à la communion, il n'y avait pas souvent vingt-quatre heures de distance, et leurs bourreaux étaient leurs conducteurs et leurs témoins. Ceux qui, par la suite, eurent l'air d'être changés avec plus de loisir, ne tardèrent pas par leur fuite ou par leur conduite à démentir leur prétendu retour." — *St. Simon*, vol. xiii. page 113, ed. 1829.

I have now nothing further to say, my dear Lord Clinton, but to beg your pardon for having already said so much, and to express a hope that you, and the public, will deal leniently by that which is now offered you, with the highest respect and esteem, by

Yours, most faithfully,

G. P. R. JAMES.

FAIR OAK LODGE, PETERSFIELD,
17th Nov. 1838.

INTRODUCTORY PREFACE.

It has become so customary, in sending forth a new and general edition of an author's works, to make the public, as it were, a father confessor, to whom we relate all the amiable little weaknesses, of which we are usually rather vain than ashamed, that I do not scruple to acknowledge one of those little weaknesses in favour of "The Huguenot." Of course, if the book had been unfavourably received by the world, I should be the last to patronize it; for, with books as with men, we generally, sooner or later, turn on the side of the favourite, and are sure to discover excellent qualities in that which other men applaud; but as the work has been one of the most popular that I have written, I am quite safe in admitting that I myself like it well. There may be, however, several other causes for this parental fondness, besides the approbation it has received, and totally independent of any merits it may possess. In the first place, from a very early period of life, that portion of history which is comprised in the reign of Louis XIV. of France has been to me a favourite object of study. A young imagination was captivated by the many brilliant scenes and events which it offered; a more mature judgment pondered the great changes which it effected in society; and a mind, I trust, not altogether indisposed to philosophical reflection, found most interesting occupation in considering the operation, even in the present times, of causes called into activity in that remote epoch. Such speculations naturally required the careful examination of facts; and so completely were my thoughts imbued with the subject, that in writing the life of the French monarch, to whom impartial posterity has refused the title of " Great," conferred upon him by contemporary flattery, I was seldom (in comparison with the labour which I have sometimes undertaken in the composition of other works) compelled to consult the authorities of the time: almost all the particulars they mention, and frequently the very words they use, being already deeply impressed upon my mind. In the second place, as a Protestant, the fate of the unfortunate Huguenots, and the barbarous persecutions which they endured under Louis, formed, in my eyes, one of the most interesting points in the history of his reign. I had known intimately many of their direct descendants, and was familiar with most of the traditions preserved in their families; so that I had a vast store of materials which were inadmissible into the sterner fabric of history. In the third place, what between previous habits of thought and the nature of the subject, I became deeply interested in the work itself, and bestowed much pains upon it.

Nevertheless, though thoroughly acquainted with the history of the period, and with almost every locality mentioned in the work, several considerable errors found their way into the tale, some of which were almost laughable. Those errors were principally of time and distance, and in the present edition are generally removed, though in one or two instances, where not very important, I have left them untouched, because the course of the tale seemed to require a deviation from that strict accuracy which, though indispensable in history, is not required in a work of fiction. Very tolerable musicians are occasionally apt to hurry their time, and an author has the same temptation, especially where any interval to be accounted for presents no incidents worthy of record; but

I will acknowledge it was too bad to make one of my characters take a journey from Paris and back in the space of four-and-twenty hours, (especially before railroads were invented,) which would have required two days each way.   Both readers and critics, however, were generous, and this oversight past uncommented on, if not unnoticed.

In the construction of the tale, it was my object to give as much variety to the scenes and to the characters as possible, both in order to display the state of society, at the time, in several of its various aspects, and to relieve the mind of the reader; and it was for this object that I have carried my kind companions to the country-house of the French nobleman, to the provincial capital of Poitou, to Paris, to Versailles, to the Bastille, to the preaching on the moor, and to the pastor's dwelling.   I strove for the same variety in the characters and in the incidents, contrasting the Count de Morseiul with the Chevalier d'Evran; the lying, but faithful valet, Riquet, with the stern and fierce Herval, the mild and liberal-minded Papists with the furious persecutors belonging to the same sect, and the more fiery and fanatic of the Protestants with their calmer and more reasonable brethren.   With a similar view I brought into close apposition the sparkling levities of the court of Louis with the bloody tyranny which was exercised under his authority, and with the dark and fearful scenes of the famous prison which, at different times, received almost all the most noble and high-minded men in France.   In so doing I was justified by nature and by history; for, probably, at no period were levity and crime more nearly allied, luxury and want brought closer, gaiety and cruelty more intimately blended, barbarism and civilization more thoroughly mingled together.

In drawing the character of the Count of Morseiul, I was of course anxious to invest him, as the hero of the tale, with all the high qualities which any man might not unnaturally possess; but

I was by no means disposed to paint him as a perfect character—a thing which, never having seen, I could not well draw—or to represent him as exempt from the faults of the age in which he lived. Thus, though the character has been censured for the devotion and reverence which he displayed towards a vicious, voluptuous, and tyrannical monarch, at the very moment that Louis was oppressing, in the most brutal and lawless manner, his Huguenot subjects, and though it has been said, that such a man, as I have represented the Count, would have been moved by hatred and indignation to the tyrant as well as sympathy with his fellow-sufferers, yet I do not think sufficient allowance has been made by those who raised these objections, for the influence of habit upon the mind. That reverence or devotion towards the sovereign, which I have attributed to the Count of Morseiul even under oppression and wrong, had become by this time so rooted in the minds of all the French nobility, that not even the grossest acts of tyranny could tear it out; and I am thoroughly convinced, that had I depicted my hero without it, his character would not be in accordance with the age in which he lived. For this reason I have not in this edition altered one expression indicative of such feelings. Some readers have expressed regret, not unmingled with censure, that I thought fit to put to death the Chevalier d'Evran; but to this I can only reply, that his death was predetermined from the very first page of the work. An author is as great a tyrant as any despot in the world; and I must assign, as my motive for this piece of butchery, the reason not uncommonly given by despots for removing from the busy scene of earth any of their disagreeable subjects : namely, that it would have been very inconvenient to let him live.

Knowing the countries well in which I have thought fit to lay most of my romances, I believe I am generally tolerably accurate in regard to the relative position and distances of the places men-

tioned. Such, as I have before said, was not the case in the
first edition of " The Huguenot," although, perhaps, I am better
acquainted with the part of the country I have described than with
any other of which I ever wrote. This arose from that inapti-
tude to the correction of the press, which I have spoken of in the introductory preface to the " Gipsy." The truth is, the scene of the
principal events was originally laid in Brittany, and not in Poitou,
and the description of the small town of Morseiul was, in fact, that
of Dinant on the Rance. For various reasons, and, amongst the
rest, because the inhabitants of that part of France were never
very zealous Huguenots, I changed the scene from Brittany to
Poitou; but in doing so, I became too much interested in the
work, as I read, and neglected, in several instances, to make the
alterations I had proposed. This has been since amended as I best
could, and I trust that no such errors will be found in this volume.
Having now made fully as sincere a confession as is at all usual in
the confessional, I will only guard myself against one more objection, which some readers, who have not studied deeply the history
of those times, may urge. It will, perhaps, be said, that I have
at times represented Louis XIV., especially in his acts, as stern
and cruel, unmindful of either the rights or the happiness of his
subjects, and at others as a very placable, good-humoured, personage. All I can say in reply is,—was he not really so? I believe
he was. Despotism is always capricious; and Louis, like other
men in his position, was vain of his clemency, though jealous of
his authority, and suffered more acts of cruelty and oppression than
he commanded. In his own demeanour, he was generally mild,
often extremely affable, and easily led to pardon; but, at the same
time, he but too frequently countenanced and approved acts of the
most barbarous tyranny, when the painful parts of the tragedy were
not brought immediately under his own eyes. Any one who will look
into the memoirs of contemporaries, I do not scruple to say, will

find far more extraordinary contradictions in his conduct than any that are recorded in these pages. I believe that his character, and those of the other historical personages who are introduced, though not very minutely drawn, will be found consistent, as far as they go, with the known facts of history; and, indeed, I may add, that several of the scenes, both in the court, in the prisons, and in the fields of France, are simply given as they are related by eye-witnesses. I have in no degree exaggerated the cruelties perpetrated on the unoffending Protestants; I have in no degree over-stated the trickery and corruption which was employed to disunite the party, and prevent them from struggling, as one body, for the maintenance of those rights which had been secured to them by the edict of Nantes. Indeed, had I entered into all the particulars of the baseness, the knavery, the fraud, the violence, the inhuman barbarity, which accompanied the revocation of that edict, I should have been forced to extend the work to a very inconvenient size; and, to those who doubt any of the facts stated, I have only to prefer a request, that they will look into Aubigné's admirable history of the Huguenots, where they will find full confirmation of everything that is here advanced.

In regard to that which may be termed the imaginative part of the tale—comprising the incidents affecting all those personages who are not historical—I have to remark, that many of the particulars are either traditionary or founded upon recorded facts, though not perhaps related of the persons, or even of the times, under consideration. The story of the pack of cards substituted in place of an important commission is well known, especially in the Isle of Wight. The fact, too, of Louis XIV. having detained in France, sometimes as close prisoners in the Bastille, sometimes under the sharp supervision of his police, various persons, natives of other countries, who differed from him on religious subjects, for the purpose of forcing them to abjure, is also well established, and it was upon an anecdote of the kind that I founded the history of Clémence de Marly and her brother.

The scene of the marriage of Madame de Maintenon, the reader need hardly be told, is fictitious; but still there are several particulars mentioned by contemporaries which render the details here given at least probable. The customs of the court of Louis, the form of receiving prisoners at the Bastille, and the account of the trial and execution of the Chevalier de Rohan, are all, I believe, perfectly accurate; and, as I imagine that it will be easy for the reader to perceive the line of demarcation between the romantic and the historical narrative, I trust that the work will not mislead in any degree the searcher for truth, while it may please the mere seeker of amusement.

THE HUGUENOT.

CHAPTER I.

THE HERO, HIS FRIEND, AND HIS DWELLING IN THE SEVENTEENTH
CENTURY.

THERE is a small town in one of the remote provinces of France,
about ten miles from the sea shore and two or three hundred from
the capital, on the appearance of which it may be as well to dwell
for a short time ; noticing not alone its houses and its streets as
they appeared in the seventeenth century, but its inhabitants, their
feelings, and their customs, at that period.

Were we not to make this formal sort of presentation, the reader
would feel as if set down suddenly amidst a crowd of strangers with
no one to introduce him, with no one to unpadlock that barrier
which the cautious laws of society set up between man and man, for
the purpose of guarding against the wild-beast propensities of the
race of intellectual tigers to which we belong. Now, however, if
we manage skilfully, the reader may become as familiar with the
people of another day and scenes of another land, as if they had
been the playfellows of his childhood and the haunts of his youth,
and may go on calmly with those to whom he is thus introduced
through the dark and painful events which are recorded in the
pages that follow.

That part of France in which our scene is laid presents features
which differ very much from the dull and uninteresting aspect of
the land from Calais to Paris, and from Paris to the mountains of
Switzerland—the route generally pursued by our travelling coun-
trymen, whether they go forth to make what is usually called the
grand tour, or content themselves with idling away a long space of
misspent time amongst the Helvetian mountains. In the district
that I speak of, the face of the country, though it cannot perhaps
be called mountainous, is richly varied, running up into occasional
high and pointed hills, presenting frequent masses of rock and
wood, diversified by a mile or two, here and there, of soft pasture
and meadow ; with innumerable streams—some calm and peaceful,
some fierce and torrent-like, some sparkling and playful, giving an

air of life and glad activity to the scene through which they flow. These manifold streams shed also a hue of indescribable verdure, a fresh leafiness of aspect, that is most grateful to the eye; and though there is not there, as in our own land, the frequent hedge-row, with its sweet village associations, yet there is no want of high umbrageous trees scattered here and there, besides the thick woods which, in various places, occupy several leagues in extent, and the lesser copses that nest themselves in many a dell.

The district that we speak of is bright in its skies and warm in its sunshine, though it is not precisely in the region of the richest vine; and there are scarcely five days, during six months of the year, in which, on every stony bank or on the short soft turf above, the large lizards may not be seen basking in their coats of green and gold. There are not, indeed, the cloudless skies of Italy, which, notwithstanding their splendid colouring, are insipid from that very cloudlessness: no, but wreathed in grand masses by the free air, sometimes drifting from the British Channel, sometimes sweeping from the wide western ocean, the clouds and the sunshine sport together in the heaven, while shadow and light chase each other over the earth below, and ever and anon comes down a passing shower, refreshing the lands it lights upon, and leaving them brighter than before.

On the top of one of the tall rocky hills we have mentioned, in very remote feudal times,—for we find it mentioned in all the wars undertaken by the Edwards and the Henries in their vain endea-vours to grasp a crown that did not belong to them,—a town had been built and fortified, circumscribed by large stone walls flanked by round towers, and crowned by the square keep of a castle, only one wall of which has been left, for now near a century and a half. This town was of small size, occupying nothing but the summit of the hill, and was strictly confined within the walls; and, indeed, below, on three sides, were such steep ascents—in some places showing precipitous spaces of rude rock, and in others covered with short, green, slippery turf—that it was scarcely possible for the inhabitants to have built beyond the fortifications, except on one side, even if they had been so inclined.

In such times of danger, however, it had been the object of those who possessed the town to keep that fourth side, by which the ascent was more easy, clear from all houses and buildings of any kind, so that the arrows from the bow, the quarrels from the cross-bow, or the balls from the cannon—as different ages brought different inventions—might sweep down unimpeded upon any approaching enemy, and that the eye might also have a free range to discover the approach of a foe. Thus that gentler slope was not even broken by a road till the end of the sixteenth century, the way up to the town from the valley below being constructed with great skill and care upon one of the steepest sides of the hill, by means of wide short platforms, each of which was defended by some particular fortification of its own, while the whole line of the valley and the lower part of the road were commanded by the cannon of the castle of St. Anne, a rude old fortress on an inferior hill, of little or no use to any persons but those who possessed the higher and more important works above. Winding through the valley and round the foot of the hill of St. Anne was a wide, clear, beautiful stream, navigable up to that spot, which fell into the sea at the distance of ten or twelve miles in a direct line, but which contrived to extend its course, by the tortuous path that it pursued amongst the hills, to a length of nearly twenty leagues.

Such as we have described was the situation, in feudal times, of the small town that we shall call Morseiul; but ere the commencement of our tale those feudal times had passed away. Even during the wars of the League the town had remained in tranquillity and repose. It was remote from the general scene of strife; and although it had sent out many who aided, and not insignificantly, in upholding the throne of Henry IV., there was but one occasion on which the tide of war flowed near its walls, and then speedily retreated, and left it unassailed.

Under these circumstances, fortifications were soon neglected—precautions were no longer taken—the cannon for half a century remained upon the walls unused—rust and honeycomb began to gnaw into the heart of the iron—sheds were erected in the embrasures—houses succeeded—gardens were laid out in the round towers—the castle of St. Anne fell utterly into ruins—and some of the patriotic and compassionate inhabitants thought it a hard tax upon the sinews of the horses, who in those days carried from place to place the merchandise of the country, to be forced to climb the zigzag path of one of the more precipitous sides of the hill. Thus in the early part of the reign of Louis XIII. a petition was addressed by the inhabitants to their count, who still retained all his feudal rights and privileges, beseeching him to construct or permit the construction of a gate upon the southern side of the town, and a road down the easier descent.

The count, who was a good-humoured man, a nobleman of the school of Henry IV., and as fond of the people of the good town as they were of him, was quite willing to gratify them in any reasonable desire; but he was the more moved to do what they wished in the present instance, inasmuch as some ten or fifteen years before he had himself broken through the old rules and regulations established in the commune, and had not only built himself a château beyond the walls on that very side, but had laid out a space of two or three acres of ground in such a manner as to afford him shade when he wanted it, and sunshine when the shade was not agreeable.

Of the château we shall speak hereafter: but it is only here necessary to say, that in building this dwelling beyond the walls, the Count de Morseiul of that day had forgotten altogether the possibility of carrying a road down that side of the hill. He had constructed a way for himself into the town by enlarging an old postern in the walls, which he caused to open into his garden, and by this postern, whenever he sought to issue forth into the country beyond, he took his way into the town, traversed the square, and followed the old zigzag road down the steep side of the hill. The peasantry, indeed, had not failed to think of that which their lord had overlooked, and when they had a dozen or two of pigeons, or a pair of fowls, or a fat calf to present to the seigneur, they almost invariably brought it by the slope up the hill. A path had thus been worn from the valley below in the precise direction which was best fitted for the road, and whenever the good townsmen presented their petition to the count, it instantly struck him how very convenient such a road would be to himself as well as to them.

Now the count was neither a cunning nor an ungenerous man : and the moment he saw that the advantage to be derived would be to himself, he determined to open the gate, and make the road at his own expense without subjecting the commune or the peasantry to corvée or fine. He told the inhabitants so at once, and they, as they well might be, were grateful to him in consequence. He made the road, and a handsome one it was; and he threw down a part of the wall, and erected a splendid gate in its place. He gave no name, indeed, to either; but the people immediately and universally bestowed a name on both, and called them the Count's Gate, and the Count's Road, so that the act was perpetuated by the grateful memory of those whom it benefited.

As, following the example of the earth on which we live, everything upon its surface moves forward, or perhaps we may say appears to move forward, while very likely it is going but in a circle, the opening of the gate and the making of the road were speedily followed by another step, which was the building of houses by the road-side; so that at the period when our tale commences, the whole aspect, appearance, and construction of the town was altered. A long street, with gardens at the back of the houses, extended all the way down the gentle slope of the hill; the gate had been widened, the summit had been cleared of a great number of small houses, and a view was opened straight up into a fine gay-looking market square at the top, with the ruined wall of the old keep, raising its high head covered with ivy on the western side, and to the north the little church, with its tall, thin, slated spire rising high, not only above the buildings of the town itself, but the whole of the country round, and forming a remarkable object, which was seen for many leagues at sea.

We are in this account supposing the reader to be looking up the street, which was turned towards the south, and was consequently full of sunshine towards the middle of the day. It would, indeed, have been intolerably hot in the summer, had it not been that the blessed irregularity of the houses contrived to give some shade at every hour of the four and twenty. But from the bottom of that street almost up to the top were to be seen, upon the left hand, rising above the buildings in the street itself, the weathercocks, and round turrets, and pointed roofs and loopholes, and windows innumerable, which marked the château built by the count who had constructed the road; while here and there, too, were also perceived the tops of the tall limes and elms with which he had shaded his gardens, and which had now grown up into tall splendid trees, flourishing in the years which had brought him to decay and death.

Into the little town of Morseiul had been early introduced the doctrines of Calvin, and the inhabitants clung to those doctrines with peculiar pertinacity. They had constantly sent volunteers to the Protestant army; they had bestirred themselves in aid of La Rochelle, and had even despatched succour to the Protestants of the far south. The weak, bigoted, and treacherous Louis XIII. had declared that they were the most obstinate heretics in his dominions, and had threatened against them many things, which the wisdom of his great minister had prevented him from performing. But the counts of Morseiul themselves had at all times rendered great services to the state: they had proved themselves on all occasions gallant and determined soldiers and skilful politicians; and though they, too, held firm by the religion of their ancestors, and set equally at defiance both threats and seductions—which conduct formed the strongest link between them and their people—Richelieu had judged that it would be hazardous to drive them into open resistance to the crown. We may indeed surmise that he judged it unnecessary also, inasmuch as there can be no doubt that, in his dealings with the Huguenots, he treated them solely as a political party, and not as a religious sect.

Such being the case, though somewhat courting the persecutions of the times, the town of Morseiul had been left unmolested in the exercise of its religious tenets, and had enjoyed not only all the liberty which was granted to the Protestants of France by the edict of Nantes, but various other privileges, obtained perhaps by a little encroachment, and retained by right of prescription.

The inhabitants were a hardy and determined race, frank and good-humoured, and possessing from various points in their position a great degree of simplicity in manners and character, mingled with much religious fervour. They had, indeed, of late years, been somewhat polished, or perhaps one might call it, corrupted. They had acquired more wants and more wishes from the increasing luxuriousness of the day, had heard with wonder, and not perhaps without some longing, of the splendours and the marvels and the gaieties of the court of Louis XIV., then in the bright and butterfly days of its youthful ostentation; and feeling strongly and beneficially the general impulse given to every sort of commerce by the genius of Colbert, they applied themselves to derive the utmost

advantage therefrom, by pursuing with skill, activity, and perseverance, various manufactures, in which they displayed no small
ingenuity. A good number of them had become wealthy, and all
of them, indeed, were well off in the station of life in which they
were placed. The artisan was rich for an artisan, as well as the
burgess for a burgess; but they were all simple in their habits, not
without their little pride, or without their luxuries on a holiday;
but frugal and thoughtful as they were industrious. Such were the
town of Morseiul and its inhabitants in the year 168—.

We must now turn to the château of the count, and to its
denizens at the time of the opening of our tale. The château was
built, as we have said, on the outside of the walls of the town, and
was one of those odd buildings of which many a specimen has
come down to us. It seemed to have been constructed by detached
impulses, and upon no general plan, though, to admit nothing but
the truth, the edifice was attributable all to one person. The great
hall was a long, wide-spreading piece of architecture, with a high
roof, and a row of windows turned to the south side, which was the
front of the château. Then came two or three square masses of
stone-work on either side of the hall, with the gables projecting to
the front, no two of them of the same height and size; and many
of them separated either by a tall round tower, with loopholes all
the way up, like buttonholes in the front of a waistcoat, or broken
towards the roof by a turret stuck on and projecting from the rest
of the building. On the western side of the château was a large
square tower, with numerous windows, placed with some degree of
regularity; and on the eastern, was an octangular tower containing
a separate entrance of a somewhat Gothic character. Two large
wings projected behind towards the town, on which the château
unceremoniously turned its back; and the large open space of
ground thus enclosed, was again divided into two by a heavy
transverse mass of building, as irregular as the external parts of the
whole. The mansion was completed by the stables and offices for
the servants and retainers, and the whole was pitched in the centre
of a platform, which had in times past formed part of one of the
outworks of the fortification.

Behind the château, and between the building and the walls,
were numerous trees, giving that space the name of the bocage,
and through this lay the little walk that led to the postern, which
was originally the only exit from the château. In front was a
tolerably wide esplanade, extending to the edge of the outwork, and
from the terrace descended a flight of steps to the slope below, on
which had been laid out a flower-garden, separated from the rest of
the ground by a stone wall, surmounted by flower-pots in the shape
of vases. The remaining portion of the space enclosed was planted,
according to the taste of that day, with straight rows of trees, on
the beauties of which it is unnecessary to dwell.

The interior of the castle was fitted up in the taste of the reigns of

Henry IV. and Louis XIII., few changes having taken place since the time it was first furnished, immediately after it was built. Some of the rooms, indeed, contained the furniture of the older castle, formerly inhabited by the counts, which furniture was of a much more remote age, and had been condemned, by scornful posterity, to the dusty oblivion which we so fondly pile upon our ancestors. It may be as well, however, to conduct the reader into one of the rooms of that château, and, telling him that we have ourselves sat therein, furnished exactly as it was then furnished, and looking exactly as it then looked, endeavour to make him see it as the glass of memory now gives it back to us.

It was a large oblong room, with a vaulted roof: not dome-shaped, indeed, for it was flat at the top; but from the walls, towards the centre, it sloped for a considerable way before it received the flattened form which we mention. It was, indeed, a four-sided vault, with the top of the arches cut off. On two sides were windows, or perhaps we should call them easements, with the glass set in leaden frames, and opening only in part. ' The hearth and chimney were of enormous dimensions, with a seat on either side of the fireplace, which was a sort of raised platform of brick-work, ornamented with two large andirons grinning with lions' heads, for the reception of the fuel.

Over the chimney again was a wide slab of marble, supported by two marble scrolls; and a tablet, on which was recorded, with very tolerable Latinity, that that château had been built by Francis Count of Morseiul, in the year of grace one thousand five hundred and ninety. Above this marble, far blacker than the dark oak panel-ling which supported it, hung an immense ebony frame, carved with a thousand curious figures, and containing a large round mirror of polished metal, reflecting, though in a different size, all the objects that the room contained. On the two sides of the chamber were one or two fine portraits by Rubens and Vandyke, also in ebony frames, but cursed with an internal border of gold. A multitude of high-backed chairs, only fitted for men in armour, and ladies with whalebone bodices; four cabinets of ebony, chequered with small lines of inlaid ivory, with immense locks, marked out by heavy, but not inelegant, silver shields; and two or three round tables, much too small for the size of the room, made up the rest of the furniture of the apartment, if we except some fine specimens of porcelain, and one or two curiosities brought by different members of the family from foreign lands. There was also a lute upon one of the tables, and ten long glasses, with a vein of gold in their taper stalks, were ranged in battle array upon the mantelpiece.

The moment at which we shall begin our tale was about the hour of dinner in the province, at that period a very different hour from that at which we dine in the present day. The windows were all open, the bright sunshine was pouring in and throwing the small

square panes into lozenges upon the flooring; and from that room,
which was high up in the castle, might be seen as wide spread and
beautiful a landscape as ever the eye rested upon, a world of verdure,
streams, and woods; and hills, with the bright sky above.

Such was the chamber and such its aspect at the period we speak
of; and we must now turn to those who inhabited it, and, in the
first place, must depict them to the reader's eye, before we enter
into any remarks or detailed account of their several characters,
which, perhaps, we may be inclined to give in this instance, even
while we admit that in general it is far better to suffer our personages to develop themselves, and tell their own tale to the
reader.

In all, there were some seven persons in that room; but there
were only two upon whom we shall at present pause. They were
seated at a table in the midst, on which were spread forth various
viands in abundance, upon dishes of silver of a rich and handsome
form; while a profusion of the same metal in the shape of cups,
forks, spoons, and lavers, appeared upon another table near, which
had been converted into a temporary sort of buffet. Ranged on
the same buffet was also a multitude of green glass bottles, containing apparently, by their dusty aspect and well-worn corks, several
kinds of old and choice wine; and five servants in plain, but rich
liveries, according to the fashion of that day, bustled about to serve
the two superior persons at the table.

Those two persons were apparently very nearly of the same
age, about the same height; and in corporeal powers they seemed
also evenly matched; but in every other respect they were as different as can well be conceived. The one who sat at the side of the
table farthest from the door was a man of about six or seven and
twenty years of age, with a dark brown complexion, clear and
healthy though not florid, and with large, full, deep-coloured gray
eyes, fringed with long black lashes. His hair and mustaches were
jet black; and the character of his countenance, for the moment at
least, was serious and thoughtful. He was evidently a very powerful
and vigorous man, deep-chested, long in the arm; and though,
at the first look, his form seemed somewhat spare, yet every motion
displayed the swelling of strong muscles called into action; and few
there were in that day who could have stood unmoved a buffet
from his hand. Such was Albert Count of Morseiul, an officer so
distinguished during the first wars of Louis XIV., that it is only
necessary to name him to bring to the reader's recollection a long
train of splendid actions.

Opposite to him sat a friend and comrade, who had gone through
many a campaign with him, who had shared watchings, and dangers,
and toils—had stood side by side with him in the "imminent deadly
breach," and who was very much beloved by the Count, although the
other often contrived to tease and annoy that nobleman, and sometimes to give him pain, by a certain idle and careless levity which

had arisen amongst the young gentlemen of France some twenty
years before, and had not yet been put out by that great extin-
guisher, the courtly form and ceremony, which Louis XIV. placed
upon every movement of the imagination.

The friend was, as we have said, very different from his host.
Although not more than a year younger than the Count, he had a
less manly look, which might perhaps be owing to the difference of
colouring; for he was of that fair complexion which the pictures of
Vandyke have shown us can be combined with great vigour and
character of expression. His features were marked and fine, his
hazel eye piercing and quick, and his well-cut lip, varying indeed
with every changing feeling or momentary emotion, still gave, by
the peculiar bend into which it was fashioned when in repose, a
peculiar tone of scornful playfulness to every expression his countenance assumed. In form, he appeared at first sight more powerful, perhaps, than the Count; but a second glance was sufficient to
show that such was not the case; and, though there was indeed
little difference, if anything, it was not in his favour.

We must pause for an instant to notice the dress of the two
friends; not, indeed, to describe pourpoints or paint rich lace, but to
speak of their garments, as the taste thereof might be supposed to
betoken some points in the character of each. The dress of the
Count de Morseiul was in the taste of the times—which was certainly
as bad a taste, as far as it affected the habiliments of the male part
of the human race, as could be devised—but he had contrived, by
the exercise of his own judgment in the colouring, to deprive it of
a part of its frightfulness. The hues were all deep-toned, but rich
and harmonious; and though there was no want of fine lace, the
ribands, which were then the reigning mode of the day, were
reduced to as few in number as any Parisian tailor would consent
to place upon the garb of a high nobleman.

His friend, however, the Chevalier d'Evran, having opinions of
his own to which he adhered with a wilful pertinacity, did not
fully give in to the fashion of the times; and retained, as far as
possible, without making himself a spectacle, the costume of an
earlier period. If we may coin a word for the occasion, there was
a good deal of Vandykism still about it. All the colours, too, were
light and sunshiny; philomot and blue, and pink and gold; and
neither jewels nor rich lace were wanting where they could be
worn with taste; for though the liking was for splendour, and for a
shining and glittering appearance, yet in all the arrangements
there was still a fine taste visibly predominant.

Such, then, was the general appearance of the two friends; and
after partaking of the good things which both the table and the
buffet displayed,—for during the meal itself the conversation was
brief and limited to a few questions and answers,—the Chevalier
turned his chair somewhat more towards the window, and gazing out
over the prospect which was spread forth before his eyes, he said,—

"And so, Albert, this is Morseiul; and here thou art again, after an absence of five years!"

"Even so, Louis," replied the Count, "even so. This is Morseiul; and I know not whether it be from that inherent love of the place in which some of our happiest days have been spent, or whether the country round us be in reality more lovely than any other that I have seen since I left it, yet just when you spoke I was about to ask you whether you were or were not satisfied with my boasted Morseiul."

"It may well be lovelier than any you have seen since you left it," replied the Chevalier; "for, as far as I know aught of your history, and I think I could account for every day of your life since last you were here, you have seen nothing since but the flat prettiness of the Beauvoisis, the green spinach plate of the Cambresis, or the interminable flats of Flanders, where plains are varied by canals, and the only eminence to be seen for forty miles round one is the top of a windmill. Well may Morseiul be prettier than that, and no great compliment to Morseiul either; but I will tell you something more, Albert. I have seen Morseiul long ago. Ay, and sat in these halls, and drank of that wine, and looked out of that window, and thought then as I think now, that it is, indeed, as fair a land as ever I should wish to cast my eyes on."

"Indeed, Louis!" exclaimed his companion; "how happens it, then, if you know the place so well, that you have listened to all my praises thereof, and come hither with me purposely to see it, without giving me one hint that you knew of the existence of such a place upon the surface of the globe?"

"Why, it has happened from two causes," replied the Chevalier, "and perhaps from three. In the first place, did you never discover that I have the gift of secrecy in a very high degree?"

"Why, I have certainly discovered," replied the Count, with a smile, "that you are fond of a mystery; and sometimes, Louis, when there's no great need of one."

"Most cuttingly and ungenerously answered," replied the Chevalier, with a laugh; "but granting the fact, as a man does when he denies it strenuously in his mind all the time—but granting the fact, was not that one good and sufficient cause for my not saying a word about it? And in the next place, Albert, if I had told you I had been here, and knew it very nearly as well as you do yourself, it would have deprived you of the whole pleasure of relating the wonders and the marvels of Morseiul, which would have been most ungenerous of me, seeing and knowing the delight you took therein; and perhaps there might be another cause," he added, in a graver tone. "Perhaps I might hesitate to talk to you, Albert, —to you, with whom filial affection is not the evanescent thing that weeps like an April shower for half an hour over the loss of those we love, and then is wafted away in sparkling and in light— I might have hesitated, I say, to speak with you of times when one whom you have loved and lost sat in these halls and commanded in these lands."

"I thank you, Louis," replied the Count—"I thank you from my heart; but you might have spoken of him. My memory of my dead father is something different from such things in general. It is the memory of him, Louis, and not of my own loss; and, therefore, as every thought of him is pleasing, satisfying, ennobling to my heart—as I can call up every circumstance in which I have seen him placed, every word which I have heard him speak, every action which I have seen him perform with pride, and pleasure, and advantage, I love to let my thoughts rest upon the memories of his life; and though I can behold him no more living, yet I may thus enable myself to dwell with him in the past. We may be sure, Louis, that those who try to banish the loved and the departed from their thoughts and from their conversation, have more selfishness in their love, have more selfishness in their sorrow, than real affection or than real esteem. The pangs which draw tears from us over the tomb may be permitted to us as a weakness not unenviable. A lapse of sorrow for the broken tie and the loss of immediate communion is also but a just tribute to ourselves and to the gone. But those who really loved the dead, and justly loved them, will cherish memory for their sakes; while those whose love was weak, or not founded on esteem, or selfish, may well give up a time to hopeless sorrow, and then banish the painful memory from their mind for ever; but it shews either that there must have been something wrong in the affection of the past, or a want of hope in the eternal meeting of the future. No, no, Louis, I live with my dead father every hour; I call to mind his looks, his words, his gestures; and as I never think to meet a man who could speak one evil word of him, I never fear to hear him mentioned, and to dwell upon his name."

The Chevalier was silent for a moment, for the feelings of his companion were too hallowed for a jest; but he replied immediately after, "I believe you are quite right, Albert; but to banish all serious themes, which you know do not suit me, my love of mystery, which, as you well know, is a part of my nature, was quite sufficient to prevent my mentioning the subject. I wonder I was fool enough to let the whole secret out now. I should only have told you, by rights, just enough to excite your curiosity, in order that I might then disappoint you."

"As you have gone so far, however," replied the Count, with a smile, "you may as well tell the whole story at once, as it must be told sooner or later, I suppose."

"On my word, I do not know whether I can make up my mind to such unusual frankness," answered the Chevalier. "I have already done quite enough to lose my reputation. However, as you seem anxious——"

"Not in the least," answered the Count; "I am quite satisfied.

I was so before, and am so still, and shall be so if you resolutely maintain your mystery, concluding that you have some good reason for doing so."

" Oh no," answered the Chevalier, " I never had a good reason for anything I did in my life. I make a point of never having one; and the very insinuation of such a thing will make me unravel the whole matter at once, and show you that there is no mystery at all in the matter. You may have heard, perchance, that the Duc de Rouvré, who, by the way, is just appointed governor of the province, has a certain property with a certain château, called Ruffigny, which——"

" Which marches with my own," exclaimed the Count.

" Exactly what I was going to say," rejoined the Chevalier; " a certain property, called Ruffigny, which marches with your own, and a château thereupon some five leagues hence. Now, the excellent Duke, being an old friend, and distant relation, indeed, of my family, it is scarcely possible, with common decency, for me to be more than ten years at a time without visiting him; and accordingly, about ten years ago, I being then a sprightly youth, shortly about to fit on my first arms, came down and spent the space of about a month in that very château of Ruffigny, and the Duke brought me over here to dine with your father, and hunt the wild boar in the woods behind St. Anne."

" It is very odd," said the Count; " I have no recollection of it."

" How should you ?" demanded his friend, " as you were then gone upon your first campaign, under Duras, upon the Rhine. It was not, in all probability, worth your father's while to write you word that a young scapegrace had been brought to dine with him, and had run his *couteau de chasse* up to the hilt in the boar's gullet."

" Oh, I now remember," exclaimed the Count; " I heard of that, but I forgot the name. Have you not been here since then ?"

" Not I," replied the Chevalier. " The Duke asked me, indeed, to return the following year; but something prevented him from returning himself, and I believe he has never come back to Ruffigny since. A man who has so many castles as he has, cannot favour any one of them above once in six or seven years or so."

" He is coming down now, however," replied the Count; " for, of course, the affairs of his government must bring him here, if it be but to hold the states."

" Ay, but he does not come to Ruffigny," replied the Chevalier. " He goes to Poitiers. I know all about his movements; and I'll tell you what, Morseiul—take care how you go to visit him at Poitiers, for you might chance not to come back unscathed."

" How so ?" demanded the Count, turning sharply, as if with some surprise. " Is there anything new against us poor Huguenots?"

"Pool I spoke not of that," replied the Chevalier. "You sectarians seem to have a sort of hereditary feeling of martyrdom in you, as if your chief ancestor had been St. Bartholomew himself, and the saint, being skinned alive, had given the world a skinless posterity, which makes them all feel alarmed lest any one should touch them."

"It is an ominous name, St. Bartholomew, you must acknowledge, to the ears of a Huguenot," replied the Count. "But what is it I have to fear, if not that, Louis?"

"What is it you have to fear!" rejoined the Chevalier — "why, a pair of the brightest eyes in all France—I believe I might say in all Europe."

The Count shook his head, with a smile.

"Well, then," continued the Chevalier, "a pair of lips that look like twin roses; eyebrows that give a meaning to every lustrous look of the eyes; a hand small, white, and delicate, with fingers tapering and rounded like those with which the Venus of the Greeks gathers around her timid form the unwilling drapery; a foot such as no sandal-shod goddess of the golden age could match; and a form which would have left the sculptor nothing to seek in other beauties but herself."

The Count laughed aloud. "I am quite safe," he said, "quite safe, Louis, quite safe. I have nothing on earth to fear."

"Indeed!" exclaimed his companion, in the same gay tone. "Pray, what panoply of proof do you possess sufficient to resist such arms as these when brought against you?"

"Mine is twofold," answered the Count. "In the first place, your own enthusiasm cannot be misunderstood, and of course I do not become the rival of my friend. Our great hero, Condé, has set all soldiers a better example."

"What, then, do you intend to follow his example in regard to the Chatillon?" demanded the Chevalier; "to yield me the lady, and as soon as I am comfortably killed off, make love to my widow? But no, no, Albert, I stand not in your way; there are other attractions for me, I tell you fairly! Even if it were not so, let every man in love, as in war, do the best for himself. But, at all events, I warn you, take care of yourself if you go to Poitiers, unless, indeed, you have some better armour than the thought of rivalry with me."

"I must go to Poitiers, of course," replied the Count, "when the Governor comes down; but yet I shall go without fear, as I think you might by this time know. Have you not seen me amongst the fairest, and the gayest, and the sweetest of this world's daughters, and yet I do not think in all the catalogue you could find one cabalistic name sufficiently powerful to conjure up a sigh from my lips."

"Why, to say the truth," replied the Chevalier, "I have often thought you as cold as a cannon-ball before it is fired; but then, my dear Count, all that time you have had something else to do, something to excite, to interest, and to engross you. But now the stir and bustle of the camp is over,—the march, the counter-march, the advance, the retreat is done,—the fierce excitement of the battle-field does not bring forth all the energies of a fiery heart,— the trumpet no longer calls you from the ear of the fair one, before the whispered tale of love be well begun. In this piping time of peace, why, man, you have nothing for it but to make love, or die of melancholy. If you have a charm, let us hear what it is!"

"Oh, I am no man of mysteries," replied the Count, "and my tale is very soon told. It is just five years ago—I was at that time in the heyday of all sorts of passions, in love, I believe, with everything in woman's form that came in my way,—when, after spending the winter in Paris, I came down here to take leave of my father before joining the army in Flanders. It seemed as if he felt that we were parting for the last time, for he gave me many a caution, and many a warning regarding the woman that I might choose for my wife. He exacted no promise, indeed, nor gave his counsels the shape of a command; but, amongst other injunctions, which I would most unwillingly violate, he strongly advised me never to wed any one of a different religious creed from myself. About the same time, however, a little incident occurred, which fancy worked up so strongly as to have had an effect upon my whole after-feelings. You know the deep and bowery lanes and roads about the place, how beautifully the sunshine streams amongst them, how richly the song of the birds sounds in the trees above, how full of a sparkling and fanciful light is the whole scenery round us when we dive into its depths. I was always fond of wandering through these lanes, and one day about that time I was out alone, at some distance beyond the castle of St. Anne, when suddenly, as I was musing, and gazing, and drinking in, as it were, the sights and sounds around me, I heard the cry of dogs, and the blast of horns. But they were distant, and they passed away, and I went on wandering slowly, with my horse's bridle hanging loosely over my arm, till suddenly I heard the sound of galloping hoofs; and, immediately after, down the little road in which I was, came a gay wild horse of the Limousin, with a fair girl upon its back, who should hardly have been trusted to ride a fiery creature like that. She was not, indeed, a mere child, being apparently some sixteen or seventeen years of age, but extreme youth was in every feature and in every line, and, I might add, beauty also, for never in my life did I behold such vision-like loveliness as hers. The horse, with some sudden fright, must have darted away while she had laid down the rein, for at the time I met her, though not broken, it was hanging at his feet, hazarding at every instant to throw him down. She sat firmly in the seat, and rode with grace and ease; but she was evidently much frightened, and as soon as she saw some one before her in the lane, she pointed with an eager gesture to the rein, and uttered some words which I did not hear. I easily divined her meaning, however, and turning my own horse loose, knowing I could catch him again in a moment, I snatched at the rein of her horse as he passed, ran for a moment by its side, not to check it too sharply, then brought it to a halt, and asked her if she would alight. She bowed her head gracefully, and smiled most sweetly, replying, as soon as she could find breath, with many thanks for the service I had rendered her, that she was not hurt, and but a little frightened, the horse having started away when she had laid down the rein to put on her gloves. She would not alight, she said, but must return quickly to her friends, who would be frightened; and, without saying more, she again gracefully bent her head, turned her horse, and cantered rapidly away. I saw her once afterwards, riding along with a gay cortège, composed of persons whom I did not know. As we passed each other she recognised me instantly, and, with a heightened colour, noticed me by another marked inclination of the head. When I had gone on, I could judge by her own gestures and those of the persons around her, that she was telling them what had occurred, and explaining to them the sign of recognition which she had made. On this second occasion she seemed to my eyes even more lovely than before. Her voice, too, though I had heard it so little, was the most musical that ever spoke to the heart of man, and I pondered and thought over the vision of loveliness that I had just seen, till it took so strong a hold of my heart and my imagination, that I could not rest satisfied without seeking to behold it again. I rode through all the country round; I was every day, and almost all day, on horseback; I called at every neighbouring house; I inquired at every place where I was likely to meet with information, but I could never see, or speak with, or hear of that fair creature again; and the time came rapidly on when I was compelled to rejoin the army. I thought of her often, however—I have thought of her ever since; that lovely face, that sweet voice will never go from my mind, and reason and fancy combine to make me resolve never to wed any one that I do not think as lovely as herself."

"Pray, what share had reason," demanded the Chevalier, "in a business altogether so unreasonable? Poo! my dear Albert, you have worked yourself into a boyish fancy of love, and then have clung to it, I suppose, as the last bit of boyhood left about you. What had reason to do with your seeing a pretty girl in a dark lane, and fancying there was nothing like her upon earth?"

"With that, nothing certainly," replied the Count, "but with my after-determination much. Long before that time, I had began to school myself a good deal on account of a propensity, not so much to fall in love, but, as you term it, Louis, to make love to every fair creature I met with. I had found it needful to put some check upon myself; and if an artificial one was to be chosen, I did not see why this should not be selected as well as any other. I determined that, as the knights of old, and our own troubadours too, if you will, and even—as by your laughing I suppose you would have it—excellent Don Quixote himself, that pattern of all true gentlemen, vowed and dedicated themselves to some fair lady, whom they had seen even less frequently than I had her—I determined, I say, that I would encourage this fancy of loving my fair horsewoman, and would employ the image of beauty, which imagination, perhaps, had its share in framing, and the fine qualities of the mind and heart, which were shadowed out beneath that lovely exterior, as a test, a touchstone, whereby to try and to correct my feelings towards others, and to approach none with words of love who did not appear to me as beautiful in form as she was, and who did not seem at least equal to the standard which fancy had raised up under her image.   The matter perhaps was carried farther than I intended, the feeling became more intense than I had expected. For some time I sincerely and truly fancied myself in love; but even since reason has come to my aid in such a matter, and I know how much imagination has to do with the whole, yet from that one circumstance, from that fanciful accident, my standard of perfection in woman has been raised so high, that I find none who have attained it; and yet so habitual has it become with me to apply it to every one I see, that whenever I am introduced to any beautiful creature, to whom I might otherwise become attached, the fanciful image rises up, and the new acquaintance is tried, and ever is found wanting."

"Thou art a strange composition, my good friend the Count," said the Chevalier, "but we shall see, now that peace and tranquillity have fallen over the world, whether you can go on still resisting with the courage of a martyr. I don't believe a word of it, although, to say sooth, your quality of heretic is something in your favour. But, in the name of fortune, tell me what are all those loud and tumultuous sounds which are borne by the wind through the open window. Your good people of Morseiul are not in rebellion, I hope."

"Not that I know of," replied the Count, with a smile at the very idea of such a thing as rebellion under Louis XIV.; "but I will call my fellow Riquet, who ought, I think, to have been called Scapin; for I am sure Molière must have had a presentiment of the approaching birth of such a scoundrel. He will tell us all about it; for if a thing takes place on the other side of the earth, Riquet knows it all within five minutes after it happens."

Before he had well finished speaking, the person he alluded to entered. But Riquet deserves a pause for separate notice.

CHAPTER II.

THE VALET—THE TOWNSPEOPLE—THE PROCLAMATION.

THE personage who entered the room, which on that, the first actual day after his arrival at his own dwelling, the Count de Morseiul had used as a dining-room, was the representative of a race now extinct, combining in his own person all the faults and absurdities with all the talents and even virtues which were sometimes mingled together in that strange composition, the old French valet. It is a creature that we find recorded in the pages of many an antique play, now either banished altogether from the stage, or very seldom acted; but, alas! the being itself is no more to be met with; and even were we to find a fossil specimen in some unexplored bed of blue clay, we should gain but a very inadequate idea of all its various properties and movements. We have still the roguish valet in sad abundance—a sort of common house-rat; and we have, moreover, the sly and the silent, the loquacious and the lying, the pilfering and the impudent valet, with a thousand other varieties; but the old French valet, that mithridatic compound of many curious essences, is no longer upon the earth, having gone absolutely out of date and being, at the same period with his famous contemporary " *le Marquis.*"

At the time we speak of, however, the French valet was in full perfection; and, as we have said, an epitome of the whole race and class was to be found in Maitre Jerome Riquet, who now entered the room, and advanced with an operatic step towards his lord. He was a man perhaps of forty years of age, which, as experience and constant practice were absolute requisites in his profession, was a great advantage to him, for he had lost not one particle of the activity of youth, seeming to possess either a power of ubiquity, or a rapidity of locomotion which rendered applicable to him the famous description of the bird which flew so fast " as to be in two places at once." Quicksilver, or a lover's hours of happiness, a swallow, or the wind, were as nothing when compared to his rapidity; and it is also to be remarked, that the rapidity of the mind went hand in hand with the rapidity of the body, enabling him to comprehend his master's orders before they were spoken, to answer a question before it was asked, and to determine with unerring sagacity by a single glance whether it would be most for his interests or his purposes to understand or misunderstand the coming words before they were pronounced.

Riquet was slightly made, though by no means fulfilling the immortal caricature of the Gates of Calais; but when dressed in his own appropriate costume, he contrived to make himself look more meagre than he really was, perhaps with a view of rendering his person less recognisable when, dressed in a suit of his master's

c

clothes with sundry additions and ornaments of his own device, he appeared enlarged with false calves to his legs, and manifold paddings on his breast and shoulders, enacting with great success the part of the Marquis of Kerousac, or of any other place which he chose to raise into the dignity of a marquisate for his own especial use.

His features, it is true, were so peculiar in their cast and expression, that it would have seemed at first sight utterly impossible for the face of Jerome Riquet to be taken for any other thing upon the earth than the face of Jerome Riquet. The figure thereof was long, and the jaws of the form called lantern, with high cheek bones, and a forehead so covered with protuberances, that it seemed made on purpose for the demonstration of phrenology. Along this forehead, in almost a straight line drawn from a point immediately between the eyes, at a very acute angle towards the zenith, were a pair of eyebrows, strongly marked throughout their whole course, but decorated by an obtrusive tuft near the nose, from which tuft now stuck out several long grey bristles. The eyes themselves were sharp, small, and brilliant; but being under the especial protection of the superincumbent eyebrows, they followed the same line, leaving a long lean cheek on either side, only relieved by a congregation of radiating wrinkles at the corners of the eyelids. The mouth was as wide as any man could well desire for the ordinary purposes of life, and it was low down too in the face, leaving plenty of room for the nose above, which was as peculiar in its construction as any that ever was brought from " the promontory of noses." It was neither the Judaical hook nose, nor the pure aquiline, nor the semi-judaical Italian, nor the vulture, nor the sheep, nor the horse nose. It had no affinity whatever to the " nez retroussé," nor was it of the bottle, nor the ace of clubs form. It was a nose *sui generis*, and starting from between the two bushy eyebrows, it made its way out with a slight parabolic curve downwards, till it had reached about the distance of an inch and a half from the fundamental base line of the face. Having attained that elevation, it came to a sharp abrupt point, through the thin skin of which the white gristle seemed inclined to force its way, and then suddenly dropping a perpendicular, it joined itself on to the lower part of the face, at a right angle with the upper lip, with the extensive territories of which it did not interfere in the slightest degree, being as it were a thing apart, while the nostrils started up again, running in the same line as the eyes and eyebrows.

Such in personal appearance was Jerome Riquet, and his mental conformation was not at all less singular. Of this mental conformation, we shall have to give some illustrations hereafter; but yet, to deal fairly by him, we must afford some sketch of his inner man, in juxtaposition with his corporeal qualities. In the first place, without the reality of being a coward, he affected cowardice as a very convenient reputation, which might be serviceable on many occasions, and could be shaken off whenever he thought fit.

" A brave man," he said, " has something to keep up, he must never be cowardly; but a poltroon can be a brave man, without derogating from a well-earned reputation, whenever he pleases. No, no, I like variety; I'll be a coward for all the ordinary purposes of life, and a brave man only when it suits me." He sometimes, indeed, nearly betrayed himself, by burlesquing fear, especially when any raw soldier was near; for he had an invincible inclination to amuse himself with the weaknesses of others, and knew how contagious a disease fear is.

The next remarkable trait in his character was a mixture of honesty and roguery, which left him many doubts in his own mind as to whether he was by nature a knave or a simpleton. He would pilfer from his master anything he could lay his hands upon, if he thought his master did not really want it; but had that master fallen into difficulties or dangers, he would have given him his last louis, or laid down his life to save him. He would pick the locks of a cabinet to see what it contained,· and ingeniously turn the best folded letter inside out to read the contents; but no power on earth would ever have made him divulge to others that which he practised such unjustifiable means to learn.

He was also a most determined liar, both by habit and inclination. He preferred it, he said, to truth. It evinced greater powers of the human mind. Telling truth, he said, only required the use of one's tongue and one's memory; but to lie, and to lie well, demanded imagination, judgment, courage, and, in short, all the higher qualities of the human intellect. He could sometimes, however, tell the truth, when he saw that it was absolutely necessary. All that he had was a disposition to falsehood, controllable under particular circumstances, but always returning when those circumstances were removed.

As to the religion of Maitre Jerome Riquet, the less that is said upon the matter the better for the honour of that individual. He had but one sense of religion, indeed, and his definition of religion will give that sense its clearest exposition. In explaining his views one day on the subject to a fellow valet, he was known to declare, that religion consisted in expressing those opinions concerning what was within a man's body, and what was to become of it after death, which were most likely to be beneficial to that body in the circumstances in which it was placed. Now, to say the truth, in order to act in accordance with this definition, Maître Jerome had a difficult part to perform. His parents and relations were all Catholics, and having been introduced at an early age into the house of a Huguenot nobleman, and attached for many years to the person of his son, with only one other Catholic in the household, it would seem to have been the natural course of policy for the valet, under his liberal view of things, to abandon Catholicism, and betake himself to the pleasant heresy of his masters. But Riquet had a more extensive conception of things than that. He

saw and knew that Catholicism was the great predominant religion of the country; he knew that it was the predominant religion
of the court also; and he had a sort of instinctive foresight, from
the beginning, of the persecutions and severities — the dark clouds
of which were now gathering fast around the Huguenots, and were
likely sooner or later to overwhelm them.

Now, like the famous Erasmus, Jerome Riquet had no will to be
made a martyr; and though he could live very comfortably in a
Huguenot family, and attach himself to its lords, he did not think
it at all necessary to attach himself to its religion also, but, on the
contrary, went to mass when he had nothing else to do, confessed
what sins he thought fit to acknowledge or invent, once every four
or five years, swore that he performed all the penances assigned to
him, and tormented the Protestant maid-servants of the château,
by vowing that they were all destined to eternal condemnation,
that there was not a nook in purgatory hot enough to bake away
their sins, and that a place was reserved for them in the bottomless
pit itself, with Arians and Socinians, and all the heretics and here-
siarchs from the beginning of the world. After having given way
to one of these tirades, he would generally burst into a loud fit of
laughter at the absurdity of all religious contentions, and run away,
leaving his fellow-servants with a full conviction that he had no
religion at all.

He dared not, it is true, indulge in such licences towards his
master; but he very well knew that the young Count was not a
bigot himself, and would not by any means think that he served
him better if he changed his religion. In times of persecution and
danger, indeed, the Count might have imagined that there was a
risk of a very zealous Catholic being induced to injure or betray
his Protestant lord; but the Count well knew Jerome to be anything but a zealous Catholic, and he had not the slightest fear that
any hatred of Protestantism, or love for the church of Rome would
ever induce the worthy valet to do anything against the lord to
whom he had attached himself.

Such, then, was Jerome Riquet; and we shall pause no longer
upon his other characteristic qualities than to say, that he was the
exemplification of the word clever; that there was scarcely anything to which he could not turn his hand; and that though light,
and lying, and pilfering, and impudent beyond all impudence, he
was capable of strong attachments and warm affections; and if we
may use a very colloquial expression to characterize his proceedings, there was fully as much fun as malice in his roguery. A love
of adventure and of jest was his predominant passion; and although
all the good things and consolations of this life by no means came
amiss to him, yet in the illegitimate means which he took to
acquire them he found a greater pleasure even than in their enjoyment when obtained.

When the door opened, as we have said, and Riquet presented

himself, the eyes of the Count de Morseiul fixed upon him at once; and he immediately gathered, from the ludicrous expression of fear which the valet had contrived to throw into his face, that something of a serious nature had really happened in the town, though he doubted not that it was by no means sufficient to cause the astonishment and terror which Jerome affected. Before he could ask any questions, however, Jerome, advancing with the step of a ballet master, cast himself on one knee at the Count's feet, exclaiming—

"My lord, I come to you for protection and for safety."

"Why, what is the matter, Jerome?" exclaimed the Count. "What rogue's trick have you been playing now? Is it a cudgel or the gallows that you fear?"

"Neither, my good lord," replied Jerome, "but it is the fagot and the stake. I fear the rage of your excited and insubordinate people in the town of Morseiul, who are now in a state of heretical insurrection, tearing down the king's proclamations, trampling his edicts under foot, and insulting his officers; and as I happen, I believe, to be the only Catholic in the place, I run the risk of being one of the first to be sacrificed, if their insane vehemence leads them into further acts of frenzy."

"Get up, fool, get up!" cried the Count, shaking him off as he clung to his knee; "tell me, if you can speak truth and common sense, what is it you mean, and what has occasioned all those shouts that we heard just now?"

"I mean, my lord," said Riquet, starting up, and putting himself in an attitude, "I mean all that I say. There is some proclamation," he continued, in a more natural tone, "concerning the performance of the true Catholic and apostolic religion, which some of the king's officers posted up on the gate at the bottom of the Count's street, and which the people instantly tore down. The huissier and the rest were proceeding up the street to read the edict in the great square, amidst the shouts and imprecations of the vulgar; but I saw them gathering together stones, and bringing out cudgels, which showed me that harder arguments were about to be used than words; and as there is no knowing where such matters may end, I made haste to take care of my own poor innocent skin, and lay myself at your feet, humbly craving your protection."

"Then, get out of my way," said the Count, putting him on one side, and moving towards the door. "Louis, we must go and see after this. This is some new attack upon us poor Huguenots—some other Jesuitical infraction of the privileges assured to us by our good King Henry IV. We must quiet the people, however, and see what the offence is;—though, God help us," he added, with a sigh, "since the parliaments have succumbed, there is no legal means left us of obtaining redress. Some day or another these bad advisers of our noble and magnificent monarch will drive the

Protestant part of his people into madness, or compel them to raise
the standard of revolt against him, or to fly to other lands, and
seek the exercise of their religion unoppressed."

"Hush, hush, hush, Morseiul," said his companion, laying his
hand kindly on his arm, "your words are hasty. You do not
know how small a matter constitutes treason now-a-days, or how
easy is the passage to the Bastille."

"Oh! I know—I know quite well," replied the Count; "and
that many a faithful and loyal subject, who has served his king and
country well, has found his way there before me. I love and
admire my king. I will serve him with my whole soul and the
last drop of my blood; and all I claim in return is that liberty of
my own free thoughts which no man can take from me. Chains
cannot bind that down; bastilles cannot shut it in; and every
attempt to crush it, is but an effort of tyranny both impotent and
cruel. However, we must calm the people. Where is my hat,
knave?"

"I have often wished, my dear Morseiul," said the Chevalier,
as they followed the valet, who ran on to get the Count's hat—"I
have often wished that you would give yourself a little time to
think and to examine. I am very sure that if you did, you would
follow the example of the greatest man of modern times, abjure
your religious errors, and gain the high station and renown which
you so well deserve."

"What, do you mean Turenne?" exclaimed the Count. "Never,
Louis, never! I grant him, Louis, to have been one of the greatest
men of this, or perhaps of any other age, mighty as a warrior, just,
clear-sighted, kind-hearted, and comprehensive as a politician, and
perhaps as great in the noble and honest simplicity of his nature as
in any other point of view. I grant him all and everything that
you could say in his favour. I grant everything that his most
enthusiastic admirers can assert; but *God forbid that we should ever
imitate the weakness of a great man's life.* No, no, Chevalier, it is
one of the most perverted uses of example, to justify wrong because
the good have been tempted to commit it. No man's example, no
man's opinion to me is worth anything, however good or however
wise he may be, if there be stamped upon its face the broad and
unequivocal marks of evil."

By this time they had reached the vestibule, from which a little
flight of steps conducted into the garden, and Maitre Jerome stood
there with his lord's hat and polished cane in his hand. The
Count took them with a quick gesture and passed on, followed
by his friend, who raised his eyebrows a little with a look of
regret as his only answer to the last words. These words had
been heard by the valet also, and the raising of the eyebrows
was not unmarked; and Maitre Jerome, understanding the whole
train of the argument as well as if he had heard every syllable,
commented upon what he considered his lord's imbecility by

a shrug of the shoulders, in which his head almost utterly disappeared.

In the meantime, the young Count and his friend passed up the little avenue to the postern gate, opened it, and entered the town of Morseiul. Then, by a short and narrow street, which was at that moment all in shadow, they entered the market square, at which they arrived, by the shorter path they pursued, long before the officers who were about to read the proclamation. A great number of persons were collected in the square, and it was evident that by this time the whole place was in a state of great excitement. The Chevalier was in some fear for the effect of the coming scene upon his friend; and, as they entered the place, he stopped him, laying his hand upon his arm, and saying—

"Morseiul, you are a good deal heated, pause for one moment and think of what you are about. For the sake of yourself and of your country, if not for mine, neither say nor do anything rashly."

The Count turned towards him with a calm and gentle smile, and grasped his hand.

"Thank you, Louis," he said, "thank you, though your caution, believe me, is unnecessary. You will see that I act as calmly and as reasonably, that I speak as quietly and as peacefully as the most earnest Catholic could desire. Heaven forbid," he added, "that I should say one word, or make one allusion to anything that could farther excite the passions of the people than they are likely to be excited already. Civil strife, Louis, is the most awful of all things so long as it lasts, and seldom, very seldom, if ever, obtains the end for which it first commenced. But even if I did not think so," he added, in a lower voice, " I know that the Protestants of France have no power to struggle with the force of the crown, unless—" and his voice fell almost to a whisper—" unless the crown force upon them the energetic vigour of despair."

The two had paused during this short conversation; and while they heard the murmuring sounds of the people coming up the hill from the right hand, the noise of several persons running could be distinguished on the other side. Turning round towards the postern, the Count saw that, thanks to the care and foresight of Maitre Jerome, a great number of his domestics and attendants were coming at full speed to join him, so that when he again advanced he was accompanied by ten or twelve persons ready to obey without hesitation or difficulty the slightest command that he should give. As there was no telling the turn which events might take, he was not sorry that it should be so; and when he again advanced towards the centre of the square the sight of his liveries instantly attracted the attention of the people, and he was recognised with joyful exclamations of " The Count! The Count!"

Gladness was in every face at his approach, for the minds of the populace were in that state of anxious hesitation, in which the

presence and direction of any one to whom they are accustomed
to look up, is an absolute blessing. Taking off his hat and bowing repeatedly to every one around him, speaking to many, and
noticing all with whom he was personally acquainted with a frank
and good-humoured smile, the Count advanced through the people,
who gathered upon his path as he proceeded, till he reached the
top of the hill, and obtained a clear view of what was passing below.

Had not one known the painful and angry feelings which were
then excited, it would have been a pleasant and a cheerful scene.
The sun had by this time got sufficiently round to the westward to
throw long shadows from the irregular gable-ended houses more
than half way across the wide open road which conducted from the
valley to the top of the hill. The perspective, too, was strongly
marked by the lines of the buildings ; the other side of the road was
in bright light ; there was a beautiful prospect of hill and dale seen
out beyond the town ; numerous booths and stalls, kept by peasant
women with bright dresses and snowy caps, chequered the whole
extent ; and up the centre of the street, approaching slowly, were
the officers of the district, with a small party of military, followed
on either side by a much more considerable number of the lower
order of town's people and peasantry.

Such was the scene upon which the eyes of the Count de Morseiul fell ; and it must be admitted, that when he saw the military,
his heart beat with some feelings of indignation, for we must remember that, in towns like that which was under his rule, the old
feudal customs still existed to a very great extent. It was still called
his town of Morseiul. The king, indeed, ruled ; the laws of the
land were administered in the king's name ; but the custody, defence, and government of the town of Morseiul were absolutely in
the hands of the Count, or of the persons to whom he delegated his
power during his absence. It was regularly, in fact, garrisoned in
his name ; and there were many instances, scarcely twenty years
before, in which the garrisons of such towns had resisted in arms
the royal authority ; and if not held to be fully justified, at all
events had passed without punishment, because they were acting
under the orders of him in whose name they were levied. The
attempt, therefore, of any body of the king's troops to penetrate
into the Count's town of Morseiul, without his having been formally
deprived of the command thereof, seemed to him one of the most
outrageous violations of his privileges which it was possible to imagine ; and his heart consequently beat, as we have said, with feelings of high indignation. He suppressed them, however, with the
calm determination of doing what was right ; and turned to gaze
upon the people who surrounded him, in order to ascertain, as far
as possible, by what feelings they were affected.

His own attendants had congregated immediately behind him ;
on his right hand stood his friend the Chevalier ; on his left, about
half a step behind, so as to be near the Count, but not to appear

obtrusive, was a personage of considerable importance in the little town of Morseiul, though he exercised a handicraft employment, and worked daily with his own arm, even while he directed others. This was Paul Virlay, the principal blacksmith of the place. He was at this time a man of about fifty years of age, tall, and herculean in all his proportions. The small head, the broad muscular chest and shoulders, the brawny arms, the immense thick hands, the thin flanks, and the stout legs and thighs, all bespoke extraordinary strength. He was very dark in complexion, with short-cut curly black hair, grizzled with grey; and the features of his face, though short, and by no means handsome, had a good and a frank expression, though it might be somewhat stern.

At the present moment his brow was more contracted than usual; but there was not any other mark of very strongly excited passions upon his countenance; and the attitude he had assumed was one of calm and reposing strength, resting—with his right hand supported by one of the common quarter-staffs of the country, a full inch and a half thick—much in the same position which he frequently assumed when, in the pauses of his toil, he talked with his workmen, leaving the sledge hammer, that usually descended with such awful strength, to support the hand which wielded it at other times like a feather.

Behind him again, was a great multitude of the town's people of different classes, though the mayor and the municipal officers had thought fit to absent themselves carefully from the scene of probable strife. But the eyes of the Count fell, as we have said, upon Paul Virlay; and knowing him to be a man both highly respected in his own class, and of considerable wealth and importance in the city, he addressed him in the first instance, saying,—

"Good morrow, Virlay; it is long since I have seen you all. What is all this about?"

"You don't forget us, Count Albert, even when you are away," replied the blacksmith, with his brow unbending. "We know that very well, and have proofs of it, too, when anything good is to be done; but this seems to me to be a bad business. We hear that the king has suppressed 'the chamber of the edict,' which was our greatest safeguard; and now my boy tells me, for I sent him down to see when they first came to the bottom of the hill, that this is a proclamation forbidding us from holding synods; and be you sure, sir, that the time is not far distant when they will try to stop us altogether from worshipping God in our own way. What think you, my lord?" he said, in a lower tone—"were it not better to show them at once that they cannot go on?" and his looks spoke much more than even his words.

"No, Virlay," replied the Count; "no, by no means. You see the people are in tumult below, evidently. Any ill-advised and illegal resistance to the royal authority will immediately call upon us harsh measures, and be made the pretext by the bad advisers who surround the king for irritating his royal mind against us. Let us hear what the proclamation really is. Even should it be harsh and unjust, which from the king's merciful nature we will hope is not the case, let us listen to it calmly and peaceably, and after having considered well, and taken the advice and opinion of wise and experienced men, let us then make what representations to the king we may think fit, and petition him in his clemency to do us right."

" Clemency!" said the blacksmith. " However, my lord, you know better than I; but I hope they will not say anything to make our blood boil, that's all."

" Even if they should," replied the Count, " we must prevent it from boiling over. Virlay, I rely upon you, as one of the most sensible men in the place, not only to restrain yourself, but to aid me in restraining others. The king has every right to send his own officers to make his will known to his people."

" But the dragoons," said Virlay, fixing his eyes upon the soldiers; " what business have they here? Why, they might, Count Albert——"

The Count stopped him.

" They are yet without the real bounds of the town, Virlay," he said; " and they do not enter into it! Send some one you can trust for the mayor with all speed; unhook the gates from the bars that keep them back; place a couple of men behind each. I will prevent the military from entering into the town; but I trust to you, and the other men of good sense who surround me, to guard the king's officers and the king's authority from any insult, and to suffer the proclamation of his will to take place in the market-place without any opposition or tumult whatsoever."

" I will do my best, Count," replied the blacksmith, " for I am sure you are a true friend to us—and we may well trust in you."

The crowd from below had in the meantime advanced steadily up the hill, surrounding the officers of the crown and the soldiery; and by this time the whole mass was within a hundred and fifty yards of the spot where the Count and his companions stood. Their progress had been without violence, indeed, but not without hootings and outcry, which seemed greatly to annoy the officer in command of the soldiers, he having been accustomed alone to the court of the grand monarch, and to the scenes in the neighbourhood of the capital, where the people might well be said to lick the dust beneath the feet of their pageant-loving king. It seemed, then, something so strange and monstrous to his ears, that any expression of the royal will should be received otherwise than with the most deep and devoted submission, that he was more than once tempted to turn and charge the multitude. A prudent consideration, however, of the numbers by which he was surrounded, and the scantiness of his own band, overcame all such purposes; and, though furious with indignation, he continued to advance, without noticing the shouts that assailed him, but playing with the manifold ribands and pieces of silk that decorated his buff coat and his sword-knot, to conceal his vexation and annoyance.

"Who have we here at the head of them?" demanded the Count, turning to the Chevalier. "His face is not unknown to me."

"As far as I can see," replied his companion, "it is young Hericourt, a nephew of Le Tellier's—do you not remember? as brave as a lion, but moreover a young coxcomb, who thinks that he can do everything, and that nothing can be done without him —as stupid as an owl, too. I wonder you do not recollect his getting great credit for taking the little fort of the *Bec de l' Oie* by a sheer act of stupidity,—getting himself and his party entangled between the two forts, and while Lamets was advancing to extricate him, forcing his way in, from not knowing what else to do."

"I remember, I remember," said the Count, with a smile; "he was well rewarded for his fortunate mistake. But what does he here, I wonder? I thought he never quitted the precincts of Versailles, but to follow the king to the camp."

"He is the worst person who could have been sent upon this errand," replied the Chevalier; "for he is certain to make mischief wherever he goes. He has attached himself much to the Rouvrés, however, of late, and I suppose Le Tellier has given him some post about the new governor, in order that his rule may not be the most tranquil in the world."

While they were speaking, the eyes of the people who were coming up the hill fell upon the group which had assembled just in front of the gates, with the Count, his friend, and his servants, in the foreground; and immediately a loud shout made itself heard, of "The Count! the Count! Long live the Count!" followed by various other exclamations, such as "He will protect us! He will see justice done us! Long live our own good Count!"

The moment that the Count's name was thus loudly pronounced, the young officer, turning to those who followed, gave some orders in a low voice, and then, spurring on his horse through the crowd, rode directly up to the Count de Morseiul, who, as he saw him approaching, turned to the Chevalier, saying, "You bear witness, Louis, that I deal with this matter as moderately and loyally as may be."

"I trust, for the sake of all," said the Chevalier, "that you will. You know, Albert, that I do not care two straws for one religion more than the other; and think that a man can serve God singing the psalms of Clement Marot as well, or perhaps better, than it he sang them in Latin, without, perhaps, understanding them. But for Heaven's sake keep peace in the inside of the country, at all events. But here comes our bold dragoon."

As he spoke, the young officer rode up, with a good deal of irritation evident in his countenance. He seemed to be three or four and twenty years of age, of a complexion extremely fair, and with a countenance sufficiently unmeaning, though all the features were good. He bowed familiarly to the Chevalier, and more distantly to the Count de Morseiul; but addressed himself at once to the latter:—

"I have the honour," he said, "I presume, of speaking to the Count de Morseiul, and I must say that I hope he will give me his aid in causing proclamation of the king's will amongst these mutinous and rebellious people of his town of Morseiul."

"My friend the Chevalier here tells me," replied the Count, "that I have the honour of seeing Monsieur de Hericourt——"

"The Marquis Auguste de Hericourt," interrupted the young officer.

"Well, sir, well," said the Count, somewhat impatiently, "I stand corrected: the Marquis Auguste de Hericourt; and I am very happy to have the honour of seeing him, and also to inform him that I will myself ensure that the king's will is, as he says, proclaimed in my town of Morseiul by the proper officers, taking care to accompany them into the town myself for that purpose, although I cannot but defend my poor townsmen from the accusation of being mutinous and rebellious subjects, nothing being further from the thoughts of any one here present than mutiny or rebellion."

"Do you not hear the cries and shouts?" cried the young officer. "Do you not see the threatening aspect of the people?"

"I hear some shouts, certainly," answered the Count, "as if something had given offence or displeasure; but what it is I do not know. I trust and hope that it is nothing in any proclamation of the king's; and if I should find it to be so, when I hear the proclamation read, I shall take every means to put an end to such demonstrations of disappointment or grief at once. We have always the means of approaching the royal ear, and I feel sure that there will be no occasion for clamour or outcry in order to obtain justice at the hands of our most gracious and wise monarch.—But allow me to observe, Monsieur le Marquis," he continued, somewhat more quickly, "your dragoons are approaching rather too near the gates of Morseiul."

"You do not intend, I presume, sir," said the young officer, sharply, "to refuse an entrance to the officers of the king, charged with a proclamation from his majesty!"

"Not to the king's proper civil officers," replied the Count, keeping his eye, while he spoke, warily fixed upon the dragoons. "But, most assuredly, I do intend to refuse admittance to any body of military whatsoever, great or small, while I retain the post with which his majesty has entrusted me as governor of this place."

There was a pause for a single instant, and the young officer turned his head, without replying, towards the soldiers, on whom the Count's eye also was still fixed. There was something, however, suspicious in their movements. They had now reached the brow of the hill, and were within twenty yards of the gate. They formed into a double file as they came up in front of the civil officers, and the head man of each file was seen passing a word to those behind him. At the moment their officer turned his head towards them, they began to move forward in quicker time, and in a moment more would have passed the gates; but at that instant the clear full voice of the Count de Morseiul was heard exclaiming, in a tone that rose above all the rest of the sounds—

"Close the gates!" and the two ponderous masses of wood, which had not been shut for many years, swung forward, grating on their hinges, and at once barred all entrance into the town.

"What is the meaning of this, Monsieur de Hericourt?" continued the Count. "Your men deserve a severe reprimand, sir, for attempting to enter the town without my permission or your orders."

The young man turned very red, but he was not ready with a reply; and the Chevalier, willing as far as possible to prevent any unpleasant consequences, and yet not to lose a jest, exclaimed—

"I suppose the Marquis took it for the Bec de l'Oie, but he is mistaken, you see."

"He might have found it a trap for a goose, if not a goose's bill," said a loud voice from behind; but the Marquis either did not or would not hear anything but the pleasant part of the allusion, and, bowing to the Chevalier with a smile, he said, "Oh, you are too good, Monsieur le Chevalier. The affair you mention was but a trifle, far more owing to the courage of my men than to any skill on my part. But, in the present instance, I must say, Count," he added, turning towards the other, "that the king's officers must be admitted to make proclamations in the town of Morseiul."

"The king's civil officers shall, sir," replied the Count, "as I informed you before: but no soldiers, on any pretence whatsoever. However, sir," he continued, seeing the young officer mustering up a superabundant degree of energy, "I think it will be much the best plan for you to do me the honour of reposing yourself, with any two or three of your attendants you may think fit, at my poor château here, without the walls, while your troopers can refresh themselves at the little auberge at the foot of the hill. My friend, the Chevalier here, will do the honours of my house till I return, and I will accompany the officers charged with the proclamation, and see that they meet with no obstruction in the fulfilment of their duty."

"I do not know that I am justified," said the young officer, hesitating, "in not insisting upon seeing the proclamation made myself."

"I am afraid there will be no use of insisting," replied the Count; "and depend upon it, sir, you will serve the king better by suffering the proclamation to be made quietly, than even risking a disturbance by protracting, unnecessarily, an irritating discussion.

I wish to treat you with all respect, and with the distinction due to your high merit. Farther, I have nothing to say, but that I am governor of Morseiul, and as such undertake to see the king's proclamation duly made within the walls."

The hesitation of the young dragoon was only increased by the cool and determined tone of the Count. Murmurs were rising amongst the people around, and the voice of Paul Virlay was heard muttering—

" He had better decide quickly, or we shall not be able to keep the good men quiet."

The Marquis heard the words, and instantly began to bristle up, to fix himself more firmly in the saddle, and put his hand towards the hilt of his sword; but the Chevalier advanced close to his side, and spoke to him for a moment or two in a low voice. Nothing was heard of their conversation, even by the Count de Morseiul, but the words "good wine—pleasant evening—laugh over the whole affair."

At length the young courtier bowed his head to the Count, saying, " Well, then, sir, I repose the trust in you, knowing you to be a man of such high honour, that you would not undertake what you could not perform, nor fail to execute punctually that which you had undertaken. I will do myself the honour of waiting your return with the Chevalier, at your château."

After some further words of civility on both parts, the young officer dismounted and threw his rein to a page, and then formally placing the civil officers under the care and protection of the Count de Morseiul, he gave orders to his dragoons to bend their steps down the hill, and refresh themselves at the auberge below; while he, bowing again to the Count, took his way with the Chevalier and a single attendant along the esplanade which led to the gates of the château without the walls. The civil officers, who had certainly been somewhat maltreated as they came up the hill, seemed not a little unwilling to see the dragoons depart, and a loud shout of mingled triumph and seorn, with which the people treated the soldiers as they turned to march down the hill, certainly did not at all tend to comfort or reassure the poor huissiers, greffiers, and other officers. The shout caused the young marquis, who had proceeded twenty or thirty steps upon his way, to stop short, and turn round, imagining that some new collision had taken place between the town's-people and the rest; but seeing that all was quiet, he walked on again the moment after, and the Count, causing the civil officers to be surrounded by his own attendants, ordered the wicket to be opened, and led the way in, calling to Virlay to accompany him, and urging upon him the necessity of preserving peace and order, let the nature of the proclamation be what it might.

" I have given you my promise, Count," replied the blacksmith, " to do my best, and I wont fail; but I wont answer for myself or others on any other occasion."

" We are only speaking of the present," replied the Count; "for other occasions other measures, as the case may be: but at present everything requires us to submit without any opposition.—Where can this cowardly mayor be," he said, "that he does not choose to show himself in a matter like this? But the proclamation must be made without him, if he do not appear."

They had by this time advanced into the midst of the great square, and the Count signified to the officer charged with the proclamation, that it had better be made at once: but for some moments what he suggested could not be accomplished, from the pressure of the people, the crowd amounting by this time to many hundred persons. The Count, his attendants, and Virlay, however, contrived, with some difficulty, to clear a little space around, the first by entreaties and expostulations, and the blacksmith by sundry thrusts of his strong quarterstaff and menaces, with an arm which few of those there present seemed inclined to encounter.

The Count then took off his hat, and the officer began to read the proclamation, which was long and wordy; but which, like many another act of the crown then taking place from day to day, had a direct tendency to deprive the Protestants of France of the privileges which had been secured to them by Henry IV. Amongst other galling and unjust decrees here announced to the people was one which—after stating that many persons of the religion affecting the title of *reformed*, being ill-disposed towards the king's government, were selling their landed property with the view of emigrating to other lands—went on to declare and to give warning to all purchasers, that if heretical persons effecting such sales did quit the country within one year after having sold their property, the whole would be considered as confiscated to the state, and that the purchasers would receive no indemnity.

When this part of the proclamation was read, the eyes of the sturdy blacksmith turned upon the Count, who, by a gesture of the hand, endeavoured to suppress all signs of disapprobation amongst the multitude. It was in vain, however; for a loud shout of indignation burst forth from them, which was followed by another, when the proclamation went on to declare, that the mayors of towns, professing the Protestant faith, should be deprived of the rank of nobles, which had been formerly granted to them. The proclamation then proceeded with various other notices of the same kind, and the indignation of the people was loud and unrestrained. The presence of the Count, however, and the exertions of Virlay, and several influential people, who were opposed to a rash collison with the authority of the king, prevented any act of violence from being committed, and when the whole ceremony was complete, the officers were led back to the gates by the Count, who gave orders that they should be conducted in safety beyond the precincts of the place by his own attendants.

After again visiting the great square, and holding a momentary conversation with some of the principal persons present, he returned by the postern to his own abode, where he found his friend and the young officer, apparently forgetting altogether the unpleasant events of the morning, and laughing and talking gaily over indifferent subjects.

"I have the pleasure of informing you, Monsieur de Hericourt," said the Count when he appeared, "that the proclamation has been made without interruption, and that the king's officers have been conducted out of the town in safety. We have therefore nothing more of an unpleasant kind to discuss, and I trust that you will take some refreshment."

Wine, and various sorts of meats, which were considered as delicacies in those days, were brought and set before the young courtier, who did justice to all, declaring that he had never in his life tasted anything more exquisite than the produce of the Count's cellars. He even ventured to praise the dishes, though he insinuated, much to the indignation of the cook, to whom it was repeated by an attendant, that there was a shade too much of taragon in one of the ragouts, and that if a matelotte had been five minutes more cooked, the fish would have been tenderer, and the flavour more decided. The Count smiled, and apologized for the error, reminding him, that the poor rustics in the country could not boast the skill and delicacy, or even perhaps the nicety of natural taste of the artists of the capital. He then turned the conversation to matters of some greater importance, and inquired when they were to expect the presence of the Duc de Rouvré in the province.

The young Marquis opened his eyes at the question, as if he looked upon it as a sign of the most utter and perfect ignorance and rusticity that could be conceived.

"Is it possible, Monsieur le Comte," he said, "that you, so high in the service of the king, and so highly esteemed, as I may add, at court, are not aware that the duke arrived at Poitiers nearly five days ago? I had the honour of accompanying him thither, and he has himself been within the last three days as near as seven leagues to the very place where we are now sitting."

"You must remember, my good sir," replied the Count, "as some excuse for my ignorance, that I received his majesty's gracious permission to return hither upon some important affairs direct from the army, without visiting the court, and that I only arrived late last night. Pray, when you return to Monsieur de Rouvré, present my compliments to him, and tell him that I shall do myself the honour of waiting upon him, to congratulate him and the duchess upon their safe arrival in the province, without any delay."

"Wait till they are fully established at Poitiers," replied the young officer. "They are now upon a little tour through the province, not choosing to stay at Poitiers yet," he added, sinking his voice into a low and confidential tone, "because their household is not in complete order. None of the new liveries are made; the guard of the governor is not yet organized; two cooks and three servers have not arrived from Paris. Nothing is in order, in short. In a week, I trust, we shall be more complete, and then indeed I do not think that the household of any governor in the kingdom will exceed in taste, if not in splendour, that of the Duc de Rouvré."

"Which is, I presume," said the Chevalier, "under the direction and superintendence of the refined and celebrated good taste of the Marquis Auguste de Hericourt?"

"Why, to say the truth," replied the young nobleman, "my excellent friend De Rouvré has some confidence in my judgment of such things: I may say, indeed, has implicit faith therein, as he has given all that department over to me for the time, beseeching me to undertake it, and of course I cannot disappoint him."

"Of course not! of course not!" replied the Chevalier; and in such conversation passed on some time, the worthy Marquis de Hericourt, swallowed up in himself, not at all perceiving a certain degree of impatience in the Count de Morseiul, which might have afforded any other man a hint to take his departure. He lingered over his wine; he lingered over his dessert; he perambulated the gardens; he criticised the various arrangements of the château, with that minute attention to nothings which is the most insufferable of all things when obtruded upon a mind bent upon matters of deep importance.

It was thus fully five o'clock in the afternoon before he took his departure; but the Count forced himself to perform every act of civility by him to the last moment. As soon as he was gone, however, the young nobleman turned quickly to his friend, saying—

"I thought that contemptible piece of emptiness would never depart, and of course, Louis, after what has taken place this morning, it is absolutely necessary for me to consult with some of my friends of the same creed as myself. I will not in any degree involve you in these matters, as the very fact of your knowing any of our proceedings might hereafter be detrimental to you; and I only make this excuse because I owe it to the long friendship between us not to withhold any part of my confidence from you, except out of cousideration for yourself."

"Act as you think fit, my dear Albert," replied his friend; "but only act with moderation. If you want my advice on any occasion, ask it, without minding whether you compromise me or not. I am quite sure that I am much too bad a Catholic to sacrifice my friend's secrets, either to Pellisson, La Chaise, or Le Tellier. If I am not mistaken, the devil himself will make the fourth at their card-table some day, and perhaps Louvois will stand by and bet."

"Oh! I entertain no fear of your betraying me," answered the Count, with a smile; "but I should entertain great fear of embroiling you with the court."

"Only take care not to embroil yourself," replied the Chevalier. "I wish there were no such thing as sects in the world. If you could but take a glance at the state of England, which is split into more sects than it contains cities, I am sure you would be of Turenne's opinion, and come into the bosom of the mother church, if it were but for the sake of getting rid of such confusion. Nay, shake not your wise head. If the truth be told, you are a Protestant because you were bred so in your youth; and one half of the world has no other motive either for its religion or its politics. But get thee gone, Albert—get thee gone. Consult with your wise friends, and come back more Huguenotized than ever."

The Count would have made some further apologies for leaving him; but his friend would not hear them, and sending for his horse, Albert of Morseiul took his departure from his château, forbidding any of his attendants to follow him.

CHAPTER III.

THE PASTOR.

THE Count's orders were given so distinctly for no one to aecompany him on his way, that none of his domestics presumed even to gaze after him from the gate, or to mark the path he took. As he wished to call no attention, he kept under the walls of the town, riding slowly along over the green till he came to the zigzag path which we have before mentioned as being now almost entirely disused. He had cast a large cloak around him, of that kind which, at an after period, degenerated into what was called a roquelaure, and his person was thus sufficiently concealed to prevent him from being recognised by anybody at a distance.

At the foot of the zigzag which he now descended, he chose a path which led along the bank of the river for some way to the right, and then entered into a beautiful wooded lane between high banks. The sun was shining full over the world, but with a tempered and gentle light, from the point of declination at which it had arrived. The rays, however, did not in general reach the road, except where the bank sloped away; and then pouring through the green leaves and branches of the wild brier, the honeysuckle, and the hazel, it streamed upon the miniature cliffs of yellow sand on the opposite side, and chequered the uneven path which the young Count was pursuing. The birds had as yet lost little of their full song, and the deep round tones of the blackbird bidding the golden day adieu as he saw the great light-bearer descending in the heaven, poured forth from beneath the holly bushes, with a melancholy and a moralizing sound, speaking to the heart of man with the grand philosophic voice of nature, and counselling peace and affection, and meditation on the bounties of God.

It is impossible to ride through such scenes at such an hour on the evening of bright summer days, without feeling the calm and elevating influence of all things, whether mute or tuneful, taught by Almighty beneficence to celebrate, either by aspect or by song, the close of another day's being and enjoyment. The effect upon the heart of the Count de Morseiul was full and deep. He had been riding slowly before, but after passing through the lane for about a minute, he gently drew in the bridle upon his horse till the beast went slower still, then laid the rein quietly upon his neck, and gave himself up to meditation.

The chief theme in his mind at that moment was certainly the state and prospects of himself and his fellow Protestants; and per- haps—even in experiencing all the beauty and the peacefulness of the scene through which he wandered, the calm tone of enjoyment in everything around, the voice of tranquillity that spoke in every sound—his feelings towards those who unnecessarily disturbed the contented existence of an industrious and happy race, might become bitterer, and his indignation grow more deep and stern, though more melancholy and tranquil. What had the Huguenots done, he asked himself, for persecution to seek them out there in the midst of their calm and pleasant dwellings—to fill them with fiery pas- sions that they knew not of before—to drive them to acts which they as well as their enemies might bitterly repent at an after period,—and to mar scenes, which seemed destined for the purest and happiest enjoyment that the nature of man and its harmony with the other works of God can produce, by anxiety, care, strife, and perhaps with bloodshed?

What had the Huguenots done? he asked himself. Had they not served their king as loyally, as valiantly, as readily in the battle field, and upon the wide ocean, as the most zealous Catholic amongst them all? Had not the most splendid victories which his arms had obtained by land been won for him by Huguenot generals? Was not even then a Huguenot seaman carrying the thunders of his navy into the ports of Spain? Were the Huguenots less loyal subjects, less industrious mechanics, less estimable as citizens, than any other of the natives of the land? Far from it. The contrary was known to be the fact—the decided contrary. They were more peaceable, they were more tranquil, they were more industrious, they were more ready to contribute either their blood or their treasure to the service of the state than the great mass of the Catholic population; and yet tormenting exactions, insults, cavillings, inquiries, and investigations, all tending to irri- tate and to enrage, were going on day by day, and were clearly to be followed soon by the persecuting sword itself.

On such themes he paused and thought as he went on, and the first effect produced upon his mind was of course painful and gloomy. As the sweetest music sounding at the same time with inharmonious notes can but produce harsh dissonance, so the brightest scenes to a mind filled with painful thoughts seem but to deepen their sadness.

Still, however, after a time, the objects around him, and their bright tranquillity, had their effect upon the heart of the Count. His feelings grew calmer, and the magic power of association came to lay out a road whereby fancy might lead his thoughts to gentler themes. The path that he was pursuing led him at length to the spot where the little adventure had occurred which he had related in the course of the morning to his friend. He never passed by that spot without giving a thought to the fair girl he had there met; but now he dwelt upon the recollection longer than he other- wise might have done, in consequence of having spoken of her and of their meeting, that very day. He smiled as he thought of the whole, for there was nothing like pain of any kind mingled with the remembrance. It was merely a fanciful dream he had che- rished, half amused at himself for the little romance he had got up in his own mind, half employing the romance itself as a check upon the very imagination that had framed it.

"She was certainly very lovely," he thought, as he rode on, " and her voice was certainly very sweet; and unless nature, as is but too often the case, had, in her instance, become accomplice to a falsehood, that form, that face, that voice, must have betokened a bright spirit and a noble heart. Alas! why is it," he went on to ask himself—"why is it that the countenance, if we read it aright, should not be the correct interpreter of the heart? Doubtless, such was at first God's will, and it was the serpent taught us, though we could not conceal our hearts from the Almighty, to falsify the stamp he had fixed upon them, for our fellow-men. And yet it is strange—however much we may have gained from experience, however painfully we may learn that man's heart is written in his actions, not in his face—it is strange, we ever judge more or less by that same deceitful countenance, and guess by its expressions, if not by its features, though we might as well judge of what is at the bottom of a deep stream by the waves that agitate its surface."

In such fanciful dreams he went on, often turning again to the fair vision which he had there seen, sometimes wondering who she could have been, and sometimes deciding, and deciding the ques- tion wrongly, in his own mind, but never suffering the wild expec- tation which he had once nourished of meeting her again to cross his mind—for he had found that to indulge it rendered him uneasy, and unfit for more real pursuits.

At length, the lane winding out upon some hills where the short dry turf betokened a rocky soil below, took its way through a country of a less pleasing aspect. Here the Count de Morseiul put his horse into a quicker pace, and after descending into another low valley full of streams and long luxuriant grass, he climbed slowly a high hill, surmounted by a towering spire. The village

to which the spire belonged was very small, and consisted entirely
of the low houses of an agricultural population. They were neat,
clean, and cheerful, however, in aspect, and there was an attention
to niceness of exterior visible everywhere, not very frequently
found amongst the lower classes of any country.

There was scarcely any one in the street, as the Count passed,
except, indeed, a few children enjoying their evening sport, and
taking the day's last hour of happy life, before the setting sun
brought the temporary extinction of their bright activity. There
was also at the end of the town a good old dame sitting at a cottage
door, and spinning in the tempered sunshine of the evening, while
her grey cat rolled happy in the dust beside her; but the rest of
the villagers were still in the fields.

The Count rode on, giving the dame " good even" as he passed;
and, leaving what seemed the last house of the village behind him,
he took his way along a road shadowed by tall walnut trees growing upon the edge of a hill, which towered up in high and broken
banks on the left, and sloped away upon the right, displaying the
whole tract of country through which the young nobleman had
just passed, bright in the evening light below, with his own town
and castle rising upon a fellow hill to that on which he now stood,
at the distance of some seven or eight miles.

As he turned one sharp angle of the road, he suddenly drew in
his rein on seeing a carriage before him. It was stationary, however, and the two boorish-looking servants, dressed in grey, who
accompanied it, were standing at the edge of the hill, gazing over
the country, as if the scene were new to them; while the horses,
which the coachman had left to their own discretion, were stamp-
ing in a state of listless dozing, to keep off the flies which the
season rendered troublesome.

It was evident that the carriage was held in waiting for some
one, and the Count, after pausing for a single instant, rode on,
looking in as he passed it. There was no one, however, within
the wide and clumsy vehicle, and the servants, though they stared
at the young stranger, took no notice, and made no sign of reverence as he went by them; with which, indeed, he was well satisfied, not desiring to be recognised by any one who might noise his
proceedings abroad.

He rode on, then, with somewhat of a quicker pace, to a spot
where, at the side of the road, a little wicket gate led into a small
grove of old trees, through which a path conducted to a neat stone-
built house, of small size, with its garden around it—flowers on the
one hand, and potherbs on the other. Nothing could present an
aspect cleaner, neater, or more tasteful than the house and the garden.
Not a straw was out of its place in the thatch, and every flower-bed
of the little parterre was trimmed exactly with the same scrupulous
care. The door was of wood, painted grey, with a rope and handle
by the side, to which was attached a large bell; but, though at

almost all times that door stood open, it was closed on the present occasion. The young Count took his way through the grove and the garden straight to the door, as if familiar with the path of old, leaving his horse, however, under the trees, not far from the outer gate. On finding the door closed, he pulled the handle of the bell, though somewhat gently; but, for a moment or two, no one replied, and he rang again, on which second summons a maid servant, of some forty or fifty years, appeared, bearing on her head a towering structure of white linen, in the shape of a cap, not unlike in shape and snowy whiteness the covered peak of some mountain ridge in the Alps.

On her appearance, she uttered an exclamation of pleasure at the sight of the young Count, whom she instantly recognised; and, on his asking for her master, she replied, that he was busy in conference with two ladies, but that she was sure that the Conut de Morseiul might go in at any time. She pointed onward with her hand, as she spoke, down the clean, nicely sanded passage, to the door of a small room at the back of the house, looking over the prospect which we have mentioned. It was evidently the good woman's intention that the Count should go in and announce himself; but he did not choose to do so, and sent her forward to ask if he might be admitted. A full clear round voice instantly answered from within, on her application, " Certainly, certainly," and, taking that as his warrant, the Count advanced into the room at once. He found it tenanted by three people, on only one of whom, however, we shall pause, as the other two, consisting of a lady, dressed in a sort of half mourning, with a thick veil which she had drawn over her face before the Count entered, and another who was apparently a female servant of a superior class, instantly quitted the room, the lady merely saying—

" I will not forget."

The third was a man of sixty-two or sixty-three years of age, dressed in black, without sword or any ornament to his plain straight-cut clothes. His head was bare, though a small black velvet cap lay on the table beside him, and his white hair, which was suffered to grow very long at the back and on the temples, fell down his neck, and met the plain white collar of his shirt, which was turned back upon his shoulders. The top of his head was bald, rising up from a fine wide forehead, with all those characteristic marks of expansion and elevation which we are generally inclined to associate in our own minds with the idea of powerful intellect and noble feelings. The countenance, too, was remarkable, the features straight, clear, and well-defined, though the eyes, which had been originally finely formed and large, were somewhat hollowed by age, and the cheeks, sunken also, left the bones beneath the eyes rather too prominent. The chin was rounded and well shaped, and the teeth white and undecayed; but, in other respects, the marks of age were very visible. There were lines and furrows about the brow and on the cheeks; and, between the eyebrows, there was a deep dent, which might give, in some degree, an air of sternness, but seemed still more the effect of intense thought, and perhaps of anxious care.

The form of the old man bore evident traces of the powerful and vigorous mould in which it had been originally cast; the shoulders were broad, the chest deep, the arms long and sinewy, the hands large and muscular. The complexion had been originally brown, and perhaps at one time florid; but now it was pale, without a trace of colour anywhere but in the lips, which for a man of that age were remarkably full and red. The eye itself, the light of the soul, was still bright and sparkling. It gave no evidence of decay, varying frequently in expression from keen and eager rapidity of thought, and from the rapid changes of feeling in a heart still full of strong emotions.

Sueh—though the picture is but a faint one—such was the appearance of Claude de l'Estang, Huguenot minister of the small village of Auron, at equal distances from Ruffigny and Morseiul. He had played, in his youth, a conspicuous part in defence of the Huguenot cause; he had been a soldier as well as a preacher, and the sword and musket had been familiar to his hands, so long as the religion of his fathers was assailed by open persecution. No sooner, however, did those times seem to have passed away, than, casting from him the weapons of carnal warfare, he resumed the exercise of the profession to which he had been originally destined, and became, for the time, one of the most popular preachers in the south of France.

Though his life was irreproachable, his manners pure, and his talents high, Claude de l'Estang had not been without his portion of the faults and failings of humanity. He had been ambitious in his particular manner; he had been vain; he had loved the admiration and applause of the multitude; he had coveted the fame of eloquence, and the reputation of superior sanctity; youth, and youth's eagerness, joined with the energy inseparable from high genius, had carried his natural errors to an extreme: but long before the period of which we now speak, years, and still more sorrows, had worked a great and beneficial, but painful alteration. His first disappointment was the disappointment of the brightest hope of youth, complicated with all that could aggravate the crossing of early love; for there was joined unto it the blasting of all bright confidence in woman's sincerity, and the destruction of that trust in the eternal happiness of one whom he could never cease to love, which was more painful to the mind of a sincere and enthusiastic follower of his own particular creed than the loss of all his other hopes together. He had loved early, and loved above his station; and encouraged by hope, and by the smiles of one who fancied that she loved in return, his ambition had been stimulated by passion, till all the great energies of his mind were called forth to raise himself

to the highest celebrity. When he had attained all, however, when
he saw multitudes flock to hear his voice, and thousands hanging
upon the words of his lips as upon oracles, even then, at the moment when he thought everything must yield to him, he had seen
an unexpected degree of coldness come upon her he loved, and
apparent reluctance to fulfil the promises which had been given
when his estate was lowlier. Some slight opposition on the part
of noble and wealthy parents—opposition that would have yielded
to entreaties less than urgent, was assigned as the cause of the hesitation which wrung his heart. The very duties which he himself had
inculcated, and which, had there been real love at heart, would have
found a very different interpretation, were now urged in opposition to his wishes; and, mortified and pained, Claude de l'Estang
watched anxiously for the ultimate result. We need not pause
upon all the steps; the end was, that he saw her, to whom he had
devoted every affection of a warm and energetic heart, break her
engagements to him, wed an enemy of her father's creed, renounce
the religion in which she had been brought up, and after some
years of ephemeral glitter in a corrupt court, become faithless to
the husband for whom she had become faithless to her religion, and
end her days, in bitterness, in a convent, where her faith was suspected, and her real sins daily reproved.

In the meanwhile, Claude de l'Estang had wrestled with his
own nature. He had refrained from showing mortification, or
grief, or despair; he had kept the serpent within his own bosom, and
fed him upon his own heart: he had abandoned not his pulpit; he
had neglected, in no degree, his flock; he had publicly held up as
a warning to others the dereliction of her whom he most loved, as
one who had gone out from amongst them because she was not of
them; he had become sterner, indeed more severe, in his doctrines
as well as in his manners, and this first sorrow had a tendency
rather to harden than to soften his heart.

The next thing, however, which he had to undergo, was the
punishment of that harshness. A youth of a gentle but eager disposition, who had been his own loved companion and friend, whom
he still esteemed highly for a thousand good and engaging qualities, was betrayed into an error, on the circumstances of which we
will not pause. Suffice it to say, that it proceeded from strong
passion and circumstances of temptation, and that for it he was
eager and willing to make atonement. He was one of the congregation of Claude de l'Estang, however; and the minister showed
himself the more determined, on account of the friendship that
existed between them, not to suffer the fault to pass without the
humiliation of public penitence; and he exacted all, to the utmost
tittle, that a harsh church, in its extremest laws, could demand, ere
it received a sinner back into its bosom again. The young man
submitted, feeling deep repentance, and believing his own powers
of endurance to be greater than they were. But the effect was

awful. From the church door, when he had performed the act demanded of him, fancying that the finger of scorn would be pointed at him for ever, he fled to his own home, with reason cast headlong from her throne. Ere two hours were over, he had died by his own hand; scrawling with his blood, as it flowed from him, a brief epistle to his former friend, to tell him that the act was his.

That awful day, and those few lines, not only filled the bosom of the minister with remorse and grief, but opened his eyes to every-thing that had been dark in his own bosom. They showed him that he had made a vanity of dealing with his friend more severely than he would have done with others; that it was for his own reputa-tion's sake that he had thus acted; that there was pride in the severe austerity of his life; that there was something like hypocrisy in the calm exterior with which he had covered over a broken heart. He felt that he had mighty enemies to combat in himself; and, as his heart was originally pure and upright, his energies great, and his power over himself immense, he determined that he would at once commence the war, and never end it till—to use his own words—"he had subdued every strong hold of the evil spirit in his breast, and expelled the enemy of his eternal Master for ever."

He succeeded in his undertaking: his very first act was to resign to others the cure of his congregation in Rochelle; the next, to apply for and obtain the cure of the little Protestant congregation, in the remote village of Auron. Every argument was brought for-ward to induce him to stay in La Rochelle, but every argument proved inefficacious. The vanity of popularity he fancied might be a snare to him, and he refused all entreaties. When he came amongst the good villagers, he altered the whole tone and cha-racter of his preaching. It became simple, calm, unadorned, suited in every respect to the capacity of the lowest person that heard him. All the fire of his eloquence was confined to urging upon his hearers their duties, in the tone of one whose whole soul and expectations were staked upon their salvation. He be-came mild and gentle, too, though firm when it was needful; and the reputation which he had formerly coveted still followed him when he sought to cast it off. No synod of the Protestant clergy took place without the opinion of Claude de l'Estang being cited almost without appeal; and whenever advice, or consolation, or support was wanting, men would travel for miles to seek it at the humble dwelling of the village pastor.

His celebrity, joined with his mildness, gained great immunities for himself and his flock, during the early part of the reign of Louis XIV. At first, indeed, when he took upon himself the charge of Auron, the Catholic authorities of the neighbouring towns, holding in remembrance his former character, imagined that he had come there to make proselytes, and prepared to wage the strife with vehemence against him. The intendant of the province was urged to visit the little village of Auron, to cause the spire of the church—which had been suffered to remain, as all the inhabitants of the neighbouring district were Protestants — to be pulled down, and the building reduced to the shape and dimensions to which the temples of the Protestants were generally restricted: but ere the pastor had been many months there, his conduct was so different from what had been expected; he kept himself so completely aloof from everything like cabal or intrigue; he showed so little disposition to encroach upon the rights, or to assail the religion of others; that, knowing his talents and his energies when roused into action, the neighbouring Catholies embraced the opinion, that it would be better to leave him undisturbed.

The intendant of the province was a wise and a moderate man, and although, when urged, he could not neglect to visit the little town of Auron, yet he did so after as much delay as possible, and with the determination of dealing as mildly with its pastor, and its population, as was possible. When he came, he found the minister so mild, so humble, so unlike what he had been represented, that his good intentions were strengthened. He was obliged to say, that he must have the spire of the church taken down, although it was shown that there was not one Catholic family to be offended by the sight within seven or eight miles around. But Claude de l'Estang only smiled at the proposal, saying, that he could preach quite as well if it were away; and the intendant, though he declared that it was absolutely necessary to be done, by some accident always forgot to give orders to that effect; and even at a later period discovered that the spire, both from its own height and from the height of the hill on which it stood, sometimes acted as a landmark to ships at sea.

Thus the spire remained; and here, in calm tranquillity, Claude de l'Estang had, at the time we speak of, passed more than thirty years of his life. A small private fortune of his own enabled him to exercise any benevolent feelings to which his situation might give rise: simple in habits, he required little for himself; active and energetic in mind, he never wanted time to attend to the spiritual and temporal wants of his flock with the most minute attention. Though ever grave and sad himself, he was ever well pleased to see the peasantry happy and amused; and he felt practically every day, in comparing Auron with Rochelle, how much better is love than popularity. No magistrate, no judge, had any occupation in the town of Auron, for the veneration in which he was held was a law to the place. Any disputes that occurred amongst the inhabitants in consequence of the inseparable selfishnesses of our nature, were instantly referred to him; and he was sure to decide in such a way as instantly to satisfy the great bulk of the villagers that he was right. There were no recusants; for though there might be individuals who, from folly or obstinacy, or the blindness of selfishness, would have opposed his decision if it had stood unsupported, yet when the great mass of their fellow villagers were against them also, they dared not utter a word. If there was any evil committed; if youth, and either youth's passions or its follies produced wrong, the pastor had learned ever to censure mildly, to endeavour to amend rather than to punish, and to repair the evil that had been done, rather than to castigate him to whom it was attributable.

In such occupations passed the greater part of his time; and he felt to the very heart the truth of the words—even in this world—that "blessed are the peace-makers." The rest of his time he devoted either to study or to relaxation. What he called study was the deep, intense application of his mind to the knowledge and interpretation of the Holy Scriptures, whether in translation or in the original languages. What he called relaxation divided itself into two parts: the reading of that high classical literature, which had formed the great enjoyment of his youth, and by attention to which his eloquence had been chiefly formed; and the cultivation of his flower-garden, of which he was extremely fond, together with the superintendence of the little farm which surrounded his mansion. His life, in short, was a life of primeval simplicity: his pleasures few, but sweet and innocent; his course of existence, for many years at least, smooth and unvaried, remote from strife, and dedicated to do good.

From time to time, indeed, persons of a higher rank, and of thoughts and manners much more refined than those of the villagers by whom he was surrounded, would visit his retirement, to seek his advice or enjoy his conversation; and on these occasions he certainly did feel a refreshment of mind from the living communion with persons of equal intellect, which could not be gained even from his converse with the mighty dead. Still it never made him wish to return to situations in which such opportunities were more frequent, if not constant. "It is enough as it is," he said; "it now comes like a refreshing shower upon the soil of the heart, teaching it to bring forth flowers; but, perhaps, if that rain were more plentiful and continued always, there would be nothing but flowers, and no fruit. I love my solitude, though perhaps I love it not unbroken."

It rarely happened that these visits had anything that was at all painful or annoying in them, for the means of communication between one part of the country and another were in that day scanty; and those who came to see him could in no degree be moved by curiosity, but must either be instigated by some motive of much importance, or brought thither by the desire of a mind capable of comprehending and appreciating his. He seldom, we may almost say he never, went out to visit any one but the members of his own flock in his spiritual capacity. He had twice, indeed, in thirty years, been at the château of Morseiul, but that was, first, on the occasion of a dangerous illness of the Countess, the

mother of Count Albert, and then, on the commencement of those
encroachments upon the rights of the Huguenots, which had now
been some time in progress.

The Counts of Morseiul, however, both father and son, visited
him often. The first he had regarded well-nigh as a brother; the
latter he looked upon almost in the light of a son. He loved their
conversation, from its sincerity, its candour, and its vigour. The
experience of the old count, which came united with none of the
hardness of heart and feeling which experience too often brings;
the freshness of mind, the fanciful enthusiasms of the younger
nobleman, alike interested, pleased, and attached him. With both
there were points of immediate communication, by which his mind
entered instantly into the thoughts and feelings of theirs; and he
felt throughout every fresh conversation with them, that he was
dealing with persons worthy of communication with him, both by
brightness and elevation of intellect, by earnest energy of character,
by virtue, honour, and uprightness, and by the rare gem of unchangeable truth.

It may well be supposed, then, that he rose to meet the young
Count de Morseiul, of whose return to his own domains he had
not been made aware, with a smile of unmixed satisfaction.

" Welcome, my dear Albert," he said, addressing him by the
name which he had used towards him from childhood—"welcome
back to your own dwelling and your own people. How have you
fared in the wars? How have you fared in perilous camps and in
the field, and in the still more perilous court? And how long is it
since you returned to Morseiul?"

" I have fared well, dear friend, in all," replied the Count;
" have had some opportunity of serving the king, and have received
more thanks than those services deserved. In regard to the court,
where I could neither serve him nor myself, nor any one else, I
have escaped its perils this year, by obtaining permission to come
straight from the army to Morseiul, without visiting either Paris or
Versailles; and now, as to your last question, when I arrived, I
would say but yesterday afternoon, were it not that you would, I
know, thank me for coming to see you so speedily, when in truth
I only intended to come to-morrow, had not some circumstances,
not so pleasant as I could wish, though not so bad as that which
I fear may follow, brought me hither, to consult with you to-day."

A slight cloud came over the old man's countenance as his
younger companion spoke.

" Is the difficulty in regard to which you seek counsel, Albert,"
he demanded, "in your own household, or in the household of
our suffering church?"

" Alas," replied the Count, "it is in the latter, my excellent
friend; had it been in my own household, unless some urgent
cause impelled me, I should not have thus troubled you."

" I feared so, I feared so," replied the old man; " I have heard something of these matters of late.—So they will not leave us in repose!" And as he spoke he rose from the chair he had resumed after welcoming the Count, and paced the room backwards and forwards more than once.

"It is in vain," he said, at length, casting himself back into his seat, "to let such things agitate me. The disposal of all is in a better and a firmer hand than mine. ' On this rock will I found my church, and the gates of hell shall not prevail against it !' So said our divine Master; and I need not tell you, Albert of Morseiul, that when he said, ' on this rock,' he meant on the rock of faith, and did not mean the trumpery juggle, the buffoon-like playing on the name of Peter, which the disciples of a corrupt sect would attribute to him. He has founded his church upon the rock of faith, and thereon do I build my hope; for I cannot but see that the enemy are preparing the spear and making ready the bow against us. Whether it be God's will that we shall resist, as we have done in former times, and be enabled, though but a handful amongst a multitude, to smite the enemies and the perverters of our pure religion, or whether we shall be called upon to die as martyrs, and seal our faith by the pouring out of our blood, leaving another ensample to the elect that come after us, will be pointed out by the circumstances in which we are placed. But I see clearly that the sword is out to smite us, and we must either resist or endure."

"It is precisely on that point," replied the Count, "that I came to consult with you. Measures of a strong, a harassing, and of an unjust nature, are taking place against us, because we will not say we believe that which we are sure is false, and follow doctrines which our soul repudiates. Did I hope, my excellent friend, that the matter would stop here; did I expect that such measures of petty annoyance as I have heard proclaimed in the town of Morseiul to-day, or anything, indeed, similar to those measures, would be the final end and limit of the attack upon our liberties and our faith, I should be most anxious to calm the minds of the people, to persuade them to endure rather than to resist, and to remember that patience will cure many things : I should ask you, I should beseech even you, plighted as you are, to support the cause of truth and righteousness, to aid me in my efforts, and to remember at what an awful price indemnity must be bought; to remember how fearful, how terrible, must be the scenes through which we wade to the attainment of those equal rights which should be granted even without our seeking them."

"And I would aid you! and I would remember!" exclaimed the pastor, grasping his hand, "so help me the God of my trust, Albert of Morseiul," he continued, more vehemently, "as I have ever avoided, for long years, every cause of strife and dissension— every matter of offence thrown in my way by those who would persecute us. Nay, more, far more; when my counsels have been sought, when my advice has been required, the words that I have spoken have always been pacific; not alone peaceful in sound, but peaceful in spirit and in intent, and peaceful in every tendency. I have counselled submission where I might have stirred up war; I have advised mild means and supplications, when the time for successful resistance was pointed out both by just cause for bitter indignation, and by the embarrassment of our enemies in consequence of their over-ambition : and now I tell thee, Albert, I tell thee with pain and apprehension, that I doubt, that I much doubt, whether in so doing I have acted right or wrong; whether, by such timid counsels, the happy moment has not been suffered to slip; whether our enemies, more wise in their generation than we are, have not taken advantage of our forbearance, have not waited till they themselves were in every way prepared, and are now ready to execute the iniquitous designs which have only been suspended in consequence of ambitious efforts in other quarters."

" I fear, indeed, that it is so," replied the young Count; " but, nevertheless, neither you nor any other person has cause to reproach himself for such conduct. Forbearance, even if taken advantage of by insidious enemies, must always be satisfactory to one's own heart."

" I know not—I know not," replied the old man. " In my early days, Albert, these hands have grasped the sword in defence of my religion; and we were then taught that resistance to the will of those bigots and tyrants who would crush out the last spark of the pure worship of God, and substitute in its place the gross idolatry which disfigures this land, was a duty to the Author of our faith. We were taught that resistance was not optional, but compulsory; and that to our children, and to our brethren, and to our ancestors, we owed the same determined, persevering, uncompromising efforts that were required from us by the service of the Lord likewise. We were taught that we should never surrender, that we should never hesitate, that we should never compromise, till the liberty of the true reformed church of France was established upon a sure and permanent basis, or the last drop of blood in the veins of her saints was poured out into the cup of martyrdom. Such were the doctrines, Albert, that were taught in my youth—such were the doctrines under which I myself became a humble soldier of the cross. But, alas, lulled with the rest of my brethren into a fatal security, thinking that no farther infraction of our liberties would take place, believing that we should always be permitted to worship the God of our salvation according to the dictates of our own conscience—perhaps even believing, Albert, that some degree of contumely and persecution, some stigma attached to the poor name of Huguenot, might be beneficial, if not necessary, in our frail condition as mortal men, to be a bond of union amongst us to maintain our religion in its purity, and to keep alive the flame of zeal ;—believing all this, I have not bestirred myself to resist small encroachments, I have even counselled others to pass them over without notice. Now, however, I am convinced that it is the intention, perhaps not of the king, for men say that he is kind and element, but of the base men that surround him, gradually to sap the foundations of our church, and cast it down altogether. I have seen it in every act that has been taking place of late, have marked it in every proceeding of the court; and though slow and insidious, covered with base pretexts and pitiful quibbles, the progress of our enemies has been sure, and I fear that it may be too late to close the door against them: I could recall all their acts one by one, and the summing up would clearly show, that the idolatrous priesthood of this popish land are determined not to suffer a purer faith to remain any longer as an offence and reproach unto them."

"I much wish," replied the Count, earnestly, "that you would put down, in order, these encroachments. I have been long absent, serving in the field, where my faith has, of course, been no obstacle, and where we have little discussion of such matters: but if I had them clearly stated before me, I and the other Protestant noblemen of France might draw up a petition to the king, whose natural sense of right is very strong, which would induce him to do us justice——"

The old man shook his head, with a look of melancholy doubt, but the Count immediately added, repeating the words he had just used—"to do us justice, or to make such a declaration of his intentions, as to enable us to take measures to meet the exigency of the moment."

"Willingly, most willingly," said Claude de l'Estang, "will I tell you all that is done, and has been doing, by our enemies. I will tell you also, Albert, all the false and absurd charges that they urge against us, to justify their own iniquitous dealings towards us. We will consider the whole together calmly and dispassionately, and take counsel as to what may best be done. God forbid that I should see the blood of my fellow Christians shed; but God forbid, also, that I should see his holy church overthrown."

"You speak of charges against us, sir," said the Count, with some surprise in his countenance: "I knew not that even malice itself could find or forge a charge against the Huguenots of France. At the court and in the camp there is no charge; tell me what we have done in the provinces to give even a foundation for a charge."

"Nothing, my young friend," replied the clergyman; "we have done nothing but defend the immunities secured unto us by the hand of the very king who now seeks to snatch them from us. We have not even defended, as perhaps we should, the unalienable privileges given us by a greater king. No; the insidious plan of our deceitful enemies has been to attack us first, and then to lay resistance to our charge as a crime. Take but a few instances. In the towns of Tonnay and of Privas, the reformed religion was not only the dominant religion, but the sole religion, and had been so for near a century; the inhabitants were all Protestants, tranquil, quiet, industrious. There were no religious contentions, there were no jealous feuds, when some one, prompted by the fiend, whispered to the crown that means should be taken to establish, in those places, the authority of the idolatrous church; that opportunity should be given for making converts from the pure to the corrupted faith; that in the end the pillage of the Protestant congregations should be permitted to the Romish priesthood. An order was instantly given for opening a Romish church in a place where there were no papists, and for preaching against our creed in the midst of its sincere followers. The church was accordingly opened; the singing of Latin masses, and the exhibition of idolatrous processions commenced where such things had not been known in the memory of man: a few boys hooted, and instantly there was raised a cry, that the Romish priests were interrupted in their functions, that the ceremonies of the church were opposed by the whole mass of Huguenots. What was the result? The parliament of Paris gave authenticity to the calumny, by granting letters of protection to the intruding clergy; and then, taking its own act as proof of the guilt of the Huguenots, commanded our temples to be pulled down, and the free exercise of our religion in that place to be abolished. This was the case at Tonnay; and if at the same time the decree, which announced its fate to that city, had boldly forbidden our worship throughout the land, we might have displayed some union, and made some successful resistance. But our enemies were too wise to give us such a general motive: they struck an isolated blow here, and an isolated blow there ; they knew man's selfishness; they foresaw how apathetic we should be to the injuries of our fellows; and they were right. The Huguenots of France made no effort in favour of those who suffered; some never inquired into the question at all, and believed that the people of Tonnay had brought evil on their own heads; some shrugged the indifferent shoulder, and thought it not worth while to trouble the peace of the whole community for the sake of a single small town. Had it been your town of Morseiul, it would have been the same, for such has been the ease with Privas, with Dexodun, with Melle, with Chevreux, with Vitré, and full fifty more; and not one Protestant has moved to support the rights of his brother. Whenever, indeed, anything has occurred affecting the whole body, then men have flocked to us, demanding advice and assistance; they have talked of open resistance, of immediate war, of defending their rights, of opposing further aggressions; but I have ever seen, Albert, that, mingled with a few determined and noble spirits, there have been many selfish, many indifferent; and I know that, unless some strong and universal bond of union be given them, some great common motive be afforded, thousands will fall off in the hour of need, and leave their defenders in the hands of the enemy. For this reason, as well as for many others, I have always urged, peace where peace can be obtained; but I see now such rapid progress made against us, that I tremble between two terrible results."

The young Count gazed thoughtfully in the pastor's face for a few moments ere he replied. " I fear," he said at length, " that we have not yet a sufficient motive to bind all men, as is most needful in the strong assertion of a common cause.—Heaven forbid that we should do, or even think of ought that is disloyal or rebellious; but I doubt much, though the new injury we have received is gross, that it will furnish a sufficient motive to unite all our brethren in one general representation to the king of our general grievances. Yet there are many points in the edict I heard read to-day wounding to the vanity of influential men amongst us, and that motive will often move them when others fail. But listen, and tell me what you think. These were the chief heads of the proclamation:"——and he went on to recapitulate all that he had heard, the old man listening with attention while he spoke.

" I fear there is no bond of union here," replied the pastor, commenting upon some of the heads which the young Count had given him; "rather, my good young friend, matter for dissension. They have cunningly thrown in more than one apple of discord to divide the mayors of the Protestant towns from their people, ay, and even to make the pastors odious to the flock."

" Let us, however," said the Count, " endeavour to act as unitedly as possible—let us keep a wary eye upon the proceedings of our enemies—let us be prepared to seize the fit moment for opposition, that we may seize it before it be necessary to resist in a manner that may be imputed to us as disloyal. Doubtless, at the assembling of the states of the province, which will take place shortly, there will be a great number of the Protestant nobles present, and I will endeavour to bring them to a general conference, in the course of which we may perhaps——"

" Hark!" said the old man, " there is the noise of a horse's feet;" and the next instant a loud ringing of the bell was heard, followed by the sound of a voice in the passage speaking to the maid-servant in jocular and facetious tones, with which the young Count was well acquainted.

" It is my rascally valet, Riquet," he said. " He's always thrusting himself where he has no business."

" I wonder you retain him in your service," said the pastor; "I have marked him in your father's time, and have heard you both say that he is a knave."

" And yet he loves me," said the young Count; " and I do in truth believe would sooner injure himself than me."

The old man shook his head with an expression of doubt; but the Count went on: " I did not wish him to know that I came here to-night, and still less desire that he should be acquainted with the nature of my errand. He is a papist, you know, and may

E

suspect, perhaps, that we are holding a secret council with others. We had better, therefore, give him admittance at once."

There was a small silver bell stood on the table beside the pastor; and, as the maid did not come in, he rang it; and after inquiring, when she did make her appearance, who it was that had just arrived, ordered the valet to be admitted.

"What brought you here, Maitre Jerome?" demanded the young Count, somewhat sternly, as the valet entered on his tiptoes, with a look of supreme self-satisfaction.

"Why, my lord," replied the man, "scarcely had you set out when there arrived a courier from the Duc de Rouvré, bringing you a packet. He was asked to leave it, as you were absent; but he said it was of vast importance, and that he was to get your answer from your own mouth: so he would give it to nobody. I took him into what used to be called the page's room, and made him drink deep of Château Thierry, picked his pocket of the packet while he was looking out of the window, and seeing that he was tired to death, commended him to his bed, with a nightcap of good liquor, promising to wake him as soon as you returned, and then set off with the packet to seek you, Monsieur le Comte."

"And pray what was the object of all this trickery?" demanded the Count. "If you be not careful, Maitre Jerome, you will place your neck in a cord some day."

"So my mother used to say," replied the man, with cool effrontery; "but I only wished to serve your lordship, and knowing that there were difficult matters in hand, thought you might like to read the packet first, in order to be prepared to give a ready answer. We could easily seal up the letter again, and slip it into the courier's jerkin—which the poor fool put under his head when he went to sleep, thinking to secure the packet that was already gone. He would then present it to you in due form, and you might give your answer without any apparent forethought."

The Count could not refrain from turning a smiling look upon the pastor, who, however, bent down his eyes and shook his head with a disapproving sigh.

The Count at the same time tore open the packet which the servant had handed to him, with a ruthless roughness, that made good Jerome Riquet start, and cry "Oh!" with an expression of pain upon his countenance, to see not the slightest possibility left of ever patching up the letter again, so as to make it appear as if it had never been opened.

"And I suppose, Maitre Jerome," continued the Count, while making his way into the packet, "that you took the trouble of watching me when I set out this afternoon?"

"Heaven forbid, sir!" replied the man; "that would have been both very impertinent, and an unnecessary waste of time and attention, as I knew quite well where you were going. As soon as you had been out to hear the proclamation and keep the people quiet, and came home and sat witn the shuttlecock Marquis de Hericourt, and then ordered your horse, I said to myself, and I told Henriot, ' his lordship is gone to consult with Monsieur Claude de l'Estang ; and where, indeed, could he go so well as to one who is respected by the Catholics almost as much as by the Huguenots ? Whom could he apply to so wisely as to one whose counsels are always judicious, always peaceful, and always benevolent ?' " and having finished this piece of oratory, Riquet—perceiving that his master, busy in the letter, gave him no attention—made a low but somewhat grotesque reverence to the good pastor, bending his head, rounding his back, and elevating his shoulders, while his long thin legs stuck out below, so that he assumed very much the appearance of a sleeping crane.

The pastor gave no sign of approbation, replying gravely, " My good friend, I have lived more than sixty-five years in the world ; and yet I trust age has not diminished the intellect which expericuce may have tended to improve."

By the time he had said this, the young Count had read to the end of the short letter which he had received, and put it before the pastor.

" This is kind," he said, " and courteous of my good friend the duke, who, though I have not seen him for many years, still retains his regard for our family. Jerome, you may retire," he added, " and wait for me without. This letter which you have brought is of no importance whatever, a mere letter of civility, so that either you or the duke's courier have lied."

" Oh, it was the courier, sir," replied the valet, with his usual quiet impudence, " it was the courier of course ; otherwise there is no truth in the old proverb, *Cheat like a valet, lie like a courier.* I always keep to my own department, sir ;" and so saying, he marched out of the room.

In the meantime, Claude de l'Estang had read the letter, which invited the young Count to visit the Duc de Rouvré at Poitiers, and take up his abode in the governor's house some days before the meeting of the states. It went on to express great regard for the young nobleman himself, and high veneration for his father's memory ; and then, glancing at the religious differences existing in the province, and the measures which had been lately taken against the Huguenots, it went on to state that the writer was anxious to receive the private advice and opinion of the young Count as to the best means of extinguishing all irritation on such subjects.

" Were this from any other man than the Duc de Rouvré," said the pastor, " I should say that it was specious and intended to mislead ; but the duke has always shewn himself favourable to the Protestants, as a politician, and I have some reason to believe is not unfavourable to their doctrines in his heart : but go, my son, go as speedily as possible ; and God grant that your efforts may conclude with peace."

After a few more words of the same tenour, the pastor and his young friend separated, and the Count and his valet, mounting their horses, took their way back towards the château, with the shades of night beginning to gather quickly about them.

***

CHAPTER IV.

UNEXPECTED COMPANIONS.

THE two horsemen rode to the village at a quick rate, but then slackened their pace, and passed through the single little street at a walk. The scene, however, was now changed: the children were no longer playing before the doors; from out of the windows of some of the cottages streamed forth the reddish light of a resin candle; from others was heard issuing the sound of a psalm, sung before the inhabitants retired to rest; and at the doors of others, again, appeared a peasant returned late from the toil of the day, and—as is so natural to the heart of man—pausing in the thickening twilight to take one more look of the world, before the darkness of night shut it out altogether. A star or two was beginning to appear in the sky; the bats were flitting hither and thither through the dusky air; and, though it was still warm and mild, everything betokened the rapid approach of night.

From the village the Count rode on, relapsing, after having spoken a few words to his servant, into the same meditative mood which had possessed him on his way to Auron. He hastened not his pace, and after he had gone about three miles, complete darkness surrounded him. There was no moon in the sky; the road by which he had come, steep, stony, and irregular, required full light to render it safe for his horse's knees; and, after the animal had tripped more than once, the Count struck into a path to the right, which led by a little *détour* into the high road from Poitiers to Nantes.

High roads, however, in those days were very different things from those which they have now become; and there is scarcely a parish road in England, or a commercial road in France, which is not wider, more open, and better in every respect than the high road we speak of was at that time. When he had gained it, however, the Count went on more easily till he arrived at the spot where it entered one of the large woods which supplied the inhabitants with fuel in a country unproductive of coal. There, however, he met with an obstruction which he had not at all anticipated. As he approached the outskirts of the wood, there was a sudden flash to the right, and a ball whistled across the Count's path, but without hitting either himself or his servant.

He was too much accustomed to scenes in which such winged messengers of death were common, to be startled by the shot; but merely muttering to himself, " This is unpleasant; we must put a stop to this, so near Morseiul," he considered whether it would be better for him to push his horse forward or to go back upon the open road. But the matter was settled for him by others; for he was surrounded in a moment by five or six men, who speedily pulled him off his horse, though he made no effort to resist where resistance he saw would be vain, and then demanded his name in an imperative and threatening manner. He heard, however, at the same time, the galloping of the horse of Jerome Riquet, who had remained some twenty or thirty yards behind him; and perfectly certain, therefore, that very efficient aid would soon be brought to deliver him, he determined to procrastinate as far as possible, in the hopes of taking some of the plunderers who had established themselves so near his dwelling.

"I cannot see," he said, "what your business can be with my name; if it is my money that you want, any that I have upon my person you can take.—My good friend, you will oblige me by not holding my collar so tight; it gives me a feeling of strangulation, which, as you may perhaps some day know, is not very pleasant."

The man who held him, and who seemed the principal of the group, did not appear to be at all offended at being reminded of what might be the end of his exploits, but let go his collar, laughing and saying, "You are merry! however, your money we shall take, as our own right. It is fair toll, you know; and your name we must have too, as, being officers of the king's highway, if not of the king, we have certainly a right to ask for passports."

"Heaven forbid that I should deny any of your rights," replied the Count; "my money I will give you with all my heart: but my name is my own, and I do not choose to give that to any one."

"Well, then, we must take you where we can see your face," replied the other. "Then, if we know you, well and good, you shall go on; if we do not know you, we shall find means to make you speak more clearly, I will warrant."

"He is one of them! he is one of them, be you sure!" replied a second voice. "I would tie him to a tree, and shoot him at once out of the way."

"No, no," rejoined the first; "I think I know his tongue. It is Maitre Nicolas, the notary—not a bad man in his way. Bring him along, and his horse too; we shall soon see."

Though the Count, perhaps, might not consider himself flattered by being taken for Maitre Nicolas, the notary, he began to perceive that there was something more in the conduct of these men than the common desire of plunder, some personal motive either of revenge or enmity; and, as he well knew that he was generally loved throughout the neighbourhood, he had no apprehensions as to the result regarding himself. He was anxious, however, to see

more of his captors' proceedings, and therefore accompanied them
without any effort to undeceive them as to who he was. They led
him along for about a quarter of a mile down the high road through
the wood; then struck into a narrower path to the right, only in
use for wood-carts; and then again took a footpath, which brought
them to a spot where a bright light was seen glimmering through
the trees before them. It was evident that some wider road than
that which they were following at the moment led also to the point
to which it tended, for the sound of horses' feet was heard in that
direction, and a creaking as if of some heavy carriage wheels.

" There is brown Keroual," said one of the men, " come back
from the other end of the wood, and I'll bet you two louis to 'two
deniers that he has got hold of them. Don't you hear the wheels?
I think we might let you go," he added, turning towards the Count,
and trying to get a full glance of his face by the light that flashed
through the leaves.

At that moment, however, one of his companions replied, " Take
him on, take him on! You can't tell what wheels they are. They
may be sending away those women."

This seemed to decide the matter somewhat to the satisfaction of
Albert de Morseiul, who was not a little anxious to witness what
was going on; and the men accordingly led him forward through
the bushes, which partially obstructed the path, till, coming suddenly
to an open space under a high sandy bank, he found himself in the
midst of a scene, upon which we must pause for a moment.

There was a large wood fire in the midst of the open space ; and
both to the right and left led away a small road, deeply channelled
by the wheels of sand-carts. The high bank above was crowned
with the fine trees of the wood, amongst the branches and stems of
which the light of the fire and of one or two torches lost itself;
while the fuller light below shone upon three or four curious groups
of human beings. One of these groups was gathered together near
the fire, and consisted of seven men, some lying down, some standing, all of them well armed, and three with carbines in their hands.
Their dress in a great degree resembled that of the English soldiery
at the time of Cromwell, though the usurper had been dead, and
the fashion of such clothing gone out, about twenty years. A few
of them had their faces bare, but the greater part had something
drawn over their countenance so as completely to disguise it. In
general, this covering was a mere piece of silk or cloth with slits
made for the eyes, but in two instances a regular mask appeared.

At a little distance from the fire, farther under the bank, sat two
ladies, one habited as a person of high station, according to the
taste of that day, with the upper part of the face, from which a large
veil had been thrown back, covered by the then common black
velvet riding-mask, and two or three rings still upon her hands,
notwithstanding the company in which she was found. The other
was dressed more simply, but still well, and wore a large watch

hanging from her girdle. There were some large grey cloaks spread upon the ground beneath them, to protect them apparently from the damp of the grass; and standing near, leaning on a musket, apparently as a guard over them, was one of the same fraternity that appeared by the side of the fire.

At some distance up the road to the right, a carriage was seen stationary, with the horses taken out and cropping the herbage; but the eyes of the whole party under the bank were turned to the other side, where, at the entrance of the road into the open space, appeared a second carriage drawn by four mules, which had just been led up by a party of the banditti, who were the first that had appeared mounted.

From the door of the vehicle, which was now brought to a halt, its tenants were in the very act of descending, with fear and unwillingness written upon their countenances. The two first that came forth were ecclesiastics of the Catholic church. The first, a man who might well be considered as remarkably ugly, had his countenance not been expressive, and its expression indicative of considerable talent. The second was a much handsomer man in every respect, but with a keen, sly, fox-like aspect, and a constant habit of biting his nether lip, of which he could not divest himself, even at a moment when, to judge by his countenance, he was possessed by extraordinary fear. After them came another man, dressed as a layman, one or two domestics, and a fat inferior priest, with a dirty and a greasy countenance, full of nothing but large black eyes and dull stupidity.

While they were thus making their unwilling exit from the carriage, several of those who had brought them thither were seen mounted upon different parts of the vehicle, busily cutting off, opening, and emptying various valises, trunk-mails, and other contrivances for conveying luggage.

The attention of the other actors in the scene was so much taken up by this group, that no one seemed to notice the arrival of the party which brought the Count thither; and though the man who led it had resumed a grasp of his collar, as if to demonstrate that the Count was the captive of his bow and spear, he was himself so intensely occupied in looking at the proceedings round the carriage, that he paused close to the wood for several minutes. At length, however, he recollected himself, and, by advancing two or three steps with those that followed, called the attention of the rest from the carriage and its ejected tenants to the new captive who had been brought in. The light flashed full upon the Count as the man held him; but the moment the eyes of the group around the fire were turned upon him, several voices exclaimed, in a tone of surprise and consternation, "The Count! The Count! The Count de Morseiul!"

No sooner did the first of the ecclesiastics, who had descended from the carriage, hear the exclamation, than he turned his eyes in that way also, ran forward, and, catching the Count by the hand, exclaimed, " Monsieur de Morseiul, my dear friend, I claim your protection.   These men threaten to murder me !"

" Monsieur Pelisson," replied the Count, "I greatly grieve that I can give you no protection.   I am a prisoner to these men, as you see, myself, and, were I not of another creed, might, for aught I know, have to apply to you to shrive me ! for they have threatened to tie me to a tree, and shoot me likewise."

" Good God ! this is very horrible," cried Pelisson, in utter terror and consternation.   " Pray, Monsieur de St. Helie," he exclaimed, turning to the other ecclesiastic who followed—" Pray, exhort these men—you are so eloquent l"

" I—I—I—I can exhort nobody," stammered forth the other, trembling in every limb.

A change, however, was working itself in their favour ; for the moment that the Count's name had been publicly announced, a great degree of agitation and movement had taken place amongst the robbers.   Those who had been lying down started up, those who had been plundering the carriage abandoned their pillage, and joined their companions by the fire ; the man who had grasped the Count let go his hold, as if he had burnt his hand ; and a rapid consultation evidently took place amongst the rest, which the Count himself was not a little surprised to see, as, amongst those whose faces were uncovered, there was not a single individual whom he could recognise as having ever beheld before.

The movement of Pelisson, however, and the words which passed between him and the Count, again called their attention in that direction from the consultation which was going on.   Two men, both masked, separated themselves from the rest, one a very tall and powerful man, somewhat richly though not tastefully dressed ; the other a short, broad made, sturdy-looking person, who only wanted the accompaniment of a bandoleer over his buff coat to be a perfect representation of the parliamentary soldier of Great Britain.   The lesser man took upon himself to be spokesman, though they both advanced direct towards the Count.

" We are sorry for what has happened, Monsieur de Morseiul," he said ; " we had not the slightest intention of disturbing you upon your road, but this fellow's stupidity and the darkness of the night have caused the mistake.   I have only to say, as I said before, that we are sorry for it, and that you are quite at liberty to go when you like."

The Count's determination was taken in a moment.   " I am happy to hear," he replied, " that you are sorry for one offence at least against the laws of the country ; but, in regard to my going, if I go, I have not the slightest intention of going alone.   I am not a person to abandon my companions in distress, and I must insist upon some of the parties here present being liberated as well as myself."

Pelisson looked at him with an imploring glance; the Abbé de St. Helie clasped his hands together, and gazed anxiously in his face; while the man to whom he had spoken answered in a surly tone—

"We would fain treat you well, Sir Count, and do you no harm; so go your way in God's name, and do not meddle with what does not concern you, for fear worse come of it. You are not leading the forlorn hope at Maestricht now, remember."

"Oh!" exclaimed the Count, with a meaning nod of the head, as if the man's allusion had let him into some secret; but ere he could reply further, the taller and more athletic of the two whispered a few words to his companion in a low voice, and the other, after a moment's pause of hesitation, turned once more to the Count, and said, "Well, sir, what is it you would have? We respect and love you, and would do much to please you. What do you demand?"

"In the first place," replied the Count de Morseiul, speaking very slowly and distinctly, and using as many words as he possibly could, knowing that every moment was something gained by bringing succour nearer—"in the first place, as I am sure that you are too much men of honour, and too courteous in your nature a great deal——"

"Come, come, Sir Count," cried the man, interrupting him, "cut your story short. We have honour of our own particular kind; but as to our nature being courteous, it is not. We are neither fools, babies, nor frequenters of the painted chambers of Paris, but freemen of the forest. What I ask is, what do you demand?"

"In the first place," replied the Count, taking a step forward towards the spot where the two ladies were sitting, and pointing in that direction with his hand, "in the first place, I demand that you should set those two ladies at liberty!"

"They might have been at liberty long ago," the man answered, "if they had chosen to say whence they came and whither they were going. However, go they shall, as you ask it; but I should like to have those rings and that watch first."

"Fie!" said the Count, "you surely would not touch the trinkets? Their purses, I dare say, have been taken already."

"Those were given up at first," replied the man, "and we should have had the watch and rings too, if we had not been interrupted by this other affair. Come, pretty one," he added, turning to the younger of the two ladies, who had both risen when they heard the intercession that was made for them, and were gazing on the young Count with eager anxiety—"come, let us see if there be any diamonds amongst those rings, for we must not let diamonds get out of the forest. They are better than gold a great deal."

Thus saying, he advanced towards her, and took the small delicate beautiful fingers on which the rings appeared, in his rough grasp.

"I fear, lady," said the Count, who had followed him, "that I cannot protect you farther. We must feel grateful for your being permitted to go at all."

"We owe you a deep debt of gratitude as it is, sir," replied the elder lady; and the younger added immediately, "Indeed we do: but let them take the rings," she continued, drawing them from her fingers.—"All but one," she added, suddenly, "all but one."

"What, a wedding-ring," cried the man, with a loud laugh, "or a lover's token, I suppose, for I see no wedding-ring here."

"No, sir," she said, drawing up her head somewhat proudly, "but the gift of a mother who loved me, and who is most dear to me still in memory. Pray let me keep it. This is the ring."

"Why, that is worth all the rest," said the man, looking at it. "No, no, my pretty mistress, we must have this."

The Count de Morseiul had stood by, somewhat pale, and with a manner which, for the first time, betrayed some degree of agitation. But he now interposed, seeing, by the trembling of her hand, how much emotion the man's words produced in the young lady, though he could not behold her countenance.

"What is the value of the ring?" he demanded of the man.

"Why, some twenty louis, I dare say," he replied.

"Well, I will give you double the amount for it," said the Count. "I have not the money upon me, for your men have taken all I had; but you can trust me, and I will pay it to any one whom you will send to tne château of Morseiul, and pledge my honour they shall come and go in safety, and without inquiry."

"Your honour, my Lord Count, is worth the city of Poitiers," replied the man. "There is the ring," and he gave it into the Count's hand.

Albert de Morseiul took it, and gazed at it by the fire-light for a moment with some attention and with some emotion. It was formed of diamonds, and, according to a fashion common in that day, formed the initials, probably of some proper name, C. S., surmounted by a Count's coronet.

"Lady," he said, after he had looked at it, "this ring is almost as strong a temptation to me as to our friend here. I long to keep it till its fair owner, once more at liberty, may come to claim it at my hands. That would be ungenerous, however, and so I suppose I must give it back."

So saying, he replaced it on her finger, and, with an air of courteous gallantry, raised the small fair hand to his lips. She bent down her head over her hand and his, as if to gaze at the recovered ring, and he felt a warm drop fall from the bright eyes that sparkled through the mask upon it.

"And now," he continued, turning to the man who had acted as chief of the band, "and now you will let the ladies depart?"

"Yes," replied the other; "but one of our people must drive them to the place where we tied the lackeys to the trees."

"They are safe, upon your honour?" said the Count.

"Upon my honour they are," answered the man, bluffly. "I should like to see the man that would wag a finger at them when I say they are free."

"Come then, quick," said the Count, turning to her who seemed the highest in rank of the two ladies; "let us not lose the fortunate moment;" and he took her hand to lead her to the carriage, which he had remarked standing farther down the road. But both Pelisson and St. Helie threw themselves in his way, exclaiming aloud, "For God's sake do not leave us! For Heaven's sake do not abandon us!"

"No, no," replied the Count. "My good friends," he added, addressing the band, "pray offer these good gentlemen no wrong, at least till my return. Perhaps I can hit upon some terms between you and them, and also tell you a piece of news which will make you change your determination."

"Not easily," said the leader; "but we will not harm them till you come back, if you are only going to take the ladies to the carriage. You, Stephen, drive it to the place where the lackeys were left."

"I will return instantly," said the Count, and he led the younger lady on, the elder following.

Till they reached the carriage, and during a part of the time occupied in tying the horses again to it, all were silent; but at length the younger lady ventured to say, in a low voice, "How can I ever thank you, Monsieur de Morseiul?"

The Count did not reply to the question; but he asked, as he was handing her in, "Am I not right? Have we not met before?"

"It is years ago," she said, in the same low tone; "but," she added, the moment after, just as the man was about to drive away, "we shall meet again, and if we do, say nothing of this meeting, I beseech you; but remember only that I am deeply grateful."

The carriage moved along the road, and the Count remained for a moment listening. He then returned to the mixed group by the fire, where the agitation of terror, in the case of the Abbé de St. Helie, had worked itself up to such a pitch during his absence, that the tears were streaming copiously from the unhappy man's eyes, while the band which had made him captive stood round gazing upon him with some contempt, but certainly no appearance of pity. Pelisson, on his part, displayed a greater degree of firmness, remaining with his hands clasped together, and his eyes fixed upon the ground, but without any other sign of fear than some paleness of his countenance, and an occasional movement of the lips, as if he were in prayer.

The Count advanced into the midst of the group; and perceiving that the leader of the band into whose hands they had fallen looked to him to speak first, and maintained a sort of dogged silence which augured but ill for the two ecclesiastics, he said,

" Now, my good friend, what do you intend to do with these gentlemen ?"

" I intend," replied the man, in a stern tone, " to shoot the two
that are standing there, without fail, to scourge that black-faced
priest by the carriage, till he has not a bit of skin on his back, and
to send the lackeys trooping."

" You are of course jesting," said the Count. " You are not a
man, I am sure, to commit deliberate murder. But you have
frightened them enough.—Let me hear what you intend to do,
without a jest."

" There has been no jest spoken," replied the man, fiercely. " I
have told you my intentions, and I shall not change. These two
villains have come down into a peaceful province, and amongst a
happy people, to bring dissension, and persecution, and hatred,
amongst us, and they shall taste the first bitter fruits of their own
works. I shall certainly not let them escape ; and I can tell the
old Jesuit Le Tellier, and his tyrant son, Louvois, that they may
send as many of such firebrands down as they will ; I will do my
best to meet them, and extinguish them in their own blood."

" I really do not know what you mean," replied the Count.
" Monsieur Pelisson, I cannot conceive, from what I know of you,
that you are a man to undertake such evil tasks as this good
gentleman accuses you of. We of the reformed religion certainly
regretted that you had thought fit to fall back into what we consider to be a great error, but we never supposed that you would
deal hardly with your reformed brethren."

" Neither would I, Count," replied Pelisson, firmly. " It is natural
that, having abandoned errors, I should seek to lead others to follow
the same course ; but no harsh means have I ever practised, no
harsh means have I ever counselled. On the contrary, I have
advocated gentleness, peace, persuasion, exhortation, kindness,
equity, on all occasions. But it is in vain, my good young gentleman," he added, looking at his captors, " it is all in vain. These
men are determined to take our blood, and it is in vain to try to
stay them ; though the retribution which will fall upon them, and
I fear, too, upon your own sect, will be awful, when our fate reaches
the ears of the king. But it is in vain, as I have said. You have
done your best for us, and I thank you from my heart. Bear witness, every one !" he continued, raising his voice, " bear witness,
every one, that this noble gentleman, the Count de Morseiul, has
no share in the terrible act these men are going to commit, and
that he has done his best to save us."

" No one will suspect me, Monsieur Pelisson," replied the Count.
" But I must yet do something more," he added, believing, not
wrongly, that the words and demeanour of Pelisson must have had
some effect upon the body of men by whom they were surrounded,
and also having some hope that aid might now be at hand. " I
must yet do something more, and the time, I believe, is come for

doing it. Listen to me, sir," he added, addressing the man who had led the band throughout. "I beg of you instantly to set these two gentlemen at liberty. I beg of you, both for your own sake and for the sake of the reformed church, to which I belong, and to whose instigations this act will be attributed; and if you will not attend to my entreaties, you must attend to my command—I command you to set them at liberty!"

"Command!" said the man, with a scornful laugh. "Your commands are likely to be mighty potent here, in the green wood, Sir Count! Now listen to my commands to you. Make the best of your time, and get away from this spot without delay; for if you stay, you shall either see those two men shot before your face, or you shall be shot with them. So be quick!"

"Be it as you say, my good friend," replied the Count, coolly. "We shall have bloody work of it; but before you go on, remember, I tell you, you shall take my life with theirs; and let me warn you of another thing which you do not know, the first shot that is fired, the first loud word that is spoken," he added, dropping his voice, "will bring destruction on the heads of all."

The man to whom he spoke gazed in his face with some surprise, as if not clearly understanding his meaning, while the rest of the band appeared eagerly whispering together, in a manner which might be interpreted to bespeak some difference of opinion between themselves and their leader.

The ear of the Count was quick; while conducting the two ladies to their carriage, he had heard uncertain sounds at a distance, which he had little doubted were occasioned by the arrival of some party from the castle in search of him. While he had spoken to the chief of the band in favour of Pelisson and his companions, he had again caught the same sounds, but more distinctly. He had heard voices, and the trampling of horse, and taking advantage of the momentary hesitation which seemed to affect his opponent, he exclaimed, "Hark!" and lifted up his hand to enjoin silence. The sounds, though distant, were now very distinct, and he added, "You hear! They are in search of me with all the force from the castle. You did not know that my servant was behind when I was taken, and fled to seek succour."

His opponent stamped his foot upon the ground, and laid his hand upon a pistol in his belt, fingering the hammer of the lock in a very ominous manner; but the Count once more interposed, anxious on many accounts to prevent a collision.

"Come," he said, "I wish to do you no injury. Let us compromise the matter. Set the party you have taken free, and doubtless they will abandon to your care and guidance all the baggage and money that they may possess. What say you, Monsieur Pelisson?"

"Willingly, willingly!" cried Pelisson, to whom all the last words spoken had been a relief.

"Willingly, willingly!" cried the Abbé de St. Helie; the tears which had been streaming from fear changing suddenly into the tears of joy, and flowing on as rapidly as ever. Their enemy, however, seemed still to hesitate; but the taller man, whom we have before seen exercising some influence over him, pulled him by the sleeve once more, and whispered to him eagerly. He listened to him for an instant, partly turning away his head, then shook himself pettishly free from his grasp, saying, "Well, I suppose it must be so. I will set them free now; but a day of reckoning will come, if they take not a warning from what has passed. Gather all those things together, my men. Each one take something, and let us be off as fast as we can. Stand to your arms, though; stand to your arms, some of you. Those fellows are coming devilish near, and may find their way up here."

"They shall not injure you," said the Count. "I break no engagements, even when only implied."

At that moment, however, the Abbé de St. Helie, having sufficiently recovered from the terror into which he had been cast to give some thought to what he was about, exclaimed aloud, "But the king's commission—the king's commission! They must not take that;" and rushing towards the baggage, he seized a white leathern bag, which seemed to contain some especial treasure. But scarcely had he got it in his hand, when the chief of their captors snatched it violently from him, and dashed it into the midst of the fire, where he set his foot upon it, as if to insure that it should be burnt, even at the risk of injuring himself.

Albert de Morseiul was an officer in the king's service, and had been brought up in his youth with high notions of devoted loyalty and reverence for the royal authority, which even the free spirit of the reformed religion had not been able to diminish. The insult offered to the monarch's commission then struck him with indignation; and starting forward, he grasped the man who would have destroyed it by the chest, exclaiming, "Sir, would you insult the king himself?"

The man replied not, but strove to keep down his foot upon the packet. The young Count, however, was as powerful in frame as himself, and considerably taller; and, after a momentary struggle, he cast him back, while the Abbé de St. Helie snatched the packet from the flames.

What would have been the result of this strife, in which both the robber's blood and that of the young Count were heated, would be difficult to say; for the man had drawn the pistol from his belt, and the click of the lock was plainly heard as he cocked it; but just at that minute the men who had been engaged in stripping the trunk mails of their contents, caught sight of a party of horsemen coming up the road; and gathering everything that was most valuable together, they retreated quickly around their leader. Abandoning his contention with the Count, the latter now promptly formed them into line, collected all the various articles belonging to themselves which were scattered about, and retreated in the direction of the opposite road, offering a firm face of five men abreast, with their carbines cocked, and levelled at the horsemen, who were now coming up thick into the open space where all these events had passed.

At the head of the body which now appeared, was the Chevalier d'Evran, armed in haste to deliver or avenge his friend, but, as the Count saw that he was now master of the field, and that the robbers were retreating in a very threatening attitude, which might produce bloodshed if it were not immediately apparent that no molestation would be offered to them, he took a rapid step or two forward, exclaiming to his own party—

" Halt, halt! We had come to a compromise before you arrived, and are all at liberty. Thanks, Louis, a thousand thanks, however, for your succour!"

The Count's men paused promptly at his command; and the robbers retreated slowly up the other road, facing round every ten or twelve steps, fully prepared for defence, like an old lion pursued by the hunters. In the meanwhile, the Chevalier sprang from his horse, and grasped his friend's hand eagerly.

" Why, Albert," he exclaimed, " Albert, this would never do! You, one of the rashest officers in the service, who have escaped balls and pikes, and bayonets and sabres, to run the risk of being killed by a ditch-fighting freebooter, within a mile or two of your own hearth! Why, when that rascal Jerome there came and told me, I thought I should have gone mad; but I was determined to ride the rascals down like wolves, if I found they had injured you."

" Oh, no," replied the Count, " they showed no inclination to injure me; and, indeed, it would appear, as far as I am concerned, that the whole matter was a mistake, for to me they were very respectful. In truth, I seemed to be in wonderful favour with them, and my only difficulty was in saving Monsieur Pelisson and this reverend gentleman here. But notwithstanding these worthy men's reverence for myself, I must set to work to put this down as soon as I come back from Poitiers."

" I am sure, Monsieur le Comte," said the Abbé de St. Helie, " we owe you everything this night, and your conduct shall never be blotted out from our grateful remembrance."

The Count bowed low, but somewhat stiffly; then, shaking Pelisson by the hand, he said, " I am happy to have been of any service to you both, gentlemen. My good friend, Monsieur Pelisson, I trust that you will not be any the worse for this short, though unpleasant sojourn in the forest. I will not ask you and your friend to return and stop awhile at the château of Morseiul, as in all probability Monsieur de St. Helie might not relish abiding under the roof of a heretic. But besides that," he added, with a smile, " besides that, in regard to which of course I speak in jest,

I doubt not you are anxious to proceed. Morseiul is out of your way, and in an hour and a half you will reach the auberge of Quatremoulins."

" But, sir, shall we be safe—shall we be safe?" exclaimed the Abbé de St. Helie, who was now examining the vehicle in which they had been travelling, with anxious eyes—" Gracious Heaven!" he exclaimed, ere the Count could answer, " look, there is a ball which has gone through the carriage within an inch of my head!"

The Count de Morseiul looked at the Chevalier, and they both laughed.

" There is a proverb in England, my good Abbé," said the Chevalier, " that a miss is as good as a mile; but if you will take my advice you will plant yourself just in the same spot again, or put your valise to raise you just opposite the shot-hole, for there are a thousand chances to one that, if you are shot at a dozen times, no bullet ever comes there again."

The Abbé did not seem much to like the pleasantry, for in his mind the subject was far too serious a one to admit of a joke; and the Count de Morseiul replied to his former question—"Depend upon it you are in perfect safety. But to make that more sure, the Chevalier and I will return to Morseiul with only one or two attendants, and send the rest of my men to escort you to the inn. However, gentlemen, if you will take my advice, you will not travel by night any more when you are in this part of the country; for from what that fellow said, I should suppose the peasantry have got some evil notion of your intended proceedings here, and it might be dangerous to trust yourselves with them too much. There are such things, you must remember, as shooting from behind hedges, and from the tops of banks; and you must not forget that, in this part of the world, where our lanes are cut deep down between the fields, our orchards thick, and our woods many, it is no easy matter to ascertain where there is an enemy. As I take it for granted you are going towards Poitiers, Monsieur Pelisson, I shall most likely see you soon again. We will all accompany you out of the wood, and then you shall have a sufficient escort to ensure your safety."

Pelisson thanked him again and again. The trunk mails, and what portion of their contents the robbers had left, which consisted of the greater part of their apparel, were gathered together, the carriage re-loaded, and its human burden placed safely in it. Pelisson and the Abbé de St. Helie, after having ascertained that the injuries inflicted by the fire upon the precious packet in the sheepskin bag extended no farther than that outer cover, gave the word that they were ready; and moving on in slow procession, the carriage, its denizens, and their escort of cavaliers made their exit from the scene of their unpleasant adventure into the high road, after which the Count and the Chevalier took leave of the others to return to the château of Morseiul; and thus ended the events of that night.

CHAPTER V.

THE JOURNEY, AND SOME OF ITS EVENTS.

WE will pass over all comments which took place amongst the parties to the scene which we described in our last chapter, and will take up our story again with the interval of a single day.

How happy would it often be for us in life if we could thus blot out a single day! if, out of our existence as out of our history, we could extirpate one four and twenty hours, its never-to-be-recalled deeds, its thoughts affecting the mind for ever, its events influencing the whole course of after-existence! How happy would it be if we could blot it out from being! and often, too often, how happy would it be if we could take it away even from memory—from memory, the treasurer of our joys and pains—memory, whose important charge differs from the bright office of hope, in the sad particular of having to deal with nothing but realities!

However, with the Count de Morseiul and his friend the Chevalier d'Evran, that day had passed in nothing which left regret. The Count had explained to his friend that he judged it necessary to go to Poitiers at once. The Chevalier had very willingly agreed to accompany him, saying, that he would take the good old duke by surprise. They had then enjoyed everything that Morseiul afforded of enjoyable; they had wandered by the glassy stream, they had ridden through the beautiful scenes around, they had hunted the boar in the Count's green woods, they had tasted with moderation his good wine, and the rich fruits of a sunny land; and thus that day had passed over without a cloud.

Although the King of France had given over, by this time, the habit with which he set out, in the light and active days of his first manhood, and no longer made all his journeys on horseback, yet the custom was kept up by a great part of his nobility and officers, and it was very usual to ride post upon a journey: that is to say, to mount whatever horse the postmaster chose to give, and trot on to the next relay, accompanied by a postilion on another horse, carrying the baggage. The Count de Morseiul, however, did not follow this plan, as he had no inclination to appear in the city of Poitiers, which at that time boasted of being the largest city in France, except Paris, in the character of a courier. As he loved not carriages, however, and had plenty of fiery horses in his stable panting for exercise, he sent forward a relay himself to a distant inn upon the road, and, on the morning appointed, accompanied by his friend and a large body of their servants, rode calmly on upon the way, proposing to make a journey of about five and thirty miles that day.

"It is politic of me, D'Evran," he said, conversing with the Chevalier—"it is politic of me to carry you away from Morseiul so soon, as you have promised to give me one whole month, for fear you should become tired of your abode, and exhaust all its little stock of amusements and pleasures too rapidly. Satiety is a great evil, and surely one of the minor policies of life is to guard against it."

"No fear of my getting tired of Morseiul so soon," replied the Chevalier; "but I cannot agree entirely to your view of satiety. I have often had many doubts as to whether it be really an evil or not."

"I have none," replied the Count; "it seems to me the greatest of intellectual evils; it seems to me to be to the mind what despair is to the heart, and in the case of a young man is surely what premature decrepitude is to the body. Good God, Louis, how can you entertain a doubt? The idea of losing one sense, one fine perception, is surely horrible enough; but tenfold horrible must be the idea of losing them altogether; or, what comes to the same thing, of losing the enjoyment that they confer upon us!"

"Nay, but, Albert," said the Chevalier, who was fond of playing with his own wit as a bright weapon, without considering its dangerous nature, and took no little pleasure in calling forth, even against himself, the enthusiastic eagerness of his friend—"nay, but, Albert, what I contend for is, that satiety is true wisdom; that it is a perfect, thorough knowledge of all enjoyments, and a proper estimation of their emptiness."

"Hold, hold!" exclaimed the Count; "that is a very different thing; to my mind, satiety is the exhaustion of our own powers of enjoying, not the discovery of the want of a power of conferring enjoyment in other things. Because a man loses the sense of smelling, that will not deprive the rose of its sweet odour. Does a tyrant cut out my tongue? the delicious flavour of the peach will remain, though I taste it not; though he blind my eyes, the face of nature will flourish and look fair as much as ever. No, no, satiety is the deprivation, by over-enjoyment, of our own powers of receiving; and not a just estimate of the powers of other things in giving pleasure."

"But you will own," said the Chevalier, "that a deep and minute acquaintance with any source of enjoyment naturally tends to diminish the gratification that we at first received from it. You will not deny that moralist and philosopher, from Solomon down to our own days, have all been right in pointing out the vanity of all things. *Vanitas vanitatis*, my dear Count, has been the stamp fixed by every great mind that the world has yet produced upon the objects of human enjoyment. This has been the acme, this the conclusion at which wisdom has arrived; and surely the sooner we ourselves arrive at it in life the better."

"Heaven forbid," exclaimed the Count; "Heaven forbid, either that it should be so, or that such should be your real and mature opinion. You say that a minute acquaintance with the sources of enjoyment diminishes the gratification they afford. There is undoubtedly something lost in every case of such minute acquaintance; but it is by the loss of a peculiar and distinct source of pleasure accompanying every enjoyment the first time it is tasted, and never going beyond. I mean novelty—the bloom upon the ripe plum, which renders it beautiful to the eye as well as refreshing to the taste—brush away the bloom, the plum is no longer so beautiful, but the taste no less refreshing. Setting aside the diminution made for the loss of that novelty, I deny your position."

The Chevalier laughed at his friend's eagerness.

"You will not surely deny, Morseiul," he said, "that there is no pleasure, no enjoyment, really satisfactory to the human heart; and, consequently, the more intimately we become acquainted with it, the more clearly do we see its emptiness."

"Had you said at the first," replied the Count, "that our acquaintance with pleasures shows their insufficiency, I should have admitted the truth of your assertion; but to discover the insufficiency of one pleasure seems to me only a step towards the enjoyment of pleasures of a higher quality."

"But we may exhaust them all," said the Chevalier, "and then comes—what but satiety?"

"No," replied the Count, "not satiety, aspirations for and hopes of higher pleasures still; the last, the grandest, the noblest seeking for enjoyment that the universe can afford; the pursuit that leads us through the gates of the tomb to those abodes where the imperfections of enjoyment end, where the seeds of decay grow not up with the flowers that we plant, where the fruit is without the husk, and the music without the dissonance. This still is left us when all other enjoyments of life are exhausted, or have been tasted, or have been cast away, or have been destroyed. Depend upon it, Louis, that even the knowledge we acquire of the insufficiency of earth's enjoyment gives us greater power to advance in the scale of enjoyment; and that, if we choose to learn our lesson from the picture given us of the earthly paradise, we shall find a grand moral in the tree of eternal life having been planted by the tree of knowledge."

"But still, my dear Count," replied the Chevalier, "you seem still to approach to my argument, while you deny its force. If such be the result of satiety, as you say it is, namely, to lead us to the aspiration after higher enjoyments, till those aspirations point to another world, surely it is better to arrive at that result as soon as possible?"

"No," replied the Count; "in the first place, I did not say that such was the result of satiety; I said that it was the result of discovering by experience the insufficiency of all earthly enjoyments to give perfect satisfaction to a high and immortal spirit and well-regulated mind. Satiety I hold to be quite the reverse of this; I hold it to be the degradation of our faculties of enjoyment, either by excessive indulgence, or by evil direction. The man who follows such a course of life as to produce any chance of reaching satiety, tends downward instead of upward, to lower rather than to higher pleasures, and exhausts his own capabilities, not the blessings of God. The opposite course produces the opposite result; we know and learn that all God's creations afford us some enjoyment, although we know and learn, at the same time, that it has been his will that none of those enjoyments upon earth should give complete and final satisfaction. Our capabilities of enjoying by enjoying properly are not blunted, but acuminated; we fly from satiety instead of approaching it; and even while we learn to aspire to higher things, we lose not a particle of the power—except by the natural decay of our faculties—of enjoying even the slight foretaste that Heaven has given us here."

" Solomon, Solomon, Solomon !" said his companion, " Solomon was evidently a misanthrope either by nature or by satiety. He had seen everything under the sun, and he pronounced everything vanity—ay, lighter than vanity itself."

" And he was right," replied the Count; " everything is lighter than vanity itself, when comparing the things of this world with the things of eternity. But you know," he added with a smile, "that we Huguenots, as you call us, acknowledge no authority against the clear operation of reason, looking upon no man as perfect but one, who broke down the barrier of sin between God and man, and made humanity divine. If you were to tell me that it was right to put a friend in a dangerous place where he was sure to be killed for the purpose of marrying his widow, I should not a bit more believe that it was right, because David had done it; and even if you were to prove to me that through the whole writings of Solomon there was not, as I believe there is, a continual comparison between earthly things and heavenly things, I should still say that you were in the wrong; the satiety that he felt being a just punishment upon him for the excesses he committed and the follies to which he gave way, and by no means a proof of his wisdom, any more than those follies and excesses themselves. Long before we have exhausted the manifold pleasures which Heaven has given us here by moderate and virtuous enjoyment—long before we have even discovered by experience the insufficiency of one half that we may properly enjoy, the span of man's life is finished; and at the gates of death he may think himself happy, if, while he has learnt to desire the more perfect enjoyment of heavenly things, he has not rendered himself unfit for that enjoyment, by having depraved his faculties to satiety by excess."

" Well, well," said the Chevalier, seeing that his friend spoke earnestly, "I am afraid I must give up Solomon, Albert. If I remember right, the man had some hundreds of wives or so; and I am sure he might well cry out that all is vanity after that. I wonder they did not all fall upon him at once, and smother him under looking-glasses and bonbonnières."

The Count saw that his friend turned the matter into a joke, and, from his long acquaintance with him, he doubted not that he had been carrying on the discussion from first to last for sport. He was not angry or cross about it; but, of an eager and of an earnest disposition, he could not play with subjects of value, like an unconscious child tossing jewels to and fro; and he remained thoughtful for some time. While the Chevalier continued to jest upon a thousand things, sometimes connecting one joke with another in rapid and long succession, sometimes pausing for a moment or two, and taking his next subject from any accidental circumstance in their ride or feature in the scene around, the Count gradually resumed the conversation upon indifferent matters. Having only in view, however, in any extracts that we may give from their conversation, either to forward the progress of their history or to display the peculiar character of each, we shall dwell no longer upon their words during the rest of the ride to a little village, some seventeen miles from the château, where they stayed a moment to water their horses. The Count was looking down, watching the animals as they drank; but the Chevalier, who was gazing at everything in the place, suddenly exclaimed—

"Surely there cannot be two such ugly heads as that in France! The Abbé Pelisson, as I live! Why, Monsieur Pelisson," he exclaimed, advancing till he was directly under the window from which the head of the Abbé was protruded, "how have you stuck here by the way?"

"Alas! my good sir," replied the Abbé, "the fright of the day before yesterday had such an effect upon my poor companion de St. Helie, that he was quite unable to proceed. He is better this afternoon, and we shall set out in an hour, after he has taken something to refresh him and give him strength."

"You will overtake us at our next lodging," said the Chevalier.

"Oh, no, we shall pass you far," replied the Abbé. "We shall still have five hours' light, and as we travel by post, we may calculate upon going between five and six miles an hour."

The Count, on his part, made no comment, but merely nodded his head to Pelisson; and when the Chevalier's brief conversation was at an end, they rode on. The village which they had fixed upon for their resting-place that night was a large, straggling, open collection of houses, which had grown up on either side of the wide road, simply because it happened to be at a convenient distance from many other places. The buildings were scattered, and separated by large gardens or courts, and the inn itself was, in fact, the only respectable dwelling in the place, having been an old brick-built country seat in former days, with the walls that defended it from attack still standing round the court, the windows rattling and quivering with the wind and their antiquity, the rooms wide and

lofty, and perhaps a little cheerless, and the kitchen, which formed
the entrance, as black as the smoke of many generations could
render it.

The whole household was prepared to meet the Count de Morseiul, his coming having been announced by the servants sent on
with the horses; and did ducks and fowls in various countries write
the histories of their several races, that morning would have been
memorable for the massacre that took place, and only be com-
parable to the day of St. Bartholomew. But the culinary art was
great in France then as it is now, and the cook, knowing that she
had a difficult task to perform, exerted her utmost ingenuity to render
tough poultry tender, and insipid viands savoury, for the distinguished guest that was to dine and sleep within those walls. Though
the preparations had been begun at an early hour, yet they were
by no means concluded when the party arrived; and while Jerome
Riquet plunged into the kitchen, and communicated to the cook a
thousand secrets from the vast stores of his own mind, the Count
and his friend gazed forth from the window of a high square-shaped
room over the wide prospect, which lay in gentle undulations
beneath their eyes, with the road that they themselves had just
passed taking, as it were, a standing leap over each of the little hills
that it met with in its way.

The day had been remarkably fine during the earlier portion
thereof, but towards three o'clock clouds had come over, not, indeed, veiling the sky under their sheet of sombre grey, but fleeting lightly across the blue expanse, like the momentary cares of infancy, and passing away, after dropping a few large tears, which
the joyful sun dried up again the moment after. As the Count and
his friend gazed forth, however, a heavier shower was seen sweeping over the prospect, the sky became quite covered, a grey mist—
through which, however, a yellow gleam was seen, saying that the
summer night was not far off—advanced over wood and field, and hill
and dale, and dashing down with all the impetuous and short-lived
fury of an angry boy, the cloud poured forth its burden on the
earth. While yet it was raging in its utmost wrath, the plain carriage of Pelisson and his companions was seen rolling slowly onward
towards the village, with coachman and lackey holding down the
drenched head towards the storm, and shading the defenceless neck.
All the windows of the vehicle were closed, in order, if possible, to
keep out the wind and rain; but constructed as carriages were in
those days, there was no great protection to be found in them
from the breath or the drops of heaven; and, as the rumbling
vehicle approached the village, the head of Pelisson was seen suddenly thrust forth on the safest side, shouting something to the
coachman, who seemed inclined to go through all the signs in the
subjunctive mood of the verb, *not to hear*. After repeating three
times his words, the Abbé drew his head in again, and the carriage
entered the village.

" For a hundred louis," said the Chevalier, " we have the company of Messieurs Pelisson and St. Helie to-night. I beseech thee, Albert, tell them they cannot lodge here, if it be but to see their rueful faces. Look, look! There comes the vehicle, like the ark of Noah, discovered by some fortunate chance on Ararat, and set upon the wheels of Pharaoh's chariot, fished out of the Red Sea. Where could they pick up such an antediluvian conveyance? Look, the ark stops! Now, open the window, Noah. Out comes the door!" and, as he spoke, he had matter for more merriment, for the first person that issued forth was the fat black-faced priest in his greasy cassock. " The raven! The raven!" shouted the Chevalier, laughing aloud, " What beast next, Count? What beast next?"

" Hush, hush! Louis," said his friend, in a lower tone; " they will hear you, and it is a pity to give pain."

" True, oh, most sapient Albert," answered the Chevalier, " and you shall see how courteous I can be. I will even take the raven by the claw—if you give me but time to order a basin and napkin in the adjoining room for the necessary ablution afterwards. Oh, Monsieur Pelisson, enchanted to see you!" he continued, as the Abbé entered the room; " Monsieur de St. Helie, this is indeed delightful; Monsieur de Beaumanoir, allow me to take you by the hand," he added, advancing towards the greasy priest.

" You mistake me for some one else," said the priest, drawing slightly back, turning his shoulder, and speaking through his teeth like a muzzled bear: " I am the Curé de Guadrieul."

" True, true; I forgot," went on the Chevalier, in the same wild way. " Enchanted to see you, Monsieur le Curé de Guadrieul! How much we are bound to laud and love this shower for having given us the felicity of your society!"

" I am sure I have no cause to laud it," said the priest, " for all the rain has come in at that crazy window, and run into my neck, besides drenching my soutane."

The Chevalier might have gone on for an hour, but the Count came to the relief of the poor priest. He notified to Pelisson and his companions, that the house and all that it contained had been engaged by him; but he pressed them to remain as his guests so cordially, that Monsieur de St. Helie, who—though he loved not Huguenots, loved damp weather less and savoury viands more— consented readily, warned by the rising odours from the kitchen, that he might certainly go farther and fare worse. Chambers were found for the new guests, and, before an hour had passed, the whole party was seated at a groaning board, the plentiful supply on which made Monsieur de St. Helie open his eyes with well satisfied astonishment. We are not quite sure, indeed, that he did not feel a greater respect for protestantism than he had ever felt before; and so placable and mild had he evidently become, that the Chevalier whispered to his friend, while apparently speaking of something

else, " For Heaven's sake, Morseiul, never suffer your people to
give that man such a feast again! Three such dinners would make
him condemn his own soul, and turn heretic."

Pelisson was cheerful as usual, mild and gentle, a little plausible
perhaps, and somewhat too courtier-like, but still rendering himself
most agreeable, both by his manner and by a sort of indescribable
ease and grace in his conversation and language. Behind the chair
of the Count, as a sort of nomenclator of the different dishes, had
placed himself worthy Maître Jerome Riquet. Now, Heaven
knows that no person was naturally more simple in his tastes than
Albert of Morseiul; but he had left, as usual, all the minor arrangements of his comfort to others, and certainly Jerome Riquet, as
soon as he heard that two Catholic abbés and a priest were about
to dine at the table of his master, had not relaxed in any of his
efforts to excel all excellence, determined to astound the ecclesiastics by the luxury and splendour of a country inn. Had that inn
produced nothing but parchment and jack-boots, Jerome Riquet
would have discovered means of sending in entrée upon entrée in
various different forms, and under various different names. But as
it was, notice of the Count's coming having been given the day
before, and vast preparations made by the worthy aubergiste, the
suppers of Versailles were little more refined than that to which
Pelisson and his companions now sat down; while, according to
Jerome's directions, two servants stood behind every chair, and the
Count was graced by his own additional presence at the right
elbow.

Riquet himself had not only taken up that position as the *Pièce
de résistance,* but as the *Pièce de parade,* and, as was not uncus-
tomary then, he mingled with what was going forward at table
whenever it suited him. Often by a happy exhortation upon some
dish, or observation upon some wine, he contrived to turn the conversation in a different direction when it was proceeding in a way
that did not please him. About half-way through the meal, however, his attention seemed to be caught by something awkward in
the position of the Curé de Guadrieul, and from time to time he
turned a sort of anxious and inquiring glance towards him, wondering whether he sat so high in his chair from the natural conformation of short legs and a long body, or from some adventitious
substance placed beneath his nether man.

He made various movements to discover it; but, in the meantime, the conversation went on, and the Count having been naturally drawn by the observation of some other person to pay Pelisson
a compliment upon his graceful style, the Abbé replied, " Oh, my
style is nothing, Monsieur le Comte, though you are good enough
to praise it; and besides, after all, it is but style. I had a brother
once, poor fellow!" he added, " who might indeed have claimed
your praise; for, in addition to good style, which he possessed in
an infinitely higher degree than myself, he had a peculiar art of

speaking briefly, which, Heaven knows, I have not, and of leaving nothing unsaid that could be said upon the subject he treated. When he was only nineteen years of age he was admitted to the academy of Castres; but, upon his admission, they made this singular and flattering condition with him, namely, that he should never speak upon any subject till everybody else had spoken, 'for,' said the academicians, 'when he speaks first, he never leaves anybody else anything to say upon the subject, and when he speaks last he finds a thousand things to say that nobody else has said.' Besides all this," he continued, " my brother had another great and inestimable advantage over me."

" Pray what was that?" demanded the Count.

" He was not hideous," replied Pelisson.

" Oh, I do not think that such an advantage," said the Chevalier. "It is the duty of a woman to be handsome; but I think men have a right to be ugly if they like."

"So say I," replied Pelisson; " but Mademoiselle de Scudery says that I abuse the privilege; and upon my word I think so, for just before I came from Paris something happened which is worth telling. I was walking along," he continued, "quite soberly and thoughtfully down the Rue de Beauvoisis—you know that little street that leads up by the convent of St. Mary?—when, coming opposite to a large house nearly at the corner, I was suddenly met by as beautiful a creature as ever I saw, with her soubrette by her side, and her loup in her hand, so that I could quite see her face. She was extremely well dressed, and, in fact, altogether fit to be the Goddess of an Idyl. However, as I did not know her, I was passing quietly on, when suddenly she stopped, took me by the hand, and said, in an earnest voice, 'Do me the pleasure, sir, of accompanying me for one moment.' On my word, gentlemen, I did not know what was going to happen; but I was a great deal too gallant, of course, to refuse her; when, without another word, she led me to the door of the house, up the stairs, rang the bell on the first floor, and conducted me into an anteroom. A servant threw open another door for her; and then bringing me into a second room, where I found a gentleman of good mien with two sticks in his hand, she presented me to him with these singular words: ' *Line for line, sir, like that! Remember, line for line, sir, like that!* ' and then turning on her heel, she walked away, leaving me petrified with astonishment. The gentleman in whose presence I stood seemed no less surprised for a moment than myself; but the instant after he burst into a violent fit of laughter, which made me a little angry.

" 'Pray, sir, what is the meaning of all this?' I asked. 'Do you not know that lady?' he rejoined. 'No, sir,' I replied, 'I neither know her nor you.' ' Oh, as for me,' replied the gentleman, ' you have seen me more than once before, Monsieur Pelisson, though you do not know me. I am Mignard, the painter; but as

to the lady, I must either not give you the clue to her bringing you
here, or not give you her name, which you like.' 'Give me the
clue; give me the clue,' replied I; 'the lady's name I will find out
hereafter.'

"'Do not be offended, then,' he said; 'but the truth is, I am
painting for that lady a picture of the Temptation in the Wilderness.
She came to see it this morning, and a violent dispute arose between us, as to how I was to represent the devil; she contending
that he was to be excessively ugly, and I, that though disfigured by
bad passions, there was to be the beauty of an angel fallen. She
left me a minute ago in a fit of playful pettishness, when lo and behold, she returns almost instantly, bringing you in her hand, and
saying, 'Line for line, like that.' I leave you to draw your own
conclusion.'

"I did draw my own conclusion," continued Pelisson, "and got
out of the way of Monsieur Mignard's brush as fast as possible, only
saying, that I thought the lady very much in the wrong, for there
could lie no great temptation under such an exterior as mine."

His auditors laughed both at the story and at the simplicity with
which it was told, and no one laughed more heartily than the black-
faced priest. But while he was chuckling on his seat, Maitre
Jerome, who had glided round behind him, suddenly seized hold of
two leathern strings that hung down over the edge of the chair, and,
exclaiming, "That must be very inconvenient to your reverence,"
he pulled out from underneath him, by a sudden jerk which nearly
laid him at his length on the floor, the identical sheep-skin bag
which had nearly been burnt to pieces in the wood.

The priest started up with terror and dismay, exclaiming, "Give
it to me: give it to me, sirrah! How dare you take it from under
me? It is the king's commission to Messieurs Pelisson and St.
Helie for putting down heresy in Poitou."

A sudden grave look and a dead silence succeeded this unexpected announcement; but while the priest snatched the packet
from Jerome Riquet's profane hands, declaring that he had promised not to part with it for a moment, Pelisson made his voice
heard, saying—

"You mistake, my good brother; such is not the object of the
commission, as the king explained it to me On the contrary, his
majesty said that, when it was opened at Poitiers, we should find
that the whole object and scope of it was to heal the religious differences of the province in the mildest and most gentle manner
possible."

"I trust it may be found so, Monsieur Pelisson," replied the
Count, gravely, turning his eyes from the Abbé de St. Helie, who said
nothing. "I trust it may be found so;" and though it was evident
that some damp was thrown upon his good spirits, he turned the
conversation courteously and easily to other subjects: while Jerome
Riquet, satisfied in regard to the nature of the packet, made a

thousand apologies to the Curé of Guadrieul, loaded his plate with delicacies, and then returned to his master's elbow.

After supper, for so the meal was then called, the party separated. The Chevalier d'Evran, for motives of his own, attached himself closely, for the time being, to the Abbé de St. Helie, and engaged him in a party at tric-trac; the young Count strolled out in the evening light with Pelisson, both carefully avoiding any religious subjects, from the delicacy of their mutual position; the fat priest went to gossip with Maitre Jerome, and smoke a pipe in the kitchen of the inn; and the serving men made love to the village girls, or caroled in the court-yard.

Thus ended the first day's journey of the Count de Morseiul towards Poitiers. On the following morning, he had taken his departure before the ecclesiastics had risen, leaving the servants, who were to follow with the horses, to make them fully aware that they had been his guests during their stay at the inn; and on the third day, at about five o'clock in the afternoon, he came under the high rocky banks that guard the entrance to the ancient city which was to be the end of his journey.

CHAPTER VI.

THE LADY AND HER LOVERS.

THE city of Poitiers is a beautiful old town—at least it is a town in which there is much to interest; and where the memories of many remote periods cross and intersect each other, like the arches of a Gothic church, forming a fretwork over head of varied and solemn, though dim, associations. The Roman, and the Goth, and the Frank, and the Englishman, have all there left indelible traces of their footsteps; and each spot through the streets of that city, and through the neighbouring country, is shadowed or brightened by the recollection of great and extraordinary deeds in the past. There is something in it, also, unlike any other town in the world; the number and extent of its gardens, the distance between its various houses, would make it look more like an orchard than a town, did not every here and there rise up some striking edifice, some fine church, bearing in its windows the leopards, or the fleurs de lis, as the case may be, a town-house, a broken citadel, or a Roman amphitheatre in ruins, and all amidst rich green gardens, and grapes, and flowering shrubs.

The Count de Morseiul and his train, after passing the gates of the city, then duly watched and warded, rode on to the house of the governor, which was, at that time, in the great square. It had probably been a Roman building, of which part of the portico had been

preserved, forming the end of one of the wings; for, during three
or four centuries, a tall porch had remained there, supported by
three columns.   Though the principal gate was in the centre of the
house, it was usual for the people of the town to enter by this
porch ; and such was the only purpose that it served.   The whole
aspect of the place has been altered long since; the governor's
house has been changed into an inn, where I have slept on more
than one occasion; and of the three columns, nothing remains but
the name, which has descended to the hotel.   It was in that time,
however, a large brick building, with an immense arched gateway
in the centre, under which Goliath of Gath himself might have
passed on horseback with a feather in his cap.   Beyond this was
the inner court, with the usual buildings around it; but upon a
large and magnificent scale; and on the left, under the archway,
rose a wide flight of stone steps, leading to the principal apartments
above.

Throughout the whole town, and especially in the neighbourhood of the governor's house, there appeared, on the day of the
Count's arrival, a greater degree of bustle and activity than Poitiers generally displays; and as he drew up his horse under the
archway, to ascend the stairs, several peasant girls, after pausing to
look at the cavaliers, passed on into the courts beyond, loaded with
baskets full of flowers, and fruit, and green branches.

As he had sent on a messenger the day before to announce his
approach, the Count de Morseiul knew that he was expected; and
it was evident, from the sudden rushing forth of a number of servants, the rapid and long ringing of the great bell, and a thousand
other such signs, that orders had been given to treat him with
especial distinction.   While some of the masters of the stable took
possession of his grooms and horse-boys, to show them to the place
appointed for them, two other servants, in costumes which certainly
did honour to the taste of M. le Marquis Auguste de Hericourt,
marshalled the Count and the Chevalier, followed by their re-
spective valets and pages—without which appurtenances men of
their rank and fortune travelled not in that day — to the vestibule
at the top of the staircase.

A step beyond the door of the vestibule, which was also a step
beyond what etiquette required, the governor of the province was
already waiting to receive the Count de Morseiul.   He was a
frank, amiable, and kind-hearted old gentleman, as tall, and as thin,
and as brown as a cypress tree; and grasping the Count's hand, he
welcomed him to Poitiers as an old friend, and the son of an old
friend, and likewise, perhaps we might say, as one whose high character and fame, as a soldier, he greatly and sincerely admired.
While speaking to the Count so eagerly that he saw nothing else,
the governor felt a hand laid upon his arm, and, turning, beheld the
Chevalier, whom he welcomed also warmly, though in a peculiar tone
of intimacy which he had not used towards the Count de Morseiul.

" Ah, d'Evran," he said, " what brought you here, mad boy? I wanted not to see you; but I can tell you I shall put you in a garret, as you deserve, for the house is filled to the doors. This is our first grand reception, our little provincial *appartement.* All the nobility in the neighbourhood are flocking in, and, as we cannot lodge them all, we are obliged to begin our entertainment as early as possible, in order to suffer some of them to get home betimes. This must plead my apology, my dear Count, for not giving you more spacious apartments yourself, and for not taking you at once to the Duchess, who is all anxiety to see our hero. Some refreshments shall be taken to you in your own apartment, to your little salon, where, perhaps, you will give a corner to this wild Chevalier; for there is that young puppy Hericourt, who only arrived last night, up to the elbows in the dining-room, in all sorts of finery and foolery."

" But where is la belle Clémence ?" demanded the Chevalier. " Where is the beauty of beauties? Will she not give me a quarter of an hour in her boudoir, think you, Duke?"

" Go along with you," replied the Duke: " Clémence does not want to see you. Go and refresh yourself with the Count: by that time we shall have found a place to put you in; and when you have cast off your dusty apparel, ransacked the perfumers, sought out your best lace, and made yourself look as insupportably conceited as you used to do two years ago at Versailles, it will be time for you to present yourself in our reception-room, and there you can see Clémence, who, I dare say, will laugh at you to your heart's content."

" So be it — so be it," replied the Chevalier, with a well-satisfied air. " Come, Count, we must obey the governor: see if he do not make himself as despotic here as his majesty in Paris. Which is our way, Monsieur de Rouvré?" and with that appearance of indifference which has always been a current sort of affectation with men of the world, from the days of Horace downwards, he followed the servants to the handsome apartments prepared for the Count de Morseiul, which certainly needed no apology.

On the table, the Count found a packet of letters, which Monsieur de Rouvré had brought for him from Paris. They contained nothing of any great importance, being principally from old military companions; but after the Chevalier had taken some refreshments, and retired to the apartments which had been prepared in haste for him, the Count took up the letters, and, carried forward by the memory of old times, went on reading, forgetful of the necessity of dressing himself for the approaching fête. He promised himself little or no pleasure indeed therein, for he expected to see few with whom he was acquainted; and his mind was too deeply occupied with important and even painful subjects, for him to think of mingling in lighter scenes with any very agreeable sensations.

Thus he did not remember then the necessity of preparation, till he had to call for lights, and heard the roll of carriage-wheels, and the clattering of horses. He then, however, hastened to repair his forgetfulness; but Jerome was not so prompt and ready as usual, or else he was far more careful of his master's appearance. We will not, indeed, pause upon all the minute points of his toilet; but certainly, by the time the valet would acknowledge that his master was fit to go down, he had given to the Count's fine person every advantage that dress could bestow; and perhaps Albert of Morseiul did not look at all the worse for that air of high and thoughtful intelligence, which the deep interests whereon his mind was fixed, called up in a countenance, to the fine and noble features of which that expression was so peculiarly suited.

When, at length, he entered the little saloon which had been allotted to him, he found one of the officers of the governor waiting, with his own page, to conduct him to the reception-rooms; and, on asking if the Chevalier was ready, he found that he had been there seeking him, and had gone down. It was a slight reproach for his tardiness, and the Count hastened to follow. The way was not long, but the stairs had been left somewhat dark, as but little time had been given for preparation; and when the doors were opened for the young Count, a blaze of light and a scene of magnificence burst upon his eyes, which he had not been prepared to see in that remote part of France.

The rooms were brilliantly, though softly lighted, and the principal blaze came from the great saloon at the farther end. Rich hangings and decorations were not wanting, but as they were, of course, to be procured with greater difficulty than in Paris, the places where many draperies would have hung, or where gilded scrolls, trophies, and other fanciful embellishments would have appeared, were filled up with much better taste from the storehouses of nature; and garlands, and green boughs, and the multitude of flowers which that part of the country produces, occupied every vacant space. A very excellent band of musicians, which the Duke had brought with him from the capital, was posted in an elevated gallery of the great saloon; and the sweet notes of many popular melodies of the day came pouring down the long suite of apartments, softened, but not rendered indistinct by the distance. In the first chamber which the Count entered were a great number of the inferior officers of the governor, in their dresses of ceremony, giving that antechamber an air of almost regal state; and through the midst of them was passing, at the moment, a party of the high nobles of the province, who had just arrived before the Count came in.

Though not above one half of the invited had yet appeared, there were numerous groups in every part of the rooms; and at more than one of the tables, which, as customary in that age, were set out for play, the young Count found persons whom he knew, and stopped to speak with them as he advanced. The Duke and

Duchess de Rouvré had taken their station in the great saloon; but in the smaller room immediately preceding it, Albert de Morseiul paused by one of the tables, to converse for a moment with the Prince de Marsillac, who was leaning against it ; not playing, but turning his back with an air of indifference upon the scene beyond.

"Ah, Monsieur de Morseiul," he said, "it is an unexpected pleasure to meet you here ; I thought you were in Flanders."

"I was so fourteen days ago," replied the Count; "but as little did I expect to see you."

"Oh, this is in some sort my native country," replied the Prince; "and being here upon family affairs, I could not, of course, hesitate to come and grace the first entertainment of the good duke. There seems a promise of a goodly assembly; and, indeed, there are attractions enough, what between a new governor, a new governess, and a Clémence de Marly."

"And pray who is Clémence de Marly?" demanded the Count. "I am a rustic, you see, and have never yet heard of her."

"Rustic, indeed!" said the Prince; "why all the Parisian world is mad about her. She is the most admired—the most adored, I may say—of all the stars or comets, or what not, that have appeared in my day ; as beautiful as Hebe, as graceful as the brightest of the Graces, as proud as Juno, about ten times colder than Diana, and as witty as Madame de Cornuel. People began to fancy that the king himself was in love with her; only you know that now, under the domination L'Amie de l'Amie, those days of folly and scandal have gone by, and, on my word, the saucy beauty treated majesty no better than she does nobility. I myself heard her——"

"But who is Clémence de Marly?" demanded the Count again; "you have not satisfied me, Marsillac. Of what race or family is she? I know of no such name connected with the Rouvrés."

The Prince replied in a lower tone, "She is an orphan—a foundling—an anything you like. Some say," he added in a whisper, "a natural child of the king's own ; but others again, and this is the true story, say that she is a natural child of De Rouvré's. There was a tale some time ago, you know, before he married, about him and the Countess de ——, a person of very large fortune; and as this girl has wealth at command, and lives always with the Rouvrés, there can be no doubt of the matter. Madame de Rouvré, having no family, wisely treats her as her child, and spoils her as if she were her grandchild They used to say she was to be married to your friend the Chevalier d'Évran, whom I saw hanging at her elbow just now. Hericourt vows that he will cut the throat of any man who marries her without his consent; but Louvois is supposed to have laid out a match for her even nearer to his race than that ; Segnelai is not without hopes of carrying off the prize for some of his people; and they seem in these days to care no more for the bend sinister than if the Adam and Eve laws still prevailed, and we were all the children of nature together."

" This is the fair lady that d'Evran has been talking to me about," replied the Count; " but he talked of her and her beauty so coolly, that I can scarcely suppose he is much in love."

" Just come round hither and look at him, then," said Marsillac, moving a little farther down, so as to give a fuller view into the other room. " You know d'Evran's way of being in love; lying down upon a sofa and playing with a feather fan, while the lady stands at the distance of two yards from him, and he says more clever things to her in five minutes than anybody else can say in an hour. There he is doing it even now."

The Count moved slowly into the place which Marsillac had left for him, so as not to attract attention by flagrant examination of what was going on, and then raised his eyes towards the part of the great saloon at which the Prince had been looking. The group that they lighted on was certainly in every respect a singular one. In the centre of it stood or rather leaned beside a high-backed chair, in an attitude of the most perfect grace that it is possible to conceive, which could not have been studied, for there was ease and nature in every line, a young lady, apparently of one or two and twenty years of age, whose beauty was both of a very exquisite and a very singular cast. It fully justified the description which had been given of it by the Chevalier d'Evran; the eyes were deep deep blue, but fringed with long and dark lashes, thickset but smooth, and sweeping in one even graceful fringe: The lips were, indeed, what lips less lovely have been often called, twin roses; the complexion delicately fair, and yet the face bearing in the cheek the warm hue of undiminished health. Those lips, even when not speaking, were always a little, a very little, parted, showing the bright pearl-like teeth beneath; the brow was smooth and fair, and yet the eyebrow which marked the exact line of the forehead above the eyes, changed, by the slightest elevation or depression, the whole expression of the countenance with every passing emotion. With every change the other features harmonized, and there was a bright sparklingness about the face, even at that distance, which made it, to the eyes of the Count, resemble a lovely landscape in an early summer morning, where everything seems fresh life and brightness. The ear, too, which was slightly turned towards them, was most beautiful; and the form, though the dress of that day did not serve to expose it much, was seen swelling through the drapery· in every line of exquisite beauty. The hand, the arm, the foot, the neck and throat, were all perfect as any sculptor could have desired to model; and the whole, with the grace of the attitude and the beauty of the expression, formed an object that one might have well wished to look at for long hours.

On the right of the lady, precisely as the Prince had described him, lay the Chevalier d'Evran, richly dressed, and, perhaps, affecting a little more indifference than he really felt. Half kneeling, half sitting, at her feet, was the Marquis de Hericourt, saying nothing, but looking up in her face with an expression which plainly implied that he was doubtful whether she or himself were the loveliest creature upon earth. On her left hand stood a gentleman whom the Count instantly recognised as one of the highest and most distinguished nobles of the court of Louis XIV., several years older than either the Marquis or the Chevalier, but still apparently as much if not more smitten than either. Behind her, and round about her, in various attitudes, were half a dozen others, each striving to catch her attention for a single moment; but it was to the elder gentleman whom we have mentioned that she principally listened, except, indeed, when some witticism of the Chevalier caused her to turn and smile upon him for a moment. Amongst the rest of the little train behind her were two personages, for neither of whom the Count de Morseiul entertained any very great esteem: the Chevalier de Rohan, a ruined and dissipated scion of one of the first families in France, and a gentleman of the name of Hatréaumont, whom the Count had known while serving with the army in Flanders, and who, though brave as a lion, bore such a character for restless and unprincipled scheming, that the Count had soon reduced their communication to a mere passing bow.

All the rest of those who surrounded her were distinguished as far as high station and wealth went, and many were marked for higher and better qualities; but, in general, she seemed to treat them all as mere slaves, sending one hither with a message, and another thither for something that she wanted, with an air of proud command, as if they were born but to obey her will.

The group was, as we have said, an interesting and a curious one; but what was there in it that made the Count de Morseiul turn deadly pale? What was there in it that made his heart beat with feelings which he had never known before in gazing at any proud beauty of this world? What was it made him experience different sensations towards that lady, the first time that he beheld her, from those which he had ever felt towards others?

Was it the first time that he had ever beheld her? Oh, no. There, though the features were somewhat changed by the passing of a few years, though the beauty of the girl had expanded into the beauty of the woman, though the form had acquired roundness and *contour* without losing one line of grace, there, in that countenance and in that form, he beheld again the dream of his young imagination; there he saw her of whom he had thought so often, and with whose image he had sported in fancy, till the playfellow of his imagination had become the master of his feelings; and now that he did see her, he saw her in a situation and under circumstances that gave him pain. All the beauty of person, indeed, which he had so much admired, was there; but all those charms of the heart and of the mind, which his fancy had read in the book of that

G

beauty, seemed now reversed; and he beheld but a spoilt, proud, lovely girl, apparently as vain and frivolous as the rest of a vain and frivolous court.

"You are silent long, de Morseiul," said the Prince de Marsillac —"you are silent very long. You seem amongst the smitten, my good friend. What! shall we see the fair lands and châteaux of the first Protestant gentleman in France laid at the feet of yon pretty dame? Take my advice, Morseiul; take the advice of an older man than yourself. Order your horses to be saddled early to-morrow morning, and get you back to your castle or to the army. Even if she were to have you, Morseiul, she would never suit you. Her heart, man, is as cold as a Russian winter, and as hard as the nether millstone, and never in this world will she love any other thing but her own pretty self."

"I am not at all afraid of her," replied the Count; "I have seen her before, and was only admiring the group around her."

"Seen her and forgotten her!" exclaimed Marsillac, "so as not to remember her when I spoke of her! In the name of Heaven let her not hear that. Nay, tell it not at the court, if you would maintain your reputation for wit, wisdom, and good taste. But I suppose, in fact, you are as cold as she is. Go and speak to her, Morseiul; go and speak to her; for I see, indeed, you are quite safe."

"Not I, indeed," said the Count; "but I will go and speak to the Duke and his excellent lady; and, I suppose, in time, shall have to go through all sorts of necessary formalities with la belle Clémence; but till it is needful, I have no inclination to increase any lady's vanity who seems to have so much of it already."

Thus saying, he turned away, only hearing the Prince exclaim, "O mighty Sybarite!" and moving with easy grace through the room, he advanced into the great saloon, cast his eyes round the whole extent, looking for the Duke and Duchess, and passing over la belle Clémence and her party with a mere casual glance, as if he scarcely saw or noticed her. There was an immediate whisper in the little group itself. Several of those around took upon them to tell her who he was, and all eyes followed him as, with the same calm and graceful, but somewhat stately, steps he advanced to the spot where the Duke and Duchess were placed, and was warmly greeted by the latter as an old and valued friend.

She made a place for him by her side, and leaning down from time to time by the good old lady's chair, he took the opportunity of each interval between the appearance of the new guests, to address to her some little kindly and graceful observation, calling back her memory to old times, when she had fondled his boyhood, and, by mingling perhaps a little of the melancholy that adheres to the past with more cheerful subjects, rendered them thereby not the less pleasant.

The Duchess was well pleased with his attention, and for some time seemed inclined to enjoy it alone; but at length she said, " I must not keep you here, Count, all night, or I shall have the Duke jealous at sixty, which would never do. You must go and say sweet things, as in duty bound, to younger dames than I am. See, there is Mademoiselle de Fronsac, as pretty a creature as ever was seen, and our Clémence. You know Clémence, do you not?— but look, Mademoiselle de Fronsac, as if to give you a fair opportunity, has dropped her bracelet."

The Count advanced to pick up the bracelet for the young lady to whom his attention had been called, but his purpose was anticipated by a gentleman who stood near, and at the same moment the Chevalier seeing his friend detached from the side of the Duchess, crossed the saloon towards him, and took him by the arm. " Come, Albert," he said, " come; this is affectation. You must come and undergo the ordeal of those bright eyes. She has been speaking of you, and with deep interest, I assure you."

The Count smiled. " To mortify some culprit lover!" he said, " or give a pang to some young foolish heart. Was it you, Louis?" he asked, in the same tone—" was it you she sought to tease, by speaking with interest of another?"

" You are wrong, Albert," said the Chevalier, in a low voice, leading him gradually towards the spot—" you are wrong. I do not seek Clémence de Marly. My resolution has long been taken. I shall never marry—nor would any consideration upon earth lead her to marry me. I know that full well; but while I say so, I tell you, too, that you do her injustice. You must not judge of her at once."

They were now within a few steps of the spot where Clémence stood, and the Count, who had been looking down while he advanced, listening to the low words of the Chevalier, now raised his eyes as the other took a step forward to introduce him. To his surprise he saw the colour varying in the cheek of the lovely being before whom he stood, and a slight degree of flutter in her manner and appearance, which Albert de Morseiul could only account for by supposing that the scene in which they had last met, the robbers, and the wood, and the plunder of the carriage, had risen up before her eyes, and produced the agitation he saw in one who was apparently so self-possessed in her usual demeanour. There, upon her finger too, he saw the identical ring which he had saved for her from the robbers; and as he was in no way vain, he attributed the heightened colour to all those remembrances. But while he recalled that evening, his feelings towards Clémence grew less severe—he felt there was a tie between them of some interest; he felt, too, that her demeanour then had been very different from that which it appeared to be now. Though scarcely ten words had been spoken in the wood, those words had been all indicative of deep feelings and strong affections; there had been the signs of the heart, the clinging memories of love, the pure sensations of an unworldly spirit; and when he now gazed upon her, surrounded by flatterers and lovers, heartless herself, and seeming to take no delight but in sporting with the hearts of others, the ancient story of the two separate spirits in the same form seemed realized before him, and he knew not how to reconcile the opposite traits that he observed.

All this passed through his mind in a moment. Rapid thought, that, winging its way along the high road of time, can cover years in a single instant, had glanced over all that we have said, even while the words of introduction were hanging upon the tongue of the Chevalier d'Evran. The Count bowed low but gravely, met the full glance of those lustrous eyes without the slightest change of countenance, and was about to have added some commonplace and formal compliment; but Clémence de Marly spoke first.

"I sent the Chevalier to you, Monsieur de Morseiul," she said, with the same musical voice which he remembered so well, "because you seemed not to recognise me; and I wished to thank you for a service that you rendered long ago to a wild girl who might probably have been killed by a fiery horse that she was riding, had you not stopped it, and given her back the rein which she had lost. Perhaps you have forgotten it; for I hear that great acts are so common to the Count de Morseiul that he is not likely to recollect what was to him a trifling event. To me, however, the service was important; and I have not forgotten, either it or the person who rendered it."

The eye of the Chevalier d'Evran was upon the Count de Morseiul while the lady spoke, and there was a sparkling brightness in it which his friend scarcely understood. At the same time, however, it was scarcely possible for human nature to hear such words from such lips totally unmoved.

"Your pardon, madam," replied the Count, "I have never forgotten the adventure either; but I did not expect that you would have remembered so trifling a service. I recollected you the moment that I saw you; but did not of course venture to claim to be recognised on the merit of so insignificant an act."

"I can answer for his not having forgotten it," said the Chevalier d'Evran, "for it is not more than five or six days ago, Mademoiselle de Marly, that he told me the whole circumstances, and if I would, I could mention——"

The colour rose slightly in the Count de Morseiul's cheek, as the Chevalier d'Evran gazed upon him with a malicious smile; but the latter, however, paused in his career, only adding, "If I would, I could mention all this grave Count's comments upon that event;—but I suppose I must not."

"Nay, nay," exclaimed Clémence, "I insist upon your telling us. You are our bondsman and slave. As you have vowed worship and true service, I command you, Monsieur le Chevalier, to tell the whole without reserve—to give us the secrets of the enemy's camp."

"I hope, madam," said the Count, willing to turn the conversation, and yet knowing very well that he might obviate his own purpose if he shewed any anxiety to do so, "I hope, madam, that you do not class me amongst the enemy; if you do, I can assure you, you are very much mistaken."

"That is what I wish to know, Count," replied the lady, smiling; "it is for the very purpose of learning whether you are of the friends or the enemies, that I put the Chevalier here upon his honour as to your comments."

"I suppose, madam," said the elder gentleman to whom she had been speaking during the former part of the evening, and who did not seem at all well pleased with the interruption occasioned by the Count's presence, "I suppose, madam, if you put the Chevalier upon his honour, he will be obliged to keep secret that which was intrusted to him in confidence."

Clémence turned and gazed at him for a moment in silence, and then said, "You are right, Monsieur le Duc de Melcourt, though I did not think to hear you take part against me. I will find means to punish you, and to show you my power and authority in a way that perhaps you do not know. Monsieur le Chevalier, we shall excuse you for your contumacy, having the means of arriving at information by a higher power. Monsieur de Morseiul," she continued, raising her head with a look of queenly authority, "we command you to give us the information yourself; but that the ears of these worthy cavaliers and gentlemen who stand around, may not be gratified by the intelligence, we will permit you to lead us to the dance which we see they are preparing for in the other room."

She extended her hand towards him. He could not of course refuse to take it; and after giving one glance of gay and haughty irony at the group she left behind, Clémence de Marly moved forward towards the other room with Albert of Morseiul. With the same air of proud consciousness she passed through the whole of the first saloon; but the moment that she entered the second, which was comparatively vacant, as the dancers were gathering in the third, her manner entirely altered. The Count felt her hand rest somewhat languidly in his; her carriage lost a great degree of its stately dignity; the look of coquettish pride passed away; and she said, "Monsieur de Morseiul, I need not tell you that my object in exercising, in this instance, that right of doing anything that I like, unquestioned, which I have found it convenient to assume, is not to ask you any foolish question of what you may have said or thought concerning a person but little worthy of your thoughts at all. Perhaps, indeed, you may have already guessed my object in thus forcing you, as it were, to dance with me against your will; but that does not render it the less necessary for me to take the first, perhaps the only opportunity I may have of thanking you deeply, sincerely, and truly, for the great service, and the kind, the manly, the chivalrous manner in which it was performed, which you rendered me on the night of Monday last. I have my own particular reasons—and perhaps may have reasons also for many other things that appear strange—for not wishing that adventure to be mentioned anywhere. Although I had with me two servants attached to the carriage, and also my old and faithful attendant whom you saw, there was no chance of my secret being betrayed by any one but by you. I was not sure that I had made my wishes plain when I left you, and was anxious about to-night; but I saw in a moment, from your whole demeanour on entering the room, that I was quite safe, and I may add my thanks for that, to my thanks for the service itself."

"The service, lady, required no thanks," replied the Count. "I do believe there is not a gentleman in France who would not have done the same for any woman upon earth."

Clémence shook her head with a grave—even a melancholy look, replying, "You estimate them too highly, Count. We women have better opportunities of judging them; and I know that there are not three gentlemen in France, and perhaps six in Europe, who would do anything for any woman without some selfish, if not some base motive—unless his own gratification were consulted rather than her comfort."

"Nay, nay, nay; you are bitter, indeed," said the Count. "On my word I believe that there is not one French gentleman who would not, as I have said, have done the same for any woman; and certainly when it was done for you, any little merit that it might have had otherwise, was quite lost."

"Hush, hush," said Clémence, with a blush and a somewhat reproachful smile—"hush, hush, Monsieur de Morseiul; you forget that I am accustomed to hear such sweet speeches from morning till night, and know their right value. If you would prove to me that you really esteem me, do not take your tone from those empty coxcombs that flutter through such scenes as these. Be to me, as far as we are brought into communication together, the same Count de Morseiul that I have heard you are to others, frank, straightforward, sincere."

"Indeed I will," replied the Count, feeling the full influence of all his fanciful dreams in the past, reviving in the present; "but will you never be offended?"

"There is little chance," she replied, as they moved on, "that we should ever see enough of each other for me to be offended. You, I hear, avoid the court as far as possible. I am doomed to spend the greater part of my life there; and I fear there is very little chance of the Duke, my guardian, going to the quiet shades of Ruffigny, where first I had the pleasure of seeing you."

"Were you, then, at Ruffigny when I first saw you?" demanded the Count, with some surprise.

"Yes," she answered; "but I was staying there with some of my relations, who were on a visit to the duke. Do you remember—I dare say you do not—do you remember meeting me some days after with a party on horseback?"

"Yes," he replied, "I have it all before my eyes even now."

"And the lady who was upon my left hand?" she said.

"Quite well," replied the Count; "was that your mother?"

"Alas! no," replied Clémence, "that was my step-mother; my mother died three years before. But to return to what we were saying, I do not pretend to be less vain than other women, and therefore can scarcely answer for it, that, if you were to tell me harsh truths, I might not be offended; but I will tell you what, Monsieur de Morseiul, I would try—I would try as steadily as possible, not to be offended; and even if I were, I know my own mind sufficiently to say, I would conquer it before the sun went down twice."

"That is all that I could desire," replied the Count; "and if you promise me to do so, I will always be sincere and straightforward with you."

"What an opportunity that promise gives," replied the lady, "of asking you to be sincere at once, and tell me what were the comments of which the Chevalier spoke. Would that be ungenerous, Monsieur de Morseiul?"

"I think it would," replied the Count; "but I will pledge myself to one thing, that if you keep your promise towards me for one month, and take no offence at anything I may say, I will tell you myself what those comments were, without the slightest concealment whatsoever."

The eyes of Clémence de Marly sparkled, as she answered, "You shall see;" but they had lingered so long that the dance was on the eve of commencing, and they were forced to hurry on into the other room. There the Count found the eyes of the Prince de Marsillae wherever he turned; and there was a peculiar expression on his countenance—not precisely a smile, but yet approaching to it—with a slight touch of sarcastic bitterness on the lip, which was annoying. Could the Count have heard, however, the conversation that was going on amongst two or three of the group which he and Clémence had quitted shortly before, he might have felt still more annoyed. There were three persons who took but a small part in that conversation, the Chevalier, the young Marquis de Hericourt, and the Duke de Melcourt. It was one of those that stood behind who first spoke.

"How long will she be?" he demanded.

"In doing what?" said another.

"In fixing the fetters," replied the first; "in making him one of the train."

"Not two whole days," said the second.

"Not two whole hours, I say," added a third; "look at them now, how they stand in the middle chamber: depend upon it, when the Count comes back, we shall all have to make him our bow, and welcome him as one of us."

There was a little shrivelled old man who sat behind, and had, as yet, said nothing.

" He will never be one of you, gentlemen," he now said, joining in—" he will never be one of you, for he sets out with a great advantage over you."

" What is that ?" demanded two or three voices at once.

" Why," replied the old man, " he is the first man under sixty I ever heard her even civil to in my life. There is Monsieur le Duc there; you know he's out of the question, because he's past the age."

The Duke de Melcourt looked a little mortified, and said, " Sir, you are mistaken ; and at all events she never said anything civil to you, though you are so much past the age."

" I never asked her," replied the other.

" But there is the Chevalier d'Evran," replied one of the younger men, " she has said three or four civil things to him this very night: —I heard her."

" As much bitter as sweet in them," replied the old man; " but, at all events, she does not love him."

" She loves me more than you know," said the Chevalier, quietly ; and turning on his heel he went to join a gay party on the opposite side of the room, and perversely paid devoted attention to a fair lady whom he cared nothing about, and to whom the morals of any other court would have required him to pay no attentions but those of ordinary civility.

CHAPTER VII.

THE GROWTH OF LOVE.

THE entertainment was kept up late ; many of the guests scarcely departed before daylight; those who were invited to remain the night at the governor's house, retired when they thought fit; and every one acknowledged that this was the most splendid and the most agreeable fête that had been given in Poitiers for many years. What were the feelings, however, of the Count de Morseiul as, at an hour certainly not later than one in the morning, he sought his own apartments? We must not afford those feelings much space ; and we will only record what he saw before he left the hall, leaving the mind of the reader to supply the rest.

On leading back Clémence de Marly to her seat, he had entered into conversation for a moment with some persons whom he knew ; and when he turned towards her again, he saw not only that she was surrounded by almost all those who had been about her before, but that a number of young cavaliers freshly arrived had swelled her train, and that her demeanour was precisely the same as that which had, at his first entrance, removed her from the high place in which his imagination had enthroned her. Every flattery seemed to be received as merely her due—every attention but as a tribute that she had a right to command. On some of her slaves she smiled more graciously than on others, but certainly was not without giving that encouragement to many which may be afforded by saucy harshness as much as by attention and condescension. She did not, indeed, dance frequently;* that was a favour reserved for few; but the whole of the rest of her conduct displeased Albert of Morseiul; and he was grieved—very much grieved—to feel that it had power to give him pain.

Under these circumstances, then, he resolved to witness it no more, and retired to his own apartments, determined, as far as possible, to conquer his own feelings while they were yet to be conquered, and to rule his heart so long as it was his own to rule.

It was late on the following morning before any of the guests assembled at the breakfast table; but when the whole had met, the party was so large, that but little pleasant conversation could take place with any one. The Duke de Rouvré paid the greatest attention to the Count, and displayed a marked anxiety to distinguish and to please him. Clémence de Marly was entirely surrounded by her little train; and her pleasure in the homage she received seemed evident to Albert of Morseiul. The Chevalier d'Evran was somewhat thoughtful and grave, and more than once turned his eyes quickly from the face of Clémence to that of his friend. In the hours that had lately passed, however, Albert of Morseiul had practised the lesson of commanding himself, which he had learnt long before, and he was now perfect at the task. He took no notice whatsoever of the fair girl's demeanour towards others; and though, as usual, calm and grave, he bore his part in the conversation with earnestness and attention; and it so happened, that on more than one occasion something was said which called up the deep poetical fire of his nature, and led him briefly to pour forth in eloquent words the fine and high-toned feelings of his heart.

All who were present knew his high character, and all were struck with his words and with his manner; so that once or twice, even when speaking casually on things of no very great importance, he was annoyed at finding a sudden deep silence spread round the table, and every one listening to what he said. If anything could have repaid him for the annoyance, it might have been to see the lustrous eyes of Clémence de Marly fixed intent upon his countenance till they met his, and then dropped with a slight heightening of the colour, or turned sparkling to those round her, while her

* On many occasions each lady remained with her first partner during the whole of a ball night; but this was not invariable.

lips gave utterance to some gay jest, intended to cover the fit of eager attention in which she had been detected.

Alas, however, it must be owned, that to find those eyes so gazing upon him was no compensation, but rather was painful to Albert of Morseiul; for it only served to encourage feelings which he was determined to conquer. He would fain have had it otherwise; he would have felt nothing but calm indifference towards Clémence de Marly; and yet he knew, from what he had experienced on the preceding night, that he did not feel towards her entirely as he did towards other women. He thought, however, that by dedicating himself altogether to the great and important subject which had occupied his mind when he came to Poitiers, by giving up all his thoughts to that, and by making his stay as brief as possible, he should be enabled to avoid those things, both in the society of Clémence herself, and in his own inmost heart, which might become dangerous to his peace.

During the course of breakfast he revolved these matters in his mind, and before it was over his thoughts were more strongly directed than ever to the affairs of the Protestants, by the appearance of the Abbés de St. Helie and Pelisson. He determined, then, to endeavour, as far as possible, in the very first instance, to discover from them what was the nature of the measures about to be pursued by the court of France towards the Huguenots. In the next place, he purposed to inquire explicitly of the Duke de Rouvré what course of conduct he intended to follow towards the Protestants of the province; and, having ascertained these facts, to consult with all the wisest and the best of the Huguenot leaders, who might happen to be at Poitiers, to determine with them the line of action to be followed, according to circumstances, and then to return at once to Morseiul.

He took an opportunity, as soon as breakfast was over, of conversing with Pelisson and St. Helie, while the Duke and Duchess of Rouvré were busy in receiving the adieus of some of their departing guests. With the frank sincerity of his native character, he demanded, straightforwardly, of the two ecclesiastics, what was the course of conduct that their commission directed them to pursue; and Pelisson had half replied, saying, that they had better open their commission at once before the Duke de Rouvré, and see the contents, when his more cunning and politic friend interrupted him, saying that he had express orders not to open the packet till the meeting of the states, which was to take place in about eight days. This announcement differing, in some degree, from the account which he had given before, excited, not unjustly, the Count's suspicion; and, knowing that he should have a more candid reply from the Duke himself, he determined, in the next instance, to apply to him.

He did so not long after, and the Duke retired with him into his library.

" My dear Morseiul," he said, grasping the young Count's hand,
" you know that I myself am an advocate for the utmost toleration,
that I am so far from entertaining any ill will towards my brethren
who differ with me in some respects, that more than one of my
relations have married Huguenots. This is very well known at the
court also. The king is fully aware of it, and I cannot but hope
that my late appointment, as governor of this province, is a sign
that, notwithstanding all the rumours lately afloat, his majesty
intends to deal kindly and well with all denominations of his subjects. I must not conceal from you, however, that there are
rumours in Paris of a different kind; that there are not people
wanting who declare that the king and his council are determined
no longer to have any more than one religion in France, and that
the most vigorous means are to be employed to carry this resolution
into effect. Nor shall I attempt to deny to you, that the coming of
Pelisson and St. Helie here seems to me a very ominous and unpleasant occurrence. The presence of the first I should care little
about, as he is frank, and I believe sincere, wishes well, and would
always act kindly; but the other is a shrewd knave, a bigot, I
believe, more by policy than by any great devotion for our holy
church, malevolent, selfish, and cunning. They bear a commission
which, it seems, is not to be opened till the meeting of the states.
This looks like a purpose of controlling me in my own government,
of putting a power over me whereof I am to stand in awe. Now,
should I find that such is the case, I shall undoubtedly beseech his
majesty to permit me to retire from public life."

" For Heaven's sake do not do so just at present," said the
Count de Morseiul. " We have need, my dear friend, of every
moderate and enlightened man like yourself, to keep the country
quiet at a moment when affairs seem verging towards a terrible
convulsion. You must remember, and I hope the king will remember, that the Protestants are a great and important body in
France ; that there are two or three millions of us in this country;
that we demand nothing but the calm and quiet exercise of our own
religious opinions: but that, at the same time, there are many
resolute and determined men amongst us, and many eager and fiery
spirits, who may be urged into acts of resistance if they be oppressed.
All wise and sensible Huguenots will endeavour, as far as may be,
to seek peace and tranquillity; but suppose that resistance be once
begun, in consequence of an attempt to debar us of the free exercise of the rights secured to us by the edict of Nantes, can the king,
or anybody else, expect even his most loyal and best-intentioned
Protestant subjects to aid in keeping down and oppressing their
brethren ?"

" Not in oppressing, not in oppressing, my dear Count," said the
Duke; " we must not attribute to our beloved sovereign even the
thought of oppressing his subjects."

" Nothing but oppression could drive any of us to resistance," replied the Count; " and it is not from the king at all that we anticipate oppression, but from those that surround him. Need I point to Louvois, to whom the king, by his own acknowledgment, yields his own better judgment?"

The Duke was silent, and his young friend proceeded: " If we have not to fear oppression, my lord, there is nothing to be feared throughout the land; but if we have, I would fain know what shape that oppression is likely to take, both as a sincere member of what we call the reformed church, and as a loyal and devoted subject of the king. I would fain know, in order that, in my own neighbourhood, and amongst my own people, I may do all in my power to maintain peace and tranquillity; which I cannot at all answer for, if such proclamations be suddenly made amongst the people, when they are unprepared, as were made five days ago in my town of Morseiul, nearly creating a serious disturbance therein. The appearance of the military, also, did infinite harm, and the renewal of such scenes might quickly irritate a small body of the people into revolt; that small body would be joined by greater numbers; and the flame of civil war would spread throughout the country."

" The proclamation," replied the Duke, " was the king's, and of course it was necessary to make it instantly. With regard to the military, the intendant of the province demanded that a force should be sent to ensure that the proclamation was made peacefully; so having no one else in whom I could at all trust, I sent young Hericourt, with as small a force as possible, as I could not, of course, refuse the application."

" Of the intendant of the province, my dear Duke," replied the Count, " I shall say nothing, except that he is as opposite as possible in mind, in character, and manners to the Duc de Rouvré. A man of low origin, chosen from the *Maîtres des Requêtes*, as all these intendants are, cannot be supposed to view such questions in a grand and fine point of view. Individual instances certainly may sometimes occur, but unfortunately they have not occurred in Poitiers. Our only safety is in the Duc de Rouvré; but I am most anxious, if possible, to act in concert with him in keeping tranquillity throughout the province."

" I know you are, my dear young friend, I know you are," replied the Duke; " wait, however, for a few days. I expect several other gentlemen in Poitiers of your persuasion in religious matters. I will see and confer with you all as to what may be done, in the best spirit towards you, believe me. I have sent, or am sending, letters to every eminent man of the so-called reformed religion throughout this district, begging him to give me the aid of his advice. When we have others here, we can take counsel together, and act accordingly."

The young Count of course submitted, whatever were the private reasons which induced him to wish to quit Poitiers as soon as possible. He felt that a long sojourn there might be dangerous to him; he saw that the feelings of his heart might trample under foot the resolutions of his judgment. But, obliged as he was to remain, he now took the wisest course that circumstances permitted him to pursue. He saw Clémence de Marly as little as possible; and that portion of time which courtesy compelled him to give up to her, was only yielded to her society upon those public occasions when he fancied that her demeanour to others was likely to counteract the effect of her fascinations upon himself. On these occasions he always appeared attentive, courteous, and desirous to please her. Perhaps at times even, there shone through his demeanour those indications of deeper feelings, and of a passion which might have become strong and overpowering, which were not likely to escape a woman's eye. But his general conduct was by no means that of a lover. He was never one of the train. He came and went, and spoke for a few moments in his usual calm and equable manner, but nothing more; and Clémence de Marly, it must be confessed, was somewhat piqued.

It was not that she sought to display the Count de Morseiul to the world as one of the idle train of adorers that followed her, for she despised them, and esteemed him too much to wish him amongst them; but it was that she thought her beauty, and her graces, and her mind; ay! and the feeling and noble heart which she knew to exist in her own bosom—forgetting that she took pains to conceal it—might all have had a greater effect upon the Count than they had apparently produced.

She thought that she merited more than he seemed to be inclined to give; and there was something also in the little mysterious link of connexion between them, which had, in some degree, excited her imagination, and taught her to believe that the Count would take a deeper interest in her than he appeared to do. There was a little disappointment, a little surprise, a good deal of mortification.— Was there anything more? We shall see! At present, we have to deal with her conduct more than with her feelings, and that conduct, perhaps, was not such as was best calculated to win the Count's regard. It is true, she paid less attention to the train that followed her; she treated the generality of them with almost undisguised contempt. It seemed as if her haughtiness towards them in general increased; but then she was far more with the Chevalier d'Evran. She was seen walking in the gardens with him, with a single servant a step behind; and twice the Count de Morseiul entered the saloon, and found her sitting alone with him in eager conversation.

He felt more and more each day that it was time for him to quit the city of Poitiers; but still he was detained there by circumstances that he could not alter; and on the fifth day after his arrival, having passed a somewhat sleepless night, and feeling his brow hot and aching, he went down into the wide gardens of the house, to enjoy the fresh morning air in comfort. It was at an hour

when those gardens seldom possessed a tenant, but at the turn of
the first walk he met Clémence de Marly.alone.   She seemed to
be returning from the farther part of the grounds, and had her eyes
bent upon the earth, with a thoughtful—nay, with even a melancholy look.   If they had not been so near when he saw her, he
might, perhaps, have turned to avoid a meeting which he feared;
but she was within a few steps, and raised her eyes instantly as she
heard the sound of approaching feet.   The colour came into her
cheek as she saw him, but only slightly; and she acknowledged his
salutation by a graceful inclination of the head.

" You are an early riser, Mademoiselle de Marly," said the
Count, as she paused to speak with him.

" I have always been so," she answered.   " I love the soft breath
of the morning air."

" It is one of the great secrets of health and beauty," rejoined the
Count.

But she shook her head with a smile, saying, " Such are not my
objects in early rising, Monsieur de Morseiul.   Health I scarcely
value as it deserves, as I never knew the want of it; and beauty I
value not at all.—It is true! whatever you may think."

" Still, beauty has its value," replied the Count.   " It is a grand
and noble gift of God; but I acknowledge it ought to be the mint-
mark of the gold."

" It is one of the most dangerous gifts of Heaven," replied Clémence, vehemently.   " It is often one of the most burdensome!
It is dangerous to ourselves, to our own hearts, to our own eternal
happiness.   It is burdensome in all its consequences.   Too much
beauty to a woman is like overgrown wealth to a man:—with this
sad difference, that he can always do good with his possession, and
she can do none with hers.   And now Monsieur de Morseiul thinks
me a hypocrite; and, though he promised ever to be straightforward with me, he will not say so."

" Nay, indeed," replied the Count, " I am far from thinking
that there is aught of hypocrisy in what you say, lady.   I may
think such feelings and thoughts evanescent with you; but I believe you feel them at the time."

Clémence shook her head, with a melancholy—almost a reproachful look.   " They are not evanescent," she said, earnestly.   " They
are constant, steadfast; have been for years."   Even while she
spoke she turned to leave him; and he thought, as she quickly
averted her head, that there was something like a tear in her
bright eye.

He could not resist; and he followed her rapidly, saying, " I
hope I have not offended."

" Oh no!" she answered, turning to him, and letting him see
without disguise that the tear was really there—" oh no! Monsieur
de Morseiul.   There was nothing said that could offend me.   Do
you not know that, like a child putting its hand upon an instru-

ment of music without knowing he will produce any sound, a mere casual word will often be spoken unconsciously, which, by some unseen mechanism in the breast of another, will awaken emotions which we never intended to call up? Our little conversation roused the thoughts of many years in a moment, but there was nothing said that could in the least offend. You know, we vain women, Count," she added, in a lighter mood, "are only offended with our lovers. It is on them that we pour forth our caprices. So, for Heaven's sake, take care how you become my lover; for then I should certainly be offended with you every five minutes."

"Would it be so terrible to you, then, to see me your lover?" demanded the Count, in the same tone.

"To be sure," she answered, half playfully, half seriously; "it would be a sad exchange, would it not? to give a friend for a slave. Besides, I doubt not that you have loved a thousand times before. But tell me, Count, do you think any one can love more than once?"

"From my own experience I cannot speak," replied the Count, "for I am a very stony-hearted person; but I should think that a man might."

"And woman not!" she interrupted, eagerly. "Poor women! You hem us in on all sides!—But after all, perhaps, you are right," she added, after a moment's pause. "There is, there must be a difference between the love of man and the love of woman. Hers is the first fresh brightness of the heart, which never can be known again; hers is the flower which, once broken off, is succeeded by no other; hers is the intense—the deep—the all-engrossing, which, when once come and gone, leaves the exhausted heart without the power of feeling such things again. With man it is different: love has not that sway over him that it has over a woman. It is not with him the only thing, the end, the object of his being. It takes possession of him but as a part, and, therefore, may be known more than once, perhaps. But, with woman, that fire once kindled must be the funeral pile of her own heart. As the ancients fabled, flowers may spring up from the ashes, but as far as real love is concerned, after the first true affection, the heart is with the dead."

She paused, and both were silent; for there was something in the words which she spoke which had a deeper effect upon Albert of Morseiul than he had imagined anything could have produced. He struggled against himself, however, and then replied, "You took me up too quickly, lady. I was not going to say that it is impossible for woman to love twice. I do not know—I cannot judge; but I think it very possible that the ancients, to whom you have just alluded, may have intended to figure love under the image of the phœnix; and I do fully believe that many a woman may have fancied herself in love a dozen times before she was so really."

"Fancy herself in love!" exclaimed Clémence, in a tone almost indignant. " Fancy herself in love, Monsieur de Morseiul! I should think it less difficult to love twice than to fancy one's self in love at all, if one were not really so. We may, perhaps, fancy qualities in a person who does not truly possess them, and thus, adorned by our own imagination, may love him; but still it is not that we fancy we are in love, but are really in love with the creature of our fancy. However, I will talk about it no more. It is a thing that does not do to think of. I wonder if ever there was a man that was really worth loving."

The Count replied, but he could not get her to pursue the sub-jeet any farther. She studiously rambled away to other things; and, after speaking of some matters of minor import, darted back at once to the point at which the conversation had begun, as if the rest had been but a temporary dream, interpolated as it were between matters of more serious moment. The Count had been endeavouring to bring her back to the subject of the heart's feel-ings; for though he felt that it was a dangerous one—a most dangerous one—one that might well lead to words that could never be recalled, yet he longed to gain some insight into that heart which he could not but think was filled with finer things than she suffered to appear. She would not listen, however, nor be led, and replied as if she had not in the slightest degree attended to what he had been saying—

" No, Monsieur de Morseiul, no, it is neither for health's sake nor for beauty's that I rise early and seek the morning air. I will tell you why it is. In those early and solitary hours, and those hours alone, I can have some communion with my own heart—I can converse with the being within myself—I can hold conference, too, with what I never meet alone at other hours—nature, and nature's God. The soft air of the morning has a voice only to be heard when crowds are far away. The leaves of the green trees have tongues, drowned in the idle gabble of a foolish multitude, but heard in the calm quiet of the early morning. The fields, the brooks, the birds, the insects, all have their language, if we will listen to it; but what are fields, and brooks, and birds, and trees, and the soft air, when I am surrounded by a tribe of things as empty as the sounding brass or tinkling cymbal? Can I think of anything more dignified than a padusoie when one baby man is whispering softly in my ear, ' The violet, mademoiselle, suits better with your complexion than with any other that the earth ever produced, which shows that complexion's exceeding bright-ness;' and another tells me that the blackness of my hair would make a raven blush, or that my eyes are fit to people the heaven with stars ! But it is time that I should go to my task," she con-tinned ; " so adieu, Monsieur de Morseiul. If you walk on straight to the ramparts you will find the view beautiful, and the air fresh."

Thus saying, she turned and left him, and the hint not to follow was too plain to be misunderstood. He walked on then towards

the ramparts with his arms crossed upon his chest, and his eyes
bent upon the ground. He did not soliloquize, for his nature was
not one of those which frequently give way to such weaknesses.
It was his thoughts that spoke, and spoke plainly, though silently.

"She is, indeed, lovely," he thought, "and she is, indeed, en-
chanting. If she would but give her heart way, she is all that I
pictured to myself, all that I dreamed of, though with a sad mixture
of faults from which her original nature was free. But, alas! it is
evident that she either does love or has loved another; and she
herself confesses that she cannot love twice. Perhaps she has
spoken thus plainly as a warning, and if so, how much ought I to
thank her for her frankness! Besides, she is of another creed. I
must dream upon this subject no more.—Yet who can be the man
that has won that young heart, and then, perhaps, thought it not
worth the wearing? Surely, surely it cannot be D'Evran; and
yet she evidently likes his society better than that of any one.
She seeks him rather than otherwise. How can I tell what may
have passed, what may be passing between them even now? Yet
she is evidently not at ease at heart; and he, too, told me but the
other day that it was his determination never to marry. He—
made for loving and being beloved!—he never marry!—It must
be so; some quarrel has taken place between them, some breach
which they think irremediable. How often is it, when such things
are the case, that lovers will fancy they are cool, and calm, and
determined, and can live like friends and acquaintances, forgetting
the warmer feelings that have once existed between them! Yes,
it must be so," he continued, as he pondered over all the different
circumstances; "it must be so, and they will soon be reconciled.
I will crush these foolish feelings in my heart; I will banish all
weak remembrances; and to do so effectually, I will quit this place
as soon as possible, leaving Louis here, if he chooses to stay."

Thus musing, with a sad heart and bitterer feelings than he
would even admit to himself, Albert de Morseiul walked on in the
direction which Clémence had pointed out, and passing through
various long alleys, planted in the taste of that day, arrived at a
spot where some steps led up to the ramparts of the town, which
commanded a beautiful view over the gently undulating country
round Poitiers, with more than one little river meandering through
the fields around. Leaning his arms on the low breastwork, he
paused and gazed over a scene on which, at any other time, he
might have looked with feelings of deep interest, and noted every
little mound and tree, marking, as he was wont, each light and
shadow, and following each turn of the Clain or Boivre. Now,
however, there was nothing but a vague vision of green and sunny
things before his eyes, while the sight of the spirit was fixed intensely upon the deeper and darker things of his own heart.

Alas, alas! it must be said, he felt that he loved Clémence de
Marly. Notwithstanding all he had seen — notwithstanding all

he had condemned—notwithstanding the fear that she could not make him happy even if he could obtain her, the belief that it would be impossible to win her, and the conviction that she loved another—alas! he felt, and felt bitterly, that at length, indeed, he loved, and loved with the whole energy of his nature. He reproached himself with weakness; he accused himself of the follies that he had so often condemned in others. Was it her mere beauty that he loved? he asked himself. Was it the mere perfection of form and colour that, in a few short years, would fleet with fleeting seasons, and give place to irremediable decay? Was he, who had believed that loveliness could have no effect on him, was he caught by the painted glittering of a mere beautiful statue? No; he felt there was something more. He felt that she had given him sufficient insight into her original nature to show him that, though spoiled by after circumstances, she had been made by the hand of God that which he had always believed he could love, that bright being where the beautiful form, and the beautiful heart, and the beautiful mind, were all attuned together in one grand and comprehensive harmony of nature. He felt that such was the case, and his sensations were only the bitterer that it should be so.

He had thus paused and meditated some little time, full of his own thoughts and nothing else, when a hand was suddenly laid upon his shoulder, and, turning round, he saw his friend the Chevalier.

"Why, Albert," he said, "in what melancholy guise are you here meditating? I met Clémence upon the stairs just now, and she told me that I should find you here, tasting the morning air upon the ramparts. I expected to see you with your eye roving enchanted over this fine scene, looking as usual half way between a mad poet and a mad painter; and, lo! instead of that, here you are planted upon the rampart, like a dragoon officer in garrison in a dull Dutch town, with your heel beating melancholy time on the pavement, and your eyes profoundly cast into the town ditch. In the name of Heaven, why did you not make Clémence come on to enliven you?"

The Count smiled with a somewhat bitter smile. "It would have hardly been necessary, and hardly right to try," he replied; "but you miscalculate my power, D'Evran. The lady left me with an intelligible hint, not only that she was not about to follow me, but that I was not to follow her."

"What, saucy with you, too!" cried the Chevalier, laughing. "I did not think that she would have had determination enough for that."

"Nay, nay, you are mistaken, Louis," replied the Count; "not in the least saucy, as you term it, but quite mistress of herself, of course, to do as she pleased."

"And yet, Albert," said the Chevalier, "and yet I do believe that there is not a man in France with whom she would so willingly have walked through these gardens as with yourself. Nay, do not be foolish or blind, Albert. I heard her saying to Marsillac but yesterday, when he called to take his leave, that she had seen at Poitiers more than she had ever seen in her life before,—a courtier who was not a fool, a soldier who was not a libertine, and a man of nearly thirty who had some good feelings left."

The Count gazed steadfastly into the Chevalier's face for a moment, as if he would have read into his very soul, and then replied, " Come, Louis, let us go back. If she meant me, she was pleased to be complimentary, and had probably quarrelled with her real lover, and knew that he was in hearing."

The Chevalier gave himself a turn round upon his heel, without reply, sang a bar or two of a gay air, at that time fashionable in Paris, and then walked back to the governor's house with the Count, who, from everything he had seen and heard, but the more firmly determined to hasten his steps from Poitiers as fast as possible.

The hour of breakfast had not yet arrived when they entered the house, and the Count turned to his own apartments, seeking to remain in solitude for a few minutes, not in order to indulge in thoughts and reflections which he felt to be unnerving, but to make a vigorous effort to recover all his composure, and pass the rest of the two or three days which he had to remain as if nothing had given any disturbance to the usual tranquil course of his feelings. In the ante-room, however, he found Maitre Jerome, sitting watching the door, like a cat before the hole of a mouse; and the moment he entered, Jerome sprang up, saying—

" Oh, monseigneur, I have something to say to you, which may not be amiss to hear quickly. I have discovered the exact nature of the commission of Monsieur de St. Helie, which you wanted to know."

The Count beckoned him into the inner chamber, and demanded, looking at him sternly, " Truth or falsehood, Riquet? This is no joking matter!"

" Truth, upon my honour, sir," replied the man; " I would deceive you on no account whatsoever; and now, pray, sir, ask no questions, but let me tell my tale. It is truth, for once in my life, depend upon it. I can tell truth upon an occasion, sir, when it suits me."

" But how am I to be sure of the accuracy of the information, if I ask you no questions, Riquet?" said the Count.

" You may be quite sure of it, sir," replied the man, " though I must not tell you how I came at my tale. Suppose, I say, only suppose that I had heard Monsieur de St. Helie repeating it word for word to Monsieur Pelisson, and the Curé de Guadrieul had confirmed it. I say, suppose it were so, and be sure that my authority is quite as good."

" Well, well," said his master, " go on."

" Well, then, sir," continued the servant, " of course, as a good

Catholic, I hope that you and all the other Huguenots of France
may be thoroughly roasted in good time; but, nevertheless, as you
happen to be my master in this world, I am in duty bound to tell
you what I have heard. Monsieur de St. Helie, then, and Monsieur Pelisson are commanded to demand of the states of the province, effectual measures to be taken for the purpose of bringing
into the bosom of the church, without delay, all the Huguenots
within their jurisdiction. In expressing this demand, there are a
great many soft words used, and much talk of gentleness and persuasion; but Huguenots' children are to be brought over by all
means; they are to be received to renounce their errors at seven
years old. No more Huguenots are to be permitted to keep schools.
They are to be excluded from all public offices of any kind or character whatsoever. They are no longer to be allowed to call their
religion *the reformed religion*——"

"Enough, enough," said the Count, stopping him, "and more
than enough. Is this information sure?"

"Most sure, sir," replied the man, with a solemnity that admitted
no doubt of his sincerity, "and the commission ended with the
words, that these means were to be taken in preparation for those
ulterior steps which the king was determined to employ."

The Count made no reply, but paced the room for two or three
minutes in considerable agitation. "I wanted something to rouse
me," he said at length, "and I have it now, indeed! Quick,
Riquet, call Claude, and Beyhours, and Martin; tell them to
saddle their horses, for I want them to carry some notes. When
you have done that, come hither yourself, and say not a word of
this affair to any one."

When the man returned, he found three notes written and
addressed to different Protestant noblemen in the neighbourhood of
Poitiers, which his lord directed him to give to the servants named,
who were to carry them to their several destinations; and the
Count then added, "Now, Riquet, I have a commission for you
yourself; I will not give you a note, as that is useless. You would
know the contents of it before you got to the end of your journey:
of that I am well aware."

"Certainly, sir," replied the man, with his usual effrontery; "I
always make a point of that, for then I can tell the purport on my
arrival if I lose the note by the way."

"I know it," replied the Count; "but I believe you, notwithstanding, to be faithful and attached to me, and that you can be
silent when it is necessary."

"As the grave, sir," replied the man.

"Well, then," continued his master, "you know the château of
the Maille, at about two leagues' distance. Go thither—ask to
speak to Monsieur de Corvoie—tell him that I will be with him to-
morrow about mid-day—that I have matters of the deepest importance to communicate to him—and that I have asked three

other gentlemen of our own persuasion to meet me at his house to-morrow. Say nothing more and nothing less."

" Sir, I will cut it on all sides exactly as you have commanded," replied the man, " and will bear you his message back immediately, if there should be any."

These arrangements being made, the Count descended to the breakfast-table, where he found the Chevalier seated by the side of Clémence de Marly. The Count had resolved that during his stay he would notice the conduct of Clémence as little as possible ; that he would endeavour to look upon her as a being that could never be his ; but, nevertheless, he could not now help noticing that though she and the Chevalier might not converse much together, a few words passed between them in a low voice, from time to time, evidently referring to things apart from the general conversation that was going on. He steeled his heart, though with agony to himself, and pleading the necessity of visiting some friends in the neighbourhood, mounted his horse immediately after break-fast, and was absent from Poitiers the greater part of the day.

CHAPTER VIII.

THE MEETING AND THE CHASE.

On the following morning, at breakfast, some sports and diversions were proposed ; and the governor, who wished to afford amusement to all parties and to keep them in especial good humour till after the meeting of the states, proposed to set out almost immediately to force a stag in the neighbouring woods. There were several young noblemen present, swelling the train of la belle Clémence ; but she had shown herself somewhat grave, and less lively than usual; and after the proposal had been made and agreed to by almost all, she remarked the silence of the Count de Morseiul, say-ing, that she feared, from his making no reply, that they were again to be deprived of the pleasure of Monsieur de Morseiul's society, as they had been on their ride of the day before. She spoke in rather a low voice, and, perhaps one might say, timidly, for her manner was very different from that which she usually assumed.

" I fear, fair lady," replied the Count, who felt that under any other circumstances her speech would have been a sore temptation, " I fear that I have engaged myself to visit a friend in the neigh-bourhood at noon to-day."

" Oh, we will take no excuse !" cried the Duke de Rouvré; " indeed, Count, you must send a messenger to tell your friend you cannot come. You who are famed for your skill in forest sports must positively be with us."

The Count, however, remained firm, saying, that he had appointed to meet his friend on business of importance to them both ; and the Duke de Rouvré was of course silent. The young De Hericourt, who had been absent for a day or two, and had only lately returned, gazed at Clémence with a sort of ironical smile, as he saw upon her countenance a look of mortification which she could not or would not restrain ; but the Count saw it too, and was struck with it ; for, though skilful by habit in reading the hearts of those with whom he was brought into contact, he could not perfectly satisfy himself with regard to the nature of that look and the feelings from which it sprang. He felt, too, that something more than a dry refusal was, perhaps, owing in mere courtesy to Clémence for the wish she had expressed for his society, and he added—

"I do assure you, Mademoiselle de Marly, that nothing could have been so great a temptation to me as the thought of accompanying you, and our gay friends here, to wake the woods with the sounds of horns and dogs, and I grieve very much that this appointment should have been made so unfortunately."

"Indeed !" she exclaimed, brightening up, "if such be your feelings, I will coax *ma reine*, as I always call our good Duchess, to coax the governor, who never refuses anything to her, though he refuses plenty of things to me, to delay the party for an hour. Then we shall be some time getting to the woodside, you know, some time in making all our preparations ; and you shall come and join us whenever you have done. We will make noise enough to let you know where we are."

Of course there was now no refusing; the Count promised to come if the important business in which he was about to be engaged was over in time, and Clémence repaid him with a smile, such as she but rarely gave to any. It was now well-nigh time for him to depart; and after shutting himself up for a few minutes alone, in order to think over the circumstances about to be discussed, he set out, with some servants, and rode rapidly to the château of the Maille. He found several horses in the court-yard, and judged rightly, from that sight, that the others had arrived before him. He found them all assembled in the large hall, and each greeted him gladly and kindly, looking with some eagerness for what he had to communicate. But the master of the château asked him to pause for a moment, adding—

"I have a friend here who arrived last night, and whom you will all be glad to see. He will join us in a moment, as he is but writing a short despatch in another room."

"Who is he ?" demanded the Count; "is it Monsieur de l'Estang ?"

"Oh no," replied the other.   "He is a man of arms instead of a man of peace."   But almost as he spoke the door opened, and the famous Maréchal de Schomberg entered the room.

"I am happy to see you all, gentlemen," he said; " Monsieur de

Morseiul, my good friend," he continued, shaking him warmly by the hand, "I am delighted to meet you. I have not seen you since we were fellow-soldiers together in very troublous times."

"I hope, Marshal," replied the Count, "that at the present we may be fellow-pacificators instead of fellow-soldiers. We are all Protestants, gentlemen, and as what I have lately learned affects us all, I thought it much the best plan, before I took any steps in consequence, in my own neighbourhood, to consult with you, and see whether we could not draw up such a remonstrance and plain statement of our case to the king, as to induce him to oppose the evil intentions of his ministers, and once more guarantee to us the full and entire enjoyment of those rights in which he promised us security on his accession to the throne, but which have been sadly encroached upon and curtailed within the last ten years."

"They have, indeed," said the Count de Champclair; "but I trust, Monsieur de Morseiul, you have nothing to tell us which may lead us to believe that greater encroachments still are intended."

Marshal Schomberg shook his head with a melancholy smile; but he did not interrupt the Count de Morseiul, who proceeded to relate what he knew of the mission of Pelisson and St. Helie, and the further information which he had gained in regard to their commission on the preceding day. The first burst of anger and indignation was greater than he expected; and nothing was talked of for a few minutes but active resistance to the powers of the crown, of reviving the days of the League or those of Louis XIII., and defending their rights and privileges to the last. Marshal Schomberg, however eminently distinguished for his attachment to his religion, maintained a profound silence during the whole of the first ebullitions; and at length Monsieur de Champclair remarked, "The Marshal does not seem to think well of our purposes. What would he have us do, thus brought to bay?'

"My good friends," replied Schomberg, "I think only that you do not altogether consider how times have changed since the days of Louis XIII. Even then the reformed church of France was not successful in resisting the king, and now resistance, unless men were driven to it by despair, would be madness. Forced as I am to be much about the court, I have seen and known these matters in their progress more intimately than any of you, and can but believe that our sole hope will rest in showing the king the utmost submission, while at the same time we represent to him the grievances that we suffer."

"But does he not know those grievances already?' exclaimed one of the other gentlemen; "are they not his own act and deed?"

"They are, it is true," replied Schomberg, mildly, "but he does not know one half of the consequences which his own acts produce. Let me remind you that it is the people who surround the king that urge him to these acts, and it is consequently their greatest

interest to prevent him from knowing the evil consequences thereof.
Not one half of the severities that are exercised in the provinces—
indeed, I may say, no severities at all—are exercised towards the
Protestants in the immediate neighbourhood of Paris, Versailles, or
Fontainbleau. They take especial care that the eyes of majesty,
and the ear of authority, shall not be opened to the cries, groans, or
sufferings of an injured people. Louis the Great is utterly ignorant
that the Protestants have suffered, or are likely to suffer, under any
of his acts. The king has been always, more or less, a bigot, and
his mother was the same : Colbert is dead, who stood between us
and our enemies. His son is a mere boy, unable, if not unwilling,
to defend us. The fury, Louvois, and his old jesuitical father, are,
in fact, the only ministers that remain, and they have been our
enemies from the beginning. But they have now stronger motives
to persecute us. The king must be ruled by some passion; he is
tired of the domination of Louvois, and that minister seeks now for
some new hold upon his master. He supported his tottering power
for many years by the influence of Madàme de Montespan.
Madame de Montespan has fallen; and a new reign has commenced
under a woman, who is the enemy of that great bad man; but she
also is a bigot, and the minister clearly sees that if he would remain
a day in power he must link Madame Scarron to himself in some
general plan which will identify their interests together. She sees,
and he sees, that whatever be that plan it must comprise something
which affords occupation to the bigoted zeal of the king. The
Jesuits see that too, and are very willing to furnish such occupation; but the king, who thinks himself a new St. George, is tired of
persecuting Jansenism. That dragon is too small and too tenacious
of life to afford a subject of interest to the king any longer; when
he thinks it is quite dead, it revives again, and crawls feebly here
and there, so that the saint is weary of killing a creature that seems
immortal. Under these circumstances they have turned his eyes
and thoughts towards the Protestants; and what have they proposed to him which might not seduce a glory-loving monarch like
himself? They have promised him that he shall effect what none
of his ancestors could ever accomplish, by completely triumphing
over subjects who have shown that they can resist powerfully when
oppressed. They have promised him this glory as an absolute
monarch. They have promised him almost apostolic glory in converting people whom he believes to be heretics. They have promised him the establishment of one, and one only religion in
France; and they have promised him that, by so doing, he will inflict a bitter wound on those Protestant princes with whom he has
been so long contending. Such are the motives by which they
lead on the mind of Louis to severe acts against us; but there is
yet one other motive ; and to that I will particularly call your attention, as it ought, I think, greatly to affect our conduct. They
have misrepresented the followers of the reformed religion in France

as a turbulent, rebellious, obstinate race of men, who adhere to their own creed more out of opposition to the sovereign than from any real attachment to the religion of their forefathers. By long and artful reasonings they have persuaded the king that such is the case. He himself told me long ago, that individually there are a great many good men, and brave men, and loyal men amongst us; but that, as a body, we are the most stiff-necked and rebellious race he ever read of in history."

"Have we not been driven to rebellion?" demanded Monsieur de Champclair—"have we not been driven to resistance? Have we ever taken arms but in our own defence?"

"True," replied Schomberg, "quite true. But kings unfortunately see through the eyes of others. The causes of our resistance are hidden from Louis scrupulously. The resistance itself is urged upon him vehemently."

"Then it is absolutely necessary," said the Count de Morseiul, "that he should be made clearly and distinctly to know how much we have been aggrieved, how peaceably and loyally we are really idsposed, and how little but the bitterest fruits can ever be reaped from the seeds that are now sowing."

"Precisely," replied Schomberg. "That is precisely what I should propose to do. Let us present a humble remonstrance to the king, making a true statement of our case. Let us make him aware of the evils that have accrued, of the evils that still must accrue from persecution; but in the language of the deepest loyalty and most submissive obedience. Let us open his eyes, in fact, to the real state of the case. This is our only hope; for in resistance I fear there is none. The Protestant people are apathetic, they are not united—and they are not sufficiently numerous, even if they were united, to contend successfully with the forces of a great empire in a time of external peace."

"I do not know that," exclaimed Monsieur de Champclair. But he had the great majority of the persons who were then present against him, and, in a desultory conversation that followed, those who had most vehemently advocated resistance but a few minutes before, who had been all fire and fury, and talked loudly of sacrificing their lives a thousand times rather than sacrificing their religion, viewed the matter in a very different light now when the first eagerness was over. One declared that not an able-bodied man in forty would take the field in defence of his religion; another said, that they had surely had warning enough at La Rochelle; another spoke, with a shudder, of Alaix. In short, Albert de Morseiul had an epitome in that small meeting of the doubts, fears, and hesitations; the apathy, the weakness, the reniency which would affect the great body of Protestants, if called upon suddenly to act together. He was forced, then, to content himself with pressing strongly upon the attention of all present the necessity of adopting instantly the suggestion of Marshal Schomberg, and of drawing up a representation to the king, to be signed as rapidly as possible by the chief Protestants throughout the kingdom, and transmitted to Schomberg, who was even then on his way towards Paris.

Vain discussions next ensued in regard to the tone of the remonstrance, and the terms that were to be employed; and those who were inclined to be more bold in words than in deeds, proposed such expressions as would have entirely obviated the result sought to be obtained, giving the petition the character of a threatening and mutinous manifesto. Though this effect was self-evident, yet the terms had nearly been adopted by the majority of those present, and most likely would have been so, had not a fortunate suggestion struck the mind of Albert of Morseiul.

" My good friends," he said, " there is one thing which we have forgotten to consider. We are all of us soldiers and country gentlemen; and many of us have, perhaps, a certain tincture of belles lettres; but a petition from the whole body of Protestants should be drawn up by some person eminent alike for learning, wisdom, and piety, whose very name may be a recommendation to that which he produces. What say you, then, to request Monsieur Claude de l'Estang to draw up the petition for our whole body? I intend to leave Poitiers to-morrow, and will communicate your desire to him. The paper shall be sent to you all as soon as it is drawn up, and nothing will remain but to place our hands to it, and lay it before the king."

The proposal was received with joy by all; for even those who were pressing their own plans obstinately, were at heart glad to be delivered from the responsibility; and this having been decided, the meeting broke up.

The Count de Morseiul lingered for a few minutes after the rest were gone, to speak with Marshal Schomberg, who asked, " So you are not going to wait for the opening of the states?"

" I see no use of so doing," replied the Count; "now that I know the measures which the king's commission dictates, I have nothing farther to detain me. But tell me, Marshal, do you really believe that Louvois and his abettors will urge the king seriously to such steps?"

" To a thousand others," replied Schomberg—"to a thousand harsher, and a thousand more dangerous measures. I can tell you that it is already determined to prohibit for the future the marriages of Catholics and Protestants. That, indeed, were no great evil, and I think rather favourable to us, than not; but it is only one out of many encroachments on the liberty of conscience, and, depend upon it, our sole hope is in opening the king's eyes to our real character as a body, and to the awful evils likely to ensue from oppressing us."

" But should we be unable so to do," demanded the Count, " what remains for us then, my noble friend? Must we calmly submit to increasing persecution? must we renounce our faith? must we resist and die?"

"If by our death," replied Schomberg, firmly but sadly, "we could seal for those who come after us, even with our hearts' blood, a covenant of safety—if by our fall in defence of our religion we could cement, as with the blood of martyrs, the edifice of the reformed church—if there were even a hope that our destruction could purchase immunity to our brethren or our children, I should say that there is but one course before us. But, alas! my good young friend, do you not know, as well as I do, that resistance is hopeless in itself, and must be ruinous in its consequences; that it must bring torture, persecution, misery, upon the women, the children, the helpless; that it must crush out the last spark of toleration which is likely to be left; and that the ultimate ruin of our church in France will but be hastened thereby? No one deserving the title of man, gentleman, or Christian, will abandon his religion under persecution; but there is another course to be taken, and it I shall take, if these acts against us be not stayed. I will quit the land—I will make myself a home elsewhere. My faith shall be my country, as my sword has been my inheritance! Would you take my advice, my dear Count, you would follow my example, and, forming your determination beforehand, be prepared to act when necessary."

The Count shook his head. "I thank you," he said—"I thank you, and will give what you propose the fullest consideration; but it is a resolution that cannot be taken at once—at least by those who feel as I do. Oh! my good friend, remember how many ties I have to break asunder before I can act as you propose. There are all the sweet memories of youth, the clinging household dreams of infancy, the sunny home of my first days, when life's pilgrimage took its commencement in a garden of flowers. I must quit all these—every dear thing to which the remembrance of my brightest days is attached—and spend the autumn and the winter of my latter life in scenes where there is not even a memory of its spring. I must quit all these, Schomberg. I must quit more. I must quit the faithful people who have surrounded me from my boyhood—who have grown up with me like brothers—who have watched over me like fathers—who have loved me with that hereditary love that none but lord and vassal can feel towards each other—who would lay down their lives to serve me, and who look to me for direction, protection, and support. I must quit them—I must leave them a prey to those who would tear and destroy them. I must leave, too, the grave of my father—the tombs of my ancestors, round which the associations of the past have wreathed a chain of glorious memories that should bind me not to abandon them. I, too, should have my grave there, Schomberg; I, too, should take my place amongst the many who have served their country, and left a name without a stain. When I have sought the battle-field, have I not thought of them, and burned to accomplish deeds like theirs? When I have been tempted to do anything that is wrong, have I not thought upon their pure renown, and cast the temptation from me like a slimy worm? And should I leave those tombs now? Were it not better to do as they would have done, to hang out my banner from the walls against oppression, and when the sword which they have transmitted to me can defend my right no longer, perish on the spot which is hallowed by the possession of their ashes?"

"No, my friend, no," replied Schomberg, "it were not better, for neither could you so best do honour to their name, neither would your death and sacrifice avail ought to the great cause of religious liberty. But there is more to be considered, Albert of Morseiul; you might not gain the fate you sought for. The perverse bullet and the unwilling steel often, too often, will not do their fatal mission upon him that courts them. How frequently do we see that the timid, the cowardly, or the man who has a thousand sweet inducements to seek long life, meets death in the first field he enters, while he who in despair or rage walks up to the flashing cannon's mouth escapes as by a miracle? Think, Morseiul, if such were to be your case, what would be the result: first to linger in imprisonment, next to see the exterminating sword of persecution busy amongst those whom you had led on into revolt, to know that their hearths were made desolate, their children orphans, their patrimony given to others, their wives and daughters delivered to the brutal insolence of victorious soldiers; and then, knowing all this, to end your own days as a common criminal, stretched on a scaffold on the torturing wheel, amidst the shouts and derisions of superstitious bigots, with the fraudulent voice of monkish hypocrisy pouring into your dying ear insults to your religion and to your God. Think of all this! and think also, that, at that last moment, you would know that you yourself had brought it all to pass, without the chance of effecting one single benefit to yourself or others."

The Count put his hand before his eyes, but made no reply; and then, wringing Schomberg's hand, he mounted his horse and rode slowly away.

For a considerable distance he went on towards Poitiers at the same slow pace, filled with dark and gloomy thoughts, and with nothing but despair on every side. He felt that the words of Marshal Schomberg were true to their fullest extent, and a sort of presage of the coming events seemed to gather slowly upon his heart, like dark clouds upon the verge of the sky. His only hope reduced itself to the same narrow bounds which had long contained those of Schomberg; the result, namely, of the proposed petition to the king.

But there were one or two words which his friend had dropped accidently, and which it would seem, from what we have told before, ought not to have produced such painful and bitter feelings in the breast of Albert of Morseiul as they did produce. They were those words which referred to the prohibition about to be decreed against the marriages of Protestants and Catholics. What was it to him, he asked himself, whether Catholics and Protestants might or might not marry? Was not his determination taken with regard to the only person whom he could have ever loved? and did it matter that another barrier was placed between them, when there were barriers impassable before? But still he felt the announcement deeply and painfully; reason had no power to check and overcome those sensations; and, oppressed and overloaded as his mind then was, it wandered vaguely from misery to misery, and seemed to take a pleasure in calling up everything that could increase its own pain and anguish.

When he had thus ridden along for somewhat more than two miles, he suddenly heard a horn winded lowly in the distance, and, as he fancied, the cry of dogs. It called to his mind his promise to Clémence de Marly. He felt that his frame of mind was in strange contrast with a gay hunting scene. Yet he had promised to go as soon as ever he was free, and he was not a man to break his promise, even when it was a light one. He turned his horse's head, then, in the direction of the spot from which the sound seemed to proceed, still going on slowly and gloomily.

A moment after, he heard the sounds again. The memory of happy days, and of his old forest sports, came upon him, and he made a strong effort against the darker spirit in his bosom.

" I will drive these gloomy thoughts from me," he said, "if it be but for an hour; I will yet know one bright moment more. For this day I will be a boy again, and to-morrow I will cast all behind me, and plunge into the stream of care and strife!"

As he thus thought, he touched his horse with the spur; the gallant beast bounded off like lightning; the cry of the hounds, the sound of the horns, came nearer and nearer; and in a few moments more the Count came suddenly upon a relay of horses and dogs, established upon the side of a hill, as was then customary, for the purpose of giving fresh vigour to the chase when it had been abated by weariness.

" Is the deer expected to pass here?" demanded the Count, speaking to one of the *veneurs*, and judging instantly, by his own practised eye, that it would take another direction.

" The young Marquis Hericourt thought so," replied the man, " but he knows nothing about it."

At that moment the gallant stag itself was seen, at the distance of about half a mile, bounding along in the upland towards a point directly opposite; and the Count, knowing that he must come upon the hunt at the turn of the valley, spurred on at all speed, followed by his attendants. In a few minutes more, a few of the huntsmen were seen; and, in another, Clémence de Marly was before his eyes. She was glowing with exercise and eagerness, her eyes bright as stars, her clustering hair floating back from her face, her whole aspect like that which she had borne, when first he saw her in all the brightness of her youth and beauty. The Chevalier was seen at a distance amusing himself by teasing, almost into madness, a fiery horse, that was eager to bound forward before all the rest; the train of suitors, and of flatterers, that generally followed her, was scattered about the field; and, in a moment—with his hat off, his dark hair curling round his brow, his features lighted up with a smile which was strangely mingled with the strong lines of deep emotions just passed, like the sun scattering the remnants of a thunder-cloud; with his chest thrown forward, his head bending to a graceful salute, and his person erect as a column—Albert of Morseiul was by the side of Clémence de Marly, and galloping on with her, seeming but of one piece with the noble animal that bore him.

The eyes of almost all those that followed, or were around, were turned to those two; and certainly almost everything else in the gay and splendid scene through which they moved seemed to go out extinguished by the comparison. In the whole air, and aspect, and figure of each, there was that clear, concentrated expression of grace, dignity, and power, which seems almost immortal; so that the Duke de Rouvré and his train, the gay nobles, the dogs, the huntsmen, and the whole array, were for an instant forgotten. Men forgot even themselves for a time to wonder and admire.

Unconscious that such was the case, Albert de Morseiul and Clémence de Marly rode on; and he—with his fate, as he conceived, sealed, and his determination taken—cast off all cold and chilling restraint, and appeared what be really was—nay, more, appeared what he was when eager, animated, and with all the fine qualities of his heart and mind welling over in a moment of excitement. All the tales that she had heard of him as he appeared in the battle-field, or in the moment of difficulty and danger, were now realized to the mind of Clémence de Marly; and while she wondered and enjoyed, she felt that for the first time in her life she had met with one to whom her own high heart and spirit must yield. Her eyes sunk beneath the eagle gaze of his; her hand held the rein more timidly; new feelings came upon her, doubts of her own sufficiency, of her own courage, of her own strength, of her own beauty, of her own worthiness; she felt that she had admired and esteemed Albert of Morseiul before, but she felt that there was something more strange, more potent, in her bosom now.

We must pause on no other scene of that hunting. Throughout the whole of that afternoon the Count gave way to the same spirit. Whether alone with Clémence, or surrounded by others, the high and powerful mind broke forth with fearless energy. A bright and poetical imagination; a clear and cultivated understanding; a decision of character and of tone, founded on the consciousness of rectitude and of great powers; a wit as graceful as it was keen, aided by the advantages of striking beauty, and a deep-toned voice of peculiar melody, left every one so far behind, so out of all comparison, that even the vainest there felt it themselves, and felt it with mortification and anger.   The hunting was over, and by chance or by design Albert of Morseiul was placed next to Clémence de Marly at supper.   The Duke de Rouvré had noticed the brightening change which had come over his young friend, and attributing it to a wrong cause, he said, good-humouredly—

" Monsieur de Morseiul, happy am I to see you shake off your sadness.   You are so much more cheerful, that I doubt not you have heard good news to-day."

This was spoken at some distance across the table, and every one heard it; but the young Count replied, calmly, " Alas! no, my lord ; I was determined to have one more day of happiness, and therefore cast away every other thought but the pleasure of the society by which I was surrounded.   I gave way to that pleasure altogether this day, because, I am sorry to say, I must quit your hospitable roof to-morrow, in order to return to Morseiul, fearing that I shall not be able to come to Poitiers again, while I remain in this part of France."

Clémence de Marly turned very pale, but then again the blood rushed powerfully over her face.   But the Duke de Rouvré, by replying immediately, called attention away from her.

" Nay, nay, Monsieur le Comte," he said, " you promised me to stay for several days longer, and I cannot part with an old friend, and the son of an old friend, so soon."

" I said, my lord, that I would stay if it were possible," replied the Count.   " But I can assure you that it is not possible ; various important causes, of the greatest consequence, not only to me, but to the state, call me imperatively away, when, indeed, there are but too many inducements to stay here."

" I know one of the causes," said the Duke ; " I hear you have taken measures for suppressing that daring band of plunderers— *night hawks*, as they call themselves—who have for some time hung about that part of the country, and who got possession of poor Monsieur Pelisson and Monsieur St. Helie, as they were telling me the other day ; but you might trust that to your seneschals, Count."

" Indeed I cannot, my lord duke," replied the Count ; " that affair has more branches than you know of—or, perhaps I should say, more roots to be eradicated.   Besides, there are many other things."

" Well, well," said the Duke, " if it must be so, it must.   However, as soon as the states have ceased to hold their meetings, I shall come for a little repose to Ruffigny, and then, if you have not been fully successful, I will do my best to help you ; but we are not going to lose our friend Louis here, too ?   Chevalier, do you go back with your friend ?"

" Not to hunt robbers," replied the Chevalier, with a smile ; " I would almost as soon hunt rats with the dauphin.   Besides, he has never asked me ; this is the first intelligence I had of his intention."

" I only formed it this morning," replied the Count. " But you have promised me a whole month, Louis, and you shall give it me when you find it most pleasant to yourself"

" Well, I shall linger on here for a few days," replied the Chevalier, " if the governor will feed and lodge me; and then, when I have seen all the bright things that are done by the states, I will come and join you at Morseiul."

Thus ended the discussion which followed the young Count's announcement. No further conversation took place between him and Clémence, who devoted her whole attention, during the rest of the evening, either to the Chevalier, the Duke de Melcourt, or the young Marquis de Hericourt. The hour for Albert de Morseiul's departure was announced as immediately after breakfast on the following day; but Clémence de Marly did not appear that morning at the table, for the first time since his arrival at Poitiers. When the hour was come, and his horses were prepared, he took leave of the rest of the party, and, with many painful emotions at his heart, quitted the saloon, the Duke and the Chevalier, with one or two others, accompanying him to the top of the stairs. At that moment, however, as he was about to descend, Clémence appeared, as if going into the saloon. She was somewhat paler than usual; but her manner was the same as ever.

" So, Monsieur de Morseiul," she said, " you are going ! I wish you a happy journey ;" and thus treating him like a mere common acquaintance, she bowed her head and entered the saloon.

CHAPTER IX.

THE DISCOVERY.

Two days after the departure of the Count de Morseiul, the states of the province were opened in form ; but neither with the states nor with their proceedings shall we have anything to do, and will merely notice an event which occurred on the eve of their meeting.

On the day preceding, a vast number of gentlemen from all parts of the province had flocked into the city. The house of the governor was again nearly filled, and though the formal opening of the states was deferred till the succeeding day, they nominally commenced their assembly on the day after the Count's departure. The colleagues, Pelisson and St. Helie, had separated after their arrival in Poitiers, the former having gone to the bishop's palace, where he busied himself in his usual occupation at this time, namely, in diffusing large sums of money through the province by different channels, for the purpose of bribing all persons who might be found weak or wavering in the Protestant faith to abandon their religion, and profess themselves Catholics. St. Helie had remained at the house of the governor, following occupations more suited to his genius, that of watching everything that was done, of gaining information concerning the views and feelings of all persons likely to be present at the assembly of the states, and of endeavouring to form a party for his own purposes amidst the more fierce, intolerant, and bigoted of the influential Catholics of the province.

The Duke de Rouvré could not avoid showing this personage every sort of civility, for, indeed, such was the king's command; but at the same time he could not conceal from himself that the Abbé was a spy upon his actions, and was intended to be a check upon his conduct; and, as may well be supposed under such circumstances, he was not particularly pleased with his guest.

On the day preceding the regular opening of the states, then, after some of the preliminary formalities had been gone through, the Duke de Rouvré, while conversing in his saloon with twelve or fourteen of the principal Roman-catholic gentry, who had come to visit him as if by accident, but in reality by a previous arrangement with others, was not agreeably surprised to see the Abbé de St. Helie, followed by Pelisson and the Curé of Guadrieul, enter the room in somewhat a formal manner, and advance towards him with a face of business. He bowed low, however, as it was the first time he had seen the Abbé that morning, greeted Pelisson somewhat more warmly, and suffered the third personage of the party to walk up in bull-like sullenness with nothing but a formal inclination of the head.

" It is time, my lord," said the Abbé de St. Helie, " to fulfil the order of the king, and to open in your presence the commission with which he has entrusted us, of the nature of which we are ourselves in some sort ignorant up to this moment."

" I thought, gentlemen," said the Duke, " that you informed me the commission was not to be opened till after the opening of the states."

" No, my lord," replied the Abbé, " I said, till after the meeting of the states, which were convened to meet to-day."

" Well, then, gentlemen," said the Duke, " I will give you my attention in a few minutes. You see I am at present occupied with friends, but in half an hour I shall be prepared to receive you in my cabinet upon any business that may remain to be transacted between us."

" I see no reason, my lord," replied the Abbé, " why the commission should not be opened before the gentlemen here present, all of whom are sincere Christians, and zealous supporters of the true faith."

" No earthly reason whatever," replied the Duke, sharply, " except that I choose to do my own business in my own way, in my own house, and in my own government."

" I am sorry to suggest any alterations in your lordship's plans," replied the Abbé, with a cool sneer, "but I have authority for what I am doing. The king's express directions are to open the commission in presence of your lordship, *and other competent witnesses.*"

"Oh, if such be the case," said the Duke, much mortified, "there could be no witnesses more competent, and none perhaps better prepared than the present. Pray open your commission, gentlemen. My good sirs, take your seats round this table. Let us give the matter, if possible, some air of regularity. Without there! Send for my secretary. We will wait till he comes, if you please, Monsieur de St. Helie. What splendid weather this is, gentlemen. We have not had one wet day for nearly two months, and yet a gentle rain every morning."

The persons present ranged themselves round the table, the Curé de Guadrieul produced the leathern bag which contained the commission, and laid it down heavily before him, and as soon as the Duke's secretary appeared, a large knot upon the leathern strings of the bag was cut with a penknife, and the whole packet handed to the Abbé de St. Helie, who had placed himself at the governor's right hand. Opening the mouth of the bag, then, the Abbé took forth a large parchment packet, sealed up at both ends with the royal arms of France. The governor asked to look at the superscription, and finding it addressed in the usual terms to the Abbé St. Helie and Pelisson, he gave it back to the former, who, with an important countenance and slow formality, began to break the seals.

Two or three paper covers were within, in order to keep the precious document secure, and one by one the Abbé unfolded them, till he came to the last, which was also sealed, but which was much smaller than the size of the outer parcel had given reason to expect. He broke the seal himself, however, and produced the contents, when, to the astonishment of everybody, and the merriment of the younger persons present, there appeared nothing but a pack of cards.

The Duke de Rouvré looked on drily; not a smile appeared upon his countenance; and he said, gazing at the Abbé de St. Helie, who sat in stupified silence—

"I admire the sagacity and propriety with which it has been judged necessary to appoint witnesses for the opening of this commission—or of this game, perhaps I ought to say, Monsieur de St. Helie. Gentlemen, I trust that you are perfectly satisfied; but I must ask you whether it be necessary to direct my secretary to take a procès verbal of the contents, import, and extent of the Abbé's commission?"

In the meantime Pelisson had reached across, and taken up the papers which had surrounded the cards. He examined them minutely and long; but at length replied to the Duke's sneer by saying—

"Perhaps it may be more necessary, my lord, than you imagine.

It seems to me, from the appearance of these papers, that the packet has been opened before. There is a slight tear in the parchment, which tear is evidently not new."

"You must look to that yourselves, gentlemen," said the Duke de Rouvré, seriously angry; "the commission has been in your charge and custody, and in that of no one else. You best know whether you have opened it before the time or not. Secretary, as these gentlemen demand it, make a note that we have this day seen opened by the Abbé de St. Helie, in our presence, a packet addressed to him and Monsieur de Pelisson, purporting to be a commission for certain purposes addressed to them by his Most Christian Majesty; and that on the said packet being so opened, there has been found in it nothing but a pack of cards, not in the most cleanly condition."

"Pray let him add," said Pelisson, "that I have declared my opinion, from the appearance of the papers, that the said packet had been previously opened."

"Let that also be noted," said the Duke; "but it must be noted, likewise, that Monsieur de Pelisson did not make that observation till after the packet had been opened, and the cards discovered, that the seals were unbroken, and the leathern bag entire; and now, gentlemen," he continued, "after having interrupted my conversation with these noble gentlemen here present, to witness the opening of a pack of cards—which may indeed be the commencement of a game that I don't understand—perhaps you will excuse me for rising and resuming our more agreeable occupation."

Pelisson bowed his head, calm and undisturbed; the Abbe de St. Helie looked stupified, mortified, and angry beyond all measure; and the dull priest of Guadrieul, upon whom the eyes of both his superiors were turned from time to time with an expression of no very doubtful import, looked swallowed up in stolid fear and astonishment. The governor and his guests in general, had risen and scattered themselves about the room; and after speaking to the Abbé de St. Helie for a few moments, Pelisson advanced, and took his leave in a few words, saying, that of course it was their duty to inform the king of what had occurred, and that therefore they must proceed to write quickly before the ordinary set out.

The governor bowed stiffly, and merely replied that he himself could not think of troubling the king upon a trifle of such minor importance, and therefore left them to make their communication in their own terms. The three then retired, and the rest of the party soon after separated; but the worthy governor had not been left half an hour alone before he received a billet from the bishop, requesting an audience, which was immediately granted. He came, accompanied by Pelisson, St. Helie, and the Curé de Guadrieul, the latter of whom remained without while the bishop and his companions held a previous conference with the governor. The Curé was then called in, and remained some time with the others.

He **was** then sent out again to the antechamber, then recalled, and nearly two hours passed in what was apparently an unpleasant discussion, for at the end of that time, when the governor returned to the saloon from his own cabinet, Clemence de Marly, the Duchess, and the Chevalier d'Evran, all remarked that he was very much agitated and heated.

In a minute or two afterwards, his secretary followed him into the room with a note in his hand, apparently just written, and asked if that would do.

The governor read the note, and replied, " Yes! Send it off directly," he said. " Bid the messenger give my very best regards to the Count de Morseiul! Lay the strictest injunctions upon the courier also, not to stop this night till he has overtaken the Count. If the Count be in bed when he reaches the place where he is, he need not of course disturb him till the morning.—But bid him say everything that is kind from me."

Clémence de Marly rose, and with a winning grace that was more natural to her than the capricious pride she sometimes assumed, walked up to the Duke, glided her arm through his, and drew the old nobleman into one of the deep windows. She spoke with him for several minutes earnestly, and he replied as if endeavouring to parry by a jest some question he did not choose to answer.

" Nay, nay," she was heard to say at length, " my dear guardian, you *shall* tell me, and you know that Clémence is more absolute than the king."

" We will talk about it to-morrow, Clémence," replied the Duke, " and perhaps I may tell you; but you shall make your confession in return, fair lady."

She blushed a little and turned away, and thus the conversation ended.

CHAPTER X.

THE RECALL.

ALBERT of Morseiul rode on his way with a heart ill at ease. The excitement of the preceding night was gone, and the lassitude that succeeded it was like the weakness after a fever. It seemed to him that the cheerful hours of life were over, and the rest was all to be strife and anguish; that the last of all the sweet dreams, with which hope and youth deck the future, was done and passed away, and that nothing but the stern grey reality was left. It is hard and sorrowful to make up the mind to any parting, and tenfold hard and sorrowful to make up the mind to our parting with the sweet promising fancies of our early days, to put ourselves under a harsher guide for ever, and follow with him a rugged and a cheerless path, when before we had been treading on sunshiny flowers. In general, it is true, the wise beneficence of Heaven has provided that we should not lose all at once, but that the visions and the dreams, like the many gay companions of our boyhood, should either be abandoned for others, or drop away from our side, one by one, till all are gone, and we hardly mark which is the last. But there are times when all are snatched away together, or, as in the case of Albert of Morseiul, when the last that is taken is the brightest and the best, and the parting is clear, defined, and terrible.

Bitter, bitter, then, were his feelings as he rode away from Poitiers, and made up his mind that the fond dream of youth was over, that the nourished vision of long years was dissipated, that the bubble was burst, and that all was gone; that she who, half ideal, half real, had been that object round which both memory and imagination had clung as the something splendid for the future, was not what he had dreamt of, and even if she were, could never, never be his; and that at length that theme of thought was gone from him for ever. That moment and that spot seemed to form the parting place, where youth, imagination, and happiness were left behind, and care, reality, and anxiety started forward with latter life.

Though, as we have endeavoured on more than one occasion to show, the Count de Morseiul was a man of strong imagination and of deep and intense feelings, yet he possessed qualities of other kinds, which served to counterbalance and to rule those dangerous gifts, not, indeed, preventing them from having their effect upon himself, paining, grieving, and wearing him, but sufficient to prevent imagination from clouding his judgment, or strong feeling from warping his conduct from the stern path which judgment dictated. He applied himself, then, to examine distinctly what were the probabilities of the future, and what was the line of conduct that it became him to pursue. He doubted not—indeed, he felt strongly convinced, that Clémence de Marly would ultimately give her hand to the Chevalier d'Evran, to his friend and companion. He believed that, for the time, some accidental circumstance might have alienated them from each other, and that, perhaps on both sides, any warmer and more eager passion that they once had felt, might have been a little cooled; but still he doubted not, from all he saw, that Clémence would yet be his friend's bride, and the first part of his own task was to prepare his mind to bear that event with calmness, and firmness, and dignity, whenever it should happen. As his thoughts reverted, however, to the situation of his fellow Huguenots, and the probable fate that awaited them, he saw a prospect of relief from the agony of his own personal feelings, in the strife that was likely to ensue from their persecution; and perhaps he drew a hope even from the prospect of an early grave.

With such thoughts struggling in his breast, and with all the varied emotions which the imagination of the reader may well supply, Albert of Morseiul rode on till he reached the house appointed for his second resting-place. Everything had been prepared for his reception, and all the external appliances were ready to ensure comfort, so that there was not even any little bodily want or irritation to withdraw his attention from the gloomy pictures presented by his own thoughts.

With a tact in such matters which was peculiarly his own, Jerome Riquet took especial care that the dinner set before his master should be of the very simplest kind, and instead of crowding the room with servants, as he had done on a former occasion, he, who on the journey acted the part of major domo, waited upon the Count at table alone, only suffering another servant to carry in and remove the dishes. He had taken the precaution of bringing with him some wine from Poitiers, which he had induced the sommelier of the bishop to pilfer from the best bin in his master's cellar, and he now endeavoured to seduce his master, whose deep depression he had seen and deplored during their journey, into taking more of the fragrant juice than usual, not, indeed, by saying one word upon the subject, but by filling his glass whenever he saw it empty.

Now Jerome Riquet would have given the tip of one of his ears to have been made quite sure of what was the chief cause of the Count's anxiety. That he was anxious about the state of the Protestant cause, the valet well knew; that he was in some degree moved by feelings of love towards Clémence de Marly, Riquet very easily divined. But Jerome Riquet was, as we have before said on more than one occasion, shrewd and intelligent, and in nothing more so than in matters where the heart was concerned. It is true he had never been in the room five times when Clémence and his master were together, but there are such things in the world wherein we live, as half-open doors, chinks, key-holes, and garret windows; and in the arts and mysteries of all these, Jerome Riquet was a most decided proficient. He had thus seen quite enough to make him feel very sure, that whatever might be Clémence de Marly's feelings towards others, her feelings towards his master were not by any means unfavourable; and after much speculation, he had arranged in his own mind—from a knowledge of the somewhat chivalrous generosity of his master's character—that he and the Chevalier d'Evran were in love with the same person, and that the Count, even with the greater probability of success, had abandoned the pursuit of his passion, rather than become the rival of his friend.

Riquet wished much to be assured of this fact, however; and to know whether it was really and truly the proximate cause of the melancholy he beheld, or whether there was some deeper and more powerful motive still, concealed from those eyes which he thought were privileged to pry into every secret of his master. Thus, after dinner was over, and the dessert was put upon the table—though he had wisely forborne up to that moment to do, to say, or to allow anything that could disturb the train of the Count's thoughts —he could resist no longer, and again quickly filled up his young lord's glass as he saw it empty.

His master put it aside with the back of his hand, saying, " No more!"

" Oh, my lord," said Riquet, " you will not surely refuse to drink that glass to the health of Mademoiselle Clémence!"

The Count, who knew him thoroughly, and in general perceived very clearly all the turnings and windings through which he pursued his purposes, turned round, gazing in his face for a moment as he bent over his shoulder, and then replied, with a melancholy smile, " Certainly not, Riquet. Health and happiness to her!" and he drank the wine.

The look and the words were quite sufficient for Jerome Riquet, though the Count was not aware that it would be so ; but the cunning valet saw clearly, that, whatever other causes might mingle with the melancholy of his master, love for Clémence de Marly had a principal share therein ; and, confirmed in his own opinion of his lord's motive in quitting Poitiers, his first thought, when he cleared away and left him, was, by what artful scheme or cunning device he could carry him back to Poitiers against his own will, and plunge him inextricably into the pursuit of her he loved.

Several plans suggested themselves to his mind, which was fertile in all such sort of intrigues, and it is very probable that, though he had to do with a keen and a clear-sighted man, he might have succeeded unaided in his object ; but he suddenly received assistance which he little expected, by the arrival, at their resting-place, of a courier from the Duke de Rouvré, towards the hour of ten at night.

Riquet was instantly called to the messenger ; and, telling him that the Count was so busy that he could see nobody at that moment, the valet took charge of the note and the message, while the governor's servant sat down to refresh himself after a long and fatiguing ride. Riquet took a lamp with him to light himself up the stairs, though he had gone up and down all night without any ; and before he reached the door of the Count's room, he had of course made himself acquainted with the whole contents of the note, so that when he returned to the kitchen to converse with the messenger, he was perfectly prepared to cross-examine him upon the various transactions at Poitiers with sagacity and acuteness.

The whole story of the cards found in the king's packet had of course made a great sensation in the household of the governor ; and Riquet now laughed immoderately at the tale, declaring most

irreverently that he had never known Louis le Grand was such a
wag.   There is nothing like laughter for opening the doors of the
heart, and letting its secrets troop out by dozens.   The courier
joined in the merriment of the valet; and Riquet had no difficulty
in extracting from him everything else that he knew.   The after
conferences between the governor, Pelisson, and the bishop, were
displayed as far as the messenger had power to withdraw the veil;
and the general opinion entertained in the governor's household
that some suspicion attached to the young Count in regard to that
packet, and that the courier himself had been sent by the party at
Poitiers to recall him to that city, was also communicated in full to
the valet.   To the surprise of the courier, however, Riquet laughed
more inordinately than ever, declaring that the governor, and the
bishop, and St. Helie, and Pelisson, must all have been mad or drunk
when they were so engaged.

In the meantime the Count de Morseiul had opened the letter
from the governor, and read the contents, which informed him that
a pack of cards had been found, in place of a commission, in the
packet given by the king to Messieurs St. Helie and Pelisson; that
those gentlemen declared that the packet had been opened; and
that they had come with the bishop for the purpose of making
formal application to the governor to recall him, the Count de
Morseiul, to Poitiers, alleging that the only period at which the
real commission could have been abstracted, was while they were in
his company at an inn on the road.   They had also pointed out,
the Duke said, that the Count, as one of the principal Protestant
leaders, was a person more interested than any other, both to
ascertain the contents of that packet, and to abstract the commission, in case its contents were such as they imagined them to
have been; and at the same time they said, there was good reason
to believe that, in consequence of the knowledge thus obtained, he,
the Count de Morseiul, had called together a meeting of Protestant
gentlemen in the neighbourhood of Poitiers, had communicated to
them the plans and purposes of the government, and had concerted
schemes for frustrating the king's designs.   The Duke de Rouvré
then went on to say, that as he knew and fully confided in the
honour and integrity of the Count de Morseiul, and as the bishop
and Monsieur Pelisson had produced no corroborative proof of
their allegation whatsoever, he by no means required or demanded
the Count to return to Poitiers, but thought fit to communicate
to him the facts, and to leave him to act according to his own
judgment.

The Count paced the room in no slight agitation for several
minutes after he had read the letter; but it was not the abstraction
of the king's commission, if such an act had really taken place, nor
the accusation insinuated, rather than made, against himself, which
agitated him on the present occasion.   The accusation he regarded
as absurd, the abstraction of the commission merely laughable; a

suspicion, indeed, might cross his mind that Riquet had had a hand in it, but he knew well that he himself had none, and therefore he cast the matter from his mind at once. But his agitation proceeded from the thought of being obliged to go back to Poitiers,—from the fear of seeing all his good resolutions overthrown—from the idea of meeting once more, surrounded with greater difficulties and danger than ever, her whom he now but too clearly felt to be the only being he had ever loved.

To the emotions which such considerations produced, he gave up a considerable time; and then, taking up the bell, he rang it sharply, ordering the page who appeared to send Riquet to him. He simply told the valet what had occurred, and ordered his horses to be saddled to return to Poitiers the next morning at day-break. He insinuated no suspicion, though he fixed his eyes strongly upon the man's countenance, when he spoke of the abstraction of the commission; but the face of Riquet changed not in the least, except in consequence of a slight irrepressible chuckle which took place at the mention of the appearance of the cards. The Count did not wish to inquire into the matter; but, from what he saw of Riquet's manner, he judged that his servant had nothing to do with the transaction; and, setting out early the next morning, he went back to Poitiers at full speed, hiring horses when his own were too tired to proceed, so that he reached the house of the governor towards nine o'clock on the same night.

He was immediately ushered into the saloon, where the family of Monsieur de Rouvré and a very small party besides were assembled, and, apologizing for the dustiness and disarray of his appearance to the Duke, who met him near the door, he said that he had only presented himself to show that he had lost not a moment in returning to repel the false insinuations made against him. He was then about to leave the room, hastily glancing his eye over the party beyond, and seeing that his friend the Chevalier was not present; but the voice of the Duchess de Rouvré called him to her side, saying—

"We will all, I am sure, excuse dust and disarray, for the pleasure of Monsieur de Morseiul's society. Is it not so, Madame de Beaune? Is it not so, Clémence?"

Clémence had scarcely looked up since the Count's arrival; but she now did so, with a slight inclination of the head, and replied, "The Count de Morseiul, my queen, values the pleasure of his society so highly that he is disposed to give us but little of it, it would appear."

The words were scarcely spoken, when the Count, with his own peculiar, graceful, but energetic manner, walked straight up to Clémence de Marly, and stopped opposite to her, saying, gravely, but not angrily, "I assure you, dear lady, I do not deserve your sarcasm. If you knew, on the contrary, how great was the pleasure that I myself have derived from this society, you would estimate

the sacrifice I made in quitting it, and approve, rather than condemn, the self-command and resolution I have shown."

Clémence looked suddenly up in his face, with one of her bright-
beaming smiles, and then frankly extended her hand to him. " I
was wrong," she said; " forgive me, Monsieur de Morseiul! You
know a spoilt woman always thinks that she has done penance
enough when she has forced herself to say, I was wrong."

If the whole world had been present, Albert of Morseiul could
not have refrained from bending down his lips to that fair hand;
but he did so, calmly and respectfully, and then turning to the
Duchess, he said, that if she would permit him, he would but do
away the dust and disarray of his apparel, and return in a moment.
The petition was not, of course, refused: his toilet was hasty, and
occupied but a few minutes; and he returned as quickly as possible
to the hall, where he passed the rest of the evening without giving
any farther thoughts or words to painful themes, except in asking
the governor to beg the presence of the Bishop, Monsieur Pelisson,
and the Abbé de St. Helie, as early as possible on the following
morning, in order that the whole business might be over before the
hour appointed for the meeting of the states.

The Bishop, who was an eager and somewhat intolerant man,
was quite willing to pursue the matter at once; and before breakfast on the following day, he, with the two Abbés and the Curé de
Guadrieul, met the Count de Morseiul in the cabinet of the
governor.

There was something in the frank, upright, and gallant bearing
of the young nobleman that impressed even the superstitious bigots
to whom he was opposed with feelings of doubt as to the truth of
their own suspicions, and even with some sensations of shame for
having urged those suspicions almost in the form of direct charges.
They hesitated, therefore, as to the mode of their attack, and the
Count, impatient of delay, commenced the business at once by addressing the Bishop.

" My noble friend, the Duke here present," he said, " has communicated to me, my lord, both by letter and by word of mouth, a
strange scene that has been enacted here regarding a commission,
real or supposed, given by the king to the Abbés of St. Helie and
Pelisson. It seems, that when the packet supposed to contain the
commission was produced, a pack of cards was found therein,
instead of what was expected; that Monsieur Pelisson found reason
to suppose that the packet had been previously opened; and that he
then did—what Monsieur Pelisson should not have done, considering the acquaintance that he has with me and with my character—
namely, charged me with having opened, by some private means,
the packet containing his commission, abstracted and destroyed the
commission itself, and substituted a pack of cards in its place."

" Stop, stop, my dear Count," said Pelisson, " you are mistaken
as to the facts. I never made such an accusation, whatever others

did. All I said was, that you were the only person interested in the abstraction of that commission, who had possessed any opportunity of destroying it."

"And in so saying, sir, you spoke falsely," replied the Count de Morseiul; "for, in the first place, you insinuated what was not the case, that I have had an opportunity of destroying it; and, in the next place, you forgot that for three quarters of an hour, or perhaps more, for ought I know, your whole baggage was in the hands of a body of plunderers, while neither you, buried in your devotions, under the expectation of immediate death, nor Monsieur de St. Helie, weeping, trembling, and insane in the agony of unmanly fear, had the slightest knowledge of what was done with anything in your possession; so that the plunderers, if they had chosen it, might have re-written you a new commission, ordering you both to be scourged back from Poitiers to Paris. I only say this to show the absurdity of the insinuations you have put forth. Here, in a journey, in which you deviated considerably from the direct road from Paris, and which has probably taken you eight or ten days to perform, in the course of which you must have slept at eight or ten different inns upon the road, and during which you were for a length of time in the hands of a body of notorious plunderers, you only choose to fix upon me, who entertained you with civility and kindness, who delivered you from death itself, and who saved from the flames and restored to your own hands, at the risk of my life, the very commission which you now insinuate I have had some share in abstracting from the paper that contained it. Besides, sir, if I remember rightly, that packet was entrusted to the care of a personage attendant upon yourselves, and who watched it like the fabled guardian of the golden fleece."

"But the guardian of the fleece slumbered, sir," replied Pelisson, who, to say the truth, was really ashamed of the charge which had been brought against the Count de Morseiul, and was very glad of an opportunity to escape from the firm grasp of the Count's arguments by a figure of speech. "Besides, Monsieur de Morseiul," he said, "had you but listened a little longer you would have heard, that though I said yours was the only party which had an opportunity of taking it, and were interested in its destruction, I never charged you with doing so, or commanding it to be done; but I said that some of your servants, thinking to do you a pleasure, might have performed the exchange, which certainly must have been accomplished with great sleight of hand."

"You do not escape me so, sir," replied the young Count; "if I know anything of the laws of the land, or, indeed, of the laws of common sense and right reason, you are first bound to prove that a crime has been committed, before you dare to accuse any one of committing it. You must show that there ever has been, in reality, a commission in that packet. If I understood Monsieur de Rouvré's letter right, the seals of the king were found unbroken on the packet, and not the slightest appearance of its having been opened was remarked, till you, Monsieur Pelisson, discovered that there was such an appearance after the fact. The king may have been jesting with you; Monsieur de Louvois may have been making sport of you; a drunken clerk of the cabinet may have committed some blunder in a state of inebriety; no crime may have been committed at all, for ought we know."

"My good sir," said the Bishop, haughtily, "you show how little you know of the king and of the court of the king, by supposing that any such transactions could take place."

"My lord," replied the Count, gazing upon him with a smile of contempt, "when you were a little curé in the small town of Castelnaudry, my father supported the late King of France with his right hand, and with the voice of his counsel: when you were trooping after a band of rebels in the train of the house of Vendôme, I was page of honour to our present gracious monarch, in dangers and difficulties, in scantiness, and in want: when you have been fattening in a rich diocese, obtained by no services to the crown, I have fought beside my monarch, and led his troops up to the cannon of his enemies' ramparts: I have sat beside him in his council of war, and ever have been graciously received by him in the midst of his court; and let me tell you, my lord bishop, that it is not more improbable, nay, not more impossible, that Louis XIV. should play a scurvy jest upon two respectable ecclesiastics, than that the Count of Morseiul should open a paper not addressed to himself."

"Both good and true, my young friend," said the Duke de Rouvré; "no one who knows you could suspect you of such a thing for a moment."

"But we may his servants," said the Abbé de St. Helie, sharply, though he had hitherto remained silent, knowing that he himself had been the chief instigator of the charge, and fearing to call upon himself the indignation of the young Count.

"Well, gentlemen," said the Count de Morseiul, "although I should have every right to demand that you should first of all establish the absolute fact of the abstraction of this packet upon proper testimony, I will not only permit, but even demand, that all my servants who accompanied me from Morseiul shall be brought in and examined one by one; and if you find any of them to whom you can fairly attach a suspicion, I will give him up to you at once, to do what you think fit with. I have communicated to them the contents of Monsieur de Rouvré's letter, but have said nothing further to them on the subject. They must all be arrived by this time: I beg that you will call them in yourselves, in what order you please."

"By your leave, by your leave," said the Abbé de St. Helie, seeing that the Bishop was about to speak; "we will have your valet; Jerome—I think I heard him so called. Let us have him, if you please."

Jerome was accordingly brought in, and appeared with a face of worthy astonishment.

Having in this instance not to deal with the Count, of whom he stood in some degree of awe, though that awe did not in the least diminish his malevolence, the Abbé de St. Helie proceeded to conduct the examination of Riquet himself. " You, Master Jerome Riquet," he commenced, " you are, I presume, of the church pretending to be reformed ?"

" Heaven forbid !" exclaimed Riquet, in a tone of well-assumed horror. " No, reverend sir, I am of the Holy Roman and Apostolical Church, and have never yet gone astray from it."

This announcement did not well suit the purposes of the Abbé, who, judging from the intolerant feelings of his own heart, had never doubted that the confidential servant of the young Count would be found to be a zealous Huguenot. He exclaimed, however, " I am glad to hear it—I am glad to hear it ! But let us speak a little further, Monsieur Jerome. It was you, I think, who snatched from under our good brother here, Monsieur le Curé de Guadrieul, a certain sheep leather bag, containing our commission from his majesty. Was it not so ?"

" I certainly did gently withdraw from under the reverend gentleman," replied Riquet, " a bag on which he was sitting, and which he took back again, as you saw, declaring it to be the king's commission for exterminating the Huguenots, which did my soul good to hear. I gave it back with all reverence, as you saw, and had it not in my hands a minute, though I did think—though I did indeed know ——"

" Did think? did know, what ?" demanded the Abbé.

" That it could not have been in safer hands than mine," added Riquet; and though St. Helie urged him vehemently, he could get him to give him no farther explanation. Angry at being foiled— and such probably was the result which Riquet intended to produce—the Abbé lost all caution and reserve. " Come, come, Master Jerome Riquet," he exclaimed, in a sharp voice, " come, come ; remember that there is such a place as the Bastille. Tell us the truth, sir ! tell us the truth ! This paper was stolen ! You evidently know something about it ! Tell us the truth, or means shall be found to make you. Now, answer me ! If your baggage were searched at this moment, would not the packet be found therein—or have you dared to destroy it ?"

Jerome Riquet now affected to bristle up in turn. His eyes flashed, his large nostrils expanded like a pair of extinguishers, and he replied, " No, Abbé, no; neither the one nor the other. But since I, one of the king's most loyal Catholic subjects, am accused in this way, I will speak out. I will say that you two gentlemen should have taken better care of the commission yourselves, and that though not one scrap will be found in my valise, or in the baggage of any other person belonging to my lord, I would not be answerable that more than a scrap was not found amongst the baggage of some that are accusing others."

" How now, sirrah !" cried the Abbé de St. Helie, " do you dare to say that either Monsieur Pelisson or I ——"

" Nothing about either of you two reverend sirs," replied the valet, " nothing about either of you two ! But first let my valise be brought in and examined. Monsieur has been pleased to say that there is something there ; and I swear by everything I hold dear, or by any other oath your reverences please, that I have not touched a thing in it since I heard of this business about the cards. Let it be brought in, I say, and examined. May I tell the people without, my lord duke, to bring in everything I have in the world, and lay it down here before you ?"

The Duke immediately assented, and while Jerome Riquet, without entirely leaving the room, bade the attendants in the antechamber bring in everything they could find in his room, St. Helie and Pelisson looked in each other's faces with glances of some embarrassment and wonder, while the Count de Morseiul gazed sternly down on the table, firmly believing that Master Jerome Riquet was engaged in playing off some specious trick which he himself could not detect, and was not bound to expose.

The goods and chattels of the valet were brought in, and a various and motley display they made ; for whether he had ar- ranged the whole on purpose, out of sheer impudence, or had left matters to take their course accidentally, his valise presented a number of objects certainly not his own property, and to most of which his master, if he had remarked them, might have laid claim. The Count was silent, however, and though the manifold collection of silk stockings, ribands, lace, doublets, &c. &c. &c., were drawn forth to the very bottom, yet nothing the least bearing upon the question of the abstraction of the commission was found throughout the whole.

As he shook the last vest, to show that there was nothing in it, a smile of triumph shone upon the countenance of Jerome Riquet, and he demanded, " Now, gentlemen, are you satisfied that I have no share in this business ?"

The Abbé de St. Helie was hastening to acknowledge that he was satisfied, for he was timid as well as malevolent ; and having lost the hold which he thought he might have had on Jerome Riquet, the menacing words which the valet had made use of filled his mind with apprehensions, lest some suspicion should be raised in the mind of the king, or of Louvois, that he himself had had a share in the disappearance of the paper. Not so, however, Pelisson, who, though he had learnt the lesson of sycophancy and flattery with wonderful aptitude, was naturally a man of courage and resolution, and before Monsieur de St. Helie could well finish what he had to say, he exclaimed, aloud—

" Stop, stop, Master Jerome Riquet, we are undoubtedly satis-

fied that the papers are not in your valise, and I think it probable
that you have had nothing to do with the matter; but you threw
out an insinuation just now, of which we must hear more. What
was the meaning of the words you made use of, when you said that
you would not be answerable that more than a scrap was not found
amongst the baggage of some who are accusing others?"

Jerome Riquet hesitated, and either felt or affected a disinclination to explain himself; but Pelisson persisted, notwithstanding
sundry twitches of the sleeve given to him both by the Abbé de
St. Helie and the Bishop himself.

"I must have this matter cleared up," said Pelisson, "and I do
not rise till it is. Explain yourself, sir, or I shall apply both to
your lord and to the governor, to insist upon your so doing."

Jerome Riquet looked towards the Count, who immediately said,
"What your meaning was, Riquet, you best know; but you must
have had some meaning, and it is fit that you should explain it."

"Well, then," said Riquet, shaking his head upon his shoulders
with an important look, "what I mean is this; that if ever I saw a
man who had an inclination to see the contents of a packet that
did not belong to him, it was Monsieur le Curé de Guadrieul
there. He knows very well that he talked to me for half an hour,
as to how easy it would be to get the packet out of the bag; and
he seemed to have a very great inclination to do it."

While he made this insinuation, the dull, fat, leaden-looking
mass of the Curé de Guadrieul was seen heaving with some internal convulsion: his breath came thick, his cheeks and his breast
expanded, his eyes grew red and fierce, his hands trembled with
rage; and starting up from his seat, he exclaimed—

"Me?—me? By the Lord, I will strangle thee with my own
hands!" and he sprang towards Jerome Riquet, as if to execute his
threat; while the governor exclaimed, in a voice of thunder, "Sit
down, sir! and, as you have joined in accusing others, learn to bear
the retaliation, as indeed you must."

"Can he deny what I say?" demanded Riquet, stretching out
three fingers of his right hand, and shaking them in the Curé's
face; "can he deny that he talked to me for half an hour about the
easiness of purloining the commission, and told me of a thousand
instances of the same kind, which have taken place before now?
No, he cannot deny it!"

"I did talk to thee, base miscreant," said the Curé, still swelling
with rage, "but it was to show why I always sat upon the bag, and
slept with it under my head, ever after that affair with the robbers."

"Mark that, gentlemen," said the Count de Morseiul.

"Well, sir, we do mark it," said the Bishop; "that proves
nothing against the Curé but extreme care and precaution."

"Nor can I prove anything directly, monseigneur," cried Riquet;
"but still I have a strange suspicion that the very night I speak of
did not go over without the fingers of Monsieur le Curé being in

the bag. Let me ask him another question, and let him mind how
he answers it. Was he, or was he not, seen by more than one
person dabbling at the mouth of the bag?"

"That was only to see that the knot was fast," replied the Curé,
glaring round him with a look of growing bewilderment and
horror.

"Ay, ay," continued Riquet, with a glance of calm contempt
that almost drove the man mad—"ay, ay, all I wish is, that I had
an opportunity of looking into your baggage, as you have had of
looking into mine."

"And so you shall, by Heaven!" cried the Duke de Rouvré. "I
will have it brought from his chamber this instant."

"I don't care," cried the priest; "let it be brought; you will
find nothing there."

But the Abbé de St. Helie and the Bishop both interposed.
Though Pelisson said nothing, and looked mortified and pained,
the others urged everything that they could think of for the protection of the baggage of the ecclesiastic, without the slightest consideration of equity or justice whatsoever; but the governor was
firm, replying—

"Gentlemen, I will be responsible for my conduct both to the
king and to the King of kings; and, in one word, I tell you that
this baggage shall be examined. You have brought back the
Count de Morseiul, and his whole train, on charges and insinuations
which you have not been able to establish; and you would now fain
shrink from a little trouble and inconvenience, which ought to be
taken, in order to clear one of yourselves of an imputation accompanied by a few singular facts. Maitre Riquet, call one of my
servants from the door, but do not leave the room yourself."

As soon as the servant appeared, the governor, notwithstanding
the renewed opposition of the two ecclesiastics, ordered the whole
baggage and effects of the Curé de Guadrieul to be brought down
from the chamber which he inhabited. This was accordingly done,
and besides a number of stray articles of apparel, almost as miscel-
laneous in character and appearance as those which the opening of
Riquet's valise had displayed, there was a large sort of trunk-mail
which appeared to be carefully locked. The Curé had looked on,
with a grim and scowling smile, while his various goods and chattels
were displayed upon the floor of the governor's cabinet, and then
turning to St. Helie with a growl, which might have been supposed
to proceed from a calumniated bear, he said—

"Don't be afraid. They can't find anything;" and advancing to
his effects, he shook them one after the other, and turned out the
pockets, when there were any, to show that there was nothing
concealed. He then produced a large key, and opening the trunk-
mail, took out, one by one, the various things that it contained. He
had nearly got to the bottom, and was displaying a store of tobacco-
pipes, some of which were wrapped up in pieces of paper, some in

their original naked whiteness, when in the midst of them appeared what seemed a tobacco-box, also wrapped up in paper.

The moment the eyes of Riquet fell upon it, he exclaimed, " Stop, stop, what is that? There is writing on that paper. Monsieur le Duc, I pray you to examine what is on that paper."

The eyes of the Curé, who had it in his hand, fixed for an instant upon the tobacco-box and its envelope, and his fingers instantly relaxed their grasp and suffered it to drop to the ground. Well, indeed, they might do so, for the very first words that were seen were, " I pray God to have you, Messieurs Pelisson and St. Helie, in his holy care," with the signature of " Louis."

The governor unrolled the paper, which, though it was but a fragment, left not the slightest doubt that it was part either of a commission or of a letter of instructions from the king to the two ecclesiastics. With his mouth wide open, his eyes ready to start from their sockets, his face become as pale as death, and his limbs scarcely able to support him, the unfortunate Curé de Guadrieul stood gasping in the middle of the room, unable to utter a word. All eyes were fixed upon him, all brows were frowning upon him, and the only thing which could have roused him, if it had been possible for anything to rouse him at that moment, was the extraordinary face which Jerome Riquet was making, in a vain endeavour to mingle in his countenance a certain portion of compassion with contempt and reprobation. Nobody spoke for a moment or two after the governor had read the contents; but at length the Duc de Rouvré said, in a dry, severe tone—

" Secretary, you have made a note of all this? you will keep also the fragment of paper. My lord the Bishop, Messieurs Pelisson and St. Helie, after the painful and distressing event of this examination, I shall make no comment whatsoever upon what has taken place. I beg that you will remove this personage, the Curé de Guadrieul, from my house, to do with him as you think fit. You will not, of course, be surprised when you remember the threatening language which you three were pleased to use towards myself, two days ago, in order to induce me to cause the arrest of the Count de Morseiul, upon a charge of crimes of which he was not guilty— Monsieur Pelisson, do not interrupt me : I know you were more moderate than the rest ; but as you were acting together, I must look upon the words of one, your spokesman, to be the words of all —You will not be surprised, I say, recollecting these facts, that I send off a special messenger to his majesty this night, in order to give him my own statement of all these occurrences, and to beseech him to take those steps which to me seem necessary for maintaining the peace and tranquillity of the province. I, gentlemen, do not encroach upon the rights and privileges of others ; and, so long as his majesty is pleased to hold me in an official situation, I will not suffer any one to trench upon my privileges and legitimate authority. As the hour for the meeting of the states is now fast approaching,

K

however, I will bid you farewell, begging you to take this personage with you, and, as I have said, deal with him as you think fit, for I wish to exercise no severity upon any ecclesiastic."

The persons he addressed had nothing to say in reply, though the Bishop thought fit to harangue the little party for a moment upon his own authority and high dignity, and Pelisson endeavoured to involve a bad business in a cloud of words. They were all, however, desperately mortified, and not a little alarmed; for there was no doubt that they had proceeded far beyond the point where their legitimate authority ended, in pressing the governor to severe measures against the Count de Morseiul. The loss of the packet, too, might now be attributed to themselves, instead of to him; the delay in executing the king's will, as it had been expressed, would be laid to their charge; the Duc de Rouvré was evidently highly irritated against them, and his representations to the throne on the subject were likely to be listened to with peculiar attention, as they were coupled with the announcement to the king that the states, by his skilful management, had voted at once a much larger sum as a gift than any one at the court had anticipated. All these considerations alarmed the whole party, though indeed Pelisson, who had more knowledge of human nature than the other two, trusted, with some degree of hope, that the cloak of religious zeal would cover all other sins. His greatest apprehension proceeded from the supposition that the king would cast the blame of the loss of the packet on themselves, and would attribute the negligence which had caused it to want of respect towards his person. He therefore set himself straightway to consider how such a result might be obviated. The Bishop and the Abbé de St. Helie took an unceremonious leave of the governor and his friend, and pushing the culprit Curé of Guadrieul out before them, quitted the cabinet in haste. Pelisson paused for a moment to say a word or two more in order to mitigate, as far as possible, the severity of the governor's report; but Monsieur de Rouvré was in no very placable mood; and the conference soon terminated, leaving the governor and the Count to discuss the affair, half laughingly, half seriously.

The invitation of the Duc de Rouvré was now pressing and strong, that the young Count de Morseiul should remain at least two days longer at Poitiers, and he coupled that invitation with the direct intimation that it was most necessary he should do so, as he, the Duke, had yet to learn in some degree the temper of the states in regard to the important questions between the Catholics and Protestants. The young Count consequently agreed to remain; taking the precaution, however, of writing at full to Claude de l'Estang, and sending off the letter by one of his own trustworthy servants, beseeching him to draw up the petition which the Protestant gentry had agreed upon, and to have it ready by the time at which he proposed to arrive at Morseiul.

During the greater part of those two days which followed, he saw little of Clémence de Marly. Without any cause assigned, she had been absent from all the spots where he was most likely to see her, except on those occasions when she was necessarily surrounded by a crowd. After breakfast, she remained but a moment in the salle: on the first day she did not appear at dinner; and on the second, she was absent from the breakfast table. The Chevalier d'Evran was also absent, and everything tended to confirm, in the mind of the young Count de Morseiul, the impression which he had received, that his friend was the lover of her whom he himself loved, and that some cause of disagreement, either temporary or permanent, had arisen between them. Nothing, however, tended to confirm this idea more than the appearance of Clémence herself, when she was present. There was an anxiety in the expression of her eyes; a thoughtfulness about her brow; an impatience of society; an occasional absence of mind, which was hardly to be mistaken. Her whole aspect was that of a person struggling with strong feelings, which were in reality getting the mastery.

She showed no particular inclination, after his return—except as we have seen, on the first evening—to speak with the Count de Morseiul, either in public or in private. Words of civility passed between them, of course; and every little courtesy was, perhaps, more scrupulously observed, on her part, than was usual with her; but on that evening, which closed the last day of the young Count's proposed stay, a change took place.

A large party had assembled at the governor's house; and though he himself looked both grave and anxious, he was doing the honours of his dwelling to every one with as much attention as possible, when suddenly, seeing the Count de Morseiul standing alone, near the doorway of the second room, he crossed over to speak with him, saying, " Albert, Clémence was seeking for you a moment ago. Where is she? have you seen her?"

Ere the young Count could reply, Clémence de Marly herself came up, as if about to speak with the Duke, whose hand she took in hers, in the sort of daughter-like manner in which she always behaved to him.

" Monsieur de Morseiul," she said, with a thoughtful lustre shining in her eyes, and giving a deeper and brighter expression to her whole countenance, " I have come to take refuge with you from that young De Hericourt, who evidently intends to persecute me during the whole evening.—But stay, stay, monseigneur," she added, turning to the Duke, who seemed about to quit them, to speak with some one else: " before you leave us, hear what I am going to say to Monsieur de Morseiul. You are going, Count, I hear, to take your departure to-morrow morning early: if you would walk with me for half an hour in the gardens ere you leave us, you would much oblige me, as I wish to speak with you.—Now, dear King of Poitou," she continued, turning to the Duke, " you may go. I have no more secrets to make you a witness of."

The Duke replied not exactly to her words, but seemed fully to comprehend them; and saying, " Not to-night, Clémence! Remember, not to-night!" he left her under the charge of the Count de Morseiul, and proceeded to attend to his other guests.

Placed in a situation somewhat strange, and, as it were, forced to appear as one of the attendant train of the bright and beautiful girl, from whose dangerous fascinations he was eager to fly, for a single instant Albert of Morseiul felt slightly embarrassed; but unexpected situations seldom so much affected him as to produce anything like ungraceful hesitation of manner. Clémence de Marly might not, perhaps, even perceive that the Count was at all embarrassed; for she was deeply occupied with her own fancies; and though she conversed with him, not gaily, but intelligently, there was evidently another train of thought going on in her breast all the time, which sometimes made her answer wide from the mark, and then smile at her own absence of mind.

The eyes of the young Marquis de Hericourt followed her wherever she turned, and certainly bore not the most placable expression towards the Count de Morseiul; but his anger or his watching disturbed neither Clémence nor her companion, who both had busy thoughts enough to occupy them. After some time the excitement of the dance seemed to rouse Clémence from her musing fit; and, though confined to subjects of ordinary interest, the conversation between her and the Count became of a deeper tone and character, and her heart seemed to take part in it as well as her mind. Albert of Morseiul felt it far more dangerous than before ; for though they might but speak of a picture, or a statue, or a song, with which he could have conversed with a connoisseur of any kind, perhaps with more profit, as far as mere knowledge of the subject went, yet there was a refinement of taste evident in the manner in which Clémence viewed everything, a sparkling grace given by her imagination to every subject that she touched upon, when her feelings were really interested therein, which was very, very winning, to a mind like that of Albert de Morseiul.

Is it possible, under such circumstances, always to be upon one's guard? Is it possible, when the heart loves deeply, always to conquer it with so powerful an effort, as not to let it have the rule, even for an hour ? If it be, such was not the case with the young Count de Morseiul. He forgot not his resolutions, it is true ; but he gave himself up to happiness for the moment, and spoke with warmth, enthusiasm, and eagerness, which can seldom, if ever, be displayed to a person we do not love. There was a light, too, in his eye, when he gazed on Clémence de Marly—a look in which regret was mingled with tenderness, and in which the cloud of despair only shadowed, but did not darken the fire of passion—which might well show her, unless her eyes were dazzled by their own light, that she was loved, and loved by a being of a higher and more energetic character than those who usually surrounded her.

Perhaps she did see it—perhaps she did not grieve to see it—for her eyes became subdued by his; her mellow and beautiful voice took a softer tone; the colour came and went in her cheek; and before the end of the dance in which they were engaged, her whole appearance, her whole manner, made the Count ask himself, " What am I doing?"

Clémence de Marly seemed to have addressed the same question to her own heart; for as soon as the dance was over, the cloud of thoughtful sadness came back upon her brow, and she said, " I am fatigued. I shall dance no more to-night. All the people are doubtless come now, and dear Madame de Rouvré will move no more ; so I shall go and sit myself down in state beside her, and get her to shield me from annoyance to-night."

The Count led her towards the Duchess, intending himself to seek his chamber soon after; but as they went, Clémence said to him, in a low tone, " Do you see that pretty girl sitting there by her mother, old Madame de Marville, so modest, and so gentle and retiring? She is as good a little creature as ever breathed, and as pretty, yet nobody leads her out to dance. If I had a brother, I should like him to marry that girl. She would not bring him fortune, but she would bring him happiness. I wish, Monsieur de Morseiul, you would go and ask her to dance."

Though he was anxious to retire, and full of other thoughts, Albert of Morseiul would not have refused for the world ; and Clémence, leading him up to her friend, said, " Annette, here is Monsieur le Comte de Morseiul, who wishes to dance with you: I am sure you will, for your friend's sake."

The young lady bowed her head, with a slight timid blush, and, rising, allowed the Count to lead her to the dance.

No great opportunity of conversing existed; but Albert of Morseiul took especial pains to show himself as courteous and as kind as possible. Annette de Marville led the conversation herself to Clémence de Marly, and nothing could exceed the enthusiastic admiration with which she spoke of her friend. Perhaps a little to the surprise of the Count, she never mentioned Clémence's beauty, or her grace, or her wit; matters which, in those days, and at the court of Louis XIV., were the only topics for praise, the only attractions coveted. She spoke of her high and noble feelings, her enthusiastic and affectionate heart; and, in answer to something which the Count said, not quite so laudatory as she would have had it, she exclaimed—

" Oh ! but Clémence does not do herself justice in the world. It is only to those who know her most intimately, that her shy heart will show itself."

The words sunk into the mind of the Count de Morseiul; and when the dance was concluded, and he had led back his fair companion to her seat, he retired speedily to his own apartments, to meditate over what he had heard, and what had taken place.

CHAPTER XI.

THE EXPLANATIONS.

SILENT and lonely thought is a sad dispeller of enchantments. Under its power, the visions, and hopes, and indistinct dreams, which had fluttered before the eyes of the Count de Morseiul during the magic moments he had passed with Clémence de Marly, fled like fairies at the approach of the sun, within a very short period after he had retired to his chamber; and all that remained was a sort of self-reproachful mournfulness, when he thought over his own conduct and the indulgence of those feelings which he feared he had displayed but too plainly. With such thoughts he lay down to rest; but they were not soothing companions of the pillow, and it was long ere he slept. From time to time he heard the sound of music from the halls below; and in the intervals, when some open door gave a freer passage to the sound, gay laughing voices came merry on the ear, speaking cheerfulness, and happiness, and contentment, and ignorance, of the cares and sorrows and anxieties of life.

"Alas!" thought the Count, as he lay and listened, "alas! that such bright illusions should pass away, and that those should ever learn the touch of grief and anguish and despair, who are now laughing in the heedless merriment of youth, unconscious of danger or of sorrow. And yet, perhaps," he continued, "could we lay bare the hearts now seemingly so gay—could we examine what is their ordinary state, and what their feelings were, even a few short moments before they entered those saloons—we might find there also, as much care and pain as in any other scene of life, and bless the glad merriment that lulls human pangs and anxieties for a time, though it cannot quench them altogether."

Though he went to sleep late, he rose early on the following morning, not forgetful of his appointment with Clémence de Marly. Fearful, however, that she might be in the gardens before him, he dressed himself, and hastened out without the loss of a single minute, not a little desirous of knowing what was the nature of the communication which she had to make to him, and with which the Duc de Rouvré was evidently acquainted. He was, in truth, anxious in regard to every part of their conversation: he was anxious in regard to its result; but still he did not lay out at all the conduct he was to pursue towards her, feeling that he had awakened from the dream of the evening before, and believing that he was not likely to indulge in such visions again. There was nobody in the part of the garden near the house; and he walked on in the direction which she had pointed out to him, till he had nearly reached the rampart, and thus satisfied himself that she had not yet arrived. He then turned back by the same path, and before he had gone half way down, he beheld Clémence coming towards him, but at some distance.

She was certainly looking more lovely than ever; and he could not but feel that, even in her very gayest and most sparkling moods, there was a charm wanting in comparison with her more serious and thoughtful aspect. Clémence was now evidently a good deal agitated. It often happens, when we have an act of importance to perform, especially when that act is unusual to us, that even in re- volving it in our own minds, and preparing for the moment, we overpower ourselves, as it were, by the force of our own thoughts, and, by guarding against agitation, give agitation the better oppor- tunity to assail us.

Albert of Morseiul saw that Clémence was much moved, and he prepared to soothe her by every means in his power. The only efficacious means being to draw her attention to ordinary things— " Let me offer you my arm," he said, in a kindly tone; and leading her on, he spoke of the beauty of the morning, and then of Annette de Marville, and then of other indifferent things. Clémence seemed to understand his object; and though she at first smiled, as if to in- timate that she did so, she gave her mind up to his guidance, and for five or ten minutes touched upon no subject but the most ordinary topics of conversation. As they approached the rampart, however, and she had an opportunity of looking along it, and ascer- taining that there was no one there, she said—

" Now I am better—now I can speak on other subjects. Mon- sieur de Morseiul," she continued, " although I am accustomed to do extraordinary things, and to behave, in many respects, unlike other people, I dare say you do not suppose that I would have taken the very bold step of asking any gentleman to meet me here, as I have done with you this day, without a motive sufficient to justify me, even in your sight."

" I am quite sure of it," replied the Count; " and though you may think me, perhaps, a harsh censor, I am not at all inclined to be so in your case."

" Indeed?" she said, with a somewhat mournful shake of the head; " indeed?—But, however, Monsieur de Morseiul, what I have to tell you is substantial, real, and more important than any feelings or inclinations. I shall have to pain you—to grieve you— to call up apprehensions—to prepare you, perhaps, for suffering!— Oh God!" she cried, bursting suddenly into tears, " that I should have to do this!"

The Count took her hand and pressed it to his lips, and be- sought her to be calm and soothed. " Do not be apprehensive, do not be grieved," he said: " calm yourself, dear lady, calm yourself, Clémence! I am prepared for much sorrow; I am prepared for danger and anxiety. I have for some time seen nothing but clouds and storms in the future!"

" Not such as these," replied Clémence, " not such as these.

But I will not keep you in suspense; for that is worse than all. The task, though a painful one, has been of my own seeking. First, Monsieur de Morseiul, to speak of that which I know is dearest to your heart—your religious liberty is in danger—it is more than in danger—it is at an end. The whole resolutions of the court are now made known—at least, amongst the principal Catholics of France. The reformed church is to be swept away—there is no longer to be any but one religion tolerated throughout the kingdom—your temples are to be overthrown—your ministers to be forbidden, on pain of death, to worship God as their fore-fathers have done—the edict of Nantes is to be revoked entirely;" and, clasping her hands together, she gazed in his face, while she added, in a low, tremulous, but distinct, voice, " you are to be driven to the mass at the point of the pike—your children are to be taken from you to be educated in another faith !"

Till she uttered the last words, Albert de Morseiul had remained with his eyes bent upon the ground, though deep feelings of agita-tion were evident in every line of his fine countenance. But when she spoke of the Protestants being driven to mass at the point of the pike, and their children being taken from them to be educated in the Catholic religion, he threw back his head, gazing up to heaven with a look of firm determination, while his left hand, by an involuntary movement, fell upon the hilt of his sword.

Clémence de Marly, as he did so, gazed upon him earnestly through the tears that were still in her eyes, and then exclaimed, as she saw how terribly moved he was, " These are dreadful tidings for me to tell, Monsieur de Morseiul: you must hate me—I am sure you must hate me !"

" Hate you?" exclaimed the Count, clasping both her hands in his, while, in that agitating moment—carried away by the strength of his own feelings, and by the tokens she displayed of deep in-terest in him and his—every barrier gave way before the passion of his heart. " Hate you? oh God! I love you but too well, too deeply—better, more deeply, than you can ever know, or divine, or dream of !"

Clémence turned away her head, with a face glowing like the rose; but she left her hands in his, without an effort to withdraw them, though she exclaimed, " Say not so! say not so!—Or at least," she added, turning round once more towards him—" say not so till you have heard all; for I have much, much more to tell, more painful, more terrible still. Let me have one moment to recover," and, withdrawing her hands, she placed them over her eyes for an instant. After a very brief pause she added, " Now, Monsieur de Morseiul, I can go on. You are here in great danger. You have been in great danger ever since you returned hither; and it has only been the power and authority of the Duke that has pro-tected you. After your first interview with the governor, the bishop and the two ecclesiastics, a party has been made in the

town, in the states, and in the province, against you, and, alas!
against the good Duc de Rouvré too. Finding that they were
likely to incur the anger of the king for something that had happened, if they did not make good their own case against you, they
have laboured, I may say night and day, to counteract the measures of the Duke with the states, so as to make him obnoxious to
his sovereign. They have pretended that you—while you were
here before—held illegal meetings with Huguenots in the neighbourhood, in order to oppose and frustrate the measures of the
king. They have got the intendant of the province upon their
side, and they insisted, to Monsieur de Rouvré, on your being
instantly arrested, they having proffered distinct information of
your having held a meeting with other Protestant noblemen, about
three miles from this place, on the day of the hunting. Do you
remember that day?"

" I shall never forget it!" replied the Count, gazing upon her
with a look that made her eyes sink again.

" Well," she continued, " Monsieur de Rouvré would not consent; and when the intendant threatened to arrest you on his own
responsibility, the governor was obliged to say that he would defend you, and protect you, if necessary, by the interposition of the
military force at his command. This created a complete breach,
which is now only apparently healed. Both parties have applied
to the king, and Monsieur de Rouvré entertained the strongest
hopes till yesterday that the decision would have been in his favour,
both inasmuch as justice was on his side, and as he had obtained
from the states a large supply, which he knew would be most grati-
fying and acceptable to the court; but suddenly, yesterday morning, news arrived of the general measures which the council
intended to pursue. These I have already told you, and they
showed the Duke that everything would give way to bigotry and
superstition. Various letters communicated the same intelligence
to others as well as to the Duke, but I having——"

She paused and hesitated, while the colour came and went
rapidly in her cheek. " Speak, dear lady, speak," said the Count,
eagerly.

" I believe I may speak," she said, " after something that you
said but now. I was going to say that, I having before taken upon
me, perhaps sillily, when first these men brought their false charge
against you, to meddle with this business, from feelings that I must
not and cannot explain, and having then made the Duke tell me
the whole business, by earnest prayers and entreaties—he seeing
that I was—that I was interested in the matter, told me all the rest,
and gave me permission to tell you the whole this morning, in
order that you may guard against the measures that he fears are
coming; ' I must not tell him myself,' the Duke said; ' and, as
the business has been communicated alone to Catholics, he is not
likely to hear it, till too late. Nevertheless, it is no secret, the

matter having been mentioned openly to at least twenty people in this town.   You can therefore do it yourself, Clémence, that he may not say I have lured him back here into the jaws of his enemies.'   Thus, then, Monsieur de Morseiul," she continued, more collectedly, " thus it is that I have acted as I have acted; and oh, if you would take my advice, painful as I acknowledge it is to give it, you would proceed instantly to Morseiul, and then either fly to England, or to some other country where you will be in safety."

" How shall I thank you," replied Albert of Morseiul, taking her hand, and casting behind him all consideration of his own fate and that of his fellow Protestants, to be thought of at an after moment, while, for the time, he gave his whole attention to the words which he had himself just spoken with regard to his love for Clémence de Marly—" how shall I ever thank you for the interest you have taken in me—for your kindness, for your generous kindness, and for all the pain that this, I see, has caused you!   Pray, Clémence, pray add one more boon to those you have conferred—forgive the rash and presumptuous words I spoke just now—and forget them a so."

" Forget them!" exclaimed Clémence, clasping her hands and raising her bright eyes to his; " forget them! Never, as long as I have being! Forgive them, Monsieur de Morseiul! that were easily done—if I could believe them true."

" They are as true as Heaven!" replied the Count; "but oh, Clémence, Clémence, lead me not away into false dreams! lead me not away to think that possible which is impossible.—Can it—ought it to be ?"

" I know not what you mean," replied Clémence, with a look somewhat bewildered, somewhat hurt.   " All I know is, Monsieur de Morseiul, that you have spoken words which justify me to myself for feelings—ay, and perhaps for actions,—in regard to which I was doubtful—fearful—which sometimes made me blush when I thought of them.   The words that you have spoken take away that blush. I feel that I had not mistaken you; but yet," she added, " tell me before you go, for I feel that it must be soon—what is it that you mean?   What is the import of your question ?"

" Oh, it means much and many things, Clémence," replied the Count: " it takes in a wide range of painful feelings; and when I acknowledge, and again and again say, that the words I have spoken are true as Heaven—when, again and again, I say that I love you deeply, devotedly, entirely, better than ought else on earth, I grieve that I have said them, I feel that I have done wrong."

Clémence de Marly withdrew her hand, not sharply, not coldly, but mournfully, and she raised her fair countenance towards the sky, as if asking, with apprehension at her heart, " What is thy will, oh Heaven ?"—" Albert of Morseiul," she said, " if you have any cause to regret that those words have been spoken, let them be for ever between us as if unspoken.   They shall never, by me, be repeated to any one. You may perhaps one day, years hence,"—and as she spoke her eyes filled with tears,—" you may, perhaps, regret what you are now doing; but it will be a consolation to you then to know, that even though you spoke words of love, and then recalled them, they were ever, as they ever shall be, a consolation and a comfort to me. The only thing on earth that I could fear was the blame of my own heart for having thought you loved me, —when, perhaps," she added, while a deep blush again spread over all her countenance, " when perhaps you did not. You have shielded me from that blame: you have taken away all self-reproach; and now God speed you, Albert! Choose your own path, follow the dictates of your own heart and your own conscience, and farewell!"

" Stay, stay, Clémence," said the Count de Morseiul, detaining her by the hand. " Yet listen to me; yet hear me a few words farther!"

She turned round upon him, with one of her former smiles. " You know how easily such requests are granted," she said; " you know how willingly I would fain believe you all that is noble, and just, and honourable, and perfectly incapable of trifling with a woman's heart."

" First, then," said the Count, " let me assure you that the words I have spoken were not, as you seemed to have imagined, for your ear alone, to be disavowed before the world. Ever shall I be ready, willing, eager, to avow those words; and the love I feel, and have spoken of, will never, can never die away in my heart. But oh, Clémence, do you remember all that passed between us in this very garden, as to whether a woman could love twice? Do you remember what you acknowledged yourself on that occasion?"

" And do you believe, then," said Clémence, " after all that you have seen, that I have ever loved? Do you believe," she said, with the bright but scornful smile that sometimes crossed her lip, " that because Clémence de Marly has suffered herself to be surrounded by fools and coxcombs, the one to neutralize and oppose the other —whereas, if she had not done so, she must have chosen one from the herd to be her lord and master, and have become his slave—do you imagine, I say, that she has fallen in love with pretty Monsieur de Hericourt, with his hair frizzled like a piece of pastry, his wit as keen as a baby's wooden sword, and his courage of that high, discriminating quality, which might be well led on by a child's trumpet? Or, with the German prince, who, though a brave man, and not without sense, is as courteous as an Italian mountebank's dancing bear, that thinks itself the pink of politeness when it hands round a hat to gather the sous, growling between its teeth all the time that it does so? Or with the Duc de Melcourt, who, though polished and keen, and brave as his sword, is as cold-hearted as the iron that lies within that scabbard, and in seeking Clémence de Marly seeks three requisite things to accomplish a French nobleman's household,—a large fortune, which may pay cooks and serving men, and give at

least two gilded coaches more ; a handsome wife, that cares nothing
for her husband, and is not likely to disturb him by her love; and
some influence at court, which may obtain for him the next blue
riband vacant ?—Out upon them all!" she added, vehemently;
" and fie, fie, fie, upon you, Albert of Morseiul! If I thought that
you could love a person of whom you judged so meanly, I should
believe you unworthy of another thought from me."

It is useless to deny, that every word she spoke was pleasant to
the ear of the Count de Morseiul; but yet she had not exactly
touched the point towards which his own apprehensions regarding
her had turned, and though he did not choose to name the Chevalier, he still went on.

" I have thought nothing of the kind you speak of, Clémence,"
he replied; " but I may have thought it possible for you to have
met with another more worthy of your thoughts and of your affection than any of these; that you may have loved him; and that on
some quarrel, either temporary or permanent, your indignation towards him, and your determination not to let him see the pain he
has occasioned, may have made you fancy yourself in love with another. May not this be the case? But still, even were it not so,
there is much—But I ask," he added, seeing the colour of Clémence fluttering like the changing hues on the plumage of a bird,
" but I ask again, may it not have been so ?"

Clémence gazed at him intently and steadfastly for a moment, and
there was evidently a struggle going on in her breast of some kind.
Perhaps Albert of Morseiul might misunderstand the nature of that
struggle; indeed, it is clear he did so in some degree, for it certainly confirmed him in the apprehensions which he had entertained. The air and the expression of Clémence varied considerably
while she gazed upon him. For a moment there was the look of
proud beauty and careless caprice with which she treated the
lovers of whom she had just spoken so lightly; and the next, as
some memory seemed to cross her mind, the haughty expression
died away into one of subdued tenderness and affection. An instant after, sadness and sorrow came over her face like a cloud, and
her eyes appeared to be filling with irrepressible tears. She conquered that, too ; and when she replied, it was with a smile so
strangely mingled with various expressions, that it was difficult to
discern which predominated. There was a certain degree of pride
in her tone ; there was sorrow upon her brow ; and yet there was
a playfulness round her eyes and lips, as if something made her
happy amidst it all.

" Such might be the case," she replied—" such is very likely to
be the case with all women. But pray, sir,—having settled it all
so well and so wisely,—who was the favoured person who had thus
won Clémence de Marly's love, while some few others were seeking
for it in vain ? Your falcon, Fancy, was certainly not without a
lure. I see it clearly, Monsieur de Morseiul."

"It might be one," replied the Count, "whose rival I would never become, even were other things done away; it might be one long and deeply regarded by myself."

"The Chevalier—the Chevalier!" exclaimed Clémence, with her whole face brightening into a merry smile. "No, no, no! You have been deceiving yourself. No, no, Count, the Chevalier d'Evran never has been—never will be, anything to me but that which he is now; we have had no quarrel—we have had no coldness. It is quite possible, Monsieur de Morseiul, believe me, even for a weak woman like myself to feel friendship and place confidence without love."

She strove in some degree to withdraw the hand that the Count had taken, as if she were about to leave him; but the Count detained it gently, saying, "Stay yet one moment, Clémence; let us yet have but one word more of explanation before we part."

"No," she replied, disengaging her hand—"no; we have had explanations enough. Never wed a woman of whom you have a single doubt, sir. No, no," she added, with a look slightly triumphant, perhaps somewhat sorrowful, but somewhat playful withal; "no, no! Clémence de Marly has already, perhaps, said somewhat too much! But one thing I will tell you, Albert of Morseiul—You love her! She sees it—she knows it, and from henceforth she will not doubt it—for a woman does not trust by halves, like a man. You love her!—You will love her! and, though you have perhaps somewhat humiliated her—though you have made the proud humble and the gay melancholy, it is, perhaps, no bad lesson for her; and she will now make you sue, before you gain, as a pressing lover, that which you now seem to require some pressing to accept. Adieu, Monsieur de Morseiul; there is, I see, somebody coming; adieu!"

"Stay yet a moment, Clémence; hear me yet urge something in my defence," exclaimed her lover. But Clémence proceeded down the steps from the rampart, only pausing and turning to say, in a tone of greater tenderness and interest—

"Farewell, Albert, farewell; and for God's sake forget not the warning that I gave you this morning, nor any of the matters so much more worthy of attention than the worthless love of a gay capricious girl."

Thus saying, she hastened on, and passing by the person who was coming forward from the house—and who was merely a servant attached to the Count de Morseiul, hunting out his master, as is usual with servants, to interrupt him at the most inappropriate time—she hurried towards a small door to the left of the building, entered, and mounting a back staircase which led towards her own apartments, she sought shelter therein from all the many eyes that were at that time beginning to move about the place; for her face was a tablet on which strong and recent emotion was deeply and legibly written.

Nor had that emotion yet passed away, indeed; but, on the contrary, new and agitating thoughts had been swelling upon her all the way through the gardens, as she returned alone—the memories of one of those short but important lapses of time which change with the power of an enchanter the whole course of our being, which alter feelings and thoughts, and hope and expectation, give a different direction to aspiration and effort and ambition, which add wings and a fiery sword to enthusiasm, and turn the thread of destiny upon a new track through the labyrinth of life.

There was in the midst of those memories one bright and beautiful spot; but it was surrounded by so many contending feelings—there was so much alloy to the pure gold—that, when at length she reached her dressing-room and cast herself into a chair, she became overpowered, and, bursting into tears, wept bitterly and completely.

The old and faithful attendant whom Albert of Morseiul had seen with her in the forest, and who was, indeed, far superior to the station which she filled, both by talents, education, and heart, now witnessing the emotion of her young mistress, glided up and took her hand in hers, trying by every quiet attention to tranquillize and soothe her. It was in vain, for a long time, however, that she did so; and when, at length, Clémence had recovered in some degree her composure, and began to dry her eyes, the attendant asked, eagerly, "Dear, dear child, what is it has grieved you so?"

"I will tell you, Maria,—I will tell you in a minute," replied Clémence. "You who have been a sharer of all my thoughts from my infancy—you who were given me as a friend by the dear mother I have lost—you who have preserved for me so much, and have preserved me myself so often—I will tell you all and everything. I will have no concealment in this from you; for I feel, as if I were a prophet, that terrible and troublous times are coming; that it is my fate to take a deep and painful part therein; and that I shall need one like you to counsel, and advise, and assist, and support me in many a danger, and, for ought I know, in many a calamity."

"Dear Clémence—dear child," said the attendant, "I will ever do my best to soothe and comfort you; and what little assistance I can give shall be given. But, both from what I have seen and what I have heard, I have trusted and I have hoped for many days, that a stronger hand than that of a weak old woman was soon about to be plighted to support and defend you for life."

"Who do you mean?" exclaimed Clémence, eagerly; "who are you speaking of, Maria?"

"Can you not divine?" demanded the old lady; "can you not divine that I mean him whom we saw in the forest—him, who seemed to my old eyes to wed you then, with the ring that your mother gave you, when she told you never to part with it to any one but to the man who was to place it again on your finger as your husband?"

Strange how the human heart will catch at any trifle to justify its own wishes, its own hopes, or its own fears.

"Good Heaven!" exclaimed Clémence, in answer to what the servant said, "I never thought of that! I am his wife, then, Maria,—at least, I shall ever consider myself such."

"But will he consider you so, too?" demanded the attendant; "and do you love him enough to consider him so, dear child? I have never seen you love any one yet; and I only began to hope that you would love him, when I saw your colour change as often as his name was mentioned."

"I have said I would tell you all, Maria," replied Clémence, "and I will tell you all. I never have loved any one before; and how could I? surrounded as I have been by the empty, and the vain, and the vicious,—by a crowd so full of vices, and so barren of virtues, that a man thought himself superior to the whole world, if he had but one good quality to recommend him; and what were the qualities on which they piqued themselves? If a man had wit, he thought himself a match for an empress; if he had courage, though that, to say the truth, was the most general quality, he felt himself privileged to be a libertine, and a gamester, and an atheist; and, instead of feeling shame, he gloried in his faults. How could I love any of such men? How could I esteem them—the first step to love? I have but heard one instance of true affection in the court of France—that of poor Conti to the king's daughter; and I never fancied myself such a paragon as to be the second woman that could raise such attachment. Nothing less, however, would satisfy me, and therefore I determined to shape my course accordingly. I resolved to let the crowd that chose it, follow, and flatter, and affect to worship, as much as ever they so pleased. It was their doing, not mine. I mean not to say that it did not please and amuse me: I mean not to say that I did not feel some sort of satisfaction—which I now see was wrong to feel—in using as slaves, in ordering here and there, in trampling upon and mortifying a set of beings that I contemned and despised, and that valued me alone for gifts which I valued not myself. Had there been one man amongst them that at all deserved me—that gave one thought to my mind or to my heart, rather than to my beauty or my fortune— he would have hated me for the manner in which I treated him and others; and I might have learned to love him, even while he learned to contemn me. Such was not the case, however, for there was not one that did so. Had I declared my determination of never marrying, to be the slave of a being I despised, they would soon have put me in a convent, or at least have tried to do so; and I feared they might. Therefore it was I went on upon the same plan, sitting like a waxen virgin in a shrine, letting adorers come and worship as much as they pleased, and taking notice of none. There is not one of them who can say that I ever gave him ought but a cutting speech, or an expression of my contempt. It is now several

years ago, but you must remember it well, when we were first with
the Duke at Ruffigny——"

" Oh, I remember it well," replied the attendant, "and the hunting, and your laying down the bridle like a wild, careless girl, as
you then were, and the horse running away with you, and this very
Count de Morseiul saving you by stopping it. Ay, I remember it
all well, and you told me how gallant and handsome he looked, and
all he had said ; and I laughed, and told you you were in love with
him."

" I was not in love," replied Clémence, with the colour slightly
deepening in her cheek—" I was not in love ; but I might soon have
been so, even then. I thought a great deal about him. I was
very young, had mixed not at all with the world, and he was certainly at that time, in personal appearance, what might well realize
the dream of a young and enthusiastic imagination.—He is older·
and graver now," she added, musing, " and time has made a change
on him ; but yet I do not think he is less handsome. However, I
thought of him a good deal then, especially after I had met him the
second time, and discovered who he was : and I thought of him often
afterwards. Wherever there was any gallant action done, I was
sure to listen eagerly, expecting to hear his name. And how often
did I hear it, Maria l Not a campaign passed but some new praises
fell upon the Count de Morseiul. He had defended this post like
some ancient hero, against whole legions of the enemy. He had
thrown himself into that small fort, which was considered untenable,
and held an army at bay for weeks. He had been the first to
plant his foot on the breach; he had been the last in the rear upon
a retreat. The peasant's cottage, the citizen's fire-side, owed their
safety to him; and the ministers of another religion than his own
had found shelter and protection beneath his sword. I know not
how it was, but when all these tales were told me, his image always
rose up before me as I had seen him, and I pictured him in every
action. I could see him leading the charging squadrons. I could
see him standing in the deadly breach. I could see the women
and the children, and the conquered and the wounded, clinging to
his knees, and could see him saving them. I did not love him,
Maria, but I thought of him a great deal more than of any one else
in all the world. Well, then, after some years, came the last great
service that he rendered us, not many weeks ago, and was not his
demeanour then, Maria—was not his whole air and conduct in the
midst of danger to himself and others—was not the peremptory
demand of our liberation—the restoration of the ring I valued—
the easy, unshaken courtesy, in a moment of agitation and risk,—
was it not all noble, all chivalrous, all such as a woman's imagination might well dwell upon ?"

" It was, indeed," replied Maria, " and ever since then, I have
thought that you were inclined to love him."

" In the meantime," continued Clémence, "in the meantime, I

had also become sadly spoilt. I had grown capricious, and vain, and haughty, by indulging such feelings for several years, in pursuit of my own system; and when the Count appeared at Poitiers, I do not know that I was inclined to treat him well. Not that I would ever have behaved to him as I did to others; but I scarcely knew how to behave better. I believed myself privileged to say and do anything I thought right, to exact anything, nay, to command anything. I was surprised when I found he took no notice of me—I was mortified, perhaps. I determined, if ever I made him happy at last, to punish him for his first indifference,—to punish him, how think you? To make him love me, to make him doubtful of whether I loved him, and to make him figure in the train of those whom I myself despised. But, oh, Maria, I soon found that I could not accomplish what I sought. There was a power, a command in his nature, that overawed, that commanded me. Instead of teaching him to love me, and making him learn to doubt that I loved him, I soon found that it was I that loved, and learned to doubt that he loved me. Then came restlessness and disquietude. From time to time I saw—I felt that he loved me; and then again I doubted, and strove to make him show it more clearly, by the very means best calculated to make him crush it altogether. I affected to listen to the frivolous and the vain, to smile upon the beings I despised, to assume indifference towards the only one I loved. Thus it went on till the last day of his stay, when he refused to accompany us on our hunting party, but left me with a promise to join us if he could. I was disappointed, mortified. I doubted if he would keep his promise. I doubted whether he had any inclination to do so; and I strove to forget, in the excitement of the chase, the bitterness of that which I suffered. Suddenly, however, I caught a glance of him riding down towards us. He came up to my side, he rode on by me, he attended to me, he spoke to me alone; there was a grace, and a dignity, and a glory about his person, that was new and strange; he seemed as if some new inspiration had come upon him. On every subject that we spoke of, he poured forth his soul in words of fire. His eyes and his countenance beamed with living light, such as I had never before beheld. Everything vanished from my eyes and thoughts but Albert of Morseiul; everything seemed small and insignificant, and to bow before him; the very fiery charger that he rode seemed to obey, with scarcely a sign or indication of his will. The cavaliers around looked but like his attendants, and I—I, Maria—proud, and haughty, and vain, as I had encouraged myself to be—I felt that I was in the presence of my master, and that, there, beside me, was the only man on earth that I could willingly and implicitly obey. I felt subdued, but not depressed—I felt, perhaps, as a woman ought to feel towards a man she loves: that I was competent to be his companion and his friend, to share his thoughts, to respond to all his feelings, to enter into his views and opinions, to meet him, in short, with a mind yielding, but scarcely to be called inferior, different in quality, but harmonious in love and thought. I felt that he was one who would never wish me to be a slave; but one that I should be prompt and ready to bend to and obey. Can I tell you, Maria, all the agony that took possession of my heart when I found that the whole bright scene was to pass away like a dream? Since then many a painful thing has happened. I have wrung my heart, I have embittered my repose, by fancying that I have loved where I was not loved in return, that I have been the person to seek, and he to despise me. But this day, this day, Maria, has come an explanation. He has told me that he loves me, he has told me that he has loved me long; he has taken away that shame; he has given me that comfort. We both foresee many difficulties, pangs, and anxieties; but, alas! Maria, I see plainly, not only that he discovers in the future far more difficulties, and dangers, and obstacles between us, than I myself perceive, but also that he disapproves of much of my conduct—that doubts and apprehensions mingle with his love—that it is a thing which he has striven against —not from his apprehension of difficulties, but from his doubts of me and of my nature: that love has mastered him for a time; but still has not subdued him altogether.—It is a bitter and a sad thing," she added, placing her hands over her eyes.

"But, dear child," said the attendant, "it will be easy for you to remove all such doubts and apprehensions."

"Hush, hush," replied Clémence, "let me finish, Maria, and then say no more upon this score to-day. I will hear all you can say to-morrow. He is gone by this time; God knows whether we shall ever meet again. But, at all events, my conduct is determined; I will act in every respect, whether he be with me or whether he be absent from me, whether he still misunderstands me or whether he now conceives my motives exactly—I will act as I know he would approve, if he could see every action and every movement of my heart. I will cast behind me all those things which I now feel were wrong; though, Heaven knows, I did not see that there was the slightest evil in any of them, till love for him has, with the quickness of a flash of lightning, opened my eyes in regard to my conduct towards others. I will do all, in short, that he ought to love me for; and, in doing that, I will in no degree seek him, but leave fate and God's will to work out my destiny, trusting that, with such purposes, I shall be less miserable than I have been for the last week. And now, Maria," she added, "I have given you the picture of a woman's heart. Let us dwell no more upon this theme, for I must wash away these tears, these new invaders of eyes that have seldom known them before, and go as soon as possible to Monsieur de Rouvré, to inform him of a part, at least, of my conversation with the Count."

CHAPTER XII.

THE RETURN.

SOMETIMES, amidst the storms and tempests of life, when the rain of sorrow has been pouring down amain, and the lightning of wrath been flashing on our path, the clouds overhead, heavy, and loaded with mischief to come, and the thunder rolling round and round after the flash, there will come a brief, calm moment of sweet tranquillity, as if wrath and enmity, and strife and care, and misfortune, had cast themselves down to rest, exhausted with their fury. Happy is the man who in such moments can throw from him remembrance of the past, and apprehension of the future, and taste the refreshing power without alloy. But seldom can we do so: the passed-by storm is fresh on memory, the threatening aspect of the sky is full before our eyes; and such was the case with Albert of Morseiul, as, on the third day after leaving Poitiers, he rode on towards his own abode.

The degree of impatient anxiety under which he had laboured had caused him to make the first two days' journeys as long as possible, so that, although it was late when he set out from Poitiers, not above ten or twelve miles, or at most fifteen, lay between him and his own château when he took his departure on that third morning from the inn.

Nothing occurred to disturb his journey; everything passed in peace and tranquillity; known, loved, and respected in that part of the country, the people vied with each other as to which should show him the most affectionate civility; and no news either from the capital or Poitiers had reached him to dissipate the apparent calm around. Everything wore the aspect of peace throughout the country. The peasant's wife sunned herself at the door of her cottage, with distaff and spindle in hand, plying lightly her daily toil, while her children ran or crawled about before her, full of enjoyment themselves, and giving enjoyment to her who beheld them. The peasant pursued his labour in the fields, and cheered it by a song; and although the Count knew many of those whom he saw to be Protestants, there was no appearance of anxiety or apprehension amongst them. Everything was cheerful, and contented, and tranquil, and the peace of the scene sank into his heart. Angels may be supposed to look upon this earth's pleasures with a feeling of melancholy though not sadness, from a knowledge of their fragility; and so Albert of Morseiul, though he felt in some degree calmed and tranquillized by what he saw, yet could not prevent a sensation of deep melancholy from mingling with his other feelings, as he thought, " This can but last for a very, very little time."

He was now pursuing the high road from Poitiers to Nantes, and at length turned into the very wood where he had encountered the robbers, which now bore, of course, a different aspect, in the full daylight, from that which it had borne in the depth of the night. The summer sunshine was streaming through the green leaves ; and far away, between the wide bolls of the trees, the mossy ground might be seen carpeted with velvet softness, and chequered with bright catches and streams of light. The road, too, though not in the full day, was crossed here and there by long lines of radiance, and the sky overhead was seen clear and blue, while every project-ing branch of the tall trees above caught the beams, and sparkled with a brighter green.

The aspect of this scene was more tranquillizing still than the last ; but it did not chase the Count's deep melancholy ; and, finding that he was riding very slow, which only afforded time for thought when thought was useless, he turned round to see if his attendants were near, intending to ride on faster, if they were within sight. The road was very nearly straight ; and, at the distance of four or five hundred yards, he saw the body of servants riding gaily on after him, and conversing together. Between him and them, however, just issuing from one of the green wood paths, which joined the high road, was another figure, that immediately called the Count's attention. It was that of an old man, plain and simple in his own appearance, but mounted on a mule, gaily tricked and caparisoned, as was the universal custom in those days, with fringes and knobs of red worsted, and bells of many a size and shape about its collar and head-stall. The rider was not one of those whom men forget easily ; and, though he was at a con-siderable distance as well as the attendants, the Count instantly recognised good Claude de l'Estang.

Seeing the young lord pause, the old man put his mule into a quicker pace, and rode on towards him. When he came near, he wished his friend joy of his return, but his own face was anything but joyful.

"Every one here will indeed be glad to see you, my dear Albert," he said, "for we have very great need of your return, on every account. Besides all these grievous and iniquitous proceed-ings against the Protestants, we have in our own bosom men, who I hear had the impudence even to attack you, but who have since committed various other outrages of a marked and peculiar cha-racter. One man, I learn, has been shot dead upon the spot, another has been wounded severely, a third has been robbed and maltreated. But I cannot discover that any one has met with such treatment, except those who are distinguished for a somewhat inordinate zeal in favour of the Romish church. Not a Protestant has been attacked, which marks the matter more particularly ; and the peasantry themselves are beginning to remark the fact, so that it will not be long before their priests take notice of it, and the eyes of the state will be turned angrily upon us."

"I fear, indeed, that it will be so," replied the Count; "but whether the result will or will not be evil, God in his wisdom only knows."

"How is this, my dear Albert?" exclaimed the clergyman. "You sent to ask that I should draw up a humble petition to the king, representing the Protestants as peaceful, humble, and obedient subjects, and surely we must take every measure that is possible, to ensure that by our own actions we do not give the lie to our own words."

"I will certainly, my dear friend," replied the Count, "take every measure that it is possible for man to take, to put down this evil system of plunder and violence, whether it be carried on by Protestants or Catholics. There is a notorious violation of the law; and I am determined to stop it, without making any distinction whatsoever between the two religions. The petition to the king was necessary when I wrote about it, and is so still, for it was then our only hope, and it may now be taken as a proof that even to the last moment we were willing to show ourselves humble, devoted, and loyal. I expect nothing from it but that result; but that result itself is something."

"I fear, my son," said the old man, "that you have heard bad news since you wrote to me."

"The worst," replied the Count, with a melancholy shake of the head, "the very worst that can be given. They intend, I understand from authority that cannot be doubted, to suppress entirely the free exercise of our religion in France, and to revoke the edict of our good King Henry which secured it to us."

The old man dropped the reins upon his mule's neck, and raised his eyes appealingly to Heaven. "Terrible, indeed!" he said; "but I can scarcely credit it."

"It is but too true—but too certain!" replied the Count; "and yet, terrible as this is—horrible, infamous, detestable as is the cruelty and tyranny of the act itself, the means by which it is to be carried into execution are still more cruel, tyrannical, and detestable."

The old man gazed in his face, as if he had hardly voice to demand what those means were; but, after a brief pause, the Count went on: "To sum up all in one word, they intend to take the Protestant children from the Protestant mother, from the father, from the brother, and, forbidding all intercourse, to place them in the hands of the enemies of our faith, to be educated in the superstitions that we abhor."

"God will avert it!" said the old man; "it cannot be that even the sins and the follies of him who now sits upon the throne of France should deserve the signal punishment of being thus utterly given up and abandoned by the Spirit of God to the tyrannical and brutal foolishness of his own heart. I cannot believe that it will ever be executed. I cannot believe that it will ever be attempted. I doubt not they will go on as they have begun; that they wil send smooth-faced priests with cunning devices, as they have done, indeed, since you went hence, to bribe and buy to the domination of Satan the weak and wavering of our flocks, and to despatch lists of them to the king, to swell his heart with the pride of having made converts. I can easily conceive that they will be permitted to take from us places and dignities, to drive us, by every sort of annoyance, so that the gold may be purified from the dross, the corn may be winnowed from the chaff. All this they will do; for all this undoubtedly we sinners have deserved. But I do not believe that they will be permitted to do more, and my trust is not in man, but in God. For the sins that we have committed, for the weakness we have displayed, for murmurs and rebellion against his will, for sinful doubts and apprehensions of his mercy, from the earthliness of our thoughts, and the want of purity in all our dealings, God may permit us to be smitten severely, terribly; but the fiery sword of his vengeance will not go out against his people beyond a certain point. He has built his church upon a rock, and there shall it stand; nor will I ever believe that the reformed church of France shall be extinguished in the land, nor that the people who have sought God with sincerity shall be left desolate. We will trust in him, my son! We will trust in him!"

"Ay," said the Count; "but, my excellent old friend, it now becomes our duty to think seriously what means, under God's will, we may use in defence of his church. I myself have thought upon it long and eagerly; but I have thought of it in vain, for the subject is so difficult and so embarrassed, that without some one to counsel me, some one to aid me, I can fix upon no plan that offers even a probability of success. I must speak with you before to-morrow be over, long and earnestly. I know not why I should not turn to your dwelling with you even now," he added; "I know not when I may be taken away from the midst of you, for much personal danger threatens myself. But, however, what I have to say must be said alone, and in private. The man Riquet is behind, and though I believe he is faithful to me, and holds but loosely by his popish creed, I must not trust too far. Let us turn towards your dwelling."

"Be it so, be it so," replied the old man; and wending on their way through the forest for some distance farther, they took the first road that turned to the left, and pursued the forest path that ran along through the bottom of the deep valleys, in which some part of the wood was scattered.

It had been a bright and a beautiful day, but the air was warm and sultry; and the horses of the Count looked more fatigued than might have been expected from so short a journey. The old clergyman and his young friend spoke but little more as they went along; and it was only to comment upon the tired condition of the horses, and the oppressive state of the atmosphere, that they did so.

"It is as well, my son," said Claude de l'Estang, at length, "it is as well that you have turned with me, for depend upon it we shall have a storm. Do you not see those large harsh masses of cloud rising above the trees?"

"I have remarked them some time," replied the Count, "and twice I thought I saw a flash."

"Hark!" exclaimed the clergyman, and there was evidently a sound of thunder not very distant. "Let us ride a little quieker," the old man continued; "we are just coming to the slope of the hill where the wood ends, and then we are not far from Auron."

The Count did as the pastor asked him, and the moment after they issued from the wood, upon the shoulder of a gentle eminence, from either side of which, green slopes declined into the valleys. A tall hill rose gradually to their left, along the side of which the highway was cut; and full in their view, to the right,— but two or three miles on, across the low ground, at the foot of the eminence along which they rode—appeared the high conical hill of Auron, crowned, as we have before described it, by the little village spire.

Though there were some detached masses of cloud sweeping over the sky above them, and twisting themselves into harsh, curious forms, the sun was still shining warm and strong upon the spot where they were, while the storm, the voice of which they had heard in the wood, was seen treading the valleys and hills beyond towards Auron, wrapped in a mantle of dark vapours and shadows. The contrast between the bright sunshine and sparkling light around them, and the sweeping-thunder clouds that were pouring forth their mingled wrath upon the beautiful country beyond, was very fine, and the Count drew in his horse for a moment to gaze upon it more at ease.

"You see, though they have been busy in seducing my flock, over there," said the pastor, fixing his eyes with a look of affection upon Auron, "you see they have still left me my spire to the church. I fear, not from any good-will to me or mine," he added, "but because they say it acts as a sort of landmark at sea."

The Count made no reply, for he thought that the time was not far distant when that peaceful village would be the scene of persecution, if not of desolation, and the building where a quiet and industrious population had worshipped God for ages, according to the dictates of their own consciences, would be taken from them. His only answer then was a melancholy smile, as he rode slowly on again, still gazing on the village and the storm, the flashes of the lightning blazing across the path from time to time, as brightly as if the cloud from which they issued had been close above the travellers. Scarcely, however, had the Count and his companion gone a hundred yards along the side of the hill, when a bright fitful line of intense light darted across the curtain of the dark cloud before their eyes, aimed, like a fiery javelin cast by the unerring hand of the destroying angel, at the pointed spire of the village church. The shape of the spire was instantly changed; a part evidently fell in ruins; and, the next moment, the whole of that which remained, blazed forth in flames,—like a fiery beacon raised on the highest hill of an invaded land to tell that strife and bloodshed have begun.

"It is accomplished!" cried the pastor, as he gazed upon the destruction of the spire. "It is accomplished! Oh, Albert, how natural is weakness and superstition to the human heart! Can we see the fall of that building, in which for many a long year our pure faith has offered up its prayers, unmingled with the vanities of a false creed, and not feel as if the will of God were against us—as if that were a sign unto us that his favour had passed from us, at least in this land—as if it were a warning for us to gird ourselves, and, shaking off the dust of our feet, to seek another place of abiding?"

He paused not while he spoke, however, but rode on quickly, in order to aid and direct in saving any part of the building that yet remained; but as they went, he still continued to pour forth many a sorrowful ejaculation, mingling, with personal grief for the destruction of an object which had for long years been familiar with his eye, and associated with every feeling of home, and peace, and of happy dwelling amongst his own people, and of high duties well performed, vague feelings of awe, and perhaps of superstition, as he read in that sight a warning, and a sign, and a shadowing forth of the Almighty will, that the church whereof he was a member was destined to destruction also.

Before the party reached the village, the spire had been completely consumed; but the peasantry had fortunately succeeded in preventing the fire from reaching the body of the building, and the rain was now pouring down in torrents, like the tears of an angel of wrath over the accomplishment of his painful mission; so that all that remained was to ascertain what damage had been done. Both the clergyman and the Count remarked several strangers standing round the church, offering no assistance to any one, and only communing together occasionally, in a low voice, on the proceedings of the Protestant population. Albert of Morseiul gazed upon them with some surprise, and at length said, "I think, gentlemen, you might have given some little aid and assistance in this matter."

"What!" cried one of the men, "aid in upholding a temple of heretics! What, keep from the destruction with which God has marked it, a building which man should long ago have pulled down!"

"I did not know you, gentlemen," replied the Count, in a cold, calm tone. "There are some circumstances in which people may be expected to remember that they are fellow-men and fellow-Christians, before they think of sects or denominations."

Thus saying, he turned and left them, accompanying Claude de l'Estang to his dwelling.

"Never mind them, Albert—never mind them," said the pastor, as they walked along. "These are the men who are engaged daily

in seducing my flock. I have seen them more than once, as I have
been going hither and thither amongst the people; but I have
heeded them not, nor ever spoken to them. Those who can sell
themselves for gold—and gold is the means of persuasion that these
men are now adopting—are not steadfast or faithful in any religion,
and are more likely to corrupt others, and to lead to great defection,
by falling away in a moment of need, than to serve or prop the
cause to which they pretend to be attached. I trust that God's
grace will reach them in time; but in a moment of increasing
danger like this, I would rather that they showed themselves at
once. I would rather, if they are to sell themselves, either for
safety or for lucre, that they should sell themselves at once, and let
us know them before the fiery ordeal comes. I would rather have
to say, they went forth from us, because they were not of us, than
think them children of light, and find them children of darkness."

"I fear," said the Count, in a low voice—"I fear that they are
waging the war against us, my good friend, in a manner which will
deprive us of all unanimity. It is no longer what it was in former
times, when the persecuting sword was all we had to fear and to resist. We have now the artful tongues of oily and deceitful dispu-
tants. We have all the hellish cunning of a sect which allows every
means to be admissible, every falsehood, every misstatement, every
perversion, every deceit, to be just, and right, and righteous, so that
the object to be obtained is the promotion of their own creed. Thus
the great mass of the weak or the ill-informed may be affected by
these teachers; while at the same time gold is held out to allure the
covetous—the deprivation of rank, station, office, and emolument,
is employed to drive the ambitious, the slothful, and the indifferent;
and threats of greater severity of persecution, mental torture, insult,
indignity, and even death itself, are held over the heads of the
coward and the fearful."

They thus conversed as they went along; and the opinion of
each but served to depress the hopes of the other more and more.
Both were well acquainted with the spirit of doubt and disunion
that reigned amongst the Protestants of France, a spirit of disunion
which had been planted, fostered, and encouraged by every art that
a body of cunning and unscrupulous men could employ to weaken
the power of their adversaries. On arriving at the house of Claude
de l'Estang, the pastor put into the hands of his young friend the
petition to the king which he had drawn up, and which, perfectly
meeting his views, was immediately sent off for general signature,
in order to be transmitted to Paris, and presented to the monarch.
Long before it reached him, however, the final and decisive blow
had been struck, and, therefore, we shall notice that paper no more.

A long conversation ensued between the pastor and his young
friend; and it was evident to the Count de Morseiul, that the
opinions of Claude de l'Estang himself, stern and fervent as they
had been in youth, now rendered milder by age, and perhaps by

sorrow, tended directly to general and unquestionng submission, rather than to resistance: not, indeed, to the abandonment of any religious principle, not to the slightest sacrifice of faith—not to the slightest conformity to what he deemed a false religion. No; he proposed himself, and he advised others, to suffer in patience for the creed that he held; to see even the temples of the reformed church destroyed, if such an extreme should be adopted; to see persons of the purer faith excluded from offices and dignity, and rank and emoluments; even to suffer, should it be necessary, plunder, oppression, and imprisonment itself, without yielding one religious doctrine; but, at the same time, without offering any resistance to the royal authority.

"But should they go still farther," said the Count, "should they attempt to interdict altogether the exercise of our religion; should they take the child from the mother, the sister from the care of the brother; should they force upon us Roman rites, and demand from us confessions of papistical belief, what are we to do then, my good old friend?"

"Our religious duties," replied the pastor, "we must not forbear to exercise, even if the sword hung over us that was to slay us at the first word. As for the rest, I trust and believe that it will not come to pass; but if it should, there will be no choice left us but resistance or flight. Ask me not, Albert, to decide now upon which of the two we should choose. It must ever be a dark, a painful, and a terrible decision, when the time comes in which it is necessary to make it; and perhaps the decision itself may be affected far more by the acts of others than by our own. We must determine according to circumstances; but, in the meantime, let us, as far as possible, be prepared for either of the two painful alternatives. We must make great sacrifices, Albert, and I know that you are one of those who would ever be ready to make such for your fellow-Christians. If we are driven to flee from the land of our birth, and to seek a home in other countries; if by the waters of Babylon we must sit down and weep, thinking of the Jerusalem that we shall never behold again, there will be many, very many of our brethren compelled to fly with but little means of support, and perhaps it may be long before, in distant lands, they obtain such employment as will enable them to maintain themselves by the work of their own hands. Those who are richer must minister unto them, Albert. Luckily, I myself can do something in that sort, for long ago, when there was no thought of this persecution, I sold what little land I had, intending to spend the amount in relieving any distress that I might see amongst my people, and to trust to the altar that I served for support in my old age. But little of this sum has been as yet expended, and if I did but know any hands in which I could trust it in a foreign land, either in England or in Holland, I would transmit it thither instantly. You too, Albert, if I heard right, derived considerable wealth in money from some distant relation lately. For your own sake as well as others, it were better to place that in safety in foreign lands, for I find that it would be dangerous now to attempt to sell any landed possessions, and if you were forced to leave this country, you might find yourself suddenly reduced to want in the midst of strangers."

" I have not only thought of this before," replied the Count, " but I have already taken measures for transmitting that sum to Holland. As soon as I heard of the unjust prohibitions regarding the sale of lands by Protestants, I wrote to Holland to a banker, whom I knew there in days of old, an honest man and a sincere friend, though somewhat too fond of gain. The sum I can thus transmit is far more than enough to give me competence for life, and if you please I can transmit thither the little store you speak of also."

" Willingly, willingly," replied the pastor; " it may be a benefit to others, if not to me.—Albert," he added, " I shall never quit this land! I feel it, I know it! My ministry must be accomplished here till the last: and whether I shall be taken from you by some of the ordinary events of nature, or whether God wills it that I should seal with my blood the defence of my faith and my testimony against the church of Rome, I cannot tell; but I am sure—I feel sure, that I shall never quit the land in which I was born."

Albert of Morseiul did not attempt to argue with Claude de l'Estang upon this prejudice, for he knew it was one of those which, like some trees and shrubs, root themselves but the more firmly from being shaken, and from an ineffectual endeavour being made to pluck them out.

For nearly two hours the young Count remained at the house of the clergyman, discussing all the various topics connected with their situation, while his servants were scattered about in different dwellings of the village. At the end of that time, however, Master Jerome Riquet made his appearance at the pastor's house, to inform his lord (from a participation in whose actions he judged he had been too long excluded) that the storm had passed away; and, ordering his horses to be brought up, after a few more words with Claude de l'Estang, the Count mounted, and pursued his way homeward to the château of Morseiul.

Throwing his rein to the groom, the young nobleman walked on through the vestibule, and entered the great hall. It was calm and solitary, with the bright evening sunshine streaming through the tall windows and chequering the stone floor. Nothing was moving but a multitude of bright motes dancing in the sunbeam, and one of the banners of the house of Morseiul, shaken by the wind as the door opened and closed on the Count's entrance. The whole aspect of the place told that it had not been tenanted for some time. Everything was beautifully clean indeed, but the tall-backed chairs ranged straight along the walls, the table standing exactly in the midst, the unsullied whiteness of the stone floor, not even marked with the print of a dog's foot, all spoke plainly that it had been long untenanted. The Count gazed round it in silent melancholy, marked the waving banner and the dancing motes, and, if we may use the term, the solemn cheerfulness of that wide hall; and then said to himself, ere he turned again to leave it—

"Such will it be, and so the sun will shine, when I am gone afar—or in the grave."

CHAPTER XIII.

NEW ACQUAINTANCES.

WE will now lead the reader to another and very different scene from any of those into which we have as yet conducted him. It is a small but cheerful sitting-room, or parlour, in the house of a comfortable citizen of the town of Morseiul. There was everything that could be required for comfort, and a little for show. The corner cupboard, which protruded its round stomach into the room, like that of some fat alderman of the olden time, was ornamented with a variety of little gewgaws, and nic-nacs of silver, displayed in quaint array upon the shelves; and, besides several brass lamps and sconces wonderfully well polished, which were never lighted, were a number of articles of porcelain, of a kind which was then somewhat rare, and is now nearly invaluable. The two windows of this little parlour looked out upon the great square or market-place, towards the southern corner of which it was situated, and commanded a view of a large blacksmith's forge on the opposite side, close by the gate leading down to what was called the Count's Road. There was a door out of this parlour, a black oaken door, with panels richly carved and ornamented, which appeared to lead into a room at the back, and another similar door at the side, opening into the passage which went straight through the house from the square into the garden behind.

The table in the midst of this room, which table, at the moment we speak of—that is, half-past eight o'clock in the morning—was decorated with a large pewter dish, containing a savoury ragout of veal, flanked by two bottles of cider and four drinking-cups. At this well supplied board sat the burly person of good Paul Virlay, the rich blacksmith, who being well to do in the world, and enabled by competence to take his ease, had not yet gone out to superintend the work which his men were carrying on at the forge opposite.

Another effect of his easy situation in life was, that he had time to perform those necessary ablutions too much required by the faces and hands of all blacksmiths, but which, alas! all blacksmiths are but too apt to neglect. It is true that, had he washed his face and hands for ever, or, after the prescribed rule of the Arabian Nights, had scoured them "forty times with alkali, and forty times with the ashes of the same plant," his face and hands would still have retained a certain glowing, coppery brown hue, which they had acquired by the action of sun, and air, and fire, and hard work, and which they likewise possessed, it must be confessed, in some degree from nature.

At the table with Paul Virlay were three other personages. The first was his daughter, a sweet little girl of thirteen or fourteen years of age; and the second, his wife, a goodly dame, perhaps two or three years older than himself, and who, being terribly marked with the small-pox, had never possessed any beauty. Thus, at his marriage, Virlay, who had been in much request amongst the young ladies of Morseiul, declared that he had taken the good working horse instead of the jennet. She had always been extremely careful, laborious, active, and economical; somewhat given to smartness of apparel, indeed, but by no means to extravagance, and though decorating herself with black velvet riband, and large ornaments of gold, yet careful that the riband was not worn out too soon, and the gold ornaments neither bruised nor broken.

On her right hand, between herself and her husband, sat the fourth person of the party, who was no other than the lady's brother, a stout, broad-made, determined-looking man, who had served long in the army, under the Count; and had risen as high, by his daring courage and somewhat rash gallantry, as any person not of noble blood could rise, except under very extraordinary circumstances. He had accumulated, it was said, a considerable sum of money—perhaps not by the most justifiable of all dealings with the inhabitants of conquered districts—so that Armand Herval was an object of not a little attention, and what we may call cupidity, to the unmarried ladies of Morseiul.

That place was not, indeed, his regular dwelling, for his abode was at a small town nearer to the sea-coast, some five or six miles off; but he frequently came to visit his sister and brother-in-law, over both of whom he exercised very considerable influence, although, as frequently is the case, the latter was naturally a man of much stronger natural sense than himself. It is in almost all instances, indeed, energy that gives power; and, with persons not well educated, or not very highly endowed by nature, that energy loses none of its effect from approaching somewhat towards rashness. Such, then, was the case with Paul Virlay and his brother-in-law. When unmoved by any strong passions, however, Armand Herval was quite the man to lead and to seduce. He was gay, blithe cheerful, full of frolic, fearless of consequences, specious in reasoning, possessing much jest and repartee, overflowing with tales, or anecdotes, of what he had seen, or heard, or done in the wars; and it was only when crossed, or opposed, or excited by wine or anger, that the darker and more fiery spirit of the somewhat ruthless trooper would break forth and overawe those that surrounded him.

On the present morning there was a strange mixture in his demeanour, of a sad and serious thoughtfulness with gaiety and even merriment. He laughed and jested with his niece, he took a pleasure in teasing his sister, but he spoke, once or twice, in a low and bitter tone, to Paul Virlay, upon various matters which were taking place in the neighbourhood, and did not even altogether spare the Count de Morseiul himself. At that, however, Virlay bristled up; and his brother-in-law, who had done it more from a spirit of teasing than ought else, only laughed at his anger, and turned the discourse to something else. He ate and drank abundantly of the breakfast set before him; laughed at the cleanness of Virlay's face and hands, and the smartness of his brown jerkin, and insisted that his little niece should run to the window to see whether the men were working properly, saying that her father was no longer fit for his trade.

The girl did as she was bid, and replied immediately, "I do not see the men at all; but I see the young Count, just turning the corner."

"That is early!" cried Virlay, laying down his fork. "Is he on horseback?"

"No, he is on foot," replied the girl, "and nobody with him. —He is coming over here! I declare he is coming over here!" cried the girl, clapping her hands.

"Nonsense!" cried Virlay, starting up, as well as his wife and brother-in-law.

"Not nonsense at all, Paul!" cried Herval. "He is making straight for the house, so I shall be off as fast as I can, by the back door. I am not fond of making low bows, and standing with my hat in my hand, when I can help it."

"Stay, stay!" cried Virlay; "do not go yet, Armand; I have much to talk with you about."

But his brother-in-law shook his head, and darted through the oak door we have mentioned, into the room beyond. Madame Virlay bestirred herself to give order and dignity to the breakfast table; but before she could accomplish that purpose, the Count was in the open passage, and knocking at the door of the room for admission.

Virlay opened it immediately, and the young nobleman entered, with that frank and graceful bearing which was part, indeed, of his inheritance, but which secured to him the hereditary love for his race, which the virtues and kindness of his forefathers had established amongst the people.

"Good morrow, Virlay," he said. "Good morrow, Madame

Virlay! Oh, my pretty Margette, why you have grown so great a
girl that I must call you so no longer, lest the people say that I
am making love to you.—Virlay," he added, in a graver tone, "I
would fain speak a word or two with you on business. I would not
send for you to the château, for various reasons; but cannot we go
into the next room for a moment or two?"

Virlay made a sign to his wife and daughter to retire, and placed
a seat for the Count. "No, my lord," he said, "you shall not give
yourself that trouble. Shut the door, wife, and remember, no
eaves-dropping!"

"Bless thee, Paul!" exclaimed his wife, bridling with a little
indignation; "do you think I would listen to what my lord the
Count says to you? I know better, I trust;" and she shut the door.

Perhaps neither the Count, however, nor Virlay was quite certain of the lady's discretion under such circumstances, and they,
therefore, both remained near the window, and conversed in low
tones.

"I come to speak to you, Virlay," said the Count, in somewhat
of a grave tone, "both as an influential man and as a sensible man
—though he may have his little faults," he added, fixing his eyes
somewhat meaningly upon the blacksmith's face, "and who may
suffer himself to be a little too much led by others; but who, nevertheless, has the best intentions, I know, and who will always,
sooner or later, remember that one must not do wrong that right
may come of it."

The blacksmith replied nothing, but kept his eyes fixed upon
the ground, though the red became somewhat deeper in his brown
cheek, and an expression of consciousness was to be seen in every
feature of his countenance.

"What I want to speak with you about is this," continued the
Count: "since I have been away, during this last campaign, there
has sprung up, it seems, a dangerous band in this part of the province; consisting of men who are carrying on a system of violence,
depredation, and intimidation, which must be put a stop to; and
I want to consult you in regard to the best means of putting down
this band, for put down I am determined it shall be, and that right
speedily."

"You will not be able to put them down, my lord!" replied the
blacksmith. "If mere simple plunder were the object of these
persons, the thing would be easily done. You would have the
whole people to aid you, and nothing would be more easy. But,
my lord, such is not the case. The men may plunder—I do not
say that it is not so—but they only plunder their enemies. It has
always been so in this part of the country, as the good Count, your
father, well knew; and it always will be so to the end of the world.
People have given these bands different names, at different times,
and from different circumstances. Once they were called *les
Faucons*, because, at that time, the minister was sending down men

into the country, taxing the salt and the fish, and when any of
them came, one of these bands stooped upon him, like a falcon,
carried him off, and he was never heard of more.   At another time
they were called *les Eperviers,* because they hovered over all the
country and caught what they could.   That was the time when the
king brought so many soldiers into the province, that our people
could not carry off the collectors without hovering round them for
a long time.   Now they call them *les Chauve-souris,* because they
fly about just at the setting in of night, and woe be to the persecuting papist that falls in their way.   To-morrow, if obliged to do
the work later at night, they may be called *les Hiboux ;* and the
time may come, perhaps, when they will be called *les Loups* or *les
Chouettes,* the wolves or the screech-owls : but they will do no harm
to any one but their enemies.   An honest man, who seeks to harm
nobody, may go from one end of the province to another,—ay, and
through all Brittany, too, as well as Poitou, without meeting with
the least annoyance.   But if it be different, if he be an oppressor
of the people, a seller of men's souls, let him see that he travels by
daylight only, and even then he wont be very safe."

"I do not know," said the Count, "that I am either an oppressor
of the people or a buyer and seller of men's souls; and yet, my good
friend Virlay, these Chauve-souris, as you call them, fastened their
claws upon me, and put me to no slight inconvenience and discomfort.   They might have shot me, too, for they fired at my horse.
You may have heard of all this before, I dare say," he added, with
a smile.

The blacksmith did not reply for a moment; but then he said,
"I dare say, my lord, it was some mistake.   I doubt not that they
did not know you; or that some foolish fellow, as will happen sometimes, went beyond his orders."

"But then, again," said the Count, "they both attacked and
plundered two ladies, defenceless women, who could have given
them no offence."

"Some hangers-on of a governor that was sent down to oppress
the province," replied the blacksmith.   "These bands, my lord,
know all that is passing throughout the country better than you do
yourself."

"But in this instance," said the Count, "they certainly knew
not what they were about, for instead of a governor sent down to
oppress the province, Monsieur de Rouvré is the very man to stand
between the province and oppression ; and, from all I hear, is likely
to give up his post and the court, and retire to Ruffigny, if the
measures of the council are what he judges unfair towards us."

"If he do that," said the blacksmith, "he will have a better
body-guard at Ruffigny than ever he had at Poitiers.   But what is
it you want me to do, Monsieur le Comte ?   I have no power to
put down these bands.   I have no sway with them or against them."

"What I want you to do," replied the Count, "is to use your

whole power and influence in every way, to put a stop to a system which cannot be suffered to go on. Sorry should I be to draw the sword against these mistaken people, but I must have them no more on the lands and lordships of Morseiul, where they have quartered themselves, I find, during my absence. I must have my forests free of such deer, and you know, Virlay, when I say anything I will keep my word. I have been in their hands, and they were civil to me, respected my person, did something towards obeying my directions; and, although I know two of them, however well concealed they might be," he added, laying strong emphasis on the words, "I will in no degree betray the knowledge I acquired. I only wish to make it fully understood, that I wish this band to be dispersed. I am well aware of the evil custom that you allude to, and how deeply it has rooted itself in the habits of the people; but I tell you, Virlay, that this is likely to produce more evil to the cause of the reformed church than anything that could be devised. At all events, it is contrary altogether to the laws of the land, and to civil order; and whatever be the pretext, I will not tolerate it on my lands. I wish the bands to be dispersed, the night meetings to be abandoned, the men to pursue their lawful employments, and in other hours to take their necessary rest. But, at all events, as I have said before, within my jurisdiction they shall not remain. If they go to the lands of other lords, I cannot, of course, help it; but I trust that those other lords will have spirit and decision enough to drive them off their territories. Let us say no more about it, Virlay. You understand me distinctly, and know my whole meaning; and now, tell me when, and how, I may best obtain a meeting with a person called Brown Keroual, for I must make him hear reason also."

The blacksmith paused for two or three minutes before he answered. "Why, my lord," he said, at length, "I ought not to tell you anything about him, perhaps, by that name. On all accounts, perhaps I ought not; but yet I know I can trust you; and I am sure you will take no advantage. So I'll only ask you one thing, not to go down to the place where he is, with too many people about you, for fear of bad consequences, if there should be any of his folks near."

"I shall go down," said the Count, "towards the place where you may tell me he is generally to be met with, with only two servants; and when I come near enough, I shall give the horse to the servants, and walk forward on foot."

"You will be as safe as in your own château, then," said the blacksmith; "but you must not go for a couple of days, as where he will be to-morrow, and next day, I cannot tell. But if, on the day after, you will be, just at the hour when the bat begins to flit, at a little turn of the river about six miles down—you know the high rock just between the river and the forest, with the tall tree upon it, which they call the *chêne vert?*——"

M

" I know it well. I know it well," said the Count. " But on which side of the rock do you mean? The tall face flanks the river, the back slopes away towards the wood."

" At the back, at the back," replied the blacksmith. " Amongst the old hawthorns that lie scattered down the slope—you will find him there at the hour I mention."

" I will go," said the Count, in reply, " and I will allow the intervening time for the band to quit the woods of Morseiul. But if it have not done so by the morning after, there will be a difference between us, which I should be sorry for."

Thus saying, the Count left the worthy townsman, and took his way back to the château.

In the two days that intervened, nothing occurred to vary the course of his existence. He entertained some expectation of receiving letters from Poitiers, but none arrived. He heard nothing from the governor, from the Chevalier d'Evran, or from Clémence de Marly; and from Paris, also, the ordinary courier brought no tidings for the young Count. A lull had come over the tempestuous season of his days, and we shall now follow him on his expedition to the *chêne vert*—under which, be it said, we have ourselves sat many an hour thinking over, and commenting upon, the deeds we now record.

The Count, as he had promised, took but two servants with him, and rode slowly on through the evening air, with his mind somewhat relieved by the absence of any new excitement, and by the calm, refreshing commune of his spirit with itself. On the preceding day, there had been another thunder-storm; but the two which had occurred had served to clear and somewhat cool the atmosphere, though the breath of the air was still full of summer.

When at the distance of about a mile from the spot which the blacksmith had indicated, the Count gave his horse to the servants, and bade them wait there for his return. He wandered on slowly, slackening his pace, as much to enjoy the beauty and brightness of the scene around, as to let the appointed time arrive for his meeting with the leader of the band we have mentioned. When he had gone on about a hundred yards, however, he heard, in the distance, the wild but characteristic notes of a little instrument, at that time, and even in the present day, delighted in throughout Poitou, and known there by the pleasant and harmonious name of the musette. Sooth to say, it differs but little, though it does in a degree, from the ordinary bagpipe; and yet there is not a peasant in Poitou, and scarcely a noble of the province either, who will not tell you that it is the sweetest and most harmonious instrument in the world. It requires, however, to be heard in a peculiar manner, and at peculiar seasons: either, as very often happens in the small towns of that district, in the dead of the night, when it breaks upon the ear, as the player walks along the street beneath your window, with a solemn and plaintive melody, that seems scarcely of the earth; or else in the

morning and evening tide, heard at some little distance amongst
the hills and valleys of that sunny land, when it sounds like the
spirit of the winds, singing a wild ditty to the loveliness of the
scene.

The Count de Morseiul had quite sufficient national, or perhaps
we should say provincial, feeling to love the sound of the musette;
and he paused to listen, as, with a peculiar beauty and delicacy of
touch, the player poured forth the sounds in the very direction in which
he was proceeding. He did not hasten his pace, however, enjoying
it as he went; and still the nearer and nearer he came to the *chêne
vert*, the closer he seemed to approach to the spot whence the notes
issued. It is true the player could not see him, as he came in an
oblique line from the side of the water, to which, at various places,
the wood approached very near. But the moment that the Count
turned the angle of the rock which we have mentioned, and on the
top of which stood the large evergreen oak, from which it took its
name, he beheld a group that might well have furnished the picture
of a Phyllis and a Corydon to any pastoral poet that ever penned
an idyl or an eclogue.

Seated on a little grassy knoll, under one of the green hawthorns,
was a girl apparently above the common class, with a veil, which
she seemed to have lately worn over her head, cast down beside her,
and with her dark hair falling partly upon her face, as it bent over
that of a man, seated, or rather stretched, at her feet, who, supporting himself on one elbow, was producing from the favourite instrument of the country the sounds which the Count had heard.

Lying before them, and turning its sagacious eyes from the face
of the one to the face of the other, was a large rough dog, and the girl's
hand, which was fair and small, was engaged in gently caressing
the animal's head, as the Count came up. So occupied were they
with each other, and so full were the tones of the music, that it was
the dog who first perceived the approach of a stranger, and bounded,
barking, forward towards the Count, as if the young nobleman were
undoubtedly an intruder. The girl and her lover—for who could
doubt that he was such?—both rose at the same time, and she, casting her veil over her head, darted away with all speed towards the
wood, while her companion called after her, " Not far, not far !"

The Count then perceived, somewhat to his surprise, that the
veil was one of those which were usually worn by novices in a convent. Notwithstanding the barking of the dog, and the somewhat
fierce and uncertain aspect of his master, the Count advanced with
the same slow, steady pace, and in a minute or two after, was standing within five steps of Armand Herval. That good personage had
remained fixed to his place, and for some time had not recognised
the young Count; but the moment he did so, a change came over
his countenance, and he saluted him with an air of military respect.

" Good day, Armand," said the Count; " I am afraid I have
disturbed your young friend; but pray go after her, and tell her

that I am neither spy nor enemy, so she need not be alarmed. Come back and speak to me, however, for I want a few minutes' conversation with you.—Have you seen your brother-in-law Virlay, lately?"

" Not for several days," replied Armand; " but I will go after her, my lord, and see her safe, and come back to you in a minute."

" Do so," replied the Count, " and I will wait for you here. Will you not stay with me, good dog?" he added, patting the dog's head, and casting himself down upon the ground; but the dog followed his master, and the Count remained alone, thinking over the little picture which had been so unexpectedly presented to his eyes.

" This lets me into much of the history," he thought. " Here is a motive and an object, both for accumulating wealth and intimidating the papists!   But how can he contrive to get the girl out of a convent to sit with him here, listening to him playing the musette, while it is yet the open day?   It is true, we are at a great distance from any town or village.   The only religious house near, either, is that upon the hill two miles farther down.—Though I cannot prevent this business, I must give him some caution;" and then he turned his mind to consider the whole affair again, endeavouring in vain to account for an event which was less likely, perhaps, to take place in that province, in the midst of a Protestant population, than in any other part of France.

Some time passed ere Armand Herval returned, and by this time the twilight was growing thick and grey.

" It is later than I thought, Herval," said the young Count, rising from the ground, on which he had been stretched, as the other came up; " I should hardly have time to say all I had to say, even if the person were here whom I came to converse with."

" Then you did not come to see me, my lord?" demanded Herval, in a tone perhaps expressive of a little mortification.

" No, Herval," replied the Count, with a slight smile; "I came to see a person called Brown Keroual: but," he added, after a moment's pause, " if you are likely to stay here, I will leave the message with you."

The Count stopped, as if for a reply, and his companion answered, " Speak, speak, my lord Count! your message will not fail to reach him."

" Well then, Armand," replied the nobleman, " tell Keroual this for me: first, that I know him—that I recognised him the moment he spoke when last we met; but that, having some regard for him, I do not intend to take any advantage whatever of that knowledge to his prejudice, although he be engaged in wrong and unlawful deeds. However, I came here to meet him, in order to reason with him on his conduct, for he is a good and a gallant soldier, and would now have been an officer—for I recommended him for advancement—had it not been for that plundering of the priory of

St. Amand, which was thrown in my teeth by Monsieur de Louvois, whenever I mentioned his name."

" If Louvois had been in it," replied his companion, " it would not have escaped half as well as it did; for I think, according to the very doctrines of their popish church, the good act of burning one Louvois would be quite enough to obtain pardon for the sin of burning a whole score of monks along with him. But what were you going to say farther, sir?"

" Why, to Brown Keroual," continued the Count, " I was going to say, that he is engaged in a matter contrary to all law and order, heading a band of robbers which must be——"

" I beg your pardon, sir," interrupted Herval, somewhat impatiently, " not robbers! If you please, a band of *chauve-souris*. They rob no man: they only plunder the enemy; and let me tell you, my lord Count, that there is many a man more or less joined with that band, who would just as soon think of robbing another as you would.—Has anything been asked for the ring, though it was the ring of a papist? Was not the money that was taken from you restored?"

" It was," replied the Count; " but we must not be too nice about our terms, Herval. I do not know any law, human or divine, that allows a man to pick and choose at his own will and pleasure whom he will rob, and whom he will murder."

" Ay, my noble lord," answered the man, getting warm; " but there is a law of nature, which, after all, is a law of God, and which not only justifies but requires us to destroy him who would destroy us; and, whether it be straightforwardly that he is seeking our destruction, or by cunning and crooked paths, it matters not, we have a right to prevent him by every means in our power, and if we catch hold of him, to knock him on the head like a viper or any other noxious vermin."

" In all cases but direct attack," answered the Count, " civil society gives our defence into the hands of the law."

" But when the law and its ministers are leagued with the destroyers, with the real plunderers, with the real disturbers of the public peace," exclaimed the man vehemently, " we must make a new law for ourselves, and be its officers also."

The Count did not interrupt him, as he was very well pleased to be made acquainted clearly with all the views and opinions of that body of men whom Armand Herval might be supposed to represent; and the soldier went on with great volubility, and some eloquence, to defend the right of resistance with all the well-known arguments upon the subject, which have been repeated and combated a thousand times; but he came not a bit nearer than any who had gone before him to the real question at issue, namely, where the duty of submission ceased and the right of resistance began. We must remember that not only the higher orders, but also the lower classes of French Protestants, were at that time much more

generally enlightened and accustomed to the use of their own
reason than the Catholics, and the natural consequence of any
attempt to oppress them, was to render such arguments as those
used by Herval very common amongst them.   Neither was the
Count de Morseiul prepared to oppose the general scope of the man's
reasoning, though he was determined to resist the practical mis-
application of it, which was then actively going on in the province.

" I will not argue with you, Herval," he said, " nor will I
attempt to persuade you that what the council is doing now, and
may do against us poor Protestants, is right, feeling it, as I do, to
be wrong.   But, nevertheless, I think—nay, I am sure—that such
proceedings, as those of the band we speak of, are perfectly incom-
patible with our duty to the king and our fellow-subjects, and
likely to produce infinitely greater evil to the reformed religion
than good.   The existence of such bands will give an excuse for
sending a large military force into the province, for persecuting
the Protestants still farther, and for taking such precautions that
even, if a crisis were to come, in which the resistance to oppression which you speak of would be necessary, that resistance would
be rendered hopeless by the prepared state of the enemy.   In the
meantime it is wrong, because, at the best, it is carrying on what
you call hostilities without a declaration of war; it is dangerous to
the peaceful even of our own friends, as has been shown in my
case, and in that of two ladies of the governor's family, who is most
warmly interested in our behalf; and it is degrading a powerful
and just cause in the eyes of all men, by giving its supporters the
air of night plunderers."

" As for a declaration of war," replied Herval, " they have made
that themselves by their own acts, and as to the rest of what you
say, sir, there are objections, certainly.   Did I but see our noblemen like yourself, and our ministers preparing a good resistance to
tyranny and injustice, I would be as quiet as a lamb.   But I see
nothing of the kind; you are all sitting still in your houses, and
waiting till they come to cut your throats.   So, as there must and
shall be resistance of some kind, and it must begin by the lower
instead of the higher, we must even take the lesser of two evils,
and go on as we have done."

Armand Herval spoke, as was common with him when at all
heated, with very little reverence or respect in his tone; but
Albert of Morseiul was not of a character to suffer himself to be
irritated in the slightest degree by any want of formal respect.
No man knew better how to preserve his own dignity without
making any exaction, and he accordingly replied, with perfect
calmness—

" I should be sorry, Armand, that our good friend Brown
Keroual should persist in conduct which may make a division
amongst different classes of the Protestants, at the very moment
that we require union for our common safety.   You will, therefore,

let him know at once, that I am determined, upon my own lands, to put an end to this system; that my forest and my moors shall no longer hold these *chauve-souris*. The day after to-morrow I shall begin my operations, and as I know the country as well as any man in it, shall have no difficulty in putting my plans in execution. Keroual knows me for a man of my word, and I must not have one single man disguised and in arms anywhere within my jurisdiction at the end of three days from this time."

The man smiled, with a grim but less dissatisfied look than the Count had expected. " They none of them wish to give you offence, sir," he replied, " and can easily move off your lands to others."

" That they *must* do," replied the Count; " but there is something more still to be said. When once off my lands, they may doubtless consider that the matter is at an end; but such is not the case."

" My lord, if you follow us off your lands," said Armand, dropping farther disguise, and making use of the pronoun of the first person—" if you follow us off your own lands, you must take the consequences."

" I am always prepared to do so," replied the Count. " My purpose is not, of course, to follow any of you off my own lands, unless I am summoned to do so; but if I am summoned, which will immediately be the case if there be any renewal of outrages whatsover, I shall most assuredly use my whole power, and employ my whole means, to put down that which I know to be wrong."

The man to whom he spoke gazed sternly upon the ground for a moment or two, and seemed to be struggling with various contending feelings. " Come, my lord Count," he said, at length, " I will tell you what. Every one who has served under you knows that you are as brave a man, as kind an officer, and as skilful a commander, as any that ever lived, and we are all willing to do what we can to please you in your own way. If you would put yourself at our head, there is not a man amongst us that would not follow you to death itself.—No, but hear me out, my lord; don't answer till you have heard.—We get quicker information than even you can get, for with us it flies from mouth to mouth like lightning. We have no long written letters, but, as soon as a thing is known, one man tells it to another, and so it comes down here. Now, we know, what most likely you don't know, that everything is settled in Paris for putting down the reformed religion altogether. We are aware, too, of that which I see you have not heard, that the Duc de Rouvré has received orders to resign the government of the province, and retire to Ruffigny, without presenting himself at the court. Now, depend upon it, my lord, before a fortnight be over, you will have to rouse yourself against this oppression, to make the voice of remonstrance heard in firmer tones, and with arms in your hand. You know it as well as I do; and I know you are no more afraid of doing it than I am; but only, like all the rest of the people about the court, you have gone mad concerning a thing called loyalty, and have got your head filled with ideas of respect and veneration for the king—simply because he is the king, and wears a crown—when, if the truth were known, he is not so much worthy of respect and veneration as any of our peasants who drive a team of oxen, with a whip of sheep leather, from one end of the field to the other. A selfish, voluptuous, adulterous tyrant——"

" Hush, hush!" exclaimed the Count, " I can neither stay nor hear, if you proceed in such terms as those."

" Well, well," said the man, " though what I say is true, and you know it, my lord Count, I wont go on, if it offends you. But what I was going to say besides, is this. You have got your head filled with these ideas; you wish to do everything respectfully and loyally; you wish to show the most profound respect for the law, and be compelled to resist before you do resist. But are our enemies doing the same towards us? Are they showing any respect for the law, or for justice, or good faith, honour, honesty, or treaties? No, no, they are taking step by step, and ruining us piecemeal! My lord, you are like a man in a fortress, with a truce between him and a perfidious enemy, who takes advantage of his good-nature to get possession of one outpost after another, then marches over the glacis, lodges himself on the counterscarp, erects his batteries, points his cannon, and says, ' Now, surrender, or I'll blow you to pieces!' This is what you are suffering to be done, my lord; and, at one word, if you, Count, will come and put yourself at our head, to resist oppression, you shall have two hundred men, at one whistle; and ere five days be over, you shall have two thousand; before ten days, ten thousand. Will you do it?"

" Undoubtedly not," replied the Count. " Were the time to come when, all other means having failed, I should be forced to draw the sword in my own defence, and the defence of my fellow-Protestants, I would openly plant my banner on the hill of Morseiul, stand upon the straightforward righteousness of my cause, point to the unvarying loyalty of my life, and demand simple justice for myself and my brethren."

" And you would find all confusion and consternation in your own party," replied the man; " not a skeleton even of a regiment ready to support you, the timid abandoning you, and the brave unprepared. You would find, on the other side, the enemy upon you before you knew where you were; instead of justice, you would get persecution, and, before a fortnight was over, your head would be rolling about the Place de Grève. Well, well, be it so!—I will help you yet, my lord, whether you like it or not, and when the day of danger comes, you may find Brown Keroual and his band nearer to your hand than you imagine. In the meantime we will keep as quiet as may be. But if you hear of a few Jesuits and Lazarites being hung, you must not be surprised, that's all.—Have you anything farther to say to me, my lord? for it is now quite dark; and, like a sober, peaceable man," he added, with a laugh, " I must be going home to supper. One or two of my companions may come to fetch me, too."

" I have nothing farther to say, Armand," replied the Count, " except, perhaps, it were a word of caution about that young person I saw with you just now; and who, I must say, I was sorry to see with you."

" Why, my lord, why?" demanded the man, quickly; " you don't suppose I would do her hurt. I would not injure her, so help me God! for the whole world. If you had not come up, I should have taken her back in five minutes."

"I do not suppose you would wrong her, Herval," said the Count; " by no means do I suppose such a thing; but she was out here, with you, with a novice's veil on! She is evidently some Roman-catholic girl in a convent, and I would have you cautious on that account."

" Oh, my lord," replied the man, " the time for caution is all over now. We are soon coming to a setting to rights of all those things. Quiet cannot be kept above a fortnight longer, and then the doors of more than one convent will be as wide open as the sea. One of three things must then happen. We shall either have established our rights, and my little novice will be out of her fetters; or we shall be defeated, and I killed, and that matter over; or I shall be defeated, yet living, and flying away with her, pretty soul, to some country where we may be united in peace."

" Yes, yes," replied the Count; " but you do not reflect what you may bring upon her head in the meantime. She may be removed from that convent to another, where you can never reach her. If these wanderings with you are detected, she may be subjected, too, to punishments and penances such as you have no idea of."

The man laughed aloud. " No fear, my lord, no fear," he said; " the good mothers dare no more send her away than they dare lose their right hand. They would fancy the convent in flames the very first night she slept out of it. Why, she is their guardian angel, at least, so they think; and she is specially appointed to bring their tribute, consisting of a silver crown and a flask of wine, twice in the week, to Brown Keroual, in virtue of which they obtain his protection against all bands and companies whatsoever. The only stipulation they made, when the tribute was demanded, was, that he was on no account to tell the director; and when the director, who is a greater old woman than any one amongst them, heard it in confession, he added a fifteen sous piece once a week for himself, with no other stipulation than that Brown Keroual was not to tell the bishop; so that twice in the week the dear child brings me the tribute—ay, and the real tribute for which I sought—her own sweet company. Nobody dares watch her, nobody dares follow her; and as she is always absent the same time, and always back again before the bat's wing is to be seen flitting in the air, they ask no questions, but judging the distance long, exempt her from vespers, that she may accomplish it more easily. And now, my lord Count," he continued, "I must leave you; for my people will be waiting for me. I think where we now stand is off your lordship's ground, for I could not well give up this meeting place. But farther than this, I shall not come, till the time when you shall be very willing to thank Brown Keroual for his help."

The Count made no reply to his words, but wishing him good night, left him, and rejoined his servants. He then rode quickly homeward, but was somewhat surprised, as he climbed the steep towards the castle, to see a full blaze of light pouring through the windows of the lesser hall. On entering the gates, however, he saw several horses and servants in the liveries of the Chevalier d'Evran, and found his friend seated at supper in the hall above.

"You see, Albert," said the Chevalier, rising, and grasping his hand, as he came in—"you see what liberties I take, and what account I make of your friendship. Here I come, and order all sorts of viands without ceremony, simply because I have ridden hard, and am desperately an hungered."

His countenance was frank and open, though not perhaps so cheerful in its expression as usual; his manner was free and un-embarrassed, and seemed not as if anything that had occurred at Poitiers would have the slightest tendency to diminish the friend-ship and intimacy which existed between him and the Count. Albert of Morseiul, however, could not feel exactly the same. He could not divest his mind of a vague feeling of jealous disquietude in regard to the confident intimacy which seemed to exist between the Chevalier d'Evran and Clémence de Marly. However hope-less might be his own love towards her—however much he might have taught himself that despair was in his case wisdom—how-ever strong might be his resolutions to resist every temptation to seek her society any more, there was something painful to him that he could not overcome, in the idea of the Chevalier being constantly at her side; and although his regard and affection for his friend were not diminished, yet there was an unpleasant feeling at his heart when he saw him, which perhaps might make some differ-ence in his manner.

"Many thanks for doing so, Louis," he answered, struggling hard against such sensations, "many thanks for doing so. What news bring you from Poitiers?"

The Chevalier did not appear to feel any change in the manner of his friend, and replied, "But little news, Albert, and that not good. I was but one day in Poitiers before I set off in haste. I found everything in confusion and derangement. The states split into factions; the governor, the intendant, and the bishop, at open war with each other; cabals of the basest and blackest character going on in every quarter of the town; good Madame de Rouvré wishing her husband anything but a governor; and Clémence de Marly looking pale, ill, and sorrowful. I stayed but a sufficient time," he continued, not giving the Count an opportunity to make any observations, "I stayed but a sufficient time to make myself thoroughly acquainted with all that was proceeding, and then set off at once for the purpose of proceeding to Paris. As I had promised to return to your hall, I came to spend two or three hours with you, Albert, at the most, for I must hurry on without delay. The king, you know, is my godfather, and I trust that my representation of what is taking place at Poitiers may do some good. If it do not, de Rouvré is ruined, and a most pitiful intrigue triumphant."

"I trust in Heaven that you may be successful," replied the Count; "but proceed with your supper, d'Evran."

"I will, I will," replied the Chevalier, "but will you let me give you one more proof of how much at home I can make myself in your house, by giving an order to your servants?"

"Most assuredly," replied the Count; "you have nothing to do but to speak."

"It is this, then," said the Chevalier: "you will be good enough, Master Jerome Riquet, to make all these worthy gentlemen who are assisting you to serve my supper, march out of the room in single file. Now, come, Master Riquet, do it in an officer-like way. You have seen service, I know."

Riquet seemed well pleased at the honourable task conferred upon him, and, according to the Chevalier's direction, made the servants troop out of the room one by one, he himself preparing to remain as a confidential person to serve the Count and his friend during the conversation which he doubted not was to ensue. The Chevalier, however, as soon as he saw himself obeyed so far, again raised his voice, saying—

"Now, Master Riquet, you have executed the manœuvre so well, that it is a pity your men should be without their officer. You will be good enough to follow them."

Riquet made a sort of semi-pirouette on the tips of his toes, and disappointed, though perhaps not surprised, marched out of the room, and shut the door.

"Albert," said the Chevalier, as soon as he was gone, "I am afraid, very much afraid, that all is lost for the cause of you Huguenots. There are people about the king, who must be mad to counsel him as they do. All the news I have, which perhaps you know already, is as sad as it can be. There wants but one more step to be taken for the utter abolition of what you call the reformed religion in France—I mean the abolition of the privileges granted by the edict of Nantes—and perhaps that step will be taken before I can reach Paris."

"So quickly!" exclaimed the Count.

" Even so !" rejoined his friend. " All the mad-like steps which have been taken by the council have been applauded by one general roar of the whole clergy of France. Petition after petition has come in from every Catholic body through the land, beseeching the king to do you every sort of injustice; and I feel convinced that they are persuading him, while he is risking a civil war, ruining his provinces, and exasperating some of his most faithful subjects, that he is acting justly, politically, and religiously, and is, in short, a saint upon earth, notwithstanding all his mistresses. I pretend to no power over the king or influence with him, except inasmuch as I can often say to him, in my wild, rambling way, things that nobody else could say, and dare to tell him, under the same cloak, many an unpleasant fact that others will not tell him. However, my object now is to open his eyes about de Rouvré, to whom I am too deeply bound by ties of gratitude to see him injured and calumniated, if I can help it. I would fain ask you, Albert, what you intend to do, how you intend to act, when these rash measures are pushed to the extreme against you; but yet it is unfair to give you the pain of refusing me, and perhaps unwise to seek a share in secrets which I ought not to know, or, knowing, to reveal."

" As far as anything has yet passed," replied the Count, " there is nothing either to conceal or to reveal, Louis. It will be difficult for the king to tire out my loyalty. I am determined to bear to the very utmost. What I shall do, when the very utmost bound of endurance is passed, I do not know, having as yet settled nothing in my own mind."

" I cannot think," continued the Chevalier, " that the king will individually treat you ill, who have served him so well; but with regard to your religion, depend upon it the utmost extremes are determined upon already."

" I grieve to hear it," replied the Count; " but it is not more than I expected. The rapidity of these measures gives no time for calm and loyal remonstrance or petition to make the king aware of the real truth."

" Such is indeed the case," said the Chevalier. " Couriers are arriving at Poitiers, and taking their departure again, five or six times in the day, killing the horses on the road, setting off fat men themselves and returning thin.—I know this is no joking matter, Albert, and I am anxious to do what little good I can. I am there-fore going to follow the example of these couriers; and as soon as I have seen the king, and obtained some satisfaction on these matters, I shall return hither with all speed to watch the progress of events, and, if possible, to shield and protect my friends. In this quarter of the world," he added, holding out his hand to the Count, with a frank smile, " in this quarter of the world are all those for whom I entertain any very sincere affection; de Rouvré, who has befriended me from my youth, and never lost an opportunity of serving me; you, Albert, who have been my companion for many years in perils and dangers, to whom I owe the immense benefit of a good example, and the no less inestimable blessing of a noble mind to communicate with under all circumstances."

"And Clémence de Marly," said the Count, with a melancholy smile, "of course, you will add Clémence de Marly, Chevalier?"

"Assuredly," replied the Chevalier, "assuredly, Albert, I will add Clémence de Marly. I will not ask you, Albert, why you look at me reproachfully. Clémence, I believe from my heart, loves you, and I scruple not to tell you so. If it were not for the obstacle of your religion, you might both be happy. That is a terrible obstacle, it is true; but were it not for that—I say—you might both be happy; and your example and her love for you might do away the only faults she has, and make her to you a perfect angel, though there is not one other man in France, perhaps, whom she could endure or render happy. She also, and her fate, are amongst the objects of my journey to Paris; but of that I shall tell you nothing till I can tell you all."

"I know you are a man of mysteries," said the Count, with a faint smile, "and therefore, I suppose, I must neither attempt to investigate this, nor to inquire how it is, that the gay and gallant Chevalier d'Evran is in one way insensible to charms which he is so sensible of in other respects."

"You are right, Albert, not to make any such attempt," replied the Chevalier. "With respect to love for Clemence, a thousand causes may have produced the peculiar feelings I entertain towards her. I may *have loved* and been cured, though I say not that it is so."

The Count made no reply, but fell into a reverie; and after gazing on him for a minute or two, the Chevalier added, "You, Albert, love her, and are not cured, nor ever will be."

His friend, however, was still silent; and, changing the conversation, the Chevalier talked of indifferent things, and did not return to subjects of such painful interest, till midnight came, and he once more took his departure from the château of Morseiul.

CHAPTER XIV.

THE PREACHING IN THE DESERT.

AGAIN we must pass over a brief space of time, comprising about ten days; and we must also somewhat change the scene, but not very far. In the interval, the acts of a bigoted and despotic monarch had been guided by the advice of cruel and injudicious ministers, till the formal prohibition of the opening of any place of worship throughout France, for the service of God, according to the con-

sciences of the members of the reformed church, had been proclaimed throughout the land.   Such had been the change, or rather
the progress, made in that time ; and the falling off of many leading
Protestants, the disunion which existed amongst the others, the
overstrained loyalty of some, and the irresolution of many, had
shown to even the calmer and the firmer spirits, who might still
have conducted resistance against tyranny to a successful result,
that though, perhaps, they might shed oceans of blood, the Protestant cause in France was lost, at least for the time.

The scene, too, we have said, was changed.   It was no longer
the city of Poitiers, with its multitudes and its gay parties ; it was
no longer the château, with its lord and his attendants ; it was no
longer the country town, with its citizens and its artizans ; but it
was an elevated spot upon one of those dark brown moors of which
so many are to be found on the borders of Brittany and Poitou,
under the canopy of heaven alone, and with nothing but the bleakest
objects of nature round about.

The moor had a gentle slope towards the westward.   It was
covered with gorse and heath, interspersed with old ragged hawthorns, stunted and partly withered—as we often see some being
brought up in poverty and neglect, without ever knowing care or
shelter, become stinted and sickly, and shrivelling with premature
decay.   Cast here and there amongst the thorns, too, were large
masses of rock and cold grey stone, the appearance of which in that
place was difficult to account for, as there was no higher ground
around from which such masses could have fallen.   A small wood
of pines had been planted near the summit of the ground, but that,
too, had decayed prematurely in the ungrateful soil ; and though
each tree presented here and there some scrubby tufts of dark green
foliage, the principal branches stood out, white and blasted, skeleton
fingers pointing in despairing mockery at the wind that withered
them.

The hour was about six o'clock in the evening ; and as if to accord with the earth below it, there was a cold and wintry look about
the sky which the season did not justify ; and the long blue lines of
dark cloud, mingled with streaks of yellow and orange towards the
verge of heaven, seemed to bespeak an early autumn.   There was
one little pond in the foreground of the picture, sunk deep amongst
some banks and hawthorn bushes, and looking dark and stern as
everything around it.   Flapping up from it, however, scared by the
noise of a horse's feet, rose a large white stork, contrasting strangely
with the dim shadowy waters.

The person who startled the bird by passing nearer to him than
anybody else had done, rode forward close by the head of the pond
to a spot about three hundred yards farther on, where a multitude
of people were assembled, perhaps to the number of two thousand.
He was followed by several servants ; but it is to be remarked, that
both they and their lord were unarmed.   He himself did not even

wear the customary sword, without which not a gentleman in France was seen at any distance from his own house; and no apparent weapons of any kind, not even the small knife, or dagger, often worn by a page, was visible amongst the attendants. There was a buzz of many voices as he approached, but it was instantly silenced, when, dismounting from his horse, he gave the rein to a servant, and then advanced to meet one or two persons who drew out from the crowd, as if privileged by intimacy to speak with him. The first of these was Claude de l'Estang, whose hand he took and shook affectionately, though mournfully. The second was a tall, thin, ravenous-looking personage, with sharp-cut lengthened features, a keen, but somewhat unsettled—we might almost use the word frenzied—eye, and an expression of countenance altogether neither very benevolent nor very prepossessing. He also took the Count's hand, saying, " I am glad to see thee, my son; I am glad to see thee! Thou art somewhat behind the time, and in this great day of backsliding and falling off, I feared that even thou, one of our chief props and greatest lights, might have departed from us into the camp of the Philistines."

" Fear not, Monsieur Chopel," replied the Count; " I trust there is no danger of such weakness on my part. I was detained to write a letter in answer to one from good Monsieur de Rouvré, who has suffered so much in our cause, and who, it seems, arrived at Ruffigny last night."

" I know he did," said Claude de l'Estang; " but pray, my dear Albert, before I and our good brother, Monsieur Chopel, attempt to lead the devotions of the people, do you speak a few words of comfort and consolation to them, and, above all things, counsel them to peace and tranquil doings."

The Count paused, and seemed to hesitate for a moment. In truth, the task that was put upon him was not pleasant to him, and he would fain have avoided it; but, accustomed to overcome all repugnance to that which was right, he conquered himself, with scarcely a struggle, and advanced with Claude de l'Estang into the midst of the people, who made way with respectful reverence, as he sought for some slightly elevated point from which to address them more easily. Chopel and l'Estang, however, had chosen a sort of rude rock for their pulpit before he came, and having been led thither, the Count mounted upon it, and took off his hat, as a sign that he was about to speak. All voices were immediately hushed, and he then went on.

" My brethren," he said, " we are here assembled to worship God according to our own consciences, and to the rules and doctrines of the reformed church. In so doing, we are not failing in our duty to the king, who, as sovereign of these realms, is the person whom, under God, we are most bound to obey and reverence. It has seemed fit to his majesty, from motives, upon which I will not touch, to withdraw from us much that was granted by his predecessors. He has ordered the temples in which we are accustomed to worship to be closed, so that on this, the Sabbath day, we have no longer any place of permitted worship but in the open air. That, however, has not been denied us; there is no prohibition to our meeting and praising God here, and this resource at least is allowed us, which, though it may put us to some slight inconvenience and discomfort, will not the less afford the sincere and devont an opportunity of raising their prayers to the Almighty, in company with brethren of the same faith and doctrines as themselves. We know that God does not dwell in temples made with hands; and I have only to remind you, my brethren, before giving place to our excellent ministers, who will lead our devotions this day, that the God we have assembled to worship is also a God of peace, who has told us, by the voice of his Son, not to revile those who revile us, nor smite those that smite us, but to bear patiently all things, promising that those who endure to the last shall be saved. I appointed this place," he continued, " for our meeting, because it was far from any town, and consequently we shall have few here from idle curiosity, and afford no occasion of offence to any man. I begged you earnestly to come unarmed also, as I myself have done, that there might be no doubt of our views and purposes being pacific. I am happy to see that all have followed this advice, I believe without exception ; and also that there are several women amongst us, which, I trust, is a sign that, in the strait and emergency in which we now are, they will not abandon their husbands, their fathers, and their brothers, for any inducement, but continue to serve God in the faith in which they have been brought up."

Having thus spoken, the Count gave place, and descended amongst the people, retiring several steps from the little sort of temporary pulpit, and preparing to go through the service of the reformed church, as if he had been within the walls of the temple which his father had built in Morseiul, and which was now ordered to be levelled with the ground.

After a few words between Claude de l'Estang and Chopel, the latter mounted the pulpit and gave out a psalm, the ——, which he led himself, in a voice like thunder. The whole congregation joined; and though the verses that they repeated were in the simple, unadorned words of the olden times, and the voices that sung them not always in perfect harmony, yet the sound of that melody in the midst of the desert had something strangely impressive—nay, even affecting. The hearts of a people that would not bow down before man, bowed down before God; and they who in persecution and despair had lost all trust on earth, in faith and hope raised their voices unto heaven with praise and adoration.

When the psalm was over, and the minds of all men prepared for prayer, the clergyman who had given out the psalm, closing his eyes and spreading his hands, turned his face towards the sky, and began his address to the Almighty. We shall not pause upon the words that he made use of here, as it would be irreverent to use them lightly; but it is sufficient to say, that he mingled many themes with his address which both Claude de l'Estang and the Count de Morseiul wished had been omitted. He thanked God for the trial and purification to which he had subjected his people: but in doing so, he dwelt so long upon, and entered so deeply into, the nature of all those trials and grievances, and the source from which they sprang, pointed out with such virulent acrimony the tyranny and the persecution which the reformed church had suffered, and clothed so aptly, nay, so eloquently, his petitions against the persecutors and enemies of the church, in the sublime language of Scripture, that the Count could not but feel that he was very likely to stir up the people to seek their deliverance with their own hand, and think themselves fully justified by holy writ; or, at all events, to exasperate their already excited passions, and render the least spark likely to cast them into a flame.

Albert of Morseiul was uneasy while this was proceeding, especially as the prayer lasted an extraordinary length of time, and he could not refrain from turning to examine the countenances of some of the persons present, in order to discover what was the effect produced upon them, especially as he saw a man, standing between him and the rock on which the preacher stood, grasp something under his cloak, as if the appearance of being unarmed was, in that case, not quite real. Near to him were one or two women, wrapped up in the large grey cloaks of the country, and they obstructed his view to the right; but at some distance straight before him he saw the burly form of Virlay, the blacksmith, and close by him again the stern, but expressive, countenance of Armand Herval. Scattered round about, too, he remarked a considerable number of men with a single cock's feather stuck in the front of the hat, which, though bands of feathers and similar ornaments were very much affected, even by the lower classes of that period, was by no means a common decoration in the part of the country where he then was.

Everything, indeed, was peaceable and orderly in the demeanour of the crowd: no one pressed upon the other, no one moved, no one spoke, but each and all stood in deep silence, listening to the words of the minister; but they listened with frowning brows, and stern, dark looks, and the young Count felt thankful that the lateness of the hour, and the distance from any town, rendered it unlikely that the proceedings would be interrupted by the interference, or even appearance, of any of the Catholic authorities of the province.

The prayer of the clergyman Chopel at length came to an end; and, as had been previously arranged between them, Claude de l'Estang, in turn, advanced. Another hymn was sung; and the ejected minister of Auron commenced, what was then called, amongst the Huguenots of France, " the preaching in the desert." On mounting the rock that served them for a pulpit, the old man

N

seemed a good deal affected; and twice he wiped away tears from his eyes, while he gazed round upon the people with a look of strong interest and affection, which every one present saw and felt deeply. He then paused for a moment in silent prayer, and, when that was concluded, took a step forward, with the Bible open in his hand, his demeanour changed, the spirit of the orator upon him, and high and noble energy lighting up his eyes and shining on his lofty brow.

"The nineteenth verse of the twenty-first chapter of St. Luke," he said, "*In your patience possess ye your souls!*"

"My brethren, let us be patient, for to such as are so, is promised the kingdom of heaven. My brethren, let us be patient, for so we are taught by the living word of God. My brethren, let us be patient, for Christ was patient, even unto death, before us. What! shall we know that the saints and prophets of God have been scorned, and mocked, and persecuted, in all ages? what! shall we know that the apostles of Christ, the first teachers of the gospel of grace, have been scourged, and driven forth, and stoned, and slain? what! shall we know that, for ages, the destroying sword was out, from land to land, against our brethren in the Lord? what! shall we know that he himself closed a life of poverty and endurance, by submitting willingly to insult, buffeting, and a torturing death?—and shall we not bear our cross meekly? What! I ask again, shall we know that the church of Christ was founded in persecution, built up by the death of saints, cemented by the blood of martyrs, and yet rose triumphant over the storms of heathen wrath; and shall we doubt that yet, even yet, we shall stand, and not be cast down? Shall we refuse to seal the covenant with our blood, or to endure the reproach of our Lord even unto the last?

"Yes, my brethren, yes! God will give you, and me also, grace to do so; and though 'ye shall be betrayed both by parents and brethren, and kinsfolk, and friends, and some of you shall they cause to be put to death,' yet the faithful and the true shall endure unto the last, and '*in your patience possess ye your souls.*'

"But there is more required at your hands than patience, my brethren. There is constancy! perseverance in the way of the Lord! There must be no falling off in the time of difficulty or danger; there must be no hesitation in the service of our God. We have put our hands to the plough, and we must not look back. We have engaged in the great work, and we must not slacken our diligence. Remember, my brethren, remember, that the most fiery persecution is but the trial of our faith; and all who strive for a great reward, all who struggle for the glory of the kingdom of heaven, must be as gold ten times purified in the fire. Were it not so even,—were we not Christians,—had we not the word of God for our direction,—had we not the command of Christ to obey, where is the man amongst us who would falsify the truth, declare that thing wrong which he believed to be right, swear that he believed that which he knew to be false, put on the garb of hypocrisy, and clothe himself with falsehood as with a garment, to shield himself from the scourge of the scorner or the sword of the persecutor ?

"If there be such a coward or such a hypocrite here, let him go forth from amongst us, and Satan, the father of lies, shall conduct him to the camp of the enemy. Where is the man amongst us, I say, that, were there nothing to restrain him but the inward voice of conscience, would show himself so base as to abandon the faith of his fathers, in the hour of persecution ?

"But when we know that we are right, when the word of God is our warrant, when our faith in Christ is our stay, when the object before us is the glory of God and our own salvation, who would be fool enough to barter eternal condemnation for the tranquillity of a day? Who would not rather sell all that he has, and take up his cross and follow Christ, than linger by the flesh-pots of Egypt, and dwell in the tents of sin ?

"Christ foretold, my brethren, that those who followed him faithfully should endure persecution to the end of the earth. He won us not by the promises of earthly glory, he seduced us not by the allurements of worldly wealth, he held out no inducement to our ambition by the promises of power and authority, he bribed not our pride by the hope of man's respect and reverence. Oh, no; himself, *The Word of God,* which is but to say, all in one word, *Truth ;* he told us all things truly ; he laid before us, as our lot below, poverty, contempt, and scorn, the world's reproach, the calumny of the evil, chains, tortures, and imprisonment, contumely, persecution, and death. These he set before us as our fate, these he suffered as our example, these he endured with patience for our atonement ! Those who became followers of Christ knew well the burden that they took up ; saw the load that they had here to bear ; and, strengthened by faith and by the Holy Spirit, shrunk not from the task, groaned not under the weight of the cross. They saw before their eyes the exceeding great reward,—the reward that was promised to them, the reward that is promised to us, the reward that is promised to all who shall endure unto the last,—to enter into the joy of our Master, to become a partaker of the kingdom reserved for him from before all worlds.

"We must therefore, my brethren, endure ; we must endure unto the last ; but we must endure with patience, and with forbearance, and with meekness, and with gentleness; and 'it shall turn to us for a testimony,' it shall produce for us a reward. They may smite us here, and they may slay us, and they may bring us down to the dust of death ; but he has promised that not a hair of our heads shall perish, and that *in our patience shall we possess our souls.*

"The woe that he denounced against Jerusalem, did it not fall upon it ? When the day of vengeance came, that all things written were to be fulfilled, did not armies compass it about, and desolation draw nigh unto it, and was not distress great in the land, and wrath upon the people, and did not millions fall by the sword, and were not millions led away captives into all nations, and was not Jerusalem trodden down of the Gentiles, and was there one stone left upon another?

"If, then, God, the God of mercy, so fulfilled each word, when kindled to exercise wrath, how much more shall he fulfil every tittle of his gracious promises to those that serve him? If, then, the prophecies of destruction have been fulfilled, so, also, shall be the prophecies of grace and glory, by Him whose words pass not away, though heaven and earth may pass away. For sorrows and endurance in time he has promised us glory and peace in eternity; and for the persecutions which we now suffer, he gives to those, who endure unto the last, the recompence of his eternal joy.

"With endurance we shall live, and *with patience we shall possess our souls;* and we—if we so do, serving God in this life under all adversities—shall have peace, the peace of God, which passeth all understanding: joy, the joy of the Lord, who has trodden down his enemies; glory, the glory of the knowledge of God, when he cometh with clouds and great glory, and every eye shall see him, and they, also, which pierced him, and all kindreds of the earth shall wail because of him. Even so—Amen."

The words of the preacher were poured forth rather than spoken. It seemed less like eloquence than like inspiration. His full, round, clear voice, was heard through every part of his large auditory; not a word was lost, not a tone was indistinct, and the people listened with that deep stern silence which caused a general rustle, like the sighing of the wind, to take place through the multitude when he paused for a moment in his discourse, and every one drew deep the long-suppressed breath.

In the same strain, and with the same powers of voice and gesture, Claude de l'Estang was going on with his sermon, when some sounds were heard at the farther part of the crowd, towards the spot where the scene was sheltered by the stunted wood we have mentioned. As those sounds were scarcely sufficient to give any interruption to the minister, being merely those apparently of some other persons arriving, the Count de Morseiul, and almost every one on that side of the preacher, remained gazing upon him as he went on with the same energy, and did not turn their heads to see what occasioned the noise.

Those, however, who were on tne opposite side, and who, when looking towards the minister, had at the same time in view the spot from which the noise proceeded, were seen to gaze sternly from time to time in that direction; and once or twice, notwithstanding the solemn words they heard, stooped down their heads together, and spoke in whispering consultation. These appearances at length induced the Count de Morseiul to turn his eyes that way; when he beheld a sight which at once made his blood boil, but made him thankful also that he had come in such guise as even to act as a restraint upon himself, having no arms of any kind upon him.

At the skirt of the crowd were collected a party of eighteen or twenty dragoons. They were forcing their horses slowly in amongst the people, who drew back, and gazed upon them with looks of stern, determined hatred. The purpose of the soldiers, indeed, seemed to be simply to insult and to annoy, for they did not proceed to any overt act of violence, and were so far separated from each other, in a disorderly manner, that it could only be supposed they came thither to find themselves sport, rather than to disperse the congregation by any lawful authority. The foremost of the whole party was the young Marquis de Hericourt; and Albert of Morseiul conceived, perhaps not unreasonably, that there might be some intention of giving him personal annoyance at the bottom of that young officer's conduct.

Distinguished from the rest of the people by his dress, the Count was very plainly to be seen from the spot where De Hericourt was; and the young dragoon slowly made his way towards him through the press, looking at the people on either side with but ill-concealed signs of contempt upon his countenance.

The Count determined, as far as possible, to set an example of patience; and when the rash youth came close up to him, saying aloud, "Ha, Monsieur de Morseiul, a lucky opportunity! I have long wished to hear a *prêche*," the Count merely raised his hand as a sign for the young man to keep silence, and pointed with his right hand to the pastor, who, with an undisturbed demeanour and steady voice, pursued his sermon as if not the slightest interruption had occurred, although the young dragoon on horseback in the midst of his people was at that moment before him.

De Hericourt was bent upon mischief, however. Rash to the pitch of folly, he had neither inquired nor considered whether the people were armed or not, but having heard that one of the preachings in the desert was to take place, he had come, unauthorized, for the purpose of disturbing and dispersing the congregation, not by the force of law, but by insult and annoyance, which he thought the Protestants would not dare to resist. He listened, then, for a moment or two to the words of Claude de l'Estang, seeming, for an instant, somewhat struck with the impressive manner of the old man; but he soon got tired, and, turning the bridle of his horse, as if to pass round the Count de Morseiul, he said again, aloud, "You've got a number of women here, Monsieur de Morseiul; pretty little heretics, I've no doubt! I should like to have a look at their faces."

So saying, he spurred on unceremoniously, driving back five or six persons before him, and caught hold of one of the women— whom we have noticed as standing not very far from the Count de Morseiul—trying, at the same time, to pull back the thick veil which was over her face.

The Count could endure no longer, more especially as, under the grey cloak and the veil—with which the person assailed by the dragoon was covered, he thought he recognised the dress of the lady he had formerly seen at the house of Claude de l'Estang.

Starting forward, then, instantly to her side, he seized the bridle of De Hericourt's horse, and forced the animal back almost upon his haunches. The young officer stooped over his saddle-bow, seeking for a pistol in his holster, and at the same moment addressing an insulting and contemptuous term to the Count. No sooner was it uttered, however, than he received one single buffet from the hand of Albert of Morseiul, which cast him headlong from his horse into the midst of the people.

Every one was rushing upon him; his dragoons were striving to force their way forward to the spot; the voice of Claude de l'Estang, though exerted to its utmost power, was unheard; and in another instant the rash young man would have been literally torn to pieces by the people he had insulted.

But with stern and cool self-possession the Count de Morseiul strode over him, and held back those that were rushing forward, with his powerful arms, exclaiming, in a voice of thunder—

"Stand back, my friends, stand back! This is a private quarrel. I must have no odds against an adversary and a fellow-soldier. Stand back, I say! We are here man to man, and whoever dares to take him out of my hands is my enemy, not my friend. Rise, Monsieur de Hericourt," he said, in a lower voice, "rise, mount your horse, and be gone. I cannot protect you a minute longer."

Some of the Count's servants, who had been standing near, had by this time made their way up to him, and with their help he cleared the space around, shouting to the dragoons who were striving to come up, and had not clearly seen the transaction which had taken place, "Keep back, keep back!—I will answer for his life! If you come up, there will be bloodshed!"

In the meantime the young man had sprung upon his feet, his dress soiled by the fall, his face glowing like fire, and fury flashing from his eyes.

"You have struck me," he cried, glaring upon the Count; "you have struck me, and I will have your blood!"

"Hush, sir," said the Count, calmly. "Do not show yourself quite a madman. Mount your horse, and begone while you may! I shall be at the château of Morseiul till twelve o'clock to-morrow," he added, in a lower voice. "Mount—mount!" he proceeded, in a quicker manner, seeing some movements on the other side of the crowd of a very menacing kind; "mount, if you would live and keep your soldiers' lives another minute!"

De Hericourt sprang into the saddle, and, while the Count, in that tone of command which is seldom disobeyed, exclaimed, "Make way for him, there—let no one impede him!" he spurred on quickly through the crowd, gathering his men together as he went.

All eyes were turned to look after him, but the moment he and his troop were free from the people at the extreme edge of the crowd, he was seen to speak a word to the man at the head of the file. The soldiers immediately halted, faced about, and, carrying fire-arms as they did, coolly unslung their carbines.

The first impulse of that part of the crowd nearest to the dragoon, was to press back, while those on the opposite side strove to get forward, headed by Virlay and Armand Herval. The crush in the centre was consequently tremendous, but the Count de Morseiul succeeded in casting himself between the female he had rescued and the troopers. At the very moment that he did so, the dragoons raised their weapons to their shoulders, and fired at once into the midst of the compact mass of the people. Every shot told; and one unfortunate young man, about two paces from the Count de Morseiul, received no less than four shots in his head and throat. A mingled yell of rage and agony rose up from the people, while a loud exulting laugh broke from the soldiery. But their triumph was only for a moment, for they were instantly assailed by a shower of immense stones, one of which knocked a trooper off his horse, and killed him on the spot.

Herval and Virlay, too, made their way round behind the rock on which the clergyman had been standing; and it now became apparent that, in that part of the crowd at least, arms were not wanting, for flash after flash broke from the dense mass of the advancing multitude, and swords and pikes were seen gleaming in the air.

The troopers at length turned their horses and fled, but not before they had suffered tremendously. The Huguenots pursued, and with peculiar skill and knowledge of the country, drove them hither and thither over the moor. Some having mounted the horses which brought them thither, drove them into spots where they could not pass, while some on foot defended the passes and ravines. The Count de Morseiul and his servants mounted instantly, and rode far and wide over the plain, attempting to stop the effusion of blood, and in many instances succeeded in rescuing some of the soldiery from the hands of the people and from the death they well deserved. Thus passed more than an hour, till, seeing that the light was beginning to fail, and that the last spot of the sun was just above the horizon, the Count turned back to the scene of that day's unfortunate meeting, in the hope of rendering some aid and assistance to the wounded who had been left behind.

He had by this time but one servant with him, and, when he came to the spot where the assembly had been held, he found it quite deserted. The wounded and the dead had been carried away by those that remained upon the ground when the dragoons fled; and, of the rest of the people who had been there, the greater part had been scattered abroad in pursuit of the fugitive soldiers, while part had hastened in fear to their own homes. There was nothing but the cold, grey rock, and the brown moor, stained here and there with blood, and the dark purple streaks of the evening sky, and the east wind whistling mournfully through the thin trees.

" I think, sir," said the servant, after his master had paused for some moments in melancholy mood, gazing on the scene around, " I think, sir, that I hear voices down by the water, where we put up the stork as we came."

The Count listened, and heard voices, too, and he instantly turned his horse thither. By the side of that dark water he found a melancholy group, consisting of Claude de l'Estang and two female figures, all kneeling round or supporting the form of a third person, also a female, who seemed severely hurt. This was the sight which presented itself to the eyes of the Count from the top of the bank above; and, dismounting, he sprang down to render what assistance he could.

His first attention was turned, of course, almost entirely to the wounded girl, whose head and shoulders were supported on the knee of one of the other women, while the pastor was pouring into her ear, in solemn tones, the words of hope and consolation—but they were words of hope and consolation referring to another world. The hand that lay upon her knee was fair and soft, the form seemed young and graceful; and, though the Count, as he descended, could not see her face, the novice's veil, that hung from her head, told him a sad tale in regard to the story of her life. He doubted not, from all he saw, that she was dying; and his heart sickened when he thought of the unhappy man who had brought her thither, and of what would be the feelings of his fierce and vehement heart when he heard the fate that had befallen her.

He had scarcely time to think of it; for, ere he had well reached the bottom of the descent, the sound of a horse, coming furiously along, was heard, and Armand Herval paused on the opposite side of the dell, and gazed down upon the group below. It seemed as if instinct told him that there was what he sought; for, without going on to the moor, he turned his horse's rein down the descent, though it was steep and dangerous, and in a moment had sprung from the beast's back and was kneeling by her he had loved.

It is scarcely to be told whether she was conscious of his presence or not, for the hand of death was strong upon her; but it is certain that, as he printed upon her hands the burning kisses of love in agony, and quenched them with his tears, it is certain that a smile came over her countenance before that last awful shudder with which the soul parted from the body for ever.

After it was all over, he gazed at her for a single instant without speaking. Every one present saw that he acted as if of right, and let him do what he would; and, unfastening the veil from her long beautiful hair, he took and steeped it in the blood which was still, notwithstanding all that had been done to stanch it, welling from a deep wound in her breast, till every part of the fabric was wet with gore. He then took the veil, placed it in his brown, scarred bosom—upon his heart;—and, raising his eyes and one hand to heaven, murmured some words that were not distinctly heard. He had not uttered one audible sentence since he came up; but he now turned, and, with a tone of intreaty, addressed Claude de l'Estang.

"The spirit will bless you, sir," he said, "for giving her comfort in the hour of death! May I bear her to your house till eleven o'clock to-night, when I will remove her to her own abode?"

"I must not refuse you, my poor young man," replied the clergyman. "But I fear that my house will be no safe resting-place, even for the dead, just now."

Herval grasped his arm, and said, in a low but emphatic tone, "It is safe, sir, against all the troops in Poitou. How long it may be so, I cannot tell; but as long as this arm can wield a sword, it shall not want defence. My lord the Count," he added, pointing to the dead body, "did I not hear that you meet her murderer to-morrow at noon?"

"I know not the hour or place he may appoint," replied the Count, in a low, deep voice; "but we do meet! and there are things that call aloud for vengeance, Herval, which even I cannot forgive."

The man laughed aloud, but that laugh was no voice of merriment. It was dreary, boding, horrible, and in good accordance with the circumstances and the scene. He replied nothing to the words of the Count, however, turning to the pastor and saying, "Now, sir, now! if you will give shelter to the dead for but an hour or two, you shall win deep gratitude of the living."

"Willingly," replied the pastor: "but then," he added, turning to one of the other two women who were present, "who shall protect you home, dear lady?"

"That will I do, at the risk of my life," said the Count; and the other woman, whom the pastor had not addressed, replied, "It will be better so. We have been too long absent already."

Armand Herval had not noticed the brief words that were spoken, for he was gazing with an intense and eager look upon the fair countenance of the dead, with bitter anguish written in every line of his face. The pastor touched his arm gently, saying, "Now, my son, let me and you carry the body. We can pass through the wood unseen."

But the other put him by, with his hand, saying, in a sad tone, "I need no help;" and then, kneeling down by her side, he placed his arms around her, saying, "Let me bear thee in my bosom, sweet child, once only, once before the grave parteth us, and ere it shall unite us again. Oh, Claire, Claire," he added, kissing her cold lips passionately, "Oh, Claire, Claire, was it for this I taught thee a purer faith, and brought thee hither to see the worship of the persecuted followers of the cross? Was it for this I bent down my nature, and became soft as a woman; to suit my heart to yours? Oh, Claire, Claire, if I have brought thee to death, I will avenge thy death; and for every drop that falls from my eyes, I will have a drop of blood."

" Vengeance is mine, saith the Lord!" the old man said, in a low tone; " but let us haste, my son, for night is coming on fast. Farewell, lady. Albert, I trust them to thee. We shall meet again—if not here, in heaven!"

Armand Herval raised the corpse of the fair girl who had fallen, in his powerful arms, and bore her after the pastor towards the wood we have mentioned, while his horse, trained so to do, followed him with a regular pace, and entered the road through the copse immediately after him

Albert of Morseiul remained alone with the two ladies, his inter-position in favour of one of whom, had brought on the sad events which we have detailed. As soon as the pastor was gone, he ad-vanced towards her, and held out both his hands with deep emo-tion. " I cannot be mistaken," he said. " The disguise might deceive any other eyes, but it cannot mine. Clémence! it must be Clémence! Am I not right?"

She put her hands in his in return, saying, " Oh yes, you are right! But what, what shall I do, Monsieur de Morseiul? I am faint and weary with agitation, and all this terrible scene. I have left the carriage which brought me hither, at two or three miles' distance; and perhaps it too has gone away on the report of the fliers from this awful place."

" I will send up my servant immediately," said the Count, " to see, and in the meantime rest here, Clémence. In this deep hollow we shall escape all passing eyes till his return, and you will have more shelter than anywhere ' else.—Where can the servant find the carriage?"

Clémence, who had raised her veil, looked towards her com-panion to explain more fully than she could do. But her at-tendant, Maria—for she was the person who accompanied her—judging, perhaps, that a word spoken at such a moment between two people, situated as were Clémence de Marly and the Count de Morseiul, might be more important than whole hours of conversa-tion at another time, took upon herself the task of telling the servant, saying, " I can direct him, my lord, better than any one. It were as well to bring your horse here before he goes."

The Count assented; and, with a slow step, she proceeded to fulfil her errand.

Clémence de Marly trembled not a little. She was terribly impressed and agitated by all that had passed; but on that we will not pause, for there were other feelings moved her. She felt that the moment for the decision of her fate for life was come. She felt that her heart and her faith must be plighted to Albert of Morseiul at that moment, or, perhaps, never. She felt that if she did so plight it, she plighted herself to care, to grief, to anxiety, to danger—perhaps to destruction—perhaps to desolation. But that very conviction took away all hesitation, all scruple, and made her, in a moment, resolve to let him see her heart as it really was, to cast away from her every vain and every proud feeling, and to stand, before him she loved, without disguise. It was, indeed, no hour for coquetry—nay, nor for hesitation. The Count, too, felt, and felt strongly, that this was a moment which must not be suffered to pass; and, the instant the attendant had quitted them, he raised the lady's hand to his lips, pressing on it a warm and passionate kiss.

"Tell me, Clémence, tell me, dear Clémence," he said, "what is the meaning of this. What is the meaning of your presence here? Is it—is it that the only barrier which existed between us is removed? Is it that you are of the same faith as I am?"

"Is that the only barrier, Albert?" she said, shaking her head somewhat reproachfully. "Is that the only barrier?—You spoke of many."

"I spoke of only one insurmountable," replied the Count, "and I believed that to be insurmountable, Clémence; for I was even then aware of the decree, which did not appear till afterwards, but which forbade the marriage of Catholics and Protestants."

"And was that the only insurmountable one?" she demanded. "Was that the only impassable obstacle to our union?—What, if I had previously loved another?"

"And is it so, then?" demanded the Count, with somewhat of sadness in his tone. "And have you before loved another?"

"No, no!" exclaimed Clémence, eagerly, and placing the hand which she had withdrawn, in his again; "no, no! The woman was coming over me once more; but I will conquer the woman. No, I never did love another. Even had I, as you say, fancied it, I should now know, Albert, by what I feel at this moment, how idle such a fancy had been. But I never did fancy it. I never did believe it, even in the least degree; and now, that I have said all that I can say, whatever may happen, never doubt me, Albert. Whatever you see, never entertain a suspicion. I have never loved another, and I can say nothing more."

"Yes, yes! Oh, yes!" he exclaimed, "you can say more, Clémence. Say that you love me."

She bent down her head; and Albert of Morseiul drew her gently to his bosom. "Say it! Say it, dear Clémence!" he said.

Clémence hesitated, but at length she murmured something that no other ear but his could have heard, had it been ever so close. But he heard, and heard aright, that her reply was, "But too well!"

The Count sealed the words upon her lips, and Clémence de Marly hid her eyes upon his shoulder, for they were full of tears. "And now," she added, raising them after a moment's pause, "and now, having said those awful words, of course I am henceforth a slave. But this is no scene for jest, Albert. Desolation and destruction is round us on every side, I fear."

"It matters not," replied the Count, "if thy faith is the same as mine is ——"

"It is, it is!" cried Clémence. "It may have wavered, Albert; but, thanks to yon good creature who has just left us, the light has never been wholly extinguished in my mind. My mother was a Protestant, and in that faith she brought me up. She then, knowing that I must fall into other hands, left Maria with me, with charges to me never to let her quit me. I was but a child then," she continued, "and they forced me to abjure. But their triumph lasted not an hour, for though I dared not show my feelings, I always felt that the path on which they would lead me was wrong, and strove, whenever I could, to return to a better way. To-day I came here at all risks; but I fear very much, Albert,—I fear that destruction, and oppression, and grief, surround us on every side."

"If thy faith be the same as mine, Clémence," said the Count—"if thy heart be united with mine, I will fear nothing, I will dare all. If they will not suffer us to live in peace in this our native land, fortunately I have just transmitted to another country enough to support us in peace, and tranquillity, and ease.—And yet, oh, yet, Clémence," he continued, his tone becoming sadder and his countenance losing its look of hope, "and yet, oh, yet, Clémence, when I think of that unhappy man who was so lately here, and of the fair girl whose corpse he has now borne away in his arms;—when I remember that, scarcely more than ten days have passed since he was animated with the same hopes that I am, founding those hopes upon the same schemes of flight, and trusting more than I have ever trusted to the bright hereafter,—when I think of that, and of his present fate, the agony that must now be wringing his heart, the dark obscurity of his bitter despair, I tremble to dream of the future, not for myself, but for thee, sweet girl. But we must fall upon some plan, both of communicating when we will, and of acting constantly on one scheme and for one object. Here comes your faithful attendant. She must know our situation and our plans—only one word more. You have promised me this," he continued, once more raising her hand to his lips.

"When and where you will," replied Clémence.

"And you will fly with me, whenever I find the opportunity of doing so?"

"I will," she answered.

The attendant had now approached; and the Count took a step towards her, still holding Clémence by the hand, as if he feared to lose the precious boon she had bestowed upon him.

"She is mine, madam," he said, addressing the attendant. "She is mine, by every promise that can bind one human being to another."

"And you are hers?" demanded the attendant, solemnly. "And you are hers, my lord Count, by the same promises?"

"I am, by everything I hold sacred," said the Count, raising his hand towards heaven, "now and for ever, till death take me from her. But ere we can be united, I fear that many things must be undergone. Alas, that I should recommend it! but she must even conceal her faith: for, from the cruel measures of the court, even now death or perpetual imprisonment in some unknown dungeon is the only fate reserved for the relapsed convert, as they call those who have been driven to embrace a false religion, and quitted it in renewed disgust. But I must trust to you to afford me the means of communicating with her at all times. The only chance for us, I fear, is flight."

"It is the only one! it is the only one!" replied the maid. "Fly with her to England, my lord. Fly with her as speedily as possible. Be warned, and neither delay nor hesitate. The edge of the net is just falling on you. If you take your resolution at once, and quit the land before a week be over, you may be safe; but if you stay longer, every port in France will be closed against you."

"I will make no delay," replied the Count. "Her happiness and her safety are now committed to my charge; inestimable trusts, which I must on no account risk. But I have some followers and dependents to provide for, even here. I have some friends to defend; and I must not show myself remiss in that, or she herself would hardly love me. It were easy, methinks, however, for you and your mistress to make your escape at once to England, and for me to join you there hereafter."

"Oh, no, my lord, I fear not!" replied the maid. "I do not think Monsieur de Rouvré himself would object to her marrying you, and flying. He shrewdly suspects, I think, that she is Protestant at heart; but he would never yield to her flying by herself. But, hark! I hear horses coming. Let us draw back and be quiet."

"There is no noise of carriage-wheels, I fear," said Clémence, listening. "Oh, Albert, all this day's sad events have quite overpowered me; and I dread the slightest sound."

The Count pressed her hand in his, and, as was usual with him in moments of danger, turned his eyes towards his sword-belt, forgetting that the blade was gone. The sound of horses' feet approaching rapidly, however, still continued; and, at length, a party of four persons, whose faces could not be well distinguished in the increasing darkness, stopped exactly opposite the spot from which a little rough road led down into the hollow where the lovers were. One of the riders sprang to the ground in a moment, and, leaving his horse with the others, advanced, exclaiming aloud—

"Hollo! Ho! Albert de Morseiul! Hollo! where are you?"

"It is the voice of the Chevalier d'Evran," cried Clémence, clinging closer to her lover, as if with some degree of fear.

"I think it is," said the Count; "but fear not! He is friendly to us all. Draw down your veil, however, my beloved; it is not necessary that he should see and know you—I knew not that he had returned."

With the same shout the Chevalier continued to advance towards them, and the Count took a step or two forward to meet him. But, shaking his friend warmly by the hand, the Chevalier passed on at once to the lady, and, to the surprise of the Count, addressed her immediately by her name: "Very pretty, indeed, Mademoiselle Clémence!" he said; "this is as dangerous a jest, I think, as ever was practised."

Clémence hesitated not a moment, but replied at once, "It is no jest, sir! It is a dangerous reality, if you will."

"Poo, poo, silly girl!" cried the Chevalier. "By the Lord that lives, you will get yourself into the castle of Pignerol, or the Bastille, or some such pleasant abode! I have come at full speed to bring you back."

"Stay yet a minute, Louis," said the Count, somewhat gravely. "There is another person to be consulted in this business, whom you do not seem to recollect. Mademoiselle de Marly is, for the time, under my protection; and you know we delegate such a duty to no one."

"My dear Count," replied the Chevalier, "the good Duc de Rouvré will doubtless be infinitely obliged to you for the protection you have given to this fair lady; but having sent me to find her and bring her back, I must do so at once; and will only beg her to be wise enough to make no rash confessions as she goes. The affair, as far as she is concerned, is a jest at present: it is likely, I hear, to prove a serious jest to others. I left your man, who directed me hither, to bring up the carriage as far as possible: and now, Mademoiselle Clémence, we will go, with your good pleasure."

The tone of authority in which the Chevalier spoke by no means pleased Albert of Morseiul, who felt strong in his heart the newly acquired right of mutual love to protect Clémence de Marly himself. He was not of a character, however, to quarrel with his friend lightly, and he replied, "Louis, we are too old friends for you to make me angry. As your proposal of conveying Mademoiselle de Marly back in her own carriage coincides with what we had previously arranged, of course I shall not oppose it; but equally, of course, I accompany her to Ruffigny."

"I am afraid that cannot be, Albert," answered the Chevalier; and the resolute words, "It must be!" had just been uttered in reply, when Clemence interfered.

"It is very amusing, gentlemen," she said, in her ordinary tone of scornful playfulness, "it is very amusing, indeed, to hear you calmly and quietly settling a matter that does not in the least depend upon yourselves. You forget that I am here, and that the decision must be mine. Monsieur le Chevalier, be so good as not to be authoritative, for, depend upon it, you have no more power here than one of these old hawthorn stumps. Monsieur de Rouvré cannot delegate what he does not possess; and as I have never yet suffered any one to rule me, I shall not commence that bad practice to-night. You may now tell me, in secret, what are your motives in this business; but, depend upon it that my own high judgment will decide in the end."

"Let it!" replied the Chevalier; and bending down his head, he whispered a few words to Clémence in a quick and eager manner. She listened attentively, and when he had done, turned at once to the Count de Morseiul, struggling to keep up the same light manner, but in vain.

"I fear," she said, "Monsieur de Morseiul, that I must decide for the plan of the Chevalier, and that I must lay my potent commands upon you not to accompany or follow me. Nay, more, I will forbid your coming to Ruffigny to-morrow; but the day after, unless you hear from me to the contrary, you may be permitted to inquire after my health."

Albert of Morseiul was deeply mortified; too much so, indeed, to reply in any other manner than by a stately bow. Clémence saw that he was hurt; and, though some unexplained motive prevented her from changing her resolution, she cast off reserve at once, and holding out her hand to him, said aloud, notwithstanding the presence of the Chevalier, "Do you forgive me, Albert?"

Though unable to account for her conduct, the Count felt that he loved her deeply still, and he pressed his lips upon her hand warmly and eagerly, while Clémence added, in a lower tone, but by no means one inaudible to those around who chose to listen, "Have confidence in me, Albert! Have confidence in me; and remember, you have promised never to doubt me, whatever may happen. Oh, Albert, having once given my affection, believe me utterly incapable of trifling with yours even by a single thought."

"I will try, Clémence," he replied; "but you must own there is something here to be explained."

"There is!" she said, "there is; and it shall be explained as soon as possible; but, in the meantime, trust me! Here comes the servant, I think: the carriage must be near."

It was as she supposed; and the Count gave her his arm to assist her in climbing back to the level ground above, saying, at the same time in a tone of some coldness which he could not conquer, "As the lady has herself decided, Chevalier, I shall not, of course, press my attendance farther than to the carriage-door; but have you men enough with you to ensure her safety? It is now completely dark."

"Quite enough!" replied the Chevalier, "quite enough, Albert;"

and he fell into silence till they reached the side of the vehicle, dropping, however, a few yards behind Clémence and her lover.

Every moment of existence is certainly precious, as a part of the irrevocable sum of time written against us in the book of life ; but there is no occasion on which the full value of each instant is so entirely felt, in which every minute is so dear, so treasured, so inestimable in our eyes, as when we are about to part with her we love.   Albert of Morseiul felt that it was so ; and in the few short moments that passed, ere they reached the carriage, words were spoken in a low murmuring tone, which, in the intensity of the feelings they expressed and excited, wrought more deeply on his heart and hers, than could the passage of long indifferent years. They were of those few words spoken in life that remain in the ear of memory for ever.

The fiery hand that, at the impious feast, wrote the fate of the Assyrian in characters of flame, left them to go out extinguished when the announcement was complete ; but the words that the hand of deep and intense passion writes upon firm, high, and energetic hearts, remain for ever, even unto the grave itself.

Those moments were brief, however ; and Clémence and her attendant were soon upon their way ; the Chevalier sprang upon his horse, and then held out his hand frankly to the Count. " Albert," he said, laughing, " I have never yet beheld so great a change of Love's making as that which the truant boy has wrought in you.   You would even quarrel with your oldest and dearest companion — you who are no way quarrelsome.   You have known me now long, Albert ; love me well still.   If you have ever seen me do a dishonest act, cast me off ; if not, as I heard Clémence say just now—Trust me !" and thus saying, he galloped off, without waiting for any reply.

CHAPTER XV.

THE REVENGE.

WHILE Clémence de Marly cast herself back in the carriage ; and, with the great excitement under which she had been acting for some time, now over, hid her eyes with her hands, and gave herself up to deep, and even to painful thought—while over that bright and beautiful countenance came unseen a thousand varied expressions as she recollected all that had passed—while the look of horror rose there as she remembered all the fearful scenes she had beheld, the murderous treachery of the dragoons, the retribution taken by the people, and the death of the unhappy girl who had received one of the random shots—while that, again, was succeeded by the expression of admiration and enthusiasm, as she recalled the words and conduct of the Protestant pastor; and while a blush, half of shame and half of joy, succeeded, as she remembered all that had passed between her and Albert of Morseiul, the Count himself was wending his way slowly homeward, with feelings different from hers, but by no means so happy ones.

She knew that difficulty and danger surrounded her, she knew that much was necessarily to be endured, much to be apprehended; but she had woman's greatest, strongest consolation. She had the great, the mighty support, that she was loved by him whom alone she loved. With her that was enough to carry her triumphant through all danger, to give her a spirit to resist all oppression, to support her under all trials, to overcome all fears.

It may be asked, when we say that Albert of Morseiul's feelings were different, if he then loved her less than she loved him, if love in his bosom was less powerful, less all-sufficing than in hers. It might seem strange to answer, no; but such certainly was not the case. He loved her as much, as deeply, as she did him; he loved her as tenderly, as truly. His love—though there must always be a difference between the love of man and the love of woman—was as full, as perfect, as all-sufficing as her own, and yet his bosom was not so much at ease as hers, his heart did not feel the same confidence in its own happiness that hers did. But there were many different causes combined to produce that effect. In the first place, he knew the dangers, the obstacles, the difficulties, far better than she did. He knew them more intimately, more fully, more completely; they were all present to his mind at once; no bright hopes of changing circumstances came to relieve the prospect; but all, except the love of Clémence de Marly, was dark, obscure, and threatening around him. That love might have seemed, however, only a brighter spot amidst the obscurity, had it not been that apprehensions for her were now added to all his apprehensions for his religion and his country. It might have seemed all the more brilliant for that obscurity had it been itself quite unclouded, had there not been some shadows, though slight, some mystery to be struggled with, something to be forgotten or argued down.

During the last few minutes that he passed with her, the magic fascination of her presence had conquered everything, and seated love triumphant above all; but as he rode on, Albert de Morseiul pondered over what had occurred—thought of the influence which the Chevalier d'Evran had exerted over her—combined it with what he had seen before at Poitiers; and pronounced it in his own heart, "Very strange." He resolved not to think upon it, and yet he thought. He accused himself—the man of all others the least suspicious on the earth, by nature—he accused himself of being basely suspicious. He argued with himself that it was impossible that, either on the part of Clémence or the Chevalier, there should be anything which could give him pain, when each, in the presence of the other, behaved to him as they had behaved that night; and yet there was something to be explained which—like one of those thin veils of cloud that sometimes cover even the summer sun, prognosticating a weeping evening to a blithe noon—which hung over the only star that fate had left to shine upon his track; and he thought of it sadly and anxiously, and longed for something to bear it far away.

He struggled with such feelings and such reflections for some time; and then, forcing his thoughts to other things, he found that there was plenty, indeed, for him to consider and to provide against, plenty to inquire into and to ponder over, ere he resolved or acted. First came the recollection of the quarrel between himself and the young De Hericourt. He knew that the rash and cruel young man had made his escape from the field; for he himself, with two of his servants, had followed him close, and, by detaining a party of the pursuers, had afforded the commander of the dragoons an opportunity to fly in the very direction of Morseiul. That he would immediately require that which is absurdly called satisfaction for the blow which had been struck there could be no earthly doubt, although the laws against duelling were at that time enforced with the utmost strictness; and there was not the slightest chance whatsoever of the king showing mercy to any Protestant engaged in a duel with a Roman Catholic.

No man more contemned or reprobated the idiotical custom of duelling than the Count himself; no man looked upon it in a truer light than he did; but yet must we not forgive him if, even with such feelings and with such opinions, he prepared, without a thought or hesitation, to give his adversary the meeting he might demand? Can we severely blame him if he determined, with his own single arm, to avenge the wanton slaughter which had been committed, and to put the barrier of a just punishment between the murderer of so many innocent people and a repetition of the crime? Can we blame him if, seeing no chance whatsoever of the law doing justice upon the offender, he resolved—risking at the same time his own life—to take the law into his hand, and seek justice for himself and others?

The next subjects that started up for consideration were the general events of that day, and the question of what colouring would be given to those events at the court of France.

A peaceful body of people, meeting together for the worship of the Almighty, in defiance of no law, (for the edict concerning the expulsion of the Protestant pastors, and prohibiting the preaching of the reformed religion at all, had not yet appeared,) had been brutally insulted by a body of unauthorized armed men, had been fired upon by them without provocation, and had lost several of their number, murdered in cold blood, and in a most cowardly manner, by the hands of the military. They had then, in their own defence, attacked and pursued their brutal assailants, and had slain several of them as a direct consequence of their own crimes.

Such were the simple facts of the ease; but what was the tale, the Count asked himself, which would be told at the court of France, and vouched for by the words of those who, having committed the great crime of unprovoked murder, would certainly entertain no scruple in regard to justifying it by the lesser crime of a false oath?

"It will be represented," thought the Count, "that a body of armed fanatics met for some illegal purpose, and intending no less than revolt against the king's government, attacked and slaughtered a small body of the royal troops sent to watch their movements. It will be represented that the dragoons fought gallantly against the rebels, and slew a great number of their body; and this, doubtless, will be vouched for by the words of respectable people, all delicately adjusted by Romish fraud; and while the sword and the axe are wetted with the blood of the innocent and the unoffending, the murderer and his accomplices may be loaded with honours and rewards!—But it shall not be so, if I can stay it," he added. "I will take the bold, perhaps the rash, resolution,—I will cast myself in the gap. I will make the truth known, and the voice thereof shall be heard throughout Europe, even if I fall myself. I, at least, was there unarmed: that can be proved. No weapon has touched my hand during this day, and therefore my testimony may be less suspected."

While he thus pondered, riding slowly on through the thick darkness which had now fallen completely around his path, he passed a little wood, which is called the wood of Jersel to this day; but, just as he had arrived at the opposite end, two men started out upon him as if to seize the bridle of his horse. Instantly, however, another voice exclaimed from behind—"Back, back! I told you any one coming the other way. He cannot come that way, fools. We have driven him into the net, and he has but one path to follow. Let him go on, whoever he is, and disturb him not." The men were, by this time, drawing back, and they instantly disappeared behind the trees; while the Count rode on his way with his servant, at somewhat a quicker pace.

On his arrival at his own dwelling, Albert of Morseiul proceeded at once to the library of the château; and, though Jerome Riquet strongly pressed him to take some refreshment, he applied himself at once to draw up a distinct statement of all that had occurred, nor quitted it till the night had two-thirds waned. He then retired to rest, ordering himself to be called, without fail, if anybody came to the château, demanding to see him. For the first hour, however, after he had lain down, as may well be supposed, he could not close his eyes. The obscurity seemed to encourage thought, and to call up all the fearful memories of the day. It was a fit canvas, the darkness of the night, for imagination to paint such awful pictures on. There is something soothing, however, in the grey twilight of the morning, which came at length; and then, but not till then, the Count slept. Though his slumber was disturbed and restless, it

was unbroken for several hours; and it was nearly eleven o'clock in
the day when, starting up suddenly from some troublous dream, he
awoke and gazed wildly round the room, not knowing well where
he was.   The sight of the sun streaming into the apartment, however, showed him how long he had slept; and ringing the bell that
lay by his bedside, he demanded eagerly of Jerome Riquet, who
appeared in an instant, whether no one had been to seek him.

The man replied, "No one," and informed his lord that the gates
of the castle had not been opened during the morning.

"It is strange !" said the Count.   "If I hear not by twelve," he
continued, "I must set off without waiting.   Send forward a
courier, Riquet, as fast as possible towards Paris, giving notice at
the post-houses that I come with four attendants, yourself one, and
ordering horses to be prepared, for I must ride post to the capital.
Have everything ready in a couple of hours at the latest; for I
must distance, if possible, this morning's ordinary courier, and get
to the court before him."

"If you ride as you usually do, my lord," replied the man, " you
will easily do that; for you seldom fail to kill all the horses and all
the postilions; and if your humble servant were composed of anything but bones and a good wit, you would have worn the flesh off
him long ago."

"I am in no mood for jesting, Riquet," replied the Count; " see
that everything is ready, as I have said, and be prepared to aecompany me."

Riquet, who was never yet known to have found too little time
to do anything on earth, took the rapid orders of his lord extremely
coolly, aided him to dress, and then left him.   He had scarcely
been gone five minutes, however, before he returned with a face
somewhat whiter than usual.

"What is the matter, sirrah ?' cried the Count, somewhat
sharply.

"Why, my lord," he said, " here is the mayor, and the adjoint,
and the counsellors, arrived in great terror and trepidation, to tell
you that Maillard, the carrier, coming down from the way of Nantes
with his packhorses, has seen the body of a young officer tied to a
tree, in the little wood of Jersel.   He was afraid to meddle with it
himself, and they were afraid to go down till they had come to
tell you."

"Send the men up," said the Count, "and have horses saddled
for me instantly.—Now, Sir Mayor," he said, as the local magistrate entered, " what is the meaning of this?   What are these
news you bring?"

To say sooth, the mayor was somewhat embarrassed in presenting
himself before the Count, as he had lately shown no slight symptoms
of cowardly wavering in regard to the Protestant cause : nor would
he have come now, had he not been forced to do so by other members of the town council.   He answered, then, with evident hesitation and timidity—

"Terrible news, indeed, my lord!—terrible news, indeed! This young man has been murdered, evidently; for he is tied to a tree, and a paper nailed above his head. So says Maillard, who was afraid to go near to read what was written; and then, my lord, I was afraid to go down without your lordship's sanction, as you are *haut justicier* for a great way round."

The Count's lip curled with a scornful sneer. "It seems to me," he said, "that Maillard and yourself are two egregious cowards. We will dispense with your presence, Mr. Mayor; and these other gentlemen will go down with me at once to see what this business is. Though the man might be tied to a tree, and very likely much hurt, that did not prove that he was dead; and very likely he might have been recovered, or, at least, have received the sacraments of the church, if Maillard and yourself had thought fit to be speedy in your measures.—Come, gentlemen, let us set out at once."

The rebuked mayor slunk away with a hanging head; and the rest of the municipal council, elated exactly in proportion to the depression of their chief, followed the young Count, who led the way with a party of his servants to the wood of Jersel. On first entering that part of the road which traversed the wood, the party perceived nothing; and the good citizens of Morseiul drew themselves a little more closely together, affected by certain personal apprehensions in regard to meddling with the night's work of one who seemed both powerful and unscrupulous. A moment after, however, the object which Maillard had seen was presented to their eyes, and, though they crowded close together, curiosity got the better of fear, and they followed the Count up to the spot.

The moment Albert of Morseiul had heard the tale, he had formed his own conclusion, and in that conclusion he now found himself right. The body that was tied to the tree was that of the young Marquis de Hericourt: but there were circumstances connected with the act of vengeance thus perpetrated, which rendered it even more awful than he had expected, to the eyes of the Count de Morseiul.

There was no wound whatsoever upon the body, and the unhappy young man had evidently been tied to the tree before his death, for his hands, clenched in agony, were full of the large rugged bark of the elm, which he seemed to have torn off in dying. A strong rope round his middle pressed him tight against the tree. His arms and legs were also bound down to it, so that he could not escape; his hat and upper garments were off, and lying at a few yards' distance; and his shoulders and neck were bare, except where his throat was still pressed by the instrument used for his destruction. That instrument was the usual veil of a novice in a Catholic convent, entirely soaked and dabbled in blood, and twisted tightly up into the form of a rope. It had been wound twice round his neck, and evidently tightened till he had died of strangulation. A piece of paper was nailed upon the tree above his head, so high up, indeed, as to be out of the reach of any one present; but on it was written, in a large bold hand which could easily be read, these words:—

" The punishment inflicted on a murderer of the innocent, by Brown Keroual."

The Count de Morseiul gazed upon the horrible object thus presented to him in deep silence, communing with his own heart; while the magistrates of the town, and the attendants, as is common with inferior minds, felt the awe less deeply, and talked it over with each other, in an under voice.

" This is very horrible, indeed!" said the Count, at length. " I think, before we do anything in the business, as this gentleman was of the Roman-catholic faith, and an officer in the king's service, we had better send down immediately to the Curé of Maubourg, and ask him to come up and receive the body."

The word of the young Count was, of course, law to those who surrounded him, and one of his own attendants having been despatched for the Curé, the good man appeared, with four or five of the villagers, in less than half an hour. His countenance, which was mild and benevolent, was very sad, for he had received from the messenger an account of what had taken place. The young Count, who had some slight personal knowledge of him, and knew him still better by reputation, advanced several steps to meet him, saying—

" This is a dreadful event, Monsieur le Curé; and I have thought it better to send for you rather than move the body of this young gentleman myself, knowing him to have been a Catholic, while all of us here present were of a different faith. Had not life been evidently long extinguished," he continued, " we should not, of course, have scrupled in such a matter; but as it is, we have acted as we have done, in the hopes of meeting your own views upon the subject."

" You have done quite well, and wisely, my son," replied the Curé. " Would to God that all dissensions in the church would cease, as I feel sure they would do, if all men would act as prudently as you have done."

" And as wisely and moderately as *you always do*, Monsieur le Curé," added the Count.

The Curé bowed his head, and advanced towards the tree, where he read the inscription over the head of the murdered man, and then gazed upon the veil that was round his throat.

He shook his head sadly as he did so; and, turning to the Count, he said, " Perhaps you do not know the key of all this sad story. I heard it before I came hither. This morning, an hour before matins, the bell of the religious house of St. Hermand—you know it well, Count, I dare say, a mile or so beyond the *chêne vert* —was rung loudly, and on the portress opening the gate, four men, with their faces covered, carried in the body of one of the novices, called Claire Duval, who had been absent the whole night, causing great alarm. There was a shot-wound in her breast; she was laid out for the grave; and though none of the men spoke a word, but merely placed the body in the lodge, and then retired, a paper was found with it afterwards, saying, 'An innocent girl, murdered by the base De Hericourt, and revenged by Brown Keroual.'—This, of course, I imagine, is the body of him called De Hericourt."

" It is indeed, sir," replied the Count, " the young Marquis de Hericourt, a relation, not very distant, of the Marquis de Louvois; and a brave, but rash, unprincipled, and weak young man he was. In your hands I leave the charge of the body; but any assistance that my servants can give you, or that my influence can procure, is quite at your service."

The Curé thanked him for his offer, but only requested that he would send him down some sort of a litter, or conveyance, to carry the body to the church. The Count immediately promised to do so; and, returning home, he fulfilled his word. He then took some refreshment before his journey, wrote a brief note to the Duc de Rouvré, stating that he would have come over to see him immediately, but was obliged to go to Paris without loss of time; and then mounting his horse, and followed by his attendants, he rode to the first post-house, where taking post-horses, he proceeded at as rapid a pace as possible towards the capital.

CHAPTER XVI.

THE COURT.

WE must once more—following the course of human nature as it is at all times, but more especially as it then was, before all the great asperities of the world were smoothed and softened down, and one universal railroad made life an easy and rapid course from one end to another—We must once more, then, following the common course of being, shift the scene, and bring before our readers a new part of the great panorama of that day. It was then, at the lordly palace of Versailles, in the time of its greatest and most extraordinary splendour, when the treasures of a world had been ransacked to adorn its halls, and art and genius had been called in to do what riches had been unable to accomplish; while yet every chamber throughout the building flamed with those far-famed groups, cast in solid gold, the designs of which had proceeded from the pencil of Le Brun, and the execution of which had employed a thousand of the most skilful hands in France; while yet marble, and porphyry, and jasper, shone in every apartment; and the rarest works, from every quarter of the world, were added to the richness of the other decorations—before, in short, the consequences of his own ambition, or his successor's faults and weaknesses, had stripped one splendid ornament from that extraordinary building which Louis XIV.

had erected in the noon of his splendour—it was then that took place the scenes which we are about now to describe.

The Count de Morseiul had scarcely paused, even to take needful rest, on his way from Poitou to Paris, and he had arrived late at night at the untenanted dwelling of his fathers in the capital. The Counts de Morseiul had ever preferred the country to the town; and though they possessed a large house in the Place Royale —which then was, though it is now so no longer, a fashionable part of the city—that house had become, as it were, merely the dwelling-place of some old officers and attendants, who happened to have a lingering fondness for the busy haunts of men, which their lord shared not in. The old white-headed porter, as he opened the gate for his young master, stared with wonder and surprise to see him there, and nothing, of course, was found prepared for his reception. But the Count was easily satisfied and easily pleased. Food could always be procured without any difficulty, in the great capital of all eating, but repose was what the young Count principally required; and, after having despatched a messenger to Versailles, to ask in due form an audience of the king as early as possible on the following morning, to cast himself on the first bed that could be got ready, and forgot in a few minutes all the cares, and sorrows, and anxieties, which had accompanied him on his way to the capital.

The request for an audience was conveyed through the Marquis of Seignelai, with whom the Count himself was well acquainted; and he doubted not that it would be granted immediately, if he had preceded, as he had every reason to believe he had, the ordinary courier from Poitou, bringing the news of the events which had taken place in that province. The letter of the young secretary, in return to his application, arrived the next morning; but it was cold and formal, and evidently written under the immediate dictation of the king. It merely notified to the Count that, for the next three days, the time appointed by his majesty for business would be fully occupied; that, in the meantime, if the affairs which brought the Count to Paris were important, he would communicate them to the minister under whose department they came. The note went on to add, that if the business were not one requiring immediate despatch, the young Couht would do well to come to Versailles, to signify the place of his abode at the palace, and to wait the monarch's leisure.

This was by no means the tone which Louis usually assumed towards one of the most gallant officers in his service; and, while the Count at once perceived that the king was offended with him on some account, he felt great difficulty in so shaping his conduct as to meet the exigency of the moment. As the only resource, he determined to see and interest Seignelai to obtain for him a more speedy audience; and he had the greater hopes of so doing, inasmuch as that minister was known to be jealous of, and inimical to, Louvois, one of the great persecutors of the Protestants.

While he was pondering over these things, and preparing to set out immediately for Versailles, another courier from the court arrived, bearing with him a communication of a very different character, which, upon the whole, surprised the Count, even more than the former one had done. It contained a general invitation to all the evening entertainments of the court; specifying not only those to which the great mass of the French nobility were admitted as a matter of course, but the more private and select parties of the king, to which none in general but his own especial friends and favourites were ever invited.

This event gave Albert of Morseiul fresh matter for meditation, but also some hope that the king, whom he believed to be generous and kind-hearted, had remembered the services he and his ancestors had rendered to the state, and had consequently made an effort to overcome any feeling of displeasure which he might have entertained in consequence of reports from Poitiers. He determined, however, to pursue his plan with regard to Seignelai, believing that it would be facilitated, rather than otherwise, by any change of feeling which had come over the monarch; and he accordingly proceeded to Versailles at once.

The secretary of state was not to be found in his apartments, but one of his attendants informed the Count that, at that hour, he would find him alone in the gardens, and he accordingly proceeded to seek him with all speed. As he passed by the orangery, however, he heard the sound of steps and gay voices speaking, and, in a moment after, stood in the presence of the King himself, who had passed through the orangery, and was now issuing forth into the gardens.

Louis was at this time a man of the middle age, above the ordinary height, and finely proportioned in all his limbs. Though he still looked decidedly younger than he really was, and the age of forty was perhaps as much as any one would have assigned him, judging from appearance, yet he had lost all the slightness of the youthful figure. He was robust, and even stout, though by no means corpulent, and the ease and grace with which he moved showed that no power was impaired. His countenance was fine and impressive, though, perhaps, it might not have afforded, to a very scrutinizing physiognomist, any indication of the highest qualities of the human mind. All the features were good, some remarkably handsome, but in most there was some peculiar defect, some slight want which took away from the effect of the whole. The expression was placable, but commanding, and grave rather than thoughtful; and the impression produced by its aspect was, that it was serious, less from natural disposition or intense occupation of mind, than from the consciousness that it was a condescension for that countenance to smile. The monarch's carriage, as he walked, also produced an effect somewhat similar on those who saw him for the first time. Every step was dignified, stately, and graceful; but there was something a little theatrical in the whole, joined with, or perhaps expressing, a knowledge that every step was marked and of importance.

The King's dress was exceedingly rich and costly; and certainly, though bad taste in costume was then at its height, the monarch and the group that came close upon his steps, formed as glittering and gay an object as could be seen.

Amongst those who followed the King, however, were several ecclesiastics, and to the surprise of the young Count de Morseiul, one of those on whom his eye first fell was no other than the Abbé Pelisson, in eager but low conversation with the Bishop of Meaux. Louis himself was speaking in a familiar tone, alternately to the Prince de Marsillac, and to the well-known financier Bechameil, whose exquisite taste in pictures, statues, and other works of art, recommended him greatly to the monarch.

No sooner did the King's look rest upon the young Count de Morseiul, than his brow became as dark as a thunder-cloud; and he stopped suddenly in his walk. Scarcely had the Count time to remark that angry expression, however, before it had entirely passed away, and a grave and dignified smile succeeded. It was a common remark, at that time, that the King was to be judged by those who sought him, from his first aspect, and certainly, if that were the test in the present instance, his affection for the Count de Morseiul was but small.

Louis was conscious that he had displayed bad feelings more openly than he usually permitted himself to do; and he now hastened to repair that fault, not by affecting the direct contrary sentiments, as some might have done, but by softening down his tone and demeanour to the degree of dignified disapprobation, which they might naturally be supposed to have reached.

"Monsieur de Morseiul," he said, as the young nobleman approached, "I am glad, yet sorry to see you. Various reports have reached me from Poitou, tending to create a belief that you have been, in some degree, wanting in due respect to my will; and I should have been glad that the falsehood of those reports had been proved before you again presented yourself. Your services, sir, however, are not forgotten, and you have, on so many occasions, shown devotion, obedience, and gallantry, which might well set an example to the whole world, that I cannot believe there is any truth in what I have heard, and am willing, unless a painful conviction to the contrary is forced upon me, to look upon you, till the whole of this matter be fully investigated, in the same light as ever."

The King paused for a moment, as if for reply; and the Count de Morseiul gladly seized the opportunity of saying, "I came up post, sire, last night, from Morseiul, for the purpose of casting myself at your majesty's feet, and entreating you to believe that I would never willingly give you the slightest just cause for offence, in word,

thought, or deed. I apprehended that some false or distorted statements, either made for the purpose of deceiving your majesty, or
originating in erroneous impressions, might have reached you concerning my conduct, as I know misapprehensions of my conduct
had occurred in Poitiers itself. Such being the case, and various
very painful events having taken place, I felt it my duty to beseech
your majesty to grant me an audience, in order that I might lay
before you the pure and simple facts, which I am ready to vouch
for on the honour of a French gentleman. I am most desirous, especially with regard to the latter events which have taken place,
that your majesty should be at once made aware of the facts as they
really occurred, lest any misrepresentations should reach your ears,
and prepare your mind to take an unfavourable view of acts which
were performed in all loyalty, and with the most devoted affection
to your majesty's person."

The young Count spoke with calm and dignified boldness.
There was no hesitation, there was no wavering, there was no apprehension, either in tone, manner, or words; and there was something in his whole demeanour which set at defiance the very thought
of there being the slightest approach to falsehood or artifice in his
nature. The King felt that it was so himself, notwithstanding many
prejudices on all the questions which could arise between the Count
and himself. But his line of conduct, by this time, had been fully
determined, and he replied, " As I caused you to be informed this
morning, Monsieur de Morseiul, my arrangements do not permit
me to give you so much time as will be necessary for the hearing
of all you have to say for several days. In the meanwhile, however, fear not that your cause will be, in any degree, prejudged.
We have already, by a courier arrived this morning, received full
intelligence of all that has lately taken place in Poitou, and of the
movements of some of our misguided subjects of the pretended reformed religion. We have ordered accurate information to be obtained upon the spot, by persons who cannot be considered as
prejudiced, and we will give you audience as soon as such information has been fully collected. In the meantime you will remain at
the court, and be treated here, in every respect, as a favoured and
faithful servant, which will show you that no unjust prejudice has
been created; though it is not to be denied that the first effect of
the tidings we received from Poitou was to excite considerable anger
against you. However, you owe a good deal, in those respects, to
Monsieur Pelisson, who bore witness to your having gallantly
defended his life from a party of robbers, and to your having
saved from the flames a commission under our hand, although that
commission was afterwards unaccountably abstracted. I hope to
hear," the King continued, " of your frequenting much the society
of Monsieur Pelisson, and our respected and revered friend, the
Bishop of Meaux, by which you may doubtless derive great advantage, and perhaps arrive at those happy results which would make

it our duty, as well as our pleasure, to favour you in the very highest degree."

The meaning of Louis was too evident to be mistaken; and, as the Count de Morseiul had not the slightest intention of encouraging even a hope that he would abandon the creed of his ancestors, he merely bowed in reply, and the King passed on. The Count was then about to retire immediately from the gardens, but Pelisson caught him by the sleeve as he passed, saying, in a low voice—

"Come on, Monsieur de Morseiul, come on after the King. Believe me, I really wish you well; and it is of much consequence that you should show, not only your attachment to his majesty, by presenting yourself constantly at the court, but also that you are entering into none of the intrigues of those who are irritating him by opposition and cabals. You know Monsieur Bossuet, of course? Let us come on."

"I only know Monsieur Bossuet by reputation," replied the Count, bowing to the Bishop, who had paused also, and at the same time turning to follow the royal train. "I only know him by reputation, as who, throughout France, nay, throughout Europe, does not?"

"The compliment will pass for Catholic, though it comes from a Protestant mouth," said one of two gentlemen who had been obliged to pause also by the halt of the party before them. Neither Bossuet nor the Count, however, took any notice, but walked on, entering easily into conversation with each other; the eloquent prelate, who was not less keen and dexterous than he was zealous and learned, accommodating himself easily to the tone of the young Protestant nobleman.

Pelisson, ere they had gone far, showed himself inclined to draw the conversation to religious subjects, and was a little anxious to prove to the Count de Morseiul that, at the bottom, there was very little real difference between the Catholic and the Protestant faith, from which starting-point he intended to argue, as was his common custom, that as there was so little difference, and as in all the points of difference that did exist the Catholics were in the right, it was a bounden duty for every Protestant to renounce his heretical doctrines, and embrace the true religion.

Bossuet, however, was much more politic, and resisted all Pelisson's efforts to introduce such topics, by cutting across them immediately and turning the conversation to something less evidently applicable to the Count de Morseiul. Something was said upon the subject of Jansenism, indeed, as they walked along; and Bossuet replied, smiling—

"Heaven forbid that those discussions should be renewed! I abhor controversy, and always avoid it, except when driven to it. I am anxious, indeed, most anxious, that all men should see and renounce errors, and especially anxious, as I am in duty bound, when those errors are of such a nature as to affect their eternal salvation. But very little good, I doubt, has ever been done by controversy, though certainly still less by persecution ; and if we were to choose between those two means, controversy would of course be the best. Unfortunately, however, it seldom ends but as a step to the other."

There was something so moderate and so mild in the language of the prelate, that the young Count soon learned to take great pleasure in his discourse; and after these few brief words concerning religion, the Bishop drew the conversation to arts and sciences, and the great improvements of every kind which had taken place in France under the government of Louis XIV.

They were still speaking on the subject when the King turned at the end of the terrace, and with surprise saw the Count de Morseiul in his train, between Pelisson and Bossuet. A smile of what appeared to be dignified satisfaction came over the monarch's countenance, and as he passed he asked—

" What are you discussing so eagerly, Monsieur de Meaux ?"

" We are not discussing, sire," replied the Bishop, " for we are all of one opinion. Monsieur de Morseiul was saying, that in all his knowledge of history—which we are aware is very great—he cannot find one monarch whose reign has produced so great a change in society as that of Louis the Great."

The King smiled graciously, and passed on. But the same sarcastic personage, who followed close behind the party to which the Count had attached himself, added to Bossuet's speech, almost loud enough for the King to hear, " Except Mahomet ! Except Mahomet, Monsieur de Meaux !"

It was impossible either for the Bishop, or the Count, or Pelisson, to repress a smile ; but the only one of the party who turned to look was the Count, the others very well knowing the voice to be that of Villiers, whose strange method of paying court to Louis XIV. was by abusing everything on which the monarch prided himself. He was slightly acquainted with the Count de Morseiul, having met him more than once on service, and seeing him turn his head, he came up and joined them.

" You spoil that man, all of you," he said, speaking of the King. " All the world flatters him, till he does not know what is right and what is wrong, what is good and what is bad, what is beautiful and what is ugly. Now, as we stand here upon this terrace," he continued, " and look down over those gardens, is there anything to be seen on the face of the earth more thoroughly and completely disgusting than they are ? Is it possible for human ingenuity to devise anything so mathematically detestable ? One would suppose that La Hire, or Cassini, or some of the other clockmakers, had been engaged with their villanous compasses in marking out all those rounds, and triangles, and squares, so that the whole park and gardens, when seen from my little room, (which the King in his immense generosity gave me in the garret story of the palace,) look exactly like a dusty leaf torn out of Euclid's Elements, with all the problems demonstrated upon it. Then, Monsieur de Morseiul, do pray look at those basins and statues. Here you have a set of black tadpoles croaking at an unfortunate woman in the midst, as black as themselves. There you have a striking represention of Neptune gone mad—perhaps it was meant for a storm at sea; and certainly, from the number of people death-sick all round, and pouring forth from their mouths into the basins, one might very easily conceive it to be so. There is not one better than another; and yet the King walks about amongst them all, and thinks it the finest thing that ever was seen upon the face of the earth, and has at this moment five-and-twenty thousand men working hard, to render it, if possible, uglier than before."

The Count de Morseiul laughed, and, although he acknowledged that he loved the fair face of the country, unshaven and unornamented, better than all that art could do, yet he said, that for the gardens of such a palace as that of Versailles, where solemn and reposing grandeur was required, and regular magnificence more than picturesque beauty, he did not see that better could have been done.

Thus passed the conversation, till the King, after having taken another turn, re-entered the building, and his courtiers quitted him at the foot of the staircase. The Count then inquired of Pelisson where he could best lodge in Versailles, and the Abbé pointed out to him a handsome house, very near that in which the Bishop of Meaux had taken up his abode for the time.

"Do you intend to come speedily to Versailles?" demanded the Bishop.

"As I understood the King," replied the Count, "it is his pleasure that I should do so; and consequently I shall merely go back to Paris to make my arrangements, and then return hither with all speed. I propose to be back by seven or eight o'clock this evening, if this house is still to be had."

"For that I can answer," replied the Bishop. "The only disagreeable thing you will find here, is a want of food," he added, "for the palace swallows up all; but if you will honour me by supping with me to-night, Monsieur le Comte, perhaps Monsieur Pelisson will join us, with one or two others, and we may spend a calm and pleasant evening, in talking over such things as chance or choice may select. We do so often in my poor abode. But indeed I forgot; perhaps you may prefer going to the theatre at the palace, for this is one of the nights when a play is performed there."

"No, indeed," replied the Count. "I hold myself not only flattered, but obliged, by your invitation, Monsieur de Meaux, and I will not fail to be with you at any hour you appoint."

The hour was accordingly named; and, taking his leave, the young Count de Morseiul sought his horses, and returned to Paris. His visit to Versailles, indeed, had not been so satisfactory as he could have wished; and while Jerome Riquet was making all the preparations for his master's change of abode, the Count himself leaned his head upon his hand, and revolved in deep thought all the bearings of his present situation.

No one knew better than he did, that appearances are but little to be trusted at any court, and as little as in any other, at the court of Louis XIV. He knew that the next word from the King's mouth might be an order to conduct him to the Bastille, and that very slight proofs of guilt would be required to change his adherence to his religion, if not into a capital crime, at least into a pretext for dooming him to perpetual imprisonment. He saw, also, though perhaps not to the full extent of the King's design, that Louis entertained some hopes of his abandoning his religion ; and he doubted not that various efforts would be employed to induce him to do so—efforts difficult to be parried, painful to him to be the object of, and which might, perhaps, afford matter for deep offence if they proved ineffectual.

He knew, too, that it was decidedly the resolution of the King and of his advisers to put down altogether the Protestant religion in France ; that there was no hope, that there was no chance of mitigating, in any degree, the unchangeable spirit of intolerance.

All these considerations urged the young Count to pursue a plan which had suggested itself at first to his mind, rather as the effect of despair than of calculation. It was to go back no more to Versailles ; to return post-haste to Poitou ; to collect with all speed the principal Protestants who might be affected by any harsh measures of the court ; to demand of Clémence de Marly the fulfilment of her promise to fly with him ; and, embarking with the rest at the nearest port, to seek safety and peace in another land.

The more he thought over this design the more he was inclined to adopt it ; for although he evidently saw that tidings of what had taken place at the preaching in the desert had already reached the King's ears, and that the first effect was passed, yet he could not rely by any means upon the sincerity of the demeanour assumed towards him, and believed that even though he — if his military services were required—might be spared, from political considerations, yet the great majority of the Protestants in his neighbourhood might be visited with severe inflictions, on account of the part they had taken in the transactions of that day.

One consideration alone tended to make him pause ere he executed this purpose, which was, that having undertaken a task, he was bound to execute it, and not to shrink from it while it was half completed ; and, anxious to do what he considered right in all things, he feared that, by flying, he might but be able to protect a few, while by remaining he might stand between many and destruction.

In this world we ponder and consider, and give time, and care, and anxiety, and thought to meditation over different lines of conduct, while calm, imperturbable Fate stands by till the appointed moment, and then, without inquiring the result, decides the matter for us. The Count had sent a servant immediately after his return from Versailles to the house of Marshal Schomberg, to ask if that officer were in Paris, and if so, at what hour he would be visible. The servant returned, bringing word that Marshal Schomberg had quitted the country, that his house and effects had been sold, and that it was generally supposed he never intended to return.

This was an example of the prompt execution of a resolution, which might well have induced the Count de Morseiul to follow it, especially as it showed Schomberg's opinion to be, that the affairs of the Protestants in France were utterly irretrievable, and that the danger to those who remained was imminent. Thus was another weight cast into the scale; but even while he was rising from the table at which he sat, in order to give directions to prepare for a still longer journey than that which he had notified to his servants before, Jerome Riquet entered the room, and placed before him a note, written in a hand with which he was not at all acquainted.

"You have thought much of my conduct strange, Albert—" it began; and turning at once to the other page, he saw the name of Clémence. "You have thought much of my conduct strange; and now will you not think it still stranger, when I tell you that I have but two moments to write to you, and not even a moment to see you? I looked forward to to-morrow with hope and expectation; and now I suddenly learn that we are to set off within an hour for Paris. The order has been received from the King: the Duke will not make a moment's delay. For me to stay here alone, is, of course, impossible; and I am obliged to leave Poitou without seeing you, without the possibility even of receiving an answer. Pray write to me immediately in Paris. Tell me that you forgive me for an involuntary fault; tell me that you forgive me for anything I may have done to pain you. I say so, because your last look seemed to be reproachful; and yet, believe me, when I assure you, upon my honour, that I could not but act as I have acted.

"Oh, Albert! if I could but see you in Paris—I, who used to be so bold, I, who used to be so fearless, now feel as if I were going into a strange world, where there is need of protection, and guidance, and direction. It seems as if I had given up all control over myself; and if you were near me, if you were in Paris, I should have greater confidence, I should have greater courage, I should have more power to act, to speak, even to think rightly, than I have at present. Come, then, if it be possible—come, then, if it be right; and if not, at all events write to me soon—write to me immediately.

"May I,—yes I may, for I feel it is true—call myself

"Your CLÉMENCE."

The letter was dated on the very day that the Count himself had set off, and had evidently been sent over to the château of Morseiul shortly after his departure. Maitre Riquet had contrived to linger in the room on one pretext or another while his master read the note, and the Count, turning towards him, demanded eagerly how it had come, and who had brought it.

"Why, monseigneur," said Riquet, "the truth is, I always love to have a little information. In going through life, I have found it like a snuff-box, which one should always carry; even if one does not take snuff one's self: it is so useful for one's friends!"

"Come, come, sir, to the point!" exclaimed his master. "How did this letter arrive? that is the question."

"Just what I was going to tell you, my lord," replied the man. "I left behind me Pierre Martin, to gather together a few stray things which I could not carry with me, and a few stray pieces of information which I could not learn myself, and to bring them after us to Paris with all speed; old doublets, black silk stockings, bottles of essence, cases of razors, true information regarding all the reports in the province of Poitou, and whatever letters might have arrived between our going and his coming."

"In the latter instance," said the Count, "you have acted wisely, and more thoughtfully than myself. I do believe, Riquet, as you once said of yourself, you never forget anything that is necessary."

"You do me barely justice, sir," answered the valet, "for I remember always a great deal more than is necessary; so, seeing that the letter was in a lady's hand, I brought it you, my lord, at once, without even waiting to look in at the end; which, perhaps, was imprudent, as very likely now I shall never be able to ascertain the contents."

"You are certainly not without your share of impudence, Maitre Jerome," replied his master; "which I suppose you would say is amongst your other good qualities. But now leave me; for I must think over this letter."

Riquet prepared to obey; but as he opened the door for his own exit, he drew two or three steps back, throwing it much wider, and giving admission to the Prince de Marsillac. The appearance of that nobleman did not by any means surprise the Count, for although he had seen him that very morning at Versailles, he had obtained not a moment to speak with him; and, as an old friend, it was natural that, if anything brought the Prince to Paris, he should call at the Hôtel de Morseiul, to talk over all that had taken place since their last meeting at Poitiers.

"My dear Count," he said, "understanding from Monsieur de Meaux that you return to Versailles to-night, I have come to offer you a place down in my carriage, or to take a place in yours, that we may have a long chat over the scenes at Poitiers, and over the prospects of this good land of ours."

"Willingly," said the Count. "I have no carriage with me, but I will willingly accompany you in yours. What time do you go?"

"As soon as you will," replied the Prince. "I am ready to set out directly. I have finished all that I had to do in Paris, and return at once."

The Count paused for a moment to calculate in his own mind whether it were possible that the Duc de Rouvré could reach Paris that night. Considering, however, the slow rate at which he must necessarily travel, accompanied by all his family, Albert of Morseiul saw that one, if not two days more, must elapse before his arrival.

" Well," he said, having by this time determined at all events to pause in the neighbourhood of the capital till after he had seen Clémence—" Well, as I have not dined, old friend, I will go through that necessary ceremony, against which my man Riquet has doubtless prepared ; and then I will be ready to accompany you."

" Nor have I dined either," replied the Prince; " so if you will give a knife and fork to one you justly call an old friend, I will dine with you, and we will send for the carriage in the meanwhile."

There was something in the Prince's tone and manner difficult to describe or to explain, which struck the Count as extraordinary. The calmest, the coolest, the most self-possessed man in France was a little embarrassed. But the Count made no remark, merely looking for a moment in his face—somewhat steadfastly, indeed, and in such a manner that the other turned to the window, saying, in a careless tone, " It was under those trees, I think, that the Duke of Guise killed Coligny."

The Count made no reply, but called some of his attendants, and bade them see what had been provided for dinner. In a few minutes it was announced as ready, and he sat down with his friend to table, doing the honours with perfect politeness and cheerfulness. Before the meal was concluded, it was announced that the Prince's carriage and servants had arrived, and, when all was ready, the Count de Morseiul proposed that they should depart, leaving his attendants to follow. Just as he had his foot upon the step of the carriage, however, the Count turned to his companion, and said, " You have forgot, my good friend, to tell the coachman whether he is to drive to the Bastille, or Vincennes, or to Versailles."

" You mistake," said the Prince, following him into the carriage : " To Versailles, of course. I will explain to you the whole matter as we go.—Within ten minutes after you left Versailles this morning," he continued, as soon as they were once fully on the way, " I was sent for to the King about something referring to my post of Grand Veneur. I found Louvois with him in one of his furious and insolent moods, and the King bearing all with the utmost patience. It soon became apparent that the conversation referred to you, Louvois contending that you should never have been suffered to quit Versailles till some affairs which have taken place in Poitou were fully examined, declaring that you had only gone to Paris in order to make your escape from the country more conveniently. The King asked me my opinion ; and I laughed at the idea to Louvois' face. He replied that I did not know all, or half indeed, for that if I did, I should not feel nearly so certain. I said I knew you better; and, to settle the matter at once, I added that, as I was going to Paris, I would undertake you came back with me in my carriage, or I in yours. The King trusted me, as you see; and I thought it a great deal better to come in this manner as a friend, than to let Louvois send you a *lettre de cachet*, which you might even find a more tiresome companion than the Prince de Marsillac."

" Undoubtedly, I should," replied the Count, " and I thank you much for the interest you have taken in the affair, as well as for the candour of the confession. But now, my friend, since you have gone so far, go a little farther, and give me some insight, if you can, into what is taking place at the court just at present—I mean in reference to myself—for my situation is, as you may suppose, not the most pleasant; and is one in which a map of the country may be serviceable to me. I see none of my old friends about the court at present except yourself. Seignelai I have not been able to find——"

" And he would give you no information, even if you did find him," replied the Prince. " I can give you but very little, for I know but little. In the first place, however, let me tell you a great secret; that you are strongly suspected of being a Protestant."

" Indeed," replied the Count; " I fear they have more than sus-picion against me there."

" Confess it not," said his friend, " confess it not! for just at present it would be much more safe to confess high treason; but, in the next place, my dear Count, a report has gone abroad—quite false, I know—that you are desperately in love with this fair Clémence de Marly."

" And pray," demanded the Count, smiling, " in what manner would that affect me at the court, even were it true ?"

" Why, now, to answer seriously," replied his friend, " though, remember, I speak only from the authority of my own imagination, I should say, that you are very likely to obtain her, with every sort of honour and distinction to boot, in spite of Hericourt and the Chevalier d'Evran, and all the rest—upon one small condition; which is, that you take a morning's walk into the Church of St. Laurent, or any other that may be more pleasant to you; stay about half an hour, read a set form, which means little or nothing, and go through some other ceremonies of the same kind."

" In fact," said the Count, " make my renunciation in form, you mean to say."

The Prince nodded his head; and Albert of Morseiul fell into thought, well knowing that his friend was himself ignorant of one of the most important points of the whole affair; namely, the faith of Clémence de Marly herself. On that subject, of course, he did not choose to say anything; but after remaining in meditation for a few moments, he demanded—

" And pray, Marsillac, what is to be the result, if I do not choose to make this renunciation ?"

" Heaven only knows," replied the Prince. " There are, at least, six or seven different sorts of fate that may befal you. Probably the choice will be left to yourself; whether you will have your head struck off in a gentlemanly way in the court of the Bastille, or be broken on the wheel; though I believe that process they are keeping for the Huguenot priests now—ministers, as you call them. If the King should be exceedingly merciful, the castle of Pignerol, or the prison in the isle St. Marguerite, may afford you a comfortable little solitary dwelling for the rest of your life. I don't think it likely that he should send you to the galleys, though I am told they are pretty full of military men now. But if I were you, I would choose the axe; it is soonest over."

" I think I should prefer a bullet," said the Count; " but we shall see, my good friend, though I can't help thinking your antici- pations are somewhat more sanguinary than just. I hear that Schomberg has taken his departure, and it must have been with the King's permission. Why should it not be the same in my case ? I have served the King as well, though, perhaps, not quite so long."

" But you are a born subject of France," replied the other; " Schomberg is not ; and, besides, Schomberg has given no offence, except remaining faithful to his religion. You have been heading preaching in the open fields, they say, if not preaching yourself."

" Certainly not the last," exclaimed the Count.

" Indeed !" said his friend ; " they have manufactured a story, then, of your having addressed the people before any one else."

" Good God !" cried the Count; " is it possible that men can pervert one's actions in such a manner? I merely besought the people to be orderly and tranquil, and added a hope that they had come unarmed as I had come."

" It would seem that a number of you were armed, however," observed the Prince, " for some of the dragoons were killed, it would appear ; and, on my word, you owe a good deal to Pelisson ; for if Louvois had obtained his way this morning, as usual, your head would have been in no slight danger. The Abbé stepped in, however, and said, that he had seen much of you in Poitou, and that from all he had heard and seen, his majesty had not a more faithful or obedient subject in those parts."

" I am certainly very much obliged to him," replied the Count. " But he has strangely altered his tone ; for at Poitiers he would fain have proved me guilty of all sorts of acts that I never com- mitted."

" Perhaps he may have had cause to change," said the Prince de Marsillac. " It is known that he and St. Helie quarrelled violently before Pelisson's return. But at all events, your great security is in the fact, that there are two factions in the party who are engaged in putting down your sect. The one would do it by gentle means —bribery, corruption, persuasion, and the soft stringents of exclusion from place, rank, and emolument. The other breathes nothing but fire and blood, the destruction of rebels to the royal will, and the most signal punishment for all who differ in opinion from themselves. This last party would fain persuade the King that the Huguenots are in arms, or ready to take arms, throughout France, and that nothing is to be done but to send down armies to subdue them. But then the others come in, and say, ' It is no such thing; the people are all quiet; they are submitting with a good grace, and if you do not drive them to despair, they will gradually return, one by one, to the bosom of the mother church, rather than endure all sorts of discomfort and disgrace !' Of this party are Pelisson, the good Bishop, and many other influential people ; but, above all, Madame de Maintenon, whose power, in everything but this, is supreme."

" Had I not better see her," demanded the Count, " and endeavour to interest her in our favour ?"

" She dare not for her life receive you," replied the Prince. " What is religion, or humanity, or generosity, or anything else, to her, if it stand in the way of ambition ? No, no, Morseiul ! the good lady may perhaps speak a kind word for you in secret, and when it can be put in the form of an insinuation; but she is no Madame de Montespan, who would have defended the innocent, and thrust herself in the way to prevent injustice, even if the blow had fallen upon herself. She dared to say to the King things that no other mortal dared, and would say them, too, when her heart or her understanding was convinced; but Madame de Maintenon creeps towards the crown, and dares not do a good action if it be a dangerous one. Do not attempt to see her, for she would certainly refuse ; and if she thought that the very application had reached the King's ears, she would urge him to do something violent, merely to show him that she had nothing to do with you."

" She has had much to do with me and mine," replied the Count, somewhat bitterly; " for, to my father, she and her mother owed support, when none else would give it."

" She owed her bread to Madame de Montespan," replied the Prince, " and yet ceased not her efforts till she had supplanted her.—But," he added, after a pause, " she is not altogether bad, either, and it is not improbable, that if there be any scheme going on for converting you by milder means than the wheel, as I believe there is, she may be the deviser of it. She was in the room this morning when the business was taking place between the King, Louvois, and Pelisson. She said nothing, but sat working at a distance, the very counterpart of a pie-bald cat that sat dozing in the corner; but she heard all, and I remarked that, when the affair was settled, and other things began, she beckoned Pelisson to look at her embroidery, and spoke to him for some minutes, in a low voice.

" Morseiul, may I advise you?" the Prince continued, after a brief interval had taken place in the conversation; " listen to me but one word! I know well that there is no chance of your changing your religion, except upon conviction. Do not, however, enact the old Roman, or court too much the fate of martyrdom; but without taking any active step in the matter, let the whole plans of these good folks, as far as they affect yourself, go on unopposed: let them, in short, still believe that it is not impossible to convert you. Listen to Pelisson—pay attention to Bossuet—watch the progress of events—be converted if you can; and if not, you, at all events, will gain opportunities of retiring from the country, with far greater ease and safety than at present, if you should be driven to such a step at last. In the meantime, this affair of the preaching will have blown over, and they will not dare to revive it against you, if they let it slumber for some time. Think of it, Morseiul!—think of it!"

" I will," replied the Count, " and thank you sincerely; and, indeed, will do all that may be done with honour, not to offend the King or endanger myself." And thus the conversation ended on that subject; the Prince having said already far more than might have been expected from a courtier of Louis XIV.

CHAPTER XVII.

THE CLOUDS AND THE SUNSHINE.

THE Count de Morseiul had just time to take possession of his new abode, and make himself tolerably at his ease therein, before the hour arrived for proceeding to the house of the Bishop of Meaux, where he was received by the prelate with every sort of kindness.

He arrived before anybody else; and Bossuet took him by the hand, saying, with a smile, " Some of our good clergy, Monsieur de Morseiul, would perhaps be scandalized at receiving in their house so distinguished a Protestant as yourself; but I trust, you know, what I have always endeavoured to prove, that I look upon all denominations of Christians as my brethren, and am only perhaps sometimes a little eager with them, out of what very likely you consider an *over-anxiety*, to induce them to embrace those doctrines which I think necessary to their salvation. Should it ever be so between you and me, Monsieur le Comte, will you forgive me?"

" Willingly," replied the Count, thinking that the work of conversion was about to begin; but, to his surprise, Bossuet immediately changed the conversation, and turned it to the subject of the little party he had invited to meet the Count.

" I have not," he said, " made it, as indeed I usually do, almost entirely of churchmen; for I feared you might think that I intended to overwhelm you under ecclesiastical authority. However, we have some belonging to the church, whom you will be glad to meet, if you do not know them already. The Abbé Renaudot will be here, who has a peculiar faculty for acquiring languages, such as I never knew in any one but himself. He understands no less than seventeen foreign tongues, and twelve of those he speaks with the greatest facility. That, however, is one of his least qualities, as you may yourself judge when I tell you, that in this age, where interest and ambition swallow up everything, he is the most disinterested man, perhaps, that ever lived. Possessed of one very small, poor benefice, which gives him a scanty subsistence, he has constantly refused every other preferment; and no persuasion will induce him to do what he terms, ' encumber himself with wealth.' We shall also have La Broue, with whose virtues and good qualities you are already acquainted. D'Herbelot also wrote yesterday to invite himself. He has just returned from Italy, where that reverence was shown to him, which generous and expansive minds are always ready to display towards men of genius and of learning. He was received by the Grand Duke at Florence, and treated like a sovereign prince, though merely a poor French scholar. A house was prepared for him, the secretary of state met him, and, as a parting present, a valuable library of oriental manuscripts was bestowed upon him by the duke himself. To these grave people we have joined our lively friend Pelisson, and one whom, doubtless, you know, Boileau Despréaux. One cannot help loving him, and being amused with him, although we are forced to acknowledge that his sarcasm and his bitterness go a good deal too far. When he was a youth, they tell me, he was the best-tempered boy in the world, and his father used to say of him, that all his other children had some sharpness and some talent, but that, as for Nicholas, he was a good-natured lad, who would never speak ill of any one. One thing, however, I must tell you to his honour. He obtained some time ago, as I lament to say has frequently been done, a benefice in the church without being an ecclesiastic. The revenues of the benefice he spent, in those his young days, in lightness, if not in vice. He has since changed his conduct and his views, and, not long ago, not only resigned the benefice, but paid back from his own purse all that he had received, to be spent in acts of charity amongst the deserving of the neighbourhood. This merits particular notice and record."

Bossuet was going on to mention several others who were likely to join their party, when two of those whom he had named arrived, and the others shortly after made their appearance. The evening passed, as such an evening may well be supposed to have passed, at the dwelling of the famous Bishop of Meaux. It was cheerful, though not gay; and subjects of deep and important interest were mingled with, and enlivened by, many a light and lively sally, confined within the bounds of strict propriety, but none the less brilliant or amusing, for it is only weak and narrow intellects that are forced to fly to themes painful, injurious, or offensive, in order to seek materials with which to found a reputation for wit or talent.

The only matter, however, which was mentioned affecting at all the course of our present tale, and, therefore, the only one on which we shall pause, was discussed between Pelisson and the Abbé Renaudot, while the Count de Morseiul was standing close by them, speaking for a moment with D'Herbelot.

" Is there any news stirring at the court, Monsieur Pelisson?" said Renaudot. " You hear everything, and I hear nothing of what is going on there."

" Why, there is nothing of any consequence, I believe," said Pelisson, in a loud voice. " The only thing now I hear of is, that Mademoiselle Marly is going to be married, at length."

" What, La belle Clémence !" cried Renaudot. " Who is the man that has touched her hard heart, at length?"

" Oh, an old lover," said Pelisson. " Perseverance has carried the day. The Chevalier d'Evran is the man. The King gave his consent some few days ago, the Chevalier having come up express from Poitou to ask it."

Every word reached the ear of the Count de Morseiul, and his mind reverted instantly to the conduct of the Chevalier and Clémence, and to the letter which he had received from her. As any man in love would do, under such circumstances, he resolved not to believe a word; but, as most men in love would feel, he certainly felt himself not a little uneasy, not a little agitated, not a little pained, even by the report. Unwilling, however, to hear any more, he walked to the other end of the room to take his leave, as it was now late.

Pelisson looked after him as he went, and seeing him bid Bossuet adieu, he followed his example, and accompanied the young Count down the stairs and throughout the few steps he had to take ere he reached his own dwelling. No word, however, was spoken by either regarding Clémence de Marly; and Albert of Morseiul retired at once, though certainly not to sleep. He revolved in his mind again and again the probability of Pelisson's story having any truth in it. He knew Clémence, and he knew the Chevalier, and he felt sure that he could trust them both; but that trust was all that he had to oppose to the very great likelihood which there existed, that the King, as he so frequently did, would take the arrangement of a marriage for Clémence de Marly into his own hands, without in the slightest degree consulting her inclination, or the inclination of any one concerned.

The prospect now presented to the mind of Albert of Morseiul was in the highest degree painful. Fresh difficulties, fresh dangers, were added to the many which were already likely to overwhelm him, if even, as he trusted she would, Clémence held firm by her plighted troth to him, and resisted, what was then so hard to resist in France, the absolute will of the King. Still this new incident would only serve to show that instant flight was more absolutely necessary than before, would render any return to France utterly impossible, and would increase the danger and difficulty of executing that flight itself. But a question suggested itself to the Count's mind, which, though he answered it in the affirmative, left anxiety and doubt behind it. Would Clémence de Marly resist the will of the King? Could she do so? So many were the means to be employed to lead or drive her to obedience, so much might be done by dragging her on from step to step, that bitter, very bitter anxiety took possession of her lover's heart. He persuaded himself that it was pain and anxiety on her account alone; but still he loved her too well, too truly, not to feel pained and anxious for himself.

On the following morning, as soon as he had breakfasted, he wrote a brief note to Clémence, telling her that he was at Versailles, was most anxious to see her and converse with her, if it were but for a few minutes, and beseeching her to let him know immediately where he could do so speedily, as he had matters of very great importance to communicate to her at once. The letter was tender and affectionate ; but still there was that in it, which might show the keen eyes of love that there was some great doubt and uneasiness pressing on the mind of the writer.

As soon as the letter was written, he gave it into the hands of Jerome Riquet, directing him to carry it to Paris, to wait there for the arrival of the family of de Rouvré, if they had not yet come, and to find means to give it to Maria, the attendant of Mademoiselle de Marly. He was too well aware of Riquet's talents not to be quite sure that this commission would be executed in the best manner; and after his departure he strove to keep his mind as quiet as possible, and occupied himself in writing to his intendant at Morseiul, conveying orders for his principal attendants to come up to join him at Versailles directly, bringing with them a great variety of different things which were needful to him, but which had been left behind in the hurry of his departure. While he was writing, he was again visited by the Prince de Marsillac, who came in kindly to tell him that the report of Pelisson, who had passed the preceding evening with him, seemed to be operating highly in his favour at court.

" I am delighted," he said, " that the good Abbé has had the first word, for St. Helie is expected to-night, and, depend upon it, his story would be very different. It will not be listened to now, however," he continued ; " and every day gained, depend upon it, is something. Take care, however, Count," he said, pointing to the papers on the table, " take care of your correspondence ; for though the King himself is above espionage, Louvois is not, I can tell you ; and unless you send your letters by private couriers of your own, which might excite great suspicion, every word is sure to be known."

"I was going to send this letter by a private courier," said the Count; "but as it is only intended to order up the rest of my train from Poitou, and some matters of that kind, I care not if it be known to-morrow."

"If it be to order up your train," replied the Prince, "send it through Louvois himself. Write him a note instantly, saying, that as you understand he has a courier going, you will be glad if he will despatch that letter. It will be opened, read, and the most convincing proof afforded to the whole of them, that you have no intention of immediate flight, which is the principal thing they seem to apprehend. With this, clenching the report of Pelisson, you may set St. Helie at defiance, I should think."

The Count smiled. "Heaven deliver me from the intrigues of a court," he said. He did, however, as he was advised; and the Prince de Marsillac carried off the letter and the note, promising to have them delivered to Louvois immediately.

Several hours then passed anxiously, and although he knew that he could not receive an answer from Clémence till two or three o'clock, and might perhaps not receive one at all that day, he could not help thinking the time long, and marking the striking of the palace clock, as if it must have gone wrong for his express torment. The shortest possible space of time, however, in which it was possible to go and come between Versailles and Paris had scarcely expired, after the departure of Riquet, when the valet again appeared. He brought with him a scrap of paper, which proved to be the back of the Count's own note to Clémence, unsealed, and with no address upon it; but written in a hasty hand within was found—

"I cannot—I dare not, see you at present; nor can I now write as I should desire to do. If what you wish to say is of immediate importance, write as before, and it is sure to reach me."

There was no signature, but the hand was that of Clémence de Marly; and the heart of Albert of Morseiul felt as if it would have broken. It seemed as if the last tie between him and happiness was severed. It seemed as if that hope, which would have afforded him strength, and support, and energy, to combat every difficulty and overleap every obstacle, was taken away from him; and for five or ten minutes he paced up and down the saloon in agony of mind unutterable.

"She is yielding already," he said, at length, "she is yielding already! The King's commands are hardly announced to her, ere she feels that she must give way. It is strange—it is most strange! I could have staked my life that with her it would have been otherwise !—and yet the influence which this Chevalier d'Evran seems always to have possessed over her is equally strange. If, as she has so solemnly told me, she is not really bound to him by any tie of affection, may she not be bound by some promise rashly given in former years? We have heard of such things. However, no promises to me shall stand in the way; she shall act freely, and at her own will, as far as I am concerned ;" and, sitting down, he wrote a few brief lines to Clémence, in which, though he did not pour out the bitterness of his heart, he showed how bitterly he was grieved.

" The tidings I had to tell you," he said, " were simply these, which I heard last night. The King destines your hand for another, and has already announced that such is the case. The few words that you have written show me that you are already aware of this fact, and that perhaps struggling between promises to me and an inclination to obey the royal authority, you are pained, and uncertain how to act. Such, at least, is the belief to which I am led by the few cold, painful words which I have received. If that belief is right, it may make you more easy to know that, in such a case, Albert of Morseiul will never exact the fulfilment of a promise that Clémence de Marly is inclined to break."

He folded the note up, sealed it, and once more called for Riquet. Before the man appeared, however, some degree of hesitation had come over the heart of the Count, and he asked him—

" Who did you see at the Hôtel de Rouvré ?"

" I saw," replied the man, " some of the servants ; and I saw two or three ecclesiastics looking after their valises in the court; and I saw Madame de Rouvré looking out of one of the windows with Mademoiselle Clémence, and the Chevalier d'Evran."

" It is enough," said the Count. " I should wish this note taken back to Paris before nightfall, and given into the hands of the same person to whom you gave the other. Take some rest, Riquet. But I should like that to be delivered before nightfall."

" I will deliver it, sir, and be back in time to dress you for the *appartement*."

" The *appartement*," said the Count, " I had forgotten that, and most likely shall not go. Well," he added, after a moment's thought, " better go there than to the Bastille. But it matters not, Riquet, Jean can dress me."

The man bowed, and retired. But by the time that it was necessary for the Count to commence dressing for the *appartement*, Riquet had returned, bringing with him, however, no answer to the note, for which, indeed, he had not waited. The Count suffered him to arrange his dress as he thought fit, and then proceeded to the palace, which was by this time beginning to be thronged with company.

During one half of the reign of Louis XIV. he was accustomed to receive all the chief nobility of his court and capital, three times each week, in the splendid public rooms of his palace ; and everything that liberal, and even ostentatious, splendour could do to please the eye, delight the ear, or amuse the mind of those who were thus collected, was done by the monarch on the nights which were marked for what was called *appartement*. At an after period of his life, when the death of almost all his great ministers had cast the burden of all the affairs of state upon the King himself, he seldom, if ever, appeared at these assemblies, passing the hours, during which he furnished his court with amusement, in labouring diligently with one or other of his different ministers.

At the time we speak of, however, he almost every night showed himself in the *appartement* for some time, noticing everybody with affability and kindness, and remarking, it was said, accurately who was present and who was not. It was considered a compliment to the monarch never to neglect any reasonable opportunity of paying court at these assemblies; and it is very certain that had the Count de Morseiul failed in presenting himself on the present occasion, his absence would have been regarded as a decided proof of disaffection.

He found the halls below filled with guards and attendants; the staircase covered with officers, and the court arriving in immense crowds; while from the saloon above poured forth the sounds of a full orchestra, which was always the first entertainment afforded during the evening, as if to put the guests in harmony, and prepare their minds for pleasure and enjoyment. The music was of the finest kind that could be found in France; and no person ever rendered himself celebrated, even in any remote province, for peculiar skill or taste in playing on any instrument, without being sought for and brought to play at the concerts of the King. The concert-room, which was the only one where the light was kept subdued, opened into a long suite of apartments, hall beyond hall, saloon beyond saloon, where the eye was dazzled by the blaze, and fatigued by the immense variety of beautiful and precious ornaments which were seen stretching away in brilliant perspective. Tables also were laid out for every sort of game that was then in fashion, from billiards to lansquenet; and the King took especial pains to make it particularly known to every person at his court, that it was not only his wish, but his especial command, if any man found anything wanting, or required anything whatever for his amusement or pleasure in the apartments, that he was to order some of the attendants to bring it.

Perfect liberty reigned throughout the whole saloons, as far as was consistent with propriety of conduct. The courtiers made up their parties amongst themselves, chose their own amusements, followed their own pursuits. Every sort of refreshment was provided in abundance, and hundreds on hundreds of servants, in splendid dresses, were seen moving here and there throughout the rooms, supplying the wants, and fulfilling the wishes of all the guests, with the utmost promptitude, or waiting for their orders, and remarking, with anxious attention, that nothing was wanting to the convenience of any one.

The whole of the principal suite of rooms in the palace was thus thrown open, as we have said, three times in the week, with the exception of the great ball-room, which was only opened on particular occasions. Sometimes, at the balls of the court, the *appartement* was not held, and the meeting took place in the ball-room itself. But at other times the ball followed the supper of the King, which took place invariably at ten o'clock, and the company invited proceeded from the *appartement* to the ball-room, leaving those whose age, health, or habits, gave them the privilege of not dancing, to amuse themselves with the games which were provided on the ordinary nights.

Such was to be the case on the present evening, and such as we have described was the scene of splendour which opened before the Count de Morseiul as he entered the concert-room, and taking a seat at the end, gazed up the gallery, listening with pleasure to a calm and somewhat melancholy, but soothing strain of music. His mind, indeed, was too much occupied with painful feelings of many kinds for him to take any pleasure or great interest in the magnificence spread out before his eyes, which he had often beheld before, but which he might have seen again with some admiration, had his bosom been free and his heart at rest.

At present, however, it was but dull pageantry to him, and the music was the thing that pleased him most ; but when a gay and lively piece succeeded to that which he had first heard, he rose and walked on into the rooms beyond, striving to find amusement for his thoughts; though pleasure might not be there to be found. Although he was by no means a general frequenter of the court, and always escaped from it to the calmer pleasures of the country as soon as possible, he was known to almost all the principal nobility of the realm, and to all the officers who had in any degree distinguished themselves in the service. Thus, in the very first room, he was stopped by a number of acquaintances ; and, passing on amidst the buzz of many voices, and all the gay nothings of such a scene, he met from time to time with some one, whose talents, or whose virtues, or whose greater degree of intimacy with himself, enabled him to pause and enter into longer and more interesting conversation, either in reference to the present—its hopes and fears,—or to the period when last they met, and the events which then surrounded them.

Although such things could not, of course, cure his mind of its melancholy, it afforded him some degree of occupation for his thoughts, till a sudden whisper ran through the rooms of " The King! The King!" and everybody drew back from the centre of the apartments to allow the monarch to pass.

Louis advanced from the inner rooms with that air of stately dignity which we know, from the accounts both of his friends and enemies, to have been unrivalled in grace and majesty. His commanding person, his handsome features, his kingly carriage, and his slow and measured step, all bespoke at once the monarch, and afforded no bad indication of his character, with its many grand and extensive, if not noble qualities, its capaciousness, its ambition, and even its occasional littleness, for the somewhat theatrical demeanour,

which we have before mentioned, was never lost, and the stage
effect was not less in Louis's mind than in his person.

He paused to speak for a moment with several persons as he
passed, stood at the lansquenet table where his brother and his son
were seated, dropped an occasional word, always graceful and agreeable, at two or three of the other tables, and then paused for a moment and looked up and down the rooms, evidently feeling himself,
what his whole people believed him to be, the greatest monarch that
ever trod the earth.   There was something, indeed, it must be acknowledged, in the mighty splendour of the scene around—in the
inestimable amount of the earth's treasures there collected—in the
blaze of light, the distant sound of the music, the dazzling loveliness of many there present—the courage, the learning, the talent,
the genius collected in those halls; and in the knowledge that there
was scarcely a man present who would not shed the last drop of his
heart's blood in the defence of his king, there was something that
might well turn giddy the brain of any man who felt himself placed
on that awful pinnacle of power and greatness.   Louis, however,
was well accustomed to it, and, like the child and the lion, he had
become familiar from youth with things which might make other
men tremble.   Thus he paused but for a moment to remark and to
enjoy, and then advanced again through the apartments.

The next person that his eye fell upon was the Count de Morseiul; and his countenance showed in a moment how true had
been the prophecy of the Prince de Marsillac, that a great change
would take place in his feelings.   He now smiled graciously upon
the young Count, and paused to speak with him.

"I trust to see you often here, Monsieur de Morseiul," he said.

"I shall not fail, sire," the Count replied, "to pay my duty to
your majesty as often as I am permitted to do so."

"Then you do not return soon to Poitou, Monsieur le Comte?"
said the King.

"I have thought it so improbable that I should do so, sire," replied the Count, who evidently saw that Louvois had not failed to
report his letter, "that I have taken an hotel here, and have sent for
my attendants this day.   If I hoped that my presence in Poitou
could be of any service to your majesty ——"

"It may be, it may be, Count, in time to come," replied the
King.   "In the meanwhile, we will try to amuse you well here.   I
have heard that you are one of the best billiard-players in France.
Follow me now to the billiard-room, and, though I am out of practice, I will try a stroke or two with you."

It was a game in which Louis excelled, as, indeed, he did in all
games; and this was one which afterwards, we are told, made the
fortune of the famous minister, Chamillart.   The Count de Morseiul, therefore, received this invitation as a proof that he was very
nearly re-established in the King's good graces.   He feared not at
all to compete with the monarch, as he himself was also out of

practice, and, indeed, far more than the King; so that, though an excellent player, there was no chance of his being driven either to win the game against the monarch, or to make use of some manœuvre to avoid doing so. He followed the King then willingly; but Louis, passing through the billiard-room, went on, in the first place, to the end of the suite of apartments, noticing everybody to whom he wished to pay particular attention, and then returned to the game. A number of persons crowded round—so closely, indeed, that the monarch exclaimed—

"Let us have room—let us have room! We will have none but the ladies so close to us—ha, Monsieur de Morseiul?"

The game then commenced, and went on with infinite skill and very nearly equal success on both parts. Louis became somewhat eager, but yet a suspicion crossed his mind that the young Count was purposely giving him the advantage, and at the end of some very good strokes he purposely placed his balls in an unfavourable position. The Count did not fail to take instant advantage of the opportunity, and had well nigh won the game. By an unfortunate stroke, however, he lost his advantage, and the King never let him have the table again till he was himself secure.

"You see, Monsieur de Morseiul," he said, as he paused for a moment afterwards, "you see you cannot beat me."

"I never even hoped it, sire," replied the Count. "In my own short day I have seen so many kings, generals, and statesmen, try to do so, in various ways, with signal want of success, that I never entertained so presumptuous an expectation."

The monarch smiled graciously, well pleased at a compliment from the young Huguenot nobleman which he had not expected; and as the game was one in which he took great pleasure, and which also displayed the graces of his person to the greatest advantage, he played a second game with the Count, which he won by only one stroke. He then left the table, and after speaking once more with several persons in the apartments, retired, not to re-appear till after his supper.

As soon as he was gone, the Prince de Marsillac once more approached the young Count, saying, in a whisper—"You have not beaten the King Morseiul, but you have conquered him: yet, take my advice, on no account leave the apartments till after the ball has begun. Let Louis see you there, for you know what a marking eye he has for every one who is in the rooms."

Thus saying, he passed on, and the Count determined to follow his advice, though the hour and a half that was yet to elapse seemed tedious, if not interminable, to him. About a quarter of an hour before the supper of the King, however, as he sat listlessly leaning against one of the columns, he saw a party coming up from the concert-room at a rapid pace, and long before the eye could distinctly see of what persons it was composed, his heart told him that Clémence de Marly was there.

She came forward, leaning on the arm of the Duc de Rouvré, dressed with the utmost splendour, and followed by a party of several others who had just arrived. She was certainly not less lovely than ever. To the eyes of Albert de Morseiul, indeed, it seemed that she was more so: but there was an expression of deep sadness on that formerly gay and smiling countenance, which would have made the whole feelings of the Count de Morseiul change into grief for her grief, and anxiety for her anxiety, had there not been a certain degree of haughtiness throned upon her brow and curling her lips, which bespoke more bitterness than depression of feeling. The Duc de Rouvré was, as I have said, proceeding rapidly through the rooms, and paused not to speak with any one. The eyes of Clémence, however, fell upon the Count de Morseiul, and rested on him with their full melancholy light, while she noticed him with a calm and graceful inclination of the head, but passed on, without a word.

The feelings of the Count were bitter indeed, as may well be imagined. "So soon," he said to himself, "so soon! By Heaven, I can understand now all that I have heard and wondered at: how, for a woman—an empty, vain, coquettish woman—a man may forget the regard of years, and cut his friend's throat as he would that of a stag or boar. Where is the Chevalier d'Evran, I wonder? He does not appear in the train to-night; but perhaps he comes not till the ball. I will wait, however, the same time as if she had not been here."

He moved not from his place, but remained leaning against the column; and, as is generally the case, not seeking. he was sought for. A number of people who knew him gathered round him; and, although he was in anything but a mood for entertaining or being entertained, the very shortness of his replies, and the degree of melancholy bitterness that mingled with them, caused words that he never intended to be witty, to pass for wit, and protracted the torture of conversing with indifferent people upon indifferent subjects, when the heart was full of bitterness, and the mind occupied with its own sad business.

At length the doors of the ball-room were thrown open, and the company poured in to arrange themselves before the monarch came. Several parties, indeed, remained playing at different games at the tables in the gallery, and the Count remained where he was, still leaning against the column, which was at the distance of ten or twelve yards from the doors of the ball-room. Not above five minutes had elapsed, before the King and his immediate attendants appeared, coming from his private supper-room to be present at the ball. His eye, as he passed, ran over the various tables, making a graceful motion with his hand for the players not to rise; and as he approached the folding-doors, he remarked the Count, and beckoned to him to come up. The Count immediately started forward, and the King demanded—

"A gallant young man like you, do you not dance, Monsieur de Morseiul?"

Taken completely by surprise at this piece of condescension, the Count replied—

"Alas, sire, I am not in spirits to dance; I should but cloud the gaiety of my fair partner, and she would wish herself anywhere else before the evening were over."

Louis smiled; and so much accustomed was he to attribute the sunshine and clouds upon his courtiers' brows to the effects of his favour or displeasure, that he instantly put his own interpretation upon the words of the Count, and that interpretation raised the young nobleman much in the good graces of a monarch, who, though vain and despotic, was not naturally harsh and severe.

"If, Monsieur de Morseiul," he said, "some slight displeasure which the King expressed yesterday morning, have rendered our gay fellow-soldier of Maestricht and Valenciennes so sad, let his sadness pass away, for his conduct here has effaced unfavourable reports, and if he persevere to the end in the same course, he may count upon the very highest favour."

Almost every circumstance combines on earth to prevent monarchs hearing the truth, even from the most sincere. Time, place, and circumstance, is almost always against them; and in the present instance, the Count de Morseiul knew well, that neither the spot nor the moment were at all suited to anything like an explanation. He could but reply, therefore, that the lightest displeasure of the King was of course enough to make him sad, and end his answer by one of those compliments which derive at least half their value, like paper money, from the good will of the receiver.

"Come, come," said the King, gaily; "shake off this melancholy, fellow-soldier. Come with me; and if I have rightly heard the secrets of certain hearts, I will find you a partner this night, who shall not wish herself anywhere else while dancing with the Count de Morseiul."

The Count gazed upon the King with utter astonishment; and Louis, enjoying his surprise, led the way quickly on into the ball-room, the Count following, as he bade him, close by his side, and amongst his principal officers. As soon as they had entered the saloon appropriated to the dance, Louis paused for an instant, and every one rose. The King's eyes, as well as those of the Count de Morseiul, ran round the vast space seeking for some particular object. To Albert of Morseiul that object was soon discovered, placed between the Duchess de Rouvré and Annette de Marville, at the very farthest part of the room. Louis, however, who was in good spirits, and in a mood peculiarly condescending, walked round the whole circle, pausing to speak to almost every married lady there, and twice turning suddenly towards the Count, perhaps with the purpose of teasing him a little, but seemingly as if about to point out the lady to whom he had alluded. At length, however, he reached the spot where the Duchess de Rouvré and her party were placed; and after speaking for a moment to the Duchess, while the cheek of Clémence de Marly became deadly pale and then glowed again fiery red, he turned suddenly towards her, and said—

"Mademoiselle de Marly, or perhaps as I in gallantry ought to say, *Belle Clémence*, I have promised the Count de Morseiul here to find him a partner for this ball, who will dance with him throughout to-night, without wishing herself anywhere else. Now, as I have certain information that he is very hateful to you, there is but one thing which can make you execute the task to the full. Doubtless you, as well as all the rest of our court, feel nothing so great a pleasure as obeying the King's commands—at least, so they tell me—and therefore I command you to dance with him, and to be as happy as possible, and not to wish yourself anywhere else from this moment till the ball closes."

He waited for no reply, but making a sign to the Count to remain by the side of his fair partner, proceeded round the rest of the circle. Nothing in the demeanour of Clémence de Marly but her varying colour had told how much she was agitated while the King spoke; but the words which the monarch had used were so pointed, and touched so directly upon the feelings between herself and Albert of Morseiul, that those who stood around pressed slightly forward as soon as Louis had gone on, to see how she was affected by what had passed. To her ear those words were most strange and extraordinary. It was evident that by some one the secret of her heart had been betrayed to the King, and equally evident that Louis had determined to countenance that love which she had fancied would make her happy in poverty, danger, or distress, announcing his approbation at the very moment that a temporary coldness had arisen between her and her lover, and that her heart was oppressed with those feelings of hopelessness, which will sometimes cross even our brightest and happiest days.

On the Count de Morseiul the King's words had produced a different, but not a less powerful effect. The surprise and joy which he might have felt at finding himself suddenly pointed out by the monarch as the favoured suitor for the hand of her he loved, was well nigh done away by the conviction that the price the King put upon his ultimate approbation of their union was such as he could not pay. But nevertheless those words were most joyful, though they raised up some feeling of self-reproach in his heart. It was evident that the tale told by Pelisson regarding the Chevalier was false, or perhaps, indeed originated in some pious fraud devised for the purpose of driving him more speedily to acknowledge himself a convert to the church of Rome. Whatever were the circumstances, however, it was clear that Clémence was herself unconscious of any such report, and that all the probabilities which imagination had built up to torment him were but idle dreams. He had pained himself enough indeed; but he had pained Clémence also, and his first wish was to offer her any atonement in his power.

Such were the feelings and thoughts called up in the bosom of the young Count by the events which had just occurred. But the surprise of Clémence and her lover was far outdone by that of the Duke and Duchess de Rouvré, who, astonished at the favour into which their young friend seemed so suddenly to have risen, and equally astonished at the intimation given by the King of an attachment existing between the Count and Clémence, overflowed with joy and satisfaction as soon as the monarch left the spot, and expressed many a vain hope that, after all, the affairs which had commenced in darkness and shadow, would end in sunshine and light. Ere the Count could reply, or say one word to Clémence de Marly, the *bransle* began, and he led her forth to dance. There was but a moment for him to speak to her; but he did not lose that moment.

" Clémence," he said, as he led her forward, " I fear I have both pained you and wronged you."

A bright and beautiful smile spread at once over her countenance. " You have," she said; " but those words are enough, Albert! Say no more! the pain is done away; the wrong is forgotten."

" It is not forgotten by me, sweet girl," he replied, in the same low tone; " but I must speak to you long, and explain all."

" Come to-morrow," she answered; " all difficulties must now be done away. I, too, have something to explain, Albert," she added, " but yet not everything that I could wish to explain, and about that I will make you my only reproach. You promised not to doubt me.—Oh, keep that promise!"

As she spoke, the dance began, and their conversation for the time concluded. All eyes were upon the young Count—so rare a visiter at the palace, and upon her—so admired, so courted, so disdainful, as she was believed to be by every one present, but whose destiny seemed now decided, and whose heart every one naturally believed to be won. Graceful by nature as well as by education, no two persons of the whole court could have been better fitted than Albert of Morseiul and Clémence de Marly to pass through the ordeal of such a scene as a court ball in those days; and though every eye was, as we have said, upon them, yet they had a great advantage on that night, which would have prevented anything like embarrassment, even had not such scenes been quite familiar to them. They scarcely knew that any eyes were watching them, they were scarcely conscious of the presence of the glittering crowd around. Engrossed by their own individual feelings—deep, absorbing, overpowering, as those feelings were,— their spirits were wrapt up in themselves and in each other; they thought not of the dance, they thought not of the spectators, but left habit, and natural grace, and a fine ear, to do all that was requisite as far as the minuet was concerned. If either thought of the dance at all, it was only when the eyes of Albert of Morseiul rested on Clémence, and she seemed to him certainly more lovely and graceful than ever she had before appeared, or when his hand touched hers, and the thrill of that touch passed to his heart, speaking of love, and hope, and happiness to come. The effect was what might naturally be supposed—each danced more gracefully than, perhaps, they had ever done before; and one of those slight murmurs of admiration passed through the courtly crowd, accustomed to look upon every act as an exhibition, which was confirmed by a gracious smile and gentle inclination of the head from the King himself.

"We must not let him escape us," said the monarch, in a low voice, to the Prince de Marsillac. "Certainly he is worthy of some trouble in recalling from his errors."

"If he escape from the fair net your majesty has spread for him," replied the Prince, "he will be the most cunning bird that ever I saw. Indeed, I should suppose he has no choice, when, if caught, he will have to thank his king for everything, for honour, favour, distinction, his soul's salvation, and a fair wife that loves him. If he be not pressed till he takes fright, he will entangle himself so that no power can extricate him."

"He shall have every opportunity," said the King. "I must not appear too much in the matter. You, Prince, see that they be left alone together, if possible, for a few minutes. Use what manœuvre you will, and I will take care to countenance it."

At the court balls of that day, it was the custom to dance throughout the night with one person, and the opportunity of conversing between those who were dancing was very small. A few brief words at the commencement, or at the end of each dance, was all that could be hoped for, and Clémence and her lover were fain to fix all their hopes of explanation and of longer intercourse upon the morrow. Suddenly, however, it was announced, before the hour at which the balls usually terminated, that the King had a lottery, to which all the married ladies of the court were invited.

The crowd poured into the apartment where the drawing of this lottery was to take place; every lady anxious for a ticket where all were prizes, and the tickets themselves given by the King; while those who were not to share in this splendid piece of generosity were little less eager, desirous of seeing the prizes, and learning who it was that won them. All, then, as we have said, poured out of the ball room, through the great gallery and other state-rooms in which the *appartement* was usually held.

There were only two who lingered—Clémence de Marly and Albert of Morseiul. They, however, remained to the last, and then followed slowly, employing the few minutes thus obtained in low-spoken words of affection, perhaps all the warmer and all the tenderer for the coldness and the pain just passed. Ere three sentences, however, had been uttered, the good Duc de Rouvré approached, saying, "Come, Clémence, come quick, or you will not find a place where you will see."

The eye of the Prince de Marsillac, however, was upon them; and, threading the mazes of the crowd, he took the Duke by the arm; and, drawing him aside, with an important face, told him that the King wanted to speak with him immediately. The Duc de Rouvré darted quickly away to seek the monarch: and the Prince paused for a single instant ere he followed, to say in a low voice to the Count—

"You will neither of you be required at the lottery, if you think that the lot you have drawn already is sufficiently good."

The Count was not slow to understand the hint, and he gently led Clémence de Marly back into one of the vacant saloons.

"Surely they will think it strange," she said; but, ere the Count could reply, she added, quickly; "but, after all, what matters it if they do?—I would have it so, that every one may see and know the whole so clearly, that all persecution may be at an end. Now, Albert, now," she said, "tell me what could make you write me so cruel a letter."

"I will in one word," he replied; "but remember, Clémence, that I own I have been wrong, and in telling you the causes, in explaining the various circumstances which led me to believe that you were wavering in your engagements to me, I seek not to justify myself, but merely to explain."

"Oh never, never think it!" she exclaimed, ere she would let him go on; "whatever may happen, whatever appearances may be, never, Albert, never for one moment think that I am wavering! Once more, most solemnly, most truly, I assure you, that though perhaps fate may separate me from you, and circumstances, over which we have no control, render our union impossible, nothing— no, not the prospect of immediate death itself, shall ever induce me to give my hand to another. No circumstances can effect that, for that must be my voluntary act; and I can endure death, I can endure imprisonment, I can endure anything they choose to inflict, except to wed a man I do not love. Now, tell me," she continued, "now, let me hear what could make you think I did so waver."

The Count related all that had taken place, the words which he had heard Pelisson make use of in conversation with an indifferent person, the mortification and pain he had felt at the few lines she had written in answer to his note, the confirmation of all his anxious fears by what Jerome Riquet had told him, and all the other probabilities that had arisen to make him believe that those fears were just.

Clémence heard him sometimes with a look of pain, sometimes with a reproachful smile. "After all, Albert," she said, at length, "perhaps you have had some cause—more cause, indeed, than jealous men often have, and yet you shall hear how simply all this may be accounted for. The day after we parted in Poitou, the Abbé de St. Helie arrived at Ruffigny, with several other persons of the same kind, and Monsieur de Rouvré found his house filled with spies upon his actions. He received, however, in the evening of the same day, an order to come to the court immediately, to give an account of the events which had taken place in his government. The same spies of Louvois accompanied us on the road, as well as the Chevalier d'Evran,—who was the person that had obtained from the King an order for the Duke to appear at court, rather than to remain in exile at Ruffigny, while his enemies said what they chose of him in his absence. We had not arrived in Paris ten minutes at the time your servant came. We were surrounded by watchful eyes of every kind; the good Duke was in a state of agitation impossible to describe, and so fearful that anything like a Protestant should be seen in his house, or that anything, in short, should occur to give probability to the charges against him, that I knew your coming would be dangerous both to yourself and to him, the house being filled with persons who were ready not only to report, but to pervert everything that took place. On receiving your note, Maria called me out of the saloon; but my apartments were not prepared; servants were coming and going: no writing-paper was to be procured; a pen and ink were obtained with difficulty. I knew if I were absent five minutes, in the state of agitation that pervaded the whole household, Madame de Rouvré would come to seek me, and I was consequently obliged to write the few words I did write in the greatest haste, and under the greatest anxiety. Maria was not even out of the room conveying those few words to your servant, when the Duchess came in, and I was glad hypocritically to affect great activity and neatness about the arrangement of my apartments, to conceal the real matter which had employed me. Such is the simple state of the case; and I never even heard of this other marriage, about which Pelisson must have made some mistake. Had I heard of it," she added, "it would only have made me laugh."

"I see not why it should do so," replied the Count. "Surely, Louis d'Evran is—as I well know he is considered by many of the fair and the bright about this court—a person not to be despised by any woman. He evidently, too, exercises great influence over you, Clémence; and therefore the report itself was not such as I, at least, could treat as absurd, especially when, in addition to these facts, it was stated that the King had expressed his will that you should give him your hand."

"To me, however, Albert," she replied, "it must appear absurd, knowing and feeling as I do know and feel, that were the Chevalier d'Evran the only man I had ever seen, or ever were likely to see, that I should never even dream of marrying him. He may be much loved and liked by other women; doubtless he is, and sure I am he well deserves it. I like him, too, Albert. I scruple not to own it—I esteem him much; but that is very different from loving him as I love—as a woman should love her husband, I mean to say. And now, Albert," she continued, "with regard to the influence he has over me, I will tell you nothing more. That shall remain as a trial of your confidence in me. This influence will never be exerted but when it is right. Should it be exerted wrongly, it is at an end from that moment. When you wished to accompany me to Ruffigny, from that terrible scene in which we last parted, he represented to me in few words how Monsieur de Rouvré was situated. He showed me, that by bringing you there at such a time from such a scene, I should but bring destruction on that kind friend who had sheltered and protected my infancy and my youth, when I had none else to protect me. He showed me, too, that I should put an impassable barrier between you and me, for the time at least. He told me that no one but himself was aware of where I was, but that your accompanying me would instantly make it known to the whole world, and most likely produce the ruin of both. Now, tell me, Albert, was he not right to say all this? Was not his view a just one?"

"It was," replied the Count; "but yet he might have urged it in another manner. He might have explained the whole to me as well as to you: and still you leave unexplained, Clémence, how he should know where you were, when you had concealed it so well, so unaccountably well, from the family at Ruffigny."

"Oh! jealousy, jealousy," said Clémence, playfully; "what a terrible and extraordinary thing jealousy is! and yet, Albert, perhaps a woman likes to see a little of it when she really loves. However, you are somewhat too hard upon the Chevalier, and you shall not wring from me any other secret just yet. You have wrung from me, Albert, too many of the secrets of my heart already, and I will not make you the spoilt child of love, by letting you have altogether your own way. As to my concealing from the family of Ruffigny, however, where I was going on that occasion, or on most others, it is very easily explained. Do you not know that, till I was foolish enough at Poitiers to barter all the freedom of my heart, for love with but little confidence it would seem, I have always been a tyrant instead of a slave? Are you not aware that I have always done just as I liked with every one? and one of my reasons for exercising my power to the most extreme degree was, that my religious faith might never be controlled? Till this fierce persecution of the Protestants began, and till the King made it his great object, and announced his determination of putting down all but the Roman-catholic faith in the realm, Monsieur de Rouvré himself cared but little for the distinction of Protestant and Catholic,

and even had he known what I was doing, though he might have
objected, would not have strongly opposed me.   I established my
right, however, of doing what I liked, and going where I liked, and
acting as I liked, on such firm grounds, that it was not easily
shaken.   Even now, had I chosen to see you to-day in Paris, I
might have done it; but would you have thought the better of
Clémence if she had risked the fortunes of him who has been more
than a father to her?   Nobody would, and nobody should have
said me nay, if I had believed that it was just and right to bid you
come.   But I thought it was wrong, Albert.   Now, however, I may
bid you come in safety to all; and now that I have time and opportunity to make any arrangements I like, I may safely promise, that
should any change come over the present aspect of our affairs,
which change I fear must and will come, I will find means to see
you at any time, and under any circumstances.   But hark! from
what I hear, the lottery is over, and the people departing.   Let us
go forward and join them, if it be but for a moment."

Thus saying, she rose, and the Count led her on to the room
where the distribution of the prizes had just taken place.   Every
one was now interested with another subject.   A full hour had been
given at the beginning of the evening to the affair of the Count de
Morseiul and Mademoiselle de Marly, which was a far greater space
of time, and far more attention than such a court might be expected
to give, even to matters of the deepest and most vital importance.
But no former impression could of course outlive the effect of a
lottery.   There was not one man or woman present whose thoughts
were occupied by anything else than the prizes and their distribution; and the head of even the good Duchess de Rouvré herself,
who was certainly of somewhat higher character than most of those
present, was so filled with the grand engrossing theme, that nothing
was talked of, as the party returned to Paris, but the prize which
had fallen to the share of Madame de This, or the disappointment
which had been met with by Madame de That; so that Clémence
de Marly could lean back in the dark corner of the carriage, and
enjoy her silence undisturbed.

CHAPTER XVIII.

THE HOUR OF HAPPINESS.

At the levée of the King, on the succeeding morning, the young
Count de Morseiul was permitted to appear for a few minutes.
The monarch was evidently in haste, having somewhat broken in on
his matutinal habits in consequence of the late hour at which he
had retired on the night before.

" They tell me you have a favour to ask, Monsieur de Morseiul," said the King. "I hope it is not a very great one, for I have slept so well and am in such haste, that, perhaps, I might grant it, whether it were right or wrong."

"It is merely, sire," replied the Count, "to ask your gracious permission to proceed to Paris this morning, in order to visit Mademoiselle de Marly. Not knowing when it may be your royal pleasure to grant me the longer audience which you promised for some future time, I did not choose to absent myself from Versailles without your majesty's consent."

Louis smiled graciously, for no such tokens of deference were lost upon him. "Most assuredly," he said, "you have my full permission: and now I think of it—Bontems," he continued, turning to one of his *valets de chambre*, "bring me that casket which is in the little cabinet below—now I think of it, the number of our married ladies last night fell short at the lottery, and there was a prize of a pair of diamond ear-rings left. I had intended to have given them to La belle Clémence; but, somehow," he added, with a smile, "she did not appear in the room. Perhaps, however, you know more of that than I do, Monsieur de Morseiul!—Oh, here is Bontems—give me the casket."

Taking out of the small ebony box which was now presented to him, a little case, containing a very handsome pair of diamond ear-rings, the King placed it in the hands of the young Count, saying, "There, Monsieur de Morseiul, be my messenger to the fair lady. Give her those jewels from the King; and tell her, that I hope ere long she will be qualified to draw prizes in some not very distant lottery by appearing as one of the married ladies of our court. She has tortured all our gallant gentlemen's hearts too long, and we will not suffer our subjects to be thus ill treated. Do you stay in Paris all day, Monsieur de Morseiul, or do you come here to witness the new opera?"

"I did not propose to do either, sire," replied the Count: "I had, in fact, engaged myself to pass another pleasant evening at the house of Monsieur de Meaux."

"Indeed!" said the King, evidently well pleased. "That is all as it should be. I cannot but think, Monsieur de Morseiul, that if you pass many more evenings so well, either you will convert Monsieur de Meaux—which God forbid, or Monsieur de Meaux will convert you—which God grant."

The Count bowed gravely; and, as the King turned to speak with some one else who was giving him a part of his dress, the young nobleman took it as a permission to retire; and, mounting his horse, which had been kept ready saddled, he made the best of his way towards the capital.

That gay world, with its continual motion, was as animated then as now. Though the abode of the court was at Versailles, yet the distance was too small to make the portion of the population absolutely withdrawn from the metropolis at all important while all the other great bodies of the kingdom assembled, or were represented there.   Thousands on thousands were hurrying through the streets ; the same trades and occupations were going on then as to-day, with only this difference, that, at that period, luxury, and industry, and every productive art had reached, if not its highest, at least, its most flourishing point ; and all things presented, even down to the aspect of the city itself, that hollow splendour, that tinselled magnificence, that artificial excitement, that insecure prosperity, the falseness of all and each of which had afterwards to be proved, and which entailed a long period of fresh errors, bitter repentance, and terrible atonement.

But through the gay crowd, the Count de Morseiul passed on, noticing it little, if at all.   He was urged on his way by the strongest of all human impulses, by love—first, ardent, pure, sincere, love—all the more deep, all the more intense, all the more overpowering, because he had not felt it at that earlier period, while the animal triumphs over the mental in almost all the affections of man. His heart and his spirit had lost nothing of their freshness to counterbalance the vigour and the power they had obtained, and at the age of seven or eight and twenty he loved with all the vehemence and ardour of a boy, while he felt with all the permanence and energy of manhood.

Though contrary, perhaps, to the rules and etiquette of French life at that period, he took advantage both of the message with which he was charged from the King, and the sort of independence which Clémence de Marly had established for herself, to ask for her instead of either the Duke or the Duchess.   He was not, indeed, without a hope that he should find her alone, and that hope was realized.   She had expected him, and expected him early ; and, perhaps, the good Duchess de Rouvré herself had fancied that such might be the case, and, remembering the warm affections of her own days, had abstained from presenting herself in the little saloon where Clémence de Marly had usually fixed her abode during their residence in Paris.

Had Albert of Morseiul entertained one doubt of the affection of Clémence de Marly, that doubt must have vanished in a moment— must have vanished at the look with which she rose to meet him.   It was all brightness—it was all happiness.   The blood mounted, it is true, into her cheeks, and into her temples; her beautiful lips trembled slightly, and her breath came fast; but the bright and radiant smile was not to be mistaken.   The sparkling of the eyes spoke what words could not speak ; and, though her tongue for a moment refused its office, the smile that played around the lips was eloquent of all that the heart felt.

Not contented with the hand she gave, Albert of Morseiul took the other also ; and not contented with the thrilling touch of those small hands, he threw his arms around her, and pressed her to his heart ; and not contented—for love is the greatest of encroachers

—with that dear embrace, he made his lips tell the tale of their own joy to hers, and once and again he tasted the happiness that none had ever tasted before: and then, as if asking pardon for the rashness of his love, he pressed another kiss upon her fair hand, and leading her back to her seat, took his place beside her.

Fearful that he should forget, he almost immediately gave her the jewels which the King had sent. But what were jewels to Clémence de Marly at that moment? He told her, also, the message the King had given, especially that part which noted her absence from the room where the lottery had been drawn.

" I would not have given those ten minutes," she replied, eagerly, " for all the jewels in his crown."

They then forgot the King, the court, and everything but each other, and spent the moments of the next half hour in the joy, in the surpassing joy, of telling and feeling the happiness that each conferred upon the other.

Oh ! those bright sunny hours of early love, of love in its purity and its truth, and its sincerity—of love, stripped of all that is evil, or low, or corrupt, and retaining but of earth sufficient to make it harmonize with earthly creatures like ourselves—full of affection— full of eager fire, but affection as unselfish as human nature will admit, and fire derived from heaven itself! How shall you ever be replaced in after life? What tone shall ever supply the sound of that master chord after its vibrations have once ceased?

As the time wore on, however, and Albert of Morseiul remembered that there were many things on which it was necessary to speak at once to Clémence de Marly, the slight cloud of care came back upon his brow, and reading the sign of thought in a moment, she herself led the way, by saying—

" But we must not forget, dear Albert, there is much to be thought of. We are spending our time in dreaming over our love, when we have to think of many more painful points in our situation. We have spoken of all that concerns our intercourse with each other; but of your situation at the court I am ignorant; and am not only ignorant of the cause, but astonished to find, that when I expected the most disastrous results, you are in high favour with the King, and apparently have all at your command."

" Not so, dear Clémence—alas ! it is not so," replied the Count; " the prosperity of my situation is as hollow as a courtier's heart— as fickle as any of the other smiles of fortune."

Before he could go on, however, to explain to her the real position in which he stood, Madame de Rouvré entered the room, and was delighted at seeing one whom she had always esteemed and loved. She might have remained long; but Clémence, with the manner which she was so much accustomed to assume, half playful, half peremptory, took up the little case of ear-rings from the table, saying, " See what the King has sent me ! and now, dear Duchess, you shall go away, and leave me to talk with my lover.—It is so new a thing for me to have an acknowledged lover, and one, too, that I don't despise, that I have not half tired myself with my new plaything. Am not I a very saucy demoiselle?" she added, kissing the Duchess, who was retiring, with laughing obedience. " But take the diamonds, and examine them at your leisure. They will serve to amuse you in the absence of your Clémence."

" If I were a lover now," said the Duchess, smiling, " I should say something about their not being half as bright as your eyes, Clémence. But words vary in their value so much, that what would be very smart and pleasant from a young man, is altogether worthless on the lips of an old woman. Let me see you before you go, Count. It is not fair that saucy girl should carry you off altogether."

" Now, now, Albert," said Clémence, as soon as the Duchess was gone, " tell me before we are interrupted again."

The Count took up the tale, then, with his last day's sojourn in Brittany, and went on to detail minutely everything that had occurred since his arrival in the capital ; and, as he told her, her cheek grew somewhat paler, till, in the end, she exclaimed, " It is all as bad as it can be.—You will never change your faith, Albert ?"

" Could you love me, Clémence," he asked, " if I did ?"

She put her hand before her eyes for a moment, then placed one of them in his, and replied, " I should love you ever, Albert, with a woman's love, unchangeable and fixed. But I could not esteem you, as I would fain esteem him that I must love."

" So thought I," replied the Count, "so judged I of my Clémence ; and all that now remains to be thought of is, how is this to end, and what is to be our conduct to make the end as happy to ourselves as may be ?"

" Alas !" replied Clémence, "I can answer neither question. The probability is that all must end badly, that your determination not to yield your religion to any inducements must soon be known ; for depend upon it, Albert, they will press you on the subject more closely every day ; and you are not made to conceal what you feel. The greater the expectations of your conversion have been, the more terrible will be the anger that your adherence to your own faith will produce ; and depend upon it, the Prince de Marsillac takes a wrong view of the question ; for it matters not whether this affair in Poitou have passed away, or be revived against you,— power never yet wanted a pretext to draw the sword of persecution. Neither, Albert, can my change of faith be long concealed. I cannot insult God by the mockery of faith in things, regarding which my mind was long doubtful, but which I am now well assured, and thoroughly convinced, are false. In this you are in a better situation than myself, for you can but be accused of holding fast to the faith that you have ever professed : me they will accuse of falling into heresy with my eyes open. Perhaps they will add, that I have done so for your love."

" Then, dear Clemence," he answered, " the only path for us is the path of flight, early and rapid flight. I have already secured for us competence in another land; wealth I cannot secure, but competence is surely all that either you or I require."

"All, all," replied Clémence; "poverty with you, Albert, would be enough. But the time, and the manner of our flight, must be left to you. The distance between Paris and the frontier is so small, that we had better effect it now, and not wait for any contingency. If you can find means to withdraw yourself from the court, I will find means to join you anywhere within two or three miles' journey of the capital. But write to me the place, the hour, and the time; and, as we love each other, Albert, and by the faith that we both hold, and for which we are both prepared to sacrifice so much, I will not fail you."

" What if it should be to-morrow?" demanded the Count.

Clémence gazed at him for a moment with some agitation. " Even if it should be to-morrow," she said, at length, " even if it should be to-morrow, I will come. But, oh, Albert," she added, leaning her head upon his shoulder, " I am weaker, more cowardly, more womanly than I thought. I would fain have it a day later: I would fain procrastinate, even by a day. But never mind, never mind, Albert; should it be necessary, should you judge it right, should you think it requisite for your safety, let it be to-morrow."

" I cannot yet judge," replied the Count; " I think, I trust that it will not be so soon. I only put the question to make you aware that such a thing is possible, barely possible. In all probability the King will give me longer time. He cannot suppose that the work of conversion will take place by a miracle. I do not wish to play a double game with them, even in the least, Clémence, nor suffer them to believe that there is a chance even of my changing, when there is none; but still I would fain, for your sake as well as mine, delay a day or two."

" Delays are dangerous, even to an old proverb," said Clémence; but ere she could conclude her sentence, the Duc de Rouvré entered the room; and not choosing, or perhaps not having spirits at the moment to act towards him as she had done towards his wife, Clémence suffered the conversation to drop, and proceeded with him and her lover to the saloon of the Duchess.

In that saloon there appeared a number of persons, amongst whom were several that the Count de Morseiul knew slightly; but the beams of royal favour having fallen upon him with their full light during the night before, all those who had ever been introduced to him were eager to improve such an acquaintance, and vied with each other in smiles and looks of pleasure on his appearance. Amongst others was the Chevalier de Rohan, whom we have noticed as forming one of the train of suitors who had followed Clémence de Marly to Poitiers; but he was now satisfied, apparently, that not even any fortunate accident could give the bright prize to him, and he merely bowed to her on her entrance, with the air of a worshipper at the shrine of an idol, while he grasped the hand of his successful rival, and declared himself delighted to see him.

After remaining there for some time longer, lingering in the sunshine of the looks of her he loved, the Count prepared to take his departure, especially as several other persons had been added to the circle, and their society fell as a heavy weight upon one whose whole thoughts were of Clémence de Marly. He had taken nis leave and reached the door of the apartment, when, starting up with the ear-rings in her hand, Clémence exclaimed—

"Stay, stay, Monsieur de Morseiul, I forgot to send my thanks to the King.—Pray tell him," she added, advancing across the room to speak with the Count in a lower tone, "Pray tell him how grateful I am to his majesty for his kind condescension; and remember," she said, in a voice that could be heard by no one but himself, "to-morrow, should it be needful:—I am firmer now."

Albert of Morseiul dared not speak all that he felt, with the language of the lips; but the countenance of her lover thanked Clémence de Marly sufficiently.

He, on his part, left her with feelings which the bustle and the crowd of the thronged capital struggled with and oppressed; and he rode quick, in order to make his way out of the city as fast as possible; but ere he had passed the gate, he was overtaken by the Chevalier de Rohan, who came up to his side, saying, "I am delighted to have overtaken you, my dear Count. Such a companion on this long, dry, tiresome journey to Versailles, is indeed a delight; and I wished also particularly to speak to you regarding a scheme of mine, which I trust, may bring me better days."

Now, the society of the Chevalier de Rohan, though his family was one of the highest in France, and though he held an important place at the court, was neither very agreeable nor very reputable; and the Count, therefore, replied briefly, "I fear that, as I shall stop at several places, it will not be in my power to accompany you, Monsieur le Chevalier; but anything I can do to serve you will give me pleasure."

"Why, the fact is," replied the Chevalier, "that I was very unfortunate last night at play, and wished to ask if you would lend me a small sum till I receive my appointments from the King. If you are kind enough to do so, I doubt not before two days are over to recover all that I have lost, and ten times more ; for I discovered the fortunate number last night when it was too late."

A faint and melancholy smile came over the Count's face, at the picture of human weakness which his companion's words displayed; and as the Chevalier was somewhat celebrated for borrowing without repaying, he asked what was the sum he required.

"Oh, a hundred louis will be quite enough," answered the Chevalier, not encouraged to ask more by his companion's tone.

"Well, Monsieur de Rohan," said the Count, "I have not the sum with me, but I will send it to you on my arrival at Versailles, if that will be time enough."

"Quite! quite!" replied de Rohan; "any time before the tables are open."

"Indeed—indeed! my good friend," said the Count, "I wish you would abandon such fatal habits; and, satisfied with having lost so much, live upon the income you have, without ruining yourself by trying to make it greater.—However, I will send the money, and do with it what you will."

"You are a prude! you are a prude!" cried De Rohan, putting spurs to his horse; "but I will tell you something more in your own way, when we meet again."

CHAPTER XIX.

THE UNKNOWN PERIL.

DARK and ominous was the prospect of everything around the Count de Morseiul: the blessings of his bright days were passing away, one by one, and his best hope was exile. Yet the interview which had just taken place between him and Clémence de Marly was like a bright summer hour in the midst of storms, and even when it was over, like the June sun, it left a long twilight of remembered joy behind it. But there are times in human life when dangers are manifold, when we are pressed upon by a thousand difficulties, and when, nevertheless, though the course we have determined on is full of risks and perils, sorrows and sufferings, we eagerly, perhaps even imprudently, hurry forward upon it, to avoid those very doubts and uncertainties, which are worse than actual pains.

Such was the case with the Count de Morseiul; and he felt within him so strong an inclination to take the irrevocable step of quitting France for ever, and seeking peace and toleration in another land, that, much accustomed to examine and govern his own feelings, he paused, and pondered over the line of conduct he was about to pursue, during his visit to the Bishop of Meaux, perceiving in himself a half-concealed purpose of forcing on the conversation to the subject of religion, and of showing Bossuet clearly, that there was no chance whatever of inducing him to abandon the religion of his fathers. Against this inclination, on reflection, he determined to be upon his guard, although he adhered rigidly to his resolution of countenancing, in no degree, a hope of his becoming a convert to the Roman-catholic faith; and his only doubt now was, whether his passing two evenings so close together with the Bishop of

Meaux, with whom he had so slight an acquaintance, might not afford some encouragement to expectations which he felt himself bound to check.

Having promised, however, he went, but at the same time made up his mind not to return to the prelate's abode speedily. On the present occasion, he not only found Bossuet alone, but was left with him for more than an hour, without any other visiter appearing. The good Bishop himself was well aware of the danger of scaring away those whom he sought to win; and, sincerely desirous, for the Count's own sake, of bringing him into that which he believed to be the only path to salvation, he was inclined to proceed calmly and gently in the work of his conversion.

There were others, however, more eager than himself; the King was as impetuous in the apostolic zeal which he believed himself to feel, as he had formerly been in pursuits which, though certainly more gross and sensual, would perhaps, if accurately weighed, have been found to be as little selfish, vain, and personal as the efforts that he made to convert his Protestant subjects. The hesitation, even, in regard to embracing the *King's creed*, was an offence; and and he urged on Bossuet eagerly to press the young Count, so far, at least, as to ascertain if there were or were not a prospect of his speedily following the example of Turenne, and so many others. The Bishop was thus driven to the subject, though against his will; and shortly after the young Count's appearance, he took him kindly and mildly by the hand, and led him into a small cabinet, where were ranged in goodly order, a considerable number of works on the controversial divinity of the time. Amongst others, appeared some of the good prelate's own productions, such as, " L'Exposition de la Doctrine Catholique," the " Traité de la Communion sous les deux Espèces," and the " Histoire des Variations." Bossuet ran his finger over the titles as he pointed them out to the young Count.

" I wish, my young friend," he said, " that I could prevail upon you to read some of these works: some perhaps even of my own, not from the vanity of an author alone,—though I believe that the greatest compliment that has ever been paid to me was that which was paid by some of the pastors of your own sect, who asserted when I wrote that book," and he pointed to the Exposition, " that I had altered the Catholic doctrines in order to suit them to the purposes of my defence. Nor, indeed, would they admit the contrary, till the full approbation of the head of our church stamped the work as containing the true doctrines of our holy faith. But, as I was saying, I wish I could persuade you to read some of these, not altogether to gratify the vanity of an author, which is always great, nor even simply to make a convert, but because I look upon you as one well worthy of saving, as a brand from the burning—and because I should regard your recall to the bosom of the mother church as worth a hundred of any ordinary conversions. In short, my dear young friend, because I would save you from much unhappiness, in life, in death, and in eternity."

" I owe you deep thanks, Monsieur de Meaux," said the Count, " for the interest that you take in me ; and I will promise you most sincerely to read, with as unprejudiced an eye as possible, not only any but all of the works you have written on such subjects. I have already read some ; and it is by no means too much to admit, that if any one could induce me to quit the faith in which I have been brought up, it would be Monsieur de Meaux. He will not think me wrong, however, when I say, that I am, as yet, unconvinced. Nor will he be offended if I make one observation, or, rather, ask one question, in regard to something he has just said."

" Far, far from it, my son," replied the Bishop. " I am ever willing to explain anything, to enter into the most open and candid exposition of everything that I think or feel. I have no design to embarrass, or to perplex, or to obscure ; my whole view is to make my own doctrine clear and explicit, so that the mind of the merest child may choose between the right and the wrong."

" I merely wish to ask," said the Count, " whether by the words ' unhappiness in life, and in death,' you meant to allude to temporal or spiritual unhappiness ?—whether you meant delicately to point out to me that the hand of persecution is likely to be stretched out to oppress me ? or——"

" No! no!" cried Bossuet, eagerly. " Heaven forbid that I should hold out as an inducement the apprehension of things that I disapprove of ! No, Monsieur de Morseiul, I meant merely spiritual happiness and unhappiness, for I do not believe that any man can be perfectly happy in life while persisting in a wrong belief ; certainly I believe that he must be unhappy in his death ; and, alas ! my son, reason and religion both teach me that he must be unhappy in eternity."

" The great question of eternity," replied the Count, solemnly, " is in the hands of God. But the man, and the only man, who, in this sense, must be unhappy in life, in death, and in eternity, seems to me to be the man who is uncertain in his faith. In life and in death I can conceive the deist, or (if there be such a thing) the atheist—if perfectly convinced of the truth of his system—perfectly happy and perfectly contented. But the sceptic can never be happy. He who, in regard to religious belief, is doubtful, uncertain, wavering, must assuredly be unhappy in life and in death, though to God's great mercy we must refer the eternity. If I remain unshaken, Monsieur de Meaux, in my firm belief that what we call the reformed church is right in its views and doctrines, the only thing that can disturb or make me unhappy therein is temporal persecution. Were my faith in that church, however, shaken, I would abandon it immediately. I could not, I would not, remain in a state of doubt."

" The more anxious am I, my son," replied the Bishop, " to

R

withdraw you from that erroneous creed, for so firm and so decided a mind as yours is the very one which could the best appreciate the doctrines of the church of Rome, which are always clear, definite, and precise, the same to-day as they were yesterday, based upon decisions that never change, and not, as your faith does, admitting doubts and fostering variations. You must listen to me, my young friend. Indeed, I must have you listen to me. I hear some of our other friends in the next room; but we must converse more, and the sooner the better. You have visited me twice, but I will next visit you, for I think nothing should be left undone that may court a noble spirit back to the church of God."

Thus saying, he slowly led the way into the larger room, the young Count merely replying, as he did so—

" Would to God, Monsieur de Meaux, that, by your example and by your exhortations, you could prevent others from giving us Protestants the strongest of all temporal motives to remain attached to our own creed."

" What motive is that?" demanded Bossuet, apparently in some surprise.

" Persecution!" replied the Count; " for, depend upon it, to all those who are worthy of being gained, persecution is the strongest motive of resistance."

" Alas! my son," replied Bossuet, " that you should acknowledge such a thing as pride to have anything on earth to do with the eternal salvation of your souls. An old friend of mine used to say, ' It is more often from pride than from want of judgment that people set themselves up against established opinions. Men find the first places occupied in the right party, and they do not choose to take up with back seats.' I have always known this to be true in the things of the world; but I think that pride should have nothing to do with the things of eternity."

Thus ended the conversation between the Count and Bossuet on the subject of religion for that night. Two guests had arrived; more soon followed, and the conversation became more general. Still, however, as there were many ecclesiastics, the subject of religion was more than once introduced, the restraint which the presence of a Protestant nobleman had occasioned on the first visit of the Count having now been removed. The evening passed over calmly and tranquilly, however, till about ten o'clock at night, when the Count took his leave, and departed. The rest of the guests stayed later; and on issuing out into the street the young nobleman found himself alone in a clear, calm, beautiful night, with the irregular shadows of the long line of houses chequering the pavement with the yellow lustre of the moon.

Looking up into the wide, open square beyond, the shadows were lost, and there the bright planet of the night seemed to pour forth a flood of radiance, without let or obstruction. There was a fountain in the middle of the square, casting up its sparkling

waters towards the sky, as if spirits were tossing about the moon-
beams in their sport, and casting the bright rays from hand to
hand.   As the Count gazed, however, and thought that he would
stroll on, giving himself up to calm reflection at that tranquil hour,
and arranging his plans for the momentous future without disturbance from the bum of idle multitudes, a figure suddenly came
between the fountain and his eyes, and crept slowly down on the
dark side of the street towards him.   He was standing at the
moment in the shadow of Bossuet's porch, so as not to be seen:
but the figure came down the street to the door of the Count's
own dwelling, paused for a minute, as if in doubt, then walked
over into the moonlight, and gazed up into the windows of the
prelate's hotel.   The Count instantly recognised the peculiar form
and structure of his valet, Jerome Riquet, and, walking out from
the porch towards his own house, he called the man to him, and
asked if anything were the matter.

" Why, yes, sir," said Riquet, in a low voice, " so much so that
I thought of doing what I never did in my life before—sending in
for you, to know what to do.   There has been a person seeking
you twice or three times since you went, and saying he must speak
with you immediately."

" Do you know him ?" demanded the Count.

" Oh, yes, I know him," answered Riquet; " a determined
devil he is, too; a man in whom you used to place much confidence in the army, and who was born, I believe, upon your own
lands—Armand Herval—you know him well.   I could give him
another name if I liked."

" Well," said the Count, as tranquilly as possible; " what of
him, Riquet?   What does he want here ?"

" Ay, sir, that I can't tell," replied the man: " but I greatly
suspect he wants no good.   He is dressed in black from his head
to his feet; and his face is black enough, too, that is to say, the
look of it.   It was always like a thunder-cloud, and now it is like a
thunder-cloud gone mad.   I don't think the man is sane, sir; and
the third time he came down here, about ten minutes ago, he said
he could not stop a minute, that he had business directly; and so
he went away, pulling his great dark hat and feather over his head,
as if to prevent people from seeing how his eyes were flashing;
and then I saw that the breast of his great heavy coat was full of
something else than rosemary or honeycomb."

" What do you mean? what do you mean?" demanded the
Count.   " What had he in his breast?"

" Why, I mean pistols, sir," said the man; " if I must speak
good French, I say he had pistols, then.   So, thinking he was
about some mischief, I crept after him from door to door, dodged
him across the square, and saw him go in by a gate which I
thought was shut, into the garden behind the château.   I went in
after him, though I was in a desperate fright for fear any one

should catch me; and I trembled so, that I shook three crowns in my pocket till they rang like sheep-bells. I thought he would have heard me; but I watched him till he planted himself under one of the statues on the terrace, and there he stood like a statue himself. I defy you to have told the one from the other, or to have known Monsieur Herval from Monsieur Neptune. Whenever I saw that, I came back to look for you, and tell you what had happened; for you know, sir, I am awfully afraid of fire-arms; and I had not even a pair of curling-irons to fight him with."

" That must be near the apartments of Louvois," said the young Count, thoughtfully. " This man may very likely seek to do him some injury."

" More likely the King, sir," said the valet, in a low voice. " I have heard that his majesty walks there on that terrace every fine night after the play, for half an hour. He is quite alone, and it would be as much as one's liberty is worth to approach him at that time."

" Come with me directly, Riquet," said the Count, " and show me where this is. Station yourself at the gate you mention, after I have gone in, and if you hear me call to you aloud, instantly give the alarm to the sentries. Come, quick, for the play must soon be over."

Thus saying, the young Count strode on, crossed the place, and, under the guidance of Riquet, approached the gate through which Herval had entered. The key was in the lock on the outside, and the door ajar; and, leaving the man in the shadow, the Count entered alone. The gardens appeared perfectly solitary, sleeping in the moonlight. The principal water-works were still; and no sound or motion was to be seen or heard, but such as proceeded from the smaller fountains that were sparkling on the terrace, making the night musical with the plaintive murmur of their waters, or from the tops of the high trees as they were waved by the gentle wind. The palace was full of lights, and nothing was seen moving across any of the windows, so that it was evident that the play was not yet concluded; and the young Count looked about for the person whom he sought, for a moment or two in vain.

At length he saw the shadow cast by one of the groups of statues, alter itself somewhat in form; and instantly crossing the terrace to the spot, he perceived Herval sitting on the first step which led from the terrace down to the gardens, his back leaning against the pedestal, and his arms crossed upon his chest. He did not hear the step of the young Count till he was close upon him; but the moment he did so, he started up, and drew a pistol from his breast. He soon perceived who it was, however; and the Count, saying, in a low voice, " My servants tell me you have been seeking me," drew him, though somewhat unwilling, apparently, down the steps.

" What is it you wanted with me?" continued the Count, gazing in his face, to see whether the marks of insanity which Riquet had spoken of were visible to him. But there was nothing more in the man's countenance than its ordinary fierce and fiery expression when stimulated by high excitement.

" I came to you, Count," he said, " to make you, if you will, the sharer of a glorious deed; and now you are here, you shall at least be the spectator thereof—the death of your great enemy—the death of him who tramples upon his fellow-creatures as upon grapes in the wine-press—the death of the slayer of souls and bodies."

" Do you mean Louvois?" asked the Count, in a calm tone.

" Louvois!" scoffed the man. " No! no! no! I mean him who gives fangs to the viper, and poison to the snake! I mean him without whom Louvois is but a bundle of dry reeds to be consumed to light the first fire that wants kindling, or to rot in its own emptiness! I mean the giver of the power, the lord of the persecutions: the harlot-monger, and the murderer, who calls himself King of France; and who, from that holy title, which he claims from God, thinks himself entitled to pile sin upon folly, and crime upon sin, till the destruction which he has so often courted to his own head shall this night fall upon him. The first of the brutal murderers that he sent down to rob our happy hearths of the jewel of their peace, this hand has slain; and the same that crushed the worm shall crush the serpent also."

The Count now saw that there was, indeed, in the state of Herval's mind, something different from its usual tone and character. It could hardly be said that the chief stay thereof was broken, so as to justify the absolute supposition of insanity; but it seemed as if one of the fine filaments of the mental texture had given way, leaving all the rest nearly as it was before, though with a confused and morbid line running through the whole web. It need not be said that Albert of Morseiul was determined to prevent, at all or any risk, the act which the man proposed to commit; but yet he wished to do so, without calling down death and torture on the head of one who was kindled almost into absolute madness, by wrongs which touched the finest affections of his heart, through religion and through love.

" Herval," he said, calmly, " I am deeply grieved for you. You have suffered, I know how dreadfully; and you have suffered amongst the first of our persecuted sect: but still you must let me argue with you; for you act regarding all this matter in a wrong light; and you propose to commit a great and terrible crime."

" Argue with me not, Count of Morseiul!" cried the man; " argue with me not, for I will hear no arguments. Doubtless, you would have argued with me, too, about killing that small pitiful insect, that blind worm, who murdered her I loved, and three or four noble and brave men along with her."

" I will tell you in a word, Herval," replied the Count, " had you not slain him, I would have done so. My hand against his alone, and my life against his. He had committed a base, foul, ungenerous murder, for which I knew that the corrupted law would give us no redress; and I was prepared to shelter under a custom which I abhor and detest in general, the execution of an act of justice which could be obtained by no other means. Had it been but for that poor girl's sake, I would have slain him like a dog."

"Thank you, Count, thank you!" cried the man, grasping his hand in his with the vehemence of actual frenzy. "Thank you for those words, from my very soul. But he was not worthy of your noble sword. He died the death that he deserved: strangled like a common felon, writhing and screaming for the mercy he had never shown."

To what he said on that head the Count did not reply; but he turned once more to the matter immediately before them.

"Now, Herval," he said, "you see that I judge not unkindly or hardly by you. You must listen to my advice, however——"

"Not about this, not about this!" cried the man, vehemently; "I am desperate, and I am determined. I will not see whole herds of my fellow-Christians slaughtered like swine, to please the bloody butcher on the throne. I will not see the weak and the faint-hearted driven, by terror, to condemn their own souls and barter eternity for an hour of doubtful peace. I will not see the ignorant and the ill-instructed bought by scores, like cattle at a market. I will not see the infants torn from their mothers' arms to be offered a living sacrifice to the Moloch of Rome. This night he shall die, who has condemned so many others; this night he shall fall, who would work the fall of the pure church that condemns him. I will hear no advice: I will work the work for which I came, and then perish when I may. Was it not for this, that every chance has favoured me? Was it not for this, that the key was accidentally left in the door till such time as I laid my hand upon it and took it away? Was it not for this, that no eye saw me seize upon that key, this morning, though thousands were passing by? Was it not for this, that such a thing should happen on the very night in which he comes forth to walk upon that terrace? And shall I now pause, —shall I now listen to any man's advice, who tells me that I must hold my hand?"

"If you will not listen to my advice," said the Count, "you must listen to my authority, Herval. The act you propose to commit, you shall not commit."

"No?" cried he. "Who shall stop me?—Yours is but one life against mine, remember; and I care not how many fall, or how soon I fall myself either, so that this be accomplished."

"My life, as you say," replied the Count, "is but one. But even, Herval, if you were to take mine, which would neither be just nor grateful, if even you were to lose your own, which may yet be of great service to the cause of our faith, you could not, and you should not, take that of the King. If you are determined, I am determined too. My servant stands at yonder gate, and on the slightest noise he gives the alarm. Thus, then, I tell you," he continued, glancing his eyes towards the windows of the palace, across which various figures were now beginning to move ; "thus, then, I tell you, you must either instantly quit this place with me, or that struggle begins between us, which, end how it may, as far as I am concerned, must instantly ensure the safety of the King, and lead you to trial and execution. The way is still open for you to abandon this rash project at once, or to call down ruin upon your own head without the slightest possible chance of accomplishing your object."

"You have frustrated me !" cried the man—"you have foiled me! You have overthrown, by preventing a great and noble deed, the execution of a mighty scheme for the deliverance of this land, and the security of our suffering church. The consequences be upon your own head, Count of Morseiul! the consequences be upon your own head! I see that you have taken your measures too well, and that, even if you paid the just penalty for such interference, the result could not be accomplished."

"Come, then," said the Count; "come, Herval, I must forgive anger, as I have thwarted a rash purpose ; but make what speed you may to quit the gardens, for, ere another minute be over, many a one will be crossing that terrace to their own apartments."

Thus saying, he laid his hand upon the man's arm, to lead him gently away from the dangerous spot on which he stood. But Herval shook off his grasp sullenly, and walked on before, with a slow and hesitating step, as if, every moment, he would have turned in order to effect his purpose. The Count doubted and feared that he would do so, and glad was he, indeed, when he saw him pass the gate which led out of the gardens. As soon as Herval had gone forth, the young Count closed the door, locked it, and threw the key over the wall, saying, "There! thank God, it is now impossible !"

"Ay," replied the man. "But there are other things possible, Count; and things that may cause more bloodshed and more confusion than one little pistol shot.—It would have saved all France," he continued, muttering to himself, "it would have saved all France!—What a change !—But if we must fight it out in the field, we must."

While he spoke, he walked onward towards the Count's house, in a sort of gloomy, but not altogether silent reverie; for in the intervals thereof, he spoke or murmured to himself in a manner which seemed to justify the opinion expressed by Riquet, that he was insane. Suddenly turning round towards the valet, who followed, however, he demanded sharply, "Has there not been a tall man, with a green feather in his hat, asking for your lord two or three times to-day ?"

"So I have heard," replied Riquet, "from the Swiss, but I did not see him myself."

"The Swiss never informed me thereof," said the Count. "Pray, who might he be, and what was his business?"

"His name, sir," replied Herval, "is Hatréaumont, and his business was for your private ear."

"Hatréaumont!" said the Count, in return. "What, he who was an officer in the Guards?"

Herval nodded his head, and the Count went on : "A brave man, a determined man he was; but in other respects, a wild, rash profligate. He can have no business for my private ear, that I should be glad or even willing to hear."

"You know not that, Count," said Herval; "he has glorious schemes in view, schemes which perhaps may save his country."

The Count shook his head; "Schemes," he said, "which will bring ruin on himself, and on all connected with him. I have rarely known or heard of a man, unprincipled and profligate in private life, who could be faithful and just in public affairs. Such men there may be, perhaps; but the first face of the case is against them; for surely they who are not to be trusted between man and man, are still less to be trusted when greater temptations lie in their way, and greater interests are at stake."

"Well, well," said Herval, "he will not trouble you again. This was the last day of his stay in Paris; and ere to-morrow be two hours old, he will be far away."

"And pray," demanded the Count, "was it by his advice—he who owes nothing but gratitude to the King—was it by his advice that you were stationed where I found you?"

"He knew nothing of it," said the man, sharply, "he knew nothing of it; nor did I intend that he should know, till it was all over—and now," he continued, "what is to become of me?"

"Why, in the first place," replied the Count, "you had better come in with me and take some refreshment. While you are doing so, we will think of the future for you."

The man made no reply, but followed the Count, who led the way into his house, and then ordered some refreshments of various kinds to be set before his guest from Poitou, examining the man's countenance as he did so, and becoming more and more convinced that something certainly had given way in the brain to produce the wandering and unsettled eye which glared in his face, as well as the rash words and actions which he spoke and performed.

"And now, Herval," he said, as soon as they were alone, "there is but one question which you should ask yourself,—whether it is better for you to return at once to Poitou, or, since you are so far on your way to Holland, to take advantage of that circumstance, and speed to the frontier without delay. I know not what is the situation of your finances; but if money be wanting for either step, I am ready to supply you as an old comrade."

"I want no money," exclaimed the man; "I am wealthy in my station beyond yourself. What have I to do with money, whose life is not worth an hour? I have a great mind to divide all I have into a hundred portions, spend one each day, and die at the end of it.— Holland! no, no; this is no time for me to quit France. I will be at my post at the coming moment; I will set off again to-night for Poitou. But let me tell you, Count—for I had forgotten—if you should yourself wish to secure ought in Holland—and I have heard that there is a lady dearer to you than all your broad lands—remember, there is a schoolmaster living three doors on this side of the barrier of Passy, called Vandenenden, passing for a Fleming by birth, but in reality a native of Dort. He has regular communication with his native land, and will pass anything you please with the utmost security."

"I thank you for that information sincerely," replied the Count; "it may be most useful to me. But give me one piece of information more," he added, as the man rose, after having drank a glass of water, with a few drops of wine in it. "What was the state of the province when you left it?"

"If you mean, Count, what was the state of the reformed party," said Herval, gazing round with a look of wild carelessness, "it was a girl in a consumption, where something is lost every day, no one knows how, and yet the whole looks as pretty as ever, till there is nothing but a skeleton remains. But there will be this difference, Count, there will be this difference. There will be strength found in the skeleton! Have you not heard? There were three thousand men, together with women and children, all converted at once, within ten miles of Niort; and it cost the priest so many wafers giving them the sacrament, that he swore he would make no more converts unless the King would double the value of the cure—Ha! ha! ha!" and laughing loud and wildly, he turned upon his heel and left the room without bidding the Count good night.

CHAPTER XX.

THE DECISION.

ABOUT seven o'clock on the following morning, Jerome Riquet entered his master's room on tiptoe, drew the curtains of his bed, and found him leaning on his arm, reading attentively. The subject of the Count's studies matters not. They were interrupted immediately; for a note, which the valet placed in his hands, caused him instantly to spring up, to order his horses to be prepared with speed, and to set off for Paris at once, without waiting for the morning meal. The note which caused this sudden expedition contained but a few words. They were—

" Come to me immediately, if you can, for I have matter of deep moment on which I wish to speak with you. You must not come, however, to the Hôtel de Rouvré, for though it may seem strange in me to name another place to meet you, yet you will find with me one whom you will be surprised to see. I must not then hesitate to ask you to seek me towards ten o'clock, at number five in the street of the Jacobins; the house is that of a bookbinder, and in the shop you will find Maria."

It had no signature; but the handwriting was that of Clémence. All that had occurred within the last few days had shown the Count de Morseiul that the crisis of his fate was approaching, that a very few days, nay, a very few hours, might decide the fortunes of his future life for ever. The multitude of matters which had pressed for his consideration during the two or three preceding days, the various anxieties that he had suffered, the mingling of joy and hope with pain and apprehension, had all created a state of mind in which it was difficult to think calmly of the future. Now, however, he had regained complete mastery of his own mind: the short interval of repose which had taken place had removed all confusion, all agitation, from his thoughts; and as he rode on towards Paris somewhat slowly, finding that there was more than the necessary time to accomplish his journey, he revolved coolly and deliberately in his own mind the peculiar points in his situation, and questioned himself as to his conduct and his duty in regard to each.

First, then, of course, came the image of Clémence; and in regard to his love for her, and hers for him, there was many a question to be asked, which was answered by his own heart, whether altogether fairly and candidly or not, those who know love and love's nature can best declare.

In asking her to fly with him from France, then, he was going to take her from wealth, and splendour, and luxury, and soft nurture, and all the comforts and conveniences which, surrounding her from her earliest years, had made to her eyes poverty, and difficulty, and distress, seem but a recorded dream of which she knew nothing else, but that some men had felt such things.

He had to offer her in a foreign land, indeed, competence, mere competence; but would competence to her, educated as she had been educated, be anything but another name for poverty? Even that competence itself might perhaps be insecure. It depended upon the doubtful faith of foreign merchants, from whom he had no security; and if that were gone, he had nought to depend upon but his sword, and a high name in arms. Could Clémence bear all this? he asked himself. Could the gay, the admired, the adored, endure seclusion, and retirement, and almost solitude? Could the spoilt child of fortune undergo privation? Could she, who had been accustomed but to command to be obeyed, be contented with scanty service from foreign servants? Would she never repine? Would she never look back to the bright land of France, and think with regret of the high station from which she had voluntarily descended? Would she never even, by one repining thought in the depth of her heart, reproach him for having won her away, to share his exile and misery? Would he never see upon her countenance one shade of sorrow and dissatisfaction when· petty cares weighed down the mind made for greater things, when small anxieties and daily discomforts interrupted the current of finer and higher thoughts, or when disrespect and coldness made the sad change felt to her, upon whose words the brightest and the best had hung?

His heart answered, No; that none of these things would ever arise to make him feel that he should not have taken her from her high fortunes to share his reverses. What could not love do, he asked himself, to brighten the lowliest lot? The grand face of nature would be still before them inexhaustible as a store of enjoyment; the communion of two high minds, he felt, could never be wanting while they were united: if they retained competence, they had all that was needful; and if for a time worse fell upon them, love would surely be strong enough to excite them to every effort and every exertion, each for the other, to cheer, to encourage, to alleviate; and would bring, too, its own reward. Besides, he remembered that he should never have to reproach himself with having led Clémence to difficulty and to danger—a reproach which, could it have been brought against him by conscience, would have imbittered all his joys—for her own situation, her own faith, required flight as well as his; and by making her his own, he only secured to her protection, support, affection, and guidance.

Such were some of the thoughts which crossed his mind regarding Clémence; but there was another consideration of more difficulty, a question on which he was less satisfied. His fellow-Protestants throughout the land, and more especially those who looked up to him for aid and for direction, should he now leave them to their fate, even though he could not avert from them one blow, even though he could not save them from one single pang? Should he not stay to share their lot, to comfort or to fall with them?

The question would have been answered at once, had they been firm and united amongst themselves. It needed not, indeed, that they should have armed to resist the royal authority, against which they had no power to contend; it needed not that they should have attempted to build up the churches which had been thrown down, to replace the ministers who had been rejected, to petition for the restoration of rights which injustice had snatched from them: it needed none of these things to have induced him, without hesitation, to stay and partake of all that might befal them, if they had displayed a resolution of remaining calmly, firmly, though peaceably, attached to their faith, addressing their prayers to God in private, if public worship was forbidden them, and opposing to the iniquitous proceedings of their enemies that tranquil, steady resistance of endurance, which seldom fails in ultimately repelling attack.

Had they so acted, the Count de Morsciul would have had no hesitation; but such was not the case. Even before the last severe measures, which have been recorded in this book, the inconveniences attending their situation, the apprehension of worse, and the prospect of immediate gain, had caused weekly the conversion of hundreds of the Protestant population of France to the Roman-catholic faith. Nothing like a spirit of union had reigned amongst them for years; and now that danger and persecution fell upon them, each day brought to the court tidings of thousands upon thousands having at once professed conversion. Each bishop, each intendant, sent daily lists of the numbers who had quitted the religion of their fathers to embrace that of the state; and in almost all quarters, those who had courage to sacrifice something for conscience' sake, were flying from the land, or preparing for flight.

He, too, had to remember that he was himself placed in a situation more difficult and dangerous than the rest. The question was not whether he should remain adhering calmly to his own faith, and living in tranquillity, though under oppression, or should fly to a foreign country; but there was a choice of three acts before him: whether he should remain to trial and perpetual imprisonment, if not death; or retiring to Poitou, at once, raise the standard of hopeless revolt; or, seek security abroad, leaving those to whom he could render no possible service.

The voice of reason certainly said, Fly! but yet it was painful to him to do so. Independent of all thoughts of what he left behind —the dwelling of his infancy, the tombs of his fathers, the bright land of his birth—independent of all this, there was the clinging to his own people, which few can feel deeply but those circumstanced as he was; which none indeed can feel now, when the last vestiges have been swept away of a system which, though in no slight degree dangerous and evil, had nevertheless many an amiable and many an admirable point. He loved not to leave them, he loved not to leave any fellow-sufferer behind while he provided for his own safety; and though reason told him that on every motive he ought to go, yet he felt that lingering inclination to remain, which required the voice of others to conquer entirely.

Such were the principal questions which his mind had found to discuss during the last two days; but since the preceding night, a new subject for thought had arisen, a new question presented itself. It, however, was not so difficult of solution as the others. A dark attempt upon the King's life, which could hardly have failed of success, had been nearly executed; but that was not all. From Herval he had gathered, that schemes, which there was much reason to believe were dangerous to the whole state, were at that moment in agitation, if not upon the point of being accomplished. He loved not to be the denouncer of any man; and for Herval himself, he felt pity mingled with blame, which made him glad that the length of time that had elapsed, had given him an opportunity of retiring once more to Poitou.

With regard to the proceedings of Hatréaumont, however, he had no scruple and no hesitation. It was right and necessary that the King should be made acquainted with the fact of dangerous designs being in agitation; and, although he was well aware that the task of informing the monarch of the truth would be a difficult and delicate one, so as not to bring the strong and unscrupulous hand of power upon persons who might be innocent, and were only accused on the word of a man whom he sincerely believed to be partially insane, yet he resolved to undertake that task, trusting to the firmness and uprightness of his own character, to ensure that the execution of it should be such as to avoid doing injury to any one who was not guilty.

Men under such circumstances in general err from an inaccuracy or deficiency of statement, proceeding from the confusion and uncertainty of a mind oppressed and agitated by the burthen of important affairs, or difficult and intricate circumstances. The Count de Morseiul, however, saw his way clearly, and prepared to tell the King exactly the words which Herval had made use of, but at the same time to inform him, that he had much reason to believe that the man was insane, and that, therefore, but little reliance was to be placed upon his statement, except so far as the employing of precaution might be required.

The meditation over all these circumstances fully occupied the time till his arrival in Paris: and dismounting at his own house, he took his way alone and on foot towards the Rue des Jacobins. The capital at that period had but little of the light and graceful architectural beauty which the citizens have since endeavoured to give it; but there was, instead, a grey, mysterious-looking grandeur about the vast piles of building of which it was composed, peculiar and entirely characteristic of the French metropolis. The great height of the houses, the smallness, in general, of the windows, their multitude, their irregularities, the innumerable carriage entrances leading into courtyards where cities and new worlds seemed to be opening on every side, the intricate alleys and passages that were seen branching off here and there in unknown directions as the stranger took his way through the streets; everything, in short, impressed upon the mind, as a keen and sensible perception, that fact, which, though common to all great capitals, is generally unfelt: that we are walking in the midst of a world of human beings with whom we have scarcely one feeling in sympathy, of whose habits, character, pursuits, pleasures, and pains, we are utterly ignorant— who are living, moving, acting, feeling, undergoing life's great ordeal, smiling with rapture, writhing with anguish, melting with the bitter tears of sorrow and regret, inspired by hope, or palpitating with expectation around us on every side, without our having the slightest participation in any of their sensations, with scarcely a knowledge of their existence, and certainly none of their situation.

It was impossible to walk through the streets of Paris at that time—it was impossible even to walk through the older parts of the city when I myself remember it, without having that sensation strongly excited—without asking oneself, as one gazed up at the small windows of some of the many-tenanted houses, and saw the half-drawn curtain shading out even the scanty portion of sun that found its way thither: Is there sickness or death within? are there tears over the departing couch of the beloved? is there anguish over the bier of the gone?—without asking oneself, as one gazed at some wide-open casement, courting the summer air, and perhaps with some light piece of drapery floating out into the street, Is that the abode of love and joy? is happy heart there meeting happy heart? are they smiling over the birth of the first-born, or watching the glad progress of a young spirit kindred with their own?—without asking oneself, as the eye rested upon some squalid doorway, foul with uncleaned ages, or some window, thick and obscure with the dust of years, some dim alley, or some dark and loathsome passage, Is vice, and plunder, and iniquity, there? is there the feverish joy of sin mingled with remorse, and anguish, and apprehension? is there the wasting and the gnawing effects of vice, sickness, and sorrow, worn limbs, corroded heart, nights of restless watchfulness, and days of ceaseless anguish?—It was impossible to walk through that tall city, with its myriads living above myriads, house within house, and court within court, without asking one-self such questions, and without feeling that the whole intense and thrilling reality of the scene was rendered but more striking by the gay and careless multitude that tripped along, each seeming scarcely conscious that there was another being in the world but himself.

The Count de Morseiul was half an hour before his time. He walked somewhat slowly; and in picturing the feelings which a contemplative mind might experience in passing through Paris, we have pictured those which pressed for his attention, and crossed from time to time the current of his other thoughts. At length, however, he entered the Rue des Jacobins, and easily found the house to which he had been directed. It was a tall building of six stories, with a bookseller's shop upon the ground-floor. Very different indeed, however, was it from a gay dwelling such as Paris now exhibits, with every new publication in blue and yellow flaming in the windows: but, through a small door, entrance was obtained into a long dark shop, where, on shelves, and in cases, and on benches, and on counters, were piled up manifold dusty volumes, whose state of tranquil slumber seemed to have been long undisturbed. A single pale apprentice, with an apron on and a brush in his hand, walked from one end of the shop to the other, or examined with slow inactivity the sheets of some unbound work, moving about his task with the same indifference to its speedy execution, as if the years of Methuselah were bound up in his indentures.

The Count looked at the shop well, to ascertain that he was right, and then entered; but in the long dim vista of the counters and packages, the person he sought for was not to be seen; and not having contemplated such an occurrence, he was somewhat embarrassed as to the person he should ask for. To have inquired if a lady were waiting for him there, might perhaps have been received as an insult by the master of the house, and yet he thought it would be imprudent to risk the name of Clémence de Marly, when she herself might not have given it. He felt sure that had she arrived, her attendant Maria would have been at the post where she had promised to place her; and, in order to occupy the time till she came, he determined to ask for some book, and then enter into desultory conversation with the lad in the shop, after having bought it.

He had scarcely spoken, however, when from behind a pile of solid literature which obscured still farther the end of the shop, the servant Maria came forth and advanced towards him. The matter was then easily explained, and the youth seemed in no degree surprised at the appointment, but proceeded to tie up the book which the Count had demanded, while Maria told him that her young lady had only just arrived, and was waiting for him up stairs. He followed her with a rapid step as she led the way; and at the third turning of a long, dim, narrow staircase, he found Clémence waiting at a door and listening as if for his arrival.

There was something in the meeting under such circumstances which did away all feelings of reserve, such as perhaps might otherwise have still affected them towards each other; for Clémence felt that she was all his—that their fate was united for ever. She spoke not, however, but held up her finger, as if to enjoin silence, and then led him through a little anteroom into a room beyond.

There, seated at a table with some books scattered upon it, appeared the good pastor of Auron, Claude de l'Estang. He was thinner, paler, more worn, than when first we endeavoured to depict him; but the light was not gone out in the clear bright eye, the same mild but intelligent smile hung upon the lip, the same high spirit was throned upon the brow. He rose, and grasped the young Count's hands eagerly.

"Oh, my dear Albert," he said, "I am glad to see you! This sweet child," he added, after the first exclamation, "wrote to me all that was between you and her. She is dear to my heart as if she were my own; and is she not my own? Did I not bring her back to the faith of her dear mother? Did I not rescue her from the evils of a corrupt, perverted church? But of that we will speak not now, Albert. The moment I heard of it—the moment I heard that you were here, and had cast yourself, as it were, into the jaws of the lion after the fatal night when that murderous youth, like Pilate, mingled our blood with our sacrifices—I resolved at once to make my way hither, at all and any risks, to speak to you, to exhort you, to tell you what I have decided in my own mind is the only plan for you to follow. I thought, indeed, when I set out—notwithstanding all that has occurred since you left Poitou, notwithstanding the scattering of the sheep and the driving forth of the shepherd, and the falling off of many, and the wavering of all the rest—I thought that here I might learn tidings which might make a change in my opinion, but that, at all events, it was right for me to come, in order that I might consult with you and others, and take our last, final determination together. But, since I have heard from this dear child the situation in which you are placed, since I have heard from a weak brother, who has outwardly abjured the faith which he fondly clings to in his heart, things that you yourselves do not know, my opinion has been confirmed to the fullest extent, and I have only to say to you, Albert—fly! Fly with her immediately; save her from persecution, and anguish, and care; confirm her in the only true faith, and in the renunciation of every superstitious vanity of the church of Rome! Strengthen her, support her, protect her! Lose no time—no, not a day; for, if you do, danger to both, and, perhaps, everlasting separation in this world may be the consequence."

"I am most willing," replied the Count; "the hour cannot be too soon that makes her mine. It is absolutely necessary, indeed, that I should return to Versailles, but only for a few minutes. After that, I can return hither, and, without further delay, execute what I am fully convinced is the only plan for us to pursue."

"It *is* the only plan," said the clergyman. "Are you aware, Albert, that, in the short space of five days, one half of the Protestants of Poitou have bent the knee to Baal? Are you aware, that the very men who, a week ago, clung to you for aid and protection, would now fly from you, either in shame at their own degeneracy, or because you are marked out for indignation by the powers that be? Yes, Albert, they would fly from you! There is a remnant, indeed, faithful and true unto the last; but to them I shall say, as I say to you, they must go forth to other lands, and shake off the dust from their feet as a testimony against this place. There is nothing left you, Albert, but flight, and that speedy and unhesitating. I have told you, that I have heard much from a weak brother, whose renunciation of his faith weighs heavy upon him. He is in the confidence, it would seem, of those who rule; and he has informed me, that it is the determination of the monarch and his council, never to let you quit the court of France except as a follower of the popish church of Rome. Every temptation is to be held out to you to make you yield, every menace used to drive you on the way they approve; and should your resistance become strong and decided, the order for your arrest is already made out, and needs but one word to cause its execution. Fly, then, fly, Albert, and even if not for your own sake, for hers."

"I am most willing, my good friend," replied the Count. "I need no exhortation so to do. But is Clémence still willing to go with me?"

"Can you doubt it, Albert," she said, "with *his* approbation and advice?"

"Yet, dear Clémence," said the Count, "I should be wrong were I not to tell you what may happen. The danger, the risk of our escape, the fatigues, and labours, and anxieties of the journey, the perils that await us at every step, you have made up your mind to. But Clémence, have you thought of the change from affluence to mere competence, from splendour and luxury to bare necessaries, even perhaps to poverty itself, for all I have on earth depends upon the good faith of those to whom I have transmitted it, and I might arrive and find nothing. Have you thought of all this? Have you thought that it may last for years, that we may have to live, and die, and bring up our children in poverty —— ?"

"Out upon it, Albert!" exclaimed the old man, angrily: "wouldst thou take the part of the prince of this world against her better angel? But she will not doubt, she will not waver: I know she will not. Sooner than be a hypocrite, sooner than abandon truth and embrace error, she would cast herself upon the world, were it ten thousand times as bad.—Out upon it, she fears not! She will have her husband, and her faith, and her God to support her."

"I have not thought of all you suggest, Albert," replied Clémence, more mildly, but still somewhat reproachfully, "I have not thought of them, because it was unnecessary to think of them at all. Do you not love me, Albert? Do I not love you? Is not that love riches, and splendour, and luxury enough for us? But when, beside that all-sufficient love, we have the knowledge that we are doing our duty, that we are suffering for our conscience' sake, that we have left all to follow what we believe the dictates of the great Author of our faith, there will be a satisfaction, a pride, a glory, that even a woman's heart can feel. Fear not for me, Albert. I understand your scruples; and though they require forgiveness, I forgive them. Let us be guided by his advice,—I am sure that it is good,—and I am willing, most willing, to risk all and everything under such circumstances, and for such a cause."

"Well, then, so be it," said the Count; "let us consider our decision as made. This very night, Clémence, I will return to Paris. This very night I will meet you here; but oh, my good friend," he continued, turning to the pastor, "you whom I love and venerate as a father, you will easily understand what I feel when I say, that I could wish most anxiously that this dear girl, who is to accompany me through scenes of some peril, were united to me before we depart, not alone by the bonds of deep and true affection, not alone by the bonds of all the mutual promises and engagements which man and woman can plight towards each other, but by the sanction of that holy religion which first instituted such an union, and by the blessing of one of the ministers of Christ. I fear, however, it cannot be done."

"Nay, my son, it can," replied the clergyman. "Expelled from our temples, debarred from the performance of all those ceremonial rites, which are but the shadows and types of higher things, the abandonment of such ceremonies as we cannot exercise, can, in no degree, either in the sight of man or of God, as long as the side of law or justice is considered, affect the validity of such a contract, or do away, in the slightest degree, the solemn legality of an union complete in all the forms which we are enabled to give it. Even were it not so, I have power delegated to me by the synod of our church, without application to higher authorities, whose approbation, for many years, would have been difficult and embarrassing to obtain, to perform all the ceremonies of the church, upon due knowledge certified by me that they are not contrary, in the particular cases, to the law of God, or to those just ordinances of man to which we have ourselves subscribed. If you desire it, and if Clémence is willing, I will this very night, before you depart, give my blessing to your union, and doubt not that, with my certificate thereof, witnessed by proper witnesses, that union will be held good by the Protestant church throughout the world."

"Then I fear not," exclaimed the Count. "What say you, dear Clémence? Can you resolve upon this also?—Speak, dear girl," he added, as she paused in silence, covering her eyes with her hand. "Speak! oh speak!"

"What should I say, Albert?" she said. "Do you dream that I would refuse? Do you suppose that I would reject the only thing which was wanting to give me confidence, and strength, and hope, through all the perils that we may have to undergo?"

Albert gazed on her with a look that thanked her to the full; and, after a brief moment given to happiness, he asked, "But who shall be the witnesses?"

"Maria must be one," said Clémence, "for she of course goes with us."

"One of my servants may be another," said the Count. "But it is better to have several."

"The master of this house and his son," said Claude de l'Estang, "will make up a number more than sufficient; and all that remains, Albert, is for you to go and settle your affairs at Versailles, and return hither as soon as you may—though I wish, indeed, that it were possible for you not to go back to that place at all."

" Indeed, it is quite necessary," replied the Count; " not contemplating this meeting, I have left all the little store of wealth which I brought with me from Poitou in my house at Versailles. It is impossible to send for it without causing instant suspicion, and it is absolutely necessary, not only for the expenses of the journey, but in order to secure some little sum for our subsistence, for a year or two, in case we shall find that, either by misfortune or by fraud, the money which I transmitted to Holland is **not** forthcoming."

" It is, indeed, most necessary," said Claude de l'Estang. " I have heard that one of our poor ministers, who was banished some years ago from Languedoc, suffered most terribly in foreign lands before he could gain employment."

" But I can bring in my share," exclaimed Clémence, her eyes sparkling with gladness. " I have a number of jewels, of different kinds: many purchased in other days with my own money; many given me by friends of my youth long years ago. They have cost, I know, in all, many thousand livres. These are my own, and I will take them with me. Those that I have received from the Duke and Duchess, and other Roman-catholic friends, I shall leave to be given back to them again."

" Do so, do so !" said the pastor. " There are some people, my dear child, who would wring a text from Scripture to bid you do the contrary, telling you to spoil the Egyptians; but I think that such injunctions as that must ever be applicable to particular cases alone, and that the application must be made by God himself. I say, leave all that is not justly and absolutely your own : leave all that those who gave it, would not give now, if they could see the use to which you are going to apply it. We shall rarely regret, my child, if ever, having been too just; we shall never cease to regret, if we are once unjust."

The Count de Morseiul had remarked that, through the whole of this conversation, the pastor had never once mentioned himself or his own plans. It might, however, seem, that he left it to be understood that he, too, was about to fly from the land; but the Count de Morseiul knew him well, and was aware that he was one of those who would resolutely and firmly place himself in the way of perils which he would teach others to avoid. He did not choose even to suppose that the pastor was about to remain in the land which he advised them to quit; and he, therefore, demanded, " At what hour, my good friend, will you be ready to give us your blessing and to go with us ?"

" My son," replied the pastor, " I will give my blessing on your union at any hour you like, for I dare not go out during the day. But, alas ! I must not think of going with you. I say not that I will not come hereafter, if Heaven enable me to do so ; but it must be after I have seen every one of my flock, who is willing to sacrifice temporal to eternal things, in safety in another land before me.

Nay, nay, Albert," he said, seeing the Count about to reply, " urge
me not in this matter; for I am sure I am right, and when such is
the case I must be immovable. As soon as all who are willing to
go are gone, I will obey the injunction of the King, which orders
the pastors and ministers of our church to quit the realm immediately——"

" Indeed!" exclaimed the Count. " Has such an order been
issued? I never heard of it."

" You hear, my son, very little here," replied the old man.
" Care is taken to keep unpleasant things from the ears of kings
and courtiers. Pomp, and pageantry, and display, luxury and
feasting, and music, and games, and revelry: they are for palaces
and capitals: not the groans and tears of the wronged and injured,
not the cries and murmurs of the oppressed. Some days have
passed since the order appeared throughout all the provinces; and
many of my brethren have already obeyed. I will obey it, too—
but not till the last."

" Oh," cried Clémence, " dear and excellent friend, do not, do
not expose yourself too far. Remember how much we may need
your counsel and assistance hereafter. Remember what a stay and
support your presence may be to the whole of your flock in other
lands."

" Those who do not fulfil their duties now, Clémence," said the
pastor, "upon the pretext of fulfilling them better hereafter, will
fulfil none at all, my child. But say no more, either of you; my
determination is strong and fixed; and now, Albert," he added,
with a faint smile, " find some way of measuring her finger for the
ring that is to make her yours, and if you could get some friendly
notary to draw up a regular contract of marriage between you,
against this evening, all would be complete."

Albert of Morseiul took the fair hand of his promised bride,
which she gave him with a blushing cheek, to measure it for the
ring that was to be the symbol of their union. Upon the very
finger was that ring which he had rescued for her when it had
been taken away by the band of Herval, with the coronet and the
cipher in diamonds; and as he gazed upon it and tried it on his
own finger, to judge of the size, a brief feeling of curiosity passed
through his heart, and he thought, " This, indeed, is strange: I
am about to wed one, of whose history, and fate, and circumstances, both I myself, and almost every one around me, are
ignorant."

He lifted his look to her face, however, while he thus meditated.
Those large, pure, beautiful eyes were gazing upon him with
tenderness and trust; and, replacing the ring upon her finger, he
sealed his faith and confidence upon that fair hand with a kiss.

CHAPTER XXI.

THE KING'S CLOSET.

DURING the time of the young Count's absence from Versailles, while he was busied, as we have represented, with those schemes on which his future woe or welfare seemed beyond all doubt to depend, a scene was taking place in the palace of the King, in which the Count was more interested than he could have supposed possible, and which, as will be seen at the close of this history, was destined to affect him as much as any of his own proceedings.

The scene, then, was in the King's cabinet. A clock of a rich and singular construction stood exactly before the monarch, marking out to him the portions of time which he could bestow upon each separate affair as it was brought before him. A large inkstand, containing innumerable pens, and a portfolio, half filled with writing, in the King's own hand, lay upon the table; wax of four different colours, blue, red, white, and yellow, was also placed before him, in a small case of marquetry, which contained likewise several seals, and an instrument of a peculiar form for spreading the wax: the walls were ornamented with a few very choice small pictures; a number of maps were there also, and a few, but very few, books.

The monarch was seated in a large arm-chair, his right foot supported by a footstool, and his hand holding a pen as it rested on the table. The expression of his countenance was mild but intelligent, and before him stood—a little pale, indeed, and affecting, certainly, greater awe and terror than he really did feel—a man, who, as we have described him before, may be passed over in silence, as far as his personal appearance is concerned. He was no other than Jerome Riquet, the valet of the Count of Morseiul; and behind him appeared the figure of Bontems, Louis's confidential attendant, who instantly retreated in silence from the chamber, on a slow nod of the head from the King.

"Your name," said the monarch, fixing his eyes full upon Riquet, "is, I understand, Jerome Riquet, and you are valet to the young Count of Morseiul."

"I have been his faithful valet in the field, and the camp, and the court, and the castle, for these many years, sire," replied the man.

"And I hear," continued the King, "that you are a member of the holy Catholic church, while your lord is of the religion which its professors call reformed. Now, answer me truly, how have you contrived—during this long period of service, surrounded, as you were, by Huguenot fellow-servants and under a Huguenot lord—how have you contrived to fulfil the duties of your religion, I say, under such circumstances?"

" Oh, sire, nothing so easy," replied the man. " May it please your majesty, I was much better off, in most respects, than my brother Catholics; for, on a fast-day, sire, by my lord's order, on my account, there was either fish, or some other meagre dish prepared, so that I had my choice. I could fast and grow thin, or sin and grow fat, as I thought fit."

The King's countenance fell a little at an uncalled-for joke in his presence, especially on a subject which, in his eyes, was of serious importance. Louis, however, was very rarely disposed to say a harsh word, unless it was impossible to help it; and he, therefore, passed over the valet's levity with merely the reproof of that displeased look, and then again demanded—

" So, then, your lord gave you every facility of fulfilling the duties of your religion?"

" The greatest, sire," replied the man. " Except when we were in Holland, where there was no Catholic church to be found, he has always driven me to mass, as if with a scourge. Even at Morseiul, scarcely a Sunday passed without his telling me to go to mass, and asking me if I had been."

" This looks well for the young gentleman," said the King, seemingly well pleased with the account the man afforded. " We have had different stories at court—that he was rank and bigoted, and furious against the Catholic religion."

" Lord bless your majesty!" exclaimed the man, " he is more than three-quarters of a Catholic himself, and if the devil gets the other quarter it will only be because the Count is driven to him."

" Speak not profanely, sir, of things that are serious," said the King, " nor presume, in my presence, to venture upon such jests."

As he spoke, the whole aspect of his countenance changed, his brow grew dark, his lip curled, his voice became deeper, his head more erect, and that indescribable majesty, for which he was famous, took possession of his person, making the unfortunate Jerome Riquet ready to sink into the earth.

" Now, sir," continued the King, " be not frightened; but give me clear and straightforward answers in a serious tone. What you have told me of your young lord is satisfactory to me. I am most anxious to do him good and to show him favour. I have marked his gallant conduct as a soldier, and his upright and noble demeanour as a French gentleman, and I would fain save him from the destruction to which obstinacy may lead him. You say that he is three parts a Catholic already, and would be one altogether if it were not—at least, so I understand you—that some one drove him to the contrary conduct. Now, who is it drives him, sir? Speak to me plainly and explicitly, and no harm shall come to you.— Have you lost your tongue, sir, or are you struck dumb?" the King continued, seeing that Riquet remained silent, while his whole frame seemed to work with terror and agitation.

Perhaps, had his lord been there, he might have discovered, at once, that Riquet was working himself up to assume an immense deal more of terror than he really felt; but the King, conscious of having assumed an overawing look, which he had often seen produce effects somewhat similar, believed the fear of the valet to be entirely real, and was not at all surprised to see Riquet suddenly cast himself at his feet and burst into an amazing flood of tears.

"If I have offended your majesty," cried the man, with a species of orientalism which was not at all displeasing to the ears of the despotic monarch of the French, " if I have offended your majesty, take my head! But you are now proceeding to question me upon matters, in which what I have to tell and to speak of, may produce the most terrible results. I know not every word I utter that I may not be doing wrong—I know not that every word may not cost my life—and unless your majesty will deign to grant me in writing your full and free pardon for all that I have done, I dare not, indeed I dare not go on; or if I do, terror will make me prevaricate, and attempt to conceal facts that the wisdom of your majesty will soon discover."

"Nay, nay," exclaimed the King; "before I give you such pardon, my good friend, I must know to what it extends. You may have committed twenty crimes, for ought I know; you may be a relapsed heretic, for ought I know."

"So help me God, sire, no!" exclaimed the man, vehemently: "I am a sincere, devout, and zealous Catholic, and have been so all my life. Here is the certificate of the parish priest of Maubourg, sire, in order that I might have the benefit of the indulgence," and he drew forth from his pocket a small piece of written paper, which Louis read attentively, and which bestowed upon him so high a character for devotion to the Catholic faith, and for various other extraordinary virtues, that Louis thought he could not be far wrong in assuring him of the pardon he wanted, especially as Riquet, while he read, had relapsed into a passion of tears, and the moments allotted to the task of examining him were fleeting rapidly away. "Well," he said, "to put you at ease, I will grant you the pardon, under some conditions."

"And pray put in, sire," cried Riquet, with real joy sparkling in his eyes, " pray put in that you take me under your royal protection, for fear the Count should be angry, or any of the heretics should attempt to take vengeance upon me."

"That I will do also," replied Louis; and taking the pen, he wrote rapidly a paper which, according to the old English form, would have been somewhat to the following effect, though the beginning of it, "*A tous ceux*," &c., may be somewhat freely translated.

"Know all men by these presents, that we, for especial reasons thereunto us moving, have granted our full and free pardon unto the person called Jerome Hardouin Riquet, for all crimes or

offences that he may have committed up to the date of these presents, always excepted any crime which he may have committed
against the holy church or our sovereign state of which he is not at
this time charged, and which may be hereafter proved against him,
and that we do also take the said Jerome Hardouin Riquet under
our especial protection, warning all men to have regard unto the
same, for such is our will.   " Louis."

The King read the paper over, paused for a moment, as if he
yet hesitated whether he should give it or not, and then with a
sort of half smile, and a look expressive of something between
carelessness and magnanimity, he held it out to the valet, who
seized it and kissed it repeatedly.   Then standing up before the
monarch, he said—

" Now, sire, safe in your majesty's protection, I am ready and
capable of answering distinctly and clearly anything that you may
ask me."

The King took a paper up again, into which he had looked to
ascertain the various denominations of Maitre Riquet, and then
recommenced his questions as follows, returning in the first place to
the one which Riquet had left unanswered, " Who and what are
the people who are driving, or are likely to drive, your master to
remain obstinate in heresy?"

" Please your majesty," replied Riquet, " the principal persons
are, a very reverend and respectable gentleman, called the Abbé de
St. Helie; also, the intendant of the province of Poitou, our
reverend father the Bishop of Poitiers, Monsieur de Louvois, and I
am not very sure that good Monsieur de Rouvré himself has not a
part."

The King gazed at the bold speaker for a moment or two, as if
doubtful of his real intention ; asking of himself whether the man
spoke sincerely and simply, or whether a daring jest, or a still more
impudent sarcasm, lay concealed in the words he used.   The man's
previous terror, however, and the air of perfect unconsciousness of
offence with which he spoke, did much to convince Louis that he
had no double meaning.   His tone, however, was sharp and angry,
as he asked, " How now, sir ? How can some of the best and
wisest, the most prudent and the most zealous men in the realm,
drive any heretic to refuse obstinately the cup of salvation offered
to him ? I trust, you mean no offence, sirrah !"

Jerome Riquet's countenance instantly fell, and with a thousand
lamentations and professions of profound respect for Louvois and
St. Helie, and every one whom the King might trust and favour, he
declared, that his only meaning was, that he believed his master
and a great many other Protestants would have been converted
long ago, if they had been led rather than driven. He added,
that he had heard the young Count, and the old one too, say a
thousand times, that some of the gentlemen he mentioned, had

done as much to prevent the Protestants from returning to the mother church, as Monsieur Bossuet had done to bring them back to it.

Louis paused and thought; and had not his prepossessions been so complete as they were, the plain truth which the valet told him might not have been unproductive of fruit. As it was it went in some degree to effect the real object which Riquet had in view; namely, to impress the King with a notion, that there was a great probability of the young Count being recalled to the bosom of the Catholic church, provided the means employed were gentleness and persuasion.

It is very seldom, indeed, in this life, that we meet with anything like pure and unmixed motives, and such were certainly not to be expected in the bosom of Jerome Riquet. His first object and design was certainly to serve his master; but, in so serving him, he had an eye to gratifications of his own also; for to his feelings and disposition Versailles was a much pleasanter place than Morseiul, Paris a more agreeable land than Poitou. He used to declare, that he was fond of the country, but liked it paved; that his avenues should always be houses, and his flocks and herds wear coats and petticoats. He naturally calculated, then, that if the King undertook the task of converting the young Count by gentle and quiet means, he would not fail to keep him in the delightful sojourning place of Versailles, while he, Jerome Riquet, amongst all the gods and goddesses of brass and marble, which were gathered together in the gardens, might play the part of Proteus, and take a thousand shapes, as might suit his versatile genius.

The King thought over the reply of Riquet for some moments, somewhat struck by hearing that the arguments which the Protestants held amongst themselves were exactly similar to those which they had often put forth in addressing him. So much skill, however, had been employed by his council and advisers to open wide before him the path of error, and to close up the narrow footway of truth, that even when any one pulled away the brambles and briers with which the latter had been blocked up, and showed him that there was really another road, he refused to follow it, and chose the wider and more travelled way.

Thus his conclusion was, after those few minutes' thought—

"This is all very well, and very specious; but, as we do not trust to a sick man to point out the remedies that will cure him, so must we not trust to these Huguenots to point out what would be the best means of converting them. However, Master Jerome Riquet, it is not in regard to opinions that I sent for you; I want to hear facts, if you please. Now tell me: do you remember, upon a certain occasion, a proclamation having been sent down to be read in the town of Morseiul, the King's officers having been insulted, and, I believe, pelted with stones, and the proclamation torn down?'

"No, sire," replied Riquet, boldly—for he was telling a lie, and

therefore spoke confidently. " I remember my master going out
in haste one day to prevent, he said, any bad conduct on the part
of the people, and I remember hearing that he himself had caused
the proclamation to be made in the market-place, in spite of some
riotous folk, who would willingly have opposed it."

" High time that such folk should be put down," said the King.
" These are the peaceable and obedient subjects, which the advo-
cates of the Huguenots would fain persuade me that they are. But
one question more on this head: did you see the young Count
of Morseiul cause the gates of the town to be shut in the face of
my officers, or did you hear that he had done so, upon good
authority?"

" No, sire, I neither heard nor saw it," replied Riquet; " and,
for myself, I was safely in the château during the whole day."

" Do you remember," continued the King, looking at the paper,
" having carried notes or letters from your master to different
Protestant gentlemen in the neighbourhood of Poitiers, calling
upon them to assemble and meet him at the house of another
Huguenot, named M. de Corvoie?"

" No, sire, oh no!" replied the man. " While we were at Poitiers, I only carried one note, and that was to the saddle-maker,
who, in repadding one of my lord's saddles, had done it so as to
gall the horse's back."

" Sir, you are lying," said the King, sternly.

Riquet once more cast himself upon his knees before the monarch, clasping his hands, and exclaiming, " May I lose your majesty's favour for ever, if I am not telling you the exact truth! Let
any one who dares to say that I carried any other note than that
which I have mentioned be confronted with me this moment;
and I will prove, that he is shamefully deceiving your majesty,
for no other note did I carry—no, not even a love-letter. Otherwise, I could and would, not only tell your majesty the fact, but
every word that the notes contained."

" This is very extraordinary," said the King, " and I shall take
care to inquire into it."

" I trust your majesty will," replied the man, boldly; for it may
be recollected that he had not carried any note, but had been merely
charged with a message to M. de Corvoie: " I trust that your
majesty will; for I assure you, on the faith of a valet-de-chambre,
that no such transaction ever occurred. Did not they want to
charge me—the very men who I dare say have brought this accusation—did they not want to charge me with having abstracted
your majesty's commission to Messieurs de St. Helie and Pelisson,
and with having placed a pack of cards in its stead? and were they
not brought to shame, by its being found out, that they themselves
had done it, by fragments of the commission being found in one of
their valises, wrapped like a dirty rag about an old tobacco box?"

" How is this? How is this?" exclaimed the King. " I heard

that the commission had been abstracted, but I heard not this result—fragments of the commission wrapping a tobacco-box found in their own valises l"

" Ay, sire," replied the man, " 'tis all too true ; for the examination was conducted in presence of Monsieur de Rouvré ;" and with earnest volubility Maitre Jerome set to work, and, in his own particular manner, gave the monarch a long and detailed, but rapid account, of what had taken place on the return of the Count de Morseiul to Poitiers, adding cunning commentaries in words, gesticulations, and grimaces, which scarcely left the King the power of retaining his due gravity, especially when Riquet personated to the life, the worthy Curé of Guadrieul, on the discovery of the paper in his valise.

While he was in the very act of concluding this detail, however, the door of the royal cabinet was opened, and a man of a harsh and disagreeable countenance, with a face somewhat red and blotched, but with great fire and intelligence in his eyes, entered the room, pausing for a single moment at the door, as if for permission.

" Come in, Monsieur de Louvois, come in," said the King. " This is Jerome Riquet, the valet of the Count de Morseiul, whom I told you I intended to examine. He puts a very different face upon several matters, however, from that which we expected to find ;" and the King briefly recapitulated to his famous minister the information he had received from Riquet, leaving out, however the first part of the conversation between them, which contained matter that could not be very agreeable to the minister.

A somewhat sneering smile came upon Louvois' countenance as he listened ; and he replied, " I am very happy to hear, sire, that the Count de Morseiul is so good and faithful a servant to your majesty. May I be permitted to ask this worthy person a question or two in your presence ?"

The King bowed his head, and the minister, turning to Riquet, went on: " Although we have much more reason to think favourably of your master," he said, "than we had at first, yet there is one point in regard to which, though he did not actually commit a fault, he greatly neglected his duty, at least, so we are led to believe. We are assured, that shortly before he came up to Versailles, a great meeting of Huguenots, in the open air, took place upon a wild moor within the limits of the young Count's lands, which meeting, though held for the peaceful purpose, we are told, of merely preaching in the open air, terminated in bloodshed, and an attack upon a small body of the King's dragoons, who were watching the proceedings.

Louvois' eye was fixed upon the valet all the time he spoke, and Jerome Riquet was making up his mind to deny steadily any knowledge of the transaction ; but suddenly his whole views upon the subject were changed by the minister apparently coming to the head and front of the Count's offence.

" Now," continued Louvois, "although there was certainly no law to compel the Count to be present on such an occasion, yet, when he knew that a meeting of this kind was about to take place on his own estates, and that dangerous consequences might ensue, he would but have shown his zeal and duty in the service of the King by going to the spot, and doing all that he could to make the proceedings tranquil and inoffensive."

" But the Count did go, sir !" exclaimed Riquet ; " the Count did go, and I remember the fact of his going particularly."

" Are you ready to swear that he was there?" demanded Louvois.

" All I can say," replied the valet, " is, that he left home for the purpose of going there. I was not present myself, but I heard from every one else that he was."

" And pray at what hour did he return that night ?" demanded Louvois, " for the events that I speak of did not take place till near nightfall, and if the Count had been there till the whole assemblage had dispersed, a thousand to one no harm would have ensued."

" I cannot exactly tell at what hour he returned," said the valet, who was beginning to fancy that he was not exactly in the right road. " It was after nightfall, however."

" Recollect yourself," said Louvois, " was it nine—ten o'clock ?"

" It might be nearly ten," said the man.

" And, I think," said Louvois, his lip curling with a smile, bitter and fiend-like, " I think you were one of those, were you not, who went down on the following morning to the spot where the young Marquis de Hericourt had been murdered? Your name is amongst those who were seen there ; so say no more. But now, tell me, where is your master at this moment ?"

Jerome Riquet smarted under a strong perception of having been outwitted; and the consequence was, that knowing, or at least believing, that when a man falls into one such piece of ill luck, it generally goes on, with a sort of run against him; he made up his mind to know as little as possible about anything, for fear of falling into a new error, and replied to Louvois' question, that he could not tell.

" Is he in his hotel at Versailles, or not, sir?" said the minister, sternly ; " endeavour to forget for once that you are professionally a liar, and give a straightforward answer, for on your telling truth depends your immediate transmission to the Bastille or not. Was your master at home when you left the house, or out?"

" He was out then, sir, certainly," replied Riquet.

" On horseback, or on foot ?" demanded Louvois.

" On horseback," replied the man.

" Now, answer me one other question," continued the minister. " Have you not been heard, this very morning, to tell the head groom to have horses ready to go to Paris?"

" Sir," said Jerome, with a look of impudent raillery that he dared not assume towards the King, but which nothing upon earth could have repressed, in addressing Louvois at that moment, " Sir, I feel convinced that I must possess a valet-de-chambre without knowing it, for nobody on earth could repeat my words so accurately, unless I had some scoundrel of a valet to betray them as soon as they were spoken."

" Sir, your impudence shall have its just punishment," said Louvois, taking up a pen and dipping it in the ink; but the King waved his hand, saying, " Put down the pen, Monsieur de Louvois! You forget that you are in the King's cabinet, and in his presence! —Riquet, you may retire."

Riquet did not need a second bidding, but, with a look of profound awe and reverence towards Louis, laid his hand upon his heart, lifted up his shoulders, like the jaws of a crocodile ready to swallow up his head, and bowing almost to the ground, walked backward out of the room. Louvois stood before the King for an instant, with a look of angry mortification, which he suppressed with difficulty. Louis suffered him to remain thus, and, perhaps, did not enjoy a little the humiliation he had inflicted upon a man whom he, more than once in his life, declared to be perfectly insupportable, though he could not do without him. At length, however, he spoke in a grave but not an angry tone, saying—

" From the questions that you asked that man just now, Monsieur de Louvois, I am led to believe that you have received some fresh information regarding this young gentleman—this Count de Morseiul. My determination up to this moment, strengthened by the advice of Monsieur de Meaux, Monsieur Pelisson, and others, is simply this: to pursue to the utmost the means of persuasion and conciliation in order to induce him, by fair means, to return to the bosom of the Catholic church."

" Better, sire," replied Louvois, " far better, cut him off like a withered and corrupted branch, unfit to be grafted on that goodly tree."

" You know, Marquis," said the King, " that I am always amenable to reason. I have expressed the determination which I had taken under particular circumstances. If you have other circumstances to communicate to me which may make me alter that opinion, do so straightforwardly. Kings are as liable to error as other men,—perhaps, indeed, more so; for they see truth at a distance, and require perspective glasses to examine it well, which are not always at hand. If I am wrong, I am ready to change my resolution; though it is always a part of a king's duty to decide speedily when he can do so wisely."

" The simple fact, sire," replied Louvois, with the mortification under which he still smarted affecting his tone of voice—" the simple fact is, as your majesty must have divined from the answers that the man gave me, I have now clear and distinct proof that this Count de Morseiul has, throughout the insignificant but annoying troubles occasioned by the Huguenots in Poitou, been the great fomenter of all their discontent, and their leader in actual insurrection. He was not only present at this preaching in the desert, as these fanatics call it, and led all the proceedings, by a speech upon the occasion highly insulting to your majesty's authority and dignity; with all which your majesty has already been made acquainted——"

"But upon not very clear and conclusive evidence," said the King. "Upon evidence, Monsieur de Louvois, which would condemn none of my subjects before a court of law, and, therefore, should not before his sovereign. That he made a speech is clear; but some of the witnesses deposed, that it was only to recommend moderation and tranquillity, and to beseech them, on no account, to appear on such occasions with arms."

"All hypocrisy, sire," replied Louvois. "I have had two of the dragoons with me this morning, who were present with my unfortunate cousin, young de Hericourt; and they are quite ready and willing to swear that he, this Count de Morseiul, began the affray by striking that young officer from his horse."

"Without provocation?" demanded the King, his brow growing somewhat cloudy.

"They saw none given," replied Louvois, "and they were close to him. Not only this, but, as it is shown that he did not himself return to his own house till late at night, that de Hericourt never returned at all; and that the two were angry rivals for the hand of this very Mademoiselle de Marly, there is strong reason to believe that they met after the affair on the moor, and that the unhappy young man was slain by the hand of the Count of Morseiul."

"This is something new, indeed," said the King. "Have you any further information, Monsieur de Louvois?"

"Merely the following, sire," replied the minister, "that, in the course of yesterday evening, the famous fanatic minister, Claude de l'Estang, the great stay of the self-styled reformed church, who, on more than one occasion, in his youth opposed your royal father in arms, and has, through life, been the great friend and adviser of these Counts of Morseiul, arrived in Paris last night, sent a billet down to the Count this morning, and further, that the Count immediately went up to visit him. Unfortunately, the news was communicated to me too late to take measures for tracking the Count from Versailles to the hiding-place of the minister, whom it is desirable to lay hands upon if possible. The Count was tracked, indeed, to his own hotel in Paris; but, just before I came hither, the messenger returned to tell me, that as soon as Monsieur de Morseiul had arrived at his own house, he had gone out again on foot, and all further trace of him was lost. What I would urge upon your majesty's attention, then, is this, that if you suffer him to trifle away many days, persuading you and good Monsieur Bossuet that he intends to yield, and return to the church, you will suffer this affair of the preaching, the tumult, the murder of some of your loyal subjects, and the previous factious conduct of this young man, to drop, and be forgotten; and you cannot well revive it after any length of time, as it is known, already, that full information has been laid before you on the subject. It does seem to me, sire," continued the minister, seeing that Louis was much moved by his reasonings, "it does seem to me, that you have but one choice. You must either, believing as I do, that the Count de Morseiul has not the slightest intention of ever becomine a convert from the heresy which he now professes, determing upon arresting him, and punishing him for the crimes with which he is charged, should they be proved; or else you must grant him your royal favour and pardon, put it out of your own power to investigate further the matter, bestow upon him the hand of Mademoiselle de Marly, and leave fate, and his own inclinations, to convert him to the Catholic faith, or not, as may happen."

"I certainly shall not take the latter alternative," replied the King. "The circumstances you have brought forward are extremely strong, especially this renewed visit to Claude de l'Estang. I am not one to show indecision where firmness is necessary, Louvois. In an hour or two, whenever I think it probable that he is returned to Versailles, I will send to require his presence. I will question him myself upon his belief, ascertain the probability of his conversion, and determine at once. If I find your statement correct ——"

"Sire," cried Louvois, interrupting the King, as was too often his custom to do, "there is little use of your asking him any questions but one simple one; the answer to which must, at once, satisfy so great and magnanimous a mind as yours; and you will see that I entertain no feeling of personal enmity to the young man by the question that I am about to suggest. If he answer that question candidly, straightforwardly, and at once, in the manner and sense which your majesty can approve, give him your favour, raise him high, distinguish him in every manner; but if he prevaricates, hesitates, or answers in a sense and manner which your majesty cannot approve, send him to the Bastille."

"But what is the question?" demanded the King, eagerly. "What is the question, Monsieur de Louvois?'

"This, sire," replied Louvois: "Monsieur de Morseiul, I beg and command of you, as your king and your benefactor, to tell me whether there is, or is not, really any chance of your ever becoming a convert to the true Catholic faith of this realm?"

Louvois, by putting such a question into the King's mouth, showed not only how intimately he was acquainted with Louis's weaknesses, but also, how well he knew the firmness and candour of the young Count de Morseiul. He knew, in short, that the latter would tell the truth, and that the former would condemn it.

"Nothing can be fairer," replied the King; "nothing can be

fairer, Monsieur de Louvois. I will put that question to him exactly; and, upon his answer to it, he shall stand or fall."

"So thoroughly am I convinced, sire, of what the result will be," continued Louvois, "that I will beseech your majesty to give me authority to have him arrested immediately after he leaves you, in case you send me no order to the contrary."

"Certainly," replied the King, "certainly. I will sign the order immediately."

"Allow me to remind you, sire," replied Louvois, "that you signed one the other day, which is already in the hands of Cantal, only you ordered me to suspend the execution. That will do quite well; and Cantal will be at hand to put it in force."

"Be it so," said the monarch, "be it so; but let Cantal be in the way at the time I send for the young Count, that I may signify to him, that he is not to arrest him, if the answer I receive satisfies me. And now, Monsieur de Louvois, what news regarding this business of Dunkirk?"

The King and his minister then turned to other matters; and, having concluded the principal part of the affairs they had in hand, they were talking somewhat lightly of other matters, when one of the attendants, who knew that the hour of Louvois was over, opened the door and interrupted their further conversation, by announcing, to the surprise of both, that the Count de Morseiul was in waiting, beseeching, earnestly, a moment's audience of the monarch. The King turned his eyes upon Louvois, as if to inquire, "What is the meaning of this?" but a moment or two after, he bade the attendant give the Count admission.

"Then I had better take my leave, sire," said the minister, "and give Cantal a hint to be in readiness;" and taking up the papers, from which he had been reading some extracts to the monarch, Louvois bowed low, and quitted the room.

CHAPTER XXII.

THE UNFORESEEN BLOW.

To have judged by the affable and agreeable smile which Louvois bore upon his countenance as he passed the young Count de Morseiul in one of the anterooms, a stranger to that minister would have imagined that he was extremely well disposed towards the gentleman whom he was in fact labouring to ruin. No such error, however, could have taken place with regard to the aspect with which the King received the young Count, which, though not frowning and severe, was grave and somewhat stern.

The countenance and conduct of Albert of Morseiul, calm, tranquil, and serene; and Louis, who, intending to cut the interview as short as possible, had risen, could not help saying within himself, "That looks not like the face of a man conscious of crime."

As the King paused while he made this remark to himself, the Count imagined that he waited for him to begin and open the cause of his coming; and, consequently, he said at once, " Sire, I have ventured to intrude upon your majesty, notwithstanding your intimation that you would send for me when your convenience served, inasmuch as I have matters of some importance to lay before you, which would bear no delay."

"Pray," demanded Louis, " pray, Monsieur de Morseiul, before you proceed further, be so good as to inform me whether the matters to which you allude refer to yourself or to the state."

"By no means to myself," replied the Count, who was not altogether satisfied with the King's tone and manner. "They refer entirely to the safety of the state and your majesty. On my own affairs I would not have presumed to intrude upon you again."

"Very well, then," said the King, drily, "since such is the case, you will be good enough to communicate whatever you may have to say upon such subjects to Monsieur de Louvois, Monsieur de Seignelai, or Monsieur Colbert de Croissy, as the case may be ; such being the usual course by which matters of importance are brought to my ears. And now, Monsieur de Morseiul, though I have but a single moment to attend to anything at this particular time, let me ask you one question,—Is there or is there not any hope of my receiving the great gratification of being enabled to show you as much favour and distinction as I could wish, by your abjuring the heresy in which you have been unfortunately brought up, and seeking repose in the bosom of the Catholic church?"

The Count de Morseiul felt that a crisis in his fate had arrived ; but, with the question put to him so simply and straightforwardly, he felt that he could not evade the decision, and he would not prevaricate, even for safety.

"If, sire," he said, " what your majesty demands is to know my own opinion upon the subject at this moment——"

"I mean, sir," said the King, "plainly, Do you believe that there exists a likelihood of your becoming converted to the Catholic faith ?"

"I do not believe so, sire," replied the Count. " With deep and profound respect for your majesty, with much veneration and regard for Monsieur Bossuet, and with all the advantage of reading, as I am doing even now, some of his works upon religion, I should be deceiving your majesty, I should be wronging myself, I should be showing myself unworthy of the high opinion which Monsieur de Meaux has expressed of me, if I did not clearly and distinctly state that I see no likelihood whatsoever of my changing opinions instilled into me in infancy."

"Nay, nay !" cried the King, considerably moved and struck by the calm, yet respectful dignity of the young Count's demeanour. "Think better of it!—in God's name, think better of it! . Let me hope that the eloquence of Bossuet will prevail—let me hope that I may yet have the opportunity of conferring upon you all those favours that I am most eager to bestow."

There was an eagerness and sincerity in the King's manner which affected the Count in turn. "Alas, sire," he said, "what would I not do to merit the favour of such a king! but still I must not deceive you. Whatever hopes your majesty is pleased to entertain of my conversion to the established religion of the realm may be derived from the knowledge—from the powerful gratitude—which your majesty's generosity and high qualities of every kind must call up in your subjects and your servants; or they may arise from your knowledge of the deep and persuasive eloquence of the Bishop of Meaux: but they must not arise from anything that I have said, or can say, regarding the state of my mind at this moment."

"I grieve, Monsieur de Morseiul, I grieve bitterly to hear it," replied the King; and he then paused, looking down thoughtfully for some moments; after which he added, "Let me remonstrate with you, that nothing may be left undone, which I can do, to justify me in treating you as I could wish. Surely, Monsieur de Morseiul, there can be nothing very difficult to believe in that which so many—nay, I may say all the holiest, the wisest, and the best, have believed, since the first preaching of our religion. Surely, the great body of authority which has accumulated throughout ages, in favour of the Catholic church, is not to be shaken by such men as Luther and Calvin. You yourselves acknowledge that there are —as there must ever be when heavenly things are revealed to earthly understanding—mysteries which we cannot subject to the ordinary test of human knowledge, in the whole scheme of our redemption—you acknowledge it; and yet with faith you believe in those mysteries, rejecting only those which do not suit you, and pretending that the Scripture does not warrant them. But let me ask you, upon what authority we are to rely for the right interpretation of those very passages? Is it to be upon the word of two such men as Luther and Calvin, learned though they might be, or on the authority of the church, throughout all ages, supported by the unbiassed opinions of a whole host of the learned and the wise in every century? Are we to rely upon the opinion of two men, originally stirred up by avarice and bad passions, in preference to the whole body of saints and martyrs, who have lived long lives of piety and holiness, meditating upon those very mysteries which you reject? I am but a weak and feeble advocate, Monsieur de Morseiul, and should not, perhaps, have raised my voice at all, after the eloquence of a Bossuet has failed to produce its effect; but my zealous and anxious wish both to see you re-united to the church, and to show you that favour which such a conversion would justify, have made me say thus much."

The young Count was too prudent by far to enter into any theological discussions with the King, and he therefore contented himself with replying, " I fear, sire, that our belief is not in our own power. Most sincerely do I hope and trust that, if I be now in the wrong, God may open my eyes to the truth. At present, however——"

" Say no more, sir! say no more!" said the King, bending his head as a signal that the young nobleman might retire. " I am heartily sorry for your state of mind! I had hoped better things. As to any other information you may have to communicate, you will be pleased to give it to one of the secretaries of state, according to the department to which it naturally refers itself."

The King once more bowed his head, and the Count, with a low inclination, retired. " I had better go at once to the apartments of Louvois," he thought; " for this affair of Hatréaumont may be already on the eve of bursting forth, and I would fain have the last act of my stay in my native land one of loyalty to the king who drives me forth."

When he reached the open air, then, he turned to the right, to seek the apartments of Louvois; but, ere he reached them, he was met by the Chevalier de Rohan, whom we have already mentioned, who stopped him, with a gay and nonchalant air, saying, " Oh, my dear Count, you have made my fortune! The hundred louis that you lent me have brought good luck, and I am now a richer man than I have been for the last twelve months. I won ten thousand francs yesterday."

" And, doubtless, will lose them again to-day," answered the Count. " I wish to Heaven you would change this life—but, my dear Chevalier, I must hasten on, for I am on business."

" When shall I have an hour to talk with you, Count?" exclaimed the Chevalier de Rohan, still detaining him. " I want very much to explain to you my plan for raising myself—I am down low enough, certainly, just now."

" When next we meet, Chevalier—when next we meet!" said the Count, smiling, as he thought of his approaching departure. " I am in great haste now."

But, ere he could disengage himself from the hold of the persevering Chevalier de Rohan, he felt a hand laid gently upon his arm, and, turning round, saw a gentleman whose face was not familiar to him.

" Monsieur le Comte de Morseiul, I believe?" said the stranger; and, on the Count bowing his head, he went on. " I have to apologize for interrupting your conversation; but I have a word for your private ear of some importance."

The Chevalier de Rohan had by this time turned away, with a nod of the head; and the Count replied to the other, " I am in some haste, sir. Pray, what may be your pleasure?"

" I have an unpleasant task to perform towards you, Monsieur

de Morseiul," said the stranger; " but it is my wish to execute it
as gently and delicately as possible. My orders are to arrest and
convey you to the Bastille."

The Count de Morseiul felt that painful tightening of the heart
which every man, thus suddenly stopped in the full career of
liberty, and destined to be conveyed to long and uncertain imprisonment, to be shut out from all the happy sounds and sights of
earth, to be debarred all the sweet intercourses of friendship and
affection, has felt, and must feel. At the same time all the various
points of anxiety and difficulty in his situation rushed through his
mind with such rapidity as to turn him dizzy with the whirling
multitude of painful thoughts. Clémence de Marly, whose hand
was to have been his that very night, the good old pastor, his
friends, his servants, all might, for ought he knew, be kept in utter
ignorance of his fate for many days. The hands, too, of the unscrupulous and feelingless instruments of despotic power, would be
in every cabinet of his house and his château, invading all the little
storehouses of past affections, perhaps scattering to the winds all
the fond memorials of the loved and dead. The dark lock of his
mother's hair, which he had preserved from boyhood—the few
fragments of her handwriting, and some verses that she had composed shortly before her death—all his father's letters to him, from
the time when he first sent him forth, a gallant boy girt with the
sword of a high race, to win renown, through all that period when
the son, growing up in glory, shone back upon his father's name
the light which he had thence received, and repaid amply all the
cares which had been bestowed upon him, by the joy of his great
deeds, up to that sad moment, when, with a trembling hand, the
dying parent announced to his son the commencement and progress of the fatal malady that carried him to the grave.—All these
were to be opened, examined, perhaps dispersed by the cold, if not
the scornful; and all the sanctities of private affection violated.

Such, and a thousand other feelings, rapid, innumerable, and, in
some instances, contradictory to and opposing each other, rushed
through his bosom in a moment at the announcement of the
officer's errand. The whole facts of his situation, in short, with
every minute particular, were conjured up before his eyes, as in a
picture, by those few words; and the first effort of deliberate
thought was made while de Cantal went on to say, " As I have
said, Monsieur de Morseiul, it is my wish to save you any unnecessary pain, and therefore I have ordered the carriage, which is to
convey you to the Bastille, to wait at the further end of the first
street. A couple of musketeers and myself will accompany you
inside; so that there will be no unnecessary parade about the
matter: and I doubt not that you will be liberated shortly."

" I trust it may be so, sir," replied the Count; " and am obliged
to you for your kindness. I have violated no law, divine or
human; and though, of course, I have many sins to atone towards

my God, yet I have none towards my king. I am quite ready to accompany you; for I suppose that I shall not be permitted to return to my own house, even to seek those things which may be necessary for my comfort in the Bastille."

"Quite impossible, sir," replied the officer. "It would be as much as my head is worth to permit you to set foot in your own dwelling."

The thoughts of the young Count, as may well be supposed, were turned, at that moment, particularly to Clémence de Marly; and he was most anxious, on every account, to make his servants acquainted with the fact of his having been arrested, in the hope that Riquet would have the good sense to convey the tidings to the Hôtel de Rouvré. To have explained this, in any degree, to the officer who had him in charge, would have been to frustrate his own purpose; and therefore he replied—

"Far be it from me, sir, to wish you to do anything but your duty: but you see, as I have been accustomed, throughout my life, to somewhat, perhaps, too much luxury, I should be very desirous of procuring some changes of apparel. That, I am aware, may be permitted to me, unless I am to be in the strictest and most severe kind of imprisonment which the Bastille admits of. You know by the orders you have received whether such is to be the case or not, and, of course, I do not wish you to deviate from your orders. Am I to be kept *au secret?*"

"Oh dear no, not all," replied the officer. "The order merely implies your safe custody; and, probably, unless some private commands are given farther, you will have what is called the great liberties of the Bastille: but still that would not, by any means, justify me in permitting you to go to your own house."

"No," replied the Count; "but it renders it perfectly possible—if you are, as I believe, disposed to treat a person in my unfortunate situation with kindness and liberality—for you to send down one of your own attendants to my valet, Jerome Riquet, with my orders to send me up, in the course of the day, such clothes as may be necessary for a week. Let the message be verbal, so as to guard against any dangerous communication; and let the clothes be addressed to the care of the governor of the prison, in order that they may be inspected before they are given to me."

"Oh, to that, of course, there can be no objection," replied the young officer. "We will do it immediately. But we must lose no time, Monsieur de Morseiul, for the order is countersigned by Monsieur de Louvois, and you know he likes prompt obedience."

The Count accompanied him at a rapid pace, deriving no slight consolation under the unhappy circumstances in which he was placed, from the certainty that Clémence would be fully informed of the cause of his not appearing at the time he had promised. At the spot which Monsieur de Cantal had mentioned, was found a plain carriage, with a coachman and lackey in grey, and two

musketeers of the guard seated quietly in the inside. While the
Count was entering the vehicle, the officer called the lackey to his
side and said, " Run down as fast as possible to the house of the
Count de Morseiul, and inquire for his valet. What did you say
his name is, Monsieur de Morseiul ?"

" Jerome Riquet," said the Count.

" Ay, Jerome Riquet," said the officer. " Inquire for his valet,
Jerome Riquet: tell him that the King has judged it right that his
master should pass a short time in the Bastille, and that, therefore,
he must send up thither to-night, addressed to the care of the
governor, what clothes he judges the Count may require. The
house is next door but one to that of Monsieur de Meaux. Return
as fast as possible, and take the little alley at the end of the street,
so that you may join us at the corner of the road."

The young officer then entered the carriage, and the coachman
drove on; but before they proceeded along the high road, they
were obliged to pause for a moment or two, in order to give time
for the arrival of the lackey, who, when he came, spoke a few
words through the window to Monsieur de Cantal, in the course of
which the word "Exempt" was frequently audible.

" That is unpleasant," said the young officer, turning to the
Count: "I find that an exempt has been sent to your house
already,—to seal up your papers, I suppose; and, on hearing the
man give the message to one of your servants, he was very angry,
it seems, sending word to wait for him here; but, as I am not
under his orders or authority, I think I shall even tell the coachman to go on."

He said this in a hesitating tone, however, evidently afraid that
he had done wrong; and before he could execute his purpose of
bidding the carriage proceed, the lackey said, " Here comes the
Exempt, sir. Here he is !"

In a moment after, a tall, meagre, gaunt-looking man, dressed in
the peculiar robes of an Exempt of the court, with a nose extraor-
dinarily red, scarcely any eyebrows, and a mouth which seemed
capable of swallowing the vehicle that he approached and all that
it contained, came up to the side of the carriage, and spoke to the
young officer through the window. The words that passed between them seemed to be sharp; and at length the Exempt exclaimed, in a louder tone, so as to be completely audible to the
Count—although his articulation was of that round spluttering
kind which rendered it very difficult to make out what he said—
" I shall do so, however, sir; I shall do so, however. I have authority for what I do. I will suffer no such communications as these,
and I will not quit the carriage till I have seen the prisoner safely
lodged in the hands of the governor of the Bastille."

" Well, sir," replied the officer, a little heated, "if you choose
to overstep your duty I cannot help it, and certainly shall not attempt to prevent your going with the coachman, if you think fit.

In the inside of the carriage you shall not come, for there I will guard my prisoner myself."

" That you may do, sir, if you like," cried the Exempt, shaking the awful mass of wig in which his head was plunged : " but I will take care that there shall be no more communications.—Linen! What the devil does a prisoner in the Bastille want with linen? Why, in the very first packet sent to him there might be all sorts of treasonable things written upon the linen. Have we not heard of ink of sympathy and all manner of things ? "

" Well, well, sir," exclaimed the young officer : " I saw no harm in what I was doing, or else I should not have done it. But get up, if you are going to get up ; for I shall order the coachman to go on."

The Exempt sprang up the high and difficult ascent which led to a coachbox of those days, with a degree of activity which could hardly have been expected from a person of his pompous dignity, and the coach then drove on upon its weary way to Paris.

" A very violent and self-conceited person, indeed, that seems to be," said the Count. " Do you know him ? "

" Not I," replied the young officer, " though he threatens to make me know him pretty sufficiently, by complaining to Louvois of my sending for those cursed clothes of yours."

The officer was evidently out of temper; and the Count, therefore, left him to himself, and fell into a fit of musing over his own situation. That fit of musing, dark and painful as it was, lasted, without cessation, till the vehicle entered one of the suburbs of the great city of Paris. There, however, it met with an interruption of a very unexpected kind; for, in trying to pass between two heavy carts, which were going along in opposite directions, the coachman contrived to get the wheels of the carriage locked with those of both the other vehicles; and with such force was this done, that the lackey behind was thrown down and hurt, the Exempt himself nearly pitched off the coachbox, and obliged to cling with both his hands, while the coachman lost his hat and the reins.

The idea of making his escape crossed the mind of the Count de Morseiul; but he evidently saw that, even if he were out of the carriage, surrounded, as he was, by a great number of people, without any large sum of money upon his person, and with the eyes of the officer, the musketeers, and the Exempt upon him, it would be vain to hope for a successful result.

To render the situation of the vehicle as bad as possible, one of the horses, either irritated by the uncouth and not very gentle terms with which the coachman attempted to back out of the difficulty, or galled by part of the cart pressing upon it, began to kick most vehemently; and Monsieur de Cantal, the officer, having previously sent the two musketeers to aid the coachman and the Exempt in disentangling the carriage, now showed a strong inclination to go himself. After looking anxiously at the Count de Morsciul for a moment, he at length said, " I must either go and set those men right, or suffer the carriage to be kicked to pieces. If I go, Monsieur de Morseiul, will you give me your word not to try to escape?"

The Count paused for an instant; but then the same considerations returned upon him, and he replied, " Go, sir, go: I do give you my word."

The officer then sprang out; but scarcely had he been away a moment, when the head of the Exempt appeared looking in at the window. " Hist, hist, Monsieur de Morseiul!" he said, in a voice totally different from that which he had used before, and which was wonderfully familiar to the ears of the Count; "hist, hist! On the very first linen you receive, there will be information written for you. It will be invisible to all eyes till it is held to the fire. But the flame of a strong lamp will do, if you cannot sham an ague and get some wood to warm you."

" I can scarcely believe my eyes," said the Count, in the same low voice.

" Do not doubt them, do not doubt them," said the Exempt. " I knew of your arrest before you knew of it yourself, but could not warn you, and was making all ready when the man came to the hotel. I have sacrificed much for you, Count; as goodly a pair of eyebrows as ever valet had in this world; and I dare not blow my nose for fear of wiping off the paint: Louvois outwitted me this morning, and now I'll outwit him, if I have but time. Heavens, how that beast is plunging and kicking! The pin I ran into its stomach is sticking there yet I suppose; ay, she's quieter now; here they come, and I must splutter.—Monsieur," he said, as the officer now returned to the side of the carriage, " Monsieur, this is guarding your prisoner securely, is it not? Here I come to the window, and find not a single soul to prevent his escaping, when he might have got out in a moment, and run up the Rue de Bièvre, and passed through the Rue de l'Ecole, and across the Place de l'Université, and then down to the river ——"

" Psha!" said the officer, impatiently; " let me have no more of this impertinence, sir. The Count gave me his word that he would not escape. If I deliver my prisoner safely at the Bastille, that is sufficient, and I will not have my conduct questioned. If you have any complaint to make, make it to Monsieur de Louvois. Come, get up, sir, don't answer; the carriage is now clear, and enough of it left together to carry us to the Bastille. Go on, coach-man "

The coachman, however, pertinaciously remained in a state of tranquillity, till the Exempt was once more comfortably seated by his side : and then the carriage, rolling on through the back streets of the capital, made a little turn by the Rue de Jean Beausire, into the Rue St. Antoine, and approached the gates of that redoubted prison, in which so many of the best and noblest in France have lingered out, at different times, a part of their existence. To few, to very few, have the tall gloomy towers of that awful fortress appeared without creating feelings of pain and apprehension; and however confident he might be of his own innocence, however great might be his trust in the good providence and protection of God, however strong he might be in a good cause and a firm spirit, it cannot be denied that Albert of Morseiul felt deeply and painfully, and with an anxious and a sickening heart, his entrance into that dark, solitary abode of crime, and sorrow, and suffering.

The carriage drew up just opposite the drawbridge, and Monsieur de Cantal getting out, left his prisoner in charge of the two musketeers, and went forward to speak to the officer on guard at the gates. To him he notified, in due form, that he had brought a prisoner, with orders from the King for his incarceration; but the carriage was kept for some time standing there, while the officer on guard proceeded to the dwelling of the governor, to demand the keys of the great gates. When he had obtained them and returned, the doors were opened; the guard was turned out under arms; the great drawbridge let down; the bell which communicated with the interior of the building rang; and the vehicle containing the Count slowly rolled on into the outer court, called the Cour du Gouvernement.

There the carriage paused, the governor of the prison having expressed his intention of coming down to receive the prisoner from the hands of the officer who brought him: otherwise, the carriage would have gone on into the inner court. A short pause ensued, and at length the well-known Besmaux was seen approaching, presenting exactly that appearance which might be expected from his character; for the traits of debauchery, levity, and ferocity, which distinguished his actual life, had stamped themselves upon his countenance in ineffaceable characters.

" Ah, good day, Monsieur de Morseiul," he said, as the door of the carriage opened, and the Count descended. " Monsieur de Cantal, your very humble servant. Gentlemen, both, you had better step into the Corps de Garde, where I will receive your prisoner, Monsieur de Cantal, and read the letters for his detention.

Thus saying, with a slow and important step he walked into the building, seated himself, called for pen and ink, and a light, and then read the King's letter for the arrest and imprisonment of the Count de Morseiul.

" Monsieur de Louvois is varying these letters every day," he said; " one never knows what one is doing. However, there stands the King's name, and that is quite enough; so, Monsieur de Morseiul, you are welcome to the Bastille. You are to have our great liberties, I suppose. I must beg you to give me your sword, however, and also everything you have about your person, if you please; letters, papers, money, jewels, and everything else, in short, except your seal, or your signet-ring, which you keep for the purposes about to be explained to you."

With very painful feelings the Count unbuckled his sword, and laid it down upon the table. He then gave up all the money that he possessed, one or two ordinary papers of no import, and some other articles of the same kind, which are borne about the person. The note which he had received from Clémence in the morning, he had luckily destroyed. While this was doing, the governor continned to write, examining the different things which were put down before him, and he then said, " Is this all, sir?"

" It is," replied the Count, " upon my word."

" One of the men must put his hands in your pocket, Count," said the governor; " that is a ceremony every one has to undergo here." The prisoner shut his teeth hard, but made no remark, and offered no resistance, though, if he had given way to his feelings, he would certainly have dashed the man to the ground at once, who, with unceremonious hands, now searched his person. When that also was over, Besmaux wrote down a few more words at the end of the list of things he had made out, and handed it to the Count to read. The only observation that the young nobleman made, was, that the governor had put down his sword as having a silver hilt, when the hilt was of gold.

" Ah, it is of gold, is it?" said de Besmaux, taking it up and looking at it, while several of the attendants who stood round grinned from ear to ear. " Well, we will alter it, and put it down gold. Now, Monsieur de Morseiul, will you have the goodness to sign that paper, which, with these letters, we fold up thus? and now, with the seal which you retain, you will have the goodness to seal them, and write your name round the seal."

With all these forms the Count complied, and the governor then intimated to him, that he was ready to conduct him into the interior of the Bastille, the spot were they then were, though within the walls and drawbridge, being actually considered as without the château.

" Here, then, I take leave of you, Monsieur de Morseiul," said the officer who had brought him thither, " and I will do my best, on my return to Versailles, to ensure that the clothes you want shall be sent, notwithstanding the interference of that impertinent exempt, who took himself off on the outside of the drawbridge, and has doubtless gone back to lay his complaint against me before Louvois. I know the King, however; and knowing that he wishes no one to be treated with harshness or severity, have therefore no fear of the consequences."

The Count held out his hand to him frankly. " I am very much obliged to you, Monsieur de Cantal," he said, "for the kindness and politeness you have shown me. It is at such moments as these, that kindness and politeness become real benefits."

The officer took his hand respectfully, and then, without more words, retired; the carriage passed out; the gates creaked upon their hinges; and the heavy drawbridge swung slowly up, with a jarring sound of chains, and heavy iron-work, sadly harmonious with the uses of the building, which it shut out from the world.

The governor then led the way towards the large and heavy mass of gloomy masonry, with its eight tall gaunt towers, which formed the real prison of the Bastille, and approached the gate in the centre, looking towards the gardens and buildings of the arsenal. The drawbridge there was by this time down, and the gates were open for the admission of the prisoner; while what was called the staff of the Bastille stood ready to receive him, and the guard of the grand court was drawn up in line on either side.

"You see we have an extensive court here," said the governor, leading the way. "It is somewhat dark, to be sure, on account of the buildings being so high; but, however, some of our people, when they have been accustomed to it for a year or two, find it cheerful enough. We will put you, I think, Monsieur de Morseiul, into what is called the Tower of Liberty, both because the name is a pleasant name—though it is but a name after all, either here or elsewhere—and also, because it is close to the library, and as long as you have the great liberties, as they are called, you may go in there, and amuse yourself. Most of you Huguenots, I believe, are somewhat of bookworms, and when a man cannot find many of the living to talk to, he likes just as well to talk to the dead. I do not suppose, that, like some of our inmates here on their first arrival, you are going to mope and pine like a half-starved cat, or a sick hen. It is hard to bear at first, I acknowledge; but there's nothing like bearing a thing gaily, after all. This way, Monsieur de Morseiul, this way, and I will show you your apartment."

He accordingly led him to the extreme angle of the grand court on the left hand, where a large transverse mass of architecture, containing the library, the hall of the council, and various other apartments, separated that part from the lesser court, called the Court of the Well. A small stone doorway opened upon a narrow spiral staircase, which made the head dizzy with its manifold turnings; and about half way up the steps the governor paused, and pushed back a door which communicated by a narrow, but crooked passage, with a single tolerable sized chamber, handsomely furnished.

"You see, we treat you well, Monsieur de Morseiul," said Besmaux; "and if anything can be done to make your residence here pleasant, we shall not fail to do it. There is but little use, if any, of causing doors to be locked or sentries to be placed. Some of the guards, or some of the officers of the staff, will be very willing to show you as much as is right of the rest of the building: and, in the meantime, can I serve you?"

"In nothing, I am afraid," replied the Count. "I have neither clothes, nor baggage, nor anything else with me, which will put me to some inconvenience till they send it to me; but I understand that orders have been given to that effect already; and I should only be glad to have any clothes and linen that may arrive as soon as possible."

"I will see to it, I will see to it," replied Besmaux. "You have dined of course, Count; but to-night, you will sup with me."

"If my stay here is to be long," said the Count, after thanking the governor for his invitation, "I should, of course, be very glad to have the attendance of a domestic. I care not much, indeed, whether it be one of my own, or whether it be one with whom you can supply me for the time, but I am not used to be without some sort of attendance."

The governor smiled. "You must not be nice in the Bastille, Monsieur de Morseiul," he said; "we all do with few attendants here, but we will see what can be done for you. At present, we know nothing, but that here you are. The order for your reception is of that kind which leaves everything doubtful but the fact that, for the time, you are not to be confined very strictly ; and, indeed, as the letter is somewhat informal, as everything is that comes from the hands of Monsieur de Louvois, I must write to him again for farther information. As soon as I receive it, the whole shall be arranged as far as I can to your satisfaction. In the meantime we will give you every indulgence, as far as our own general rules will allow, though, perhaps, you will think that share of indulgence very small."

The Count expressed his thanks in commonplace terms, well knowing the character of Besmaux, and that his fair speeches only promised a degree of courtesy, which his actions generally failed to fulfil.

After lingering for a moment or two, the governor left his prisoner in the abode assigned to him, and returned to his own dwelling, without locking the door of the apartment.

There are states of mind in which the necessity of calm contemplation is so strong and overpowering, that none of the ordinary motives which affect our nature have any influence upon us for the time,—states in which even vanity, the most irritable, and curiosity the most active of our moral prompters in this world, slumber inert, and leave thought and judgment paramount. Such was the case with the Count de Morseiul. Although he had certainly been interested with everything concerning the prison, which was to be his abode for an undefined length of time ; although all that took place indicative of his future destiny was, of course, not without attraction and excitement, he had grown weary of the formalities of his entrance into the Bastille, less because they were wearisome in themselves, than because he longed to be alone, and to have a few minutes for calm and silent reflection.

When he did come to reflect, however, the prospect presented was dark, gloomy, and sad. He was cut off from the escape he had meditated. The only thing that could have saved him from the most imminent dangers and difficulties, the only scheme which he had been able to fall upon to secure even the probability of peace and safety upon earth, had been now frustrated. The charges likely to be brought against him, if once averred by the decision of a court of justice, were such as, he well knew, could not and would not be followed by pardon; and when he looked at the chances that existed of those charges being sanctioned, confirmed, and declared just, by any commission that might sit to try him, he found that the probabilities were altogether against him; and that if party feeling biassed the opinion of one single magistrate, his cause was utterly lost. In cases where circumstantial evidence is everything—and therein lies the horror and danger of judging by circumstantial evidence alone—ever so light a word, so small a turn, given by advocate, judge, or witness, will cast upon the whole circumstances of any case so different a light, will so completely prejudice the question, and bias the minds of hearers, that he was quite aware, if any zealous Catholics should be engaged in the task of persecuting him to the last, that he could scarcely hope to escape from such serious imputations as would justify, perhaps, his permanent detention, if not his death. He had been at the meeting of the Protestants on the moor, which, though not illegal at the time, had been declared to be so since. He had then addressed the people, and had exhorted them to tranquillity and to peace; but where were the witnesses to come from, in order to prove that such was the case? He had gone unarmed to that meeting; but others had been there in arms, and with arms concealed. He, himself, with his own hand, had struck the first blow, from which such awful consequences had sprung; but how was he to prove the provocation which he had, in the first instance, received; or the protection which he had afterwards given to the base and unworthy young man, who had escaped from death by his means, to become a murderer the moment after? The only witnesses whom he could call were persons of the party inimical to the court, who might now be found with difficulty—when emigration was taking place from every part of France,—who would only be partially believed if they could be heard, and who would place themselves in imminent danger by bearing testimony on his behalf.

The witnesses against him would be the hired miscreants who had fired into a body of unoffending people, but who were of the religion of the judges, the unscrupulous adherents of the cause to which those judges were bound by every tie of interest and of prejudice, and serving under a monarch who, on one terrible occasion, had stepped in to overrule the decision of a court of justice, and to inflict severer punishment than even his own creatures had dared to assign. Death, therefore, seemed to be the only probable end of his imprisonment, death, or eternal loss of liberty! and the Count knew the court, and the character of those with whom he had to deal, too well, to derive any degree of consolation from the lenity with which he was treated at first.

Had he been now, in heart and mind, the same as he had been not very long before, when, quitting the army on the signature of the truce, he had returned to the home of his ancestors, the prospect would have been far less terrible to him—far less painful. His heart was then in some degree solitary, his mind was comparatively alone in the world.   He had spent the whole of his active life in scenes of danger and of strife.   He had confronted death so often, that the lean and horrid monster had lost his terrors, and become familiar with one who had seemed to seek his acquaintance as if in sport.   His ties to the world had been few; for the existence of bright days, and happy, careless moments, and splendid fortune, and the means of luxury and enjoyment at command are not the things that most strongly bind and attach us to life.   The tie, the strong, the mighty tie of deep and powerful affection to some being, or to beings, like himself, had been wanting.   There were many whom he liked; there were many whom he esteemed; there were many he protected and supported even at that time; but he knew and felt that if he were gone the next moment, they would be liked, and esteemed, and supported, and protected by others, and would feel the same, or nearly the same, towards those who succeeded as towards him, when he had passed away from the green and sunny earth, and left them to the care of newer friends.

But now other ties had arisen around him—ties, the strength, the durability, the firm pressure of which he had never known before.   There was now a being on the earth to whom he was attached by feelings which can only once be felt—for whom he, himself, would have been ready to sacrifice everything else— who for him, and for his love, had shewn herself willing to cast from her all those bright and pageant-like days of splendour, in which she had once seemed to take so much delight.   The tie, the strong tie of human affection—the rending of which is the great and agonizing pang of death—had twined itself round his heart, and bound every feeling and every thought.   The great, the sur- passing quality of sentient being, the capability of loving, and being loved, had risen up to crush and to leave void all the lesser things of life, but also to give death terrors that it knew not before; to make the grave the bitter parting place where joy seems to end for ever; and to poison the shaft that lays us low with venom that is felt in agony, ere the dark, dreamless sleep succeeds and extin- guishes all.

But was this all that rendered his situation now more terrible than it had been before?   Alas, no!   The sense of religion was strong, and he might confidently trust, that though earthly passion ended with the grave, and the mortal fire of his love for Clémence de Marly would there become extinct—he might confidently trust that, in another world, with his love for her exalted as well as purified, rendered more intense and sublime, though less passionate and human, they would meet again, known to each other, bound together by the immortal memory of vast affection, and only dis- tinct from other spirits, bright and happy as themselves, by the glorious consciousness of love, and the intense happiness of having loved well, loved nobly, and to the last.

Such might have been his consolation in the prospect of parting with her who had become so dear to him, if he had left her in calm and peaceful security, in a happy land, and without danger or difficulty surrounding her. But when he thought of the religion she had embraced, of the perils which surrounded her at every step, of the anguish which would fall upon her at his fate, of the utterly unprotected, uncomforted, unconsoled state in which she must remain, the heart of the strong warrior failed, and the trust of the Christian was drowned in human tears.

CHAPTER XXIII.

THE CONSPIRATORS.

In such dark anticipations and gloomy reflections, as we have mentioned in the end of the last chapter, the Count de Morseiul passed the solitary hours, till a servant appeared to conduct him to the supper table of the governor. Had he not wished to think, indeed, he might long before have found amusement, either in the court below, where a number of the other prisoners were walking, or in the small library of the château; but he did wish to think; and however sad and sombre the stream of thought might be at that moment, its course only seemed too soon interrupted.

The governor was civil, and even intended to be very affable; but Albert of Morseiul was not of a character to be amused with the anecdotes of a debauched soldier's life; and the only variety which the conversation of Besmaux afforded were tales of the regency of Anne of Austria, which, though they might at any other moment have served to entertain an idle hour, were too light and insignificant to take hold of a mind agitated and writhing like that of the Count.

The governor thought his guest very dull, but for three nights, during which he continued to entertain him at supper (not without private purposes of his own) he let him have his own way. His whole conduct continued courteous; he once or twice walked with him in the court; he led him to the library; and, as nothing had yet arrived from Jerome Riquet, he supplied him with some clothes from his own wardrobe. On the fourth night the Count supped with the governor again; and, after having made various essays to enliven him, Besmaux proposed that they should sit down to play for sums, written upon pieces of paper, which were to be accounted for after the Count's liberation. The young nobleman would have certainly lost the good graces of the governor for ever by declining this proposal, had it not so occurred that two incidents intervened which prevented him from pressing it. The first was the arrival of a large packet of linen and other clothes for the use of the Count; and Besmaux, who found a real pleasure in the execution of the task of a gaoler, proceeded to examine with his own eyes and hands every separate article which had been sent. It may be supposed that, after the intimation which he had received on the road, the young Count's heart felt no slight agitation and interest during the scrutiny; but he had the pleasure of seeing that, if anything was written in the manner which Riquet had stated, no discovery thereof was made; and, having completely satisfied himself, Besmaux ordered the packet to be carried to the chamber of the Count.

The little excitement thus produced had scarcely worn away, when the great bell was heard to ring, and shortly after the officer upon guard appeared to demand the keys. According to the usual form the governor inquired—" For whose admission?"

" For the admission," said the officer, reading from a scrap of paper, " of Louis de Rohan, called the Chevalier de Rohan."

The governor started up in some surprise—" On what charge?" he demanded.

" For high treason," replied the officer; and Besmaux immediately gave orders for the Chevalier to be brought to his apartments. " Monsieur de Morseiul," he said, " you will be good enough to follow that porte-clef, who will conduct you back to your chamber. Do you feel it cold?— for the King allows firing."

" I have felt it slightly cold," the Count replied, " and of course the state of a prisoner does not tend to warm the heart."

" Give wood to the Count in his chamber," said Besmaux, to one of the turnkeys, who had entered at the same time with the officer on guard; " and now, good night, Count. No word to the prisoner, if you pass him below!"

The Count rose and departed; and, as the governor had anticipated, met the Chevalier de Rohan at the foot of the stairs. That unfortunate gentleman was guarded by a musketeer on either side, and a man holding a torch preceding him. The moment that his eye fell upon the Count de Morseiul, he stopped, and appeared as if he were about to speak: but an officer who was behind, and in whom the Count de Morseiul instantly recognised the Marquis of Brissac, major of the king's guard, exclaimed aloud, " Pass on, Monsieur de Rohan!"

The Count, who certainly had no desire to hold any communications with him, merely bowed his head, and, followed by the turnkey, walked into the court. Though Brissac knew him well, he took not the slightest notice of him as he passed, and the Count was conducted to his chamber in the Tower of Liberty, as it was called, where firing and lights were almost immediately afterwards brought him. On leaving him, however, the turnkey showed, by locking the heavy door without, that the name of the tower had but little real meaning; and the harsh sound of the grating iron fell heavy and painfully upon the Count's ear.

There was, however, the hope before him of receiving some intelligence from his friends without; and, as soon as he had made sure that the turnkey was gone for the night, he eagerly opened the packet of clothes which had been sent, and endeavoured, by the means which had been pointed out, to discover anything which might be written on them. At first he was disappointed, and was beginning to fear that Riquet had been prevented from executing the purpose which he had entertained. At length, however, as he held one of the handkerchiefs before the fire, some slight yellow lines began to appear, grew gradually darker and darker, and assumed the form of letters, words, lines, and sentences. The first thing that was written at the top was in the hand of the valet himself, and contained words of hope and encouragement. It was to the following effect:—

" Fear not; you shall soon be free. The lady has been told of all. The priest has gone safely back to Poitou. No suspicion attaches to any one, and means are taking to do away the evil."

The next sentences were in a different hand-writing; and perhaps the young Count might not have been able to recognise whose it was—so different did it seem upon the linen, and in that ink, from the usual writing of Clémence—had not the words been sufficient to show him from whom it proceeded.

" Fear not, dear Albert," the writing went; " I have heard all, and grieve, but do not despond. I have been sent for to see a person to-morrow morning early, who is all-powerful. She loved me in my childhood; she promised me many things in my youth, which I was too proud to accept; but I will now cast all pride away, for the sake of him I love."

A few lines more were written still further down, but, as the Count was turning eagerly to read them, numerous sounds were heard from the court below, the clang of soldiers grounding their arms, and voices speaking, and, the moment after, various footsteps might be distinguished ascending the staircase which came towards the room. Fearful that he should be discovered, the Count concealed the handkerchief in his bosom; but the steps passed by the door of his apartment, and, immediately after, heavy footfalls were heard in the room above, with voices speaking in sharp and angry tones. Those sounds soon ceased, however; four or five persons were heard to descend the stairs; and then all became quiet, except that a quick footstep was still heard pacing backwards and forwards in the apartment overhead.

" That is the Chevalier de Rohan," thought the Count. " What crime, I wonder, can that weak libertine have committed to deserve the rigorous imprisonment to which it seems he is to be subjected?"

With such brief thought, however, be dismissed the subject from his mind, and turned once more to the writing. By this time it had nearly vanished; but, being again exposed to the fire, it reappeared, though more faintly than before. Fearful of interruption, the Count turned to the last lines which he had not read. They seemed to him, as far as he could judge, to be written in the hand of the Chevalier d'Evran, whom, to say sooth, in the joys and fears and agitations of the few preceding days, he had nearly forgotten.

"I have just returned to Paris, dear Albert," it said, " having gone down to Poitou to secure evidence, which they would never have suffered to transpire, if some friend of yours had not been upon the spot. I have secured it. Fear not, therefore, for I and your belle Clémence are labouring together to set you free."

Oh, human nature, strange and extraordinary state of existence, how many contradictions dost thou contain! Although filled with such good hopes, although containing such proofs of friendship, although conveying such important intelligence, the lines written by the Chevalier d'Evran were not altogether pleasing to the Count de Morseiul, and he felt sensations that he was angry with himself for feeling, but which all his schooling of his own heart could scarcely banish.

"I shall hate myself," he continued, "if I feel thus. Must there ever be some counterbalancing thing in life and in feeling, to poise the bad against the good, and to make us less happy, less wise, less generous than we otherwise might be? Here new sensations have sprung up in my bosom, of a deeper and a finer kind than I ever knew before; and must there come some petty jealousy, some small, low, mean want of confidence, even in persons I most esteem and love, to debase me as much as those other feelings might elevate me? I will think of such things no more; and will only think of Louis with gratitude and affection."

Thus saying, or rather thus thinking, he re-read the lines that had been written by Clémence, and found therein a balm and a consolation which healed all the evil of the other. Having done so, his next care was to efface the writing; but that he found by no means difficult, damping the handkerchief in the cruise of water which had been left for him, and which, in a few minutes, left not a vestige of the lines which had been traced for his eye alone. He sat up for some time after this examination, soothed and calmed by the tidings he had received, and certainly far more tranquil in every respect than during the first few hours of his confinement.

The waning of the lights, however, which had been given to him, warned him, at length, that it was time to retire to rest, and after some brief prayers to the Almighty for guidance, protection, and deliverance, he undressed himself, extinguished the lights, and lay down to seek repose. But it was in vain that he did so: the words of those who were most dear to him, the last that for months, perhaps, or years, might reach him, had awakened all the thoughts of

freedom : and as he lay on the small prison bed which was allotted
to him, and gazed round upon the massy walls of the chamber in
which he was confined, with the flickering light of the half-
extinguished fire flashing from time to time on all the various objects round about, the sensation of imprisonment, of the utter loss
of liberty, of being cut off from all correspondence or communication with his fellow-men, of being in the power and at the mercy
of others, without any appeal against their will, or any means of
deliverance from their hands, came upon him more strongly, more
forcibly than ever, and made a heart, not easily bent or affected
by any apprehensions, sink with a cold feeling of deep and utter
despondency.

Thus passed several hours, till, at length, weariness overcame
thought, and he obtained sleep towards the morning. He was
awakened by the entrance of one of the turnkeys, accompanied by
the major of the Bastille ; but the tidings which the latter officer
brought to the Count de Morseiul were by no means pleasant, or
calculated to confirm the hopes that the words of Clémence and
the Chevalier d'Evran had held out to him.

"I am sorry to tell you, Monsieur de Morseiul," he said, "that
the governor last night received orders from Monsieur de Louvois
to place you in stricter confinement, and he is, therefore, obliged to
say that you can no longer be permitted to quit your chamber.
Anything that can be done, consistent with his duty, to render
your confinement less painful to you, shall be done, depend
upon it."

The officer was then bowing, as if to retire ; but the Count
stopped him by asking, "Is there any objection to my inquiring,
sir, whether there is a cause assigned for this new order ?"

"In regard to that I am as ignorant as yourself," replied the
major. "All I can tell is, that the order was brought by Monsieur
de Brissac, at the same time that he conveyed hither the Chevalier
de Rohan ;" and, without waiting for any further questions, he
quitted the room in haste ; and the turnkey, having brought the
Count his breakfast, and, as far as possible, arranged the room with
some degree of neatness, followed the major and locked the door.

The full horrors of imprisonment now fell upon the Count de
Morseiul, and the day wore away without his holding any further
intercourse with any human being, except when his dinner and his
supper were brought to him by one of the turnkeys. We need not
pause upon his sensations, nor describe minutely all the dark and
horrible anticipations which rose, like phantoms, to people his
solitary chamber. Night came at length, and this night, at least,
he slept ; for the exhaustion of his corporeal frame, by the intense
emotions of his mind, was far greater than that which could have
been produced by a day of the most unusual exercise.

Day had scarcely dawned on the following morning, however,
when he was roused by two of the officers of the prison entering

his chamber, and desiring him to rise, as an officer from the King
was waiting to convey him to the royal chamber, at the arsenal,
where a commission was sitting for the purpose of interrogating him
and his accomplices. The Count made no observation, but hastened
to do as he was directed; and, as soon as he was dressed, he descended the narrow and tortuous staircase into the great court of
the Bastille, where he found the soldiers of the garrison drawn up
in arms on either side, together with a number of officers belonging
to the staff of the garrison, various turnkeys and other gaolers, and
in their hands, evidently as prisoners, the unfortunate Chevalier de
Rohan, and an old white-headed man, apparently of seventy years
of age, with a shrewd and cunning countenance, more strongly expressive of acuteness than vigour of mind. ·

Without suffering him to speak with any one, the officers of the
prison placed him in file after the Chevalier de Rohan—a gaoler,
however, interposing between each of the prisoners and the one
that followed;—and thus between a double row of soldiery, they
marched on into the *Cour du Gouvernement,* as if they were about
to be conducted to the house of the governor. When they reached
that court, they turned at once to the left, mounted a flight of steps
leading to a raised terrace which overlooked the water, and then
passing onward, approached the grating which separated that court
from the gardens of the arsenal.

At the grating appeared a large body of musketeers, commanded
by an officer of the name of Jouvelle, who had served under the
Count de Morseiul himself, and into his hands the officers of the
Bastille delivered their prisoners, who were then marched, under
a strong escort, to the arsenal, where the commission was sitting.
All the gates of the gardens and of the building itself, the Count
remarked were in the hands of the musketeers of the King, and
not another individual was to be seen besides the soldiery, in the
gardens usually so thronged with the good citizens of Paris.

Passing through several of the narrow and intricate passages of
the building, the three prisoners were placed in a room which
seemed to have been destined for a military mess-room; and, while
they were kept separate by their guards, an inferior officer was sent
out to see whether the commission was ready to proceed. In a few
minutes he returned with two officers of the court, who demanded
the presence of Louis Chevalier de Rohan.

The interrogation of this prisoner lasted for a great length of
time; but, at the end of about an hour and a half, the same officers
re-appeared, demanding the presence of Affinius Vandenenden, upon
which the old man, whom we have mentioned, rose and followed
them out of the room. The Chevalier, however, had not returned
with the officers, and during the space of half an hour longer the
Count de Morseiul remained in suspense, in regard to what was
proceeding. At length the officers once more appeared, and with
them the captain of the musketeers, de Jouvelle, who, while the

ushers pronounced the name of "Albert Count of Morseiul," passed by the prisoner, as if to speak to one of the soldiers, saying, in a low voice, as he did so, " Be of good cheer, Count; they have confessed nothing to criminate you."

The Count passed on without reply, and followed the ushers into another chamber at the farther end of the passage, where he found a number of lawyers and counsellors of state assembled as a royal commission, and presided by the well-known La Reynie. The aspect of the room was not that of a court of justice, and it was evident that the commissioners met simply for the purpose of carrying on the preliminary interrogatories. The Count was furnished with a seat, and after a whispering consultation, for a moment, between La Reynie and one of his brethren, the former commenced the interrogation of the Count by assuring him of the clemency and mercy of the King's disposition, and adjuring him to tell, frankly and straightforwardly, the whole truth, as the only means of clearing his reputation, and re-establishing himself in the royal favour.

To this exordium the Count de Morseiul merely replied by an inclination of the head, very well knowing that with some of the gentlemen whom he saw before him it was advisable to be as niggardly of speech as possible. La Reynie then proceeded to ask how long he had been acquainted with the Chevalier de Rohan, and the Count replied that he had known him for many years.

" When did you see him last?" demanded the judge, "and where ?"

" In the gardens of Versailles," answered the Count, calmly, "at the very moment when I was myself arrested."

" And upon what occasion," demanded the judge, " did you see him previously ?"

" I saw him," replied the Count, " when I visited the Duc de Rouvré, at Poitiers, at the house of the same nobleman in Paris, and once also upon the road between the capital and Versailles, about five or six days ago."

" Are you sure that these are the only days when you have seen him ?" demanded the judge. " Recollect yourself, Monsieur le Comte. I think you must have forgotten."

" No, I have not," replied the Count. " I have only seen him on these two occasions since I arrived in Paris, and two or three times during my stay at Poitiers."

" Ay, there is the fact," said La Reynie. " You saw him frequently at Poitiers."

" I also saw various blacksmiths, and lackeys, and horse-boys," said the Count, unable to conceive what connexion there could exist between any charges against himself and those against the Chevalier de Rohan, who was known to be a zealous Catholic, " and with them, the blacksmiths, lackeys, and horse-boys, I had as much to do as I had with the Chevalier de Rohan, and no more."

" And pray," continued La Reynie, in the same tone, " what

private conversations took place between you and the Chevalier at Poitiers? To the best of your recollection repeat the substance thereof."

The Count smiled. "To the best of my recollection, then," he said, "the substance was as follows: 'Good day, Count de Morseiul. Good morning, Monsieur de Rohan. What a beautiful day it is, Monsieur de Morseiul! It is the most charming weather I remember. There is a sad want of rain, Monsieur le Chevalier, and I fear the poor peasantry will suffer. Do you go out with the duke to hunt to-day? I think not, for my horses are tired.' Such, sir, is the substance of the only private conversations that took place between myself and the Chevalier at Poitiers."

"Was that all, Monsieur de Morseiul?" demanded La Reynie, with tolerable good humour. "Are you sure you have forgot nothing of equal importance?"

"I believe I have not forgot one word," replied the Count, "except that, on one occasion, Monsieur de Rohan said to me, 'Your hat is unlooped, Count:' when, I am afraid, I looped it without thanking him."

"Well, then, now to somewhat longer and more important conversations, my good young gentleman," said La Reynie. "What has passed between you and the Chevalier de Rohan, when you have met him since your arrival at the court?"

"Why, sir," replied the Count, with a grave and somewhat grieved air, "I give you my word that nothing passed between the Chevalier de Rohan and myself which at all affected his majesty's service, and I would fain, if it were possible, avoid entering into particulars which, if told to everybody, might be painful to a gentleman of my acquaintance, who, I trust, may yet clear himself of any serious charge."

"Monsieur le Comte de Morseiul," said the Counsellor Ormesson, "we respect your motives, and have regard to the manner in which you have expressed them; but the Chevalier de Rohan, I am sorry to inform you, stands charged with high treason upon very strong presumptive evidence. There are particular circumstances which induce a belief that you may have had something to do with his schemes. We trust that such is not the case; but it is absolutely necessary that you should clearly and explicitly state the nature of any transactions which may have taken place between you and him, both for your own safety, for his, and out of respect and duty to the King."

"Then, sir, I have no other choice," replied the Count, "but to yield to your reasons, and to beg that you would put your questions in such a shape that I may answer them distinctly and easily."

"Very well, Monsieur de Morseiul," said La Reynie; "we have always heard that you are a gentleman of honour, who would not prevaricate even to save his own life. Pray inform us what was the nature of the conversation between you and the Chevalier de Rohan, on the morning of the 23rd of this month."

"It was a very short one," replied the Count, somewhat surprised to see what accurate information of his proceedings had been obtained. "The Chevalier overtook me as I was going to Versailles, and on that occasion Monsieur de Rohan informed me that he had lost a large sum at the gaming-table on the night before, and begged me to lend him a hundred louis, in the hopes of recovering it by the same means. I advised him strongly to abstain from such proceedings, but of course did not refuse to lend him what he asked."

"Then did you lend him the hundred louis on the spot?" demanded La Reynie.

"No," replied the Count; "I told him that I had not such a sum with me, but promised to send it to him at his lodgings in the course of the afternoon, which I did as soon as ever I arrived at Versailles."

"Pray, how happened it, Monsieur de Morseiul," demanded Ormesson, "that as you were going to Versailles, and the Chevalier overtook you going thither also, you did not ride on together, as would seem natural for two gentlemen like yourselves?"

"Nay," replied the Count, smiling, "that I think is pressing the matter rather too far, monsieur. My society might not be pleasant to the Chevalier, or the reverse might be the case; or we might have other business by the way. A thousand circumstances of the same kind might occur."

"Well, then, I will put the question straightforwardly and at once," said Ormesson. "Had you, or had you not, any reason to believe that the Chevalier de Rohan was at that time engaged in schemes dangerous to the state?"

"None in the world," replied the Count, "and no such feeiings or ideas whatsoever had any share in preventing my riding on with the Chevalier de Rohan."

The commissioners looked at each other for a moment with an inquiring glance, and then La Reynie placed before the Count a note, which was to the following effect:—

"MY DEAR COUNT,

"I have received what you sent me, for which I return you many thanks, and I have not the slightest doubt, by your assistance, to be able to accomplish the purpose I have in view.

"Your devoted,

"THE CHEVALIER DE ROHAN."

"Pray, Monsieur de Morseiul," said the Counsellor, "do you recognise that note?"

"Most assuredly," replied the Count. "I received that note from the Chevalier de Rohan, on the very evening of the day we have just mentioned."

"And pray, what is the interpretation you put upon it?" demanded La Reynie.

"Simply," replied the Count, "that he had received the hundred louis which I sent him, and hoped by employing them at the gaming-table, to be enabled to win back the sum which he had lost."

"It seems to me," said the Judge, "that the note will very well bear two interpretations, Count, and that, supposing a gentleman unfortunate enough to have laid schemes for introducing a foreign enemy into the country, or for causing any of the provinces of the kingdom to revolt, and supposing him, at the same time, to be greatly straitened for money and assistance—it seems to me, I say, that the note before us is just such a one as he would write to a friend who had come to his aid at the moment of need, either by giving him aid of a pecuniary or of any other kind."

"All I can say, sir," replied the Count, "is, that the note before you I received from the Chevalier de Rohan, and that no other interpretation than the one I have given was, or could be put upon it by me. I knew of no schemes whatsoever against the state, and the Chevalier himself had certainly no other meaning than the one I have assigned. It will be very easy for you, however, gentlemen, to place the note before the Chevalier, and make him explain it himself. Though an unfortunate gentleman, he is still, I believe, a gentleman of honour, and will tell you the truth. We have had no conversation together upon the subject. We have not even interchanged a word as we came hither, and you can compare his statement with mine."

"Perhaps that may have been done already, Monsieur de Morseiul," said Ormesson, "but at all events we think we may close your examination for to-day. The interrogation may be resumed at a future period, when other things have become manifest; and we have only, at present, to exhort you, on all occasions to deal frankly and openly with the court."

"Such is always my custom, sir," replied the Count. "I stand before you conscious of my innocence of any crime whatsoever; and, having nothing to conceal, am always ready to state frankly and truly what I know, except when by so doing I may wound or injure others."

Thus saying, he bowed to the commissioners and retired. At the door of the chamber, he found two musketeers waiting for his coming out, and, being placed between them, he was once more conducted back to the Bastille. He was then led by the turnkeys, who were in waiting to receive him, to the same apartment which he had previously occupied; but before nightfall, it was notified to him that the liberties of the Bastille were restored to him, and he received some slight solace from knowing that he should not, for some time at least, be confined to the solitary discomfort of his own apartment, with no better occupation than that of striding from one side to the other, or gazing out of the narrow window, and endeavouring to gain a sight of what was passing in the Rue St. Antoine.

CHAPTER XXIV.

THE EXECUTION.

WITHIN the walls of the Bastille, some weeks passed over almost without incident, though not without pain to the Count de Morseiul; but it would be tedious to detail all the feelings and the thoughts that crossed each other in his bosom during that period. He was still allowed a great degree of liberty, was permitted to take exercise in the great court, to converse with many of the other prisoners, and to hear whispers of what was taking place in the world without. But none of those whispers gave him any tidings of those he loved, any indication of his own probable fate, or any news of the church to which he belonged: and he remarked with pain, that while many of the other prisoners received visits from their friends and acquaintances, either no one sought to see him, or else those who did so were excluded by some express order.

He grieved over this, and perhaps felt, with some degree of bitterness of spirit, that the iron of captivity might not only enter into the soul, but might wear and corrode the mind on which it pressed. Such feelings made him at once apply himself eagerly to everything that could occupy his thoughts, and turn them from contemplations which he knew to be not only painful, but hurtful also; and he soon created for himself a number of those occupations which many an unhappy man besides himself has devised at different times for the solace of captivity.

The library, however, was his greatest enjoyment. Though so fond of all manly exercises, and famous for his skill therein, he had from his youth loved the communing with other minds, in the pages which the hand of genius has traced, and which have been given forth as the deliberate effort of the writer's spirit. He loved, I say, that communing with other men's hearts and minds which is undisturbed by discussion, or wordy dispute, or any of the petty vanities that creep into the living conversation even of the great, the learned, and the good; and now, though the library was small, and perhaps not very well selected, yet there was many a book therein which afforded him sweet occupation during some, at least, of the melancholy hours of imprisonment.

At other times he walked the length of the court-yard, gaining where he could a gleam of sunshine; and rather than suffer his thoughts, as he did so walk, to dwell upon the painful theme of his own fate, he would count the very stones of the pavement, and moralize upon their shapes and colours. Almost every day, during the period we have mentioned, the guard was turned out, the prisoners having the liberties were ordered to keep back, and a train of others in the stricter state of imprisonment were marched out to the arsenal. Amongst these was usually the unhappy Chevalier de Rohan; and the wistful, longing gaze with which one day he looked round the court as he passed through, seeming to envy the other captives the sort of freedom they enjoyed, caused the Count de Morseiul to task severely his own heart for the repinings which he felt at his own situation.

Various little occurrences of the same kind took place from time to time, affording a momentary matter of interest in the midst of the dark sameness of the prison life. At one period, during the whole of several nights, the Count de Morseiul heard at intervals voices which seemed to be shouting through speaking-trumpets. The place from which the sound proceeded varied constantly; and the young prisoner could only conclude that some friends of one of the sad inhabitants of the Bastille were prowling round it, endeavouring to communicate intelligence. He listened eagerly, in the supposition that those sounds might be addressed to him; but though from time to time he could catch a single word, such as "dead," "told," &c., he could make no continuous sense of what was said.

The first time this occurred was shortly after his examination before the commission; and it continued, for three or four nights, to be repeated at different hours; but still the sounds were too distant for him to ascertain the meaning of the speakers; and he was obliged to content himself with believing that this intelligence was not intended for himself, and hoping that it had been more distinct to the unfortunate person for whose ears it was designed.*

After having listened during the whole of one night, without hearing the words repeated, he determined to ask one of his fellow-prisoners, who had the liberty like himself of walking in the court, whether he had noticed the occurrence, and had been able to make out what was said.

The personage whom he fixed upon in his own mind for that purpose, was a tall, upright, elderly man, with a soldier-like air, and a good deal of frankness of manner, approaching perhaps to what is called bluffness, without being in the slightest degree rude or uncivil. He seemed to seek nobody, but to converse willingly with any one when he was sought—gave his opinion in few words, but distinctly, accurately, and positively—bore his imprisonment with perfect lightness and indifference—never referred in the slightest degree to the cause thereof or to his own history, though without appearing to avoid the subject at all—and, in short, impressed strongly on the minds of those who saw him, and were accustomed to judge of the world, that he was a frank, upright,

---

* The words were intended for the unfortunate Chevalier de Rohan, and were "Hatréaumont est mort, et n'a rien dit." The unhappy prisoner, like the Count de Morseiul, was not able to distinguish the meaning of his friends; otherwise those words, if he had shaped his course accordingly, would have insured his safety.

straightforward soldier, accustomed to various kinds of endurance, and bearing all with manly firmness and resolution.

He spoke French with great fluency and accuracy; but at times, in conversing with him, the Count de Morseiul had fancied he could remark a foreign accent, though very slight, and he was inclined to believe that the old officer was one of the Weimerians who had served so long in the pay of France. His countenance, indeed, was not like that of a German; there was more quickness and brightness of the eye, and the features were more elongated, and somewhat sharper than is common amongst the Teutonie races. But still a great part of the Weimerian troops had been levied on the borders of the Rhine, where the mixture of French and other blood often marks itself strongly amongst the German population. His ordinary walk was from one corner of the court-yard to the opposite angle, which gave the utmost extent of space that could be had; and there the young Count, on descending the staircase, found him pacing up and down with his usual quick step and erect carriage. Though the old man neither paused nor noticed him further than by a passing "Good morning, sir," the Count joined him, and at once spoke of the matter in question.

"Have you heard," he said, "during this last night or two, some people shouting, apparently through speaking-trumpets, as if they wished to convey intelligence to one of us prisoners?"

"Once or twice very faintly," replied the other. "But I am on the opposite side of the prison to you, you know, and the sounds I heard seemed to come from your side, or, at all events, not further round than the Well Tower. Do you think they were addressed to you?"

"I think not," replied the Count; "and, if they were, I certainly could make nothing of them. I looked out of my window to get a sight, as far as possible, of the speakers by the moonlight the other night, but I was not successful; for I can see, as I am placed, into the little Place St. Antoine, but no further. However, I tried to distinguish the voices, and certainly they were not those of any one I know."

"A speaking-trumpet makes a great difference," replied his companion. "I should have liked to hear them more distinctly."

"Do you think they were intended for you?" said the Count.

"Oh dear no," replied the other; "nobody can have anything to tell me. If ever my liberty comes, it will come at once; and as to either trying me or punishing me in any other way than by imprisonment, that they dare not do."

"That is in some degree a happy situation," said the Count. "But I scarcely know how that can be, for judging by my own case, and that of many others, I have no slight reason to believe that they dare try or punish any man in France, whether guilty or not."

" Any Frenchman, you mean, Count," replied the stranger;
" but that does not happen to be my case; and though my own
king may be rascal and fool enough to let me stay here wearing
out the last days of a life, the greater part of which has been devoted to the service of himself and his ungrateful ancestors, yet I
do not believe that he dare for his life suffer me to be publicly
injured. A trial would, as a matter of course, be known sooner or
later. They may poison me, perhaps," he continued, " to keep me
quiet, though I do not think it, either. Your king is not so bad as
that. Though he is a great tyrant, he is not bloody by his nature.
However, Monsieur de Morseiul, as I am not in here for any crime,
as I never had anything to do with a conspiracy of any kind, as I
am not a native of this country, nor a subject of your king, as I
have not a secret in the world, and little more money than will
serve to feed and clothe me, I do not see that any one can have
either object or interest in hallooing at me through a speaking-
trumpet."

" You have excited my curiosity," said the Count, " and a
Frenchman's curiosity, you know, is always somewhat intrusive;
but, as you have just said that you have not a secret in the world, it
will seem less impertinent than it otherwise would be if I ask what,
in the name of fortune, you can be here for?"

" Not in the least impertinent," replied the other. " I am in here
for something of the same kind that they tell me you are in here for:
namely, for differing from the King of France in regard to transub-
stantiation; for thinking that he'll go to the devil at once when he
dies, without stopping half-way at a posthouse, called Purgatory,
which a set of scoundrels have established to suit their own particular
convenience; and for judging it a great deal better that people should
sing psalms, and say their prayers, in a language that they understand, than in a tongue they know not a word of. I mean, in short,
for being a Protestant; for if it had not been for that, I should not
have been in here. The fact was, I served long in this country in
former times, and having taken it into my head to see it again, and
to visit some old friends, I undertook a commission to bring back a
couple of brats of a poor foolish relation of mine, who had been left
here for their education. Louis found out what I was about, declared that I came to make Protestant converts, and shut me up in the
Bastille, where I have been now more than nine months. I sent a
message over to the King of England by a fellow-prisoner who was
set at liberty some time ago. But every one knows that Charles
would have sold his own soul by the pound, and thrown his father
and mother, and all his family, into the scale, for the sake of a few
crowns, at any time. This popish rascal, too, who is now on the
throne, doubtless thinks that I am just as well where I am, so I
calculate upon whistling away my days within the four walls of
this court.—I don't care, it can't last very long. I was sixty-five
on the third of last month, and though there feels some life in

these old limbs, the days of Methuselah, thank God, are gone by, and we've no more kicking about now for a thousand years. I shouldn't wonder," he continued, "if the people you heard were hallooing to that unfortunate Chevalier de Rohan, whom they dragged through this morning to be interrogated again. They say he'll have his head chopped off to a certainty. If we could have found out what the people said we might have told him, for prisouers will get at each other, let them do what they like."

"I listened for one whole night," said the Count, "but found it quite in vain. The judges, I suppose, are satisfied that I had nothing to do with this business of the Chevalier de Rohan's, otherwise they would have had me up again for examination?"

"God knows," replied his companion. "Tyranny is like an actor at a country fair, and one never knows which way he will kick next."

Thus passed the conversation between the Count and the old English officer, whose name, somewhat disfigured indeed, may be found written in the registers of the Bastille, as arrested on suspicion; for which crime he, like many others, was subjected to imprisonment for a lengthened period. He and the Count de Morseiul now usually took their walk together, and in his society the young nobleman found no small delight, for there was a sort of quaint indifference, which gave salt and flavour to considerable good sense and originality of thought. The old man himself, also, seemed to take a pleasure in conversing with the young Count; which was evidently not the case with the generality of his fellow-prisoners. One morning, however, towards the end of the period we have mentioned, the sound of the falling drawbridge was heard; the soldiers drew up in double line; the order for all the captives in the court to fall back, was given; and the Chevalier de Rohan, followed by two or three other prisoners, amongst whom were Vandenenden and a lady, were brought in as if from examination.

The countenances of almost all were very pale, with the exception of that of the Chevalier de Rohan, which was inflamed with a fiery spot on either cheek, while his eyes flashed fire, and his lips were absolutely covered with foam. Four times between the great gate of the court and the tower in which he was confined, he halted abruptly, and turning round with furious gestures to the guards and gaolers who surrounded him, poured forth a torrent of fierce and angry words, exclaiming that he had been deceived, cheated, that the King's name had been used to assure him of safety, and that now the King had retracted the promises, and was going to murder him.

It was in vain that the guards tried to stop him, and endeavoured to force him onward. Still he turned round, as soon as he had an opportunity, and shouted forth the same accusation with horrible imprecations and even blasphemies. The second prisoner, who seemed to be a military man, paused, and regarded the Chevalier with a stern and somewhat scornful air; but the lady and the old man, Vandenenden, were drowned in tears, and from all the Count saw, he concluded that the trial of the Chevalier and his accomplices had either terminated in their condemnation, or else had taken such a turn as showed that result to be inevitable.

From that time none of the prisoners who had the liberties of the Bastille were allowed to remain in the court when the Chevalier and his accomplices passed through it, an order being given, before the gates were opened, for every one to retire to his own apartments. Three days after this new regulation, such a command having issued, the Count obeyed it willingly, for the weather had become cold and damp, and the court of the Bastille felt like a well. He had obtained permission to take some books out of the library, in which no fire was allowed, and, sitting by the embers in his own apartment, he was endeavouring to amuse himself by reading, when the sound of what seemed to him carts, in greater numbers than usual, mingled with the tongues of many persons speaking, called him to the little window of his chamber.

He saw that the small Place St. Antoine was filled with a crowd of people surrounding two or three large wagons as they seemed, but he could not make out what the persons present were about, and, after looking on for a few minutes, he returned to his book.

Everything within the walls of the Bastille seemed to be unusually still and quiet, and for rather more than an hour and a half he read on, till some sound of a peculiar character, or some sudden impression on his own mind which he could not account for, made him again rise and hasten to the window. When he did so, a sight was presented to his eyes, of which it would have required long years to efface the recollection. The carts which he hàd seen, and the materials they contained, had been by this time erected into a scaffold; and in the front thereof, turned towards the Rue St. Antoine, which, as well as the square itself, was filled with an immense multitude of people, was a block with the axe leaning against the side.

At one corner of the scaffold was erected a gibbet; and in the front, within a foot or two of the block, stood the unfortunate Chevalier de Rohan, with a priest, on one side of him, pouring consolation or instruction into his ear, while the executioner, on the other side, was busily cutting off his hair to prepare his neck for the stroke. Two or three other prisoners were behind, with several priests and the assistants of the executioner; and amongst them again were seen the forms of Vandenenden and the lady whom the Count had beheld pass through the court of the castle.

The aged man seemed scarcely able to support himself, and was upheld near the foot of the gallows by two of the guards; but the lady, with her head uncovered and her fine hair gathered together in a knot near the top of her head, stood alone, calm, and, to all appearance, perfectly self-possessed; and as she turned, for a moment, to look at the weak old man, whose writhing agitation at parting with a life that he could not expect to prolong for many years, even if pardoned, was truly lamentable, she showed the Count de Morseiul a fine, though somewhat faded countenance, with every line expressive of perfect resolution and tranquillity.

The Count de Morseiul was a brave man, who had confronted death a thousand times, who had seen it in many an awful shape, and accompanied by many a terrible accessory; but when he looked at the upturned eyes of the multitude, the block, the axe, the gibbet, the executioners, the cold, grey sky above that spoke of hopelessness, the thronged windows all around teeming with gaping faces, and all the horrible parade of public execution, he could not but wonder at the self-possession and the calmness of that lady's aspect and demeanour, as one about to suffer in that awful scene.

His, however, was no heart that could delight in such spectacles, and withdrawing almost immediately from the window, he waited in deep thought. In about a minute after, there was a sort of low murmur, followed by a heavy stroke; and then the murmur sounded like the rushing of a distant wind. In a few moments after that, again came another blow, and the Count thought that there was a suppressed scream, mingled with the wave-like sound of the multitude. Again came that harsh blow, accompanied by a similar noise, and, lastly, a loud shout, in which were mingled tones of ferocity and derision, very different from any which had been heard before. Not aware of what could have produced the change, the Count was once more irresistibly led to the window, where he beheld swinging and writhing on the gibbet, the form of the old man Vandenenden, whose pusillanimity seemed to have excited the contempt and indignation of the populace. On the other parts of the scaffold, the executioner and his assistants were seen gathering up the bloody ruins of the human temples they had overthrown. Sickened and pained, the Count turned away, and covered his eyes with his hands, asking himself, in the low voice of thought, "When will this be my fate also ?"

CHAPTER XXV.

THE WOMAN'S JUDGMENT.

WE must now, for a little while, change the scene entirely ; and, as we find often done most naturally, both in reality and poetry, bring the prison and the palace side by side. It was in one of the smaller chambers, then, of the palace at Versailles—exquisitely fitted up with furniture of the most costly, if not of the most splendid materials, with very great taste shown in every particular, grace in all the ornaments, harmony in all the colours, and a certain sort of justness and appropriateness in each object around, which rendered the whole very pleasing to the eye. It was in this chamber that there sat a lady, late on the evening of an autumnal day, busily reading from a book, illustrated with some of the richest and most beautiful miniatures that the artists of the French capital could then produce.

She was, at the time we speak, of somewhat past the middle period of life,—that is to say, she was nearly approaching to the age of fifty; but she looked considerably younger than she really was, and forty was the very extreme at which any one, by the mere look, would have ventured to place the number of her years. The rich worked candelabra of gold, under which she was reading, cast its light upon not a single grey hair. The form was full and rounded; the arms white and delicate; the hand, which in general loses its symmetry sooner than ought else, except, perhaps, the lips, was as tapering, as soft, and as beautiful in contour as ever. The eyes were large and expressive, and there was a thoughtfulness about the whole countenance which had nothing of melancholy in its character, perhaps a little of worldliness, but more of mind and intellect than either.

After she had been reading for some time, the door was quietly opened, and the King himself entered, with a soft and almost noiseless step. The lady immediately laid down her book and rose ; but Louis took her by the hand, led her back to her chair, and seated himself beside her.

" Still busy, reading?" he said.

" I am anxious to do so, your majesty," she answered, " at every moment that I can possibly command. In the sort of life which I am destined to lead, and in your majesty's splendid court, temptations to forget what is right, and to think of nothing but pleasures and enjoyments, are so manifold, that one has need to have recourse to such calmer counsellors as these," and she laid her hand upon the book; " counsellors who are not disturbed by such seductions, and whose words have with them a portion of the tranquillity of the dead."

The words were of a soberer character than Louis had been accustomed to hear from the lips of woman, during the greater part of his life; but still they did not displease him, and he replied only by saying—

" But we must have a few more living counsels at present, madam, for the fate of Louis—— "

" Which is the fate of France," she murmured, in so low a voice that it could scarcely be termed an interruption.

" For the fate of Louis and of his domestic happiness—a word, alas! which is so little known to kings—is even now in the balance. Madam," he continued, taking that fair hand in his, " Madam, it is scarcely necessary at this hour to tell you that I love you; it is scarcely necessary to speak what are the wishes and the hopes of the King; scarcely necessary to say what would be his conduct, were not motives, strong and almost overpowering, opposed to all that he most desires."

Madame de Maintenon, for she it was, had risen from her seat, had withdrawn her hand from that of the King, and for a moment pressed both her hands tightly upon her heart, while her countenance, which had become as pale as death, spoke that the emotion which she felt was real.

"Cease, sire; oh, cease," she exclaimed, "if you would not have me drop at your feet!—Indeed," she continued, more vehemently, "that is my proper place," and she cast herself at once upon her knees before the King, taking the hand from which she had just disengaged her own, to bend her lips over it with a look of reverence and affection.

"Hear me, sire, hear me," she said, as the King endeavoured to raise her, "hear me even as I am; for notwithstanding the deep and sincere love and veneration which are in my heart, I must yet offend in one person the monarch whom every voice in Europe proclaims the greatest on the earth, and the man whom my own heart tells me is the most worthy to be loved. There is one, however, sire, who must be loved and venerated first, and beyond all— I mean the Almighty; and from his law and from his commands, nothing on earth shall ever induce me to swerve. Now, for more than a year, such has been my constant reply to your majesty on these occasions. I have besought you, I have intreated you never to speak on such subjects again, unless that were possible which I know to be impossible."

"Nay," replied the monarch, interrupting her, and raising her with a little gentle force, "nay, nothing is impossible, but for me to see you kneeling there."

"Oh yes, indeed, indeed, it is, your majesty!" she said; "I have long known it, I have long been sure of it. You once condescended to dream of it yourself; you mentioned it to me, and I for a single instant was deceived by hope; but as soon as I came to examine the whole, I became convinced, fully convinced, that such a thing was utterly and entirely impossible, that your majesty should descend from your high station, and that you should oppose and overrule the advice and opinion of courtiers and ministers, who, though perhaps a little touched with jealousy, can easily find sound and rational reasons enough to oppose your will in this instance. Oh, no, no, sire! I know it is impossible. For Heaven's sake do not agitate me by a dream of happiness that can never be realized!"

"So little is it impossible, dear friend," replied the King, "that it is scarcely half an hour ago that I spoke with Louvois upon the subject."

"And what did he say?" exclaimed Madame de Maintenon, with an eagerness that she could not master. "He opposed it, of course—and doubtless wisely. But oh, sire, you must grant me a favour: the last of many, but still a very great one. You must let me retire from your court, from this place of cruel and terrible temptation, where they look upon me, from the favour which your majesty has been pleased to show me, in a light which I dare not name. No, sire, no, I will never have it said, that I lived on at your court, knowing that I bore the name of your concubine. However false, the imputation is too terrible to be undergone—I, who have ever raised my voice against such acts, I, who have risked offending your majesty by remonstrances and exhortations. No, sire, no! I cannot, indeed I cannot, undergo it any longer. It is terrible to me, it is injurious to your majesty, who has so nobly triumphed over yourself in another instance. It matters not what Monsieur de Louvois has said, though I trust he said nothing on earth to lead you to believe that I am capable of yielding to unlawful love."

"Oh no," replied the King; "his opposition was but to the marriage, and that, as usual, was rude, gross, and insulting to his King. I wonder that I have patience with him. But it will some day soon give way."

"I hope and trust, sire," cried Madame de Maintenon, clasping her hands earnestly, "I hope and trust that your majesty has not suffered insult on my account. Then, indeed, it were high time that I should go."

"No," replied Louis, "not absolute insult. Louvois means but to act well. He said everything in opposition, I acknowledge, coarsely and rudely, and in the end he cast himself upon his knees before me, unsheathed his sword, and, offering the hilt, besought me to take his life, rather than to do what I contemplated."

"He did!" cried Madame de Maintenon, with a bright red spot in either cheek. "He did! The famous minister of Louis XIV. has been studying at the theatre lately, I know! But still, sire, though doubtless he was right in some part of his view, Françoise d'Aubigné is not quite so lowly as to be an object of scorn to the son of Michael le Tellier, whose ancestors I believe sold drugs at Rheims, while my grandfather supported the throne of yours with his sword, his blood, and his wisdom. He might have spared his scorn, methinks, and saved his wit for argument. But I must not speak so freely in my own cause; for that it is my own, I acknowledge," and she wiped away some tears from her fine eyes. "It is my own, for when I beseech your majesty to let me leave you, I tear my own heart, I trample upon all my own feelings. But oh, believe me, sire," she continued, ardently, "believe me when I say, that I would rather that heart were broken, as it soon will be, than that your majesty should do anything derogatory to your crown and dignity, or, I must add, that I myself should do anything in violation of the precepts of virtue and religion."

She wept a good deal; but she wept gracefully, and hers was one of those faces which looked none the worse for tears. The King gently drew her to her seat, for she had still been standing, saying, " Nay, nay, be comforted, you have yet the King.—You think not really, then," he continued, " really and sincerely, you think not, that there is any true degradation in a monarch wedding a subject? I ask you yourself, I ask you to speak candidly ! "

" Nay, sire," cried Madame de Maintenon, " how can you ask me, deeply interested as I am—how can you ask any woman? For we all feel alike in such things, and differently from men. There is not one woman, proud or humble, in your majesty's court, that would not give you the same answer, if she spoke sincerely."

" Indeed!" exclaimed the King; " then we men must be certainly in the wrong. But what think you," he continued, " what think you, as a proof—what would yon fair girl, Clémence de Marly, say, were we to ask her? I saw her but now, as I passed, reading with the Dauphine in somewhat melancholy guise."

" Well may she be melancholy, sire !" replied the lady, somewhat sadly, " when the King hears not her prayers. But methinks it would be hardly fair to make her a judge."

" Why, why ?" demanded Louis, quickly; " because she is so proud and haughty ?—Remember, you said the proudest in our court."

" So I say still, sire," replied Madame de Maintenon, in a gentle tone ; " but I do not think her proud. She would be too favourable a judge ; that was my sole objection. Her own station in the court is doubtful : and besides, sire, you could not think of submitting that, on which none—no, not the wisest minister you have—can judge so well as yourself, to the decision of a girl."

" Fear not," replied the King ; " I will but take her voice on the matter, without her knowing ought of that on which her opinion is called for. I would fain hear what a young and unpractised tongue would say. Let her be called in."

Madame de Maintenon hesitated for a moment. The risk seemed great; the object of long years was at stake ; and her own fate, and that of France, might depend upon the words of a wild, proud girl. But she saw no means of avoiding the trial; and she rang the bell: even in the very act of doing so, remembering many a trait of Clémence, both in childhood and youth, which gave her some assurance. A page appeared instantly, and was despatched to the apartments of the Dauphine to call Mademoiselle de Marly to the presence of the King.

The feet of Clémence bore her thither like light, though her heart beat wildly with fear and agitation, and the hue of her cheek, once so bright and glowing, was now as pale as death. She was glad, however, to find the King and Madame de Maintenon alone, for she had succeeded in interesting the latter in the fate of the Count de Morseiul, and she doubted not that she would exert herself, as much as she dared to do for any one, to persuade the King to deal with him gently. So many long and weary days had

passed, however, with but little progress, that she had well nigh
sunk into despair, when the summons of this night made her
suppose that her fate, and that of her lover, were upon the eve of
being decided.

The page who conducted her closed the door as soon as she had
entered; and Clémence stood before the King with sensations of
awe and agitation, such as in former days she knew not that she
could feel towards the greatest potentate on earth: but Clémence
de Marly loved, and her whole feelings had been changed.

Not a little was her surprise, however, when the King addressed
her in a tone half playful, half serious—

" Come hither, spoiled beauty," he said, " come hither: and sit
down upon that stool—or, in truth, I should give you up this chair,
for you are going to act a part that you never performed before—
that of judge, and in a matter of taste, too."

Clémence put her hand to her brow, as if to clear away the
thoughts with which she had come thither. But, after gazing in
the King's face for a moment with a bewildered look, she recovered
herself, and replied—

" Indeed, sire, I am, of all people, the most unfit; but I will do
my best to please your majesty. What may be the question ?"

" Why," answered the King, smiling at her evident surprise and
embarrassment, the real cause of which he had quite forgotten in
his own thoughts and feelings—" Why, the matter is this: a new
play has been submitted to us for approval, by one of our best poets.
It turns upon an ancient king becoming in love with one of his own
subjects, and marrying her, while his ministers wish him to marry a
neighbouring queen. The question of the policy, however, is not
the thing. We have settled all that; but the point in dispute
between me and this fair lady is, whether the poet would have done
better to have made the heroine turn out, after all, to be some
princess unknown. I say not; but our sweet friend, whose opinion,
perhaps, is better than my own, contends that it would have been
better, in order to preserve the king's dignity."

Madame de Maintenon panted for breath, and grasped the book
that lay on the table to prevent herself from betraying her agitation;
but she dared not say a word, nor even look up.

She was almost instantly relieved, however, for Clémence exclaimed, almost before the King had done speaking,—" Oh, no, no !
Dear lady, you are wrong, believe me. Kings lose their dignity
only by evil acts; they rise in transcendent majesty when they
tread upon base prejudices. I know nothing of the policy; you tell
me that is apart; and the only question is, whether she was worthy
whom he chose. Was she, sire—was she noble and good ?"

" Most noble, and most excellent !" said the King.

" Was she religious, wise, well educated ?" continued Clémence,
eagerly.

" She was all !" answered Louis, " all in a most eminent degree."

"Was she in knowledge, demeanour, character, worthy of his love and of himself?" asked the enthusiastic girl, with her whole face glowing.

"In demeanour not inferior, in character equal, in knowledge superior—in all respects worthy!" replied the monarch, catching her enthusiasm.

But he was stopped by the agitated sobs of Madame de Maintenon, who, sinking from her chair at his feet, clasped his knees, exclaiming, "Spare me, sire! spare me, or I shall die!"

The King gazed at her tenderly for a moment, then bent down his head, kissed her cheek, and, whispering a few brief words, placed her in the chair where he himself had been sitting. He then turned to Clémence de Marly, who stood by, astonished at the agitation that her words had produced, and fearful that the consequences might be the destruction of all her own hopes.

The countenance of Louis, as he turned towards her, somewhat re-assured her; but still she could not help exclaiming, with no slight anxiety, "I hope, sire, I have not offended. I fear I have done so unintentionally."

"If you have," said the King, smiling upon her graciously, "we will find a punishment for you; and as we have made you act as a judge where you little, perhaps, expected it, we will now make you a witness of things that you expected still less, but which your lips must never divulge till you are authorized to do so. Go as fast as possible to my oratory, close by the little cabinet of audience. There you will find good Monsieur la Chaise: direct him to ring the bell, and—after having told Bontems to summon Monsieur de Montchevreuil and the Archbishop, who is still here, I think— to come hither himself as speedily as possible. You will accompany him."

What were the King's intentions Clémence de Marly scarcely could divine: but seeing that her words had evidently given happiness both to the King and to Madame de Maintenon, and judging from that fact that her own best hopes for the deliverance of him she loved might be on the eve of accomplishment, she flew rather than ran to obey the King's directions. She found the King's confessor, La Chaise, waiting, evidently for the return of the King, with some impatience. The message which she brought him seemed to excite his astonishment greatly; but after pausing for a moment to consider what kind of event that message might indicate, the old man clasped his hands, exclaiming, "This is God's work; the King's salvation is now secure!"

He then did as he had been directed, rang the bell for Bontems, gave the order as he had received it, and hurried after Clémence along the corridor of the palace. At the door of Madame de Maintenon's apartment the young lady paused, for there were voices speaking eagerly within, and she feared to intrude upon the monarch. His commands to return, however, had been distinct, and she consequently opened the door and entered. Madame de Maintenon was standing by the table, with her eyes bent down, and her colour much heightened. The King was also standing, and with a slight frown upon his countenance was regarding a person who had been added to the party since Clémence had left it. This was no other than the minister Louvois, whose coarse, harsh features seemed filled with sullen mortification, which even the presence of the King could scarcely restrain from breaking forth in angry words. His eyes were bent down, not in humility, but in stubbornness, his shoulders a little raised, and he was muttering, rather than speaking, when Clémence entered. The only words, however, that were audible were, " Your majesty's will must be a law to yourself as well as to your people. I have ventured, in all sincerity, to express my opinion, and have nothing more to say."

The opening of the door caused Madame de Maintenon to raise her eyes; and, when she saw Clémence and the confessor, a glad and relieved smile played over her countenance, which was greatly increased by the words which La Chaise addressed to the King immediately on his entrance.

" Sire," he said, without waiting for Louis to speak, " from what I have heard, and from what I see, I believe—nay, I am sure, that your majesty is about to take a step which will, more than any that I know of, tend to ensure your eternal salvation. Am I not right?" and he extended his hand towards Madame de Maintenon, as if that gesture were quite sufficient to indicate his full meaning.

" You are, my good father," replied the King; " and I am happy to find that so wise and so good a man as yourself approves of what I am doing. Monsieur Louvois here still seems discontented, though I have conceded so much to his views of policy as to promise that this marriage shall remain for ever private."

" What are views of policy," cried Père la Chaise, " to your majesty's eternal salvation? There are greater, there are higher considerations than worldly policy, sire; but, even were worldly policy all, I should differ with Monsieur Louvois, and say that you were acting as wisely in the things of this world as in reference to another."

" God knows, and this lady knows," said Louvois, " that my only opposition proceeds from views of policy. For herself, personally"—he added, feeling that he might have offended one who was more powerful than even himself, " for herself, personally, she well knows that I have the most deep and profound respect; and, since it is to be, I trust that his majesty will allow me to be one of the witnesses."

" Assuredly," replied the King. " I had so determined in my own mind, Monsieur de Louvois; and, as we need not have more than three, we will dispense with this young lady's presence. Oh, here comes the Archbishop and Montchevreuil; my good father

La Chaise, let me beg you to prepare an altar, even here. I have determined that all doubt and discussion upon this subject shall be over to-night. Explain, I beg you, to Monsieur de Harlay what are my views and intentions. One word, belle Clémence," he added, advancing to Clémence, and speaking to her with a gracious smile, " we shall not need your presence, fair lady," but you shall not want the bridemaid's presents. Come hither to-morrow half an hour before I go to the council; and, as you have judged well and wisely in this cause to-night, we will endeavour to judge leniently on any cause that you may bring before us to-morrow."

Although the King spoke low, his words did not escape the keen ear of Louvois; and when Clémence raised her eyes to reply, they met those of the minister, gazing upon her with a look of fiend-like anger, which seemed to imply, " You have triumphed over me for the time, and have thwarted me in a matter of deep moment. You think at the same time you have gained your own private end, but I will disappoint you."

Such at least was the interpretation that Clémence put upon that angry glance. For an instant it made her heart sink, but, recollecting her former courage the next instant, she replied boldly to the King, " My trust is always in your majesty alone. I have ever had that trust; and what I have seen to-night would show me clearly, that let us expect what we may of your majesty's magnanimity and generosity, no disappointment will await us."

Thus saying, she retired; and what farther passed in the chamber that she quitted—though it affected the destinies of Louis, and of France, and of Europe, more than any event which had taken place for years—remains in the records of history amongst those things which are known though not proved, and are never doubted, even though no evidence of their reality exists.

CHAPTER XXVI.

THE ESCAPE

THE hope delayed, which maketh the heart sick, had its wearing effect upon the Count de Morseiul. His countenance showed it in every line; the florid hue of strong health was beginning to pass away; and one morning, in taking his usual walk up and down the court of the Bastille, in company with the bluff old English officer we have mentioned, his companion, after gazing in his face for a moment, as if something therein had suddenly struck him, said, " You look ill, young gentleman; what is the matter?"

" How is it possible that I can be otherwise," replied the Count, " confined as I am here, and lingering on from day to day, without any knowledge of what is passing regarding myself, or of the fate of friends whom I love, or of the condition of all those in whose happiness I am interested?"

" Poo! you must bear things more lightly," answered the old soldier. " Why here, you, a youth, a mere boy, have plenty of time before you, to spare a year or two for imprisonment. Think of what a difference there is between you and I : here am I without a day too much in life; while to you, neither months nor years are anything. As to your friends without, too, trouble not your brain about them. The world would go on just as well without you and I, if we were put out of it to-morrow. Friends would find new friends, sweethearts gain new lovers, servants betake them to new masters, and the roses would grow, and the birds would sing, and love, and war, and policy, and the wind of heaven, would have their course as if nothing had happened. There might be a few drops in some eyes which would fall like a spring-shower, and be dried up again as soon. However," he added, seeing that his philosophy was not very much to the taste of the young Count, " you must live in the world as long as I have done ere you can take such hard lessons home : and if it be but communication with your friends without that you want, I should think that might be obtained easily."

" I see not how that is to be done," replied the Count. " If they had allowed me to have my valet here, there would have been no difficulty, for I do not think that even stone walls would keep in his wit."

" Oh, we can do without him, I dare say," replied the old man. " If you write me down a note, containing few words, and no treason, doubtless I can find means, perhaps this very day, of sending it forth to any one that you will. In my apartment we shall find paper, which I got not long ago; some sort of ink we will easily manufacture for ourselves. So, come: that will revive hope a little for you; and though I cannot promise you an answer, yet, perhaps, one may be obtained too. There are old friends of mine that sometimes will drop in to see me; but what I propose to do is, to give your note to one of the prisoners I have spoken with, who expects to be liberated to-day or to-morrow, and direct the answer to be sent by some one who is likely to come to see me."

The young Count gladly availed himself of this proposal; and the means of writing having, by one prison resource or another, been obtained, he wrote a few brief words, detailing the anxiety and pain he suffered, and begging some immediate information as to the probability of his obtaining his freedom, and regarding the situation of those whom he loved best. He couched his meaning in language as vague as possible, and addressed the note to his valet, Jerome Riquet, fearing to write to Clémence, lest he should by any means draw suspicion and consequent evil upon her. The old English officer undertook to give all the necessary directions for its delivery; and when they met again in the evening, he assured him that the note was gone.

At an early hour on the following morning the Englishman was called away from him to speak with some one admitted by an order from the minister; and in about ten minutes after he joined the Count, and slipped a small piece of folded paper into his hand, saying, in a low voice, " Neither look at it now, nor leave me immediately, for there are several of these turnkeys about, and we must not create suspicion." After a few more turns, however, the old man said, " Now, Monsieur de Morseiul," and the Count hastening to his chamber, opened the note, which was in the handwriting of Riquet.

" I have been obliged," it said, " to keep out of the way, and to change my shape a dozen times, on account of the business of the Exempt; but—from what the Count says, and from hearing that Monsieur de Louvois swore last night by all the gods he worships, that, on account of some offence just given, he will bring the Count's head to the block within a week, as he did that of Monsieur de Rohan—a bold stroke will be struck to-day. The Count will be set at liberty about two o'clock, and the moment he is at liberty he must go, neither to king nor ministers, nor to his own house, either in Paris or at Versailles, but to the little inn called the Golden Cock, in the Rue du Faubourg St. Antoine, call himself Monsieur du Sac, and ask for the horse his servant brought. Having got it, let him ride on for Poitou as fast as he can go. He will meet friends by the way."

This was all that the note contained; and what was the bold stroke that Riquet alluded to the Count could not divine. He judged, indeed, that perhaps it was quite as well he should be ignorant of the facts; and after having impressed all the directions contained in the note upon his mind, he destroyed the paper, and was preparing to go down again into the court.

It so happened, however, that he paused for a moment, and took up one of the books upon the table, which he was still reading, when an officer, who was called the Major of the Bastille, entered the room, and summoned him to the presence of the governor. The Count immediately followed, and passing through the gate into the Court of Government, he found Besmaux waiting in the corps de garde, with a blithe and smiling countenance.

" Good morning, Monsieur de Morseiul," he said; " I have got some good news for you, which perhaps you do not expect."

He fixed his eyess crutinizingly upon the Count's face, but all was calm. "Here is an order for your liberation," he continued, " which, doubtless, you will be glad to hear."

" Most glad !" exclaimed the Count; " for, to say the truth, I am growing both sick and weary of this imprisonment, especially as I know that I have done nothing to deserve it."

" That is better than being imprisoned, knowing you have done

something to deserve it," observed Besmaux. " However, here is
the order; and though it is not exactly in accurate form, I must
obey, I suppose, and set you at liberty, for here is the King's hand-
writing in every line."

" That you must judge of yourself, Monsieur de Besmaux," replied the Count. " But I hope, of course, that you will not detain
me any longer than is necessary."

" No, no," said Besmaux; " I must obey the order, for it is in the
King's hand distinctly. Here are all the things that were upon
your person, Monsieur de Morseiul. Be so good as to break the
seal yourself, examine them, and give me an acknowledgment — as
is usual here — that they have been returned to you. There is the
ordinary form; you have nothing to do but to sign it."

The Count did as he was required to do, and the governor then
restored to him his sword, saying, " There is your sword, Monsieur
le Comte. It is customary to give some little acknowledgment to
the turnkeys, if you think fit; and now, Monsieur le Comte, you
are free. Will you do me the honour of supping with me again
to-night ? "

" I fear not to-night, Monsieur de Besmaux," he answered;
" some other time I will have that pleasure. But, of course, after
this unexpected and sudden enlargement, there is much to be
done."

" Of course," replied the governor; " you will have to thank
the King, and Monsieur de Louvois, and all that. Some other
time, then, be it. It is strange they have sent no carriage or horse
for you. Perhaps you would like to wait till they arrive ? "

" Oh, no," said the Count. " Freedom before everything,
Monsieur de Besmaux. By your permission I will send for the
apparel I have left in my chamber. But now, to set my foot beyond the drawbridge is my great ambition."

" We will conduct you so far," replied Besmaux, and led the
way towards the gate. The drawbridge was lowered, the gates
opened, and the Count, distributing the greater part of the money
which had been restored to him amongst the turnkeys, turned and
took leave of the governor, and issued forth from the Bastille.
He remarked, however, that Besmaux, with the major of the prison,
and two or three others, remained upon the bridge, as if they felt
some suspicion, and were watching his farther proceedings. He,
accordingly, rendered his pace somewhat slow, and turned towards
his own hotel in Paris, while two or three boys, who hung about
the gates of the Bastille, followed, importunately looking up in his
face. He passed along two streets before he could get rid of them;
but then, suddenly turning up one of the narrow lanes of the city,
he made the best of his way to the little inn, or rather public house,
which Jerome Riquet had pointed out to him in his letter, where a
bright golden cock, somewhat larger than life, stood out into the
street upon a pole thrust into the front of the house. Before he

turned in, he looked down the street towards the Bastille, but saw no cause for suspicion, and entered the narrow entrance. As was not uncommon in such houses at that time, no door on either hand gave admission to the rooms of the inn till the visiter had threaded half way through the small ill-lighted passage. At length, however, doors appeared, and the sound of a footstep instantly called out a stout, jovial-looking personage, with a considerable nose and abundance of cheek and stomach, who, without saying anything, merely planted himself directly in the Count's way.

"Are you the landlord?" demanded the Count.

"Yes, sir," replied the cabaretier, much more laconically than might have been expected from his appearance. "Who are you?"

"I am Monsieur du Sac," answered the Count.

"Oh, oh!" cried the host, laying his forefinger on the side of his face. "If you are Monsieur du Sac, your horse will be ready in a crack. But you had better come into the stable; there are people drinking in the hall."

The Count followed him without saying any more, and found three horses standing ready saddled, and wanting only the girths tightened, and the bridles in their mouths. The centre one he instantly recognised as one of his own finest horses, famous for its great strength and courage. The other two were powerful animals, but of a different breed; and the Count was somewhat surprised when the landlord ordered a stable-boy, who was found waiting, to make haste and girth them all up. The boy began with the farther horse; but the landlord then exclaimed, "No, no! the gentleman's first, the others will do after;" and in a moment the Count's horse was ready to set out.

"Better go by the back gate, sir," said the host; "then if you follow round by the gardens of the convent of St. Mary, up the little lane to the left, you will come into the road again, where all is clear.—Where's the bottle, boy, which I told you to have ready? Monsieur du Sac will want a draught before he goes."

A large bottle was instantly produced from a nook in the stable, and a tumbler full of excellent wine poured out. The Count took it, and drank, for excitement had made him thirsty; and he might well want that support which the juice of the grape or any other thing could afford, when he reflected that the die was now cast; that he had been liberated from prison, as he could not doubt, by some counterfeit order; and that he was flying from the court of France, certainly never to return, unless it were as a captive brought back probably to death.

The blow being struck, however, he was not a man to feel regret or hesitation, and there was something in the sensation of being at liberty, of having cast off the dark load of imprisonment, which was in itself inspiring. He sprang upon his horse, then, with joyful speed, cast the landlord one of the few gold pieces that remained in his purse, and while the boy held open the back gates of the inn court,

he rode out, once more free to turn his steps whithersoever **he**
would.   That part of the city was not unknown to him, and passing round the gardens, and through the narrow lanes which at that
time were intermingled with the Faubourg St. Antoine, he entered
the high road again, just where the town ended and the country
began; and putting his horse into a quick pace, made the best of
his way onward toward Poitou.

As he now went forth, he looked not back; and he had gone on
for five or six miles, when the belief that he heard the feet of horses
following fast, made him pause and turn.   He was not mistaken in
the supposition.   There were two horsemen on the road, about five
or six hundred yards behind him; but they slackened their pace as
soon as he paused; and remembering the words written by Jerome
Riquet, that he would find friends upon the road, he thought it better not to inquire into the matter any further, but make the most of
his time, and go on.   He thus proceeded without drawing a rein for
about five-and-thirty miles, the men who were behind him still
keeping him in sight, but never approaching nearer than a certain
distance.

The road which he had chosen was that of Orleans, though not
the most direct; but by taking it, he avoided all that part of the
country through which he was most likely to be pursued if his flight
were speedily discovered.   At length, in the neighbourhood of the
little town of Angerville, a man appeared on horseback at the turning of one of the by-paths.   He was evidently waiting for some one,
and rode up to the Count as soon as he appeared, saying merely
" Monsieur du Sac."

" The same," replied the Count; and the stranger immediately
said, " This way, then, sir."

The Count followed, without any reply, and the man rode on
at a quick pace for the distance of fully three miles further.   The
horsemen turned as the Count had turned, but the road had become
tortuous, and they were soon lost to his sight.   At length, however,
the high stone walls, overtopped with trees, and partly covered with
ivy, which usually surrounded the park of an old French château,
appeared; and making a circuit round three sides of this inclo-
sure, the Count and his guide came suddenly to the large iron
gates, which gave admission to a paved court leading to another
set of gates, with a green esplanade and a terrace above, the summit
of which was crowned by a heavy mass of stonework, referable to
no sort of architecture but itself.   Round these courts were various
small buildings, scarcely fitted indeed for human habitation, but
appropriated to gardeners and gatekeepers, and other personages of
the kind; and from one of these, as soon as the Count appeared,
instantly rushed forth Jerome Riquet, kissing his master's hand
with sincere joy and affection, which was not at all decreased by a
consciousness that his liberation had been effected by the skill,
genius, and intrigue of the said Jerome Riquet himself.

"Dismount, my lord, in all safety," he said; "we have taken measures to ensure that you should not be traced. Refreshments of every kind are ready for you; and if you so please, you can take a comfortable night's repose before you go on."

"That were scarcely prudent, Riquet," replied the Count; "but I will, at all events, pause for a time; and you can tell me all that has happened. First, whose dwelling is this?"

"The house of good Monsieur Perault, at Angerville," replied the valet. "He has been dead for about two months, and his old maitre d'hôtel, being a friend of mine, and still in the family, gave me the keys of the château, that it might be your first resting-place."

On entering the château, Albert of Morseiul found it completely thronged with his own servants; and the joyful faces that crowded round, some in smiles and some in tears, to see their young lord liberated, was not a little sweet to his heart. Some balm, indeed, was necessary to heal old wounds before new ones were inflicted; and though Riquet moved through the assembled attendants with the conscious dignity of one who had conferred the benefit in which they rejoiced, yet he hastened to lead his young lord on, and to have the room cleared, having much indeed to tell. His tale was painful to the Count in many respects; but, being given by snatches, as the various questions of his master elicited one fact after another, we will attempt to put it in more continuous form and somewhat shorter language, taking it up at events which, though long past, were now first explained.

From an accidental reference to the Count's journey from Morseiul to Poitiers, Riquet was led to declare the whole facts in regard to the commission which had been given by the King to Pelisson and St. Helie. The insatiable spirit of curiosity by which Maitre Jerome was possessed, never let him rest till he had made the unhappy Curé of Guadrieul declare, by a manœuvre before related, what was in the sheepskin bag he carried; and, as soon as the valet heard that it was a commission from the King, his curiosity was still more strongly excited tc ascertain the precise contents. For the purpose of so doing, he attached himself firmly to the Curé during the rest of the evening, made him smoke manifold pipes, induced him to eat every promotive of drinking that he could lay his hands upon, plied him with wine, and then, when half besotted, ventured to insinuate a wish to peep into the bag. The Curé, however, was firm to his trust, even in the midst of drunkenness; he would peep into the bag with curious longings himself, but he would allow no one else to do so, and Riquet had no resource but to finish what he had so well commenced by a bottle of heady Burgundy, in addition, which left the poor priest but strength enough to roll away to his chamber, and, conscious that he was burthened with matters which he was incompetent to defend, to lock the door tight behind him before he sunk insensible on his bed.

He forgot, however, one thing, which it is as well for every one to remember—namely, that chambers have windows as well as doors; and Jerome Riquet, whose genius for running along house gutters was not less than his other high qualities, found not the slightest difficulty in effecting an entrance, and spending three or four hours in the examination of the sheepskin bag and its contents. With as much skill as if he had been brought up in the French post-office of that day, he opened the royal packet without even breaking the seals, only inflicting a very slight and accidental tear on one part of the envelope, which the keen eyes of Pelisson had afterwards discovered.

As soon as he saw the nature of the King's commission, Riquet, —who was no friend to persecution of any kind, and who well knew that all his master's plans would be frustrated, and the whole province of Poitou thrown into confusion, if such a commission were opened on the first assembling of the states—determined to do away with it altogether, and substitute an old pack of cards which he happened to have in his valise, in place of that important document. He then proceeded to examine minutely and accurately the contents of the Curé's trunk mail, and more from a species of jocose malice than anything else, he tore off a piece of the King's commission, which could do no harm to any one, and folded it round the old tobacco box, which he had found, wrapped up in a piece of paper very similar, amongst the goods and chattels of the priest.

Besides this adventure, he had various others to detail to the Count, with the most important of which—namely, his interview with the King and Louvois, at Versailles—the reader is already acquainted. But he went on from that point to relate, that, lingering about in the neighbourhood of the King's apartments, he had heard the order for his master's arrest given to Monsieur de Cantal. He flew home with all speed, but, on arriving at the Count's hote., found that he had already gone to the palace, and that his arrest was certain.

His next question to himself was, how he might best serve him, under such circumstances; and, habituated from the very infancy of his valet-hood to travesty himself in all sorts of disguises, he determined instantly on assuming the character of an Exempt of one of the courts of law, as affording the greatest probability of answering his purpose. He felt a degree of enjoyment and excitement in every species of trick of the kind, which carried him through, when the least timidity or hesitation would have frustrated his whole plans. The fact is, that, although it may seem a contradiction in terms, Maitre Jerome was never so much in his own character as when he was personating somebody else.

The result of his acting on this occasion we already know, as far as the Count was concerned; but the moment that he had seen him lodged in the Bastille, the valet, calculating that his frolic might render Versailles a dangerous neighbourhood, retired to the Count's hotel in Paris, where a part of his apparel was still to be found, compounded rapidly the sympathetic ink from one of the many receipts stored up in his brain, and then flew with a handkerchief, properly prepared, to seek Clémence de Marly. Several days passed ere he could obtain an interview with her; for immediately after the Count's arrest the system of espionage, then common, was established upon the Hôtel de Rouvré, and he could only inform her attendant, Maria, of the fact of her lover's imprisonment. When at length he obtained audience, he found her alone with the Chevalier d'Évran. But as his master had not made him acquainted with the occasional feelings of jealousy which he had experienced towards that gentleman, Jerome believed he had fallen upon the two persons from whom, out of all the world, his master would be most delighted to hear. The whole facts of the Count's arrest then were detailed and discussed, and the words written, which, as we have seen, were received by Albert of Morseiul in prison.

Afraid to go back to Versailles, Riquet hastened away into Poitou, leaving to Clémence de Marly and the Chevalier d'Evran the task of liberating his lord, of which they seemed to entertain considerable hopes. On his return, however, he found, first, that all his fellow-servants having been faithful to him, the investigations regarding the appearance of the Exempt had ended in nothing being discovered, except that somebody had profanely personated one of those awful personages, and, secondly, that the Count was not only still in durance, but that little, if any, progress had been made towards effecting his liberation. The Duc de Rouvré, who seemed to be restored to the King's favour, was now a guest at the palace of Versailles: with Clémence de Marly the valet could not obtain an interview, though he daily saw her in company with the Chevalier d'Evran; and the report began to be revived that the King intended to bestow her hand upon that gentleman, who was now in exceedingly high favour with the monarch.

A scheme now took possession of the mind of Riquet, which only suggested itself in utter despair of any other plan succeeding; and as, to use his own expression, the very attempt, if frustrated, would bring his head under the axe, he acknowledged to his lord that he had hesitated and trembled even while he prepared everything for its execution. He went down once more into Poitou; he communicated with all the friends and most favoured vassals of his master; he obtained money and means for carrying every part of his scheme into effect, as soon as his lord should be liberated from the Bastille, and for securing his escape into Poitou, where a choice of plans remained before him, of which we shall have to speak hereafter.

The great point, however, was to enable the Count to make his exit from the prison; and it was at this that the heart of Jerome Riquet failed. His was one of those far-seeing geniuses that never forget, in any situation, to obtain, from the circumstances of the present, anything which may be, however remotely, advantageous in the future.   Upon this principle he had acted in his conference with the King; and without any definite and immediate object but that of obtaining pardon for himself for past offences, he had induced the monarch, we must remember, to give him a document, of which he now proposed to take advantage.   By a chemical process, very easily effected, he completely took out the ink in those parts of the document where his own name was written, and then, with slow and minute labour, substituted the name of his master in the place, imitating, even to the slightest stroke, the writing of the King.   The date underwent the same change, to suit his purpose, so that a complete pardon, in what appeared the undoubted hand of the King himself, was prepared for the Count de Morseiul.

This step having been taken, Riquet contemplated his work with pride, but fear; and the matter remained there for the whole day. By the next morning he had become habituated to daring; and, resolved to make the document complete, he spent eight hours in forging, underneath, an order, in due form, for the Count's liberation; and the most practised eye could hardly have found any difference between the lines there written and those of the King himself. In all probability, if Riquet could have obtained a scrap of Louvois' writing, he would have added the countersign of the minister, but, as that was not to be had, he again laid the paper by, and was seized with some degree of panic at what he had done.

He had brought up, however, from Poitou his lord's intendant, and several others of his confidential servants and attendants, promising them, with the utmost conceit and self-confidence, to set the Count at liberty.   They now pressed him to fulfil his design, and while he hesitated, with some degree of tremour, the note which the old English officer had conveyed to him was put into his hands, and decided him at once.   He entrusted the forged order, he said, to a person whom he could fully rely upon to deliver it at the gates of the Bastille, stationed his relays upon the road, and prepared everything for his master's escape.

Such was the account which he gave to his young lord, as he sat in the château of Angerville, and though he did not exactly express all that he had heard in regard to Clémence de Marly and the Chevalier d'Evran, he told quite enough to renew feelings in the bosom of the Count which he had struggled against long and eagerly.

"Who were the men," demanded the Count, "that followed me on horseback?"

"Both of them, sir," replied the man, "were persons who would have delayed any pursuit of you at the peril of their own lives.   One of them was your own man, Martin, whom you saved from being hung for a spy, by the night attack you made upon the Prince of Orange's quarters.   The other, sir, was poor Paul Virlay, who came up with the intendant, of his own accord, with his heart well nigh broken, and with all the courage of despair about him."

"Poor Paul Virlay!" exclaimed the Count—"his heart well nigh broken! Why, what has happened to him, Jerome? I left him in health and in happiness."

"Ay, sir," replied the man, "but things have changed since then. Two hellish priests—I've a great mind to become a Huguenot myself—got hold of his little girl, and got her to say, or at least swore that she said, she would renounce her father's religion. He was furious; and her mother, who had been ill for some days, grew worse, and took to her bed. The girl said she never had said so: the priests said she had, and brought a witness; and they seized her in her father's own house, and carried her away to a convent. He was out when it happened; and, when he came back, he found his wife dying and his child gone. The mother died two days after; and Paul, poor fellow, whose brain was quite turned, was away for three days, and his large sledge-hammer with him, which nobody but himself could wield. Everybody said that he was gone to seek after the priests, to dash their brains out with the hammer; but they heard of it, and escaped out of the province; and at the end of three days he came back, quite calm and cool, but everybody saw that his heart was broken. I saw him at Morsciul, poor fellow, and I have seldom seen so terrible a sight. The mayor, who has turned Catholic, you know, sir, asked him if he had gone after the priests, to which he said ' No ;' but every one thinks that he did."

While Riquet was telling this tale, the Count had placed his hands before his eyes; and it was evident that he trembled violently, moved by terrible and strongly conflicting feelings, the fiery struggle of which might well have such an influence on his corporeal frame. He rose from his seat slowly, however, when the man had done, and walked up and down the room more than once, with a stern, heavy step. At length, turning to Riquet again, he demanded—

"And in what state is the province?"

"Why, almost in a state of revolt, sir," replied Riquet. "As far as I can hear, there are as many as a couple of thousand men in arms, in different places. It is true, they are doing no great things; and the intendant of the province, sometimes with the Bishop, sometimes with the Abbé St. Helie, marches hither and thither, with a large body of troops, and puts down the revolt here, or puts down the revolt there. Till he hears that it has broken out in another place, he remains where it last appeared, quartering his soldiers upon the inhabitants, and, according to the order of the day, allowing them *to do every thing but kill.* Then he drives the people by thousands at a time to the churches of our religion, makes them take the mass, and breaks a few of them on the wheel when they spit the host out of their mouths. He then writes up to the King that he has made wonderful conversions; but before his letter can well reach Paris, he is obliged to march to another part of the province, to put down the insurrection there, and to make converts, and break on the wheel as before."

"Say no more, say no more!" cried the Count. "Oh, God! wilt thou suffer this to go on?"

Again he paced the room for several minutes, and then turning suddenly to Riquet, he said—"Riquet, you have shown yourself at once devoted, courageous, and resolute in the highest degree—"

"Oh, sir," interrupted the man, "you mistake: I am the most desperate coward that ever breathed."

"No jesting now, Riquet," said the Count, in a sorrowful tone; "no jesting now. My spirits are too much crushed, my heart too much torn, to suffer me to hear one light word. After all that you have done for me, will you do one act more? Have you the courage to return to Paris this night, and carry a letter for me to Mademoiselle de Marly, and to bring me back her reply?"

"Well, sir, well," said Riquet, rubbing his hands, and then putting his forefinger under his collar, and running it round his neck with a significant gesture, "a man can be hanged but once in his life, at least as far as I know of; and, as Cæsar said, 'A brave man is but hanged once, a coward is hanged every day;" therefore, as I see no other object that my father and mother could have in bringing me into the world, but that I should be hanged in your service, I will go to Paris, at the risk of accomplishing my destiny, with all my heart."

"Hark you, Riquet," replied the Count, "I will give you a means of security. If by any means you should be taken, and likely to be put to death for what you have done, tell those who take you, that, upon a distinct promise of pardon to you, under the King's own hand, the Count of Morseiul will surrender himself, in your place. I will give you that engagement in writing, if you like."

"That is not necessary, sir," replied Riquet. "Everybody in all France knows that you keep your word. But, pray, write the letter quickly; for, ride as hard as I will, I shall have scarce time to reach Paris before bed-time; and I suppose you would not have the young lady wakened."

There was a degree of cold bitterness in Riquet's manner when he spoke thus of Clémence, which made the Count of Morseiul feel that the man thought he was deceived. But still, after what had passed before, he felt that he was bound to be more upon his guard against himself than against others; and he resolved that he would not be suspicious, that he would drive from his bosom every such feeling, that he would remember the indubitable proofs of affection which she had given him, and that he would act toward her as if her whole conduct had been under his eye, and had been such as he could most approve. The materials for writing were instantly procured; and while Riquet caused a fresh horse to be saddled, and prepared for his journey, the Count sat down and wrote as follows:—

" MY BELOVED CLÉMENCE,

" Thank God, I am once more at liberty; but the brightness of that blessing, great as it is under any circumstances, would be nearly all tarnished and lost if I had not the hope that you would share it with me. I am now some way on the road to Poitou, where I hear that the most horrible and aggravated barbarities are daily being committed upon my fellow Protestants. My conduct there must be determined by circumstances; but I will own that my blood boils at the butchery and persecution I hear of. I remember the dear and cheering promises you have made—I remember the willingness and the joyfulness with which those promises were uttered, and that recollection renders it not madness—renders it not selfishness to say to you, Come to me, my Clémence—come to me as speedily as possible; come and decide for me, when perhaps I may not have calmness to decide for myself! Come, and let us unite our fate for ever, and so far acquire the power of setting the will of the world at defiance. Were it possible, I would trust entirely to your love and your promises, in the hope that you would suffer the bearer of this, most faithful and devoted as he has shown himself to be, to guide you to me; but I fear that the little time he dare stay in Paris would render it impossible for you to make your escape with him. Should this, as I fear, be the case, write to me, if it be but a few lines, to tell me how I can assist or aid you in your escape, and when it can be made. Adieu! Heaven bless and guard you."

Before he had concluded, Riquet had again appeared, telling him that he was ready to set out; and taking the somewhat useless precaution of sealing his letter, the Count gave it into the valet's hands, and saw him depart.

It was now about five o'clock in the evening; and, as he knew that many a weary and expectant hour must pass before the man could return, the Count conferred with all the various attendants who had been collected at Angerville, and found that the account which Riquet had given him of the state of Poitou was confirmed in every respect. Each had some tale of horror or of cruelty. Paul Virlay, however, whom he had asked for more than once, did not appear; and it was discovered, on inquiry, that he had not even remained at Angerville, but, with the cold and sullen sort of despair which had fallen upon him, had ridden on, now that he judged the Count was in safety.

After a time, the young nobleman, anxious for some repose both of mind and of body, cast himself upon a bed, in the hope of obtaining sleep; but it visited not his eyelids. Dark and horrible and agitating visions peopled the hours of darkness, though slumber had no share in calling them up. At length, full two hours before he had expected that Riquet could return, the sound of a horse's feet, coming at a rapid pace, struck the Count's ear, as he lay and listened to the howling of the November wind; and, starting up, he went to the window of the room, and gazed out. It was a clear night, with the moon up, though there were some occasioual clouds floating quickly over the sky, and he clearly saw that the horseman was Riquet, and alone. Proceeding into the other room, where he had left a light, he hastened down to meet him, asking whether he had obtained an answer.

"I have, sir," replied the man; "though I saw not the fair lady herself: yet Maria, the waiting woman, brought it in no long time. There it is;" and, drawing it from his pocket, he gave it into the Count's hand. Albert of Morseiul hastened back with the letter, and tore it eagerly open; but what were the words that his eyes saw?

"Cruel and unkind," it began, "and must I not add—alas! must I not add, even to the man I love—ungenerous and ungrateful? What would I not have sacrificed, what would I not have done, rather than that this should have occurred, and that the first use you make of your liberty, should be to fly to wage actual war against the crown! How shall I dare look up? I, who for weeks have been pleading that no such thought would ever enter into your noble and loyal nature. No, Albert, I cannot follow the messenger you send; or, to use the more true and straightforward word, I *will* not; and never by my presence with you, however much I may still love you, will I countenance the acts to which you are now hurrying."

It was signed "Clémence;" but it fell from the Count's hand ere his eye had reached that word; and he gazed at it fixedly as it lay upon the ground for several moments, without attempting to raise it; then, turning with a sudden start to Riquet and another servant who stood by, as if for orders, he exclaimed—"To horse!"

CHAPTER XXVII.

THE PASTOR'S PRISON.

THE pillow of Clémence de Marly was wet with her tears, and sleep had not visited her eyes, when a quick knocking was heard at her door, and she demanded timidly who was there.

"It is I, madam," replied the voice of the Duchess de Rouvré's maid.

"Then wait a moment, Mariette," replied Clémence, "and I will open the door. She rose, put on a dressing-gown, and by the light of the lamp, which still stood unextinguished on the table, she raised and concealed, in a small casket, two letters which she had left open, and which bore evident signs of having been wept over before she retired to rest. The one was in the clear, free hand-writing of youth and strength; the other was in characters, every line of which spoke the feeble hand of age, infirmity, or sickness. When that was done, she opened the door, which was locked, and admitted the Duchess's maid, who was followed into the room by her own attendant, Maria, who usually slept in a little chamber hard by.

"What is the matter, Mariette?" demanded the young lady. "I can scarcely say that I have closed my eyes ere I am again disturbed."

"I am sorry, mademoiselle, to alarm you," replied the woman; "but Maria would positively not wake you, so I was obliged to do it, for the Duke was sent for just as he was going to bed, and after remaining for two hours with the King has returned, and given immediate orders to prepare for a long journey. The Duchess sent me to let you know that such was the case, and that the carriages would be at the door in less than two hours."

"Do you know whither they are going," asked Clémence, "and if I am to accompany them?"

"I heard nothing of the part of the country from the Duke or the Duchess, mademoiselle," replied the woman, "but the Duke's valet said that we were going either to Brittany or Poitou, for my lord had brought away a packet from the King, addressed to somebody in those quarters; and you are certainly to be one, mademoiselle, for the Duchess told me to tell you so, and the valet says, that it is on account of you we are going; for that the Chevalier came back with my lord the Duke, and when he parted with him, said, ' Tell Clémence she shall hear from me soon.' "

Clémence mused, but made no answer; and when, about an hour after, she descended to the saloon of the hotel, she found everything in the confusion of departure, and the Duc de Rouvré standing by the table, at which his wife was seated, waiting for the moment of setting out, with a face wan, indeed, and somewhat anxious, but not so sorrowful or dejected, as, perhaps, Clémence expected to see.

"I fear, my dear Duke," she said, approaching him, and leaning her two hands affectionately upon his arm, "I fear that you, who have been to your poor Clémence a father indeed, are destined to have even more than a father's share of pains and anxieties with her. I am sure that all this to-night is owing to me, or to those who are dear to me, and that you have fallen under the King's displeasure, on account of the rash steps of him whom I cannot yet cease to love."

"Not at all, my sweet Clémence; not at all, my sweet child," said the old nobleman, kissing her hand with that mingled air of gallant respect and affection which he always showed towards her. "I do not mean to say, that your fair self has nothing to do with this business in any way, but certainly not in that way. It is about another business altogether, Clémence, that **we** are ordered to retire from the court; but not in disgrace, my dear young friend,— we are by **no** means in disgrace. The King is perfectly satisfied that you have had no share in all the business of poor Albert of Morseiul; and when I told him how bitterly and deeply grieved you were, and how struck to the heart you seemed to have been, when you heard that the Count had fled to join the rebels in Poitou, he told me to bid you console yourself, saying, that he would find you another and a better husband soon."

Clémence's eyes were bent down upon the ground with an expression of grief and pain; but she looked up in a moment, and said, " Is it permitted me to ask you, my lord, how I am connected with this sudden removal?"

" Nay," he replied, " nay, sweet Clémence, that I must not tell you. I scruple not to say, that I think his majesty is acting without due consideration; but, of course, my first duty, like that of all his other subjects, is to obey ; and he particularly wishes that nothing should be reported to you on the subject, as it might render one duty difficult by opposing to it another. At present the whole matter is quite simple; we have nothing to do but to set out as soon as these villanous lackeys have got the carriages ready."

Thus saying, the Duke turned away, evidently wishing to avoid further inquiries ; and in about half an hour after, Clémence was rolling away from Versailles with the Duke and Duchess de Rouvré, followed by a long train of carriages and attendants.

It is needless to trace a melancholy journey in the darkest and gloomiest weather of the month of November; but it was evident that the Duc de Rouvré was in haste, travelling early and late ; and it also appeared, from his conversation as they went, that, though he was charged with no special mission from the King, he proposed only to pause for a short time in Poitou, and then to bend his steps to some of his other estates. Indeed, he suffered it to be understood, that, in all probability, for many months he should take but little repose, frequently changing his place of abode, and travelling from one city to another. Although the health of Madame de Rouvré was by no means vigorous, and though far and rapid travelling never, at any time, had agreed with her, she made no objection, but seemed contented and happy with the arrangement, and even suggested that a journey to Italy might be beneficial to them all.

Clémence wondered, but was silent; and at length, late on the afternoon of the sixth day after their departure, they arrived at the small town of Thouars, over which was brooding the dark grey fogs of a November evening. Not very many miles remained to travel from Thouars to Ruffigny ; and the Duke, who was of course well known in that part of the country, received visits of congratulation on his arrival from the principal officers and inhabitants of the town. At these visits, however, Clémence was not present.

She sent down an excuse for not appearing during the evening; and when the Duke sent up to say he wished to see her for a moment, she was not to be found, nor had she, indeed, returned at the end of an hour.

Where was Clémence de Marly? it may be asked. She was in the dark and gloomy abode, often of crime and often of innocence, but ever of anguish and of sorrow. She was in the prison of the old château of Thouars. Not, indeed, as one of those unfortunate beings, the involuntary inmates. of the place, but as one coming upon the sad and solemn errand of visiting a dear and well-beloved friend for the last time. The office of governor of the prison, as it was seldom if ever used for the confinement of state offenders, had been suffered to fall into the hands of the mayor of the place, who delegated his charge to an old lieutenant, who again entrusted it to two subordinate gaolers, antique and rusty in their office as the keys they carried. It was with one of these that Clémence was speaking eagerly in the small, dark passage that led into the interior of the building. She was habited in the ordinary grey cloak in which we have seen her twice before, and had with her still, on this occasion also, the faithful servant who had then attended her.

" Come, come, pretty mistress," said the man, thrusting himself steadfastly in the way, "I tell you it is as much as my head is worth. He is condemned to be broken on the wheel to-morrow, and I dare admit nobody to him."

" Look at these," said Clémence, pouring some gold pieces from her purse into her open hand. " I offer you these if you will allow me to speak with him for an hour, and if you refuse I shall certainly insist upon seeing the lieutenant of the governor himself. You know what manner of man he is, and whether he will reject what I shall offer him ; so he will get the money, and you will not, and I shall see the prisoner notwithstanding."

The man's resolution was evidently shaken to the foundation. He was an old man, and fond of gold. The sight was pleasant to him, and, putting forth his hand, he lifted one piece between his finger and thumb, turned it over, and dropped it back again upon the others. The sound completed what the touch had begun.

" Well," he said, at length, " I do not see why he should get it, and I not. He is asleep, too, now, in the arm-chair; so it were a pity to wake him. You want to be with the old man an hour, do you, young woman? Well, you must both go in, then ; and I must go away and be absent with the keys, for fear the lieutenant should wake, and go to see the prisoner."

" Do you mean to lock us in with him, then ?" exclaimed the maid, in some terror.

" Fear not, Maria !" said her mistress. " You, who have ever given me encouragement and support, must not fear now. There is God even here."

" Be quick, then, and come along," said the gaoler, " but first give me the money." Clémence poured it into his hand; and when he had got it, he paused, hesitating as if he were tempted by the spirit of evil to keep the gold and refuse her admission. But if such were the case, a moment's reflection showed him that to attempt it would be ruinous; and he therefore led the way along the passage in which they were, putting his finger upon his lips to enjoin silence, as they passed by a part of the prison which seemed to be inhabited by those who had some means of obtaining luxuries. At length, however, he lowered the lantern which he carried, and pointed to two or three steps leading into a second passage, narrower, damper, and colder than the former. At the distance of about fifty feet from the steps, this corridor was crossed by a third; and turning to the right, over a rough, uneven flooring of earth, with the faint light of the lantern gleaming here and there, on the damp, green, glistening mould of the walls, he walked on till he reached the end, and then opened a low heavy door.

All within was dark, and, as the man drew back to let his female companions pass, the attendant, Maria, laid her hand upon the lantern, saying, "Give us a light, at least!"

"Ah! well, you may have it," grumbled forth the gaoler; and Clémence, who, though resolute to her purpose, still felt the natural fears of her sex and her situation, turned to him, saying, "I give you three more of those pieces when you open the door again for me."

"Oh, I'll do that—I'll do that!" replied the man, quickened by the gold; and while Maria took the lantern and passed the door, Clémence gazed down the step or two that led into the dungeon, and then with a pale cheek and wrung heart followed. The door closed behind them; the harsh bolt of the lock grated as the man turned the key; and the power of retreat being at an end, the beautiful girl threw back the hood of the cloak, and gazed on before her into the obscure vault, which the feeble light of the lantern had scarcely deprived of any part of its darkness. The only thing that she could perceive, at first, was a large heavy pillar in the midst, supporting the pointed vault of the dungeon, with the faint outline of a low wooden bed, with the head thereof resting against the column.

No one spoke; and nothing but a faint moan broke. the awful silence. It required the pause of a moment or two, ere Clémence could overcome the feelings of her own heart sufficiently to take the lantern and advance—opening a part of the dim horn as she did so, in order to give greater light. A step or two farther forward brought her to the side of the bed; and the rays of the candle now showed her distinctly the venerable form of Claude de l'Estang, stretched out upon the straw with which the pallet was filled. A heavy chain was round his middle, and the farther end thereof was fastened to a stanchion in the column.

The Protestant minister was dressed in a loose grey prison gown; and, although he saw that some one approached him in the abode of misery in which he was placed, he moved not at all, but remained with his arm bent under his head, his eyes turned slightly towards the door, his lower lip dropping, as if with debility or pain, and his whole attitude displaying the utter lassitude and apathy of exhaustion and despair. When Clémence was within a foot or two of his side, however, he slowly raised his eyes towards her; and in a moment, when he beheld her face, a bright gleam came over his faded countenance, awakening in it all those peculiar signs and marks of strong intellect and intense feeling which the moment before had seemed extinct and gone. It was like the lightning flashing over some noble ruin in the midst of the deep darkness of the night.

"Is it you, my sweet child?" he cried, in a faint voice that was scarcely audible even in the midst of the still silence. "Is it you that have come to visit me in this abode of wretchedness and agony? This is, indeed, a blessing and a comfort; a blessing to see that there are some faithful even to the last, a comfort and a joy to find that she on whose truth and steadfastness I had fixed such hopes, has not deceived me ;—and yet," he exclaimed, while Clémence gazed upon him with the tears rolling rapidly over her cheeks, and the sobs struggling hard for utterance, "and yet, why, oh why have you come here? why have you risked so much, my child, to soothe the few short hours that to-morrow's noon shall see at an end?"

"Oh, dear friend," said Clémence, kneeling down beside the pallet, "could I do otherwise, when I was in this very town, than strive to see you, my guide, my instructor, my teacher in right, my warner of the path that I ought to shun? Could I do otherwise, when I thought that there was none to soothe, that there was none to console you, that in the darkness and the agony of these awful hours there was not one voice to speak comfort, or to say one word of sympathy?"

"My child, you are mistaken," replied the old man, striving to raise himself upon his arm, and sinking back again with a low groan. "There has been one to comfort, there has been one to support me. He, to whom I go, has never abandoned me : neither in the midst of insult and degradation; no, nor in the moment of agony and torture; nor in those long and weary hours that have passed since they bore these ancient limbs from the rack on which they had bound them, and cast them down here to endure the time in darkness, in pain, and in utter helplessness, till at noon to-morrow the work will be accomplished on the bloody wheel, and the prisoner in this ruined clay will receive a joyful summons to fly to his Redeemer's throne."

The tears rained down from the eyes of Clémence de Marly like the drops of a summer shower; but she dared not trust herself to speak : and after pausing to take breath, which came evidently with difficulty, the old man went on, "But still I say, Clémence, still I say, why have you come hither? You know not the danger, you know not the peril in which you are."

"What!" cried Clémence, "should I fear danger, should I fear peril, in such a case as this? Let them do to me what they will, let them do to me what God permits them to do! To have knelt here beside you, to have spoken one word of comfort to you, to have wiped the drops from that venerable brow in this awful moment, would be a sufficient recompence to Clémence de Marly for all that she could suffer."

" God forbid," cried the pastor, " that they should make you suffer as they can. You know not what it is, my child—you know not what it is! If it were possible that an immortal spirit, armed with God's truth, should consent unto a lie, that torture might well produce so awful a falling off! But you recall me, my child, to what I was saying. I have not been alone, I have not been uncomforted, even here. The word of God has been with me in my heart, the Spirit of God has sustained my spirit, the sufferings of my Saviour have drowned my sufferings, the hope of immortality has made me bear the utmost pains of earth. When they had taken away the printed words from before mine eyes, when they had shut out the light of heaven, so that I could not have seen, even if the holy book had been left, they thought they had deprived me of my solace. But they forgot that every word thereof was in my heart; that it was written there, with the bright memories of my early days; that it was traced there with the calm recollections of my manhood; that it was printed there with sufferings and with tears; that it was graven there with smiles and joys; that with every act of my life, and thought of my past being, those words of the revealed will of God were mingled, and never could be separated; and it came back to me even here, and blessed me in the dungeon; it came back to me before the tribunal of my enemies, and gave me a mouth and wisdom; it came back to me on the torturing rack, and gave me strength to endure without a groan; it came back to me even as I was lying mangled here, and made the wheel of to-morrow seem a blessed resting-place."

" Alas, alas !" cried Clémence, " when I see you here ; when I see you thus suffering; when I see you thus the sport of cruelty and persecution, I feel that I have judged too harshly of poor Albert, in regard to his taking arms against the oppressors; I feel that perhaps, like him, I should have thus acted, even though I called the charge of ingratitude upon my head."

" And is he free, then? is he free?" demanded the pastor, eagerly.

" He is free," replied Clémence, "and, as we hear, in arms against the King."

" Oh, entreat him to lay them down !" exclaimed the pastor; " beseech him not to attempt it. Tell him that ruin and death can be the only consequences : tell him that the Protestant church is at an end in France: tell him that flight to lands where the pure faith is known and loved is the only hope : tell him that resistance is destruction to him, and to all others. Tell him so, my child, tell him so from me: tell him so—but hark!" he continued, "what awful sound is that?" for even while he was speaking, and apparently close to the spot where the dungeon was situated, a sharp explosion took place, followed by a multitude of heavy blows given with the most extraordinary rapidity. No voices were distinguished for some minutes; and the blows continued without a moment's cessation, thundering one upon the other with a vehemence and force which seemed to shake the whole building.

"It is, surely," said Clémence, "somebody attacking the prison door. Perhaps, oh, Heaven! perhaps it is some one trying to deliver you."

"Heaven forbid!" exclaimed the old man; "Heaven forbid that they should madly rush to such an attempt for the purpose of saving, for a few short hours, this wretched frame from that death which will be a relief. Hark, do you not hear cries and shouts?"

Clémence listened, and she distinctly heard many voices, apparently elevated, but at a distance, while the sound of the blows continued thundering upon what was evidently the door of the prison, and a low murmur, as if of persons speaking round, joined with the space to make the farther cries indistinct. A pause succeeded for a moment or two; but then came the sound of galloping horse, and then a sharp discharge of musketry, instantly followed by the loud report of fire-arms from a spot immediately adjacent to the building. Clémence clasped her hands in terror, while her attendant, Maria, filled with the dangerous situation in which they were placed, ran and pushed the door of the dungeon, idly endeavouring to force it open.

In the meanwhile, for two or three minutes nothing was heard but shouts and cries, with two or three musket shots; then came a volley, then another, then two or three more shots, then the charging of horse mingled with cries, and shouts, and screams, while still the thundering blows continued, and at length a loud and tremendous crash was heard shaking the whole building. A momentary pause succeeded, the blows were no longer heard, and the next sound was the rush of many feet. A moment of doubt and apprehension, of anxiety, nay, of terror, followed. Clémence was joyful at the thought of the pastor's deliverance; but what, she asked herself, was to be her own fate, even if the purpose of those who approached was the good man's liberation. Another volley from without broke in upon the other sounds; but in an instant after the rushing of the feet approached the door where they were, and manifold voices were heard speaking.

"It is locked!" cried one; "where can the villain be with the keys?"

"Get back!" cried another loud voice; "give me but a fair stroke at it."

A blow like thunder followed; and, seeming to fall upon the locks and bolts of the door, dashed them at once to pieces, driving a part of the wood-work into the dungeon itself. Two more blows cast the whole mass wrenched from its hinges to the ground. A multitude of people rushed in, some of them bearing lights, all armed to the teeth, some bloody, some begrimed with smoke and gunpowder; fierce excitement flashing from every eye, and eager energy upon every face.

"He is here, he is here!" they shouted to the others without. "Make way—make way—let us bring him out!"

"But who are these women?" cried another voice.

"Friends, friends,—dear friends, come to comfort me!" cried the pastor.

"Blessings on the tongue that so often has taught us!" cried other voices, while several ran forward and kissed his hands with tears; "blessings on the heart that has guided and directed us!"

"Stand back, my friends,—stand back!" cried a gigantic man, with an immense sledge-hammer in his hand, "let me break the chain!" and at a single blow he dashed the strong links to atoms.

"Now bring them all along." he cried, "now bring them all along! Take up the good man on the bed, and carry him out."

"Bring them all along! bring them all along!" cried a thousand voices, and without being listened to in anything that she had to say, Clémence, clinging as closely as she could to her attendant, was hurried out along the narrow passages of the prison, which were now flashing with manifold lights, into the dark little square, which was found filled with people. Multitudes of lights were in all the windows round; and, covering the prison, a strong band of men was drawn up facing the opposite street. A number of persons on horseback were in front of the band, and, by the lights which were flashing from the torches, one commanding figure appeared to the eyes of Clémence at the very moment she was brought forth from the doors of the prison, stretching out his hand towards the man behind him, and shouting, in a voice that she could never forget, though now that voice was raised into tones of loud command, such as she had never heard it use. "Hold! hold! the man who fires a shot, dies! Not one unnecessary shot, not one unnecessary blow!"

Clémence strove to turn that way, and to fly towards the hotel where Monsieur de Rouvré lodged; but she was borne away by the stream, which seemed to be now retreating from the town. At the same moment an armed man laid gently hold of her cloak, seeing her efforts to free herself, and said—

"This way, lady, this way. It is madness for you to think to go back now. You are with friends. You are with one who will protect you with his life, for your kindness to the murdered and the lost."

She turned round to gaze upon him, not recollecting his voice; and his face, in the indistinct light, seemed to her like a face remembered in a dream, connected with the awful scene of the preaching on the moor, and the dark piece of water, and the dying girl, killed by the shot of the dragoons. Ere she could ask any questions, however, the stream of people hurried her on, and in a few minutes she was out of Thouars, and in the midst of the open country round.

CHAPTER XXVIII.

THE DEATH OF THE PERSECUTED.

WHEN the flight had been conducted for about two miles in the midst of the perfect darkness which surrounded the whole scene—for the lights and torches which had appeared in the town had been extinguished, with the exception of one or two, on leaving it—the voice which had before addressed Clémence de Marly again spoke nearer, apparently giving command, as some one in authority over the others.

" Where is the litter ?" he exclaimed—" where is the litter that was brought for the good minister? Bring it hither: he will be more easy in that."

Clémence had kept as near as she could to the spot where Claude de l'Estang was carried, and she now heard him answer, in a faint and feeble voice—

" Do not move me : in pity do not move me. My limbs are so strained and dislocated by the rack, that the slightest movement pains me. Carry me as I am, if you will; but move me not from this bed."

" Well, then, place these two ladies in the litter," said the same voice. " We shall go faster then."

Without asking her consent, Clémence de Marly was placed in the small hand-litter which had been brought for the pastor; her maid took the place by her side, and, lifted on the shoulders of four men, she was carried on more quickly, gaining a faint and indistinct view of what was passing around, from the more elevated situation in which she now was.

They were mounting slowly the side of the hill, about two miles from the town of Thouars, and she could catch a distant view of the dark towers and masses of the town as it then existed, rising above the objects around. From thence, as far as her eye was able to distinguish, a stream of people was flowing on all along the road to the very spot where she was, and several detached parties were seen here and there, crossing the different eminences on either side, so that the force assembled must have been very considerable. She listened eagerly for any sound from the direction of Thouars, apprehensive at every moment that she would hear the firing renewed ; for she knew, or at least she believed she knew, that Albert

of Morseiul, with the better disciplined band which he seemed to
command, would be the last to leave the city he had so boldly entered.   Nothing, however, confirmed her expectation.   There was
a reddish light over the town, as if there were either fires in the
streets, or that the houses were generally lighted up; but all was
silent, except a dull distant murmur, heard when the sound of the
marching feet ceased from any cause for a moment.   Few words
passed between Clémence and her attendant; for though Maria
was a woman of a calm determined spirit in moments of immediate danger, and possessed with a degree of religious zeal, which
was a strong support in times of peril and difficulty, yet the scenes
in the prison and the dungeon, the horrors which she had only
dreamt of before brought actually before her eyes, had not precisely
unnerved her, but had rendered her thoughtful and silent.   The
only sentence which she ventured to address to her mistress, without being spoken to, was—

" Oh, madam, is the young Count so much to blame, after all ?"

" Alas, Maria," replied Clémence, in the same low tone, " I
think that all are to blame, more or less.   Deep provocation has
certainly been given; but I do think that Albert ought to have
acted differently.   He had not these scenes before his eyes when
he fled to put himself at the head of the insurgents; and, ere he
did so, he certainly owed something to me and something to the
king.   Nevertheless, since I have seen what I have seen, and heard
what I have heard, I can make excuses which I could not make
before."

The attendant made no answer, and the conversation dropped.
The march continued rapidly for three or four hours, till at length
there was a short halt; and a brief consultation seemed to take
place between two or three of the leaders on horseback.   The
principal part of the men on foot, exhausted, as it appeared, by
great exertion, sat or lay down by the road side; but ere the conference had gone on for above five minutes, a cavalier, followed by
several other men on horseback, came up at the full gallop; and
again the deep mellow tones of that remarkable voice struck the
ear of Clémence de Marly, and made her whole frame thrill.   His
words, or, as they appeared, commands, were but few; and, without either approaching the side of Claude de l'Estang or herself, he
rode back again in haste, and the march was renewed.

Ere long a fine cold rain began to fall, chilling those it lighted
on to the very heart; and Clémence thought she perceived that as
they advanced the number of people gradually dropped away.   At
length, after a long and fatiguing march through the night, as the
faint grey of the dawn began to appear, she found that, at the very
utmost, there were not above a hundred of the armed Protestants
around her.   The party was evidently under the command of a
short but powerfully made man, on horseback, whom she recognised
as the person who had carried the unfortunate novice Claire in his

arms to the house of Claude de l'Estang. He rode on constantly by the side of the bed in which the good pastor was borne on men's shoulders, and, bowing down his head from time to time, he spoke to him with what seemed words of comfort and hope. They were now on a part of the road from Tbouars towards Nantes, which passed through the midst of one of those wide sandy tracts called in France *landes*, across which a sort of causeway had been made by felled trees, rough and painful of passage, even to the common carts of the country. This causeway, however, was soon quitted by command of Armand Herval. One party took its way through the sands to the right; and the rest, following the litters, bent their course across the country, towards a spot where a dark heavy line bounded the portion of the *landes* within sight, and seemed to denote a large wood of the deep black pine, which grows better than any other tree in that sandy soil. It was near an hour before they reached the wood; and even underneath its shadow the shifting sand continued, only diversified a little by a few thin blades of green grass, sufficient to feed the scanty flocks of sheep, which form the only riches of that tract.

In the midst of the wood—where they had found or formed a little oasis around them—were two shepherds' cottages; and to these the party commanded by Armand Herval at once directed its course. An old man and two boys came out as they approached, but with no signs of surprise; and Claude de l'Estang was carried to one of the cottages, into which Clémence followed. She had caught a sight of the good man's face as they bore him past her; and she saw that there was another sad and painful task before her, for which she nerved her mind.

" Now, good Antoine," said Armand Herval, speaking to one of the shepherds, " lead out the sheep with all speed, and take them over all the tracks of men and horses that you may meet with. You will do it carefully, I know. We have delivered the good man, as you see; but I fear—I fear much, that we have after all come too late, for the butchers have put him to the question, and almost torn him limb from limb. God knows I made what speed I could, and so did the Count."

The old shepherd to whom he spoke made no reply, but listened, gazing in his face with a look of deep melancholy. One of the younger men who stood by, however, said, " We heard the firing. I suppose they strove hard to keep him."

" That they assuredly did!" replied Herval, his brows knitting as he spoke; " and, if we had not been commanded by such a man, they would not only have kept him, but us too. One half of our people failed us. Boursault was not there. Kerac and his band never came. We were full seven hundred short, and then the petard went off too soon, and did no good, but brought the whole town upon us. They had dragoons, too, from Niort; and tried first to drive us back, then to take us in flank by the Tower-street,

then to barricade the way behind us; but they found they had to
do with a Count de Morseiul, and they were met everywhere, and
everywhere defeated.—Yet, after all," continued the man, " he will
ruin us from his fear of shedding any blood but his own.   But I
must go in and see after the good man; and then speed to the
woods.   We shall be close round about, and one sound of a conch *
will bring a couple of hundred to help you, good Antoine."

Thus saying, he went into the cottage, where Clémence had
already taken her place by the side of the unhappy pastor's bed;
and, on the approach of Herval, she raised her finger gently to
indicate that he slept.   He had, indeed, fallen into momentary
slumber, utterly exhausted by suffering and fatigue; but the fallen
temples—the sharpened features—the pale ashy hue of the countenance, showed to the eyes of Clémence, at least, that the sleep
was not that from which he would wake refreshed and better.
Herval, less acute in his perceptions, judged differently; and, after
assuring Clémence, in a whisper, that she was quite in safety there,
as the woods round were filled with the band, he left her, promising
to return ere night.

Clémence would fain have asked after Albert of Morseiul, and
might, perhaps, have expressed a wish to see him; but there were
strange feelings of timidity in her heart which kept her silent till
the man was gone, and then she regretted that she had not spoken,
and accused herself of weakness.   During the time that she now
sat watching by the pastor's side, she had matter enough for
thought in her own situation.   What was now to become of her,
was a question that frequently addressed itself to her heart; and,
more than once, as she thus sat and pondered, the warm ingenuous
blood rushed up into her cheek at thoughts which naturally arose
in her bosom, from the consideration of the strange position in
which she was placed.   Albert of Morseiul had not seen her, she
knew.   He could not even divine or imagine that she was at
Thouars at all, much less in the prison itself; but yet she felt
somewhat reproachfully towards him, as if he should have divined
that it was she whom he saw borne along, not far from the unhappy pastor.   Though she acknowledged, too, in her own heart,
that there were great excuses to be made for the decided part
which her lover had taken in the insurrection of that part of the
country, still she was not satisfied, altogether, with his having
done so; still she called him, in her own heart, both rash and
ungrateful.

On the other hand, she remembered, that she had written to him
in haste, and in some degree of anger, or, at least, of bitter dis-

---

* This large shell is used in many of the sea-coast districts of France still, for
the purpose of giving signals.   The sound, when properly blown, is very powerful
and peculiar.   They assert that across a level country it can be heard six miles.
I have. myself heard it more than two, and so distinctly, that it must have been
audible at a much greater distance

appointment; that she had refused, without explaining all the circumstances which prevented her, to share his flight as she had previously promised; that, hurried and confused, she had neither told him that, at the very time she was writing, the Duchess de Rouvré waited to accompany her to the court, and that to fly at such a moment was impossible; nor that, during the whole of the following day, she was to remain at Versailles, where the eyes of every one would be upon her, more especially attracted towards her by the news of her lover's flight, which must, by that time, be generally known. She feared, too, that in that letter she had expressed herself harshly, even unkindly; she feared that those very words might have driven the Count into the desperate course which he had adopted, and she asked herself, with feelings such as she had never experienced before, when contemplating a meeting with Albert of Morseiul, how would he receive her?

In short, in thinking of the Count, she felt that she had been somewhat in the wrong in regard to her conduct towards him. But she felt also, at the same time, that he had been likewise in the wrong, and, therefore, what she had first to anticipate were the words of mutual reproach, rather than the words of mutual affection. Such was one painful theme of thought; and how she was to shape her own immediate conduct, was another. To return to the house of the Duc de Rouvré seemed utterly out of the question. She had been found in the prison of Claude de l'Estang. Her religious feelings could no longer be concealed; her renunciation of the Catholic faith was sure, at that time, to be looked upon as nothing short of treason; and death or eternal imprisonment was the only fate that would befall her, if she were once cast into the hands of the Roman-catholic party.

What, then, was she to do? Was she to throw herself at once upon the protection of Albert of Morseiul? Was she to bind her fate to his for ever, at the very moment when painful points of difference had arisen between them? Was she to cast herself upon his bounty as a suppliant, instead of holding the same proud situation she had formerly held,—instead of being enabled to confer upon him that which he would consider an inestimable benefit, while she herself enhanced its value beyond all price, by the sacrifice of all and everything for him? Was she now, on the contrary,—when it seemed as if she had refused to make that sacrifice for his sake,—to come to him, as a fugitive claiming his protection, to demand his bounty and his support, and to supplicate permission to share the fate in which he might think she had shown a disinclination to participate, till she was compelled to do so?

The heart of Clémence de Marly was wrung at the thought. She knew that Albert of Morseiul was generous, noble, kind-hearted. She felt that, very likely, he might view the case in much brighter hues than she herself depicted it to her own mind: she felt that, if she were a suppliant to him, no reproach would ever spring to his lips, no cold averted look would ever tell her, that he thought she had treated him ill. But she asked herself whether those reproaches would not be in his heart; and the pride, which might have taken arms and supported her under any distinct and open charge, gave way at the thought of being condemned, and yet cherished.

How should she act, then? how should she act? she asked herself; and as Clémence de Marly was far from one of those perfect creatures who always act right from the first impulse, the struggle between contending feelings was long and terrible, and mingled with some tears. Her determination, however, was right at length.

"I will tell him all I have felt, and all I think," she said. "I will utter no reproach: I will say not one word to wound him: I will let him see once more, how deeply and truly I love him. I will hear, without either pride or anger, anything that Albert of Morseinl will say to me, and then, having done so, I will trust to his generosity to do the rest. I need not fear! Surely, I need not fear!" and, with this resolution, she became more composed, the surest and the strongest proof that it was right.

But, to say the truth, since the perils of the night just passed, since she had beheld him she loved in a new character; since, with her own eyes, she had seen him commanding in the strife of men, and everything seeming to yield to the will of his powerful and intrepid mind, new feelings had mingled with her love for him, of which, what she had experienced when he rode beside her at the hunting party at Poitiers, had been but, as it were, a type. It was not fear, but it was some degree of awe. She felt that, with all her own strength of mind, with all her own brightness of intellect and self-possession, there were mightier qualities in his character to which she must bow down: that she, in fact, was woman, altogether woman, in his presence.

As she thus thought, a slight motion on the bed where Claude de l'Estang was laid, made her turn her eyes thither. The old man had awoke from his short slumber; and his eyes, still bright and intelligent, notwithstanding the approach of death and the exhaustion of his shattered frame, were turned towards her with an earnest and a melancholy expression.

"I hope you feel refreshed," said Clémence, bending over him. "You have had some sleep; and I trust it has done you good."

"Do not deceive yourself, my dear child," replied the old man. "No sleep can do me good, but that deep powerful one which is soon coming. I wait but God's will, Clemence, and I trust that he will soon give the spirit liberty. It will be in mercy, Clémence, that he sends death: for were life to be prolonged, think what it would be to this torn and mangled frame. Neither hand nor foot can I move, nor would it be possible to give back strength to my limbs or ease to my body. Every hour that I remain, I look upon but as

a trial of patience and of faith; and I will not murmur: no, Clémence, not even in thought, against His almighty will, who bids me
drag on the weary minutes longer. But yet, when the last of those
minutes has come, oh! how gladly shall I feel the summons that
others dread and fly from! I would fain, my child," he said, "I
would fain hear, and from your lips, some of that blessed word
which the misguided persecutors of our church deny unmutilated
to the blind followers of their faith, though every word therein
speaks hope, and consolation, and counsel, and direction to the
heart of man."

"Alas! good father," replied Clémence, "the Bible which I always carry with me, was left behind when I came to see you in
prison, and I know not where to find one here."

"The people in this, or the neighbouring cottage, have one,"
said the pastor. "They are good honest souls, whom I have often
visited in former days."

As the good woman of the cottage had gone out, almost immediately after the arrival of the party, to procure some herbs, which
she declared would soothe the pastor greatly, Clémence proceeded
to the other cottage, where she found an old man with a Bible in
his hand, busily reading a portion thereof to a little boy who stood
near. He looked up, and gave her the book as soon as she told
him the purpose for which she came, and then, following into the
cottage where the pastor lay, he and the boy stood by, and listened
attentively while she read such chapters as Claude de l'Estang expressed a wish to hear.

Those chapters were not, in general, such as might have been
supposed. They were not those which hold out the glorious promises of everlasting life to men who suffer for their faith in this
state of being. They were not such as portray to us, in its real
and spiritual character, that other world, to which the footsteps of
all are tending. It seemed as if, of such things, the mind of the pastor was so fully convinced, so intimately and perfectly sure, that
they were as parts of his own being. But the passages that he
selected were those in which our Redeemer lays down all the bright,
perfect, and unchangeable precepts for the rule and governance
of man's own conduct, which form the only code of law and philosophy that can indeed be called divine. And in that last hour it
seemed the greatest hope and consolation which the dying man
could receive, to ponder upon those proofs of divine love and wisdom which nothing but the Spirit of God himself could have dictated.

Thus passed the whole of the day. From time to time Clémence
paused, and the pastor spoke a few words to those who surrounded
him: words of humble comment on what was read, or pious exhortation. At other times, when his fair companion was tired, the
attendant Maria would take the book and read. No noises, no visit

from without, disturbed the calm. It seemed as if their persecutors were at fault; and though from time to time one of the different members of those shepherd families passed in or out, no other persons were seen moving upon the face of the *landes;* no sounds were heard but their own low voices throughout the short light of a November day. To one fresh from the buzz of cities, and the busy activity of man, the contrast of the stillness and the solitude was strange; but doubly strange and exceeding solemn were they to the mind of her who came, fresh from the perturbed and fevered visions of the preceding night, and saw the day lapse away like a long and quiet sleep.

Towards the dusk of the evening, however, her attendant laid her hand upon Mademoiselle de Marly's arm, as she was still reading, saying, "There is a change coming;" and Clémence paused and gazed down upon the old man's countenance. It looked very grey; but whether from the shadows of the evening, or from the loss of whatever hue of living health remained, she could hardly tell. But the difference was not so great in the colour as in the expression. The look of pain and suffering which, notwithstanding all his efforts to bear his fate with tranquillity, had still marked that fine expressive countenance, was gone, and a calm and tranquil aspect had succeeded, although the features were extremely sharpened, the eye sunk, and the temples hollow. It was the look of a body and a soul at peace; and, for a moment, as the eyes were turned up towards the sky, Clémence imagined that the spirit was gone: but the next moment he looked round towards her, as if inquiring why she stopped.

"How are you, sir?" she said. "You seem more at ease."

"I am quite at ease, Clémence," replied the old man. "All pain has left me. I am somewhat cold, but that is natural; and for the last half hour the remains of yesterday's agony have been wearing away, as I have seen snow upon a hill's side melt in the April sunshine. It is strange, and scarcely to be believed, that death should be so pleasant; for this is death, my child, and I go away from this world of care and pain with a foretaste of the mercies of the next. It is very slow, but still it is coming, Clémence, and bringing healing on its wings. Death, the messenger of God's will, to one that trusts in his mercy, is indeed the harbinger of that peace of God which passes all understanding."

He paused a little, and his voice had grown considerably weaker, even while he spoke. "God forgive my enemies," he said, at length, "and the mistaken men who persecute others for their soul's sake. God forgive them, and yield them a better light; for, oh how I wish that all men could feel death only as I feel it!"

Such were the last words of Claude de l'Estang. They were perfectly audible and distinct to every one present, and they were spoken with the usual calm, sweet simplicity of manner which had characterized all the latter part of his life. But after he had again paused for two or three minutes, he opened his lips as if to say something more; but no sound was heard. He instantly felt that such was the case, and ceased the effort; but he feebly stretched forth his hand toward Clémence, who bent her head over it, and dewed it with her tears.

When she raised her eyes, they fell upon the face of the dead.

CHAPTER XXIX.

THE DISCOVERY OF ERROR.

WE must now, once more, change the scene and time, though the spot to which we will conduct the reader is not situated more than ten miles from that in which the events recorded in the last chapter took place, and though only one day's interval had elapsed since those events occurred. Considerably more inland, the country presented none of that sandy appearance which characterises the *landes*. The vegetation also was totally different, the rich, even rank, grass spreading under the tall trees of the forest, and the ivy covering those which had already lost their leaves.

There was a little château, belonging to an inferior noble of the province, situated in the midst of one of those wide woods which the French of that day took the greatest pains to maintain in a flourishing condition, both for the sake of the fuel which they afforded, and the cover that they gave to the objects of the chase. The château itself was built, as usual, upon an eminence of considerable elevation, overlooking the forest world around; and in its immediate neighbourhood the wood was cleared away, so as to leave an open esplanade, upon which, on the present occasion, some fifteen hundred or two thousand men had passed the preceding day and night: having liberated the poor pastor of Auron on the night before. Some few tents of rude construction, some huts hastily raised, had been their only shelter; but they murmured not; and indeed it was not from such causes that any of those who deserted the body of Protestant insurgents quitted the standard of their leader. It was, that the agents of the governing priesthood had long been busy amongst them, and had sapped the principles and shaken the resolution of many of those who even showed themselves willing to take arms, but who soon fell away in the hour of need, acting more detrimentally on their own cause than if they had absolutely opposed it, or abandoned it from the first. Doubts of each other, and hesitation in their purposes, had thus been spread through the Protestants; and though of the number assembled there, few existed who had now either inclination or opportunity to turn back, yet they thought with gloomy apprehension upon the defection that was daily taking place in the great body of Huguenots throughout France; and their energies were chilled even if their resolution was not shaken.

The day of which we now speak rose with a brighter aspect than the preceding one, and it was scarcely more than daylight when the gates of the castle were opened, the horses of the Count de Morseiul and his immediate officers and attendants were brought out; and in a minute after, he himself, booted and spurred, and bearing energetic activity in his eye, came forth upon the esplanade, surrounded by a number of persons, who were giving him information, or receiving his orders. The men who were gathered in arms on the slope of the hill, gazed up towards him with that sort of expectation which is near akin to hope; and the prompt rapidity of his gestures, the quickness with which he was speaking, the ease with which he seemed to comprehend everybody, and the readiness and capability, if we may so call it, of his own demeanour, were marked by all those that looked upon him, and gave trust and confidence even to the faintest heart there.

" Where is Riquet?" the Count said, after speaking to some of the gentlemen who had taken arms; " where is Riquet? He told me that two persons had arrived from Paris last night, and were safe in his chamber. Where is Riquet?"

" Riquet! Riquet!" shouted several voices, sending the sound back into the castle; but in the meantime the Count went on speaking to those around them in a sorrowful tone.

" So poor Monsieur de l'Estang is dead!" he said. " That is a shining light, indeed, put out. He died yesterday evening, you say? God forgive me that I should regret him at such a moment as this, and wish that he had been left to us! There was not a nobler or a wiser, or, what is indeed the same thing, a better man in France. I have known him from my childhood, gentlemen, and you must not think me weak that I cannot bear this loss as manly as might be," and he dashed a tear away from his eye. " That they should torture such a venerable form as that!" he added; " that they should stretch upon the rack him who never pained or tortured any one! These things are too fearful, gentlemen, almost to be believed. The time will come when they shall be looked upon but as a doubtful tale. Is it not six of our pastors, in Poitou alone, that they have broken on the wheel? Out upon them, inhuman savages! Out upon them, I say! But what was this you told me of some ladies having been freed from the prison?—Oh, here is Riquet! Now, sirrah, what are your tidings? Who are these personages from Paris?"

" One of them, sir," replied Riquet, whose tone was changed in no degree by the new situation in which he was placed, " one of them is your lordship's own man, or rather your lordship's man's man, Peter. He is the personage that I left in Paris to give the order for your liberation that you wot of."

" Ay!" said the Count; " what made him so long in following us? He was not detained by any chance, was he?"

" Oh no, my lord," answered the valet, " he was not detained; only he thought—he thought—I do not know very well what he thought. But, however, he stayed for two or three days, and is only just come on hither."

" Does he bring any news?" demanded the Count.

" None, but that the Prince de Conti is dead—very suddenly, indeed—of the small pox, caught of his fair wife," was the man's reply; " that all Protestants are ordered to quit Paris immediately; and that the Duke of Berwick has made formal abjuration."

" I grieve for the Prince de Conti," said the Count; " he was promising and soldier-like; though the other, the young Prince de la Roche-sur-Yon, is full of still higher qualities. So, the boy Duke of Berwick has abjured? That might be expected. No other news?"

" None, my lord, from him," replied the man, who evidently was a little embarrassed in speaking on the subject of his fellow-servant; and he added, immediately, " The other gentleman seems to have news; but he will communicate it to none but yourself."

" I will speak with them both," rejoined the Count. " Bring them hither immediately, Riquet."

" Why, my lord," said the valet, " as to Peter, I do not well know where——"

" You must know where, within three minutes," answered the Count, who, in general, interpreted pretty accurately the external signs and symbols of what was going on in Riquet's heart. " You must know where, within three minutes; and that where, must be here, by my side. Maitre Riquet, remember, though somewhat indulgent in the saloon or the cabinet, I am not to be trifled with in the field. Now, gentlemen, what were we speaking of just now?— Oh, these ladies.—Have you any idea of what they were in prison for? Doubtless, for worshipping God according to their consciences. That is the great crime now. But I did not know that they had begun to persecute poor women;" and a shade of deep melancholy came over his fine features, as he thought of what might be the situation of Clémence de Marly.

" Why, it would seem, sir," replied one of the gentlemen, " from what I can hear, that the ladies were not there as prisoners; but were two charitable persons of the town of Thouars, who had come to give comfort and consolation to our poor friend, Monsieur de l'Estang."

" God's blessing will be upon them!" replied the Count; " for it was a noble and a generous deed in such times as these. But,

lo! Master Riquet, with our two newly-arrived friends! Good
Heaven, my old acquaintance of the Bastille! Sir, I am very glad to
see you free, and should be glad to greet you in this poor province
of Poitou, could we but give you any other entertainment than bullets and hard blows, and scenes of sorrow or of strife."

" No matter, no matter, my young friend," replied the old Englishman; " to such entertainment I am well accustomed. It has
been meat and drink to me from my youth; and though I cannot
exactly say that I will take any other part in these transactions,
being bound in honour, in some sense, not to do so, yet I will take
my part in any dangers that are going, willingly. But do not let
me stop you, if you are going to ask any questions of that fellow,
who came the last five or six miles with me; for if you don't get
him out of the hands of that rascal of yours, there will be no such
thing as truth in him in five minutes."

" Come hither, Peter," cried the Count. " Maitre Riquet, you
have face enough for anything; so stand here. Now, Peter, the
truth at one word! What was it that Riquet was telling you not
to tell me?"

" Why, my lord," replied the man, glancing his eye from his
master to the valet, and the awe of the former in a moment overpowering the awe of the latter, " why, my lord, he was saying,
that there was no need to tell your lordship that I never delivered
the order that he gave me to deliver at the gates of the Bastille."

The Count stood for a moment gazing on him, thunderstruck.
" You never delivered the order!" he exclaimed. " Do you mean
to say you never delivered the order he gave you for my liberation?"

" No, my lord," answered the man, beginning to quake in every
limb for fear that he had done something wrong. " I never did
deliver the order. But I'll tell your lordship why. I thought
there was no use of delivering it; for just as I was walking up to
do so, and had made myself look as like a courier of the court as I
could, I saw you yourself going along the Rue St. Antoine, with
two boys staring up in your face, and I thought I might only make
mischief for myself or you, if I went and said anything more about
the matter. When I knew you were free, I thought that was quite
enough."

" Certainly, certainly," replied the Count; " but, in the name
of Heaven, then, by whom have I been delivered?"

" Why, my lord, that is difficult to say," replied Riquet, " but
not by that fellow, who has brought me back the order as I gave it
to him; and now—as very likely your lordship would wish to
know—I told him not to tell you, simply because it would tease you
to no purpose, and take away from me the honour of having set
your lordship free, without doing you any good."

" You are certainly impudent enough for your profession," replied the Count, " and in this instance as foolish as knavish. The

endeavour and the risk were still the same, and it is for that I owe you thanks, not for the success or want of success."

"Ah, sir," replied Riquet, "if all masters were so noble and generous, we poor valets should not get spoilt so early. But how you have been liberated, Heaven only knows."

"That's a mistake," replied the old English officer; "everybody at the court of France knows. The King was in a liberating mood one week; and he himself gave an order for the Count's liberation one day, and for mine two days afterwards. I heard of it when I went to present myself before the King; and the whole court was ringing with what they called your ingratitude, Count; for by that time it was known on what errand you had set off hither."

The Count clasped his hands together, and looked down upon the ground. "I fear," he said, in a low voice, "that I have been sadly misled."

"Not by me, my lord, upon my honour!" cried Riquet, with an earnest look. "I did my best to serve you, and to deliver you; and I fully thought that, by my means, it had been done. The man can tell you that he had the order from me: he can produce it now——"

"I blame you not, Riquet," said his master; "I blame you not; you acted for the best; but most unhappily has this chanced to bring discredit on a name which never yet was stained. It is now too late to think of it, however. My part is chosen, and there is no retracting."

"When on my visit to the court," said the old English officer, "in order to return thanks for my liberation, and to demand certain acts of justice, I heard you blamed; I replied, my good sir, that we in England held that private affections must never interfere with public duties, and that doubtless you felt the part you had chosen to be a public duty. They seemed not to relish the doctrine there —nor you fully to feel its force, I think."

"My dear sir," said the Count, "I have not time to discuss nicely all the collateral points which affect that question. All I will say is, that in following such a broad rule, there is much need to be upon our guard against one of man's greatest enemies—his own deceitful heart—and to make sure that, in choosing the seeming part of public duty, we be not as much influenced by private affections—amongst which I class vanity, pride, anger, revenge— as in adopting the opposite course."

"That is true, too; that is true, too," replied the other. "Man puts me in mind of an ape I once saw, whose greatest delight was to tickle himself; but if any one else tried to do it, he would bite him to the bone. But I see you are about to march—and some of your people have got their troops already in motion. If you will allow me half an hour's conversation as we ride along, I shall be glad. I will get my horse, and mount in a minute."

" The horse that brought you here must be tired," replied the Count; " my people have several fresh ones. Riquet, see that a horse be saddled quickly for—this gentleman. A strange piece of ignorance, sir," he continued, " but I am still unacquainted with your name."

" Oh, Thomas Cecil, my good Count," replied the old officer, " Sir Thomas Cecil; but I will go get the horse, and be with you in a moment."

The Count bowed his head, and while the Englishman was away, proceeded to conclude all his arrangements for the march. In something like regular order, but still with evident symptoms of no long training in the severe rules of military discipline, the Count's little force began to march, and a great part thereof was winding down the hill when the old Englishman returned.

" That is a fine troop," he said, "just now getting into motion. If you had many such as that, you might do something."

" They are a hundred of my own Protestant tenantry and citizens," replied the Count. " They have all served under me long in the late war, and were disbanded after the Truce of twenty years was signed. There is not a braver or a steadier handful in Europe ; and since I have been placed as I am, I make it a point to lead them at the head in any offensive operations on our part, and to follow with them in the rear in the event of retreat, which you see is the case now. We will let them precede us a little, and then we can converse at leisure."

Thus saying, he mounted his horse, and after seeing the little body, which he called his legion, take its way down the hill, he followed, accompanied by Sir Thomas, with a small party of attendants fifty yards behind them.

" And now, my good sir," said the young nobleman, " you will not think me of scanty courtesy if I say that it may be necessary to tell me in what I can serve you, or, in fact, to speak more plainly, if I ask the object of your coming to my quarters, at once ; for I am informed that the intendant of the province, with what troops he can bring together from Berry and Rouergue, forming altogether a very superior force to our own, is marching to attack us. If he can do so in our retreat, of course he will be glad to avail himself of the opportunity, especially as I have been led away from the part of the country which it is most easy to defend with such troops as ours, in order to prevent an act of brutal persecution which they were going to perpetrate on one of the best of men. Thus our time for conversation may be short."

" Why, you have not let him surprise you, I hope?" exclaimed the old officer.

" Not exactly that," replied the Count ; " but we are come into a part of the country where the people are principally Catholic, and we find a difficulty in getting information. I am also obliged to make a considerable movement to the left of my real line of retreat, in order to prevent one of our most gallant fellows, and his band of nearly three hundred men, from being cut off. He is, it is true, both brave and skilful, and quite capable of taking care of himself; but I am sorry to say grief and excitement have had an effect upon his brain, and he is occasionally quite insane, so that without seeming to interfere with him too much, I am obliged, for the sake of those who are with him, to give more attention to his proceedings than might otherwise have been necessary."

The Count paused, and the old officer replied, in a thoughtful tone, "I am in great hopes, from what I hear, that you will find more mild measures adopted towards you than you anticipate. Are you aware of who it is that has been sent down to command the troops in this district, in place of the former rash and cruel man?"

" No," answered the Count; " but, from what I have heard during these last four days, I have been led to believe that a man of far greater skill and science is at the head of the King's troops. All their combinations have been so much more masterly, that I have found it necessary to be extremely cautious; whereas a fortnight ago, I could march from one side of the country to the other without any risk."

" The officer," replied Sir Thomas Cecil, "was raised to the rank of major-general for the purpose, and is, I understand, an old friend of yours, the Chevalier d'Evran."

The Count suddenly pulled up his horse, and gazed for a moment in the old man's face. " Then," said he, "the Protestant cause is ruined.—It is not solely on account of Louis d'Evran's skill," he added, "that I say so: though if ever any one was made for a great commander, he is that man; but he is mild and moderate, conciliating and good-humoured; and I have remarked that a little sort of fondness for mystery which he affects,—concealing all things that he intends in a sort of dark cloud, till it flashes forth like lightning,—has a very powerful effect upon all minds that are not of the first order. The only bond that has kept the Protestants together has been the sharp and bitter persecution lately endured. If any one equally gentle and firm, powerful and yet conciliating, appears against us, I shall not have five hundred men left in two days."

' And perhaps, Count," said the old man, " not very sorry for it?"

The Count turned his eyes upon him, and looked steadily in his face for a moment. "That, I think," he said, "is hardly a fair question, my good friend. I believe you, sir, from all I have seen of you, to be an upright and honourable man; and I have looked upon you as a sincere Protestant, and one suffering, in some degree, from your attachment to that faith. I take it for granted, then, that nothing which I have said to you this day is to be repeated."

"Nothing, upon my honour," replied Sir Thomas Cecil, frankly. "You are quite right in your estimation of me, I assure you. If I ask any question, it is for my own satisfaction, and because, sir, I take an interest in you. Nothing that passes your lips shall be repeated by me without your permission: though I tell you fairly, and at once, that I am going very soon to the head-quarters of the Chevalier d'Evran, to fulfil a mission to him, which will be unsuccessful I know, but which must still be fulfilled. Will you trust me so far as this, Count? Will you let me know, whether you really wish this state of insurrection to go on; or would not rather, if mild—I will not call them equitable—terms could be obtained for the Protestants of this district, that peace should be restored and a hopeless struggle ended? I do not say hopeless," he continued, "at all to disparage your efforts; but——"

"My dear sir," replied the Count, "act as bluntly by me as you did in the Bastille; call the struggle hopeless if you will. There are but ten men in my little force who do not know it to be hopeless, and those ten are fools. The sole choice left, sir, to the Protestants of this district when I arrived here, was between timid despair and courageous despair; to die by the slow fire of persecution without resistance, or to die with swords in our hands in a good cause. We chose the latter, which afforded, indeed, the only chance of wringing toleration from our enemies by a vigorous effort. But I am as well aware as you are that we have no force sufficient to resist the power of the crown; that in the mountains, woods, and fastnesses of this district and of Brittany, upon which I am now retreating, I might, perhaps, frustrate the pursuit of the royal forces for months, nay, for years; living, for weeks, as a chief of banditti, and only appearing for a single day, from time to time, as the general of an army. Day by day my followers might decrease; for the scissors of inconvenience often shear down the forces of an insurgent leader more fatally than the sharp sword of war. Then, a thousand to one, no means that I could take would prevent all my people from committing evil acts. I, and a just and holy cause, would acquire a bad name; and the whole would end, by the worst of my people betraying me to death upon the scaffold. All this, sir, was considered before I drew the sword; but you must remember that I had not the slightest idea whatsoever that the King had shewn any disposition to treat me personally with anything but bitter severity. —To return to your former question, then, and to answer it candidly and straightforwardly, but merely, remember, between ourselves, I should not grieve on such reasonable terms being granted to the generality of Protestants as would enable them to live peacefully, adhering to their own religion, though it be in private; to see my men reduced, as I have said, to five hundred, ay, or to one hundred: provided those gallant men, who, with firm determination, adhere to the faith of their fathers, and are resolved neither to conceal that faith nor submit to its oppression, have the means of seeking liberty of conscience in another land. As for myself," he continued, with a deep sigh, " my mind is at present in such a state, that I should little care, if once I saw this settled, to go to-morrow and lay my head at the foot of the King's throne. Abjure my religion I never will; live in a land where it is persecuted I never will; but life has lately become a load to me ; and it were as well for all, under such circumstances, that it were terminated. This latter part of what I have said, sir, you may tell the Chevalier d'Evran : namely, that, on the government granting such terms to the Protestants of this district as will insure the two objects I have mentioned, the Count of Morseiul is willing to surrender himself to the pleasure of the King ; though, till such terms are granted, and my people so secured, nothing shall induce me to sheath the sword: —and yet I acknowledge that I am bitterly grieved and mortified that this error has taken place in regard to the order for my liberation, and that thus an imputation of ingratitude has been brought upon me which I do not deserve."

The old officer held out his hand to him, and shook that of the Count heartily, adding, with a somewhat profane oath, which characterises the English nation, " Sir, you deserve your reputation."

He went on a minute or two afterwards to say, " I have been accustomed, in some degree, to such transactions ; and I will report your words and nothing more : but, by your leave, I think you had better alter the latter part, and stipulate that you shall be allowed yourself to emigrate with a certain number of your followers. Louvois is extremely anxious to keep from the King's ears the extent of this insurrection, having always persuaded him that there would be none. He will, therefore, be extremely glad to have it put down without more noise, on easy terms; and doubtless he has given the Chevalier d'Evran instructions to that effect."

" No, no," replied the Count; " I must endeavour, sir, to wipe away the stain that has been cast upon me. Do you propose to go to the Chevalier's head-quarters at once ?"

" Not exactly," replied the old Englishman. " I am first going to Thouars, having some business with the Duc de Rouvré."

" Good God !" exclaimed the Count ; " is the Duc de Rouvré at Thouars ?" and a confused image of the truth, that Clémence de Marly had been one of the two persons found in the prison with Claude de l'Estang now flashed on his mind. Ere the old man could reply, however, two of the persons who were following, and who seemed to have ridden some way to the left of the direct road, rode up as fast as they could come, and informed the Count de Morseiul, that what seemed a large body of men was marching up towards their flank by a path which ran through the hollow-way between them and the opposite hills.

The little force of the Count had by this time emerged from the woods, and was marching along the side of the hill, which gradually sank away into those *landes*, across which Armand Herval had, as we have seen, led Clémence de Marly. Up the valley, on the left, lay a deep ravine, bringing the cross road from Thouars into the road in which the Huguenots then were, so that the flank of the Count's force was exposed to the approach of the enemy on that side, though it had somewhat the advantage of the ground. No other line, however, had been open for him, the country on the other side leading into tracts much more exposed to attack; and, in fact, on that morning no choice had been left, but either to run the risk of what now appeared to have happened, or to leave Herval and his men to their fate, they not having joined the main force on the preceding day, as they had been directed to do.

The Count instantly turned his horse's head, galloped to the spot from whence the men had seen the head of the enemy's column, paused for a single instant, in order, if possible, to ascertain their force, and then riding back, commanded the small troop, which he called his legion, to face about. While, by his orders, they traversed a piece of broken ground to the left, so as to approach a spot where the hollow-way debouched upon the open country, he sent five or six of his attendants with rapid orders to the different noblemen who were under his command, in regard to assuming a position upon the hill.

" Tell Monsieur du Bar," he said to one of the men, " to march on as quickly as possible till he reaches the windmill, to garnish that little wood on the slope with musketeers, to plant the two pieces of cannon by the mill so as to bear upon the road, to strengthen himself by the mill and the walls around it, and to hold that spot firm to the very last. Jean, bid the Marquis send off a man instantly to Herval, that he may join us with his Chauve-souris, and, in the meantime, ask him to keep the line of the hill from the left of Monsieur du Bar to the cottage on the slope, so that the enemy may not turn our flank. If I remember right, there are two farm roads there, so that all movements will be easy from right to left, or from front to rear. As soon as Herval comes up, let the Marquis throw him forward, with his marksmen, to cover my movements, and then commence the general retreat by detachments from each flank, holding firm by the mill and the wood to the last; for they dare not advance while those are in our hands. I can detain them here for a quarter of an hour, but not longer.—Sir Thomas Cecil," he added, " take my advice, and ride off for Thouars with all speed. This will be a place for plenty of bullets, but no glory."

Thus saying, he galloped down to his troop; and in a moment after the old English officer, who stood with the utmost sang-froid to witness the fight, saw him charge into the hollow-way at the head of his men.

CHAPTER XXX.

THE BATTLE AND THE RETREAT.

WE must now return to the small shepherd's cottage in the *landes;* and, passing over the intervening day which had been occupied in the burial of the good pastor, we must take up the story of Clémence de Marly on the morning of which we have just been speaking. At an early hour on that day, Armand Herval came into the cottage, where the people were setting before her the simple meal of ewe milk and black bread, which was all that they could afford to give; and, standing by her side with somewhat of a wild air, he asked her if she were ready to go. She had seen him several times on the preceding day, and his behaviour had always been so respectful, his grief for the death of Claude de l'Estang so sincere, and the emotions which he displayed at the burial of the body in the sand so deep and unaffected, that Clémence had conceived no slight confidence in a man, whom she might have shrunk from with terror, had she known that in him she beheld the same plunderer, who, under the name of Brown Keroual, had held her for some time a prisoner in the forest near Auron.

"To go where, sir?" she demanded, with some degree of agitation. "I knew not that I was about to go anywhere."

"Oh yes!" replied the man, in the same wild way. "We should have gone yesterday; and I shall be broke for insubordination. You do not know how stern he is, when he thinks fit, and how no prayers or entreaties can move him."

"Whom do you speak of, sir?" demanded Clémence. "I do not know whom you mean."

"Why, the General to be sure," replied the man; "the Commander-in-Chief—your husband—the Count de Morseiul."

The blood rushed up into the cheek of Clémence de Marly. "You are mistaken," she said; "he is not my husband."

"Then he soon will be," replied the man with a laugh; "though the grave is a cold bridal bed.—I know that, lady!—I know that full well; for when I held her to my heart on the day of our nuptials, the cheek that used to feel so warm when I kissed it, was icy as stone; and when you come to kiss his cheek, or brow, too, after they have shot him, you will find it like clay—cold—cold—with a coldness that creeps to your very soul; and then all the heat that used to be in your heart goes into your brain, and there you feel it burning like a coal."

Clémence shuddered, both at the evident insanity of the person who was talking to her, and at the images which his words called up before her eyes. He was about to go on; but a tall, dark, powerful man came in from the cottage door where he had been previously standing, and laid hold of Herval's arm, saying, " Come, Keroual, come. You are only frightening the lady; and, indeed, you ought to be upon the march. What will my lord say? The fit is upon him now, Madam," he continued, addressing Clémence in a low voice; " but it will soon go away again. They drove him mad, by shooting a poor girl he was in love with at the preaching on the moor, which you may remember.—I am not sure, but I think you were there too.—If I could get him to play a little upon the musette at the door, the fit would soon leave him. He used to be so fond of it, and play it so well.—Poor fellow, he is terribly mad! See how he is looking at us without speaking.—Come, Keroual, come ; here is the musette at the door;" and he led him away by the arm.

" Ay," said the old shepherd, as they went out, " one is not much less mad than the other. There, they ought both to have gone to join the Count last night. But the burying of poor Monsieur de l'Estang seemed to set them both off; and now there are all the men drawn out and ready to march, and they will sit and play the musette there, Lord knows how long!"

" But what did they mean by asking if I were ready?" said Clémence. " Do they intend to take me with them?"

" Why, yes, Madam," replied the old man ; " I suppose so. The litter was ready for you last night, and as the army is going to retreat, I hear, it would not be safe for you to stay here, as the Catholics are coming up in great force under the Chevalier d'Evran."

Clémence started and turned round, while the colour again rushed violently into her cheeks; and then she covered her eyes with her hands, as if to think more rapidly by shutting out all external objects. She was roused, however, almost immediately, by the sound of the musette, and saying, " I will go! I am quite ready to go!" she advanced to the door of the cottage.

It was a strange and extraordinary sight that presented itself. Herval and Paul Virlay, dressed in a sort of anomalous military costume, and armed with manifold weapons, were sitting together on the stone bench at the cottage door, the one playing beautifully upon the instrument of his native province, and the other listening, apparently well satisfied; while several groups of men, of every complexion and expression, were standing round, gazing upon the two, and attending to the music. The air that Herval or Keroual was playing was one of the ordinary psalm tunes in use amongst the Protestants, and he gave it vast expression ; so that pleasure in the music and religious enthusiasm seemed entirely to withdraw the thoughts of the other men from the madness of the act at that moment. Paul Virlay, however, was mad in that kind, if mad at all, which is anxious and cunning in concealing itself; and the moment he saw Clémence, he started up with somewhat of shame in his look, saying—

" He is better now, madam ; he is better now.—Come, Herval," he continued, touching his arm, " let us go."

Herval, however, continued till he had played the tune once over again, and then laying down the musette, he looked in Virlay's face for a moment, without speaking; but at length replied—

" Very well, Paul; let us go. I am better now. Madam, I beg your pardon ; I am afraid we have hurried you."

Even as he spoke, a messenger came up at full speed, his horse in a lather of foam, and eagerness and excitement in his countenance.

" In the name of Heaven, Keroual, what are you about?" he cried. " Here are the Count and Monsieur du Bar engaged with the whole force of the enemy within two miles of you. In Heaven's name, put your men in array, and march as fast as possible, or you will be cut off, and they defeated."

The look of intelligence and clear sense came back into Herval's countenance in a moment.

" Good God! I have been very foolish," he said, putting his hand to his head. " Quick, my men : each to his post : sound the conch there! But the lady," he continued, turning to the man who had ridden up, " what can we do with the lady?"

" Oh, she must be taken with you, by all means," replied the man. " We can send her on from the cross road into the front. They will sweep all this country, depend upon it; and they are not men to spare a lady."

Clémence turned somewhat pale as the messenger spoke; and though, in fact, her fate was utterly in the hands of those who surrounded her, she turned an inquiring look upon Maria, who stood near, as if asking what she should do.

" Oh, go, lady! go !" cried the attendant, in a language which the men did not understand, but which Clémence seemed to speak fluently; and after a few more words, she retired into the cottage, to wait for the litter, while the band of Brown Keroual, some on horseback and some on foot, began to file off towards the scene of action. In a few minutes after, the litter appeared; but by this time two mules had been procured for it; and, with a man who knew the country well for their driver, Clémence and Maria set off with the last troop of the Huguenots, which was brought up by Herval himself. He was now all intelligence and activity; and no one, to see him, could have conceived that he was the same man, whose mind but a few minutes before seemed totally lost. He urged on their march as fast as possible, pressing the party of foot which was attached to his mounted band; and in a few minutes after, a sharp fire of musketry met the ear of Clémence as she was borne forward. This continued for a little time, as they passed

A A

round the edge of a low wood, which flanked the hills on one side and seemed the connecting link between the *landes* and the culti-·vated country. About five minutes after, however, louder and more rending sounds were heard; and it was evident that cannon were now employed on both sides. The voices of several people shouting, too, were heard, and a horse without a rider came rushing by, and startled the mules that bore the litter.

Clemence de Marly could but raise her prayers to God for his blessing on the right cause. It was not fear that she felt, for fear is personal. It was awe. It was the impressive consciousness of being in the midst of mighty events, which sometimes in her moments of wild enthusiasm she had wished to witness, but which she now felt to be no matter for sport or curiosity.

Another instant she was out upon the side of the hill beyond the wood; and the whole scene was laid open before her. That scene was very awful, notwithstanding the confusion which prevented her from comprehending clearly what was going on. A large body of troops was evidently marching up the valley to the attack of the heights. A windmill surrounded by some low stone walls, not a hundred yards to the left of the spot where she was placed, appeared, at the moment she first saw it, one blaze of fire, from the discharge of musketry and cannon, which seemed to be directed, as far as she could judge, against the flank of a body of cavalry coming up a road in the valley. On the slope of the hill, however, to the right, a considerable body of infantry was making its way up to the attack of the farther angle of the wood, round which she herself had just passed; and from amongst the trees and brushwood, nearly stripped of their leaves as they were, she could see poured forth an almost incessant torrent of smoke and flame upon the assailing party, seeming at every other step to make them waver, as if ready to turn back.

The object, however, which engaged her principal attention was a small body of horsemen, apparently rallying, and reposing for a moment, under shelter of the fire from the hill. Why, she knew not,—for the features of none of those composing that party were at all discernible,—but her heart beat anxiously, as if she felt that there was some beloved being there.

The next instant that small body of men was again put in motion; and, galloping down like lightning, it might be seen, though half hidden by the clouds of dust, to hurl itself violently against the head of the advancing column, like an avalanche against some mighty rock. Almost at the same moment, however, an officer rode furiously up to Herval, and gave him some directions in a quick and eager voice. Herval merely nodded his head, then turned to the driver of the mules, and told him to make as much haste as he could towards Mortagne, along the high road.

" Remain with the head of the column," he said ; " and, above all things, keep your beasts to the work, for you must neither embarrass the march nor let the lady be left behind."

The man obeyed at once; but before he had left the brow of the hill, Clémence saw the band of Keroual begin to descend towards the small body of cavaliers we have mentioned, while a company of musketeers, at a very few yards' distance from her, began to file off as if for retreat.

All the confusion of such a scene succeeded, the jostling, the rushing, the quarrels, the reproaches, the invectives, which take place upon the retreat of an irregular force. But several bodies of better disciplined men, taking their way along the road close to Clémence, preserved some order, and gave her some protection; and as they passed rapidly onward, the sounds of strife and contention, the shouts and vociferations of the various commanders, the rattle of the small-arms and the roar of the artillery, gradually diminished; and while Clémence hoped in her heart that the battle was over, she looked round for some one from the rear, to inquire for the fate of him for whom her heart had beat principally during that morning.

For about half an hour, however, nobody came; the retreat assumed the appearance of an orderly march; and all was going on tranquilly, when a horseman came up at a quick pace, and pulled in his charger beside the litter. Clémence looked towards him. It was not the face that she expected to see, but, on the contrary, that of a tall, thin, hale old man, perfectly a stranger to her. He pulled off his hat with military courtesy, and bowed low.

" I beg your pardon, madam," he said, " but I have just been informed of your name, quality, and situation, and also with the circumstances of your being brought from Thouars hither. I come to say," he added, lowering his voice and bending down, " that I am just going to visit an old friend, the Duke de Rouvré, who, I understand, is your guardian. Now, I do not know whether you are here of your own good will, or whether there be any degree of force in the matter. Should you, however, be disposed to send any message to the Duke, I am ready to take it."

" I give you many thanks, sir," replied Clémence, " but, of course, I can send no long message now, nor detailed explanation of my situation. Assure him only, and the Duchess, who has been a mother to me, of my deep love, and gratitude, and respect."

" But shall I tell them," said the old man, " that you are here with your consent, or without your consent ? "

" You may tell them," replied Clémence, " that I was brought here, indeed, without my consent, though being here, I must now remain voluntarily. My fate is decided."

" Do you mean to say, madam ? " demanded the old gentleman, bluffly, " that I am to tell them you are married ? That is the only way in general that a woman's fate can be decided which I know of."

"No, sir," replied Clémence, colouring, "there is in this country a different decision of one's fate. I am a Protestant! It must no longer, and it can no longer be concealed."

A bright and noble smile came upon the old man's countenance. "I beg your pardon, madam," he said. "I have spoken somewhat rudely, perhaps; but I will deliver your message, and at some future time may ask your pardon, if you will permit me, for having called the colour into a lady's cheek, a thing that I am not fond of doing, though it be beautiful to see."

Thus saying, and bowing low, he was about to turn his horse and canter back again, when an eager look that lighted up Clémence's features, made him pause even before she spoke, and ride on a little further beside her.

"You came from the rear, sir, I think," she said, in a low and faltering voice. "May I ask how has gone the day?—Is the Count de Morseiul safe?"

The old man smiled again sweetly upon her. "Madam," he said, "did not sad experience often show us that it were not so, I should think, from the fate of the Count of Morseiul this day, that a gallant and all daring heart is a buckler which neither steel nor lead can penetrate. I myself have sat and watched him, while in six successive charges he attacked and drove back an immensely superior force of the enemy's cavalry, charging and retreating every time under the most tremendous and well-sustained fire of the light infantry on their flanks that ever I saw. Scarcely a man of his whole troop has escaped without wounds, and but too many are killed. The Count himself, however, is perfectly unhurt. I saw him five minutes ago bringing up the rear, and as by that time the enemy were showing no disposition to pursue vigorously, he may be considered as safe, having effected his retreat from a very difficult situation in the most masterly manner. Is there any one else, madam, of whom I can give you information?"

"I fear not," replied the lady. "There is, indeed, one that I would fain ask for; but as you have been with the Count de Morseiul, probably you do not know him. I mean the Chevalier d'Evran."

"What, both the commanders!" exclaimed the old gentleman, with a smile which again called the colour into Clémence's cheek. "But I beg your pardon, madam," he added; "I have a better right to tell tales than to make comments. In this instance I cannot give you such accurate information as I did in the other, for I do not know the person of the Chevalier d'Evran. But as far as this little perspective glass could show me, the gentleman who has been commanding the royal forces, and whom I was informed was the Chevalier d'Evran, is still commanding them, and apparently unhurt. I discovered him by his philomot scarf, and sword-knot, after losing sight of him for a time. But he was still upon horseback, commanding in the midst of his staff, and has the credit of having won the day, though the immense superiority of his forces rendered any other result out of the question, even if he had not acted as well and skilfully as he has done. I will now once more beg pardon for intruding upon you, and trust that fair fortune and prosperity may attend you."

Thus saying, he turned and cantered away, and on looking round to her maid, Clémence perceived that Maria had drawn the hood of her grey cloak over her head.

CHAPTER XXXI.

THE LOVERS' RE-UNION.

THE march was over, the pursuers left behind, and the Count of Morseiul had pitched his tents in a strong position, with some shepherds' huts and one or two cottages and farm-houses in the midst of his camp. A nunnery of no great extent, situated upon a little eminence, was within the limits of his position, and a small chapel belonging thereunto, nearly at the bottom of the hill, and commanding the passage of a stream and morass, was occupied by a strong body of his followers, under Herval and Virlay; while the Marquis du Bar, who had been slightly wounded in the course of that day's strife, insisted upon fixing his quarters on the most exposed side of the camp, where any attack was likely to take place.

No attempt had been made to take possession of the nunnery, as it was only occupied by women, and as the Count was aware that in case of need, he could obtain entrance in a moment. At the same time he could fully depend not only upon the courage and firmness, but upon the vigilance of Du Bar, and he therefore looked upon his small force as completely in security, for that night at least. Provisions, too, had been found in abundance; and the people of the neighbouring country were somewhat better disposed towards the Huguenot cause than those of the district which they had just left.

His men, however, had suffered tremendously, even in the brief struggle which had taken place with the overpowering force of the Catholics. Of his own troop, not more than thirty men were found capable of action at the end of that day, and, at least, one-third of the whole Huguenot force was unfit for service. This was a lamentable prospect, as the insurgents had no points of strength to fall back upon; and had not the leaders been animated by the consciousness of having performed great actions in that day's contest, and having held at bay a royal army of six times their own number, the proposal of dispersing and carrying on the warfare by desultory efforts in the woods, which was suggested in one of their little councils, would certainly have been adopted.

In the meantime, however, the spirit of the men was kept up, and their resolution fortified, by the prayers and exhortations of the various ministers who accompanied the camp; and on going round to the different quarters just after nightfall, the Count found some bodies of the Protestants still engaged in their religious exercises, some just concluded, but all less depressed at heart than he was himself.

When he had done his round, he paused before the door of one of the farm-houses—the best and most comfortable—and dismissing the men who had followed, he turned to go in. A slight degree of hesitation, however, seemed to come over him as he did so, and he remained for some moments with his hand upon the latch. He at length raised it, and entered the kitchen of the farm-house, where the family of the proprietor were assembled round the ample hearth, on which was a full supply of blazing wood. At that very moment, speaking to the mistress of the house, was Clémence's attendant, Maria; but Clémence herself was not present, and on inquiring for her, the Count was told that she was in an upper chamber, to which the woman immediately led him.

Albert of Morseiul followed her step by step, and when the door opened he beheld Clémence sitting at the table, with her head resting on her hand, and her eyes turned towards the fire; but with such a look of deep sadness and painful thought, as made his heart ache to see it, and to know that he could not change it.

"Here is the Count de Morseiul," said the maid; and instantly Clémence started up, and turned towards the door, while the Count entered, and the maid retired. The face of Clémence de Marly assumed two or three different expressions in a moment. There was joy to see him, there was doubt, there was apprehension; but she advanced towards him at once, and the look of love was not to be doubted. He took the hands that she held out to him, he kissed them tenderly and often: but still there was deep sadness on his brow, as there was in his heart, and his first words were, " Oh, Clémence, at what a moment have you come to me at last ! "

"Albert," she said, in reply, "I have much to say to you. Since I have been here, and seen what I have seen, I have found many excuses for your conduct; and I have learned to think that what I wrote briefly I may have written harshly and unkindly, and to blame myself as much, nay more than you: believing that though I had no time to explain why I could not come at the moment, as I could have wished, yet, that I should still have added such words as might show you that I was yours unchanged, however much I might judge that you had acted rashly, unadvisedly, and unlike yourself. I have determined to tell you all this at once, Albert, and, acknowledging that I blame myself, to shelter myself from all reproaches on your part in your kindness and generosity."

" Thanks, thanks, dearest Clémence," replied the Count, pressing her to his heart; " this is, indeed, balm after such a day as this: but I think, my Clémence, when you hear all, you will yourself exculpate me from blame,—though I fear that the charge of ingratitude which others may bring against me, will never be done away in the less generous minds of the world in general,—without a terrible sacrifice. You, I know, Clémence, will believe every word I tell you."

" Oh, every word!" she exclaimed; " to doubt you, Albert, were to doubt truth itself."

" Well, then, believe me, Clemence," he said, " when I tell you, that till this morning,—till this very morning,—I had not the slightest idea whatsoever that my liberation was attributable to the King. Not only I, but all my domestics, every attendant that I have, my man Riquet himself, all supposed that it was through an artifice of his that I had been set at liberty. Had I thought otherwise, upon my word, my first act would have been to fly to Versailles, in order to express my thanks, whatever my after conduct might have been."

He then explained to her everything that had taken place, and the mistake under which he had himself laboured throughout.

" What confirmed me in the belief that the whole of Riquet's story was perfectly correct," he said, " was the fact that Besmaux, when he set me at liberty, had observed that the order under which he did it, was not quite in the usual form, together with some remarks that he made upon there being no carriage sent for me with the order."

" Alas! alas!" cried Clémence, wringing her hands, " it was my weakness; it was my foolish fears and anxiety, that produced all this mischief. Listen to my tale now, Albert, and forgive me, forgive me for what I have done."

She then related to her lover almost all that had taken place between the King, herself, and Madame de Maintenon. We say almost, because she did not relate the whole; but though Albert of Morseiul saw that she concealed a part, he divined from what she did tell, that there were matters which she was bound not to divulge. Perhaps he divined the important truth itself; and at all events he did not love her a bit the less for a concealment which had no want of confidence in it.

" On the following morning," she said, " at the hour that the King had appointed, I did not fail to be in attendance. I found him writing; but it was soon over, and he handed me the paper, saying, ' There, lady, we have judged the cause that you have at heart as favourably as you judged ours last night. Tell him,' he added, " when you see him, that—though we cannot alter the strict laws, which we have found it necessary to make, for his sake—we will grant him all that may reasonably render him happy, either in our own land, or in another ! "

" And I have borne arms against him ! " cried the Count, clasping his arms together.

" Yet hear me out, Albert," continued Clémence, " for the fault is mine. The order was for your immediate liberation. I took it eagerly, thanked the King, and retired, well knowing that it ought to be countersigned by Louvois, and sent through his office. But during the evening before, on the occasion of something that was said, he gave me such a fiend-like look of revenge, that I knew he would seek your destruction, if not mine. I was well aware, too, that in many an instance he has intercepted the King's clemency, or his bounty ; and weakly, most weakly, I sent the order without his signature—ay, and without a moment's delay, by a servant belonging to the Duc de Rouvré. Thus, thus it was, that I, in my eagerness for your safety, have plunged you into new dangers,— dangers from which, alas ! I fear that there is scarcely a possible means of escape."

The Count looked down upon the ground for a moment, and he then replied, " I will write to the King myself, Clémence. It is very possible that he will not even read the letter of a rebel with arms in his hand. But still it will be a satisfaction to me to do so. I must first get to the sea side, however, in order that I may place poor Riquet in security, for were the tale told, and he afterwards discovered, I fear that no tortures would be considered too horrible to punish the daring act that he committed."

" I, too, will write," replied Clémence. " I will write and tell the whole to one, who, though she will refuse at first, I know, to do anything in our behalf, yet will not fail, calmly and quietly, to labour in our favour, thinking that she owes something to me. I will tell her the whole ; I will tell her distinctly, Albert ; and, if you will procure it for me, I will send her even the forged order that you mention, with the attestation of the man who brought it back from Paris."

Albert of Morseiul pressed her to his heart ; and she added, " At all events, Albert, we shall be able to fly. We are now not far from the sea ; ships can easily be procured, and we may be happy in another land."

Albert of Morseiul kissed her cheek for his only reply : but his heart was sad, and he could scarcely command even a smile to countenance the false hope she had expressed. His own determinations were taken, his own resolutions formed ; but he thought it better and more kind not to make them known to Clémence de Marly till the moment arrived for putting them in execution.

While they were yet speaking, the attendant again came into

the room to inform the Count that three persons waited below to see him, and on going down he found Riquet, with one of the Protestants attached to the Marquis du Bar, and a gentleman, who appeared to be an inferior officer in the royal service. The two latter instantly stepped forward when the Count appeared.

"Monsieur du Bar," said the Protestant soldier, "has sent you this gentleman, bearing a flag of truce, from the Chevalier d'Evran. He carries a letter to yourself, and a letter to the lady from Thouars."

The Count bowed to the stranger, and begged to see the letter to himself. It was simply addressed to the Count de Morseiul, and he opened it with some emotion, for it was strange to see the hand of Louis d'Evran, writing to him as from one adversary to another. The style and tone of the letter, however, though it was very short, were precisely as if nothing had occurred to interrupt their intimacy, or array them hostilely against each other. It ran—

"DEAR ALBERT,

"I write to you simply to know whether I am to regard the communication made to me, on your part, by an English gentleman, called Sir Thomas Cecil, as formal and definitive, as I must be made aware of that fact before I can transmit it to the court. I trust and hope that good results may proceed from it: but you must not forget that it is an awful risk. For my part, I will do my best to quiet the province with as little harshness as possible, and with that object I accepted, or rather may say, solicited this command. In every respect, however, my duty must be done to the king, and shall be so done to the utmost. You never in your life fought better than you did this morning. Your defence of the heights was quite a Turenne affair; but you made a mistake in your morning movement to the left, which shewed me your flank. Perhaps, however, you had some reason for it, for I think there was a fresh corps came up towards the close of the affair. Look to yourself, dear Albert, for be you sure that I shall give you no breathing time; and so God speed you!

"LOUIS D'EVRAN.

"Post Scriptum. I find myself called upon by my duty, to require you formally to send back la belle Clémence to her good friend de Rouvré, and to address a letter to her upon the subject of her return."

The Count had read this epistle with a thoughtful and a somewhat frowning brow. It was quite characteristic of the Chevalier d'Evran, but yet there was something in it that did not please him. He turned, however, to the officer, courteously saying—

"The Chevalier d'Evran notifies to me, that he has sent a letter to Mademoiselle de Marly, and seems to leave it to me to deliver it.

I would rather, however, that you did so yourself, if that lady will permit me to introduce you to her, when you can bear her answer from her own mouth. Riquet," he said, " go up and inquire whether Mademoiselle de Marly will grant this gentleman a few minutes' audience."

A short pause ensued: for Clémence hesitated for some time. At length, however, Riquet returned with an answer in the affirmative, and the Count led the officer to her presence.

"I am commanded, Madam," said the stranger, "by Monsieur le Chevalier d'Evran, lieutenant-general of the province, to deliver you this letter, and to say, that, at any time to-morrow which you will name, he will send a proper carriage and attendants, to convey you back to the town of Thouars, from which he understands that you were forcibly carried away, some nights ago."

Clémence merely bowed her head, and held out her hand for the letter, which she opened and read. A faint smile came over her countenance as she proceeded; and when she had done, she handed the epistle to her lover, asking, " What shall I do or say?"

" Nay, I can give you no advice," replied the Count. " In this matter, Clémence, you must act by your own judgment: advice from me, situated as you are now, would bear somewhat the character of dictation. Do you wish me to read the letter?"

" Certainly," she replied. " My mind will be easily made up as to the answer."

The Count then proceeded to read the letter, which was merely one of form; and began—

" MADEMOISELLE,

" I am urged by Monsieur le Duc de Rouvré, and feel it a part of my duty, to apply to you immediately to return to the care and protection of that gentleman and the duchess, under whose charge and guardianship you have been placed by the king. Although we are fully informed that you were carried away from the town of Thouars without your own consent and approbation, we feel sure, from the high character and reputation of the Count de Morseiul, though now unfortunately in open rebellion, that he will be most anxious you should return, and will do all that he can to facilitate the arrangements for that purpose. Such being the case, let me exhort you, mademoiselle, to make all haste to quit the camp of a body of men in open insurrection, and to place yourself under the protection of legitimate authority.

" I have the honour to be, mademoiselle, your devoted servant,
" LOUIS D'EVRAN."

The Count returned the letter with no other comment than, " It is strange;" and Clémence paused for a moment, gazing upon the back of the letter, but evidently occupied by deep thoughts.

She then turned to the officer, who had remained standing, and said, " I will not detain you, sir, to write, as my answer must be merely what the Chevalier d'Evran expects. You will inform him—notwithstanding that it may seem bold of me to say so—that although I was certainly not brought here with my consent, I, nevertheless, am here by my consent; and as I have long been disposed to return to that faith in which I was originally instructed, and have for some time embraced it upon sincere conviction, I cannot consent to place myself in a situation where the exercise of the reformed religion will be denied to me; but must, on the contrary, remain with those who will protect and support me in my adherence to what I consider the only pure and true faith."

" In short, madam," replied the officer, " I am to tell the Chevalier that you are a Huguenot?"

" Exactly, sir," replied Clémence; " and that I have been so for some time."

The officer shewed an inclination to pause, and to add something to what had been said; but the Count stopped him.

" You are, sir," he said, " I think, but the bearer of a letter. There is nothing in that letter giving you at all the title of an envoy. You have, therefore, but to bear back the reply which this lady has given."

" And your own, sir," said the officer, " which I have not received."

" It is as simple as hers, sir," replied the Count. " Assure the Chevalier d'Evran of my best regard; tell him he may trust entirely and fully to the proposal made to him on my part, to which he alludes, as far, at least, as I myself am concerned. In respect, however, to what will satisfy the other leaders, who are in arms for the maintenance of their just liberties, and for the attainment of immunity in worshipping God according to their own consciences, he must deal with themselves. In that I cannot, and do not interfere, and have only to support them with my sword and counsels till such time as they have obtained their rights, or are satisfied with any arrangement proposed."

" I shall not fail," replied the officer, " to convey these messages distinctly;" and thus saying, he bowed, and left the room, followed by the Count of Morseiul, who, giving directions that his eyes should be properly bandaged, placed him in the hands of the Protestant soldier who had accompanied him, and of the guard which was waiting without. He then made a sign to Riquet to follow him up stairs, and bade his valet repeat to Clémence de Marly all that had occurred respecting his liberation from the Bastille.

" And now, Riquet," he said, when the man had given a much more straightforward and decided statement than he usually made, " it is my intention, as soon as possible, to lay the whole of these facts before the King, feeling it due to my own honour to shew him that I have not been so ungrateful as he thinks. As the act, however, which you have committed might prove very dangerous to you, if you should fall into the hands of the Catholic party, I shall take care, before I give this account, that you have an opportunity of seeking refuge in another land. I know that all countries are to you alike; and I will ensure that you shall be provided with full means of obtaining for yourself comfort and repose."

" Sir," said the man, with some feeling, " all countries, as you say, are to me alike. But such is not the case with regard to all masters. Please God, I will never serve another but yourself. If you quit the country, I will quit it with you; if you remain, I will remain. I am already—am I not?—in arms against the crown. I am just as much a rebel riding after you from place to place, and every now and then firing a musket when I think nobody sees me, as if I were at the head of the whole business, and people called it the rebellion of Riquet. You may therefore lay the whole statement before the King if you please, and I will myself write down the plain facts, in fewer words than a paper drawn up by a notary's clerk without a fee. I have no fear, sir, of gathering together upon my shoulders a few more stray crimes and misdemeanours. That does not lie in the way of my cowardice. My neck is thin and long, and whether it be the axe or the rope that has to do with it, it will neither give the cord nor the edge much trouble; while I have always one consolation, which is, that if the experiment of hanging should prove disagreeable, it cannot be tried upon me twice. I will go and get the paper directly, sir, which the man Peter brought back again. I will put down all his sayings and doings, and all my own; and the King, who is said to have a high taste in all branches of skill, ought to declare when he sees the order for your liberation which I manufactured, that there is not a piece of mosaic like it in all Versailles, and grant me a high reward for such a specimen of dexterity in my art."

" I fear you deceive yourself, Riquet," replied the Count; but the man shook his head. " No, sir, I do not," he said, " I assure you. All things considered and well weighed, I do not think that I run a bit more risk by this matter being told to the King, than if it never reached his ears."

Thus saying he left the room, and Albert of Morseiul turned to other and sweeter thoughts. " Dear, dear Clémence," he said, gazing tenderly upon her, " you have now, indeed, chosen your part as I could expect Clémence to do; and by the words that you have this day spoken, you have swept away every feeling in my bosom that could give me a moment's pain."

" Hush, Albert, hush !" said Clémence; " I know the kind of pain to which you allude. But you should never have entertained it. Love, Albert—the love of a heart such as yours ought never to doubt."

" But, dear Clémence," replied the Count, " is it possible for love to be satisfied while there is anything touching its affection concealed ?"

Clémence smiled, but shook her head ; and as she was about to reply, a single musket-shot was heard disturbing the tranquillity which had fallen over the camp. The Count listened, and his ear caught the distant sounds of " Alerte ! Alerte !" followed almost immediately afterwards by a more general discharge of musketry. Clémence had turned very pale.

" Fear not, dear Clémence," he said, " this is merely a night attack upon some of our quarters which will soon be repelled, for I have taken sufficient precautions. I will see what it is, and return immediately."

Thus saying he left her, and Clémence, with a heart full of strong and mingled emotions, leaned her head upon the little table and wept.

CHAPTER XXXII.

THE NIGHT ATTACK.

PARTICULAR orders had been issued by the Count de Morseinl that no offence should be given to the religious feelings of the Catholics; and, in issuing his commands for the occupation of the little chapel at the bottom of the hill, he had directed that the building appropriated to the ceremonies of the church should not be entered, except in case of necessity ; the porch and the sacristy being taken possession of, and the piece of consecrated ground around it, which was strongly walled, affording a sort of fort, in which the men constructed huts, or set up their tents.

They were accustomed, indeed, to abide in the forest, and found no difficulty or discomfort in taking their night's rest where they were. Three fine spreading yew trees, of unknown age and immense thickness, afforded a pleasant shelter to many ; and wine, which had been found plentifully in the hamlet above, as well as in a little town at no great distance, flowed liberally amongst a body of men who had fought hard and marched long since the morning.

There was a great difference, however, to be remarked between them and the religious insurgents of more northern countries ; for, though both the sterner fanaticism which characterised Scotland and England not long before, and the wilder imaginations and fanciful enthusiasms of the far south were occasionally to be found in individuals, the great mass were entirely and decidedly French, possessing the character of light, and somewhat thoughtless gaiety, so peculiar to that indifferent and laughter-loving nation.

Thus, though they had prayed earnestly, after having fought with determination in the cause which to them was the cause of conscience, they were now quite ready to forget both prayer and strife, till some other cause should reproduce the enthusiasm which gave vigour to either.

They sat in groups, then, round fires made out of an old apple tree or two, which they had pulled down, and drank the wine, which they had procured, it must be acknowledged, by various different means; but though they sang not, as perhaps they might have done under other circumstances, nothing else distinguished them from any other party of gay French soldiers carousing after a laborious day.

Herval and Virlay, as the commanders of that peculiar body, had taken possession of the little sacristy, and made themselves as comfortable therein as circumstances admitted. They were both somewhat inclined to scoff at, and do dishonour to everything connected with the church of Rome; but the commands of the Count were still sufficiently potent with them to prevent their indulging such feelings; and they remained conversing both over the events of the day, and also over past times, without any farther insult to the Roman-catholic faith than merely a scornful glance towards the vestments of the priests, the rich purple and lace of which excited their indignation even more than many articles of faith.

Several hours of the evening had thus worn away, and their conversation, far from being like that of their men without, was sad, dark, and solemn. The proximity of the convent had recalled to the mind of Herval the situation of her he had loved; and though they talked much of her fate, yet by some peculiar accident, which we shall not attempt to explain, that subject, dark and painful as it was, did not disturb his mental faculties as might have been expected. It produced, however, both on him and on Virlay, that dark and profound gloom, from which actions of a fierce and cruel nature more frequently have birth, than even from the keen and active excitement of strife and anger.

" Ay, and your child, too, Virlay," said Herval: " it is strange, is it not, that we have not yet found her? I should not wonder if she were in this very convent, up here upon the hill. The Count will not surely want you to leave it unsearched, when we march to-morrow?"

" It matters little whether he do or not," replied Virlay. " Search it I will; and that as soon as it be grey day-light. My child I will have, if she be in France: and, oh, Herval, how often, when we are near a monastery or a convent, do I long to put a torch to the gate of it, and burn it all to the ground!"

" No, no," cried Herval, " that would not do; you would be burning the innocent with the guilty."

" Ay, true," answered Virlay, " and thus I might burn my own poor child."

" Ay, or my Claire," replied Herval,—" that is to say, if she had been living, poor thing! You know they shot her, Paul. They shot her to the heart. But as I was saying, you might burn your own poor child, or the child of many a man that loves his as well as you do yours."

" I wonder if she be in there," said Paul Virlay. " Why should I not take ten or twelve men up, and make them open the gates, and see ?"

" Better wait till day," replied Herval; " better wait till day, Virlay. They have thousands of places that you might miss in the night. Hark! some one knocked at the door—Who is it? Come in !"

" Only a poor old woman," replied a voice from without, half opening the door; " only a poor old woman soliciting charity and peace ;" and a minute after, with timid and shaking steps, a woman, dressed in a grey gown like the portress of some convent, gradually drew herself within the doorway, and crossed herself twenty times in a minute, as she gazed upon the two Protestants sitting with the gloom of their late conversation still upon their faces.

" What do you want, old woman?" said Herval, sharply. " Don't you know that you risk a great deal by coming out at this hour? My men are not lambs, nor wood pigeons, nor turtle doves."

" Oh, Heaven bless you, Sir, I know that," replied the old lady, " and in a great fright I am too : but after all, I am the least in a fright of all the convent; and Sister Bridget—when she came to me with her teeth chattering in her head just after the men had come round and knocked at the door, and swore they would burn the place to the ground before morning—she talked so much about my courage, that I thought I had some, and agreed to come down; and then when she had got me out, she locked the wicket, and vowed I should not come in till I had been down to do the errand. So I came quietly on, and through the little gate, and got out of the way of the great gate, because I saw there were a number of fires there; and when I saw a light under the sacristy door, I said to myself, the officers will be in there, and they will be gentler and kinder——"

" Well, and what was your errand when you did come?" demanded Herval, sharply.

" Why, Sir," replied the old woman, " we have a young lady amongst us—" Paul Virlay started suddenly on his feet—" and a sweet young lady she is, too," continued the poor old nun, " as sweet a young lady and as pretty as ever I set my eyes on, and she told our good lady mother, the superior——"

" What is her name, woman?" cried Paul Virlay, advancing upon the poor sister, who retreated before him, but who still, with

woman's intuitive tact in such things, saw that she had got the
advantage. "What is her name, woman? It is my child! Oh,
Herval, it is my child!"

"So she said to my lady mother," continued the good nun, as
soon as she could make her voice heard; "so she said to my lady
mother, that she was sure that if her father was in the Count of
Morseiul's camp, he would come up in a minute with a guard of
men to protect the convent—especially if he knew that we had
been kind and good to her."

"Where is she?—Take me to her," cried Paul Virlay. "Woman,
take me to my child!—I will bring a guard,—I will protect you.
Where is my poor Margette?"

"Are you her father, then, Sir?" demanded the old woman.
"Is your name Monsieur Virlay."

"Yes, yes, yes!" cried he, impetuously: "I am Paul Virlay,
woman."

"Then, sir," she replied, "if you will bring up a guard and
undertake to protect the convent, you can have the young lady,
only pray ——"

"I will take a guard," cried he; "do not be afraid, woman!
Nobody shall hurt you. I will take a guard," he continued,
speaking to Herval, as if in excuse for taking away part of the men
from an important post, "I will take a guard for fear there should
be men up there, and they should want to keep Margette. The
Count said, too, that the only reason he did not occupy the
convent was, that he did not like to disturb the nuns. Now, when
they ask it themselves, I may well go. You can send for me in a
moment if I be wanted."

"There is no fear of that," replied Herval; "go, in God's name,
and see your child."

Paul Virlay hastened away, drawing the old woman by the arm
after him, while Herval remained behind shaking his head, with a
melancholy motion, and saying, "He will see his child again, and
she will cling round his neck and kiss his cheek, and they will be
happy: but I shall never see my poor Claire, as long as I linger on
upon this dull earth." He paused, and leaning his head upon his
hand, plunged into melancholy thought.

There was a little bustle without, while Virlay chose out such
men as he thought he could best depend upon, and then, that part
of the camp did not exactly sink into tranquillity, but the general
noise of the party became less. There was still loud talking
amongst the men; and wine seemed to have done its work too,
as in one or two instances, especially near the little sacristy, where
the wilder and less tractable of Herval's band had been placed,
that they might be under his own eye, the psalms with which the
evening had begun had now deviated into gayer songs; and he
sat and listened gravely, while one of the men near the door
carolled to his comrades a light ditty.

SONG.

In the deep woods, when I was young,
　Sly the happy, happy sunshine stole,
Under the green leaves, where the birds sung,
　And merry, merry music filled the whole;
　　　For Mary sat there,
　　　And all her care
Was to outsing the linnet,—Dear little soul!

Through the long grass, then would I steal,
　In music and sunshine to have my part.
That no one was coming, seemed she to feel,
　Till the warm kiss made the sweet maid start.
　　　Then would she smile,
　　　Through her blushes the while,
And vow she did not love me,—Dear little heart!

The sunshine is stealing still through the trees,
　Still in the green woods the gay birds sing,
But those leaves have fall'n by the wintry breeze,
　And many birds have dropped, that were then on the wing,
　　　All, all alone,
　　　Beneath the cold stone,
Lies my sweet Mary!—Poor little thing!

Herval wept bitterly. It was one of the songs of his own youth, which he had himself sung in many a joyous hour—a song which was the master-key to visions of early happiness, and touching in its light emptiness upon all the most painful themes of thought. The song, the dear song of remembered happiness, sung at that moment of painful bereavement, was like a soldier's child springing to meet a father returning from the wars, and unconsciously plunging the arrow head deeper into the wound from which he suffered.

As he thus sat and wept, he was suddenly roused by the sound of a single musket-shot at no great distance, and starting up, he listened, when loud cries from the other side of the chapel caught his ear, and he rushed out. All was dark; not a star was in the sky; but the air was free from vapour, and looking in the direction whence the sounds proceeded, he could see a dark body moving rapidly along the side of the hill, beyond the enclosure round the chapel. The shot which had been fired was not returned, and hurrying up to the spot as fast as possible, he clearly distinguished a column of infantry marching along at a quick pace in that direction, and evidently seeking to force its way between the convent and the chapel. There was none but a single sentry near—the man who had discharged his musket—and Herval exclaimed in agony, "Good God! how is this? They have been suffered to pass the morass and the stream!"

"I fired as soon I saw them," replied the man; "but Virlay

carried off all the men from down below there, and marched them up to the convent."

Herval struck his clenched hand against his brow, exclaiming, " Fool that I was to suffer him !" Then rushing back as fast as possible, he called all the rest of his troop to arms, and with the mere handful that assembled in a moment, rushed out by the gate through which the portress of the convent had entered, and attempted to cast himself in the way of the head of the enemy's column.

It was in vain, however, that he did so. A company of light infantry faced about, and met his first furious attack with a tremendous fire, while the rest of the force moved on. The sound, however, of the combat thus commenced, roused the rest of the camp : and the Count of Morseiul, himself on foot, and at the head of a considerable body of the most determined Huguenots, was advancing, ere five minutes were over, not to repel the attack of the enemy—for, by what he saw, Albert of Morseiul instantly became aware that, his camp being forced at the strongest point, it was in vain to hope that the King's army could be repulsed—but at least to cover the retreat of his troops with as little loss as possible.

All the confusion of a night combat now took place ; the hurrying up by the dull and doubtful light ; the cowardice that shows itself in many men when the eye of day is not upon them ; the rashness and emotion of others, who indeed are not afraid, but only agitated ; the mistakes of friends for foes, and foes for friends ; the want of all knowledge of which party is successful in those points where the strife is going on at a distance.

As far as it was possible in such circumstances, Albert of Morseiul restored some degree of order and regularity to the defence. Relying almost altogether upon his infantry, he held the royalists in check, while he sent orders to some of the inferior commanders to evacuate the camp in as orderly a manner as possible, gathering the horse together upon the brow of the hill, so as to be ready when the occasion served to charge and support the infantry. His particular directions were despatched to Monsieur du Bar to maintain his post to the last, as the Count well knew that the forces of the Chevalier d'Evran were sufficient to attack the Huguenot camp on both sides at once.

Such, indeed, had been the plan of the Chevalier ; but it was not followed correctly. He had placed himself at the head of the attack upon the side of the convent, as by far the most hazardous and difficult. The officer who commanded the other attack was a man of considerable skill, but he had with him the Intendant of the province, a personage as weak and presumptuous as he was cruel and bigoted : and insisting upon it, that the officer had made a mistake in regard to the way, he entangled him in the morass, and delayed him for more than an hour.

Had the attack on that side succeeded, as well as that on the side of the chapel, the little force of the Huguenots must have been absolutely annihilated; and had the attack there even commenced at the same time that it began on the other side, the disasters of that night must have been tenfold greater than they proved. As it was, the Count de Morseiul had time to offer at least some resistance, and to organize his retreat. A horse was soon brought to him, and perceiving by the firing on the flank of the enemy's column that Herval and his men were striving desperately to retrieve the error which had been committed, he called up a small body of cavalry, and making a gallant charge at their head, drove back some of the infantry companies that interposed between himself and the chapel, and opened a communication with Herval and the men. Giving orders to the officer in command of the horse to make another rapid charge, but not to entangle his men too far, the Count himself rode down to Herval, to ascertain what was proceeding in that quarter. He found the man covered with blood and gunpowder, raging like a wolf in the midst of a flock.

"Herval," he exclaimed, "a great mistake has been committed. A handful of men could have defended that bridge against an army."

"I know it, Count—I know it," replied Herval. "I have been a fool. Virlay has been a madman. I should never have trusted him by himself. It is time I should die."

"It is rather time, Herval," replied the Count, "that you should live, and exert your good sense to remedy what is amiss. Do you not see that by spending your strength here you are doing no good, and losing your men every minute? Gather them together: quick! and follow me. We want support, there, upon the hill. The chapel is untenable now. Quick! lose not a moment. Good God!" he said, "they are not charging as I ordered, and in another moment we shall be cut off!"

It was indeed as he said. The young officer, to whom he had given the command, was shot through the head at the very moment that he was about to execute it. The charge was not made; the body which had been driven back by the Count were rallied by the Chevalier d'Evran; the infantry of the Huguenots, which had been guarding the heights, wavered before the superior force brought against them; and by the time that Herval's men were collected, a large body of foot interposed between the Count de Morseiul and the spot where he had left his troops. Nothing remained but to lead round Herval's little force by the hollow way on the edge of the morass, and climbing the steeper part of the hill, by the road that led to the little hamlet and farm-houses, to rejoin the principal body of the Protestants there, and to make one more effort to hold the hamlet against the advancing force of the royalists, till Monsieur du Bar had time to draw off his troops.

Ere the Count, however, could reach the ground where he had fixed his own head-quarters, both the infantry and cavalry, which he had left, had been driven back, and, by a terrible oversight, instead of retiring upon the hamlet, had taken the way to the right, along which the other bodies of troops had been ordered to retreat. The royalists thus, at the time that the Count arrived, were pouring in amongst the cottages and farm-houses; and when he reached the little knoll immediately behind the house, where he had left Clémence de Marly, he was instantly assailed by a tremendous fire from behind the walls of the court-yard, and the lower windows of the house itself. He had no troops with him but Herval's band, and a small body of foot which arrived at that moment to his assistance from the Marquis du Bar, and he paused for an instant in agony of heart, knowing and feeling that it was utterly hopeless to attempt to retake the farm-house, and enable Clémence to effect her escape. The grief and pain of a whole life seemed summed up in that one moment.

"I will not," he cried, in the rashness of despair—"I will not leave her without an effort!"

Herval was by his side. "Sir," he said, "I must not live over this night. Let us advance at all risks."

The Count gave the order, and the men advanced gallantly, though the enemy's fire was terrible. They were actually scaling the wall of the court-yard, when suddenly a fire was opened upon them from the houses and walls on either side. Herval fell over, amidst the enemy; the Count's horse dropped at once under him, and he felt himself drawn forcibly out from beneath the dying animal, and carried along by the men in full retreat from that scene of slaughter.

"Here is a horse, Count,—here is a horse!" cried a voice near him. "Mount, quick, and oh, take care of my poor girl! She is on with the troops before. I have lost you the battle, and know what must come of it."

The Count turned, and saw Paul Virlay by his side; but before he could reply, the man left the bridle in his hand, and rushed into the midst of the enemy.

Springing on the charger's back, the Count gazed round him. Herval's band was all in confusion; but beginning to rally upon the body of infantry sent by Du Bar. The hamlet was in full possession of the enemy: the only means of communication between Du Bar and the troops that were retreating was along the hill side. Albert of Morseiul saw that if he did not maintain that line, his gallant friend would be cut off, and, for the moment, casting from his mind all the other bitter anxieties that preyed upon it, he hastened to occupy a little rising ground, terribly exposed, indeed, to the enemy's fire, but which would protect the flank of his friend's little corps, while they joined the rest who were in retreat. That he was just in time was proved to Albert of Morseiul, by the sound of a loud cannonade, which commenced from the very direction of Du Bar's quarters; and, sending that officer orders to retreat directly, he remained, for twenty minutes, repelling every charge of the enemy; and, by the example of his own desperate courage and perfect self-command, seeming to inspire his men with resolution unconquerable. In the meantime, the Marquis du Bar retreated before the other body of royalists which had now come up, and having seen his men in comparative safety, rode back, with a small troop of horse, to aid the Count in covering the retreat. The royalists now, however, had gained their object; the camp of the Huguenots was in their hands; the slaughter on both sides had been dreadful, considering the short space of time which the strife had lasted; the country beyond was difficult and defensible, and the order for stopping further pursuit was given as soon as no more resistance was made in the Huguenot camp.

CHAPTER XXXIII.

THE ROYALIST CAMP.

" I am astonished, sir, that you should presume to interfere," said the Chevalier d'Evran, speaking to the Intendant of the province, whom he had found on riding down to the post of the second in command, in order to ascertain what was the cause of the attack having been so long delayed in that quarter—" I am astonished that you should presume to interfere at all. The weak gentlemen who have hitherto been commanding in this country, have been indulgent to such insolence: but you will find very different consequences if you attempt to practise it upon me."

" Insolence, sir!—Insolence!" exclaimed the Intendant, foaming with rage and mortified pride at being thus addressed in the presence of many hundreds of witnesses. " Insolence in me!—Why, who am I, sir? Am I not the intendant of justice, police, and finance in this province?"

" Yes, sir, insolence!" replied the Chevalier d'Evran, sternly. " You are the intendant of justice, police, and finance; but before I assumed the command of the King's forces in this province, you yourself had required martial law to be proclaimed, so that you not only put every one else under the authority of the military power, but yourself also; and, by Heaven, if you stare in my face in that manner one moment longer, I will have you hanged up to yonder tree.—Bring a drum hither," he continued, turning to an officer who stood near, " and summon four competent persons from the regiments of Lorraine and Berry.—We will soon see who is to command here."

The unfortunate intendant turned as pale as ashes; for the gallantry and decision which the Chevalier d'Évran had shewn since he assumed the command, were of a very impressive character, and gave weight to his threats. The officer who had laid the complaint against him, however, now interfered. "For God's sake, General," he said, "have mercy upon this poor man, and consider what will be the result of calling a drum-head court-martial."

"I should always be very willing, sir," replied the Chevalier, drawing up his fine person to its full height, to attend to your recommendations; but, sir, in the course of this night and the preceding day, I have obtained two great and signal successes over the great body of insurgents; and I think that those successes will fully justify me in the eyes of the King, for punishing, with such authority as is vested in my hands, the person to whom we may attribute that our success was not completed by the annihilation of the Huguenot party in the province. If the intendant chooses immediately to make a humble apology for what has passed, and to promise in the most solemn manner never to interfere in any one thing in my camp, or under my command, I will so far overlook the matter for the time, as not to carry this extreme measure into execution against him at once. But, in the meantime, I will hold it suspended over his head, and if required, execute it on the moment."

The apologies and promises were as full and ample as the Chevalier could demand; and, leaving strict orders that the worthy intendant should be kept in a sort of honourable surveillance in the camp, the Chevalier turned his horse's head, and rode back with his staff towards the village, smiling slightly over what had just passed, for, to say the truth, he had been acting a part much more harsh and severe than he was inclined to pursue in reality. The truth is, that after the engagement of the preceding morning, the intendant had shewn some disposition to take possession of one or two prisoners who had fallen into the royalists' hands, for the purpose of employing the rack and the wheel in their conversion; but the Chevalier, having determined from the first to put a stop to such measures, had evaded all discussion for the time, very sure that ere long the intendant would give him an opportunity of depriving him, at least for the time, of all authority in the province.

The smile, however, was soon succeeded by a somewhat more anxious expression; for knowing as he did that Clémence de Marly was in the camp of the Huguenots, he was not a little apprehensive of what might have been her fate in the course of the struggle of that night. He had given particular instructions regarding her, had made it so fully understood, that he would have no unnecessary bloodshed, and had exhorted his troops and inferior officers so eloquently to regard the Protestants merely as erring brothers, as soon

as the arms were out of their hands, that he felt little or no apprehension of any excesses being committed after the engagement. As
soon, then, as he had ascertained that Mademoiselle de Marly was
in the farm-house on the top of the hill, and was perfectly safe, he
contented himself with sending a message to her, telling her that he
would visit her in the morning, and begging her in the meantime
to put her mind completely at ease. He then proceeded to investigate the amount of his own loss, and that of the Huguenots. Nearly
an equal number had fallen on each side; but the army of the Chevalier d'Evran could afford to lose a thousand men without any
serious diminution of its strength, while the same loss on the part
of the Protestant force, reduced it in a lamentable degree.

"Now," thought the Chevalier, when he heard the result of the
inquiries which he had caused to be made, "if I can but drive
Albert of Morseiul to the sea, and force him to embark with the
most determined of his sect, while the others lay down their arms
and conform, we shall do very well. These battles were necessary
to dishearten the desperate fellows, and to give me power to do
them good, and treat them mercifully. But we may change our
system now, and press them hard without losing the lives of gallant
men. What this old Cecil tells me of the mistake about the liberation, may, if properly shewn, mitigate a part of the King's anger towards Albert; but it will never do the whole, and I fear flight is his
only resource. This offer that he has made, however, stands desperately in the way; and yet, it must be communicated to the King.
I dare not conceal it."

While he thus thought, sitting in the room of one of the cottages,
information was brought him that one of the wounded Huguenots,
who was kept with other prisoners in a barn hard by, was very
anxious to see him.

"I will come immediately," he replied to the officer; and then
sitting down, he wrote a brief despatch to Louvois, in which he detailed all the events which had occurred; but at the same time,
knowing the views of the minister, he intimated that the only means
of keeping the extent of the insurrection from the King's knowledge, and from general publicity throughout the whole of Europe,
would be to give him the full power of pardoning all men on laying
down their arms. He begged the minister to believe that he had
not the slightest desire whatsoever that the little services he had
performed should be reported to Louis XIV.; but at the same time
he pointed out that those services could not be ultimately beneficial,
unless the power which he demanded was granted to him, and all
other authority in the province superseded for at least one month.
He felt very sure that this would be acceded to by Louvois, as that
minister had become greatly alarmed, and had openly expressed to
the young commander his anxiety lest the extent of the revolt which
had taken place in consequence of measures he had advised, should

ruin him for ever with the King. The Chevalier trusted, also—although he was obliged, in the end of his epistle, to state the proposal made by the Count de Morseiul—that the powers granted by the minister would be such as to enable him to serve that nobleman.

When this despatch was concluded, and sent off, he inquired where the person was who had expressed a wish to see him, and was led to a small out-house close by the farm in which Clémence abode. The door, which was padlocked, and at which a sentry appeared, was opened to give him admission, and he found, stretched upon piles of straw on the floor of the building, two or three men, apparently in a dying state, and another seated in a somewhat extraordinary attitude in one corner of the shed. The sight was very horrible; the straw in many parts was stained with blood, and anguish was legibly written on the pale countenances of the dying.

" Who was the prisoner that wished to speak with me?" said the Chevalier, going in; but they each answered by claiming to be heard: one demanding a little water, one asking to be taken into the open air, and one, who before the words had fully passed his lips lay a corpse upon the straw, asking pardon and life, and promising obedience and conversion. The Chevalier ordered everything that could make them comfortable to be supplied as far as possible, adding some sharp reproaches to his own people for the state in which he found the wounded; and he then said, " But there was some one who, as I understood, wished to speak with me more particularly."

" It was I," said the man who was sitting down in the corner, at once starting up into the likeness of Jerome Riquet; while at the same moment, another faint voice from the farther part of the building, said, " It was I, General. I told the officer who came here, that I would fain see you about the Count de Morseiul."

" Riquet," said the Chevalier, " I will attend to you presently. You seem well, and unhurt; answer me three questions, and I may say something that will satisfy you in return. Have you been engaged in this unfortunate business simply as the servant of the Count de Morseiul?"

" As nothing else, upon my word, sir," replied Riquet.

" Are you a Catholic or a Protestant?"

" As Catholic as salt fish on a Friday," replied Riquet. " Surrounded on all sides by heretics, I was at one time in great fear for myself, like a man in a city where there is a plague. But bless you, sir, I found it was not catching, and here I am, more Catholic than ever."

" Have you, then, in any instance, borne arms in this war?" demanded the Chevalier.

" No, on my honour, Chevalier," replied the valet. " No arms have I borne except a shaving-brush, a razor, a pair of tweezers, and a tooth-pick."

" Well, then," replied the Chevalier, " I can promise you pardon ; but remember you are a prisoner on parole. Do you give me your word that you will not try to escape ?"

" Lord bless you, sir," replied the man, " I would not escape for the world. I am with the winning side. You don't suppose Riquet's a fool, to go over to the poor devils whom you're driving into the sea !"

" Scoundrel !" said a deep but faint voice from the other-side of the building; and, telling Riquet to bring the light with him, the Chevalier advanced to the spot, where, stretched upon the straw, in the most remote corner of the shed, lay the unfortunate Armand Herval, dying from the effects of at least twenty wounds. As soon as the eyes of the wounded man fell upon Riquet, he exclaimed, angrily,—" Get thee hence, traitor!—Let me not see your face, scoundrel!—To abandon thus your noble lord at the first moment of misfortune !"

" You mistake, monsieur," replied Riquet, quietly—" I am not a bit more of a scoundrel than you are, Monsieur Herval, nor, indeed, of a traitor either. Every one serves his lord in his own way, Master Herval, that's all. You in your way, and I in mine. If you had waited a little, to hear what I had to say to the Chevalier, you would have seen that I was quite as ready to make sacrifices for my lord as yourself."

" Herval !" said the Chevalier, as he listened to their conversation; " that name is surely familiar to me."

" Well it might be," answered Riquet; " for I dare say, my lord must have told you, Monsieur le Chevalier, this man, or I am much mistaken, would have killed the King himself, if my lord had not prevented him."

" Indeed !" demanded the Chevalier. " Can we get any proof of this ?"

" Proof, sir !" replied the dying man ; " it was on that account I sent for you. The Count de Morseiul is ruined ; and the cause of the reformed church is over; and all this evil has happened through my fault. I have heard, too, that he has offered to surrender himself to the axe, in order to buy safety for the rest of us. But surely the King—let him be as great a tyrant as he may—will not murder the man that saved his life."

" The King, sir, is no tyrant," replied the Chevalier; " but a generous and noble master to those who are obedient and loyal: even to the disobedient he is most merciful; and if this fact could be made known to him, and proved beyond all doubt, I feel perfectly convinced that he would not only pardon the Count de Morseiul for his past errors, but shew him some mark of favour, in gratitude for what he has done."

" The King does know it," replied Herval, sharply; " the King must know it; for I have heard that the whole papers of Hatréaumont fell into the hands of Louvois; and I have myself seen that foul tiger's name written to an order for my arrest, as one of Hatréaumont's accomplices."

"But that does not prove," replied the Chevalier, "that either the King or Louvois knew of this act of the Count's."

"It does prove it," replied the dying man; "for the only letter I ever wrote to Hatréaumont in my life was to tell him that I had failed in my purpose of killing the tyrant; that everything had gone fair till the Count de Morseiul came in between me and him, and declared, that I should take his life first. I told him all, everything—how I got into the gardens of Versailles at night, and hid under the terrace where the King walked alone—how yon babbling fool betrayed my purpose to the Count, and he came and prevented me doing the deed I ought to have done, even if I had taken his life first. I told him all this, and I cursed the Count of Morseiul in my madness, over again and again—and now the man whose life he saved, is seeking to bring him to the block."

"This is extraordinary and important," said the Chevalier: "I cannot believe that the King knows it. Louvois must have kept it from his ears. Will you make a deposition of this, my good fellow, as early to-morrow as we can get proper witnesses and a notary?"

"Early to-morrow?" said the man, faintly—"early to-morrow, Chevalier? I shall never see a to-morrow. Now is your only moment, and as for witnesses, quick, get paper and pen and ink. There is not half-an-hour's life in me. If you had come when first I sent, there would have been plenty of time, but now every moment is a loss."

"Quick, Riquet," cried the Chevalier, "bid the officer at the door run to my quarters, and bring down pen and ink and paper, without a moment's delay."

Riquet lost no time, and the Chevalier endeavoured, as far as possible, to keep Herval quiet till the means of writing were brought. The dying man would go on speaking, however, but with his voice becoming lower and lower, and his ideas evidently in some degree confused. Once or twice he spoke as if he were at Versailles, and in the presence of the King; then seemed as if he fancied himself conversing with Hatréaumont; and then again pronounced the name of Claire more than once, and talked of happiness. When Riquet returned, however, with the materials for writing, he had still strength and recollection enough to commence his declaration in a formal manner.

"I, Armand Herval," he said, "do hereby declare, and on the bed of death affirm most solemnly, that had it not been that the Count de Morseiul prevented me, I would have shot the King of France, upon the terrace at Versailles, after the play, on the night before the arrest of the Chevalier de Rohan, and that all I said was perfectly true, in a letter which was written by me to Monsieur de

Hatréaumont, dated on the—I cannot recollect the day," he added, in a lower tone; "it seems as if a mist had come over that part of my memory."

"Never mind," said the Chevalier; "go on, my good friend, go on; the date is unimportant."

"Was it the twenty-fourth or the twenty-fifth?" continued the man. "I cannot recollect for the life of me, your majesty. It's a short life, too. Mine will soon be spent, and Claire's is all gone——"

He spoke very faintly indeed; and the Chevalier said, "You forget, my friend—you forget. We were talking of the Count de Morseiul."

"Ah!" cried the man, with a greater effort, and starting up on the straw—"ah, so we were! What a fool I am! Write it down quick—write it down quick! but take your fingers off my throat—take your fingers off my throat! I cannot speak if you stop my breath! What's the use of putting out the light? Why do you put out the light? Oh, Heaven, it is death—it is death!" and falling back upon the straw, the strong frame shook for a moment, as if an ague had seized him, and then all was still.

The Chevalier d'Evran shut his teeth close, saying, "This is unfortunate. However, you are a witness, Riquet, to all that he said."

"Lord bless you, noble sir," replied the valet, "nobody will believe a word that I say. I should consider my character ruined for ever if there was anybody in all Europe that would believe me upon my oath."

"I had forgot," said the Chevalier, drily; "your character is in no danger, I believe, on that score. But my word will be believed, and my voice, at least, shall be heard."

"Well, sir," replied Riquet, perhaps a little piqued at the Chevalier's reply, "let me add my voice too; for, though they may believe me in nothing else, they may, perhaps, believe me in a confession which will go to twist my own neck. I wish to be sent to the King, sir; though if you can find out when he is in a good humour, I should prefer it. But my object is to inform him that it was altogether my fault, and my foolishness, and my crime, that prevented the Count de Morseiul from going to Versailles as soon as he was liberated from the Bastille to throw himself at the King's feet. If it had not been for that aforesaid foolishness of mine, he would never have come hither—would never have led the rebels at all, and, most likely, by this time, would have been as high in the King's good graces as ever."

"I have heard all this before," said the Chevalier. "But are you positively resolved, my good friend, to go voluntarily and make confession of all these things? Do you remember the consequences?—do you think of the risks?"

"No, sir," replied Riquet, "I do quite the contrary. I try to forget them all as fast as possible, being resolved to go at any rate; and therefore judging that the less I think about risks and consequences, the better."

"By Heaven, thou art right," replied the Chevalier; "and thou shalt have a bottle of Burgundy, if there be one in the camp, to keep warm thy good philosophy. See, there is the grey of the morning coming in, and I may well go away satisfied with having found one man in the world who is not so great a scoundrel as I thought him."

The Chevalier returned to the hut in which he had established his quarters, and cast himself down for an hour's repose; but before the daylight had been long in the sky, he was on foot again, and at the door of the farm-house which contained Clémence de Marly. He was immediately admitted; and, strange as it may seem, if the Count de Morseiul had witnessed that meeting, it would certainly have wrung his heart more than the loss of a great battle. The royalist commander advanced at once to his fair prisoner, and putting his arms slightly round her, kissed her cheek without any apparent reluctance on her part; and her first exclamation was— "Oh, Louis, I am glad to see you safe! You know not how my heart is torn!"

"I dare say it is, my pretty Clémence," replied the Chevalier, in his usual light tone; "but you, who have been doing nothing else but tearing other people's hearts for the last five years, must take your turn now. You have placed me in a terrible predicament, however, thoughtless girl," he added. "You are obstinate as an Arragonese mule about this matter of religion, and will not be contented till you have got yourself roasted in this world as preparatory to——"

"But tell me, Louis—tell me about him!" demanded Clémence. "Is he safe? Has he escaped from this awful night?"

"I suppose you mean Morseiul, by he and him," said the Chevalier; "and if so, he is safe, as far as I know. He has escaped— that is to say, he has not been taken, thank God, though one time he was very near it; for, by the flash of the guns, I saw his face in the middle of our men: but I dare say now, Clémence, that you would a thousand-fold rather have me killed than this heretic of yours?"

"Do not be unkind, Louis," replied Clémence. "I would of course rather have neither of you killed; but now that you have got me, tell me what is to be my fate?"

"Why, that question is difficult to answer," said the Chevalier. "Heaven knows I did not want you, madam. I was obliged to write you a formal summons to return, for mere decency's sake; but I certainly never expected you would obey it. You might have said, No, silly girl, without telling all the world that you had turned Huguenot—all for the love of a gallant knight."

" Nonsense, Louis! Do speak seriously," replied Clémence: " you very well know I was what you call a Huguenot long before."

" Not quite, Clémence—not quite!" cried the Chevalier: " you were what may be called Huguenoting. But this rash and imprudent determination of declaring your feelings, doubts, or whatever they may be, at the very moment when the sword of persecution is drawn, was, indeed, very silly, Clémence. What is to be done now is rendered doubly difficult, and I suppose I must of course connive at your escape. We must take means to have an intimation conveyed for some trading vessels to hover about the coast, to give you an opportunity of getting away till this fierce bigotry has gone by. It will not last long; and, in a year or two, I doubt not, exiles will be permitted to return. The only difficulty will be to have the ships opportunely; but I think I can manage that."

" Oh, do, do, Louis!" exclaimed Clémence, eagerly. " That is all that can be desired; and pray try to persuade Albert to fly at once."

" Nay, nay," replied the Chevalier, laughing, " that must not be my task, Clémence. On that subject I dare not say a word. But you may well do what you will. I will take care that the means of flight to another country shall be provided for you, and you may take with you any one who is willing to go."

" But then," exclaimed Clémence, " I must have the opportunity of persuading him."

" Certainly," exclaimed the Chevalier: " the first thing you have to do is to get out of my camp as fast as you can. I would not have you three days here for the world; for, as affairs go at present, I cannot answer that the power of protecting you will be left to me for three days. However," he added, after a moment's thought, " to-day you must stay and march on with us, and before to-morrow, I trust I shall be able to put you under such protection as will ensure you safety and support in your flight; and now, pretty maid, I must leave you. We shall begin to march about noon. In the meantime, there is a courier going to Montaigu, so send off thither for whatever you may need to make you comfortable. An easy horse shall be ready for you; and if at any time you may feel yourself inclined to gallop away, you may take him with you as a present from me. By the way, little heretic," he added, when he got to the door, " you will want money for your peregrinations."

" Oh, no," replied Clémence, " I have plenty—I have plenty, I assure you. I have near two hundred double louis which I took to the prison in hopes——."

" Little do you know what you may want, silly girl," replied the Chevalier. " Why, one of these very merchant ships may demand the half of that for carrying you over. " Here," he added, drawing forth a leathern purse embroidered in gold, " I am not aware how

much there is here; but you must take it too; and if by any un-
foreseen circumstance you should need more when in England,
draw on me what they call a bill of exchange."

Clémence took the money without ceremony, as if it were a
mere matter of course, and only added, "Come and see me again
before we march, Louis."

The Chevalier nodded his head, and left her.

CHAPTER XXXIV.

THE LAST EFFORTS.

To describe the military manœuvres which took place during the
three or four following days, would be neither amusing nor instructive to the reader. Suffice it to say, that the small force of
the Count de Morseiul diminished as he retreated, while the army
of the Chevalier d'Evran was increased by the arrival of two new
regiments. The latter had thus an opportunity of extending his
line, and frustrating a vigorous attempt on the part of the Count to
cut his way into Brittany. Every effort that the Protestant leader
made to bring to his aid the various nobles who had promised very
soon to join him, only showed him that the estimation which he
had formed of the degree of vigour and unanimity to be expected
from the Huguenots was but too accurate. Almost all those determined and daring leaders of the lower orders, who had given
energy and activity to all the movements of the insurgents, had
fallen in the preceding skirmishes. Herval was heard of no more;
Paul Virlay had been seen by one of the soldiers to fall by a shot
through the head towards the close of the last affair; and at length,
with not more than five hundred men under his command, Albert
of Morseiul found himself shut in between a force of eight thousand
men and the sea. The only consolation that he had, was to hear
that Clémence de Marly was safe; and his only hope, that some
vessels from Rochelle, for which he had despatched a shallop in
haste, might be tempted by the large sum he offered, to hasten
round and carry off a certain portion of his troops, comprising the
principal leaders, while the rest laid down their arms, and he himself surrendered to the fate that awaited him.

Such were his plans and purposes when the last day of the insurrection dawned upon the world; and we must pause for an
instant to describe the situation of his little force on that eventful
morning.

There is upon that coast a small rocky island, not so high as the
celebrated Mont so Michel, which is on the opposite side of the

peninsula of Brittany, but in almost every other respect similar to that famous rock. At the time we speak of, this island was fortified, and the guns of the castle commanded almost entirely the small bay in which it was situated. At low water the island becomes a peninsula, being joined to the land, like the Mont St. Michel, by a narrow neck of land, along the top of which there ran a paved causeway, covered entirely by the sea to the depth of five or six feet at the time of high water. The commandant of the fort was a Protestant gentleman who had distinguished himself in some degree in the service. He had been raised, and greatly favoured by the influence of the Counts of Morseiul, and owed his post to them. He had not only promised to co-operate with the young Count in the commencement of the unfortunate revolt, but he had sent him some assistance, and a large quantity of ammunition; and when the Count found that he was cut off from forcing his way into Brittany on the one hand, or reaching Saintonge on the other, he had shaped his course past Montaigu, towards the little bay in which this island was situated, and had succeeded in reaching it, notwithstanding the efforts of the royalist corps to prevent him.

Opposite to the island was a small village, on a high bank above the sea-shore. It possessed a large church, and two or three walled farm-houses; and during one half of the night after his arrival, the Count toiled with the country people, who were principally Protestants, to throw up breastworks and plant palisades, so as to fortify the village in as strong a manner as possible. Four cannon, which were all that he possessed, were planted to command the principal road leading to the village; and ere morning, the whole defences were brought to such a condition as to enable the little band of Protestants to offer a determined and lengthened resistance, should they be driven to do so.

Was it then, it may be asked, the purpose of the Count to offer that resistance? It certainly was not; but feeling perfectly sure that the Chevalier d'Evran was disposed to grant the Protestants the most lenient terms consistent with his duty, he took these measures in order to give him the best excuse for treating with the insurgents, and granting them a favourable capitulation. "If," he thought, "the Chevalier can show to the King that it would have cost him two or three thousand of his best troops to overcome or slaughter a poor body of five hundred men, Louis is too wise and too good a soldier himself not to hold him perfectly justified in granting the mildest terms."

When all was completed, the Count cast himself down to rest, and slept for some time from utter exhaustion. By the first ray of morning, however, he was upon the shore, looking towards the sea, and beheld, to his no small joy and satisfaction, three vessels, at the distance of about four or five miles, standing off and on, as if waiting for the tide to enter the bay. The tide, however, though not quite at the ebb, had sunk so low that there was no chance of their being able to come in till it had quite gone down and risen again; and Albert of Morseiul looked with anxiety for the passing of six or seven hours, which must thus elapse.

His anxiety now led him to the other side of the village; and going to one of the farm houses, situated at the corner of a small cart-road, which he had barricaded, he went up to a window on the first floor, and looked over the wide view that sloped away below. There he beheld what he had expected to find, the camp of the Chevalier d'Evran, hemming him in on all sides. The distance between the village and the first tents was about two miles, so that at any time, without more than half an hour's notice, the attack upon his little fortress might commence. He was quite prepared, it is true, and doubted not to be able to maintain his post for many hours, knowing that his men would fight with the energy of despair. But no movement whatsoever in the royalist camp indicated any great haste to attack him. There were no groups of officers busily reconnoitring; there were no regiments drawn up as if to march to the assault; and the only moving objects within sight were two files of soldiers marching along to relieve the guard at different points of the camp. All this was satisfactory to an experienced eye like that of the Count de Morseiul; and well knowing his opponent, he judged that the Chevalier was waiting for some reply from Paris, ere he gave any answer to the terms which he, the Count, had suggested.

He paused, therefore, for nearly twenty minutes, gazing over the scene, when suddenly, from a point of the camp where nothing seemed stirring before, a little group of persons on horseback drew out, and rode swiftly towards the village. The moment after the Count perceived that two of those persons were clad in women's garments; and the rapidity with which they came, showed him that they were fearful of being stopped. Going down from the window in haste, he sprang upon horseback, and with the attendants, who were waiting for him below, rode out upon the side of the hill, in order to assist the fugitives in case of need; but no sign of pursuit took place till one half of the distance or more had been passed by the little party; and the Count dismounting about a quarter of a mile from the village, watched their coming with eager eyes and a beating heart, as he recognised the form of Clémence de Marly. When she was beyond all risk of being overtaken, a small party of cavaliers issued forth from another part of the camp, and rode on towards the village, but slowly; but they were still at more than a mile's distance when Clémence was in the arms of her lover, and weeping upon his bosom. He led her in as fast as possible, followed by the maid Maria, and no less a person than Jerome Riquet, who seemed to have found the breaking of his word so strong a temptation, that he could not resist it.

A rumour had spread amongst the Protestants in the place, that something of interest was proceeding without; and when the Count and Clémence turned towards the village, they found that their meeting had been witnessed by many eyes. But in the faces of those they passed, Albert of Morseiul read courage brightened, and resolution strengthened, by that which they had just seen; and there was not a man within that little encampment whose heart did not feel elevated and confirmed by witnessing the bursting forth of those tender and ennobling feelings, which ever, when pure and true, dignify man's spirit, and brighten his mind.

When they were within the barriers, the Count turned for a moment to look at the other group which had drawn out from the camp; but it did not seem that they were in pursuit of Clémence, for they shaped their course along the road towards the principal entrance of the village; and when the Count turned, he clearly saw them displaying a flag of truce. He led Clémence into the house where he had taken up his head-quarters, however, and saying a few soothing words, left her, to see what was the intelligence which the Chevalier's envoys conveyed. As he walked down, he met a messenger coming to demand his presence at the barrier; and on approaching it, he found waiting, in the guard-house, the old English officer, Sir Thomas Cecil, with one or two French gentlemen, with whom he was slightly acquainted.

"Monsieur de Morseiul," said the old Englishman, "I have been charged by Major-General the Chevalier d'Evran to communicate to you the only terms which he is permitted by the King to grant under the circumstances in which you respectively stand. He was long in hopes that those terms would have been more favourable than they are, and they are very painful to me to announce. But as you conveyed to him a message through me, he thought that I ought to undertake to bear the reply."

"I thank you, my dear sir," replied the Count, "most sincerely for undertaking the task. But, as a preliminary, let me tell you before these gentlemen who have come with you, as well as before Monsieur du Bar here, and my own friends around me, that the only terms which I will accept are those which I notified to the Chevalier d'Evran through you—namely, permission for any one hundred of my friends of the reformed religion to retire from France numolested; a free pardon to all the rest, except myself, on laying down their arms; and a promise that they shall be permitted to exercise their religion in private without annoyance. On these conditions, we will immediately lay down our arms, and I will surrender myself at discretion to his majesty's pleasure."

"No, no!—No, no!" cried several voices amongst the Protestants; "we cannot submit to that. We will die at our post with arms in our hands, rather than that the Count shall be sacrificed."

"My good friends," replied the Count, "that is a personal matter altogether. I have made the best terms that I can for you, and I

c c

have done what I judge right for myself; knowing that the only
way of dealing with his majesty is to throw myself upon his magnanimity."

The old Englishman wiped away a tear from his eye. "I am
sorry to say, sir," he rejoined, "that I cannot even mention such
favourable terms as those. On condition of your immediately
laying down your arms, the Chevalier d'Evran, in the name of the
King, offers the following:—Permission for every one not absolutely a subject of France to leave the country unmolested. Free
pardon to all but the actual leaders of the revolt, specified in the
following list. They must unconditionally surrender to the King's
pleasure, and trust to his mercy."

The list apparently contained about fifty names; at the head of
which stood that of the Count of Morseiul. The Count looked
round upon the Protestant gentlemen by whom he was surrounded.
On the countenances of all but one or two there was awe, but not
fear. As the only reply needful, the Marquis du Bar laid his finger
upon the hilt of his sword; and the Count, turning to Sir Thomas
Cecil, said, "You perceive, sir, that it is utterly impossible we can
accede to this demand. I know not whether it has been made
under any mistaken impression; but when I offered what I did
offer through you to the Chevalier d'Evran, I was just as certain
that we should be reduced to the situation in which we are at
present as I am now—nay, expected it to be worse than it is. We
can but die, sir; and I have not the slightest objection to lead you
round the preparations which I have made for resisting to the last;
so that if our blood must be shed, and the Chevalier is determined
to sacrifice the lives of a large body of our royal master's troops, he
may be satisfied that he cannot carry this position without the loss
of two or three thousand men."

"It is not necessary, Count. It is not necessary," replied the
old officer. "The Chevalier has no choice; the terms are dictated
by higher authority; and all that he can do farther than signify
those terms to you, is to grant you five hours to consider of them.
If you like to accept a truce for that time you may take it."

The Count felt not a little surprise at this indulgence, but he
took care to express none; and accepting the truce willingly,
suffered the old officer to depart. Several of the young royalist
officers, whom he had known in the army, wrung his hand as they
went away, and besought him, with kindly feelings, to think well of
what he was about. One of them, however, ere he went, whispered
a more important word in his ear.

"There are ships out at sea," he said. "You and the other
leaders may get off before the five hours are out."

The Count took no notice, but wished him Good-bye; and
returning with Monsieur du Bar and the rest of the officers, he
held a brief consultation with them in the saloon of the little inn.

"Had we more boats," he said, "the matter would be easily managed. But there are but two on the shore, which will not carry out above twenty of us. However, my good friends, it becomes necessary to take some prompt resolution. I have begun to be somewhat doubtful to-day of Le Luc, who commands in the fort. He has sent me no answer to my note of last night; and though I do not believe that he would be so great a scoundrel, after all his promises, as to turn against us, yet I must ascertain decidedly what are his intentions; for he might sink the boats as they passed under his guns. If he be still friendly to us, and willing really to aid us, we are safe; for while the soldiery lay down their arms and surrender upon promise of free pardon, you, gentlemen, who all of you, I find, are upon this long list of proscription, can march along the causeway into the fort, and embark in the ships that lie out there. If, on the contrary, we find him a traitor, we must make the boats hold as many as they will, and take the chance of the scoundrel firing upon them. I shall only claim to have one place reserved in one of the boats."

"Two," said Du Bar; "surely two, Morseiul. Did I not see a lady?"

"It is for her I speak," replied the Count. "Du Bar, in pity do not urge me in matters where my resolution is taken. I have pangs and agony at my heart sufficient at this moment, believe me, to be spared that of refusing a friend.—Now then, gentlemen," he added, after a moment's pause, "let five of you accompany me along the causeway—which must be passable by this time—to speak to Monsieur Le Luc. If you will mount your horses, I will be down with you in an instant," and he went up to take one hurried embrace of her he loved, and to explain to her what had happened, and what was proposed, concealing from her, as far as he could, the dangers and difficulties of their situation; but concealing from her still more carefully his own purpose of surrendering at discretion.

When this was done, he went down, and finding the other gentlemen ready, sprang upon his horse, without noticing that a multitude of the inferior Protestants had gathered round, and seemed to be watching them with somewhat suspicious eyes.

The sea had not quite left the causeway dry, except in one or two places, and the sands were still quite covered. But the only result of this was to force the Count and his train to proceed slowly, and one by one, while he himself led the way, the white stone pavement being clearly discernible through the thin water.

In the meantime, however, the Protestants who had been gazing at him as be mounted, gathered into knots together, and seemed to be speaking hastily and discontentedly. Some of the inferior officers joined them, and a great deal of tumult and talking ensued, which called out several of the gentlemen of the party to remonstrate. But remonstrance seemed in vain, and the crowd soon after trooped away out of the little open space where they had assembled, in the direction of the corps de garde, where the small battery of cannon was placed. Various broken sentences, however, were heard from time to time, such as, " I would hardly have believed it. To take care of themselves, and leave us to perish. I always said, we should be made the sacrifice. Better be a Catholic and at peace, than that."

" Ride after the Count and tell him what is going on," said one of the gentlemen to another, " while I go to our good minister, Monsieur Vigni, and get him to reason with them. You see they are mistaking the matter altogether, and think that we are going to abandon them. Make haste, or it will be too late."

The suggestion was instantly followed ; but ere the officer could get his horse and ride down to the sea-shore, the Count and his party were nearly at the fort, and to them we must now turn.

The progress of the young general of the Huguenots had been slower than it might have been, not only on account of the causeway being partially covered with water, but also because the stone, of which it was composed, had in some places been broken up or carried away. He at length reached, however, the fortified head of the causeway at the foot of the rock, and then demanded admission to speak with the governor.

This was refused him ; but as such might naturally be the case, his suspicions were but little increased by that event. He, however, directed the officer in command immediately to send up and inform the governor Le Luc of his being there, and of his desire to see him.

After keeping him some time, the officer returned, saying, " that Monsieur le Luc would come down himself to speak with the Count," and during the period that the leaders were thus occupied in waiting for the appearance of the governor, the Protestant officer arrived from the village, bringing news that the soldiery which had been left behind were in a state of actual mutiny, having entirely mistaken the object of the Count and his companions, and imagined that they were engaged in seeking their own safety, leaving the soldiers to meet whatever fate might befal them."

" In the name of Heaven, ride back, Du Bar," said the Count, " and quiet them till I return. It is better for me to stay and talk personally to this worthy gentleman, who seems to be showing us a cold face, for you know he owes everything to my house. I will return instantly, as soon as he condescends to favour us with his presence."

Du Bar did not reply, but turned his horse ; for they were still kept on the outside even of the causeway head, and rode back as fast as he could go, accompanied by one of the other officers.

The Count remained, growing more and more impatient every

moment; and the governor, perhaps thinking that he would get
tired of waiting, and retire without an answer, kept him nearly half
an hour before he made his appearance. He then come down
with that dull and dogged look, which generally accompanies the
purpose of disgraceful actions; and the Count, restraining his indignation, called to him to cause the drawbridge to be lowered, in
order that he might speak to him more privately.

"No, indeed," replied the governor, in a scoffing tone; "with
the little force I have in here, I shall not think of causing the drawbridge to be lowered, when I know that the village is occupied by
a large party of armed traitors."

"Traitors!" exclaimed the Count; but again overcoming his
anger, he added, "Monsieur le Luc, up to this moment I have
believed you to be of the reformed church."

"I am so no longer," muttered the governor.

"Well, Sir," continued the Count, "there are other things which
may have influence upon men of honour and good feeling besides
their religion. There is at the village, as you say, a large party of
Protestant gentlemen, assembled in defence of their liberty and
freedom of conscience. They find themselves unable to resist the
power of those that would oppress them; but terms are proposed
for extending a free pardon to all but some thirty or forty; and
those thirty or forty are desirous of obtaining shelter in this fortress
for one or two hours at the utmost, till they can embark in those
ships, which are waiting for the rising of the tide. Now, Monsieur
le Luc, my father gave you the first commission that you held
under the crown. He obtained for you your first promotion, and
I bestowed upon you the post in this fortress which you now
hold. Will you, Sir, grant us the shelter that we demand at your
hand?"

"Very pretty," replied Le Luc, "to talk of honour, and ask me
to betray the trust that the King reposes in me."

Still the Count kept his temper. "You refuse, then?" he
demanded.

"Yes, that I do," answered the governor, in a rude tone; "and
the sooner you take yourself back to the land the better, for I am
in no humour to be trifled with."

It was with difficulty that the Count restrained himself; but
there was one chance more, and he tried it.

"Yet another word, my good friend," he said. "There is a
matter in which you can favour us without endangering your own
safety, or getting into discredit with the government. If we
attempt to pass to the ships in what boats we can find, will you
pledge me your word that you do not fire into them?"

"If you do not make haste away from the gates of this fortress,"
replied the governor, who saw, by the quivering of the Count's lip,
the contempt that he could not help feeling, "I will fire upon you

where you are, and will sink the boat of every traitor that comes within shot."

" Sir," said the Count, " you are a dastardly, pitiful, contemptible scoundrel. It is only happy for you that the drawbridge is between us, or I would treat you like an ill-conditioned hound, and lash you within an inch of your life under my horse's feet."

" You shall hear more, traitor; you shall hear more in a minute," replied the governor. " And mind I tell you, the faster you go, the better for you."

Thus saying, he darted away, and mounted the zigzag staircase in the rock with a rapid step. The Count paused, and turned his horse; but at that very moment he saw a party of horsemen at the other end of the causeway apparently coming towards him with great speed, part of them upon the sands, which by this time had been left dry, part of them following the road in the midst.

" It is Du Bar and the rest," he said, in a low voice, to one of the gentlemen near him. " I have a very great mind to stay here, and try to punish that fellow for his insolence. I could swim that little space of sea in a moment, and the drawbridge once in our possession, the castle would be ours."

" Count, Count," shouted the officer of the guard from the fortress-side of the drawbridge, " for God's sake, make haste and ride back. I hear that governor of ours giving orders for charging the cannon with grape. He will fire upon you, as sure as I am alive, for he sent word to the Chevalier d'Evran last night, that he would do so."

" I thank you, Sir, for your courtesy," replied the Count, calmly. " Under these circumstances, my friends, it is better for us to go back."

The other officers put their horses into a quick pace; and they rode on; but they had barely gone a hundred yards, when the cannon of the castle opened a fire of grape upon them. The shot, however, flew over their heads; for they were too near the walls to be easily hit from any point but the tête du pont, where the Count could see preparations being made for following up the same course. At the same moment, however, he pulled up his horse, exclaiming, " Good Heaven, that is not the Marquis Du Bar! It is the Chevalier D'Evran!"

The officers who were with him paused also, and, to their surprise, and somewhat to their consternation, perceived that, shut in as they were by the sea on two sides, and by the fortress on another, the only open ground before them was occupied by the Commander-in-chief of the royalist forces, with a numerous staff, and a small escort of cavalry.

" We have nothing for it, my friends," said the Count de Morseiul, in a low, calm tone, " but to surrender. It is evident our men have capitulated in the village. Let us onward and meet them, however."

Thus saying, he spurred on his horse, while the Chevalier d'Evran galloped forward on his side, waving his hat, and shaking his clenched fist towards the people on the walls of the fort. They either did not recognise him, or did not choose to obey his commands; and before he and the Count de Morseiul met, a second discharge of grape-shot took place from the cannon of the castle. At the same moment, the Count de Morseiul beheld the Chevalier d'Evran suddenly check up his horse, press his hand upon his side, and fall headlong to the ground, while one of the horses of the Count's party was killed upon the spot, and an officer of the Chevalier's staff fell wounded, but sprang up again immediately.

The Count galloped eagerly on to the spot where he had seen the Chevalier d'Evran fall, and the memory of long friendship came painfully back upon his heart. Before he had reached the group of royalist soldiers and officers, however, five or six men had raised the unfortunate commander from the ground, and were bearing him rapidly back towards the village. So eagerly were those who remained conversing together, and so fully occupied with their own thoughts, that the Count de Morseiul might, to all appearance, have passed by them without opposition or inquiry; but he himself drew in his rein, demanding, " Is he much hurt?"

" Alas! Monsieur de Morseiul," replied the officer, who seemed to be next in command, " he is dead! Killed on the spot by that infernal shot! And a nobler gentleman, or better soldier, never lived. But some of your own people are killed also, are they not?"

" One of the horses only, I believe," replied the Count. " Pray, may I ask how all this has happened?—Poor Louis!"

" Ride on, ride on, Charliot," said the officer, speaking to one of his own men, before he answered the Count; " that scoundrel will fire upon us again. Tell him I will hang him over the drawbridge if he fires another shot. Monsieur de Morseiul, I will explain all this as we ride back; for you will have but little time to make your arrangements. Scarcely half an hour ago, as Monsieur d'Evran and the rest of us were reconnoitring pretty close to your camp, a party of your men came out and offered to capitulate on certain terms, which the Chevalier instantly agreed to, and they gave us possession of the gate and the corps de garde. Just at that moment, however, came up Monsieur du Bar, who remonstrated somewhat angrily with the Chevalier on signing a capitulation with the men, when he had given the officers a truce of five hours to consider of his terms. He represented that in those five hours all the gentlemen named in the proscribed list might have made their escape. On that, the Chevalier replied, that he intended to take no advantage; that the truce should be held to exist, notwithstanding the capitulation; and that every gentleman on that list might act exactly as he pleased, without

any one trying to impede him. He could not suffer them, he said, of course, to pass through our camp; but if they could escape by sea, they might. He added, however, that he wished to speak with this Le Luc, and that he would take the liberty of riding down through the village. Du Bar then asked if he intended to bid Le Luc fire on the boats or ships. He answered, quite the contrary, that his only intention was to supersede him in his command, and put an officer in his place who would keep the truce to the letter. You have, therefore, yet four hours nearly, in which to do what you will, Monsieur de Morseiul; for I, of course, taking the Chevalier's command, shall maintain all his arrangements, and act in their full spirit."

The Count had listened sadly and attentively; and when the royalist officer had done speaking, he replied, that by his leave he would ride on as fast as possible to the village, and consult with his companions.

" Do so! do so!" answered the other; "and now I think of it, I had better go on to the fort, and put the Chevalier's intentions in execution. For this firing upon you may be considered already a breach of the truce. I shall find you on my return; and at the little auberge you will meet with an English gentleman very anxious to speak with you." Thus saying, he turned again towards the fort, and the Count, with a sad heart, rode back to the village.

CHAPTER XXXV.

THE BITTER PARTING.

JUST at the entrance of the village, the Count met with his companion, Du Bar.

" Have you heard all?" demanded that officer. " What is to be done?"

" Get the boats ready with all speed," replied the Count. " The tide will turn within half an hour, the ships will be able to come farther in. Twenty or thirty persons may get off in the first boats, which must come back again for a second freight. I see clearly, my friend, that there is no intention of dealing harshly with us. All the officers wish us to escape, and there will be no more firing from the castle. I must leave the embarkation, and all that, to you, Du Bar, for I have things to go through that will try my heart to the utmost. I must have a few minutes to make up my mind to parting with my friends and companions, and all that I love on earth, for ever.—Du Bar," he continued, while the other wrung his hand affectionately, " there will be a young lady who will aecompany you, and that girl, the daughter of poor Virlay. You have a wife and children yourself, whom you love, I know, fondly and devotedly. They are in safety, you told me, on those opposite shores which I shall never see. But let me beseech you,—by the memory of these dark and terrible days, when the hand that now presses yours is laid in the dust, as I know too well must soon be the case,— let me beseech you, I say, to give every aid and assistance to those two whom I now commit to your charge. Be to the one as a brother, Du Bar, and to the other as a father. I know you to be honest and true as you are brave and wise; and I shall lay my head upon the block with more peace at my heart, if you promise me that which I now ask."

"I do, I do," replied the Marquis, with the tears standing in his eyes. "I do promise you, from my heart; but I would fain persuade you even now to consider——"

But the Count waved his hand, and rode on.

There was a considerable crowd round the entrance of the little inn, and he had some difficulty in making his way in. At the door of the room where he had fixed his own quarters, he found two or three of the royalist soldiers; but, passing by them, he entered the room, when a sight met his eye which might well chill and wring his heart.

The room was nearly empty; but stretched upon the long table, which occupied the midst, was the fine noble form of the Chevalier d'Evran, now still in death. Standing near the head of the body, was the old English officer, Sir Thomas Cecil, with an air of deep, stern grief upon his fine and striking countenance. His hat was off, shewing his white hair, his arms were crossed upon his chest, his head was erect as ever, and nothing like a tear was in his eye: but there was no mistaking the expression of his countenance. It was that of intense sorrow. But on the other side of the table, grief was displaying itself in a different manner, and in a different form. For there knelt Clémence de Marly, with her beautiful head bent down over the dead body; her hair, fallen from its bindings, scattered wildly, partly over her own shoulders, partly over the breast of the Chevalier; her left hand clasping that of the dead man, and her eyes and face buried on his bosom, while the convulsing sobs that shook her whole frame, told how bitterly she was weeping.

The Count paused with a look of deep sadness; but there was no anger or jealousy in his countenance. The old English officer, however, as soon as he perceived him, hurried forward, and took both his hands, saying, in a low and solemn voice, "You must let her weep, Count, you must let her weep!—It is her brother!"

"I have been sure of it for several days," replied the Count. "She told me not; but I knew it from what she did tell me. This day of agony, however, sir, is not yet over. I must disturb her grief but to waken her to more. You know the short time that is allowed for flight. You know the fate that would await her here, if she were to remain in this country as what is called a relapsed heretic, by the cruel persecutors of this land. Within two hours from this time, my good sir, she must take her departure for ever. The boats will be ready, and not a moment must be lost; and in those two short hours she must part with one who loves her as well as ever woman yet was loved, with one who truly believes she loves him as well as woman's heart can love—and who shall say where is the boundary of that boundless affection? She must part with him, sir, for ever, and with her native land."

"This is not her native land," replied the old officer. "The Lady Clémence Cecil, sir, is an English woman. But in one respect you say true. My poor niece must go, for I have experienced in my own person, as you know, how daring is the injustice of arbitrary power in this land, in the prisons of which, I, an English subject, have been detained for more than a year, till our own papistical and despotic king chose to apply to your despot for my liberation, and for the restoration of my brother's children. She must leave this land, indeed. But your words imply that you must stay behind. Tell me, tell me, my noble friend, is this absolutely necessary, in honour and in conscience?"

The Count grasped his hand, and pointed to the dead body. "I promised him," he said, "who lies there, that I would surrender myself to the King's pleasure. I have every reason to believe, that, in consideration of that promise, he dealt as favourably with us as he was permitted; that he even went beyond the strict line of his duty to give us some facilities of escape; and I must hold my promise to the dead as well as if he were here to claim it."

"God forbid," said Sir Thomas Cecil, "that I should say one word against it, terrible as is your determination—for you must well know the fate that awaits you. It seems to me that there was only that one act wanting, to make you all that our poor Clémence ought to love on earth, at the very moment she is to lose you for ever. See, she is raising her head. Speak to her, my friend, speak to her!"

The Count advanced and threw his arms round her. He knew that the grief which she felt was one that words could do nothing to mitigate, and the only consolation that he offered was thus by pressing her fondly to his heart, as if to express that there was love and tenderness yet left for her on earth. Clémence rose and wiped away her tears, for she felt he might think that some doubt of his affection mingled with her grief for her brother, if she suffered it to fall into excess.

"Oh, Albert," she said, "this is very terrible. I have but you now ——"

A hesitation came over the Count de Morseiul as she spoke those words, gazing tenderly and confidingly upon him: a hesitation, as to whether he should at once tell her his determination, or not let her know that he was about to remain behind, till she was absolutely in the boat destined to bear her away. It was a terrible question that he thus put to his own heart. But he thought it would be cruel not to tell her, however dreadful might be the struggle, to witness and to share.

"Alas, Clémence," he replied, "I must soon trust you, for a time at least, to other guidance, to other protection than my own. The boats are preparing to carry off a certain number of our friends to England. You must go in one of them, Clémence, and that immediately. Your noble uncle here, for such I understand he is, Sir Thomas Cecil, will protect you, I know, and be a father to you. The Marquis du Bar, too, one of the noblest of men, will be to you as a brother."

Clémence replied not, but gazed with a look of deep, earnest, imploring inquiry on the countenance of her lover, and after a moment he answered that look by adding, "I have given my promise, Clémence, to remain behind!"

"To death, to death!" cried Clémence, casting herself upon his bosom, and weeping bitterly, "you are remaining to die. I know it. I know it, and I will never quit you!"

The Count kissed her tenderly, and pressed her to his heart; but he suffered not his resolution to be shaken. "Listen to me, my Clémence," he said. "What may be my fate I know not: but I trust in God's mercy, and in my own uprightness of intentions. But think, Clémence, only think, dear Clémence, how terrible would be my feelings, how tenfold deep and agonizing would be all that I may have to suffer, if I knew that, not only I myself was in danger, but that you also were in still greater peril. If I knew that you were in imprisonment, that the having followed the dictates of your conscience was imputed to you as a crime ; that you were to be tormented by the agony of trial, before a tyrannical tribunal, and doomed to torture, to cruel death, or to eternal imprisonment. Conceive, Clémence, conceive how my heart would be wrung under such circumstances. Conceive how to every pang that I may otherwise suffer would be added the infinite weight of grief, and indignation, and suspense on your account. Conceive all this, and then, oh, Clémence, be merciful, be kind, and give me the blessing of seeing you depart in safety, as a consolation and a support under all that I may have myself to endure."

Clémence wept bitterly upon his bosom ; and the Count soothed her by every endearing and tender word. At length, she suddenly raised her head, as if some new idea had struck her, and she exclaimed, "I will go, Albert. I will go, upon one condition, without torturing you more by opposition."

"What is that condition, dear Clémence ?" demanded the Count, gazing on her face, which was glowing warmly even through her tears. " What is that condition, dearest Clémence ?"

Clémence hid her face again upon his breast, and answered, " It is, that I may become your wife before I quit this shore. We have Protestant ministers here ; the ceremony can be easily performed. My uncle, I know, will offer no opposition ; and I would fain bear the name of one so noble and so beloved, to another land, and to the grave, which may, perhaps, soon re-unite us."

The Count's heart was wrung, but he replied, " Oh, beloved Clémence, why, why propose that which must not—which cannot be ? why propose that which, though so tempting to every feeling of my heart, would cover me with well-deserved shame if I yielded to it ?—Think, think, Clémence, what would deservedly be said of me if I were to consent—if I were to allow you to become my wife, to part with you at the altar, and perhaps, by my death as a condemned criminal, to leave you an unprotected widow within a few days."

Clémence clasped her hands, vehemently exclaiming, " So help me Heaven, as I would rather be the widow of Albert of Morseiul than the wife of any other man that ever lived on earth !"

Sir Thomas Cecil, however, interposed. " Clémence," he said, " your lover is right: but he will not use arguments to persuade you that I may use. This is a severe and bitter trial. The Almighty only knows how it will terminate: but, my dear child, remember that this is no ordinary man you love. Let his character be complete to the last ! Do not—do not, by any solicitation of yours, Clémence, take the least brightness from his bright example. Let him go on, my child, to do what he believes his duty, at all risks, and through all sacrifices. Let there not be one selfish spot from the beginning to the end for man to point at ; and the Almighty will protect and reward him to whom he has given power to act uprightly to the last ;—if not in this world, in another he will be blest, Clémence, and to that other we must turn our hopes of happiness, for here it is God's will that we should have tribulation."

Clémence clasped her hands, and bent down her eyes to the ground. For several minutes she remained as if in deep thought, and then said, in a low but a firmer voice, " Albert, I yield ; and knowing, from what is in my own heart, how dreadful this moment must be to you, I will not render it more dreadful by asking you anything more that you must refuse. I will endeavour to be as calm as I can, Albert ;—but weep I must. Perhaps," she added, with a faint, faint smile upon her lips, " I might weep less, if there were no hope ; if it were all despair: but I see a glimmering for exertion on my part, if not exactly for hope ; and that exertion may certainly be better made in another land than if I were to remain here ; —and now for the pain of departure. That must be undergone, and I am ready to undergo it rather at once than when I may have

forgotten my faint resolution. Do you go with me?" she con-
tinned, turning to her uncle; "if it be needful that you stay, I fear
not to go alone."

Sir Thomas Cecil, however, replied that he was ready to accompany her. Her maid, Maria, was warned to prepare with all speed;
and by the time that a few more sentences had been spoken on
either part, the Marquis du Bar came to inform the Count that the
boats were afloat, and the vessels standing in as far as they could
into the bay. The Huguenot gentlemen mentioned in the list of
proscription were already on the shore, not a little eager to be in
the first boats to put off; and the soldiery were drawn up under
arms to await the expiration of the truce. The Count and Sir
Thomas Cecil led down Clémence, weeping bitterly, to the sands;
and, as they passed, a murmur of sympathy and compassion ran
through the crowd, and through the ranks of the troops, while the
gentlemen drew back to give her the first place in the boats. Before they reached the edge of the bay, however, the Count, whose
eye had been raised for a moment to the vessels, pointed towards
them with a smile of satisfaction.

"Gentlemen," he said, looking round, "I am happy to see that
you will all be able to get off without risk. Do you not perceive
they are sending off their boats for you?—Clémence," he added, in
a lower voice, "will you go at once, or will you wait till the other
boats arrive, and all go together?"

"Let me wait—let me wait," said Clémence, in the same low
tone. "Every moment that my hand touches yours is a treasure."

The other boats came in rapidly with the returning tide; and as
soon as their keels touched the sand, and a few words had been
spoken to ascertain that all was right and understood, the Count
turned and said—

"Now, gentlemen."

There were some twenty or thirty yards of shallow water between the dry sands and the boats; and Albert of Morseiul raised
Clémence in his arms, and carried her to the edge of the first.
Neither of them spoke a word; but as leaning over, he placed her
in the little vessel, she felt his arms clasp more tightly round her;
and his lips were pressed upon hers.

"The Almighty bless thee!" and, "God protect and deliver
thee!" was all that was said on either side; and the Count turned
back to the shore.

One by one the different officers advanced to him in silence, and
grasped his hand before they proceeded to the boats. When they
were all embarked, and the boats began to push off, the Count
pulled off his hat, and stood bareheaded, looking up to heaven.
But at that moment, a loud shout burst from the soldiery, of "The
Count—the Count! They have forgotten the Count!"

But the Count of Morseiul turned round towards them, and

said aloud, in his usual calm, firm tone, " They have not forgotten me, my friends. It was you who were mistaken when you thought that I had forgotten you. I remain to meet my fate, whatever it may be."

A number of men in the ranks instantly threw down their muskets, and rushing forward, clasped his knees, beseeching him to go. But he waved his hand, saying gently, " It is in vain, my friends! My determination has been taken for many days. Go back to your ranks, my good fellows—go back to your ranks! I will but see the boats safe, and then join you, to surrender the village and lay down our arms."

The Count then turned again to the sea, and watched the four boats row onward from the shore. They reached the vessels in safety in a few minutes; in a few minutes more the boats belonging to the village began to row back empty. After a little pause, some more canvas was seen displayed upon the yards of the vessels. They began to move; they sailed out of the harbour; and, after gazing down upon the sand fixedly and intently while one might count a hundred, the Count of Morseiul, feeling himself solitary, turned, gave the word of command, and marched the men back into the village. He entered immediately into the room where the Chevalier d'Evran lay; and although by this time all the principal officers of the royalist force were there, with several other persons, amongst whom was his own servant Riquet, he walked silently up to the head of the corpse, and gazed for several minutes on the dead man's face; then lifting the cold hand, he pressed it affectionately in his.

" God receive thee, Louis—God receive thee!" he said, and his eyes filled with the first tears which they had shed that day.

" I see no use now, sir," he continued, turning to the officer who had taken the command of the royal forces, " of delaying any longer the surrender of the village. I am ready in person to give it up to you this moment, and also to surrender my sword. The only favour I have to ask is, that you will make it known to his majesty that I had no share in the event by which my unhappy friend here fell. The shot which slew him was intended for me, as you are doubtless aware."

" Perfectly," replied the commander; " and I have already sent off a despatch to the King, giving him an account of the events of this morning. I myself, joined with all the officers here present, have not failed to testify our sense of the noble, upright, and disinterested conduct of the Count of Morseiul. I would fain speak with him a word alone, however;" and he drew him aside to the window. " Count," he said, " I shall not demand your sword, nor in any way affect your liberty, if you will promise to go to Paris immediately, and surrender yourself there. If you would take my advice, you would go at once to the King, and cast yourself at his feet. Ask for no audience, but seek admission to him at some public moment. If fortune favours you, which I trust it will, you may have an opportunity of explaining to his majesty many things that have probably been misrepresented."

"I shall certainly follow your advice," said the Count, "since you put it in my power to do so."

"Ah, gentlemen," cried Riquet, who had been listening unperceived to all they said, "if the poor Chevalier had lived, the Count would have been quite safe; for he had the means of proving that the Count saved the King's life not long ago, of which his majesty knows nothing. I heard the man Herval make his confession to the Chevalier with my own ears, of how monsieur prevented him from killing the King, and how he had written the whole story to Hatréaumont; but the Chevalier could not take it down, for the man died before pen and ink could do their work."

"That is unfortunate, indeed," said the commander; "but still you can give your testimony of the facts, my good friend."

"Bless you, sir," replied Riquet, "they will never believe anything I can say."

"I fear not, indeed," replied the Count. "Besides, sir, my good friend Riquet, if he went to Paris, would have so much to confess on his own account, that they would not mind what he said in regard to the confessions of others."

"Unfortunately, too," said the commander, "all the papers of Hatréaumont, if I remember right, were ordered to be burnt by the common hangman. Such was the sentence of the court, I think, and it must have been executed long ago. However, Count, the plan that I have proposed is still the best. Speed to Paris with what haste you may; cast yourself upon the King's mercy; tell him all and everything, if he will permit you to do so, and engage all your friends to support your cause at the same moment. Take your way at once into Brittany," he added, dropping his voice, "and from thence to Paris, for I very much fear that the result would be fatal if you were to fall into the hands of the intendant of Poitou. He is exasperated to the highest degree. You have surrendered at discretion, taken with arms in your hand. He has already broken on the wheel two or three under the same circumstances; and I dare not deal with him in the same way that the Chevalier d'Evran did, for I have not sufficient power."

The Count thanked him for his advice, and followed it; and, as we must not pause upon such small circumstances as the surrender of the village, we shall let that event be supposed to have taken place; and, in our next chapter, shall, if possible, pursue this sad history to its conclusion.

CHAPTER XXXVI.

THE END.

It was in the great reception room at Versailles, an hour after the
King had held the usual council, which failed not to meet every
day.   His mood was neither more nor less severe than ordinary;
for if, on the one hand, events had taken place which had given
him pleasure, other events had reached his ears from the south of
France, which showed him, notwithstanding all Louvois' efforts to
conceal the extent of the evil, that serious disturbances in the
Cevennes and other parts of France, near the mouth of the Rhone,
were likely to follow the measures which had been adopted against
the Protestants.

Louvois himself was present, and in no very placable mood, the
King having replied to him more than once during the morning
haughtily and angrily, and repressed the insolence by which his
demeanour was sometimes characterized, with that severe dignity
which the minister was very willing to see exercised towards any
one but himself.

Louis, who was dressed in the most sumptuous manner, held in
his hand a roll of papers, which had been given him just before his
entrance into the chamber; but he did not read them, and merely
turned them round and round from time to time, as if he were
handling a truncheon.   Many eyes were fixed upon him, and
various were the hopes and fears which the aspect of that one man
created in the breasts of those who surrounded him.   All, however,
were silent at that moment; for an event was about to take place
highly flattering to the pride of the ostentatious King of France,
and the look of all was soon fixed upon the doors at the end of the
hall, in the expectation of what was to come.

At length those doors were opened, and a fine-looking middle-
aged man, dressed in a robe of red velvet, followed by four others
clothed in black velvet, was led into the apartment, and approached
the King.   He bowed low and reverently, and then addressed the
French sovereign without embarrassment, and with apparent ease,
assuring the monarch in vague, but still flattering terms, that the
republic of Genoa, of which he was Doge, had entertained no feeling, throughout the course of events lately passed, but profound
respect for the crown of France.

Somewhat to the left of the King, amongst the multitude of
French princes and officers, appeared one or two groups, consisting of the ambassadors from different barbarous nations; and while
the Doge of Genoa spoke, offering excuses for the conduct of the
state he ruled, the eye of Louis glanced from time to time to the

Indian envoys in their gorgeous apparel, as they eagerly asked questions of their interpreter, and were told that it was the prince of an independent state come to humble himself before the mighty monarch whom he had offended.

When the audience of the Doge of Genoa was over, and he withdrew, a multitude of the courtiers followed, so that the audience hall was nearly clear, and the King paused for a moment, talking over the Doge's demeanour to those who surrounded him, and apparently about to retire immediately. He had taken a step forward, indeed, to do so, when the Prince de Marsillac, who certainly dared to press the King upon disagreeable subjects, when no one else would run the risk, advanced, and, bowing low, pointed to the papers in the King's hand.

"I ventured, sire," he said, "before your majesty came here, to present to you those papers, which you promised to look at."

The King's brow instantly darkened. "I see at once, Prince," he said, "that they refer to the Count of Morseiul, a rebel, as I am informed, taken with arms in his hand, in regard to whom the laws of the land must have their course."

The Prince was somewhat abashed, and hesitated; but another gentleman stepped forward with stern and somewhat harsh features, but with a noble air and look that bespoke fearless sincerity.

"What is it, Montausier?" said the King, sharply, addressing that celebrated nobleman, who is supposed to have been represented by Molière under the character of the misanthrope.

"Merely to say, sire," replied the Duke, in a firm, strong tone of voice, "that some one has falsified the truth to your majesty. My nephew, in command of the troops to whom the Count surrendered, informs me that he was not taken with arms in his hand, as you have said, but, on the contrary, (and here lies a great difference,) surrendered voluntarily, when, according to the truce of five hours granted to the Huguenots by the Chevalier d'Evran, he had every opportunity of escaping to England had he so pleased, as all the rest of the leaders on that occasion did."

"How is this, sir?" demanded the King, turning to Louvois. "I speak from your statements, and I hope you have not made me speak falsely."

"Sire," replied Louvois, with a look of effrontery, "I have just heard that what the Duke says is the case; but I judged that all such points could naturally be investigated at the Count's trial."

The King seemed struck with this observation; but Montausier instantly replied — "Monsieur de Louvois, if his majesty will permit me to tell you so, you have been, for the first time in your life, sadly tardy in receiving information; for my nephew informs me that he gave you intelligence of this fact no less than three days ago; and, in the next place, you are very well aware of what you have not thought fit to say, that by investigating such things at a trial, you would directly frustrate the express object for which the Count de Morseiul surrendered himself when he might have escaped, which was to cast himself at the King's feet, and explain to him the strange and extraordinary misconception by which he was thrown into rebellion, and to prove that as soon as ever he discovered the mistake which had been committed, he had expressed himself ready to surrender, and trust to his majesty's clemency, which is as great a quality as his justice."

Louvois's face had grown fiery red. "Expressed his readiness to surrender!" he cried, with a scoff. "Did he not fight two battles after that?"

"How, sir?" exclaimed the King. "I had understood from you that no battles had been fought at all. Mere skirmishes, you said—affairs of posts—that the insurrection was nothing but the revolt of a few peasants."

Louvois stammered forth some excuse about the numbers being insignificant, and the whole business crushed within nine days after the Chevalier d'Evran took the command; but the King turned away angrily, saying, "Monsieur de Louvois, no more interruption. I find in my middle age, as I found in my youth, that a king must see with his own eyes. Now, Marsillac, what is it you wish? What is it you desire of me, Montausier?"

"For my part, sire," replied the Prince de Marsillac, "I only desire that your majesty should run your eyes over those papers. They are very brief, and to the point; and every fact that is therein stated, I can assure you, may be proved on indisputable authority."

"And I," said the Duke of Montausier, "have only to beg that your majesty would see and hear the Count de Morseiul. From him, as every man here present knows, you will receive the pure and simple truth, which is a thing that happens to your majesty perhaps once in five or six years, and will do you good."

The King smiled, and turned his eyes upon the papers; and when he had read them nearly through, he smiled again, even more gaily than before.

"It turns out, gentlemen," he said, "that an affair has happened to me, which I fancy happens to us all more than once in our lives. I have been completely cheated by a valet. I remember giving the villain the paper well, out of which it seems he manufactured a free pardon for his master. At all events, this exculpates the Count from the charge of base ingratitude which has been heavily urged against him. Your statement of his willing surrender, Montausier, greatly diminishes his actual and undoubted crime; and as I have complied with the request of the Prince de Marsillac, and looked at the papers, I must not refuse you yours. Either to-day, if the Count have arrived, or to-morrow, I will hear his story from his own lips."

"Sire," answered the Duke of Montausier, "I have been daring enough to receive him in my apartments."

The cloud came slightly again over Louis's countenance; but though he replied with dignified gravity, yet it was not with anger. "You have done wrong," he said; "but since it is so, call him to my presence. All you ladies and gentlemen around shall judge if I deal harshly with him."

There was a pretty girl standing not far from the King, and close between her own mother and the interpreter of the ambassadors from Siam. We have spoken of her before, under the name of Annette de Marville; and while she had remained in that spot, her eyes had more than once involuntarily filled with tears. She was timid and retiring in her nature; and as the Duke of Montausier turned away to obey the King, every one was surprised to hear her voice raised sufficiently loud to reach even the ear of Louis himself, saying to the interpreter, "Tell them, that they are now going to see how magnanimously the King will pardon one who has offended him."

The King looked another way; but it was evident to those who were accustomed to watch his countenance, that he connected the words he had just heard with the humiliation he had inflicted on the Doge of Genoa, and that the contrast struck and pleased him not a little.

In a very short time—before this impression had at all faded away—the door again opened, and the Duke of Montausier re-entered with the Count of Morseiul. The latter was pale, but perfectly firm and composed. He did not wear his sword, but carried it sheathed in his hand; and advancing directly towards Louis, he bent one knee before the King, at the same time laying down the weapon at the monarch's feet.

"Sire," he said, without rising, "I have brought you a sword, which for more than ten years was drawn in every campaign in your majesty's service. It has, unfortunately, been drawn against you; and that it has been so, and at the very moment when your majesty had a right to expect gratitude at my hands, is the bitterest recollection of my life; so bitter indeed, so horrible, so painful, that the moment I discovered the terrible error into which I had been hurried, the moment that I discovered that I owed my liberation to your majesty, I instantly determined, whatever might be the result of the events that were then taking place, to surrender myself, unconditionally, to your majesty's pleasure, to embrace no means of escape, to reject every opportunity of flight; and if your indignation so far overcame your mercy as to doom me to death, to submit to it, not alone with courage, which every man in your majesty's service possesses, but with perfect resignation to your royal will."

The words, the manner, the action, all pleased the King, and the countenance with which he looked upon the young nobleman was by no means severe.

"You have, I fear, greatly erred, Monsieur de Morseiul," he

replied. " But still I believe you have been much misled. Is there any favour that you have to ask me?"

The Count gazed up in the King's face, still kneeling; and every head was bent forward, every ear listened eagerly. A momentary pause followed, as if there was a great struggle within him; and then he answered, " Sire, I will not ask my life of your majesty;—not from any false pride, for I feel and acknowledge that it is yours to give or to take,—but because my conduct, however much it might originate in mistake, must appear so ungrateful to you that you cannot, at this moment, feel I deserve your mercy. The only favour I will ask, then, is this: that should I be brought to a trial, which must end, as I know, inevitably in my fall, you will read every word of my deposition, and I therein promise to give your majesty a full and true account, without the falsification of a single word, of all that has taken place in this last lamentable business."

Louvois took a half step forward, as if to speak, and not a little anxiety was upon his countenance. But, contrary to the general impression of those present, all that the Count had said had pleased the King; though his latter words had not a little alarmed the minister, who knew that truths must be displayed in the young nobleman's deposition, which he had studiously concealed from the monarch, and which would prove his own ruin if they should be revealed.

" Monsieur de Morseiul," replied the King, " I will promise what you ask, at all events. But what you have said has pleased me, for it shows that you understand my spirit towards my subjects, and that I can grant without being asked. Your life, sir, is given to you. What punishment we shall inflict may, perhaps, depend upon the sentence of a judicial court, or of our council."

" May it please your majesty," said Louvois, stepping forward, " to hear me one moment. You have, perhaps, thought me inimical to Monsieur de Morseiul, but such, indeed, is not the case; and I would propose, that instead of subjecting him to any trial at all, you, at once, pronounce sentence of banishment upon him, which is all the mercy that he can expect. His estates, as ought to be the case, must be forfeited to the crown."

" And he driven forth," observed the King, drily, " to employ his military talents in the service of our enemies."

" Never, never, never, sire!" exclaimed the Count, clasping his hands eagerly. " Never should my sword be drawn against my native land. I would rather beg my bread in misery, from door to door: I would rather live in want, and die in sorrow, than do so base an act!"

There was truth and zeal upon his countenance, and Louvois urged what he had proposed; but while he was addressing the monarch, in a lower tone, one of the side doors of the hall opened, and a lady came partly in, speaking to some one behind her, as if she knew not that any one was in the hall. The moment that she perceived her mistake, Madame de Maintenon drew back; but the King advanced a step, and besought her to enter.

"We want your presence much, madam," he said, with a smile, "for we cannot decide upon what is to be done with this young culprit. But you seem in haste, and who is this with you? I have somewhere seen his face before."

The King might well fail to recognise the countenance of Jerome Riquet; for it was at that moment actually cadaverous in appearance, from the various emotions that were going on in his heart.

"I was at that moment seeking your majesty," said Madame de Maintenon, advancing with her usual calm grace, "and was passing this way to your cabinet, to crave an audience ere you went out. But I thought the ceremony of the day was over."

"What are your commands, madam?" inquired the King. "Your wishes are to be attended to at all times."

"You know, sire," she said, "that I am not fond of ever asking one, who is only over generous to his servants, for anything. But I was eager at that moment to beseech your majesty to grant at once your pardon to this unfortunate man, who some time ago committed a great crime in misapplying your majesty's hand-writing, and who has now just committed another, for which I understand the officers of justice are in pursuit of him, though the swiftness of the horse which brought him here has enabled him to escape for the moment. He found out my apartments, I know not how, and I brought him instantly to your majesty, as soon as I had heard his story, and read this paper?"

"What is this paper?" demanded the King, taking it: "ticketed I see in the hand of Monsieur de la Reynie, 'Letter from the said Herval to the Sieur de Hatréaumont!' How come you possessed of this, sirrah?"

Riquet advanced and knelt before the King, while Louvois suddenly seemed to recollect some business, and retired from the circle. "Sire," said the valet, in the briefest possible terms, "in serving my master I was taken by your majesty's forces, shut up in a barn with some wounded prisoners, heard the well known leader, Herval, confess to the Chevalier d'Evran, that he had written a letter to the traitor Hatréaumont, regarding his having been prevented from murdering your majesty, by the Count de Morseiul, (in which prevention I had some little share.) The man died before his words could be taken down. The Chevalier d'Evran said it did not signify, for you would believe his evidence. But the Chevalier d'Evran was killed. My word I knew would not be believed; but I heard that the papers of Hatréaumont were to be burnt this day by the common hangman, opposite the Bastille.*

---

* The papers of Hatréaumont were preserved for some time after his death, in order to give light in regard to the guilt of his accomplices.

I had a swift horse saddled. I got close to the fire. I fixed my eyes upon the papers one by one as they were thrown in, till, seeing the writing of Herval, I seized the letter, and galloped hither as hard as I could. This is my tale, sire, and on my word it is true."

The King hastily opened the paper, and read the contents, the expression of his countenance changing several times as he proceeded. But when he had done, he turned towards the Count, saying, "Monsieur de Morseiul, I require no one now to advise me how to act towards you. You are freely and entirely pardoned. I have given up the hope of ever seeing you cast away the errors of your faith. But even that must not make me harsh towards the man who has saved my life. I would only fain know how it was that you did not inform me of this at the time?"

"Sire," replied the Count, "I came to your majesty for the purpose. Your majesty must remember, that I told you that I had matters of deep importance to communicate. You referred me to Monsieur de Louvois, and as I was proceeding to seek him, I was arrested. In the Bastille I was allowed to communicate with no one, and the rest you know."

"We have been all very unfortunate, Count," answered the King. "However, I trust, that these embarrassments are at an end. You have your free pardon for the past; and now for the future. I cannot violate in your favour the laws that I have laid down for the regulation of the land, and for the establishment of one general religion throughout the country. If you stay in France, you, with others, lose the means of exercising the ceremonies of your sect. But, as I said to the Count de Schomberg, I say to you: in consideration of the great services that you have rendered, I will allow you to sell all your possessions, if you choose to retire to another land, and this is, I fear, all I can do."

"Your majesty overwhelms me with bounty," said the Count, "but there are yet two favours that I would ask."

"What more?" asked the King.

"One request is, sire," answered the Count, "to be allowed once in every year to present myself before your majesty; and the other, that I may retain the château and the immediate grounds around it belonging to my ancestors. Thus every fond recollection that I have attached to France will still be gratified; and though in exile, I shall live a Frenchman to the last."

"Your request is granted," replied the King, with a smile. "And now, gentlemen and ladies, as by your faces round I judge you are all well satisfied, we will not detain you longer."

Thus saying, Louis turned and withdrew.

Ere the Count of Morseiul retired from the room, and before any of his friends therein could speak with him, Madame de Maintenon said a word in his ear in a low voice.

" Go to the hotel of the British ambassador," she said. " You will there find those whom you do not expect."

The heart of the Count of Morseiul beat high. He had words of gratitude to speak to many there present; but as soon as that was done, he hurried to Paris without a moment's pause, and in a few minutes clasped Clémence de Marly to a joyful heart.

We need not tell here the brief story she related of her flight from the coast of France to London; and of her having found an affectionate parent in one who, by the wiles of an artful second wife, and an intriguing priest, had been persuaded to leave his children, by a first marriage with a Protestant lady, to the charge of her Catholic relations in France, and to the care of the king of that country. Louis had become the godfather of the eldest, (known to us as the Chevalier d'Evran,) while the earl himself was in exile during the troubles of the great rebellion. A Catholic himself, the earl had been easily induced to believe that his children's salvation depended upon their being educated in a Catholic country; even though concealed there from Protestant relations by assumed names. But on the death of his second wife, all his feelings of natural affection returned, and during an illness, which made him believe that he was on his death-bed, he sent his brother to seek and bring back his children. We need not enter into the detail any farther. The reader can and will imagine it all. All that remains to be said is, that Clémence, in her eagerness, had easily persuaded that parent, whose only child she now was—for the three which had sprung from the second marriage had not survived—to hasten over to Paris, invested with every authority from King James II., with whom his religion rendered him a favourite, to solicit the pardon of the Count of Morseiul. In consequence of the considerable round which the Count was obliged to take in his journey to the capital, and the difficulty of obtaining an audience of the King, she had arrived the day before his fate was finally decided.

The only part of that fate which could yet be doubtful, was now in her hands; and, if the King of France had shown himself merciful to the Count de Morseiul, she showed herself devoted to him through life, making him as happy, as the combination of the rarest qualities of mind and person with the noblest, and the deepest, and the dearest qualities of the heart, could render such a man as we have endeavoured to depict the Huguenot.

THE END.

T. C. Savill, Printer, 107, St. Martin's-lane.

A New Edition, in demy 8vo, price 16s. *boards,*

THE

HISTORY OF CHARLEMAGNE

WITH

𝕬 𝕾𝖐𝖊𝖙𝖈𝖍 𝖔𝖋 𝖙𝖍𝖊 𝕾𝖙𝖆𝖙𝖊 & 𝕳𝖎𝖘𝖙𝖔𝖗𝖞 𝖔𝖋 𝕱𝖗𝖆𝖓𝖈𝖊

FROM

THE FALL OF THE ROMAN EMPIRE TO THE RISE OF THE
CARLOVINGIAN DYNASTY.

BY

G. P. R. JAMES, ESQ.

" To that first great merit, veracity, our author may well lay claim; and we say first great merit, for what is the ingenious hypothesis, if the fact on which it is founded be untrue? And yet for the sake of favourite theory how often is the truth wilfully concealed. Now it is but justice to Mr. James when we observe, that he takes no position without most carefully giving his reasons of preference, and referring to the various authorities. His style is at once animated and clear." *Literary Gazette.*

" It is filled to overflowing with erudition; the facts are carefully sifted and correctly stated, and the language is in general moderate, and suited to the dignity of history. This is high praise, and Mr. James must feel it to be so. We go further, and say that this work displays talent of a very high order, and that it supplies an important *desideratum* in English literature." *Athenæum.*

" Out of the mass of contradictions and difficulties which lay at the very threshold of his task, Mr. James has produced a luminous and impartial work, which will confer lasting honour on his name." *Atlas.*

" It is eloquent, interesting, and instructive in no common degree. It stands out from the flimsy and elementary literature of the day, a monument of great erudition and high talent." *Scots Times.*

" Mr. James manifests throughout great patience in research, scrupulous regard to truth, a sound discriminating judgment, and that happy combination of narrative and reflective talent which communicates at once liveliness and dignity to history. His style is clear, vigorous, and classical."—*Scotsman.*

" We rise from it as from the contemplation of a magnificent picture, and our admiration is divided between the subject itself and the artist."
Doncaster, Notts, and Lincoln Gazette.

LONDON: SMITH, ELDER AND CO., CORNHILL.

1845.

CPSIA information can be obtained
at www.ICGtesting.com
Printed in the USA
LVHW08*1626230818
587900LV00011B/174/P